The sublime poetry and superb theater of *Doctor Faustus,*

The savagely funny skewering of greed and hypocrisy of *Volpone,*

The grandeur of a woman'
Malfi,

The sense of infinite corru
Women,

The evil spawned by love in *'Tis Pity She's a Whore,* are all part of the wealth of genius in—

FIVE PLAYS OF THE ENGLISH RENAISSANCE

Professor Bernard Beckerman teaches in the departments o literature and drama at Columbia University. He is the autho of numerous articles and books, including the classic study o the performance aspects of Elizabethan drama, SHAKE SPEARE AT THE GLOBE, and is counted today among th world's leading scholars of the English Renaissance.

FIVE PLAYS OF THE ENGLISH RENAISSANCE

Edited
and with an Introduction
by

Bernard Beckerman

A MERIDIAN BOOK

MERIDIAN
Published by the Penguin Group
Penguin Books USA Inc., 375 Hudson Street,
New York, New York 10014, U.S.A.
Penguin Books Ltd, 27 Wrights Lane,
London W8 5TZ, England
Penguin Books Australia Ltd, Ringwood,
Victoria, Australia
Penguin Books Canada Ltd, 10 Alcorn Avenue,
Toronto, Ontario, Canada M4V 3B2
Penguin Books (N.Z.) Ltd, 182–190 Wairau Road,
Auckland 10, New Zealand

Penguin Books Ltd, Registered Offices:
Harmondsworth, Middlesex, England

Published by Meridian, an imprint of Dutton Signet, a division of Penguin Books USA Inc. Previously published in a Meridian Classic Books edition.

First Meridian Printing, July, 1993
First Meridian Classic Printing, November, 1983
10 9 8 7 6 5 4 3 2 1

Library of Congress Catalog Card Number: 83-61422

Printed in the United States of America

CONTENTS

quintum sed ~~dispari et structura~~, bestiarum conflictati-oni destinatum, in quo multi ursi, Tauri, et stupendae magnitudinis canes, discretis caveis et septis aluntur, qui ad.

Interior of the Swan Playhouse (1596)

The drawing of the Swan Playhouse is the only contemporary illustration we have of the interior of an Elizabethan public playhouse. It is a sketch made by Arend van Buchell based on information he received from his friend Johannes DeWitt, who visited the Swan in 1596. Theaters similar to the Swan housed such plays as *Doctor Faustus, Volpone,* and *The Duchess of Malfi.* The features common to the Swan, the Rose, the Globe, and several other playhouses include (1) a ring of galleries around a yard open to the sky, (2) a large platform connected to one side of the inner galleries and extending to the middle of the yard, (3) two pillars holding up a "shadow" or "heavens" over half the stage platform, and (4) a facade with doors at platform level and a balcony for actors or audience on a second, higher level. In respect to the Swan, however, we should note that the facade, as shown, does not satisfy the staging requirements for all scenes. In many plays, a third entrance or a curtained area is needed, as is probably the case in *Doctor Faustus,* in which the stage direction for the first scene states, "Enter Faustus in his study." The sketch of the Swan Playhouse, therefore, while it represents the general appearance of an Elizabethan public playhouse stage, should not be regarded as definitive in all details.

INTRODUCTION

A good play has a double life. First, it has a stage life. However noble its intentions or profound its philosophy, a play, before it can be anything else, must be a show. Most often, it is a show of strange events made familiar or familiar events made strange. Through the magic of acting, successive passages of dialogue and monologue become the ebb and flow of human behavior. Words come out as thoughts, phrases as impulses. The script, which is so often regarded as the entire play, turns out to be only a blueprint for possible performances.

But if a play's first life is its stage life, its second life is literary. However much the lines depend on actor and setting, they are also full of intricate ideas, provocative signs, and multilevel actions. To read a play as though its stage life were incidental is to ignore its very nature. On the other hand, to ignore the second, more rarefied existence of the written text is to miss the contemplation of life in all its allusiveness. As theater, the play immerses us in the turbulence of experience; as literature, it permits us the leisure to understand that experience and ponder its implications.

The plays in this volume have such a double existence. They share with Shakespeare's work the rare quality of lively action worthy of steady reflection. At the same time the plays possess incomplete thoughts and feelings waiting to burst into life on a stage. It is this duality that makes them at once ancient and modern, well-worn and fresh, vestiges of the past and yet untapped treasures for the present.

At their best the literary and theatrical aspects of a play are only reciprocal sides of a single full life. Yet it often happens that the snobberies and biases of an age idolize one side of the drama and not the other. In European culture it is usually the literary side that receives praise. This was true in the Elizabethan age and, until recently, largely true in our own day. Then as now, influential people admired literary drama at the expense of the common garden variety found on the popular stage. Yet this habit flies in the face of history. Theatrical tradition shows that "literary" drama, however greatly admired and patiently nurtured, seldom if ever achieves theatrical distinction, while popular drama, from time to time, becomes the literature of a nation.

No time was this more true than in sixteenth-century England. Not until Christopher Marlowe had conquered London with his "mighty line" and Shakespeare, Jonson, and others had produced a body of drama to challenge the Greek tragedians did the new plays in English win respect as works of literature. In the generation before Marlowe's mastery of the stage, men like George Gascoigne and Sir Philip Sidney encouraged the composition of classically correct art. They favored the unified action, the circumscribed scale, and the limited cast of characters found in Senecan and Italian example. For them the far-ranging adventures and long-running histories of the popular stage violated the appropriate dimensions of dramatic poetry.

Yet though the popular dramatists rejected the literary models favored by the elite, they were not unaware of classical forms. Whether they came to London from a university, as did Marlowe, or were self-educated, as was Jonson, they knew the ancient playwrights; above all, they knew Seneca and Plautus thoroughly. Jonson, the finest classicist of his age, met the challenge by striking a balance between Latin models and contemporary taste. He was in the vanguard of those who insisted on the literary distinction of the new drama, especially of his own. Other dramatists were less concerned with ancient models, although they were no less interested than Jonson in creating a poetic drama of high quality. And though formal literary criticism was rudimentary, there were commentators like Francis Meres who were ready to match English writers favorably against the masters of Greek and Latin. Thus, while taking what they could from the past, the Elizabethan dramatists were primarily concerned with satisfying the practical conditions of their own theater, and, as a result, created a body of plays that possess the double vitality of stage and page.

It is rare for literature and performance to fuse so richly as they did in the Elizabethan age. By chance or historical circumstance there was a happy concurrence of rhetorical, narrative, and emblematic influences with hospitable theatrical conditions. Sixteenth-century England had a delayed response to the Renaissance ideas and art that had dominated Italian court life for a century. While native traditions of morality and thought continued to affect intellectual and artistic practice, those traditions did not hinder new growth. In poetry no single writer in English dominated the imagination. Familiar though Chaucer's poetry was to the Elizabethan, Chaucer had written in a language that was no longer vital. Nor was there any later poet of like stature to set standards. Poetic form itself was in flux, and aspiring poets were open to new challenges. Stimulated by ancient Latin and contemporary Italian poets, invigorated by the task of translating the work of these poets into a vivid, unaffected English, a new generation of poets played with stanzaic shapes and metric variation. Eschewing slavish imitation, they nevertheless refashioned alien expressions into native art. Finding their language unsettled, they made it supple.

The refinement of poetry did not have an immediate parallel in the cultivation of prose. The English lacked a vital tradition of nonpoetic literature, and only with the growth of preaching in the reformed churches did there emerge a vigorous polemical prose. Though English writers, like English poets, drew inspiration and materials from the Italian, they did not immediately produce a vigorous and original narrative art comparable to the dazzling poetry of Spenser or Sidney. The romances and tales collected by such men as William Painter served more as raw material for later poets and dramatists rather than achieving distinction in their own right. Even where an elegant prose appeared, as in the proto-novels of Euphues by John Lyly, the effect was precious rather than profound, tributary rather than autonomous. Lyly's prose plays helped to shape the course of future drama and impelled Shakespeare to sharpen his own prose, yet in his own work, Lyly did not succeed in blending literature and theater as effectively as the poets. Verse thus continued to be the principal vehicle of theatrical expression.

But vibrant and promising as poetry was, the poets had to experiment throughout the last half of the sixteenth century to blend image, accent, and beat into fresh forms. In the course of this period the Greco-Roman gods were naturalized, becoming the familiar inhabitants of English rhetoric and poetry. Yet the best poetry never lost its ties to nature or to the moral architecture that rested on Christian example. However tempted the poets might be by one or another literary tradition, their overriding impulse was to mix ancient and contemporary, native and foreign images together. Concurrently, the poets reacted against the stiff and encrusted meters and rhyme schemes that characterized English tradition. From the Italians they learned a looser rhythm and a form more responsive to private feelings. The sonnet gave them the technique and rhetorical theory gave them the rationale for what they sought: a firm yet flexible means for expressing high-flying thoughts and intense, highly colored passions.

All of these changes influenced dramatic writing. While poets explored the lyric and made it an instrument of sustained emotion, playwrights searched for a rhythmic instrument to present lamentation, romantic love, heady fantasies, moral attitudes. They played with various meters and verse forms. As early as *Gorboduc* in 1561, the two Thomases, Norton and Sackville, had tried blank verse, with limited success. Nevertheless, for nearly thirty years after that, dramatists experimented with quite different meters and with various combinations of rhymed verse. Long favored was the seven-foot line, mockingly known as the "galloping fourteener." Though Shakespeare satirizes it as "Cambises' vein" in the first part of *Henry IV* and parodies it in the play of Pyramus and Thisby in *A Midsummer Night's Dream,* serious playwrights used it repeatedly to convey the most tragic emotions until Marlowe swept it away in the 1580s. Only then, when he showed what a poet could do with a five-foot line of blank verse, did Elizabethan drama find its voice. Yet it was in the course of these experiments and prior to the full popularization of the public playhouse that dramatists absorbed and refined the manifold literary influences of the time.

But if literary developments supplied a language for drama, theatrical conditions helped mold that language into an art. Unlike the case of Italy and, later, France, the conditions in England did not favor ancient example. Classical models were plentiful, and for a time they promised to set the style for English drama. Had they done so, tragedy would have surrendered to rhetorical recital, and the bustling world of diverse characters have yielded to the austerity of the few. But for the classical model to have prevailed, it would have needed a sponsor. One potential—and in part actual—sponsor was the school or university. Several of the most influential early plays, such as *Ralph Roister-Doister* and *Gammer Gurton's Needle,* were school plays. Yet the educational institutions could only encourage the drama; they could not promote a continuing repertory. Nor was the church in a better position to act. Because of the Reformation and the consequent prohibition of religious plays, the church was barred from supporting drama, and indeed the Calvinist sects vigorously opposed theatrical shows, so much so that it took the determined intervention of the court to protect the nascent theater.

Actually, the only institution that could have decisively influenced the course of drama was the court. In Tudor England, virtually all the agencies of the state were arms of the Crown. Queen Elizabeth seldom called—or needed to call—Parliament into session. She reigned through ministers chosen by her personally and responsible to her alone. To her very substantial political powers, furthermore, she imparted an aura of dedication and romance that ultimately made her court the cynosure of the nation. Through the court's control over public entertainment and Elizabeth's cultivation of a public image, the drama could very well have become an extension of the nobility, as it did to a considerable extent in the city-states of Italy. But for that to have happened, Elizabeth would have had to finance plays and shows more extensively, and the court would have had to become the major locus for stage performance.

For a short time it appeared that Elizabeth was prepared to take this route, to foster the theater under her own aegis. She encouraged or at least tolerated the expansion of stage performances by boy choristers and grammar-school students. Dependent on the favor of the Queen, they played frequently at the court. Moreover, the choristers, because of their choral duties, were on an intimate footing with the royal household. In 1583 Elizabeth seemed ready to extend her patronage to adult players. In that year she authorized the formation of a new acting company under her patent. It was named the Queen's men. Composed of the leading actors chosen from existing troupes, the Queen's men appears to have received a monopoly on stage performance, or at least so elevated a status that the company name alone became an assurance of welcome throughout the kingdom. Fortunately for the course of English drama, no such monopoly took hold. The Queen's men had only a brief glory. Within a few years the company lost its principal players through death or retirement, and a remnant was reduced to provincial touring.

This abortive patronage was typical of Elizabeth. In this instance as in so many of her contacts with her subjects, Elizabeth lent her name and her authority to an enterprise, but not very much hard cash. Aside from bringing them to court for occasional performances, she did not single out the Queen's men for special support. Nor did she ever again take players under her wing. Thereafter she left patronage to her nobles. They in turn followed her practice in their own patronage. The great men of her court, the Lord Chamberlain and the Lord Admiral in particular, gave the name of their offices to the actors, but left them to earn a living as best they could. As a result, the players, however much they depended on the goodwill of the court, had to survive by appealing to the public at large rather than to a select clientele.

This dependence on the public coincided with the expansion of London's social and economic life. Even before the defeat of the Spanish Armada in 1588, London had become sufficiently populous and prosperous to warrant the erection of a playhouse devoted solely to stage performance. This occurred in 1576, and the playhouse was named the Theatre. One year later a second playhouse, the Curtain, was constructed nearby. By the end of Elizabeth's reign in 1603, four more playhouses rose on the south banks of the Thames or, in the case of the Fortune, north of the city. These playhouses are the best testimony to the importance that theater had for the metropolis. Thriving trade had made London a lively center for merchants from the city and from abroad. Also contributing to the bustle of the city was the rising prosperity of nobles around Elizabeth who flourished at court by the privileges that the Queen granted them, privileges that were often commercial in nature. Each nobleman was a little monarch, socially, at least. He was the hub of a household that mirrored the court. In his wake came a shoal of attendants: lesser peers, gentry, servants, and hangers-on. Together these households comprised a small city.

The end of the sixteenth century also saw the first signs of a London season. Drawn to London partly by the quarter terms of the law courts, partly by the pleasures of the town, country gentry began to make annual sojourns in the capital. They carried on business, followed the fashions, and tasted the pleasures. In all likelihood they helped to swell the audience for the various playhouses. To them were added visitors from abroad, official and otherwise, who found London a lively city, full of formal and informal entertainment, not the least of which was playgoing. It is from two of these visitors, Johannes deWitt, a Dutchman, and Thomas Platter, a Swiss, that we get the fullest description we have of what occurred in these public playhouses. Apparently it was customary then for a tourist to go to the theater in the same way that today a tourist in Spain attends a bullfight. From these various populations, native and foreign, the theater drew its audience. Given moral but only marginal support from the Crown and having a favorable climate for commercial development, the theater evolved along pragmatic lines as a prosperous business.

The men who forged and benefited from this prosperity were of two kinds: actors and theater owners. The latter were closely connected to the business, but with the possible exception of one of them, Philip Henslowe, the playhouse owners did not influence the art of the English theater significantly. The actors, on the other hand, were directly and fully involved in all phases of production. As members of an acting company, they constituted the core of the English theater. They were the ones who held the patent from one of the great lords. After Elizabeth's death, when they finally came under royal patronage, they were the ones to bear the name of the King or Queen, the Prince or Princess. As His Majesty's servants or the Prince's men, as Queen Anne's men or Lady Elizabeth's servants, they had an immediate link to the royal household.

However much an acting company might depend on a playhouse owner or need the playwrights, the company was the only organization capable of producing plays regularly. Two exceptions should be noted, however. First, during the two brief periods when troupes of boy players were active (before 1590 and between 1599 and 1608), the choral master or theater manager controlled the company. The boys were their wards. Second, after 1605 when the Jacobean court annually sponsored theatrical masques, it was usually the Crown through its representative, principally the designer Inigo Jones, who supervised production. But for the production of the kinds of plays represented in this volume, plays that distinguish English drama to this day, the acting company was responsible. Several of them, including the Lord Admiral's men, performed *Dr. Faustus;* the King's men played *Volpone* and *The Duchess of Malfi;* and the Queen's Majesty's servants, *'Tis Pity She's a Whore.*

An acting company consisted of sharers and hired workers. The sharers were partners, usually the leading actors of the company. They in effect owned the company, or rather its assets: costumes, furniture, and play books. Usually there were ten or twelve sharers in a troupe. Distinct from the sharers were the salaried men and apprentice boys. Most of these were actors too, responsible for the smaller roles and women's parts. The boys, who played the women, were trained by and apprenticed to sharers, although their services were engaged by the company. Besides the actors, there were book-keepers, tire men (costumers), and musicians. As for the playwrights, they were not usually members of a company. None of the playwrights here represented ever became a sharer. Ben Jonson began his career as a hired actor, but he never rose to partnership in one of the companies for which he wrote. Only Shakespeare and Thomas Heywood achieved that position. But these two were sharers by virtue of being actors first and playwrights second. Otherwise, the playwright was a free-lance writer who sold his work to the actors. Once sold, the play no longer belonged to the playwright. It was the property of the company, and as such could be used as the actors saw fit without consulting the original author. They could cut or alter the text or, as happened fairly often, they could hire another writer to revise the play. That was the case with Marlowe's *Dr. Faustus,* which underwent reworking at the hands of Samuel Rowley.

As a free-lance writer, the dramatist could make a living composing plays only if he worked steadily. Sometimes he would write on commission. Sometimes he would collaborate with other writers. Although with few exceptions the best drama was the work of a single poet, nevertheless a loose community of writers did exist who often cooperated on a single play. In actuality, all the major dramatists wrote plays in collaboration at one time or another. What effect that had upon their writing as a whole is hard to say. Yet the fact that three or four men could divide a commission among them suggests that there was rough agreement on how to make a play.

Like the actors, most playwrights came from the middle or lower middle class. Some of them studied at the university —hence the name "University Wits" given to the first generation of popular dramatists, which included Marlowe, George Peele, and Robert Greene. Rather than go into the church (for which the university prepared them) or law (for which they needed money), they sought other means of employment. Unfortunately, men of intellect and talent lacking position and patronage had few outlets. For the would-be writer, opportunities were meager. Although London housed an active publishing industry, much of what was published came from the pens of genteel amateurs. While one could earn a few pence turning out pamphlets and perhaps a little more devising romances and tales, to find continuous employment as a writer one had to turn to the stage.

Again, the peculiar circumstances of the London theater created a huge demand for plays. Despite a substantial playgoing public, the size of the playhouse kept down the number of performances of any one play. Each building held two to three thousand people. Even for an exceptionally popular play, ten or twelve performances a year were the most the actors could reasonably expect. Nor did plays remain long in the repertory. A play that continued to be performed after eighteen months was a runaway hit. Consequently, the actors required a constant supply of new material. At the time Jonson wrote *Volpone* in 1606, three men's companies were performing in London. Among them they needed something like fifty new plays a year. It is this kind of demand that gave rise to the profession of dramatist and created conditions in which a great art could thrive.

To generalize about how these authors satisfied the demand is hazardous. Each man was so different in style and temperament. Yet they shared some common assumptions and practices not only among themselves but with so extraordinary a poet as Shakespeare. We cannot, however, appreciate their achievements by measuring them against Shakespeare's. Though we cannot help but read their plays in his shadow, we must realize that they did not write in that shadow. Undoubtedly Shakespeare's greatness was apparent. But it did not overwhelm or overawe them. Jonson, who claimed to "love the man this side idolatry," certainly did not think himself inferior to Shakespeare. And Webster, at the point that Shakespeare's career was ending, created a tragedy that is strikingly individual in conception and diction. Where there are crosscurrents of influence, as between Marlowe and Shakespeare, it is not at all certain that they all flow one way. It is more likely that Marlowe influenced Shakespeare than that Shakespeare influenced Marlowe. Altogether then, though we may pay more acute attention to the plays by Marlowe, Jonson, and Webster because of Shakespeare, the plays deserve our attention for themselves.

What all the playwrights of the period shared was the need to be storytellers. Elizabethan taste favored a loosely connected, many-scened narrative, full of adventure and variety. That encouraged the dramatists to mix comedy with tragedy, pastoral with farce, one story line with another. Given the size of the acting company and the practice of doubling, dramatists could introduce as many characters as they wanted as long as they did not bring more people onstage for any one scene than the company could muster. This ample and adventurous form, moreover, was housed in a suitable yet deceptive building, a building full of contradictions. Though the Elizabethan playhouse was the first permanent structure for regular performance in Europe, not a single board of one remains, unlike the ruins of Greece and Rome or the preserved jewels of Renaissance Italy. Renowned as a gorgeous place in its own day, to the contemporary mind it is bare and neutral. Graced by costly and magnificent costumes, the stage was open to the foulest weather. Most important, while the playhouse held several thousand people, it was surprisingly compact. Its three rings of galleries hugged an open yard at one end of which was set a large platform. No auditor was very far from a speaker. That is one of the reasons why, proceeding from a long-standing oral tradition familiar to the audience, the playwrights did not hesitate to introduce complex verse into the swift flow of their stories.

These theatrical conditions encouraged and favored a mixture of exciting storytelling and lyric dramatic poetry. Like film and television writers at present, the early English playwrights usually adapted material from other literary or historical sources. In no other way could they meet the demand for so many plays. Furthermore, in the absence of copyright, nothing prevented a dramatist from using any story he found as the basis for a play. Most of Shakespeare's plays derive from another source. The same is true of Marlowe's, Webster's, and Middleton's work. Marlowe drew the raw material of *Doctor Faustus* from the English *Faust Book*. Webster based *The Duchess of Malfi* on the version of actual events recorded by Painter in his collection *The Palace of Pleasure*. Only Jonson persistently sought to devise original events and characters, and then only in his comedies. In his two tragedies, *Sejanus* and *Cataline,* he painstakingly documented all the circumstances and sentiments in the scripts.

The story was not the only thing the playwright adapted. Webster kept a commonplace book into which he copied snatches from his reading so that he could later weave them into his dialogue. He may be an extreme case of phrase gatherer, but he illustrates a general truth about the playwrights. They were omnivorous readers. They plundered classics and modern literature, and they extracted from these sources not only the main lines of a story but the finest details of poetic expression. Despite his striving for originality, Jonson was no less assiduous than Webster in panning for golden thoughts.

But even though there was widespread acceptance of imitation, adaptation, and revision in playwriting, there was equally forceful insistence on invention. The playwright's goal was to fuse the many sources of a play into a coherent work. However much Webster's tragedies may appear to be pastiches of events, phrases, and images gathered from dozens of sources, the final effect is unmistakably and brilliantly Websterian.

This individuality is nowhere more evident than in the imaginative worlds that these playwrights create. They take the entire universe as their province. Faustus' cosmology, whereby he seeks to encompass all climes and all realms, may well stand for the ambition of the poets. In his half-dozen plays Marlowe bestrides Asia and Malta, England and France, Africa and Rome. This readiness to parade the monarchs of the world before the xenophobic Londoners epitomizes the audacity and daring of the writers. For them the stage was a place where one could join the familiar and the exotic. Like Othello telling stories to Desdemona, the dramatists localized tales of wonder, winning admiration by enabling the audience to feel the pulse of rare adventures.

Of all places that sparked the English imagination, Italy was the most exotic. It exerted fear and fascination. It is no coincidence that three of the five plays in this volume are set in the Italian cities of Venice, Parma, and Florence, and yet another one ranges throughout the country. For the English, Italy was a land of intrigue, sensuosity, elegance, and grotesquerie. The few Elizabethan tragedies set in England lack the luxury or mystery found in the southern landscape, and while many plays unfold in France or Spain, Italy was the most frequent and thrilling locale. It is inconsequential whether the Italy of the plays is a genuine Italy verified by travelers' reports or an Italy of the mind, a projection of the erotic and myth-touching notions of English fancy. The stage image of Italy is collective projection, a giant mirror not of what is but of what the audience fantasizes. The Italies of Webster and Jonson, Middleton and Ford embody that attraction and repulsion for politico-sexual scheming in the midst of which the individual struggles, often futilely, to save his or her soul.

The five playwrights represented here span the entire period of Elizabethan and Jacobean drama. It is common to see this period as one of growth, fulfillment, and decay. But that is too simple a sequence. Admittedly, the theater goes through considerable change between 1587, when Marlowe begins writing, and 1633, when Ford publishes *'Tis Pity She's a Whore*. Yet in essentials neither the theatrical profession, the staging practice, nor the dramatic form altered radically. John Ford, whom we think of as a late dramatist, was born in 1586 and grew to maturity during the years when Shakespeare and Jonson wrote their major works. Ford's plays still belong to the stream of dramatic invention that exploded in the 1580s.

The history of English Renaissance drama is, to a large extent, the history of these men. Marlowe, dead at twenty-nine in 1593, created three enormously popular plays within the brief period of six years: *Tamburlaine, Dr. Faustus,* and *The Jew of Malta*. Jonson had his first success in 1598. More than any other poet, he wrote for many different kinds of theater and in different styles, continuing to work well into the 1630s. Paralleling him was Middleton, who turned out comedies, tragedies, and satires from early in the seventeenth century until the mid-1620s. Webster, less prolific than the others, first began collaborating on plays with various writers and then, within a few years after 1610, produced his two masterpieces, *The White Devil* and *The Duchess of Malfi*. Ford, though twenty-four by this time, did not actually begin writing plays until the early 1620s and then went on into the 1630s. Together these five men encompass the beginning, middle, and end of the Elizabethan and Jacobean ages.

Their scripts are a pale and sometimes obscure record of that creative burst. They give us literary echoes of what were once fully resonant voices. In these echoes we are left to detect—insofar as we can—the full vibrancy of the original thought and feeling. The scripts themselves convey these thoughts and feelings with varying degrees of reliability. First, play texts give us only remnants of a threatical event. The infrastructure of performance has to be reconstructed from the many signs and clues in the text. Second, an Elizabethan play text varies considerably in what it represents. It may embody the script that the poet submitted to the actors, it may reflect the play as the actors actually performed it, or it may mix original passages with later revisions. Since a play belonged to the players, the players ostensibly controlled its publication. They often withheld plays from the press to prevent theft. Therefore, printing could be the result of any number of deliberate or accidental circumstances. It might be allowed or surreptitious, carefully surpervised or haphazard. Few dramatists saw their plays through the press. Jonson was an exception, as were, to a lesser extent, Webster and Ford. Jonson, mindful of his literary aspirations and not at all backward in asserting his claims to distinction, carefully prepared the texts of his plays for publication. In 1616, he took the unprecedented step of publishing his play scripts in a folio volume under the impressive title of *The Works of Ben Jonson*. His objective in using the large folio size was not only to assure reliable copy but also to assert his literary standing as a poet. Similarly, Webster made certain that the full script of *The Duchess of Malfi* was printed. By contrast, *Doctor Faustus* was published after Marlowe's death, first in 1604 in a quarto edition that is appreciably different from a later 1616 edition. Yet neither edition is entirely reliable and both require extensive explanation. With few exceptions, then, the plays we have are working scripts that contain the action as it was realized at a certain point either in the author's mind or in the players' work. It would be inaccurate then to regard these scripts as firmly and unalterably fixed. Rather we can consider them as provisional texts with which we can build the world and action of the play. While the text should not be treated lightly or arbitrarily altered, it should also be read with allowance for theatrical flexibility.

In the intervening years between the writing of these plays and our reading of them, interest has ebbed and flowed. While the major works of Shakespeare were never long absent from the stage and never long neglected by readers, the plays of his contemporaries and successors were not so consistently appreciated. Seldom were their plays widely produced, though there were a few works, such as Philip Massinger's *New Way to Pay Old Debts,* that held the stage for many years. For most plays even their familiarity as printed drama diminished. When at last there was a revival of interest in them, it was initially literary and divorced from the theater. Though once so theatrically alive, these plays were treated as poetic literature. The philosophical content of their lines, the juxtaposition of their images, and the portrayal of character—all elements accessible to the reader—assumed first importance. But the interaction between actors-as-characters, the byplay between the spoken word and the visual response, and the give and take of player and audience received little attention. Not until these plays were revived with increasing frequency did their stage life, as distinct from their literary life, become apparent. In the course of the last generation, however, as widespread Shakespearean production has stimulated performance of plays by his contemporaries, we can more readily envision the printed text as vital play. The literary and theatrical views of a work, like separate halves of a stereoptical photograph, can now fuse into a single three-dimensional image. The lesson for the play reader is significant. It teaches that for a play to be adequately appreciated, it needs to be spoken as well as read, conceived as performance as well as imagined as fictional experience.

This flexibility of approach is what the modern imagination brings to these plays. As we have learned more about Elizabethan staging in the last half century and used that learning to produce Shakespeare's plays in new and exciting ways, we have seen contemporary life in Elizabethan shapes. Faustus continues to haunt our minds as the archetypical desire to exceed human limitation. Bertolt Brecht, the German dramatist, and W. H. Auden, the English poet, shared a fascination with the fatal love of the Duchess of Malfi, and followed Elizabethan practice in revising it for modern taste. *Volpone* too has undergone revision, by the German novelist Stephen Zweig, who adapted it in a version that was a huge theatrical success and that later gave rise to a superb French film. More recently, *Volpone* came to life on Broadway as *The Sly Fox,* testifying once again to its persistent vitality.

This contemporary interest stems from the fact that all these plays capture extraordinarily compelling situations that go to the heart of what fascinates and horrifies us in human behavior. However much habits and words have changed since the seventeenth century, the plays dramatize paradoxes that cut through time. Faustus' unbounded ambition is corroded by triviality, Volpone's masterful cleverness is defeated by a blindness to Mosca's treachery, Annabella and Giovanni's genuine love is transmogrified by its violation of a universal taboo. The plays of Webster and Middleton are particularly topical. They show the vulnerability of women who are subject to the power and ego of men, Middleton most notably showing how corrupt men can corrupt women. Remote though these plays are in setting and subject, they continue to astonish us and to address us directly.

Though presented as scripts within a book, these plays, one must remember, have a double life. They are available for reading. Yet they are always waiting to be rediscovered and raised to fresh existence by anyone who can speak and move. They are not sacred objects in danger of being damaged if treated roughly, but robust inventions, ready to be explored again, tested, and made new. They will withstand staging experiments, group readings, and mock rehearsals, not only withstand all these, but through them reveal their power. Despite passages and occasional lines that may be difficult to understand or a style of expression initially alien, the sweep of action and the bursting presence of the characters make these plays images of today as well as yesterday.

General note on play texts:
Material enclosed in square brackets [as thus] indicates passages added by the editor.

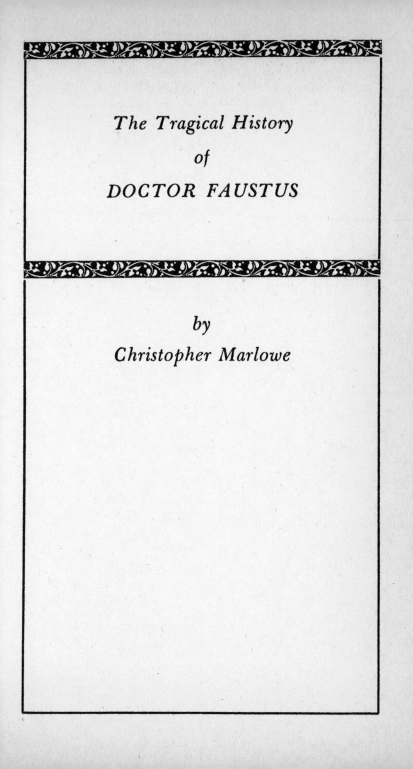

The Tragical History of DOCTOR FAUSTUS

by

Christopher Marlowe

CHRISTOPHER MARLOWE

Christopher Marlowe could well have been a hero in one of his own tragedies. In the six years between the time in 1587 that his Scythian superman, Tamburlaine, dazzled the London stage and the day of his own violent death in a tavern brawl on May 30, 1593, Marlowe lived a strange double life of dramatic poet and secret agent. Details about either life are scanty, yet so suggestive that they invite the most fanciful hypotheses. As a dramatic poet, he composed a string of fabulously successful plays. Cumulatively, they changed the course of English drama. As agent, he was entwined, so it would seem, in the government's espionage network, an involvement that may have led directly to his early death.

The first record of his role as agent appears in a notice issued by the Privy Council to the university authorities at Cambridge. Contrary to what they may have heard, the notice advised, Christopher Marlowe had "done her Majesty good service," and therefore the authorities should permit no obstacle to stand in the way of his receiving his degree as Master of Arts. That "service" seems connected to one or more trips to the Continent, where Marlowe may have spied upon the English Catholics at Rheims. Whatever the truth, it is evident that young Marlowe had friends in high places.

Marlowe had gone to Cambridge University from the city of Canterbury, where he was born in 1564, the year of Shakespeare's birth. Canterbury at that time was the religious center of England. Even before the break with the Roman church, it was the seat of one of the two principal bishoprics in the realm. Under Henry VIII, the Archbishop of Canterbury became Primate of England, and the city one of the great educational and cultural centers. Apparently Marlowe attracted attention as a promising youth. Son of a moderately prosperous shoemaker, he received the important Matthew Parker scholarship to Corpus Christi College at Cambridge. There he went early in 1580, and there he was to remain, on and off, for seven years, years during which he garnered the rich harvest of classical and Renaissance poetry and history that was later to inform his plays.

In the six years that he spent in London, whatever else he did, he seems to have continued his undercover life in some manner while, at the same time, running afoul of the authorities in other respects. Two weeks before his death, the Privy Council issued a warrant for his arrest as part of a sweeping investigation into seditious activities. The councilors, eager to question Marlowe about charges of atheism, directed the arresting officer to seek Marlowe at the home of Sir Thomas Walsingham, the chief of Queen Elizabeth's intelligence agency. For some reason, the arrest was not made, and at the end of May, Marlowe had dinner at Eleanor Bull's tavern at Deptford, where he met his death in suspicious circumstances. The coroner's inquest reported that Ingram Frizer, his killer, had acted in self-defense. Yet the details of the record are not altogether convincing, raising doubt that Marlowe's death was a mere accident.

Meanwhile, Marlowe's other life, as poet and dramatist, was full and amazingly productive. Before his death at the age of twenty-nine, he composed five full-length plays, co-authored one other, left still another unfinished, completed translations of Ovid and Lucan, and wrote a substantial portion of an amorous poem, *Hero and Leander*. In all likelihood, while still at Cambridge he made the translations and probably started, if he did not finish, his first play, *Tamburlaine*. Presumably, Part II of *Tamburlaine* followed hard upon the enthusiastic reception of Part I. In what order the rest of his plays appeared is uncertain, however. The only certainty is that sometime between 1588 and 1593, Marlowe created *Doctor Faustus, The Jew of Malta, Edward II,* and the unfinished *Massacre of Paris.*

It is customary to praise Marlowe as a poet and question his ability as a playwright. His lyric gifts receive universal adulation. Not so his dramatic talents. And yet, in light of contemporary response to his plays, this is a puzzling attitude. Of the five full plays that saw the stage, three were extraordinary hits. From allusions as well as actual theatrical records, the first part of *Tamburlaine, The Jew of Malta,* and *Doctor Faustus* were among the most popular plays of their time. According to Philip Henslowe's account books, *The Jew of Malta* had the greatest number of performances of any play then showing. Only two plays other than *The Jew of Malta* had more performances than *Doctor Faustus.* Moreover, the fifteen recorded performances of *Tamburlaine,* Part I, a hit by Elizabethan standards, came in 1594-95, at least six years after the play opened in London. Even Part II of *Tamburlaine* had a healthy run at this time. *Edward II* alone does not show evidence of wide appeal. That leaves a solid record of four warmly received plays out of five. This percentage of acceptance is remarkable for a playwright, not only of the Elizabethan but of any age. Statistically, if for no other reason, Marlowe must rank as one of the most popular playwrights in history.

But popular success was not his only achievement. Marlowe brought a stunning theatricality to the public playhouse. It was a theatricality that infused both language and action. In the few years leading to the appearance of *Tamburlaine,* English dramatic style became set, and Marlowe did much to set it. For more than thirty years before him, English playwrights and poets had experimented with stage speech. Blank verse was long available, had been used in *Gorboduc,* but languished in favor of other forms. But sometime in the mid-1580s Marlowe, and Thomas Kyd along with him, vitalized blank verse and stormed the stage with it. Whichever of these two men first showed the way, it was Marlowe with his mighty line who hypnotized the London audience. He set the course for tragedy, demonstrating how a poet could run the gamut from proud heroics to tender musing in this pliant verse.

To this powerful medium Marlowe wedded bold and vivid action: the conquest of the world in *Tamburlaine,* the Machiavellian-tinged thirst for wealth in *The Jew of Malta,* the challenge to God in *Doctor Faustus,* and the intertwining of sexual appetite and political warfare in *Edward II.* Eschewing for the most part the careful twisting and turnings of intricate plots, Marlowe aims his characters squarely at achieving the impossible, and endows them, by and large, with the audacity and imagination to pursue the impossible. This posture, though it neglected some of the conventional methods for stimulating dramatic interest, was supremely theatrical. It pitted the tragic hero against the largest forces of inevitability, morality, and fate, and in doing so, gave the stage a cosmic dimension.

This dimension achieves its grandest scale in *The Tragical History of Doctor Faustus.* It is Marlowe's boldest attempt to dramatize man as demigod. While Tamburlaine boasts that he shall rival the gods, Faustus does indeed challenge the celestial and infernal powers to match his aspirations. He draws all knowledge to him. He ranges over the earth to taste its wonders and master them. That he succumbs to powers greater than his own does not demean his attempt. Because he concentrates all the potentialities of mankind within himself, his tragedy is far from personal; his fall implicates the heady and unrestrained longing of all secret dreams. Though Faustus' destruction comes from pride, his pride is an essential and not altogether unworthy spark of the human spirit.

Marlowe drew the material for this tragedy from the half-historical, half-legendary career of a German astrologer and charlatan named John Faustus. An anonymous German writer first told the story of Faustus' compact with the devil and his subsequent exploits, serious as well as comic, in the *Historia von D. Iohan Faustun* in 1587. Five years later an English translation came out as *The Historie of the damnable life, and deserved death of Doctor Iohn Faustus.* This volume is known as the English Faust Book. It is this work that served as the immediate source for Marlowe as well as any others who contributed to the play script. Its appearance as late as 1592 would seem to determine the earliest date for the composition of Marlowe's play. There are, however, allusions and other evidence in *Doctor Faustus* that suggest an earlier date, and these have led some scholars to think that Marlowe may have seen the English Faust Book in manuscript. Be that as it may, Marlowe did utilize the story for virtually all events in the action. But in doing so, he transformed the unscrupulous and rather shallow quack into an everyman extraordinary who is tempted by the unlimited possibilities of the Renaissance imagination, yet obliged to act within the constricted boundaries of medieval morality.

This heady conception of Faustus is, unfortunately, marred by the unevenness of the available texts of the play. There are two versions that have some claim to authority. In both the action begins with Faustus meditating on his accomplishments in philosophy, medicine, law, and theology. He rejects each discipline in turn, finding one after the other superficial in purpose and unworthy of the aspiring mind. At last he turns to the metaphysics of magic. From his friends Valdes and Cornelius he learns how to raise spirits to serve him. Late one night, in a forest grove, he calls the devil Mephostophilis to him, demanding obedience. But Mephostophilis insists on a pact, and while answering some of Faustus' questions, will not heed Faustus without express approval from Lucifer. Here begins Faustus' vacillation, for his Good and Evil Angels appear, as they do repeatedly throughout the play, in order to persuade him to virtue or vice. The Evil Angel prevails, for when Faustus seeks to renege on his allegiance, Lucifer threatens to seize him immediately and then seduces him with the show of the seven deadly sins.

Interspersed among these scenes are comic parallels in which first Wagner, Faustus' student-servant, intimidates the clown Robin with his supposed magical powers. In a later scene Robin impresses his fellow servant Rafe by promising to conjure. These scenes, though they are brief, do throw the central action into relief. By exposing the triviality of Wagner's and then Robin's prospective conjurations, Marlowe, if he was indeed the writer of these scenes, qualifies the grandeur of Faustus' vision.

The action to this point is very much alike in both versions of the play. While there are textural and even scene differences between them, both editions capture the loftiness of Faustus' ideas and the boldness of Marlowe's conception. It is at the end of scene 6, or as it is marked in most contemporary editions, the end of the second act, that the texts diverge.

In the following two acts (scenes 7 through 12), the two versions show a general rather than a precise correspondence. The events themselves are very much the same in each case. But the language, characters, details, and elaboration differ considerably. In both versions Faustus visits the Pope in his papal palace at Rome, later travels to the court of Emperor Charles V, tricks a horsedealer out of his money, and then delights the Duke and Duchess of Vanholt with his art. All of these scenes show Faustus either playing practical jokes or entertaining princes. Measured against Faustus' initial vision, these amusements degrade him and the tragedy.

It is when Faustus approaches the termination of his contract with the devil, that the high seriousness of the early part of the play reappears. He meditates with his fellow scholars, is assailed by his angels, recoils from the accusation of a righteous Old Man, and finally passes through the fires of his final hour on earth. Although differences exist between the two texts in this section, in all essential respects they coincide in revealing Faustus' tragic stature. The primary Marlovian conception dominates these final events that fill scenes 13 and 14 (Act V).

Thus, it is at his beginning and at his end that Faustus

matches the near mythic figures of Tamburlaine and Barabas, the Jew of Malta. In the middle of the play, by contrast, he appears silly and sycophantic. At the Pope's he is merely a spiteful prankster and at the Emperor's a court jester. Even when he produces Alexander the Great, he does so as a performing illusionist. Nothing of the steadfastness of the opening action persists in these scenes, and little of his recurrent spasm of spiritual loss. So sharp is the contrast between the early and middle action that we are driven to account for it outside the play itself.

One of the two versions of the play was printed as a quarto in 1604; it is known as the A-text. The second version, also in quarto, was printed in 1616 and is known as the B-text. Determining which version of these two editions corresponds to Marlowe's original is complicated by the fact that in 1602 two writers, William Birde and Samuel Rowley, were paid to provide additions to *Doctor Faustus*. Since they were given the substantial sum of £4, that is, two-thirds of the amount paid for an entirely new play, we can assume that their additions were considerable. By 1602 the play was no longer new, having been completed at the latest by 1593. It may well have had additions or revisions before those of Birde and Rowley. As a result, the two printed versions may embody one or more sets of changes, and not necessarily the same changes.

With the evidence at our disposal, it is unlikely that we can ever recover the script of *Faustus* as Marlowe first conceived it. The play was too much a creature of the playhouse at a time when theatrical companies were unstable and playing conditions in flux. As a result, the contemporary reader needs to accept the provisional nature of any text of *Doctor Faustus*. Each one embodies a working state of the play. This is indeed true of most Elizabethan drama with its interdependence of playwright and actor. Added to that is the fact that the actors owned the scripts so that they largely controlled its preservation and transmission. The case of *Doctor Faustus* is only a more extreme example of the general instability of texts that prevailed in the late sixteenth century. Therefore, which version of the play we favor will depend partly on a highly technical assessment of the printed texts and partly on our criteria and preferences, whether literary or theatrical.

In assessing the rival merit of the A-text and B-text, we encounter the central complication. There is widespread agreement that the very scenes that differ most in the two versions are precisely those least likely to have been written by Marlowe. Therefore, in establishing the authenticity of one copy rather than another, we are not necessarily getting closer to the original. We should keep this fact in mind, though it does not in itself make both versions of equal reliability.

The standard work on the text of *Doctor Faustus* is W. W. Greg's parallel edition of 1950. In a brilliantly detailed examination of both quartos, he demonstrates the subtle and tantalizing relation between them. He shows that the B-text (Q 1616) was principally derived from a manuscript copy of the play, though some portions were set from one of the printed copies of the A-text (Q 1604). Clearly, the B-text is more regular in its verse and lacks the intrusive exclamations of actors. From this evidence as well as the general character of the A-text, Greg concludes that it is a memorial reconstruction of a group of touring actors. So convincing has Greg made his case that all editions since 1950 have utilized the B-text as the standard.

It is therefore necessary to explain why this edition is based on the earlier A-text, the theatrical copy. Greg argues that the A-text is a corrupt version of the manuscript copy that was preserved in the B-text. At the same time he concedes that it contains revisions, probably those made by Birde and Rowley. According to that argument, the A-text would then be a revision of a revision. It would also be a simplification, since the later copy is more spectacular in its shows and processions. Yet this view doesn't account for several distinctive features of the A-text that may originate not in textual corruption but in theatrical difference. The finale of the play is especially revealing in this respect.

The second, more spectacular version has Lucifer and his cohorts oversee the last hours of Faustus. It introduces the Good and Bad Angels so that they can take leave of Faustus, one rising to heaven, the other descending to hell. In these portions of the finale Faustus plays only a marginal part. Thus, at the climactic moments of his life, the audience is distracted by figures who impart a superficial melodrama to the central tragic action. In doing so, they dispel Faustus' terrifying isolation. This isolation, without benefit of a ring of gloating spirits, accords with those moments of existential confrontation where Tamburlaine contemplates the nature of beauty (Part I, V. ii) or the inevitability of death (Part II, V. ii). Thus, a stage free of Lucifer does not represent a poorer but a legitimate, alternate version of the same action.

In an analogous way, the elaboration of the struggle between Benvolio and Faustus at the Emperor's court (IV. i-iv), found only in the B-text, changes the shape of the entire play. By occupying over three hundred lines in the fourth act, Benvolio's mockery of Faustus, the magician's retaliation, and Benvolio's subsequent efforts at revenge go far beyond the brief illustrative actions that compose the rest of the play. This is material that Greg concedes is non-Marlovian; its retention in a modern edition serves to alter the fundamental rhythm of the tragedy.

The case for using the A-text thus rests on theatrical grounds. It is unquestionably a player's text. Its stage directions and sequence of action embody practices that agree with all we know of staging in the early 1590s. Structurally, it maintains a balance among the illustrative scenes while the B-text allows one episode to grow out of proportion. This is exactly what we find in a parallel circumstance when Ben Jonson supplied additions to Thomas Kyd's *The Spanish Tragedy*. In short, when we consider the relation of the two scripts theatrically rather than verbally, the A-text has its own measure of authority.

Admittedly, given the revisions in the B-text and the unevenness of the A-text, any printed edition is only a stab at reproducing the full glory of the play. It is desirable, therefore, that the modern text not only be flexible but also invite readers to test its qualities through oral reading and class staging. In the present edition, I have followed the A-text (Q 1604) in most respects. At two points I have modified the sequence of scenes, and these changes are noted in the text. In addition, I have included scenes from the B-text that otherwise do not appear in Q 1604. These scenes are set off by angle brackets (< >). There is one exception to this format, however. Because the Benvolio-Faustus conflict alters the structure of the play so thoroughly, the scenes containing this action (IV. i-iv) are relegated to an appendix.

To facilitate comparison between the two versions, the running heads specify which scene in one text matches which scene in the other. For example, the note [10/IV.ii] means that scene 10 in Q 1604 parallels Act IV, scene ii in Q 1616.

The power of the Faust legend is apparent not only from the play, even in its present state, but also from its later treatments, notably by Goethe. Yet Marlowe's version is the only one to hold the stage until this day. Frequently revived, it still fascinates us, even in this era of skepticism. However entrapped Faustus may be in a world of God and Lucifer, his aspiring mind speaks to us, perhaps never more poignantly than today as the contemporary world becomes acutely aware of the limits to its own vaulting ambitions.

[Cast of Characters

Chorus
Doctor Faustus
Wagner, his student-servant
Good Angel
Evil Angel
Valdes } Faustus' friends
Cornelius }
Three Scholars
Mephostophilis
Clown (Robin)
Lucifer, prince of hell
Belzebub, his companion prince
Pride } the Seven Deadly Sins
Covetousness }
Wrath }
Envy }
Gluttony }
Sloth }
Lechery }
Rafe (Dick)°[1]
Pope Adrian
Raymond, King of Hungary
Bruno, rival pope to Adrian
Two Cardinals
Archbishop of Rheims (Cardinal of Lorraine)°
Vintner
Emperor Charles V
Knight
Alexander the Great
His Paramour
Horse-courser
Carter
Hostess
Duke of Vanholt

[1] The degree sign (°) indicates a footnote, which is keyed to the text by the line number. Text references are printed in **boldface** type; the annotation follows in roman type.

Rafe (Dick) In parallel scenes, this character is named Rafe in Q 1604 (scene vii) and Dick in Q 1616 (II. iii). **Archbishop of Rheims (Cardinal of Lorraine)** Parallel characters. The Archbishop appears in Q 1616, the Cardinal in Q 1604.

Duchess of Vanholt
Old Man
Helen of Troy
Devils, Friars, Lords, Servants]
[Additional characters for scenes in appendix: Martino, Frederick, Benvolio, Duke of Saxony, Darius, Soldiers]

Prologue

Enter Chorus.°

Not marching now in fields of Thrasimen,°
Where Mars did mate° the warlike Carthagens,
Nor sporting in the dalliance of love
In courts of kings where state° is overturned,
Nor in the pomp of proud audacious deeds
Intends our muse to vaunt his heavenly verse.
Only this, gentle men: we must perform
The form of Faustus' fortunes, good or bad:
  To patient judgments we appeal our plaud,°
And speak for Faustus in his infancy.
Now is he born of parents base of stock
In Germany within a town called Rhodes;°
At riper years to Wittenberg he went
Whereas his kinsmen chiefly brought him up.
So soon he profits in divinity,
The fruitful plot° of Scholarism graced,
That shortly he was graced with doctor's name,
Excelling all, whose sweet delight disputes°
In heavenly matters of theology;
Till swoll'n with cunning° of a self-conceit,

Prologue s.d. **Chorus** (periodically a choral figure comes on stage, sometimes in the person of Faustus' servant, Wagner, to carry the narrative forward) 1 **fields of Thrasimen** i.e., the fields around Lake Trasimene where the Carthaginians under Hannibal defeated the Romans in 217 B.C. 2 **mate** (the usual sense is "checkmate = overcome" though such a reading suggests that Marlowe thought the Romans had beaten the Carthaginians) 4 **state** political stability 9 **plaud** praise, applause 12 **Rhodes** (actually Roda, a city in Germany) 16 **plot** i.e., of land 18 **whose . . . disputes** whose sweet delight it is to dispute 20 **cunning** intellectual pride

His waxen wings did mount above his reach
And melting, heavens conspired his overthrow.°
For falling to a devilish exercise,
And glutted now with learning's golden gifts,
He surfeits upon cursèd negromancy:°
Nothing so sweet as magic is to him
Which he prefers before his chiefest bliss,°
And this the man that in his study sits.

Exit.

[Scene 1]

Enter Faustus in his study.°

Faustus. Settle thy studies Faustus, and begin
To sound the depth of that thou wilt profess.°
Having commenced,° be a divine in show,
Yet level at the end of every art,
And live and die in Aristotle's works.
Sweet *Analytics,*° 'tis thou hast ravished me.
Bene disserere est finis logices.°
Is to dispute well Logic's chiefest end?
Affords this art no greater miracle?
Then read no more, thou has attained that end.
A greater subject fitteth Faustus' wit:
Bid *on kai me on*° farewell, Galen° come:
Seeing, *ubi desinit philosophus, ibi incipit medicus.*°
Be a physician Faustus, heap up gold,
And be eternized for some wondrous cure.
Summum bonum medicinae sanitas,

21-2 **waxen wings . . . overthrow** (Icarus, by means of wings held together by wax, flew too near the sun; the wax melting, he fell to his death) 25 **negromancy** black magic (also overlaps meaning of necromancy = divination by communicating with the dead) 27 **chiefest bliss** soul's salvation Sc 1 s.d. **study** (an enclosed space revealed by drawing of a curtain) 2 **that . . . profess** that subject you will teach or specialize in 3 **commenced** graduated 6 **Analytics** (two treatises on logic by Aristotle) 7 **Bene . . . logices** (usually though not always Marlowe gives the English translation after the Latin line, here line 8; this quotation actually comes from Peter Ramus, a sixteenth-century anti-Aristotelian) 12 **on kai me on** "being and not being" (Greek) 12 **Galen** Greek physician of second century A.D. 13 **ubi . . . medicus** "where the philosopher finishes, the doctor begins"

The end of Physic° is our body's health.
Why Faustus hast thou not attained that end?
Is not thy common talk sound aphorisms?
Are not thy bills° hung up as monuments
Whereby whole cities have escaped the plague
And thousand desperate maladies been eased,
Yet art thou still but Faustus and a man.
Could'st thou make men to live eternally?
Or being dead raise them to life again?
Then this profession were to be esteemed.
Physic farewell. Where is Justinian?
Si una eademque res legatur duobus, alter rem, alter valorem rei, et cetera.°
A petty case of paltry legacies.
Exhereditare filium non potest pater, nisi°—
Such is the subject of the *Institute*
And universal body of the law.
His study fits a mercenary drudge
Who aims at nothing but external trash,
Too servile and illiberal for me.
When all is done, divinity is best.
Jerome's Bible,° Faustus, view it well.
Stipendium peccati mors est. Ha! *Stipendium et cetera.* The reward of sin is death: That's hard. *Si peccasse negamus, fallimur, et nulla est in nobis veritas.* If we say that we have no sin, we deceive ourselves, and there's no truth in us. Why then belike we must sin, and so consequently die.
Ay, we must die an everlasting death.
What doctrine call you this? *Che serà, serà:*
What will be, shall be! Divinity, adieu.
These Metaphysics° of magicians
And negromantic books are heavenly;
Lines, circles, signs, letters and characters.

17 **Physic** medicine 20 **bills** prescriptions 28-9 **Si . . . et cetera** "If one and the same thing is willed to two persons, one shall have the thing, the other the value of the thing, and so forth" (cited from *Institutes,* a treatise on Roman law compiled under order of the Roman Emperor Justinian) 31 **Exhereditare . . . nisi** "A father cannot disinherit his son unless . . ." 38 **Jerome's Bible** (the Latin translation known as the Vulgate) 49 **Metaphysics** studies beyond physics or natural order

Ay, these are those that Faustus most desires.
O, what a world of profit and delight,
Of power, of honor, of omnipotence
Is promised to the studious artisan!
All things that move between the quiet° poles
Shall be at my command: emperors and kings
Are but obeyed in their several provinces:
Nor can they raise the wind, or rend the clouds.
But his dominion that exceeds in this,
Stretcheth as far as doth the mind of man.
A sound magician is a mighty god.
Here Faustus, try thy brains to gain a deity.

Enter Wagner.

Wagner, commend me to my dearest friends,
The German Valdes and Cornelius,
Request them earnestly to visit me.
Wagner. I will, sir.
Exit.
Faustus. Their conference will be a greater help to me
Than all my labors, plod I ne'er so fast.

Enter the Good Angel and the Evil Angel.

Good Angel. O Faustus, lay that damnèd book aside,
And gaze not on it, lest it tempt thy soul
And heap God's heavy wrath upon thy head.
Read, read the Scriptures; that° is blasphemy.
Evil Angel. Go forward Faustus, in that famous art
Wherein all nature's treasure is contained.
Be thou on earth as Jove is in the sky,
Lord and commander of these elements.
Exeunt.
Faustus. How am I glutted with conceit° of this!
Shall I make spirits fetch me what I please,
Resolve me of all ambiguities,
Perform what desperate enterprise I will?
I'll have them fly to India for gold,
Ransack the ocean for orient° pearl,

56 quiet motionless 73 that i.e., one of the negromantic books
78 conceit idea 83 orient precious

And search all corners of the new-found world
For pleasant fruits and princely delicates.
I'll have them read me strange philosophy,
And tell the secrets of all foreign kings;
I'll have them wall all Germany with brass,
And make swift Rhine circle fair Wittenberg;
I'll have them fill the public schools° with silk
Wherewith the students shall be bravely clad.°
I'll levy soldiers with the coin they bring
And chase the Prince of Parma° from our land,
And reign sole king of all the provinces.
Yea, stranger engines for the brunt of war
Than was the fiery keel° at Antwerp's bridge
I'll make my servile spirits to invent.
Come German Valdes and Cornelius,
And make me blest with your sage conference.

Enter Valdes and Cornelius.

Valdes, sweet Valdes, and Cornelius,
Know that your words have won me at the last
To practice magic and concealèd arts.
Yet not your words only, but mine own fantasy,
That will receive no object for my head
But ruminates on negromantic skill.
Philosophy is odious and obscure,
Both Law and Physic are for petty wits,
Divinity is basest of the three,
Unpleasant, harsh, contemptible, and vile.
'Tis magic, magic that hath ravished me!
Then, gentle friends, aid me in this attempt
And I that have with subtle syllogisms
Graveled° the pastors of the German church,
And made the flow'ring pride of Wittenberg
Swarm to my problems° as th' infernal spirits
On sweet Musaeus° when he came to hell,

90 **public schools** universities 91 **bravely clad** finely clothed 93 **Prince of Parma** Spanish governor-general of the Netherlands, 1579-92 96 **fiery keel** fireship, one of which was used in 1585 to destroy the bridge built by the Prince of Parma to blockade Antwerp 113 **Graveled** confounded 115 **problems** points of disputation 116 **Musaeus** legendary Greek poet

Will be as cunning as Agrippa was,
Whose shadows° made all Europe honor him.
Valdes. Faustus, these books, thy wit, and our experience
Shall make all nations to canonize us.
As Indian Moors° obey their Spanish lords,
So shall the spirits of every element
Be always serviceable to us three:
Like lions shall they guard us when we please,
Like Almain rutters° with their horsemen's staves,
Or Lapland giants trotting by our sides;
Sometimes like women, or unwedded maids,
Shadowing more beauty in their airy brows
Than in the white breasts of the queen of love.
From Venice shall they drag huge argosies,
And from America the golden fleece
That yearly stuffs old Philip's treasury,°
If learnèd Faustus will be resolute.
Faustus. Valdes, as resolute am I in this
As thou to live; therefore object it not.
Cornelius. The miracles that magic will perform
Will make thee vow to study nothing else.
He that is grounded in astrology,
Enriched with tongues,° well seen° in minerals,
Hath all the principles magic doth require.
Then doubt not Faustus but to be renowned
And more frequented° for this mystery°
Than heretofore the Delphian oracle.°
The spirits tell me they can dry the sea
And fetch the treasure of all foreign wracks,
Ay, all the wealth that our forefathers hid
Within the massy entrails of the earth.
Then tell me Faustus, what shall we three want?°

117-18 **Agrippa . . . shadows** Cornelius Agrippa, author of *De occulta philosophia* (1531), who described how to raise "shadows" or images of the dead 121 **Indian Moors** i.e., Indians of the Americas 125 **Almain rutters** German cavalrymen 132 **old Philip's treasury** the plate-fleet of Philip II of Spain ("old" used here familiarly and condescendingly) 139 **tongues** languages (especially the learned ones of Greek and Latin) 139 **seen** skilled 142 **frequented** resorted to 142 **mystery** mastery of an art or craft 143 **Delphian oracle** oracle of Apollo at Delphi renowned for wisdom and foresight 148 **want** lack

Faustus. Nothing, Cornelius. O, this cheers my soul.
Come, show me some demonstrations magical
That I may conjure in some lusty grove
And have these joys in full possession.
Valdes. Then haste thee to some solitary grove,
And bear wise Bacon's and Albanus' works,°
The Hebrew Psalter, and New Testament;
And whatsoever else is requisite
We will inform thee ere our conference cease.
Cornelius. Valdes, first let him know the words of art,
And then, all other ceremonies learned,
Faustus may try his cunning by himself.
Valdes. First I'll instruct thee in the rudiments,
And then wilt thou be perfecter than I.
Faustus. Then come and dine with me, and after meat
We'll canvass every quiddity° thereof
For ere I sleep I'll try what I can do:
This night I'll conjure though I die therefor.
[*Exeunt.*]

[Scene 2]

Enter two Scholars.

1 Scholar. I wonder what's become of Faustus that was wont to make our schools ring with *sic probo.*°
2 Scholar. That shall we know, for see here comes his boy.

Enter Wagner.

1 Scholar. How now sirrah, where's thy master?
Wagner. God in heaven knows.
2 Scholar. Why, dost not thou know?
Wagner. Yes, I know, but that follows not.

154 **Bacon's . . . works** books by Roger Bacon, medieval friar, whose scientific efforts were thought to be magical and by "Albanus," identified inconclusively with Albertus Magnus or Pietro d'Abano, medieval figures noted for scientific interests 164 **every quiddity** the essence of every detail Sc. 2.2 **sic probo** "thus I prove it"

1 Scholar. Go to sirrah, leave your jesting and tell us where he is.

Wagner. That follows not necessary by force of argument, that you being licentiate° should stand upon't; therefore acknowledge your error, and be attentive.

2 Scholar. Why, didst thou not say thou knew'st?

Wagner. Have you any witness on't?

1 Scholar. Yes sirrah, I heard you.

Wagner. Ask thy fellow if I be a thief.

2 Scholar. Well, you will not tell us.

Wagner. Yes sir, I will tell you. Yet if you were not dunces,° you would never ask me such a question. For is he not *corpus naturale,* and is not that *mobile?*° Then wherefore should you ask me such a question? But that I am by nature phlegmatic, slow to wrath, and prone to lechery—to love, I would say—it were not for you to come within forty foot of the place of execution,° although I do not doubt to see you both hanged the next sessions.° Thus having triumphed over you, I will set my countenance like a precisian,° and begin to speak thus: truly my dear brethren, my master is within at dinner with Valdes and Cornelius, as this wine if it could speak would inform your worships, and so the Lord bless you, preserve you, and keep you my dear brethren, my dear brethren.

Exit.

1 Scholar. Nay, then I fear that which I have long suspected,
That he is fall'n into that damnèd art
For which they two are infamous through the world.

2 Scholar. Were he a stranger, not allied to me,
The danger of his soul would make me mourn.

12 **licentiate** academic degree between the bachelor's and the master's 20 **dunces** (besides current sense, dunce retained the older meaning of "a hair-splitting reasoner") 21-2 **corpus . . . mobile** *corpus naturale seu mobile* = a body that is natural or capable of motion (scholastic expression for the subject matter of physics) 26 **place of execution** scene of action, i.e., (1) the dining room and (2) the gallows 28 **sessions** i.e., of the law courts 29 **precisian** Puritan

But come, let us go and inform the rector.°
It may be his grave counsel may reclaim him.
1 Scholar. I fear me nothing will reclaim him now.
2 Scholar. Yet let us see what we can do.
Exeunt.

[Scene 3]

Enter Faustus to conjure.

Faustus. Now that the gloomy shadow of the earth,
Longing to view Orion's drizzling look,°
Leaps from th' antarctic world unto the sky,
And dims the welkin° with her pitchy breath,
Faustus, begin thine incantations
And try if devils will obey thy hest,
Seeing thou hast prayed and sacrificed to them.
Within this circle° is Jehovah's name
Forward and backward anagrammatized,
Th' abbreviated names of holy saints,
Figures of every adjunct to° the heavens,
And characters of signs° and erring stars,°
By which the spirits are enforced to rise:
Then fear not Faustus. But be resolute
And try the utmost magic can perform.
Sint mihi dei Acherontis propitii, valeat numen
triplex Iehovae, ignei, aerii, aquatici, spiritus, salvete.
Orientis princeps, Belzebub inferni ardentis monarcha,
et Demogorgon, propitiamus vos ut appareat et surgat
Mephostophilis. Quid tu moraris? Per Iehovam,

41 **rector** chief officer of the university Sc. 3.2 **Orion's drizzling look** a common description for the constellation Orion which makes its appearance in northern latitudes at the beginning of winter 4 **welkin** sky 8 **circle** i.e., the magic circle drawn by the conjuror as a spell over spirits and a protection against them 11 **adjunct to** body fixed to 12 **signs** i.e., of the Zodiac 12 **erring stars** planets 16-23 **Sint . . . Mephostophilis** "May the gods of Acheron [the lower world] be favorable to me. Away with the triple deity of Jehovah. Hail, spirits of fire, air, and water. Prince of the fire, air, and water. Prince of the East, Belzebub monarch of burning hell, and Demogorgon, we ask your favor that Mephostophilis may appear and rise. Why do

Gehennam, et consecratam aquam quam nunc spargo,
signumque crucis quod nunc facio, et per vota nostra,
ipse nunc surgat nobis dicatus Mephostophilis.°

Enter a Devil.°

I charge thee to return and change thy shape,
Thou art too ugly to attend on me.
Go, and return an old Franciscan friar:
That holy shape becomes a devil best.

Exit Devil.

I see there's virtue in my heavenly words.
Who would not be proficient in this art?
How pliant is this Mephostophilis
Full of obedience and humility,
Such is the force of magic and my spells.
Know Faustus, thou art conjuror laureate
That canst command great Mephostophilis.
Quin redis Mephostophilis fratris imagine?°

Enter Mephostophilis.

Mephostophilis. Now Faustus, what wouldst thou have me do?
Faustus. I charge thee wait upon me whilst I live
To do whatever Faustus shall command,
Be it to make the moon drop from her sphere
Or the ocean to overwhelm the world.
Mephostophilis. I am a servant to great Lucifer
And may not follow thee without his leave.
No more than he commands must we perform.
Faustus. Did not he charge thee to appear to me?

---

you delay? By Jehovah, Gehenna, and the holy water, which now I sprinkle, and the sign of the cross which now I make, and by our vows, let Mephostophilis now arise to obey us." **24 s.d. Devil** (in Q 1616, the word dragon appears after Mephostophilis, line 20, possibly indicating that a figure of a dragon may have appeared momentarily, unseen by Faustus; Faustus' charge to the Devil, i.e., Mephostophilis, to change shape may mean that the Devil first enters as a dragon. The Admiral's men are known to have had a prop dragon for this play) **35 Quin . . . imagine** "Why do you not return, Mephostophilis, in the appearance of a friar?"

Mephostophilis. No, I came now hither of mine own accord.
Faustus. Did not my conjuring raise thee? Speak.
Mephostophilis. That was the cause, but yet *per accidens:*°
For when we hear one rack° the name of God,
Abjure the Scriptures and his savior Christ,
We fly in hope to get his glorious soul.
Nor will we come unless he use such means
Whereby he is in danger to be damned.
Therefore the shortest cut for conjuring
Is stoutly to abjure the Trinity
And pray devoutly to the prince of hell.
Faustus. So Faustus hath already done, and holds this principle,
There is no chief but only Belzebub:°
To whom Faustus doth dedicate himself.
This word "damnation" terrifies not him,
For he confounds hell in Elysium:°
His ghost° be with the old° philosophers.
But leaving these vain trifles of men's souls,
Tell me, what is that Lucifer thy lord?
Mephostophilis. Arch-regent and commander of all spirits.
Faustus. Was not that Lucifer an angel once?
Mephostophilis. Yes Faustus, and most dearly loved of God.
Faustus. How comes it then that he is prince of devils?
Mephostophilis. O, by aspiring pride and insolence,
For which God threw him from the face of heaven.
Faustus. And what are you that live with Lucifer?
Mephostophilis. Unhappy spirits that fell with Lucifer,
Conspired against our God with Lucifer,
And are forever damned with Lucifer.
Faustus. Where are you damned?
Mephostophilis. In hell.
Faustus. How comes it then that thou art out of hell?

47 **the cause . . . accidens** the immediate but not the final cause 48 **rack** torture 57 **Belzebub** (the play treats Belzebub sometimes as identical with Lucifer, sometimes as one of his companion princes in hell) 60 **confounds hell in Elysium** makes no distinction between hell and Elysium (probably with the thought that the Christian hell is as fanciful as the Grecian notion of paradise) 61 **ghost** spirit 61 **old** pagan

Mephostophilis. Why this is hell, nor am I out of it.
Think'st thou that I who saw the face of God,
And tasted the eternal joys of heaven,
Am not tormented with ten thousand hells
In being deprived of everlasting bliss?
O Faustus, leave these frivolous demands
Which strike a terror to my fainting soul.

Faustus. What, is great Mephostophilis so passionate
For being deprivèd of the joys of heaven?
Learn thou of Faustus manly fortitude
And scorn those joys thou never shalt possess.
Go bear these tidings to great Lucifer:
Seeing Faustus hath incurred eternal death
By desperate thoughts against Jove's deity,
Say he surrenders up to him his soul,
So he will spare him four and twenty years,
Letting him live in all voluptuousness,
Having thee ever to attend on me,
To give me whatsoever I shall ask,
To tell me whatsoever I demand,
To slay mine enemies and to aid my friends,
And always be obedient to my will.
Go and return to mighty Lucifer
And meet me in my study at midnight,
And then resolve me of thy master's mind.

Mephostophilis. I will, Faustus.

[*Exit.*]

Faustus. Had I as many souls as there be stars,
I'd give them all for Mephostophilis.
By him I'll be great emperor of the world,
And make a bridge through the moving air
To pass the ocean with a band of men;
I'll join the hills that bind the Afric shore
And make that country continent to° Spain,
And both contributory to my crown.
The Emperor shall not live but by my leave,
Nor any potentate of Germany.
Now that I have obtained what I desire,
I'll live in speculation of this art
Till Mephostophilis return again.

Exit.

109 **continent to** continuous with

[Scene 4]

Enter Wagner and the Clown [*Robin*].

Wagner. Sirrah boy, come hither.

Clown. How, boy? O, disgrace to my person! Swowns° boy, I hope you have seen many boys with such pickadevaunts° as I have. Boy quotha!°

Wagner. Tell me, sirrah, hast thou any comings in?°

Clown. Ay, and goings out° too, you may see else.

Wagner. Alas poor slave, see how poverty jesteth in his nakedness. The villian is bare, and out of service, and so hungry that I know he would give his soul to the Devil for a shoulder of mutton, though it were blood raw.

Clown. How, my soul to the Devil for a shoulder of mutton though 'twere blood raw? Not so, good friend. By'r lady, I had need have it well roasted, and good sauce to it, if I pay so dear.

Wagner. Well, wilt thou serve me, and I'll make thee go like *Qui mihi discipulus*?°

Clown. How, in verse?

Wagner. No sirrah, in beaten° silk and stavesacre.°

Clown. How, how, knave's acre? Ay, I thought that was all the land his father left him. Do you hear, I would be sorry to rob you of your living.°

Wagner. Sirrah, I say, in stavesacre.

Clown. Oho, oho, stavesacre. Then belike, if I were your man, I should be full of vermin.

Wagner. So thou shalt, whether thou beest with me or no. But sirrah, leave your jesting, and bind yourself presently unto me for seven years, or I'll turn all the lice about thee into familiars,° and they shall tear thee in pieces.

Clown. Do you hear, sir? You may save that labor. They

Sc.4.2 **Swowns** God's wounds 4 **pickadevaunts** pointed beards 4 **quotha** says he 5 **comings in** earnings 6 **goings out** (1) expenses, (2) flesh pepping through ragged clothing 17 **Qui mihi discipulus** "One who is my pupil," first words of a well-known poem 19 **beaten** embroidered 19 **stavesacre** seed used to kill vermin 22 **living** income derived from an estate 29 **familiars** spirits

are too familiar with me already. Swowns, they are as bold with my flesh as if they had paid for my meat and drink.

Wagner. Well, do you hear, sirrah? Hold, take these guilders.

Clown. Gridirons. What be they?

Wagner. Why, French crowns.

Clown. 'Mas, but for the name of French crowns,° a man were as good have as many English counters.° And what should I do with these?

Wagner. Why now, sirrah, thou art to be at an hour's warning whensoever or wheresoever the devil shall fetch thee.

Clown. No, no, take your gridirons again.

Wagner. Truly, I'll none of them.

Clown. Truly, but you shall.

Wagner. Bear witness, I gave them him.

Clown. Bear witness, I give them you again.

Wagner. Not I. Thou are pressèd. Prepare thyself, for I will presently raise up two devils to fetch thee away. Baliol and Belcher!

Clown. Let your Balio and your Belcher come here, and I'll knock them, they were never so knocked since they were devils. Say I should kill one of them, what would folks say? Do you see yonder tall fellow in the round slop?° He has killed the devil. So I should be called Kill-devil all the parish over.

Enter two devils, and the Clown runs up and down crying.

<*Wagner.* How now sir, will you serve me now?

Clown. Ay, good Wagner, take away the devil then.>

Wagner. Baliol and Belcher, spirits away.

[*Exeunt.*]

Clown. What, are they gone? A vengeance on them. They have vile long nails. There was a he-devil and a she-devil. I'll tell you how you shall know them. All he-devils has horns, and all she-devils has clefts and cloven feet.

39 **French crowns** heads made bald by syphilis 40 **counters** worthless objects (?) 57 **slop** wide baggy breeches

Wagner. Well sirrah, follow me.

Clown. But, do you hear? If I should serve you, would you teach me raise up Banios and Belcheos?

Wagner. I will teach thee to turn thyself to anything; to a dog, or a cat, or a mouse, or a rat, or anything.

Clown. How? a Christian fellow to a dog or a cat, a mouse or a rat? No, no sir, if you turn me into anything, let it be in the likeness of a little pretty frisking flea, that I may be here and there, and everywhere. O I'll tickle the pretty wenches' plackets.° I'll be amongst them, i'faith.

Wagner. Well sirrah, come.

Clown. But, do you hear, Wagner?

Wagner. How, Baliol and Belcher.

Clown. O Lord, I pray sir, let Banio and Belcher go sleep.

Wagner. Villian, call me Master Wagner, and let thy left eye be diametrically fixed upon my right heel, that thou mayest *quasi vestigias nostras insistere.*°

[*Exit.*]

Clown. God forgive me, he speaks Dutch fustian. Well, I'll follow him. I'll serve him, that's flat.

[*Exit.*]

[Scene 5]

Enter Faustus in his study.

Faustus. Now, Faustus, must thou needs be damned,
And canst thou not be saved?
What boots° it then to think on God or heaven?
Away with such vain fancies, and despair,
Despair in God and trust in Belzebub.
Now go not backward. Faustus, be resolute!
Why waver'st thou? O something soundeth in mine ear
Abjure this magic, turn to God again.
Ay, and Faustus will turn to God again.
To God? He loves thee not
The god thou serv'st is thine own appetite

76 **plackets** aprons or slits in them 84 **quasi . . . insistere** "as if to walk in our footsteps" (ungrammatical, thus appropriate for Wagner) Sc.5.3 **boots it** use is it

Wherein is fixed the love of Belzebub.
To him I'll build an altar and a church
And offer lukewarm blood of newborn babes!

Enter Good Angel and Evil [*Angel.*]

Evil Angel. Go forward, Faustus, in that famous art.
Good Angel. Sweet Faustus, leave that execrable art.
Faustus. Contrition, prayer, repentance: what of them?
Good Angel. O, they are means to bring thee unto heaven.
Evil Angel. Rather illusions, fruits of lunacy,
That make men foolish that do use them most.
Good Angel. Sweet Faustus, think of heaven and heavenly things.
Evil Angel. No Faustus, think of honor and of wealth.
Exeunt.
Faustus. Of wealth?
Why, the signory of Emden° shall be mine.
When Mephostophilis shall stand by me,
What God can hurt thee Faustus? Thou art safe.
Cast no more doubts. Mephostophilis, come,
And bring glad tidings from great Lucifer.
Is't not midnight? Come Mephostophilis,
Veni,° veni, Mephostophile.

Enter Mephostophilis.

Now tell me, what says Lucifer thy Lord?
Mephostophilis. That I shall wait on Faustus whilst he lives,
So he will buy my service with his soul.
Faustus. Already Faustus hath hazarded that for thee.
Mephostophilis. But now thou must bequeath it solemnly
And write a deed of gift with thine own blood,
For that security craves Lucifer.
If thou deny it I must back to hell.
Faustus. Stay Mephostophilis and tell me
What good will my soul do thy lord?
Mephostophilis. Enlarge his kingdom.
Faustus. Is that the reason why he tempts us thus?

24 **signory of Emden** lordship or state of Emden, a wealthy trading port in Germany 30 **Veni** come

Mephostophilis. Solamen miseris socios habuisse doloris.°
Faustus. Why, have you any pain that torture others?
Mephostophilis. As great as have the human souls of men.
But tell me, Faustus, shall I have thy soul?
And I will be thy slave and wait on thee,
And give thee more than thou hast wit to ask.
Faustus. Ay Mephostophilis, I'll give it thee.
Mephostophilis. Then, Faustus, stab thy arm courageously,
And bind thy soul, that at some certain day
Great Lucifer may claim it as his own.
And then be thou as great as Lucifer.
Faustus. Lo, Mephostophilis, for love of thee
I cut my arm and with my proper° blood
Assure my soul to be great Lucifer's,
Chief lord and regent of perpetual night.
View here this blood that trickles from mine arm
And let it be propitious for my wish.
Mephostophilis. But Faustus, thou must
Write it in manner of a deed of gift.
Faustus. Ay so I will. But Mephostophilis,
My blood congeals and I can write no more.
Mephostophilis. I'll fetch thee fire to dissolve it straight.
[*Exit.*]
Faustus. What might the staying of my blood portend?
Is it unwilling I should write this bill?°
Why streams it not, that I may write afresh.
Faustus gives to thee his soul. Ah, there it stayed.
Why shouldst thou not? Is not thy soul thine own?
Then write again, Faustus gives to thee his soul.

Enter Mephostophilis with a chafer° of coals.

Mephostophilis. Here's fire. Come Faustus, set it° on.
Faustus. So, now the blood begins to clear again.
Now will I make an end immediately.
Mephostophilis. O, what will not I do to obtain his soul!
Faustus. Consummatum est.° This bill is ended,
And Faustus hath bequeathed his soul to Lucifer.
But what is this inscription on mine arm?

43 Solamen . . . doloris "It is a comfort for misery to have friends in sorrow." **55 proper** own **66 bill** contract 70 s.d. **chafer** pan, saucer 71 **it** i.e., the 'saucer' with Faustus' blood 75 **Consummatum est** "It is finished," last words of Christ on the cross

Homo fuge.° Whither should I fly?
If unto God, He'll throw me down to hell.
My senses are deceived, here's nothing writ.
I see it plain. Here in this place is writ,
Homo fuge, yet shall not Faustus fly.

Mephostophilis. I'll fetch him somewhat to delight his mind. *Exit.*

Enter with Devils giving crowns and rich apparel to Faustus, and dance, and then depart.

Faustus. Speak Mephostophilis, what means this show?

Mephostophilis. Nothing Faustus, but to delight thy mind
And to show thee what magic can perform.

Faustus. But may I raise up spirits when I please?

Mephostophilis. Ay Faustus, and do greater things than these.

Faustus. Then there's enough for a thousand souls.
Here Mephostophilis, receive this scroll,
A deed of gift of body and of soul:
But yet conditionally that thou perform
All articles prescribed between us both.

Mephostophilis. Faustus, I swear by hell and Lucifer
To effect all promises between us.

Faustus. Then hear me read them.
"On these conditions following:
First, that Faustus may be a spirit in form and substance.
Secondly, that Mephostophilis shall be his servant and at his command.
Thirdly, that Mephostophilis shall do for him, and bring him whatsoever.
Fourthly, that he shall be in his chamber or house invisible.
Lastly, that he shall appear to the said John Faustus at all times in what form or shape soever he please.
I, John Faustus of Wittenberg, Doctor, by these presents, do give both body and soul to Lucifer, prince of the east, and his minister Mephostophilis, and furthermore grant unto them that four and

78 **Homo fuge** "Man, fly!"

twenty years being expired, the articles above written being inviolate, full power to fetch or carry the said John Faustus, body and soul, flesh, blood, or goods, into their habitation wheresoever.

By me John Faustus.

Mephostophilis. Speak Faustus, do you deliver this as your deed?

Faustus. Ay, take it, and the devil give thee good of it.

Mephostophilis. So now Faustus, ask me what thou wilt.

Faustus. First will I question with thee about hell.
Tell me, where is the place that men call hell?

Mephostophilis. Under the heavens.

Faustus. Ay, but whereabout?

Mephostophilis. Within the bowels of these elements
Where we are tortured and remain forever.
Hell hath no limits, nor is circumscribed
In one self place, but where we are is hell,
And where hell is there must we ever be.
And to conclude, when all the world dissolves
And every creature shall be purified
All places shall be hell that is not heaven.

Faustus. Come, I think hell's a fable.

Mephostophilis. Ay, think so still, till experience change thy mind!

Faustus. Why, think'st thou then that Faustus shall be damned?

Mephostophilis. Ay, of necessity, for here's the scroll
Wherein thou hast given thy soul to Lucifer.

Faustus. Ay, and body too, but what of that?
Think'st thou that Faustus is so fond° to imagine
That after this life there is any pain?
Tush, these are trifles and mere old wives' tales.

Mephostophilis. But Faustus I am an instance to prove the contrary,
For I am damned and am now in hell.

Faustus. Nay, and this be hell, I'll willingly be damned here.
What, sleeping, eating, walking, and disputing?
But leaving this, let me have a wife, the fairest maid in Germany, for I am wanton and lascivious and cannot live without a wife.

137 fond foolish

Mephostophilis. How, a wife? I prithee Faustus, talk not of a wife.

Faustus. Nay, sweet Mephostophilis, fetch me one, for I will have one.

Mephostophilis. Well, thou wilt have one.
Sit there till I come. I'll fetch thee a wife in the devil's name.

Enter with a devil dressed like a woman with fireworks.

Mephostophilis. Tell, Faustus, how dost thou like thy wife?

Faustus. A plague on her for a hot whore.

[*Exit devil.*]

Mephostophilis. Tut Faustus,
Marriage is but a ceremonial toy.
If thous lovest me, think no more of it.
I'll cull° thee out the fairest courtesans,
And bring them every morning to thy bed.
She whom thine eye shall like, thy heart shall have,
Be she as chaste as was Penelope,°
As wise as Saba,° or as beautiful
As was bright Lucifer before his fall.
Hold, take this book and peruse it thoroughly.
The iterating° of these lines brings gold,
The framing° of this circle on the ground
Brings whirlwinds, tempests, thunder and lightning.
Pronounce this thrice devoutly to thyself,
And men in armor shall appear to thee,
Ready to execute what thou desir'st.

Faustus. Thanks, Mephostophilis, yet fain would I have a book wherein I might behold all spells and incantations, that I might raise up spirits when I please.

Mephostophilis. Here they are in this book.

There turn to them.°

Faustus. Now would I have a book where I might see all characters and planets of the heavens, that I might know their motions and dispositions.

159 **cull** choose 162 **Penelope** Ulysses' faithful wife 163 **Saba** the Queen of Sheba 166 **iterating** repetition 167 **framing** drawing 175 s.d. **them** i.e., spells and incantations (this and the following stage directions suggest that Faustus turns the pages of several books one after the other)

Mephostophilis. Here they are too. [*Turn to them.*]
Faustus. Nay, let me have one book more, and then I have done, wherein I might see all plants, herbs and trees that grow upon the earth.
Mephostophilis. Here they be.
Faustus. O, thou art deceived.
Mephostophilis. Tut, I warrant thee. *Turn to them.*

[Scene 6°]

Faustus. When I behold the heavens, then I repent
And curse thee, wicked Mephostophilis,
Because thou hast deprived me of those joys.
Mephostophilis. Why Faustus,
Think'st thou heaven is such a glorious thing?
I tell thee, 'tis not half so fair
As thou or any man that breathe on earth.
Faustus. How prov'st thou that?
Mephostophilis. 'Twas made for man, therefore is man more excellent.
Faustus. If it were made for man, 'twas made for me.
I will renounce this magic and repent.

Enter Good Angel, and Evil Angel.

Good Angel. Faustus, repent yet: God will pity thee.
Evil Angel. Thou art a spirit: God cannot pity thee.
Faustus. Who buzzeth in mine ears I am a spirit?
Be I a devil, yet God may pity me
Ay, God will pity me, if I repent.
Evil Angel. Ay, but Faustus never shall repent.
Exeunt.
Faustus. My heart is hardened, I cannot repent.
Scarce can I name salvation, faith, or heaven,
But fearful echoes thunder in mine ears.

Scene 6/II.ii (Q 1616 inserts a speech by Wagner as a bridge between II.i and II.ii, but it is only a portion of a longer speech used between II.iii and III.i. Q 1604, however, maintains a continuous action, lines 172-185 of scene 5 appearing only in this version. For purpose of reference to other editions, I begin a new scene here)

Faustus, thou art damned: then swords and knives,
Poison, guns, halters, and envenomed steel
Are laid before me to dispatch myself,
And long ere this I should have slain myself,
Had not sweet pleasure conquered deep despair.
Have not I made blind Homer sing to me
Of Alexander's love and Oenon's° death?
And hath not he° that built the walls of Thebes
With ravishing sound of his melodious harp
Made music with my Mephostophilis?
Why should I die then, or basely despair?
I am resolved, Faustus shall ne'er repent.
Come Mephostophilis, let us dispute again
And argue of divine astrology.°
Speak, are there many spheres above the moon?
Are all celestial bodies but one globe
As is the substance of this centric earth?

Mephostophilis. As are the elements, such are the heavens,
Even from the moon unto the empyreal orb
Mutually folded in each others' spheres,
And jointly move upon one axle-tree,
Whose terminè is termed the world's wide pole.
Nor are the names of Saturn, Mars, or Jupiter
Feigned but are erring stars.

Faustus. But tell me, have they all one motion,
Both *situ et tempore?*°

Mephostophilis. All jointly move from east to west in four and twenty hours upon the poles of the world but differ in their motions upon the poles of the zodiac.

Faustus. Tush, these slender trifles Wagner can decide.
Hath Mephostophilis no greater skill?
Who knows not the double motion of the planets?
The first is finished in a natural day,°
The second thus. As Saturn in thirty years,

27 **Oenon's death** (Oenone slew herself when her lover Alexander, i.e., Paris, died; he had deserted her for Helen of Troy) 28 **he** Amphion, whose music raised the walls of Thebes 34 **astrology** (what follows is an unorthodox variation of Ptolemaic astronomy which placed the earth at the center of successive spheres of moon, planets, firmament, and finally the motionless and invisible *coelum empyreum* of God) 46 **situ et tempore** in place and in time 53 **natural day** twenty-four hours

Jupiter in twelve, Mars in four, the sun, Venus, and Mercury in a year: the moon in twenty-eight days. Tush, these are freshmen's suppositions. But tell me, hath every sphere a dominion or *intelligentia*?°

Mephostophilis. Ay.

Faustus. How many heavens or spheres are there?

Mephostophilis. Nine: the seven planets, the firmament, and the empyreal heaven.

<*Faustus.* But is there not *coelum igneum et crystallinum*?°

Mephostophilis. No Faustus, they be but fables.>

Faustus. Resolve me then in this one question. Why are not conjunctions, oppositions, aspects, eclipses all at one time,° but in some years we have more, in some less?

Mephostophilis. Per inaqualem motum respectu totius.°

Faustus. Well, I am answered. Now tell me, who made the world?

Mephostophilis. I will not.

Faustus. Sweet Mephostophilis, tell me.

Mephostophilis. Move° me not, for I will not tell thee.

Faustus. Villain, have I not bound thee to tell me anything?

Mephostophilis. Ay, that is not against our kingdom, but this is.
Think thou on hell Faustus, for thou art damned.

Faustus. Think Faustus upon God that made the world.

Mephostophilis. Remember this. *Exit.*

Faustus. Ay, go accursèd spirit to ugly hell.
'Tis thou hast damned distressèd Faustus' soul:
Is't not too late?

Enter Good Angel and Evil Angel.

Evil Angel. Too late.

Good Angel. Never too late, if Faustus can repent.

58-9 **intelligentia** guiding angelic intelligence 64-5 **coelum igneum et crystallinum** spheres of fire and of crystal 69 **at one time** according to a single measure of time 71-2 **Per . . . totius** "Because of unequal motion in respect to the whole" 76 **Move** urge

Bad Angel. If thou repent, devils will tear thee in pieces.
Good Angel. Repent, and they shall never raze° thy skin.
Exeunt.
Faustus. O Christ, my savior, my savior!
Help to save distressèd Faustus' soul.

Enter Lucifer, Belzebub,° and Mephostophilis.

Lucifer. Christ cannot save thy soul, for he is just.
There's none but I have interest in the same.
Faustus. O, what art thou that look'st so terribly?
Lucifer. I am Lucifer
And this is my companion prince in hell.
Faustus. O Faustus, they are come to fetch thy soul.
Lucifer. We come to tell thee thou dost injure us.
Thou talk'st of Christ contrary to thy promise.
Thou should'st not think of God. Think of the Devil,
And his dam too.
Faustus. Nor will I henceforth. Pardon me in this,
And Faustus vows never to look to heaven,
Never to name God, or to pray to him,
To burn his Scriptures, slay his ministers,
And make my spirits pull his churches down.
Lucifer. Do so, and we will highly gratify thee.
Faustus, we are come from hell to show thee some pastime. Sit down and thou shalt see all the Seven Deadly Sins appear in their proper shapes.

Faustus. That sight will be as pleasing unto me as Paradise was to Adam, the first day of his creation.

Lucifer. Talk not of Paradise, nor creation, but mark the show. Talk of the Devil, and nothing else. Come away.

Enter the Seven Deadly Sins.

Now Faustus, examine them of their several names and dispositions.

Faustus. What art thou? the first.

Pride. I am Pride. I disdain to have any parents. I am

90 **raze** scratch 92 s.d. **Belzebub** (in this version Belzebub has no lines; in Q 1616, he speaks the following lines: 103, part of 105, 106, 113-116, 122-23)

like to Ovid's flea,° I can creep into every corner of a wench. Sometimes, like a periwig I sit upon her brow, or like a fan of feathers, I kiss her lips. Indeed I do. What do I not? But fie, what a scent is here! I'll not speak another word, except the ground were perfumed and covered with cloth of arras.°

Faustus. Thou art a proud knave indeed. What art thou? the second.

Covetousness. I am Covetousness, begotten of an old churl in an old leathern bag;° and might I have my wish, I would desire that this house, and all the people in it were turned to gold that I might lock you up in my good chest, O my sweet gold.

Faustus. What art thou? the third.

Wrath. I am Wrath. I had neither father nor mother. I leapt out of a lion's mouth when I was scarce half an hour old and ever since I have run up and down the world with this case° of rapiers, wounding myself when I had nobody to fight withal. I was born in hell, and look to it, for some of you shall be my father.

Faustus. What art thou? the fourth.

Envy. I am Envy, begotten of a chimney-sweeper and an oyster-wife.° I cannot read and therefore wish all books were burned. I am lean with seeing others eat. O, that there would come a famine through all the world, that all might die and I live alone. Then thou should'st see how fat I would be. But must thou sit and I stand? Come down with a vengeance.

Faustus. Away, envious rascal. What art thou? the fifth.

Gluttony. Who? I sir? I am Gluttony. My parents are all dead, and the devil a penny they have left me, but a bare pension: and that is thirty meals a day and ten bevers,° a small trifle to suffice nature. I come of a

120 **Ovid's flea** (the poet of the lascivious medieval poem *Carmen de pulce,* once thought to be by Ovid, envisions a flea making free with his beloved's body) 125 **cloth of arras** tapestrylike cloth 129 **leathern bag** possibly a money bag 137 **case** pair 142-43 **chimney-sweeper and an oyster-wife** (therefore filthy and smelling bad) 153 **bevers** drinks or light meals

royal parentage. My father was a gammon of bacon, and my mother was a hogshead of claret wine. My godfathers were these: Peter Pickle-herring and Martin Martlemas-beef. O but my godmother, she was a jolly gentlewoman, and well-beloved in every good town and city. Her name was Mistress Margery March-beer. Now Faustus, thou hast heard all my progeny.° Wilt thou bid me to supper?

Faustus. No. I'll see thee hanged. Thou wilt eat up all my victuals.

Gluttony. Then the devil choke thee.

Faustus. Choke thyself, glutton. What art thou? the sixth.

Sloth. I am Sloth. I was begotten on a sunny bank, where I have lain ever since, and you have done me great injury to bring me from thence. Let me be carried thither again by Gluttony and Lechery. I'll not speak another word for a king's ransom.

Faustus. And what are you, Mistress Minx? the seventh and last.

Lechery. Who, I, I sir? I am one that loves an inch of raw mutton° better than an ell of fried stockfish,° and the first letter of my name begins with Lechery.

Lucifer. Away to hell, to hell.

Exeunt the Sins.

Now Faustus, how dost thou like this?

Faustus. O, this feeds my soul.

Lucifer. Tut Faustus, in hell is all manner of delight.

Faustus. O, might I see hell and return again, how happy were I then!

Lucifer. Faustus, thou shalt. I will send for thee at midnight.
Meantime take this book, peruse it thoroughly,
And thou shalt turn thyself into what shape thou wilt.

Faustus. Great thanks mighty Lucifer.
This will I keep as chary as my life.

Lucifer. Farewell Faustus, and think on the devil.

Faustus. Farewell great Lucifer. Come Mephostophilis.

Exeunt omnes.

160 progeny offspring (a malapropism) **174 raw mutton** here, a lewd allusion to a virile penis **174 an ell of fried stockfish** forty-five inches of dried codfish

[Scene 7]

Enter Robin° the Ostler with a book in his hand.

Robin. O, this is admirable! Here I ha' stolen one of Doctor Faustus' conjuring books, and i'faith I mean to search some circles for my own use. Now will I make all the maidens in our parish dance at my pleasure stark naked before me, and so by that means I shall see more than ere I felt or saw yet.

Enter Rafe calling Robin.

Rafe. Robin, prithee come away. There's a gentleman tarries to have his horse, and he would have his things rubbed and made clean. He keeps such a chafing with my mistress about it, and she has sent me to look thee out. Prithee, come away.

Robin. Keep out,° keep out, or else you are blown up. You are dismembered, Rafe. Keep out, for I am about a roaring piece of work.

Rafe. Come, what doest thou with that same book, thou canst not read?

Robin. Yes, my master and my mistress shall find that I can read, he for his forehead, she for her private study. She's born to bear with me, or else my art fails.

Rafe. Why, Robin, what book is that?

Robin. What book? Why, the most intolerable book for conjuring that ere was invented by any brimstone devil.

Rafe. Canst thou conjure with it?

Robin. I can do all these things easily with it: first, I can make thee drunk with ipocras° at any tavern in Europe for nothing. That's one of my conjuring works.

Rafe. Our master parson says that's nothing.

Robin. True Rafe, and more Rafe, if thou hast any mind to Nan Spit our kitchen maid, then turn her and wind

Sc. 7 s.d. **Robin** the same character as the Clown in scene 4 (this scene is numbered scene 8 in Greg) 12 **Keep out** i.e., of the magic circle that the Clown has drawn 25 **ipocras** concoction of wine and spices

her to thy own use, as often as thou wilt, and at midnight.

Rafe. O brave Robin, shall I have Nan Spit, and to mine own use? On that condition I'll feed thy devil with horsebread° as long as he lives, of free cost.

Robin. No more, sweet Rafe. Let's go and make clean our boots which lie foul upon our hands, and then to our conjuring in the devil's name.

[*Exeunt*.]

[Chorus]

Enter Wagner solus.

Wagner. Learned Faustus,
To know the secrets of Astronomy,
Graven in the book of Jove's high firmament,
Did mount himself to scale Olympus' top.
Being seated in a chariot burning bright,
Drawn by the strength of yoky dragon's necks,
He now is gone to prove Cosmography,°
And as I guess, will first arrive at Rome,
To see the Pope, and manner of his court,
And take some part of holy Peter's feast,
That to this day is highly solemnized.

[*Exit Wagner*.]

[Scene 8°]

Enter Faustus and Mephostophilis.

Faustus. Having now, my good Mephostophilis,
Passed with delight the stately town of Trier,°
Environed round with airy mountain tops,
With walls of flint, and deep-entrenchèd lakes,

34 **horsebread** bread made from beans, bran, etc. for horses
Chorus 7 **Cosmography** description of heaven and earth
Scene 8 (this scene is marked scene 7 in Greg) 2 **Trier** city in the valley of the Moselle

Not to be won by any conquering prince:
From Paris next, coasting the realm of France,
We saw the river Main fall into Rhine,
Whose banks are set with groves of fruitful vines.
Then up to Naples, rich Campania,
Whose buildings fair and gorgeous to the eye,
The streets straight forth and paved with finest brick,
Quarters the town in four equivalents.
There saw we learnèd Maro's° golden tomb,
The way he cut an English mile in length
Through a rock of stone in one night's space.
From thence to Venice, Padua, and the rest,
In midst of which a sumptuous temple stands
That threats the stars with her aspiring top,
Whose frame is paved with sundry colored stones
And roofed aloft with curious work in gold.
Thus hitherto hath Faustus spent his time.
But tell me now, what resting-place is this?
Hast thou, as erst I did command,
Conducted me within the walls of Rome?

Mephostophilis. I have, my Faustus, and for proof thereof
This is the goodly palace of the Pope,
And 'cause we are no common guests
I choose his privy chamber for our use.

Faustus. I hope his Holiness will bid us welcome.

Mephostophilis. Tut, 'tis no matter, man.
We'll be bold with his good cheer.
And now my Faustus, that thou may'st perceive
What Rome containeth to delight thee with.
Know that this city stands upon seven hills
That underprop the groundwork of the same:
Just through the midst runs flowing Tiber's stream
With winding banks that cut it in two parts,
Over the which four stately bridges lean
That make safe passage to each part of Rome.
Upon the bridge called Ponte Angelo
Erected is a castle passing strong
Within whose walls such store of ordinance are,
And double cannons, framed of carvèd brass,

13 **Maro** Virgil, considered a magician as well as a poet in the medieval period

As match the number of the days contained
Within the compass of one complete year:
Beside the gates and high pyramides°
That Julius Caesar brought from Africa.
Faustus. Now, by the kingdoms of infernal rule,
Of Styx, of Acheron, and the fiery lake
Of ever-burning Phlegethon,° I swear
That I do long to see the monuments
And situation of bright-splendent Rome.
Come therefore, let's away.
Mephostophilis. Nay stay my Faustus. I know you'd see the Pope
And take some part of holy Peter's feast,
<The which this day with high solemnity,
This day, is held through Rome and Italy
In honor of the Pope's triumphant victory.
Faustus. Sweet Mephostophilis, thou pleasest me.
Whilst I am here on earth let me be cloyed
With all things that delight the heart of man.
My four and twenty years of liberty
I'll spend in pleasure and in dalliance,
That Faustus' name, whilst this bright frame doth stand,
May be admirèd through the furthest land.
Mephostophilis. 'Tis well said, Faustus, come then, stand by me
And thou shalt see them come immediately.
Faustus. Nay stay, my gentle Mephostophilis,
And grant me my request, and then I go.
Thou know'st, within the compass of eight days
We viewed the face of heaven, of earth, and hell.
So high our dragons soared into the air
That looking down the earth appeared to me
No bigger than my hand in quantity.
There did we view the kingdoms of the world,
And what might please mine eye I there beheld.
Then in this show let me an actor be
That this proud Pope may Faustus' cunning see.
Mephostophilis. Let it be so, my Faustus, but first stay
And view their triumphs as they pass this way.
And then devise what best contents thy mind

46 **pyramides** obelisk (four syllables) 49-50 **Of Styx . . . Phlegethon** rivers in Hades

By cunning in thine art to cross the Pope
Or dash the pride of this solemnity:
To make his monks and abbots stand like apes
And point like antics° at his triple crown,
To beat the beads about the friars' pates,
Or clap huge horns upon the cardinals' heads,
Or any villainy thou canst devise—
And I'll perform it, Faustus. Hark, they come.
This day shall make thee be admired° in Rome.

Enter the Cardinals and Bishops, some bearing crosiers, some the pillars; Monks and Friars singing their procession; then the Pope and Raymond King of Hungary, with Bruno led in chains.

Pope. Cast down our footstool.
Raymond. Saxon Bruno, stoop,
Whilst on thy back his Holiness ascends
Saint Peter's chair and state° pontifical.
Bruno. Proud Lucifer, that state belongs to me.
But thus I fall to Peter, not to thee.
Pope. To me and Peter shalt thou grov'lling lie
And crouch before the papal dignity.
Sound trumpets then, for thus Saint Peter's heir
From Bruno's back ascends Saint Peter's chair.

A flourish while he ascends.

Thus as the gods creep on with feet of wool
Long ere with iron hands they punish men,
So shall our sleeping vengeance now arise,
And smite with death thy hated enterprise.
Lord Cardinals of France and Padua,
Go forthwith to our holy consistory,°
And read amongst the statutes decretal°
What by the holy council held at Trent
The sacred synod° hath decreed for him

85 **antics** grotesque creatures 90 **admired** wondered at 93 **state** chair of state, but here, authority 105 **consistory** office of the papal consistory or senate 106 **statutes decretal** laws issued by papal decree 108 **synod** general council

That doth assume the papal government
Without election and a true consent.
Away, and bring us word with speed.
1 Cardinal. We go my lord.

Exeunt [*two*] *Cardinals.*

Pope. Lord Raymond—[*Aside to him.*]
Faustus. Go haste thee, gentle Mephostophilis,
Follow the cardinals to the consistory,
And as they turn their superstitious books,
Strike them with sloth and drowsy idleness,
And make them sleep so sound, that in their shapes,
Thyself and I, may parley with this Pope,
This proud confronter of the Emperor.
And in despite of all his holiness
Restore this Bruno to his liberty
And bear him to the States of Germany.
Mephostophilis. Faustus, I go.
Faustus. Dispatch it soon.
The Pope shall curse that Faustus came to Rome.

Exit Faustus and Mephostophilis.

Bruno. Pope Adrian,° let me have some right of law.
I was elected by the Emperor.
Pope. We will depose the Emperor for that deed
And curse the people that submit to him.
Both he and thou shalt stand excommunicate
And interdict from church's privilege
And all society of holy men.
He grows too proud in his authority,
Lifting his lofty head above the clouds,
And like a steeple overpeers the church.
But we'll pull down his haughty insolence.
And as Pope Alexander° our progenitor,°
Trod on the neck of German Frederick,
Adding this golden sentence to our praise:
"That Peter's heirs should tread on emperors
And walk upon the dreadful adder's back,

127 **Adrian** a reference either to Hadrian IV or Hadrian VI; although the individuals and events in this scene are not historical, the conflict does correspond in broad outline to that between Pope and Emperor in the time of Hadrian IV, 1154-59 138 **Alexander** Alexander III excommunicated the Emperor Frederick Barbarossa in 1160 138 **progenitor** predecessor

Treading the lion and the dragon down,
And fearless spurn the killing basilisk"°
So will we quell that haughty schismatic
And by authority apostolical
Depose him from his regal government.

Bruno. Pope Julius swore to princely Sigismond,°
For him and the succeeding Popes of Rome,
To hold the emperors their lawful lords.

Pope. Pope Julius did abuse the church's rites
And therefore though we would, we cannot err.
Is not all power on earth bestowed on us?
And therefore though we would, we cannot err.
Behold this silver belt whereto is fixed
Seven golden keys fast sealed with seven seals
In token of our sevenfold power from heaven
To bind or loose, lock fast, condemn, or judge,
Resign° or seal, or whatso pleaseth us.
Then he and thou and all the world shall stoop,
Or be assured of our dreadful curse
To light as heavy as the pains of hell.

Enter Faustus and Mephostophilis like the cardinals.

Mephostophilis. Now tell me Faustus, are we not fitted well?

Faustus. Yes Mephostophilis, and two such cardinals
Ne'er served a holy Pope as we shall do.
But whilst they sleep within the consistory
Let us salute his reverend Fatherhood.

Raymond. Behold my lord, the cardinals are returned.

Pope. Welcome grave fathers, answer presently,°
What have our holy council there decreed
Concerning Bruno and the Emperor
In quittance of their late conspiracy
Against our state and papal dignity?

Faustus. Most sacred patron of the church of Rome,
By full consent of all the synod
Of priests and prelates it is thus decreed:

144 **basilisk** fabled serpent whose glance was deadly 148 **Pope Julius . . . Sigismond** (ahistorical, though the Emperor Sigismund played a role in healing a schism in the church early in the fifteenth century) 159 **Resign** unseal 169 **presently** at once

That Bruno and the German Emperor
Be held as lollards° and bold schismatics
And proud disturbers of the church's peace.
And if that Bruno by his own assent,
Without enforcement of the German peers,
Did seek to wear the triple diadem,
And by your death to climb Saint Peter's chair,
The statutes decretal have thus decreed:
He shall be straight condemned of heresy,
And on a pile of fagots burnt to death.

Pope. It is enough. Here, take him to your charge
And bear him straight to Ponte Angelo,°
And in the strongest tower enclose him fast.
Tomorrow, sitting in our consistory
With all our college of grave cardinals,
We will determine of his life or death.
Here, take his triple crown along with you,
And leave it in the church's treasury.
Make haste again,° my good lord cardinals,
And take our blessing apostolical.

Mephostophilis. So, so, was never devil thus blessed before.

Faustus. Away sweet Mephostophilis, be gone!
The cardinals will be plagued for this anon.

Exeunt Faustus and Mephostophilis [*with Bruno.*]

Pope. Go presently and bring a banquet forth,
That we may solemnize Saint Peter's feast,
And with Lord Raymond, King of Hungary,
Drink to our late and happy victory. *Exeunt.*>

<[III.ii] *A sennet° while the banquet is brought in, and then enter Faustus and Mephostophilis in their own shapes.*

Mephostophilis. Now Faustus, come prepare thyself for mirth.
The sleepy cardinals are hard at hand
To censure Bruno, that is posted hence,
And on a proud-paced steed as swift as thought

178 **lollards** heretics 188 **Ponte Angelo** i.e., the castle at Ponte Angelo 195 **again** i.e., to return III.ii.s.d. **sennet** set of notes on trumpet or cornet

Flies o'er the Alps to fruitful Germany,
There to salute the woeful Emperor.

Faustus. The Pope will curse them for their sloth today
That slept both Bruno and his crown away.
But now, that Faustus may delight his mind
And by their folly make some merriment,
Sweet Mephostophilis, so charm me here
That I may walk invisible to all
And do whate'er I please unseen of any.

Mephostophilis. Faustus, thou shalt. Then kneel down presently,
Whilst on thy head I lay my hand
And charm thee with this magic wand.
First wear this girdle, then appear
Invisible to all are here:
The planets seven, the gloomy air,
Hell, and the Furies' forkèd hair,°
Pluto's blue fire,° and Hecat's tree°
With magic spells so compass thee
That no eye may thy body see.
So Faustus, now for all their holiness,
Do what thou wilt, thou shalt not be discerned.

Faustus. Thanks Mephostophilis. Now friars, take heed
Lest Faustus make your shaven crowns to bleed.

Mephostophilis. Faustus, no more. See where the cardinals come.

Enter Pope [and Friars] and all the Lords [with King Raymond and the Archbishop of Rheims]. Enter the [two] Cardinals with a book.

Pope. Welcome lord cardinals. Come, sit down.
Lord Raymond, take your seat. Friars, attend,
And see that all things be in readiness
As best beseems this solemn festival.

1 Cardinal. First may it please your sacred Holiness
To view the sentence of the reverend synod
Concerning Bruno and the Emperor.

20 **forkèd hair** (instead of hair the Furies had forked-tongued snakes upon their heads) 21 **blue fire** i.e., flames of hell 21 **Hecat's tree** gallows tree (?)

Pope. What needs this question? Did I not tell you
Tomorrow we would sit i' th' consistory
And there determine of his punishment?
You brought us word, even now, it was decreed
That Bruno and the cursèd Emperor
Were by the holy council both condemned
For loathèd lollards and base schismatics.
Then wherefore would you have me view that book?

1 Cardinal. Your Grace mistakes. You gave us no such charge.

Raymond. Deny it not; we all are witnesses
That Bruno here was late delivered you
With his rich triple crown to be reserved
And put into the church's treasury.

Both Cardinals. By holy Paul we saw them not.

Pope. By Peter you shall die
Unless you bring them forth immediately.
Hale them to prison, lade their limbs with gyves.°
False prelates, for this hateful treachery
Cursed be your souls to hellish misery.

Exeunt Attendants with two Cardinals.

Faustus. So, they are safe. Now Faustus, to the feast.
The Pope had never such a frolic guest.>

Pope. My Lord of Lorraine,° wilt please you draw near.

Faustus. Fall to, and the devil choke you, an you spare.

Pope. How now, whose that which spake? Friars, look about.

Friar. Here's nobody, if it like your Holiness.

Pope. My Lord, here is a dainty dish was sent me from the Bishop of Milan.

Faustus. I thank you, sir. *Snatch it.*

Pope. How now, whose that which snatched the meat from me? Will no man look? My Lord, this dish was sent me from the Cardinal of Florence.

Faustus. You say true. I'll ha' it.

Pope. What again? My Lord, I'll drink to your grace.

Faustus. I'll pledge your grace.

Pope. <My wine gone too? Ye lubbers, look about
And find the man that doth this villainy,

52 **gyves** shackles 57 **Lord of Lorraine** (in Q 1604 it is the Cardinal of Lorraine who is the chief guest rather than Lord Raymond or the Archbishop of Rheims)

Or by our sanctitude you all shall die.
I pray, my Lords, have patience at this
Troublesome banquet.>

Lord. My Lord, it may be some ghost newly crept out of purgatory come to beg a pardon of your holiness.

Pope. It may be so. Friars, prepare a dirge to lay the fury of this ghost. Once again, my Lord, fall to.

The Pope crosseth himself.

Faustus. What, are you crossing yourself?
Well, use that trick no more, I would advise you.

Cross again.

Faustus. Well, there's the second time. Aware the third, I give you fair warning.

[The Pope makes the sign of the] cross again, and Faustus hits him a box of the ear, and they all run away.

Faustus. Come on, Mephostophilis, what shall we do?

Mephostophilis. Nay I know not. We shall be cursed with bell, book, and candle.°

Faustus. How? bell, book, and candle, candle, book, and bell,
Forward and backward, to curse Faustus to hell.
Anon you shall hear a hog grunt, a calf bleat, and an ass bray, because it is St. Peter's holy day.

Enter all the Friars to sing the dirge.

Friar. Come brethren, let's about our business with good devotion.

Sing this. Cursed be he that stole away his holiness' meat from the table.

Maledicat dominus.°

Cursed be he that struck his holiness a blow on the face.

Maledicat dominus.

Cursed be he that took Friar Sandelo a blow on the pate.

Maledicat dominus.

Cursed be he that disturbeth our holy dirge.

Maledicat dominus.

86 bell, book, and candle the instruments of excommunication
95 Maledicat dominus "the Lord curse him"

Cursed be he that took away his holiness' wine.
Maledicat dominus.
Et omnes sancti amen.

[*Faustus and Mephostophilis*] *beat the friars, and fling fireworks among them, and so exeunt.*

[Scene 9]

Enter Robin and Rafe with a silver goblet.

Robin. Come Rafe. Did not I tell thee, we were forever made by this Doctor Faustus' book? *Ecce signum,*° here's a simple purchase for horse-keepers. Our horses shall eat no hay as long as this lasts.

Enter the Vintner.

Rafe. But Robin, here comes the vintner.

Robin. Hush. I'll gull him supernaturally. Drawer, I hope all is paid for. God be with you. Come, Rafe.

Vintner. Soft sir, a word with you. I must have a goblet paid from you ere you go.

Robin. I, a goblet Rafe. Ay, a goblet? I scorn you. And you are but a *et cetera.* I a goblet? Search me.

Vintner. I mean so, sir, with your favor.

[*Searches him.*]

Robin. How say you now?

Vintner. I must say somewhat to your fellow. You, sir.

Rafe. Me sir? me sir? Search your fill. Now sir, you may be ashamed to burden honest men with a matter of truth.

Vintner. Well, t'one of you hath this goblet about you.

Robin. You lie, Drawer, 'tis afore me. Sirrah you, I'll teach ye to impeach honest men. Stand by. I'll scour you for a goblet. Stand aside you had best, I charge you in the name of Belzebub. Look to the goblet, Rafe.

Vintner. What mean you, sirrah?

Sc. 9.2 Ecce signum "behold the sign"

Robin. I'll tell you what I mean. *He reads.* *Sanctobulorum Periphrasticon.* Nay, I'll tickle you, Vintner. Look to the goblet, Rafe. *Polypragmos Belseborams framanto pacostiphos tostu*° *Mephostophilis, &c.*

Enter Mephostophilis, sets squibs° *at their backs; they run about.*

[*Mephostophilis exits.*]

Vintner. O nomine Domine,° what meanst thou, Robin thou hast no goblet.

Rafe. Peccatum peccatorum,° here's thy goblet, good Vintner.

Robin. Misericordia pro nobis,° what shall I do? Good devil, forgive me now, and I'll never rob thy library more.

Enter to them Mephostophilis.

Mephostophilis. Vanish villains, th'one like an ape, another like a bear, the third an ass, for doing this enterprise.
Monarch of hell, under whose black survey
Great potentates do kneel with awful fear,
Upon whose altars thousand souls do lie,
How am I vexed with these villains' charms!
From Constantinople am I hither come,
Only for pleasure of these damned slaves.

Robin. How, from Constantinople? You have had a great journey. Will you take six pence in your purse to pay for your supper, and be gone?

Mephostophilis. Well, villiains, for your presumption, I transform thee into an ape, and thee into a dog, and so be gone. *Exit.*

25-7 **Sanctobulorum . . . tostu** nonsense Latin 28 s.d. **squibs** kind of fireworks 29 **nomine Domine** "in the name of the Lord" (this and the two succeeding exclamations are feeble attempts by the Clowns to keep Mephostophilis at bay with Latin tags) 31 **Peccatum peccatorum** "sin of sins" 33 **Misericordia pro nobis** "have mercy on us"

Robin. How, into an ape? That's brave. I'll have fine sport with the boys. I'll get nuts and apples enow.

Rafe. And I must be a dog.

Robin. I'faith, thy head will never be out of the potage° pot. *Exeunt.*

[Chorus]

Enter Chorus.

When Faustus had with pleasure ta'en the view
Of rarest things, and royal courts of kings,
He stayed his course, and so returned home,
Where such as bear his absence but with grief,
I mean his friends and nearest companions,
Did gratulate his safety with kind words.
And in their conference of what befell,
Touching his journey through the world and air,
They put forth questions of Astrology,
Which Faustus answered with such learned skill,
As they admired and wondered at his wit.
Now is his fame spread forth in every land,
Amongst the rest the Emperor is one,
Carolus the fifth, at whose palace now
Faustus is feasted amongst his noblemen.
What there he did in trial of his art,
I leave untold, your eyes shall see performed.

Exit.

[Scene 10]

Enter Emperor, Faustus, and a Knight, with Attendants.

Emperor. Master doctor Faustus, I have heard strange report of thy knowledge in the black art. How that none in my empire nor in the whole world can compare with thee for the rare effects of magic. They say thou hast a

54 **potage** soup

familiar spirit by whom thou canst accomplish what thou list. This therefore is my request: that thou let me see some proof of thy skill, that mine eyes may be witnesses to confirm what mine ears have heard reported. And here I swear to thee, by the honor of mine imperial crown, that whatever thou doest, thou shalt be no ways prejudiced or endamaged.

Knight. I'faith, he looks much like a conjuror. *aside.*

Faustus. My gracious sovereign, though I must confess myself far inferior to the report men have published, and nothing answerable to the honor of your imperial majesty, yet for that love and duty binds me thereunto, I am content to do whatsoever your majesty shall command me.

Emperor. Then Doctor Faustus, mark what I shall say. As I was sometime solitary set, within my closet, sundry thoughts arose about the honor of mine ancestors. How they had won by prowess such exploits, got such riches, subdued so many kingdoms, as we that do succeed, or they that shall hereafter possess our throne, shall, I fear me, never attain to that degree of high renown and great authority. Among which kings is Alexander the Great, chief spectacle of the world's preeminence,
The bright shining of whose glorious acts
Lightens the world with his reflecting beams,
As when I hear but motion° made of him,
It grieves my soul I never saw the man.
If, therefore, thou, by cunning of thine art,
Canst raise this man from hollow vaults below
Where lies entombed this famous conqueror,
And bring with him his beauteous paramour,
Both in their right shapes, gestures, and attire
They used to wear during their time of life,
Thou shalt both satisfy my just desire,
And give me cause to praise thee whilst I live.

Faustus. My gracious lord, I am ready to accomplish your request, so far forth as by art and power of my spirit I am able to perform.

Knight. I'faith, that's just nothing at all. *aside.*

Sc. 10. 30 **motion** mention, reference

Faustus. But if it like your grace, it is not in my ability to present before your eyes the true substantial bodies of those two deceased princes which long since are consumed to dust.

Knight. Ay marry, master doctor, now there's a sign of grace in you, when you will confess the truth.

aside.

Faustus. But such spirits as can lively° resemble Alexander and his paramour shall appear before your Grace, in that manner that they best lived in, in their most flourishing estate, which I doubt not shall sufficiently content your imperial majesty.

Emperor. Go to, master doctor, let me see them presently.

Knight. Do you hear, master doctor? You bring Alexander and his paramour before the emperor?

Faustus. How then, sir?

Knight. I'faith, that's as true as Diana turned me to a stag.°

Faustus. No sir, but when Actaeon died, he left the horns for you. Mephostophilis, be gone.

Exit Mephostophilis.

Knight. Nay, and you go to conjuring, I'll be gone.

Exit Knight.

Faustus. I'll meet with you anon for interrupting me so. Here they are, my gracious lord.

Enter Mephostophilis with Alexander and his paramour.

Emperor. Master doctor, I heard this lady, while she lived, had a wart or mole in her neck. How shall I know whether it be so or no?

Faustus. Your highness may boldly go and see.

Exit Alexander.

Emperor. Sure, these are no spirits, but the true substantial bodies of those two deceased princes.

Faustus. Wilt please your highness now to send for the knight that was so pleasant with me here of late?

Emperor. One of you call him forth.

50 **lively** lifelike 59 **Diana . . . stag** (for peeping at her while she was bathing, Diana turned Actaeon into a stag to be torn to pieces by his own hunting dogs)

Enter the Knight with a pair of horns° on his head.

Emperor. How now, sir knight? Why, I had thought thou hadst been a bachelor. But now I see thou hast a wife, that not only gives thee horns, but makes thee wear them. Feel on thy head.

Knight. Thou damned wretch, and execrable dog,
Bred in the concave of some monstrous rock.
How dar'st thou thus abuse a gentleman?
Villain, I say, undo what thou hast done.

Faustus. O not so fast sir. There's no haste but good. Are you remembered how you crossed me in my conference with the Emperor? I think I have met with you for it.

Emperor. Good master doctor, at my entreaty, release him. He hath done penance sufficient.

Faustus. My gracious lord, not so much for the injury he offered me here in your presence, as to delight you with some mirth, hath Faustus worthily requited this injurious knight, which being all I desire, I am content to release him of his horns. And sir knight, hereafter speak well of scholars. Mephostophilis, transform him straight. Now, my good lord, having done my duty, I humbly take my leave.

Emperor. Farewell, master doctor. Yet ere you go, expect from me a bounteous reward. *Exit Emperor.*

[Scene 11]

[*Faustus and Mephostophilis remain on stage.*]

Faustus. Now Mephostophilis, the restless course that time doth run with calm and silent foot,
Shortening my days and thread of vital life,
Calls for the payment of my latest years.
Therefore, sweet Mephostophilis, let us make haste to Wittenberg.

Mephostophilis. What, will you go on horse back, or on foot?

Faustus. Nay 'til I am past this fair and pleasant green, I'll walk on foot.

73 s.d. **horns** the sign of a cuckold

Enter a Horse-courser.°

Horse-courser. I have been all this day seeking one master Fustian. 'Mas, see where he is. God save you, master doctor.

Faustus. What, Horse-courser, you are well met.

Horse-courser. Do you hear, sir? I have brought you forty dollars for your horse.

Faustus. I cannot sell him so. If thou lik'st him for fifty, take him.

Horse-courser. Alas sir, I have no more. I pray you speak for me.

Mephostophilis. I pray you, let him have him. He is an honest fellow, and he has a great charge, neither wife nor child.

Faustus. Well, come give me your money. My boy will deliver him to you. But I must tell you one thing before you have him. Ride him not into the water at any hand.

Horse-courser. Why sir, will he not drink of all waters?

Faustus. O yes, he will drink of all waters. But ride him not into the water. Ride him over hedge or ditch, or where thou wilt, but not into the water.

Horse-courser. Well, sir. Now am I made man forever. I'll not leave my horse for forty. If he had but the quality of hey ding, hey ding, ding, ding, I'd make a brave living on him. He has a buttock so slick as an eel. Well, god b'ye sir. Your boy will deliver him me. But hark ye sir, if my horse be sick, or ill at ease, if I bring his water to you, you'll tell me what it is?

Faustus. Away, you villain. What doest think I am a horse-doctor? *Exit Horse-courser.*
What art thou, Faustus, but a man condemned to die?
Thy fatal time doth draw to final end.
Despair doth drive distrust unto my thoughts.
Confound these passions with a quiet sleep.
Tush, Christ did call the thief upon the cross,
Then rest thee Faustus, quiet in conceit.

Sleep in his chair.

Sc. 11. 10 s.d. **Horse-courser** horse-dealer

Enter Horse-courser all wet, crying.

Horse-courser. Alas, alas, Doctor Fustian quoth 'a. 'Mas Doctor Lopus° was never such a doctor; has given me a purgation,° has purged me of forty dollars. I shall never see them more. But yet like an ass as I was, I would not be ruled by him, for he bade me I should ride him into no water. Now, I thinking my horse had had some rare quality that he would not have had me know of, I, like a ventrous youth,° rid him into the deep pond at the town's end. I was no sooner in the middle of the pond, but my horse vanished away, and I sat upon a bottle° of hay, never so near drowning in my life. But I'll seek out my doctor, and have my forty dollars again, or I'll make it the dearest horse. O, yonder is his snipper snapper. Do you hear? you, hey, pass, where's your master?

Mephostophilis. Why sir, what would you? You cannot speak with him.

Horse-courser. But I will speak with him.

Mephostophilis. Why, he's fast asleep. Come some other time.

Horse-courser. I'll speak with him now, or I'll break his glass-windows° about his ears.

Mephostophilis. I tell thee, he has not slept this eight nights.

Horse-courser. And he have not slept this eight weeks, I'll speak with him.

Mephostophilis. See where he is fast asleep.

Horse-courser. Ay, this is he. God save ye, master doctor. Master doctor, master doctor Fustian, forty dollars, forty dollars for a bottle of hay.

Mephostophilis. Why, thou seest he hears thee not.

Horse-courser. So, ho, ho: so, ho, ho.

Hallow in his ear.

47 **Doctor Lopus** the Jewish physician Roderigo Lopez, tried for treason in February 1594 and executed in June 48 **purgation** laxative 53 **ventrous youth** venturous, hence inexperienced fellow 56 **bottle** bundle 67 **glass-windows** (this suggests that Faustus is at home)

No, will you not wake? I'll make you wake ere I go.

Pull him by the leg, and pull it away.

Alas, I am undone. What shall I do?

Faustus. O my leg, my leg. Help Mephostophilis, call the officers. My leg, my leg.

Mephostophilis. Come, villain, to the Constable.

Horse-courser. O Lord sir, let me go, and I'll give you forty dollars more.

Mephostophilis. Where be they?

Horse-courser. I have none about me. Come to my hostelry, and I'll give them you.

Mephostophilis. Be gone quickly.

Horse-courser runs away.

Faustus. What, is he gone? Farewell he. Faustus has his leg again, and the Horse-courser, I take it, a bottle of hay for his labor. Well, this trick shall cost him forty dollars more.

Enter Wagner.

How now, Wagner, what's the news with thee?

Wagner. Sir, the Duke of Vanholt doth earnestly entreat your company.

Faustus. The Duke of Vanholt! An honorable gentleman, to whom I must be no niggard of my cunning. Come, Mephostophilis, let's away to him. *Exeunt.*

<[IV.vi] *Enter* [*Robin the*] *Clown, Dick, Horse-courser, and a Carter.*

Carter. Come my masters, I'll bring you to the best beer in Europe. What ho, hostess! Where be these whores?

Enter Hostess.

Hostess. How now? What lack you? What, my old guests, welcome.

Robin. [*aside*] Sirrah Dick, dost thou know why I stand so mute?

Dick [*aside*] No Robin, why is't?

Robin. [*aside*] I am eighteen pence on the score.° But say nothing. See if she have forgotten me.

IV.vi.8 on the score in debt

Hostess. Who's this that stands so solemnly by himself? What, my old guest!

Robin. O, hostess, how do you? I hope my score stands still.

Hostess. Ay, there's no doubt of that, for methinks you made no haste to wipe it out.

Dick. Why hostess, I say, fetch us some beer!

Hostess. You shall, presently.—Look up into th' hall there, ho! *Exit.*

Dick. Come sirs, what shall we do now till mine hostess comes?

Carter. Marry sir, I'll tell you the bravest tale how a conjurer served me. You know Doctor Fauster?

Horse-courser. Ay, a plague take him! Here's some on's have cause to know him. Did he conjure thee too?

Carter. I'll tell you how he served me. As I was going to Wittenberg t'other day with a load of hay, he met me and asked me what he should give me for as much hay as he could eat. Now sir, I thinking that a little would serve his turn, bad him take as much as he would for three farthings. So he presently gave me my money and fell to eating; and as I am a cursen° man, he never left eating till he had eat up all my load of hay.

All. O monstrous, eat a whole load of hay!

Robin. Yes yes, that may be, for I have heard of one that has eat a load of logs.°

Horse-courser. Now sirs, you shall hear how villainously he served me. I went to him yesterday to buy a horse of him, and he would by no means sell him under forty dollars. So sir, because I knew him to be such a horse as would run over hedge and ditch and never tire, I gave him his money. So, when I had my horse, Doctor Fauster bade me ride him night and day and spare him no time. "But," quoth he, "in any case ride him not into the water." Now sir, I thinking the horse had had some quality that he would not have me know of, what did I but rid him into a great river—and when I came just in the midst, my horse vanished away and I sate straddling upon a bottle of hay.

All. O brave doctor!

31 cursen i.e., Christian **35 eat a load of logs** been drunk (?)

Horse-courser. But you shall hear how bravely I served him for it. I went me home to his house, and there I found him asleep. I kept ahallowing and whooping in his ears, but all could not wake him. I seeing that, took him by the leg and never rested pulling till I had pulled me his leg quite off, and now 'tis at home in mine hostry.°

Dick. And has the doctor but one leg then? That's excellent, for one of his devils turned me into the likeness of an ape's face.

Carter. Some more drink, hostess!

Robin. Hark you, we'll into another room and drink awhile, and then we'll go seek out the doctor.

Exeunt omnes.>

[Scene 12]

Enter to them [*Faustus and Mephostophilis*] *the Duke, and the Duchess; the Duke speaks.*

Duke. Believe me, master doctor, this merriment hath much pleased me.

Faustus. My gracious lord, I am glad it contents you so well. But it may be, Madame, you take no delight in this. I have heard that great bellied women do long for some dainties or other. What is it, Madame? Tell me, and you shall have it.

Duchess. Thanks, good master doctor. And for I see your courteous intent to pleasure me, I will not hide from you the thing my heart desires. And were it now summer, as it is January, and the dead time of the winter, I would desire no better meat than a dish of ripe grapes.

Faustus. Alas, Madame, that's nothing. Mephostophilis, be gone. *Exit Mephostophilis.* Were it a greater thing than this, so it could content you, you should have it.

Enter Mephostophilis with the grapes.

Here they be, madame. Wilt please you taste on them?

Duke. Believe me, master doctor, this makes me wonder above the rest, that being in the dead time of winter,

60 hostry i.e., hostelry

and in the month of January, how you should come by these grapes.

Faustus. If it like your grace, the year is divided into two circles over the whole world, that when it is here winter with us, in the contrary circle it is summer with them, as in India, Saba, and farther countries in the East. And by means of a swift spirit that I have, I had them brought hither, as ye see.° How do you like them, Madame? Be they good?

Duchess. Believe me, master doctor, they be the best grapes that ere I tasted in my life before.

Faustus. I am glad they content you so, Madame.

<*The Clowns* [*Robin, Dick, Carter, and Horse-courser*] *bounce° at the gate within.*

Duke. What rude disturbers have we at the gate? Go pacify their fury, set it ope,
And then demand of them what they would have.

They knock again and call out to talk with Faustus.

A Servant. Why, how now masters, what a coil° is there!
What is the reason° you disturb the Duke?

Dick. We have no reason for it, therefore a fig for him!

Servant. Why saucy varlets, dare you be so bold!

Horse-courser. I hope sir, we have wit enough to be more bold than welcome.

Servant. It appears so. Pray be bold elsewhere
And trouble not the Duke.

Duke. What would they have?

Servant. They all cry out to speak with Doctor Faustus.

Carter. Ay, and we will speak with him.

Duke. Will you sir? Commit° the rascals.

Dick. Commit with us! He were as good commit with his father as commit with us!

Sc. 12. 21-26 **If . . . as ye see** (this passage follows the source in the English Faust Book literally, which accounts for the confusion between east-west and north-south) 30 s.d. **bounce** knock 34 **coil** noisy row 35 **reason** pronounced "raisin" 45 **Commit** put in prison

Faustus. I do beseech your Grace, let them come in.°
They are good subject for a merriment.
Duke. Do as thou wilt, Faustus, I give thee leave.
Faustus. I thank your Grace.

Enter [Robin] the Clown, Dick, Carter, and Horse-courser.

Why, how now my good friends?
'Faith, you are too outrageous; but come near,
I have procured your pardons. Welcome all.

Robin. Nay sir, we will be welcome for our money, and we will pay for what we take. What ho, give's half a dozen of beer here, and be hanged!

Faustus. Nay, hark you, can you tell me where you are?

Carter. Ay, marry can I, we are under heaven.

Servant. Ay, but Sir Sauce-box, know you in what place?

Horse-courser. Ay ay, the house is good enough to drink in. Zounds, fill us some beer, or we'll break all the barrels in the house and dash out all your brains with your bottles.

Faustus. Be not so furious. Come, you shall have beer.
My Lord, beseech you give me leave awhile;
I'll gage my credit° 'twill content your Grace.
Duke. With all my heart, kind doctor, please thyself.
Our servants and our court's at thy command.

Faustus. I humbly thank your Grace.—Then fetch some beer.

Horse-courser. Ay, marry, there spake a doctor indeed! And 'faith, I'll drink a health to thy wooden leg for that word.

Faustus. My wooden leg? What dost thou mean by that?

Carter. Ha, ha, ha, dost hear him Dick? He has forgotten his leg.

Horse-courser. Ay ay, he does not stand much upon° that.

Faustus. No, 'faith, not much upon a wooden leg.

Carter. Good lord, that flesh and blood should be so frail

48 **let . . . in** (the clowns appear to be offstage during this portion of the dialogue) 66 **gage my credit** pledge my reputation 77 **stand much upon** attach too much importance to

with your worship! Do not you remember a horse-courser you sold a horse to?

Faustus. Yes, I remember I sold one a horse.

Carter. And do you remember you bid he should not ride into the water?

Faustus. Yes, I do very well remember that.

Carter. And do you remember nothing of your leg?

Faustus. No, in good sooth.

Carter. Then I pray remember your curtsy.°

Faustus. I thank you sir.

Carter. 'Tis not so much worth. I pray you tell me one thing.

Faustus. What's that?

Carter. Be both your legs bedfellows every night together?

Faustus. Would'st thou make a colossus° of me that thou askest me such questions?

Carter. No, truly sir, I would make nothing of you, but I would fain know that.

Enter Hostess with drink.

Faustus. Then I assure thee certainly they are.

Carter. I thank you, I am fully satisfied.

Faustus. But wherefore dost thou ask?

Carter. For nothing, sir, but methinks you should have a wooden bedfellow of one of 'em.

Horse-courser. Why, do you hear sir, did not I pull off one of your legs when you were asleep?

Faustus. But I have it again now I am awake. Look you here sir.

All. O horrible! Had the doctor three legs?

Carter. Do you remember sir, how you cozened me and eat up my load of—

Faustus charms him dumb.

Dick. Do you remember how you made me wear an ape's—

[*Faustus charms him.*]

Horse-courser. You whoreson conjuring scab! Do you remember how you cozened me with a ho—

[*Faustus charms him.*]

88 **curtsy** ("make a leg" was synonymous with "curtsy") 94 **colossus** monumental statue bestriding the entrance to the harbor at Rhodes

Robin. Ha' you forgotten me? You think to carry it away with your "hey-pass" and "re-pass"?° Do you remember the dog's fa— [*Faustus charms him.*]

Exeunt Clowns.

Hostess. Who pays for the ale? Hear you master doctor, now you have sent away my guests, I pray who shall pay me for my a— [*Faustus charms her.*]

Exit Hostess.>

Duke. Come Madame, let us in, where you must reward this learned man for the great kindness he hath showed to you.

Duchess. And so I will, my lord, and whilst I live,
Rest beholding for this courtesy.

Faustus. I humbly thank your Grace.

Duke. Come, master doctor, follow us, and receive your reward. *Exeunt.*

[Scene 13]

Enter Wagner solus.

Wagner. I think my master means to die shortly,
For he hath given to me all his goods.
And yet methinks, if that death were near,
He would not banquet, and carouse, and swill
Amongst the students, as even now he doth,
Who are at supper with such belly-cheer,
As Wagner ne'er beheld in all his life.
See where they come. Belike the feast is ended.

Enter Faustus with two or three Scholars.

1 Scholar. Master Doctor Faustus, since our conference about fair ladies, which was the beautifulest in all the world, we have determined with ourselves that Helen of Greece was the admirablest lady that ever lived. Therefore master doctor, if you will do us that favor, as to let us see that peerless dame of Greece, whom all

114 "hey-pass" and "re-pass" conjuror's terms

the world admires for majesty, we should think ourselves much beholding unto you.

Faustus. Gentlemen,
For that I know your friendship is unfeigned,
And Faustus' custom is not to deny
The just request of those that wish him well:
You shall behold that peerless dame of Greece
No otherwise for pomp or majesty
Than when Sir Paris crossed the seas with her
And brought the spoils° to rich Dardania.°
Be silent then, for danger is in words.

Music sounds, and Helen passeth over the stage.

Scholar. Too simple is my wit to tell her praise,
Whom all the world admires for majesty.

3 Scholar. No marvel though the angry Greeks pursued
With ten years war the rape of such a queen,
Whose heavenly beauty passeth all compare.

1 Scholar. Since we have seen the pride of nature's works,
And only paragon of excellence,
Let us depart, and for this glorious deed
Happy and blest be Faustus evermore.

Enter an Old Man.

Faustus. Gentlemen farewell, the same I wish to you.

Exeunt Scholars.

Old Man. Ah Doctor Faustus, that I might prevail,
To guide thy steps unto the way of life
By which sweet path thou mayest attain the goal
That shall conduct thee to celestial rest.
Break heart, drop blood, and mingle it with tears,
Tears falling from repentant heaviness
Of thy most vile and loathsome filthiness,
The stench whereof corrupts the inward soul
With such flagitious° crimes of heinous sins,
As no commiseration may expel
But mercy, Faustus, of thy Savior sweet,
Whose blood alone must wash away thy guilt.

Faustus. Where art thou, Faustus? Wretch, what hast thou done?

Sc. 13. 24 **spoils** plunder 24 **Dardania** Troy 44 **flagitious** atrocious or extremely wicked

Damned art thou, Faustus, damned. Despair and die.
Hell calls for right, and with a roaring voice
Says: Faustus come, thine hour is come.
Mephostophilis gives him a dagger.
And Faustus will come to do thee right.

Old Man. Ah stay, good Faustus, stay thy desperate steps.
I see an angel hovers o'er thy head,
And with a vial full of precious grace
Offers to pour the same into thy soul:
Then call for mercy and avoid despair.

Faustus. Ah, my sweet friend,
I feel thy words to comfort my distressèd soul:
Leave me awhile to ponder on my sins.

Old Man. I go, sweet Faustus, but with heavy cheer,
Fearing the ruin of thy hopeless soul. [*Exit.*]

Faustus. Accursèd Faustus. Where is mercy now?
I do repent, and yet I do despair:
Hell strives with grace for conquest in my breast.
What shall I do to shun the snares of death?

Mephostophilis. Thou traitor Faustus, I arrest thy soul
For disobedience to my sovereign lord.
Revolt,° or I'll in piecemeal tear thy flesh.

Faustus. Sweet Mephostophilis, entreat thy lord
To pardon my unjust presumption,
And with my blood again I will confirm
My former vow I made to Lucifer.

Mephostophilis. Do it then quickly, with unfeignèd heart
Lest greater dangers do attend thy drift.

Faustus. Torment, sweet friend, that base and crookèd age
That durst dissuade me from thy Lucifer,
With greatest torment that our hell affords.

Mephostophilis. His faith is great. I cannot touch his soul.
But what I may afflict his body with
I will attempt, which is but little worth.

Faustus. One thing, good servant, let me crave of thee
To glut the longing of my heart's desire:
That I may have unto my paramour
That heavenly Helen which I saw of late,
Whose sweet embraces may extinguish clear
Those thoughts that do dissuade me from my vow,
And keep mine oath I made to Lucifer.

69 **Revolt** turn back

Mephostophilis. Faustus, this or what else thou shalt desire
Shall be performed in twinkling of an eye.

Enter Helen.

Faustus. Was this the face that launched a thousand ships
And burnt the topless towers of Ilium?°
Sweet Helen, make me immortal with a kiss.
Her lips suck forth my soul. See where it flies.
Come Helen, come, give me my soul again.
Here will I dwell, for heaven be in these lips
And all is dross that is not Helena.
I will be Paris, and for love of thee
Instead of Troy shall Wittenberg be sacked;
And I will combat with weak Menelaus°
And wear thy colors on my plumèd crest.
Yea, I will wound Achilles° in the heel
And then return to Helen for a kiss.
O, thou art fairer than the evening's air,
Clad in the beauty of a thousand stars,
Brighter art thou than flaming Jupiter
When he appeared to hapless Semele,°
More lovely than the monarch of the sky
In wanton Arethusa's azured arms,°
And none but thou shalt be my paramour.
Exeunt.

Old Man. Accursèd Faustus, miserable man,
That from thy soul exclud'st the grace of heaven,
And fliest the throne of his tribunal seat.

Enter the Devils.

Satan begins to sift me with his pride,
As in this furnace God shall try my faith.
My faith, vile hell, shall triumph over thee.
Ambitious fiends, see how the heavens smiles

92 **Ilium** Troy 100 **Menelaus** Helen's husband 102 **Achilles** famous Greek warrior, invulnerable except for a point at the back of his foot 107 **Semele** (at whose request Jupiter appeared in his full glory, the sight of which destroyed her) 108-109 **monarch . . . arms** (there is no known classical legend that fits this passage; Arethusa was a fountain nymph)

At your repulse, and laughs your state to scorn.
Hence hell, for hence I fly unto my God.

Exeunt.°

[Scene 14]

<[V.ii] *Thunder. Enter Lucifer, Belzebub, and Mephostophilis.*°

Lucifer. Thus from infernal Dis° do we ascend
To view the subjects of our monarchy,
Those souls which sin seals the black sons of hell.
'Mong which as chief, Faustus, we come to thee,
Bringing with us lasting damnation
To wait upon thy soul. The time is come
Which makes it forfeit.

Mephostophilis. And this gloomy night
Here in this room will wretched Faustus be.

Belzebub. And here we'll stay
To mark him how he doth demean himself.

Mephostophilis. How should he but in desperate lunacy?
Fond worldling, now his heart blood dries with grief,
His conscience kills it, and his laboring brain
Begets a world of idle fantasies
To overreach the devil; but all in vain:
His store of pleasures must be sauced with pain!
He and his servant Wagner are at hand.
Both come from drawing Faustus' latest will.
See where they come.

Enter Faustus and Wagner.

Faustus. Say Wagner, thou hast perused my will;
How dost thou like it?

119 s.d. **Exeunt** (ostensibly, the Old Man resists the torments of the Devils though it is not certain whether he actually rises to heaven or exis with devils in pursuit) V.ii. e.d. **Enter . . . Mephostophilis** (in Q 1616 Lucifer, Belzebub, and Mephostophilis watch Faustus pass through his last hours; in Q 1604, the Devils appear only at the last moment) **1 Dis** ruler of the underworld

Wagner. Sir, so wondrous well
As in all humble duty I do yield
My life and lasting service for your love.>

Enter the Scholars.°

Faustus. Ah gentlemen!

2 Scholar. What ails Faustus?

Faustus. Ah my sweet chamber-fellow, had I lived with thee, then had I lived still, but now I die eternally. Look, comes he not, comes he not?

2 Scholar. What means Faustus?

3 Scholar. Belike he is grown into some sickness, by being over-solitary.

1 Scholar. If it be so, we'll have physicians to cure him. 'Tis but a surfeit.° Never fear, man.

Faustus. A surfeit of deadly sin that hath damned both body and soul.

2 Scholar. Yet Faustus, look up to heaven, remember God's mercies are infinite.

Faustus. But Faustus' offense can ne'er be pardoned. The serpent that tempted Eve may be saved, but not Faustus! O gentlemen, hear with patience and tremble not at my speeches. Though my heart pant and quiver to remember that I have been a student here these thirty years, O, would I had never seen Wittenberg, never read book. And what wonders I have done, all Germany can witness, yea all the world, for which Faustus hath lost both Germany and the world, yea heaven itself—heaven, the seat of God, the throne of the blessèd, the kingdom of joy—and must remain in hell forever, hell, Ah hell forever. Sweet friends, what shall become of Faustus being in hell forever?

Scholar. Yet Faustus, call on God.

Faustus. On God, whom Faustus hath abjured? On God, whom Faustus hath blasphemed? Ah my God, I would weep, but the devil draws in my tears. Gush forth blood instead of tears, yea life and soul. O, he stays my tongue! I would lift up my hands, but see, they hold 'em, they hold 'em!

23 s.d. Enter the Scholars (in Q 1604 the scene begins here with the s.d. "Enter Faustus with the Scholars") **33 surfeit** indigestion

All. Who, Faustus?

Faustus. Lucifer and Mephostophilis. Ah gentlemen! I gave them my soul for my cunning.

All. God forbid!

Faustus. God forbade it indeed, but Faustus hath done it. For vain pleasure of four and twenty years hath Faustus lost eternal joy and felicity. I writ them a bill with mine own blood. The date is expired. The time will come, and he will fetch me.

1 Scholar. Why did not Faustus tell us of this before, that divines might have prayed for thee?

Faustus. Oft have I thought to have done so, but the devil threatened to tear me in pieces if I named God, to fetch both body and soul if I once gave ear to divinity; and now 'tis too late. Gentlemen, away, lest you perish with me.

2 Scholar. O, what shall we do to save Faustus?

Faustus. Talk not of me but save yourselves and depart.

3 Scholar. God will strengthen me. I will stay with Faustus.

1 Scholar. Tempt not God, sweet friend, but let us into the next room and there pray for him.

Faustus. Ay, pray for me, pray for me. And what noise soever ye hear, come not unto me, for nothing can rescue me.

2 Scholar. Pray thou, and we will pray that God may have mercy upon thee.

Faustus. Gentlemen, farewell. If I live till morning, I'll visit you. If not, Faustus is gone to hell.

All. Faustus, farewell. *Exeunt Scholars.*

<*Mephostophilis.* Ay, Faustus, now thou hast no hope of heaven.
Therefore, despair! Think only upon hell,
For that must be thy mansion, there to dwell.

Faustus. O thou bewitching fiend, 'twas thy temptation
Hath robbed me of eternal happiness.

Mephostophilis. I do confess it Faustus, and rejoice.
'Twas I, that when thou wert i' the way to heaven
Dammed up thy passage. When thou took'st the book
To view the Scriptures, then I turned the leaves
And led thine eye.
What, weep'st thou! 'Tis too late, despair, farewell!
Fools that will laugh on earth, most weep in hell.

Exit.

Enter the Good Angel and the Bad Angel at several doors.

Good Angel. O Faustus, if thou hadst given ear to me
Innumerable joys had followèd thee.
But thou did'st love the world.
Bad Angel. Gave ear to me,
And now must taste hell's pains perpetually.
Good Angel. O, what will all thy riches, pleasures, pomps
Avail thee now?
Bad Angel. Nothing but vex thee more,
To want in hell, that had on earth such store.
Music while the throne descends.°
Good Angel. O, thou hast lost celestial happiness,
Pleasures unspeakable, bliss without end.
Had'st thou affected° sweet divinity,
Hell or the devil had had no power on thee.
Had'st thou kept on that way, Faustus behold
In what resplendent glory thou had'st sat
In yonder throne, like those bright shining saints,
And triumphed over hell! That hast thou lost.
[*Throne ascends.*]
And now, poor soul, must thy good angel leave thee,
The jaws of hell are open to receive thee. *Exit.*
Hell is discovered.°
Bad Angel. Now Faustus, let thine eyes with horror stare
Into that vast perpetual torture-house.
There are the furies, tossing damnèd souls
On burning forks. Their bodies boil in lead.
There are live quarters° broiling on the coals,
That ne'er can die: this ever-burning chair
Is for o'er-tortured souls to rest them in.
These that are fed with sops of flaming fire
Were gluttons and loved only delicates
And laughed to see the poor starve at their gates.
But yet all these are nothing. Thou shalt see
Ten thousand tortures that more horrid be.
Faustus. O, I have seen enough to torture me.

105 s.d. **the throne descends** i.e., from the shadow or 'heavens' located above the stage platform 108 **affected** had feeling for 115 s.d. **Hell is discovered** a trap door in the stage floor opens 120 **quarters** parts of bodies

Bad Angel. Nay, thou must feel them, taste the smart of all:
He that loves pleasure must for pleasure fall.
And so I leave thee Faustus, till anon:
Then wilt thou tumble in confusion.° *Exit.*>
The clock strikes eleven.

Faustus. Faustus,
Now hast thou but one bare hour to live,
And then thou must be damned perpetually.
Stand still you ever-moving spheres of Heaven.
That time may cease, and midnight never come:
Fair nature's eye, rise, rise again and make
Perpetual day, or let this hour be but a year,
A month, a week, a natural day,
That Faustus may repent, and save his soul.
O lente lente currite noctis equi!°
The stars move still, time runs, the clock will strike,
The devil will come, and Faustus must be damned.
O, I'll leap up to my God! Who pulls me down?
See, see where Christ's blood streams in the firmament!
One drop would save my soul, half a drop. Ah, my Christ.
Ah rend not my heart for naming of my Christ.
Yet will I call on him. O spare me, Lucifer!
Where is it now? 'Tis gone: and see where God
Stretcheth out his arm and bends his ireful brows.
Mountains and hills, come, come and fall on me,
And hide me from the heavy wrath of God!
No, no.
Then will I headlong run into the earth.
Earth gape. O no, it will not harbor me.
You stars that reigned at my nativity,
Whose influence hath allotted death and hell,
Now draw up Faustus like a foggy mist
Into the entrails of yon laboring cloud
That when you vomit forth into the air,
My limbs may issue from your smoky mouths
So that my soul may but ascend to heaven!
Ah, half the hour is passed. *The watch strikes.*
'Twill all be passed anon.
O God,
If thou wilt not have mercy on my soul,

132 **confusion** ruin 142 **O . . . equi** "O run slowly, slowly, horses of the night"

Yet for Christ's sake, whose blood hath ransomed me,
Impose some end to my incessant pain.
Let Faustus live in hell a thousand years,
A hundred thousand, and at last be saved.
O no end is limited to damnèd souls.
Why wert thou not a creature wanting soul?
Or, why is this immortal that thou hast?
Ah, Pythagoras' metempsychosis,° were that true
This soul should fly from me, and I be changed
Into some brutish beast.
All beasts are happy, for when they die
Their souls are soon dissolved in elements.
But mine must live still° to be plagued in hell.
Cursed be the parents that engendered me.
No Faustus, curse thyself, curse Lucifer
That hath deprived thee of the joys of heaven.

The clock striketh twelve.

O it strikes, it strikes! Now body, turn to air,
Or Lucifer will bear thee quick° to hell.

Thunder and lightning.

O soul, be changed into little water drops,
And fall into the ocean, ne'er be found.
My God, my God, look not so fierce on me.

Enter Devils

Adders and serpents, let me breathe awhile.
Ugly hell, gape not! Come not Lucifer!
I'll burn my books, ah Mephostophilis.

Exeunt with him.

<[V.iii] *Enter the Scholars.*

1 Scholar. Come gentlemen, let us go visit Faustus,
For such a dreadful night was never seen
Since first the world's creation did begin!

175 **metempsychosis** theory of the transmigration of souls 180 **still** always, i.e., eternally 185 **quick** alive

Such fearful shrieks and cries were never heard!
Pray heaven, the doctor have escaped the danger.

2 Scholar. O, help us heaven, see here are Faustus' limbs°
All torn asunder by the hand of death!

3 Scholar. The devils whom Faustus served have torn him
thus:
For 'twixt the hours of twelve and one, methought
I heard him shriek and call aloud for help,
At which self° time the house seemed all on fire
With dreadful horror of these damnèd fiends.

2 Scholar. Well gentlemen, though Faustus' end be such
As every Christian heart laments to think on,
Yet for he was a scholar once admired
For wondrous knowledge in our German schools,
We'll give his mangled limbs due burial;
And all the students, clothed in mourning black,
Shall wait upon° his hevay funeral. *Exeunt.*

[Epilogue]

Enter Chorus.

Cut is the branch that might have grown full straight,
And burnèd is Apollo's laurel bough
That sometime grew within this learnèd man.
Faustus is gone: regard his hellish fall,
Whose fiendful fortune may exhort the wise
Only to wonder at unlawful things,
Whose deepness° doth entice such forward wits
To practice more than heavenly power permits.

[*Exit.*]

Terminat hora diem; terminat Author opus.°

V.iii. 197 **see . . . limbs** (possibly the Scholar draws a curtain to display the limbs) 202 **self** exact 210 **wait upon** attend 7 **deepness** seductive mystery 9 **Terminat . . . opus** "The hour ends the day; the Author ends his work"

Appendix to *Doctor Faustus.* Act IV, scenes i-iv (Q 1616)

[IV.i] *Enter Martino and Frederick at several° doors.*

Martino. What ho, officers, gentlemen!
Hie to the presence° to attend the Emperor.
Good Frederick, see the rooms be voided straight,°
His Majesty is coming to the hall.
Go back and see the state° in readiness.
Frederick. But where is Bruno, our elected Pope,
That on a fury's back came post from Rome?
Will not his Grace consort° the Emperor?
Martino. O yes, and with him comes the German conjurer,
The learnèd Faustus, fame of Wittenberg,
The wonder of the world for magic art:
And he intends to show great Carolus
The race of all his stout progenitors
And bring in presence of his Majesty
The royal shapes and warlike semblances
Of Alexander and his beauteous paramour.°
Frederick. Where is Benvolio?
Martino. Fast asleep, I warrant you.
He took his rouse° with stoups° of Rhenish wine
So kindly yesternight to Bruno's health
That all this day the sluggard keeps his bed.
Frederick. See, see, his window's ope. We'll call to him.
Martino. What ho, Benvolio!

Enter Benvolio above at a window, in his nightcap, buttoning.

Benvolio. What a devil ail you two?
Martino. Speak softly sir, lest the devil hear you,
For Faustus at the court is late arrived
And at his heels a thousand furies wait
To accomplish whatsoever the doctor please.

IV.i.s.d. **several** different or opposite 2 **presence** presence-chamber 3 **voided straight** cleared at once 5 **state** throne 8 **consort** attend 16 **paramour** his wife Roxana (?), his mistress Thais (?) 18 **rouse** drinking bout 18 **stoups** large cups, flagons

Benvolio. What of this?
Martino. Come, leave thy chamber first, and thou shalt see
This conjurer perform such rare exploits
Before the Pope° and royal Emperor
As never yet was seen in Germany.
Benvolio. Has not the Pope enough of conjuring yet?
He was upon the devil's back late enough!
And if he be so far in love with him
I would he would post with him to Rome again.
Frederick. Speak, wilt thou come and see this sport?
Benvolio. Not I.
Martino. Wilt thou stand in thy window and see it then?
Benvolio. Ay, and I fall not asleep i' th' meantime.
Martino. The Emperor is at hand, who comes to see
What wonders by black spells may compassed be.
Benvolio. Well, go you attend the Emperor.
[*Exit Martino with Frederick.*°]

I am content for this once to thrust my head out at a window, for they say if a man be drunk overnight the devil cannot hurt him in the morning. If that be true, I have a charm in my head shall control him as well as the conjurer, I warrant you.

[*Benvolio remains at window.*]

[IV.ii] *A sennet. Charles the German Emperor, Bruno,* [*Duke of*] *Saxony, Faustus, Mephostophilis, Frederick, Martino, and Attendants.*°

Emperor. Wonder of men, renowned magician,
Thrice-learnèd Faustus, welcome to our court.
This deed of thine in setting Bruno free
From his and our professèd enemy,
Shall add more excellence unto thine art
Than if by powerful necromantic spells
Thou could'st command the world's obedience.

31 **Pope** i.e., Bruno 42 s.d. **Exit . . . Frederick** (the only direction for exit occurs at the end of the scene. However, since Martino and Frederick appear immediately with the Emperor, and Benvolio remains at the window, Martino and Frederick probably exit at the point noted) IV.ii. s.d. **A sennet . . . Attendants** (in the absence of a specific s.d. for entrance, it may be that the characters are discovered by the drawing of a curtain)

For ever be beloved of Carolus!
And if this Bruno thou hast late redeemed
In peace possess the triple diadem
And sit in Peter's chair despite of chance,
Thou shalt be famous through all Italy
And honored of the German Emperor.

Faustus. These gracious words, most royal Carolus,
Shall make poor Faustus to his utmost power
Both love and serve the German Emperor
And lay his life at holy Bruno's feet.
For proof whereof, if so your Grace be pleased,
The doctor stands prepared by power of art
To cast his magic charms that shall pierce through
The ebon gates of ever-burning hell,
And hale the stubborn furies from their caves
To compass whatsoe'er your Grace commands.

Benvolio. Blood! He speaks terribly. But for all that I do not greatly believe him. He looks as like a conjurer as the Pope to a costermonger.°

Emperor. Then Faustus, as thou late didst promise us,
We would behold that famous conqueror
Great Alexander and his paramour
In their true shapes and state majestical,
That we may wonder at their excellence.

Faustus. Your Majesty shall see them presently.
Mephostophilis away,
And with a solemn noise of trumpets' sound
Present before this royal Emperor
Great Alexander and his beauteous paramour.

Mephostophilis. Faustus, I will. [*Exit.*]

Benvolio. Well master doctor, an° your devils come not away quickly, you shall have me asleep presently. Zounds,° I could eat myself for anger to think I have been such an ass all this while to stand gaping after the devils' governor and can see nothing.

Faustus. I'll make you feel something anon if my art fail me not!
My lord, I must forewarn your Majesty
That when my spirits present the royal shapes
Of Alexander and his paramour,

26 **costermonger** fruit-seller 38 **an** if 40 **Zounds** by God's wounds

Your Grace demand no questions of the King
But in dumb silence let them come and go.

Emperor. Be it as Faustus please; we are content.

Benvolio. Ay ay, and I am content too. And thou bring Alexander and his paramour before the Emperor, I'll be Actaeon and turn myself to a stag.

Faustus. [*aside*] And I'll play Diana and send you the horns presently.

Sennet. Enter at one [*door*] *the Emperor Alexander, at the other Darius.*° *They meet. Darius is thrown down. Alexander kills him, takes off his crown, and offering to go out, his Paramour meets him. He embraceth her and sets Darius' crown upon her head, and coming back both salute the Emperor; who leaving his state offers to embrace them, which Faustus seeing suddenly stays him. Then trumpets cease and music sounds.*

My gracious lord, you do forget yourself.
These are but shadows, not substantial.

Emperor. O pardon me, my thoughts are so ravished
With sight of this renownèd Emperor.
That in mine arms I would have compassed° him.
But Faustus, since I may not speak to them,
To satisfy my longing thoughts at full,
Let me this tell thee: I have heard it said
That this fair lady whilst she lived on earth,
Had on her neck a little wart or mole.
How may I prove that saying to be true?

Faustus. Your Majesty may boldly go and see.

Emperor. Faustus, I see it plain!
And in this sight thou better pleasest me
Than if I gained another monarchy.

Faustus. Away, be gone! *Exit show.*
See, see, my gracious lord, what strange beast is yon that thrusts his head out at the window!

Emperor. O wondrous sight! See, Duke of Saxony,
Two spreading horns most strangely fastened
Upon the head of young Benvolio.

55 s.d. **Darius** King of Persia whom Alexander defeated 60 **compassed** enclosed

Saxony. What, is he asleep or dead?

Faustus. He sleeps my lord, but dreams not of his horns.

Emperor. This sport is excellent. We'll call and wake him. What ho, Benvolio!

Benvolio. A plague upon you! Let me sleep awhile.

Emperor. I blame thee not to sleep much, having such a head of thine own.

Saxony. Look up Benvolio! 'Tis the Emperor calls.

Benvolio. The Emperor! Where? O zounds, my head!

Emperor. Nay, and thy horns hold, 'tis no matter for thy head, for that's armed sufficiently.

Faustus. Why, how now Sir Knight? What, hanged by the horns? This is most horrible! Fie fie, pull in your head for shame! Let not all the world wonder at you.

Benvolio. Zounds doctor, is this your villainy?

Faustus. Oh, say not so sir: The doctor has no skill,
No art, no cunning to present these lords
Or bring before this royal Emperor
The mighty monarch, warlike Alexander.
If Faustus do it, you are straight resolved
In bold Actaeon's shape to turn a stag.
And therefore my lord, so please your Majesty,
I'll raise a kennel of hounds shall hunt him so
As all his footmanship shall scarce prevail
To keep his carcass from their bloody fangs.
Ho, Belimote, Argiron, Asterote!°

Benvolio. Hold, hold! Zounds, he'll raise up a kennel of devils I think, anon. Good my lord, entreat for me. 'Sblood,° I am never able to endure these torments.

Emperor. Then good master doctor,
Let me entreat you to remove his horns.
He has done penance now sufficiently.

Faustus. My gracious lord, not so much for injury done to me, as to delight your Majesty with some mirth, hath Faustus justly requited this injurious° knight; which being all I desire, I am content to remove his horns. Mephostophilis, transform him. And hereafter sir, look you speak well of scholars.

102 **Belimote . . . Asterote** (corruptions of devils' names) 105 **'Sblood** by God's blood 111 **injurious** insulting

Benvolio. [*aside*] Speak well of ye! 'Sblood, and scholars be such cuckold-makers to clap horns of honest men's heads o' this order, I'll ne'er trust smooth faces and small ruffs° more. But an I be not revenged for this, would I might be turned to a gaping oyster and drink nothing but salt water. [*Exit.*]

Emperor. Come Faustus, while the Emperor lives,
In recompense of this thy high desert,
Thou shalt command the state of Germany
And live beloved of mighty Carolus.

Exeunt omnes.

[IV.iii] *Enter Benvolio, Martino, Frederick, and Soldiers.*

Martino. Nay, sweet Benvolio, let us sway thy thoughts
From this attempt against the conjurer.

Benvolio. Away! You love me not to urge me thus.
Shall I let slip so great an injury
When every servile groom jests at my wrongs
And in their rustic gambols proudly say,
"Benvolio's head was graced with horns today"?
O, may these eyelids never close again
Till with my sword I have that conjurer slain!
If you will aid me in this enterprise,
Then draw your weapons and be resolute;
If not, depart. Here will Benvolio die
But° Faustus' death shall quit° my infamy.

Frederick. Nay, we will stay with thee, betide what may,
And kill that doctor if he come this way.

Benvolio. Then, gentle Frederick, hie thee to the grove
And place our servants and our followers
Close in an ambush there behind the trees.
By this, I know, the conjurer is near.
I saw him kneel and kiss the Emperor's hand
And take his leave laden with rich rewards.
Then soldiers, boldly fight. If Faustus die,
Take you the wealth, leave us the victory.

Frederick. Come soldiers, follow me unto the grove.
Who kills him shall have gold and endless love.

Exit Frederick with the Soldiers.

118 small ruffs (worn by scholars) IV.iii.13 But unless 13 quit pay for

Benvolio. My head is lighter than it was by th' horns—
But yet my heart more ponderous than my head,
And pants until I see that conjurer dead.
Martino. Where shall we place ourselves, Benvolio?
Benvolio. Here will we stay to bide the first assault.
O, were that damnèd hell-hound but in place
Thou soon should'st see me quit my foul disgrace.

Enter Frederick.

Frederick. Close, close! The conjurer is at hand
And all alone comes walking in his gown.
Be ready then and strike the peasant down!
Benvolio. Mine be that honor then! Now sword, strike home!
For horns he gave I'll have his head anon.

Enter Faustus with the false head.

Martino. See see, he comes.
Benvolio. No words. This blow ends all!
[*Strikes Faustus.*]
Hell take his soul, his body thus must fall.
Faustus. O!
Frederick. Groan you, master doctor?
Benvolio. Break may his heart with groans! Dear Frederick, see,
Thus will I end his griefs immediately.
[*Cuts off Faustus' false head.*]
Martino. Strike with a willing hand! His head is off.
Benvolio. The devil's dead, the furies now may laugh.
Frederick. Was this that stern aspect, that awful frown,
Made the grim monarch of infernal spirits
Tremble and quake at his commanding charms?
Martino. Was this that damnèd head whose heart conspired
Benvolio's shame before the Emperor?
Benvolio. Ay, that's the head, and here the body lies
Justly rewarded for his villainies.
Frederick. Come let's devise how we may add more shame
To the black scandal of his hated name.
Benvolio. First, on his head in quittance of my wrongs
I'll nail huge forkèd horns and let them hang

Within the window where he yoked me first
That all the world may see my just revenge.

Martino. What use shall we put his beard to?

Benvolio. We'll sell it to a chimney-sweeper. It will wear out ten birchen brooms, I warrant you.

Frederick. What shall eyes do?

Benvolio. We'll put out his eyes, and they shall serve for buttons to his lips to keep his tongue from catching cold.

Martino. An excellent policy! And now sirs, having divided him, what shall the body do?

[*Faustus rises.*]

Benvolio. Zounds, the devil's alive again!

Frederick. Give him his head for God's sake!

Faustus. Nay keep it. Faustus will have heads and hands,
Ay, all your hearts, to recompense this deed.
Knew you not, traitors, I was limited
For four and twenty years to breathe on earth?
And had you cut my body with your swords
Or hewed this flesh and bones as small as sand,
Yet in a minute had my spirit returned
And I had breathed a man made free from harm.
But wherefore do I dally my revenge?
Asteroth, Belimoth, Mephostophilis!

Enter Mephostophilis and other Devils.

Go horse these traitors on your fiery backs
And mount aloft with them as high as heaven,
Thence pitch them headlong to the lowest hell.
Yet stay, the world shall see their misery,
And hell shall after plague their treachery.
Go Belimoth, and take this caitiff° hence
And hurl him in some lake of mud and dirt:
Take thou this other, drag him through the woods
Amongst the pricking thorns and sharpest briars:
Whilst with my gentle Mephostophilis
This traitor flies unto some steepy rock
That rolling down may break the villain's bones
As he intended to dismember me.
Fly hence, dispatch my charge immediately!

84 caitiff villain

Frederick. Pity us, gentle Faustus, save our lives!
Faustus. Away!
Frederick. He must needs go that the devil drives.
Exeunt Spirits with the Knights.

Enter the ambushed Soldiers.

1 Soldier. Come sirs, prepare yourselves in readiness.
Make haste to help these noble gentlemen.
I heard them parley with the conjurer.
2 Soldier. See where he comes, dispatch, and kill the slave!
Faustus. What's here, an ambush to betray my life?
Then Faustus, try thy skill. Base peasants, stand!
For lo, these trees remove° at my command
And stand as bulwarks 'twixt yourselves and me
To shield me from your hated treachery!
Yet to encounter this your weak attempt
Behold an army comes incontinent.°

Faustus strikes the door, and enter a Devil playing on a drum, after him another bearing an ensign, and divers with weapons: Mephostophilis with fireworks: they set upon the Soldiers and drive them out.

[*Exeunt all.*]

[IV.iv] *Enter at several doors Benvolio, Frederick, and Martino, their heads and faces bloody and besmeared with mud and dirt, all having horns on their heads.*

Martino. What ho, Benvolio!
Benvolio. Here! What, Frederick, ho!
Frederick. O, help me gentle friend. Where is Martino?
Martino. Dear Frederick, here,
Half smothered in a lake of mud and dirt,
Through which the furies dragged me by the heels.
Frederick. Martino, see, Benvolio's horns again.
Martino. O misery! How now Benvolio?
Benvolio. Defend me, heaven! Shall I be haunted still?
Martino. Nay fear not man, we have no power to kill.

101 remove move **105 incontinent** unrestrained and immediately

Benvolio. My friends transformèd thus! O hellish spite,
Your heads are all set with horns.
Frederick. You hit it right:
It is your own you mean. Feel on your head.
Benvolio. Zounds, horns again!°
Martino. Nay chafe not man, we all are sped.°
Benvolio. What devil attends this damned magician,
That spite of spite our wrongs are doubled?
Frederick. What may we do that we may hide our shames?
Benvolio. If we should follow him to work revenge
He'd join long asses' ears to these huge horns
And make us laughing-stocks to all the world.
Martino. What shall we then do, dear Benvolio?
Benvolio. I have a castle joining near these woods,
And thither we'll repair and live obscure
Till time shall alter this our brutish shapes.
Sith° black disgrace hath thus eclipsed our fame,
We'll rather die with grief than live with shame.
Exeunt omnes.

12 **horns again** (Benvolio's surprise at having horns after Frederick shows them to Martino in l. 6 indicates that the three men are groping about in search of each other, and that Benvolio's line "Shall I be haunted still?" is in response to Martino's ghostlike appearance) 13 **sped** beaten 24 **Sith** since

VOLPONE

or

The Fox

by

Ben Jonson

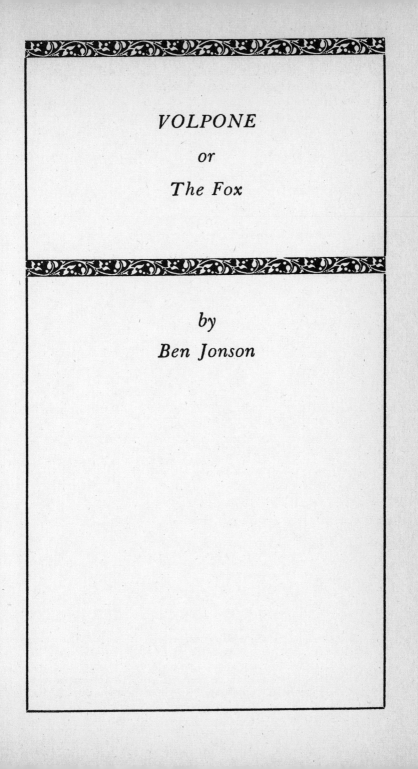

BEN JONSON

Fleeing his stepfather's trade of bricklayer, Ben Jonson first turned soldier, went to the wars in the Netherlands, fought in single combat before the gaze of opposing armies, and returned to London by 1597 to become an actor, all before the age of twenty-five. His career as an actor was brief and, if we can believe the gibes of his critics, undistinguished. But it introduced him to the bustling world of the theater just as it was exploding with fantastic creative vitality.

Like Shakespeare, Jonson combined writing with acting from the very start. While acting with major London companies, he collaborated with other writers and added scenes to the wildly popular play by Thomas Kyd, *The Spanish Tragedy*. Although his earliest plays have not survived, by 1598 Jonson was not only praised for his tragedies, whatever they were, but enjoyed his first success with his comedy *Every Man in his Humour*. Presented by the Lord Chamberlain's men, the company of Shakespeare and Burbage, *Every Man In* was the first of a number of Jonson's plays that this company produced.

Jonson was too restless, too protean a person, however, to be content with a steady—and subordinate—position with one troupe of actors. Soon after *Every Man In*, he gave up acting, it appears, and devoted his full attention to drama and poetry. More than any other playwright of the time, he composed for all types of performance. His comedies and tragedies appeared on the public stages. His satiric plays often commanded the private stages. After the accession of James I in 1603, he became the principal poet and developer of the court masque with its ornate emblems and striking spectacles. For the plays on the public stages he had little opportunity to involve himself in production. That was the province of the professional actors. But with the children of the private companies and the noble amateurs of the court masque, he could and did become immersed in every aspect of presentation. Only when his disputes with the court designer, Inigo Jones, led to an irrevocable break between them did he lose active contact with the stage.

Yet the anomaly of the man is that despite his thorough involvement with the stage, Jonson, more than any other Elizabethan dramatist, was a man of the word and the book. As a child, he came under the tutelage of the noted antiquarian and educator William Camden. With him Jonson began his long and devoted companionship with Greek and Latin authors. His poverty prevented him from going to the university, unquestionably the proper habitat for his budding genius. Nevertheless, by enormous diligence, he mastered the ancient languages to become one of the outstanding classicists of his age.

His absorption in the ancient authors, however, did not lead to slavish imitation. He read deeply, selected shrewdly, and above all invented freely, fusing passages from the Latin poets with his own pungent, lyrical fancies in fresh and seamless poetry. Attentive to the finest nuances of verbal expression, he insisted on continuous practice as a path to an effortless style. "Take care," he advises would-be authors, "in placing and ranking both matter and words, that the composition be comely; and to do this with diligence and often." This concern with polished writing is reflected in his care of play scripts. As I discussed in my general introduction, Jonson was the first of the professional playwrights to see his works through the press. In opposition to received wisdom, he did not regard his dramas as occasional pieces, deserving little or no attention in their preservation. In his opinion they had enduring value, and he took pains to see that satisfactory copies reached the printers.

His independence in this respect was at one with his larger independence of soul. Ferociously sure of his own judgment, he had a volatile temperament that often led to argument and fights, and yet it must have been a temperament easily reconciled. Never hesitant to criticize others, he nevertheless resumed friendships with men he had castigated. His life is thus a mixture of arguments and affections. In 1598 he quarreled with an actor named Gabriel Spencer and killed him in a duel. A year later he is the focus of a literary battle known as the War of the Theatres. His antagonists included Thomas Dekker, with whom he had previously collaborated, and John Marston, with whom he would collaborate in 1604. Still later he engaged in a lengthy acrimonious dispute with Inigo Jones. Aside from these personal quarrels were the occasions when he underwent public chastisement for dipping his pen too liberally in venom. For writing *The Isle of Dogs* with Thomas Nashe (1597) and *Eastward Ho!* (1605) with Marston and George Chapman, he was remanded to prison, escaping, happily, more serious punishment. This quarrelsomeness was a facet of the moral righteousness that threatened to distort his artistry, but which in actuality came to infuse his imagination in a complex and subtle manner.

Commencing with *Every Man in his Humour* and followed by its companion in title if not in reception, *Every Man Out of his Humour,* Jonson created a rich tapestry of dramatic types in works held together by the idiosyncrasies of the characters. Fascinated by the compulsions and obsessions that afflict people, he sought to dramatize their folly and demonstrate how that folly might be purged. In both of these plays he wavered between the outright depiction of contemporary English life and the conventional fiction of aesthetic distance. Thus, *Every Man In* had an Italian setting in its first form and a London locale when Jonson revised it in 1612. *Every Man Out* tried the odd combination of Italianate characters living in the London suburbs and haunting the aisles of St. Paul's Cathedral.

The plays in the War of the Theatres—*Cynthia's Revels* (1600-01) and *The Poetaster* (1601)—are satiric in tone and literary in subject matter. *The Poetaster,* for one, is set in the court of the Emperor Augustus, where Horace-Jonson fends off the carping attacks of lesser poets. These plays, given by the Children of Her Majesty's Chapel, were interesting more as ammunition than as achievement. Not until Jonson returned to the popular theater with *Volpone* did he once again win unstinting acclaim. Prior to *Volpone* came *Sejanus* (1603), Jonson's first extant tragedy, a close study of the aspiring political climber Sejanus, who sought to supplant his master, the tyrannical Tiberius. Awesome in its learning, austere in its action, *Sejanus,* despite some fine scenes, lacks the sure hand that we find in the later plays. Indeed, in the six or seven years between *Every Man In* and *Volpone,* Jonson experimented with several types of plays until in *Volpone* he realized a format and subject that suited his genius. Supposedly composed in forty days, a fantastically short time for the usually painstaking Jonson, *Volpone* bursts with a fancy that is quintessentially Jonsonian.

Epicoene, or The Silent Woman and *The Alchemist* followed in 1607 and 1610 respectively. Together with *Volpone* they constitute three recognized masterpieces of Jonson. In centering his plays on a pair or a trio of cheaters or, rather, artists of cheating, he found a way of exposing the follies and gullibilities of the populace at large. Only one other play, *Bartholomew Fair* (1614), matched or exceeded these three comedies. Save for a prologue-like opening scene, *Bartholomew Fair* unfolds entirely at the great Smithfield fair where citizen and con man—and woman—mingle. Returning to his early style of complex interweaving of many characters, Jonson creates a turbulent purgation of self-deceivers.

At the same time as he was writing *Volpone* and these later plays, Jonson was transforming the rather simple Elizabethan masque, essentially a pageant-like dance, into a dramatic entertainment celebrating the Jacobean court. For nearly twenty years Jonson regularly composed elegant libretti for this spectacular mix of song, dance, and poetry, and even returned to the genre in 1630-31. Meanwhile, between 1614 and 1625, he ceased writing for the public stages. Regrettably, when he resumed work as a dramatist, he appears to have lost his sure touch. Between 1625 and 1632, he produced *The Staple of News* (1625), *The New Inn* (1629), *The Magnetic Lady* (1632), and *The Tale of a Tub* (1633), none of which added to his fame or his purse. At his death in 1641 his worldly fortunes were low though his reputation was high; it continued to mount steeply throughout the rest of the seventeenth century.

Of all Jonson's plays, *Volpone* is easily the most popular and accessible. In it Jonson moderates his fierce impulse to cram the scene with events and observations. Rich in detail, vibrant with fancy, the comedy nevertheless follows a simple line of action from Volpone's opening celebration of gold to the final judgment of the Venetian court. Rather than create a fanciful Anglo-Italian world that never existed, in *Volpone* Jonson portrays a contemporary Venice with its Scrutineo, its Arsenale, its *magnificos*, and its mountebanks. His Venetians, though endowed with animal attributes, are nonetheless local citizens. Into this exotic atmosphere he introduces his English travelers with their news of London and their northern stolidity. But it is the last time he effectively combines these two worlds. Henceforth, Jonson places his action in his native England, usually in London.

But Jonson's Venice, in addition to being a city of wealth and fortune hunting, is also a stage for shrewd gestures. At the center of the scene are the two intriguers, patron and parasite. First there is the fox, a Venetian noble, a magnifico, dazzled by the treasures he has acquired, but even more by the pleasure of acquiring them through trickery and deception. Serving him yet outdoing him is his henchman of mixed ancestry, Mosca.

A buzzing flesh fly from the medieval bestiary, he is also a Venetian hanger-on; a Roman parasite so cleverly portrayed by Plautus, he is, as well, a native vice from the English moralities. He takes his subservience from one parent, his boastful self-love from another. Together he and his master alternate virtuoso acting with exhilarated self-congratulation. The first time we see Mosca alone on stage, he rhapsodizes,

> I could skip
> Out of my skin, now, like a subtle snake,
> I am so limber. O! Your parasite
> Is a most precious thing . . .
>
> (III. i. 5-8)

For him as for Volpone, cheating is an excuse for giving magnificent performances.

Volpone plays a dying man so to the life, if one may state such a contradiction, that he completely deceives his otherwise shrewd victims. As the excitement of the game mounts, he plays Scoto, the noted mountebank, and then the scruffy sergeant-at-law. Like a superb character actor, Volpone changes his appearance so thoroughly that he is unrecognizable in his different guises. Ironically, Mosca plays the "leading man" to Volpone's characters. Mosca never changes his role, but he slips from one mood to another, from one thought to another, so adroitly that most of his marks believe that it is they who are in control of the situations.

The objects of the intriguers' schemes are not the "fathers of poor families" nor "widows" and orphans. Instead, they are the birds of prey: the vulture, the raven, the crow, who themselves try to catch unwary victims in their claws. Only gradually, and as the game gets hot, do Volpone and Mosca seek to ravage the innocent Celia and openhearted Bonario. Lady Wouldbe, not only a would-be sophisticate but a would-be gull, thrusts herself into the plot, and Mosca, in his usual fluent manner, uses her for his own purposes. But though all these figures become grist to the mill of the intriguers, their mistreatment affects us quite differently.

The voracious bird-men collaborate in their self-deception. Believing they are more sharp-eyed than others, they are easily blinded by their greed. We rejoice in their fall. Lady Wouldbe is a victim in another way. As blind as the greedy birds, she along with her super-wise husband, Sir Politic, believe in their superior knowledge, she of the arts and fashions, he of affairs of state. Thus, the first set are deceived by their belief in knowing men, the second in their claim to know matters. Together they are exposed as either scavengers or fools. The scavengers, being vicious, are punished severely; the fools are merely unmasked, and although their exposure may not reform them, it chastens them for the time being.

The third set of victims, the innocent Celia and Bonario, are redeemed, not by their innocence but by the self-destruction of the schemers, who fall out with each other. Bonario's suspicions of Mosca do not save them. Rather, their steadfast commitment to decency is what sustains them through the horrid trials that husband and father inflict upon them respectively. Their firmness is often read as shallowness, and, no doubt, they lack the fascination of the intriguers and birds of prey. But Celia and Bonario supply a moral standard by which to judge Volpone's actions, a necessary standard lest we be seduced by Volpone and Mosca's cleverness. Volpone's attempt to rape Celia and Mosca's almost successful deception of Bonario restore perspective on their villainy.

Not to be entirely ignored are the inhabitants of Volpone's household: Nano the dwarf, Castrone the eunuch, and Androgyno the hermaphrodite. Their presence alerts us to the absence of any conventional servants. The traditional household of a nobleman is missing. All Volpone's subordinates are entertainers, Mosca especially. The others are present to supply casual diversions, and though the first of these diversions is couched in a pseudo-intellectual dialogue, this apparent sophistication cannot dissipate the discomfort of the entertainment. The performers are creatures who had entertainment value in the Renaissance primarily because of their deformations. And their diversion is nothing but a tracing of the degeneration of a soul from Apollo through that believer in transmigration of souls, Pythagoras, into the unnatural body of a fool. Coming so early in the play, this show-within-a-show warns us against the pleasures of Volpone and the perverse talents of his parasite.

The action of the play unfolds in a direct, cumulative manner. Yet its advancement is deceptive. It commences with Volpone's invocation to the primacy of gold, indeed to its godlike power, and proceeds to Mosca's celebration of how Volpone gains his gold. This scene, in effect, reveals Volpone's soul, setting the stage for all further action. How long Volpone has dangled the bait of his legacy before the eyes of his victims, we never learn. But Volpone has apparently hovered on the brink of death for some time, and the climax of his scheme is near.

Now the action is ready to move to more extravagant limits and increasingly hazardous efforts. What propels the play is Mosca's need and desire to dazzle his master more and more. Addicted to his own cleverness, he must test the edges of the impossible. Ultimately, he seeks to destroy his master and in doing so destroys them both.

In preparing his script for publication, Jonson regularized the development of the action in accord with neoclassical practice. Thus, he divides his play into the conventional five acts of Horatian theory and then marks scenes on the basis of the entrance of characters—the so-called French system. But this kind of division, which gave the printed drama a literary appearance, did not accord with English theatrical practice. However subdivided the play may be on the page, the King's men, who first performed the work, played it without intermission. In such a continuous performance, the only meaningful scene designation is determined by alterations of continuity and discontinuity. According to English practice, a scene consists of all the action between clearances of the stage. When all characters leave the stage and another set of characters enter, then a scene begins. Since the English stage relied very little on scenery, the stage clearance helped to indicate significant changes in the action. A new scene usually signaled a shift in locale, a leap in time, or a redirection of focus to a secondary plot.

The present edition follows the copy of the play as printed in the Folio of 1616. It is essentially the same copy that appeared in the quarto of 1607. Both editions embody Jonson's intentions in all essential respects. It is, therefore, one of the most reliable texts of this period. All the same, Jonson's classicizing inclinations may distort the theatrical flow of the play. Thus, the first act is divided into five scenes even though according to English practice, there is only one continuous action. The second "true" scene is Act II, scene i, when the plot shifts to a square in Venice and to the underplot of Peregrine and Sir Politic Wouldbe. The reader should therefore distinguish those scenes that merely mark the entrance of a new character from the scenes that indicate a change in the action.

Of the effervescent theatrical vitality of the play there can be little doubt. With the exception of Shakespeare's most popular works, it is the most frequently revived Elizabethan play in the twentieth century. It has been presented in its unexpurgated state, adapted to modern taste, transformed into musicals, and made into a successful film. Through all these media, Jonson's pair of sharpers continue to fascinate and entertain us.

To the
Most Noble And Most Equal° Sisters,
The Two Famous Universities,°
For Their
Love and Acceptance Shown to His Poem
In The Presentation;
Ben. Jonson,
The Grateful Acknowledger,
Dedicates Both It And Himself.
There follows an Epistle, if
you dare venture on the length.

Never, most equal Sisters, had any man a wit so presently excellent as that it could raise itself; but there must come both matter, occasion, commenders, and favorers to it. If this be true, and that the fortune of all writers doth daily prove it, it behooves the careful to provide well toward these accidents,° and, having acquired them, to preserve that part of reputation most tenderly wherein the benefit of a friend° is also defended. Hence is it that I now render myself grateful and am studious to justify the bounty of your act, to which, though your mere authority were satisfying, yet, it being an age wherein poetry and the professors° of it hear so ill on all sides, there will a reason be looked for in the subject. It is certain, nor can it with any forehead° be opposed, that the too much license of poetasters° in this time hath much deformed their mistress,° that, every day, their manifold and manifest ignorance doth stick unnatural reproaches upon her; but for their petulancy° it were an act of the greatest injustice either to let the learned suffer, or so divine a skill (which indeed should not be attempted with unclean

2 **equal** equal in merit and justice 3 **universities** Oxford and Cambridge 17 **accidents** chance occasions of positive response 19 **benefit of a friend** blessing bestowed by the universities 23 **professors** practitioners 25 **forehead** audacity 26 **poetasters** petty poets 27 **mistress** i.e., poetry 29 **for their petulancy** because of their insolence

hands) to fall under the least contempt. For, if men will impartially, and not asquint, look toward the offices and function of a poet, they will easily conclude to themselves the impossibility of any man's being the good poet without first being a good man. He that is said to be able to inform° young men to all good disciplines, inflame grown men to all great virtues, keep old men in their best and supreme state, or, as they decline to childhood, recover them to their first strength; that comes forth the interpreter and arbiter of nature, a teacher of things divine no less than human, a master in manners; and can alone, or with a few, effect the business° of mankind: this, I take him,° is no subject for pride and ignorance to exercise their railing rhetoric upon. But it will here be hastily answered that the writers of these days are other things: that not only their manners, but their natures, are inverted, and nothing remaining with them of the dignity of poet but the abused name, which every scribe usurps; that now, especially in dramatic, or, as they term it, stage poetry, nothing but ribaldry, profanation, blasphemy, all license of offense to God and man is practiced. I dare not deny a great part of this, and am sorry I dare not, because in some men's abortive features° (and would they had never boasted the light) it is overtrue; but that all are embarked in this bold adventure for hell is a most uncharitable thought, and, uttered, a more malicious slander. For my particular, I can, and from a most clear conscience, affirm, that I have ever trembled to think toward the least profaneness, have loathed the use of such foul and unwashed bawdry as is now made the food of the scene. And, howsoever I cannot escape, from some, the imputation of sharpness, but that they will say I have taken a pride, or lust, to be bitter, and not my youngest infant° but hath come into the world with all his teeth; I would ask of these supercilious politics, what nation, society, or general order, or state I have provoked? what public person? whether I have not in all these preserved their dignity, as mine own person, safe? My works are read, allowed° (I speak of those that are

36 **inform** shape 43 **effect the business** perform the proper function 43 **I take him** I understand 54 **abortive features** i.e., misshapen plays 64 **youngest infant** (Jonson's recent play, *Sejanus*) 69 **allowed** approved for performance by the Master of the Revels

entirely mine); look into them. What broad° reproofs have I used? where have I been particular? where personal? except to a mimic,° cheater, bawd, or buffoon, creatures for their insolencies worthy to be taxed? Yet to which of these so pointingly as he might not either ingenuously have confessed or wisely dissembled his disease? But it is not rumour can make men guilty, much less entitle me to other men's crimes. I know that nothing can be so innocently writ or carried,° but may be made obnoxious to construction;° marry, whilst I bear mine innocence about me, I fear it not. Application° is now grown a trade with many, and there are that° profess to have a key for the deciphering of everything; but let wise and noble persons take heed how they be too credulous, or give leave to these invading interpreters to be overfamiliar with their fames, who cunningly, and often, utter° their own virulent malice under other men's simplest meanings. As for those that will (by faults which charity hath raked° up, or common honesty concealed) make themselves a name with the multitude, or (to draw their rude and beastly claps) care not whose living faces they entrench with their petulant styles, may they do it without a rival, for me. I choose rather to lie graved in obscurity than share with them in so preposterous a fame. Nor can I blame the wishes of those severe and wiser patriots,° who, providing° the hurts these licentious spirits may do in a state, desire rather to see fools, and devils, and those antique° relics of barbarism retrieved, with all other ridiculous and exploded follies, than behold the wounds of private men, of princes, and nations. For, as Horace makes Trebatius speak, among these,

—Sibi quisque timet, quamquam est intactus, et odit.°

70 **broad** indecent 72 **mimic** actor 78 **carried** handled 79 **construction** here, misinterpretation 80 **Application** identification of dramatic fiction with fact 81 **that** i.e., those that 85 **utter** i.e., circulate the counterfeit coin of 87 **raked** covered 94 **wiser patriots** concerned fellow countrymen 94 **providing** foreseeing 96 **antique** antic, grotesque 101 **Sibi . . . odit** "Although he is unhurt, each man fears for himself, and is angry" (Horace, *Satires*, II. i, 23)

And men may justly impute such rages, if continued, to the writer, as his sports. The increase of which lust in liberty, together with the present trade of the stage, in all their misc'line° interludes, what learned or liberal soul doth not already abhor? where nothing but the filth of the time is uttered, and that with such impropriety of phrase, such plenty of solecisms, such dearth of sense, so bold prolepses,° so racked metaphors, with brothelry able to violate the ear of a pagan, and blasphemy to turn the blood of a Christian to water. I cannot but be serious in a cause of this nature, wherein my fame and the reputations of divers honest and learned are the question; when a name so full of authority, antiquity, and all great mark, is, through their insolence, become the lowest scorn of the age; and those men subject to the petulancy of every vernaculous° orator that were wont to be the care of kings and happiest monarchs. This it is that hath not only rapt me° to present indignation, but made me studious heretofore, and by all my actions to stand off from them; which may most appear in this my latest work—which you, most learned Arbitresses, have seen, judged, and to my crown, approved—wherein I have labored, for their instruction and amendment, to reduce° not only the ancient forms, but manners of the scene: the easiness, the propriety, the innocence, and last, the doctrine, which is the principal end of poesie, to inform men in the best reason of living. And though my catastrophe° may in the strict rigor of comic law meet with censure, as turning back to my promise; I desire the learned and charitable critic to have so much faith in me to think it was done of industry:° for with what ease I could have varied it nearer his scale (but that I fear to boast my own faculty) I could here insert. But my special aim being to put the snaffle in their mouths that cry out: We never punish vice in our interludes,° &c. I took the more liberty, though not without some lines of example, drawn even in the ancients themselves, the goings out of whose comedies are not always joyful, but oft times the bawds, the servants, the

105 **mis'line** miscellaneous 109 **prolepses** preparatory summaries 117 **vernaculous** scurrilous 118-19 **rapt me** carried me forcefully 124 **reduce** restore 128 **catastrophe** climax 132 **of industry** deliberately 136 **interludes** plays

rivals, yea, and the masters are mulcted, and fitly, it being the office of a comic poet to imitate justice, and instruct to life, as well as purity of language, or stir up gentle affections. To which I shall take the occasion elsewhere to speak. For the present, most reverenced Sisters, as I have cared to be thankful for your affections past, and here made the understanding° acquainted with some ground of your favors, let me not despair their continuance, to the maturing of some worthier fruits; wherein, if my muses be true to me, I shall raise the despised head of poetry again, and stripping her out of those rotten and base rags wherewith the times have adulterated her form, restore her to her primitive habit,° feature, and majesty, and render her worthy to be embraced and kissed of all the great and master-spirits of our world. As for the vile and slothful, who never affected an act worthy of celebration, or are so inward with their own vicious natures, as they worthily fear her and think it a high point of policy to keep her in contempt with their declamatory and windy invectives; she shall out of just rage incite her servants (who are *genus irritabile*) to spout ink in their faces that shall eat, farther than their marrow, into their fames, and not Cinnamus° the barber with his art shall be able to take out the brands, but they shall live, and be read, till the wretches die, as things worst deserving of themselves in chief, and then of all mankind.

From my house in the Blackfriars,
this 11th day of February, 1607°

The Persons of the Play°

Volpone, a Magnifico°
Mosca, his Parasite°

146 **the understanding** those with understanding 152 **primitive habit** original dress 162 **Cinnamus** celebrated surgeon-barber skilled at removing stigmata 166-7 **From . . . 1607** (only in quarto) **The Persons of the Play** (virtually all the characters have names that allude to animals: Volpone = fox, Mosca = fly, Voltore = vulture, Corbaccio = raven, Corvino = crow, Peregrine = hawk) **Magnifico** great magnate **Parasite** hanger-on

Voltore, an Advocate
Corbaccio, an old Gentleman
Corvino, a Merchant
Avocatori, four Magistrates
Notario, the Register°
Nano, a Dwarf
Castrone, an Eunuch
[Sir] Politic Wouldbe, a Knight
Peregrine, a Gent[leman]-traveler
Bonario, a young Gentleman [son of Corbaccio]
Fine Madame Wouldbe, the Knight's wife
Celia, the Merchant's wife
Commendatori, Officers
Mercatori, three Merchants
Androgyno, a Hermaphrodite
Servitore, a servant
Grege°
Women

The Scene

Venice

The Argument

V olpone, childless, rich, feigns sick, despairs,
O ffers his state° to hopes of several heirs,
L ies languishing; his Parasite receives
P resents of all, assures, deludes. Then weaves
O ther cross plots, which ope themselves, are told.°
N ew tricks for safety are sought; they thrive. When, bold,
E ach tempts th' other again, and all are sold.

Prologue

Now, luck God send us, and a little wit
  Will serve, to make our play hit;

Register clerk of the court **Grege** crowd **Argument** 2 **state** estate 5 **told** disclosed

According to the palates of the season,
  Here is rhyme not empty of reason.
This we were bid to credit,° from our poet,
  Whose true scope,° if you would know it,
In all his poems still, hath been this measure:
  To mix profit, with your pleasure;
And not as some, whose throats their envy failing,
  Cry hoarsely, "All he writes is railing,"°
And, when his plays come forth, think they can flout them,
  With saying, "He was a year about them."°
To these there needs no lie, but this his creature,°
  Which was, two months since, no feature;
And though he dares give them five lives to mend it,
  'Tis known, five weeks fully penned it:
From his own hand, without a coadjutor,°
  Novice, journeyman, or tutor.
Yet thus much I can give you, as a token
  Of his play's worth, no eggs are broken;
Nor quaking custards° with fierce teeth affrighted,
  Wherewith your rout° are so delighted;
Nor hales he in a gull, old ends° reciting,
  To stop gaps in his loose writing;
With such a deal of monstrous and forced action,
  As might make Bedlam° a faction:°
Nor made he 'his play, for jests, stol'n from each table,
  But makes jests, to fit his fable.
And, so presents quick° comedy, refined,
  As best critics have designed,
The laws of time, place, persons he observeth,
  From no needful rule he swerveth.
All gall, and copperas,° from his ink he draineth,
  Only a little salt remaineth;
Wherewith, he'll rub your cheeks, till (red with laughter)
  They shall look fresh, a week after.

Prologue 5 **credit** believe 6 **scope** aim 10 **railing** abusive language 12**He . . . them** (Jonson was frequently charged with being a slow writer) 13 **this his creature** i.e., *Volpone* 17 **coadjutor** collaborator 21 **quaking custards** cowards, also type of slapstick comedy 22 **rout** mob 23 **old ends** old-fashioned bits of poetry 26 **Bedlam** London insane asylum 26 **a faction** a supporting or participating group 29 **quick** lively, lifelike 33 **copperas** an acid

Act I, Scene i

Volpone, Mosca [*onstage.*]

[*Volpone.*] Good morning to the day; and next, my gold.
Open the shrine° that I may see my saint.
[*Mosca discloses piles of gold.*]
Hail the world's soul, and mine. More glad than is
The teeming earth to see the longed-for sun
Peep through the horns of the celestial Ram,°
Am I, to view thy splendor darkening his;
That lying here, amongst my other hoards,
Show'st like a flame by night, or like the day
Struck out of chaos,° when all darkness fled
Unto the center.° O thou son of Sol,°
But brighter than thy father, let me kiss,
With adoration, thee, and every relic
Of sacred treasure in this blessed room.
Well did wise poets, by thy glorious name,
Title that age° which they would have the best,
Thou being the best of things, and far transcending
All style of joy in children, parents, friends,
Or any other waking dream on earth.
Thy looks when they to Venus° did ascribe,
They should have giv'n her twenty thousand cupids,
Such are thy beauties and our loves! Dear saint,
Riches, the dumb god that giv'st all men tongues,
That canst do nought, and yet mak'st men do all things;
The price of souls; even hell, with thee to boot,
Is made worth heaven! Thou art virtue, fame,
Honor, and all things else! Who can get thee,
He shall be noble, valiant, honest, wise—
Mosca. And what° he will, sir. Riches are in fortune
A greater good than wisdom is in nature.
Volpone. True, my belovèd Mosca. Yet, I glory

I.i.2 **shrine** casket (?), recess (?) 5 **Ram** the sign of Aries (the sun enters Aries at the spring equinox) 8-9 **day . . . chaos** the light of day first created out of the darkness of chaos 10 **center** i.e., of the earth 10 **son of Sol** i.e., gold, in alchemy the child of the sun 15 **that age** i.e., the Golden Age 19 **Venus** (the Latin poets often called Venus golden) 28 **what** whatever

More in the cunning purchase° of my wealth
Than in the glad possession, since I gain
No common way: I use no trade, no venture;°
I wound no earth with ploughshares; fat no beasts
To feed the shambles;° have no mills for iron,
Oil, corn, or men, to grind 'em into powder;
I blow no subtle° glass; expose no ships
To threat'nings of the furrow-facèd sea;
I turn° no monies in the public bank,
Nor usure private°—
Mosca. No, sir, nor devour
Soft prodigals.° You shall ha' some will swallow
A melting heir as glibly as your Dutch
Will pills of butter,° and ne'er purge° for 't;
Tear forth the fathers of poor families
Out of their beds, and coffin them, alive,
In some kind, clasping prison, where their bones
May be forthcoming, when the flesh is rotten.
But, your sweet nature doth abhor these courses;°
You loathe the widow's or the orphan's tears
Should wash your pavements, or their piteous cries
Ring in your roofs, and beat the air for vengeance—
Volpone. Right, Mosca, I do loathe it.
Mosca. And besides, sir,
You are not like the thresher that doth stand
With a huge flail, watching a heap of corn,
And, hungry, dares not taste the smallest grain,
But feeds on mallows° and such bitter herbs;
Nor like the merchant, who hath filled his vaults
With Romagnìa° and rich Candian wines,°
Yet drinks the lees of Lombard's vinegar.
You will not lie in straw, whilst moths and worms
Feed on your sumptuous hangings and soft beds.
You know the use of riches, and dare give, now,

31 **purchase** acquisition 33 **venture** business speculation 35 **shambles** slaughterhouse 37 **subtle** delicate 39 **turn** exchange 40 **usure private** do not privately, i.e., secretly, lend money at exorbitant rates 41 **prodigals** spendthrifts, usually young and wealthy 42-3 **Dutch . . . butter** (Dutch were famous for devouring butter) 43 **purge** take a laxative 48 **courses** methods 56 **mallows** wild plants 58 **Romagnìa** Rumnev (Romanie), a sweet wine from Greece 58 **Candian wines** wines from Candy (Crete)

From that bright heap, to me, your poor observer,°
Or to your dwarf, or your hermaphrodite,
Your eunuch, or what other household trifle
Your pleasure allows maintenance—
Volpone. Hold thee, Mosca,
[*Gives him money.*]
Take, of my hand; thou strik'st on truth in all,
And they are envious term thee parasite.
Call forth my dwarf, my eunuch, and my fool,
And let 'em make me sport. [*Exit Mosca.*] What should
I do
But cocker up° my genius and live free
To all delights my fortune calls me to?
I have no wife, no parent, child, ally,
To give my substance to; but whom I make
Must be my heir, and this makes men observe me.°
This draws new clients,° daily, to my house,
Women and men of every sex and age,
That bring me presents, send me plate,° coin, jewels,
With hope that when I die (which they expect
Each greedy minute) it shall then return
Tenfold upon them; whilst some, covetous
Above the rest, seek to engross° me, whole,
And counterwork the one unto° the other,
Contend in gifts, as they would seem in love.
All which I suffer, playing with their hopes,
And am content to coin 'em into profit,
And look upon their kindness, and take more,
And look on that; still bearing them in hand,°
Letting the cherry knock against their lips,
And draw it by their mouths, and back again,
How now!

63 observer follower **71 cocker up** indulge **74-5 whom I make . . . observe me** whomever I designate will be my heir, and for this reason causes men to pay court to me **76 clients** followers **78 plate** dishes made of silver or gold **82 engross** absorb **83 unto** against **88 bearing . . . hand** leading them on

Act I, Scene ii

[Enter] Nano, Androgyno, Castrone [ready to perform for] Volpone. Mosca [follows.]

Nano. Now, room for fresh gamesters, who do will you to know,
They do bring you neither play nor university show;
And therefore do entreat you that whatsoever they rehearse,
May not a whit the worse, for the false pace° of the verse.
If you wonder at this, you will wonder more ere we pass,
For know, here is enclosed the soul of Pythagoras,°
[Points to Androgyno.]
That juggler divine, as hereafter shall follow;
Which soul, fast and loose,° sir, came first from Apollo,
And was breathed into Aethalides, Mercurius his son,
Where it° had the gift to remember all that ever was done.
From thence it fled forth, and made quick transmigration
To goldy-locked Euphorbus,° who was killed in good fashion,
At the siege of old Troy, by the cuckold of Sparta.°
Hermotimus° was next (I find it in my charta°)
To whom it did pass, where no sooner it was missing,
But with one Pyrrhus of Delos° it learned to go afishing;
And thence did it enter the sophist of Greece.°
From Pythagore, she went into a beautiful piece,

I.ii.4 **false pace** irregular or faulty meter (Nano and Androgyno's dialogue uses an outmoded four-stress rhythm) 6 **Pythagoras** Greek philosopher, one of whose teachings was that the soul passed from one body to another after death 8 **fast and loose** i.e., fixed yet slippery (from betting game where player bets whether or not a dagger is firmly held by a belt) 10 **it** i.e., the soul 12 **Euphorbus** the Trojan who first wounded Patroclus 13 **cuckold of Sparta** i.e., Menelaus 14 **Hermotimus** Greek philosopher 14 **charta** paper, script (possibly his source was Lucian's "Dialogue of the Cobbler and the Cock") 16 **Pyrrhus of Delos** a philosopher (?) 17 **the sophist of Greece** i.e., Pythagoras

Hight Aspasia,° the meretrix;° and the next toss of her
Was again of a whore, she became a philosopher,
Crates° the Cynic, as itself° doth relate it.
Since,° kings, knights, and beggars, knaves, lords, and fools gat it,
Besides ox and ass, camel, mule, goat, and brock,°
In all which it hath spoke, as in the Cobbler's cock.°
But I come not here to discourse of that matter,
Or his one, two, or three, or his great oath, "By Quater!"°
His musics, his trigon, his golden thigh,°
Or his telling how elements shift; but I
Would ask, how of late thou hast suffered translation,
And shifted thy coat in these days of reformation?°

Androgyno. Like one of the reformèd,° a fool, as you see,
Counting all old doctrine heresy.

Nano. But not on thine own forbid meats° hast thou ventured?

Androgyno. On fish, when first a Carthusian° I entered.

Nano. Why, then thy dogmatical silence° hath left thee?

Androgyno. Of that an obstreperous° lawyer bereft me.

Nano. O wonderful change! When Sir Lawyer forsook thee,
For Pythagore's sake, what body then took thee?

Androgyno. A good, dull moyle.°

Nano. And how! by that means
Thou wert brought to allow of the eating of beans?

Androgyno. Yes.

Nano. But from the moyle into whom didst thou pass?

19 **Hight Aspasia** named Aspasia (mistress of Pericles) 19 **meretrix** courtesan, whore 21 **Crates** a pupil of Diogenes the Cynic 21 **itself** i.e., the soul, as represented by Androgyno 22 **Since** i.e., since that time 23 **brock** badger 24 **Cobbler's cock** (the speaker in Lucian's dialogue) 26 **By Quater** by four (the principle of harmony in the universe, symbolized by the trigon, a triangle based on four dots) 27 **golden thigh** (Pythagoras' followers believed he had a golden thigh) 30 **reformation** i.e., the Protestant reformation 31 **reformèd** Puritans 33 **forbid meats** prohibited foods (Pythagoreans avoided fish and beans) 34 **Carthusian** (a member of a religious order noted for the severity of its diet, though fish was allowed) 35 **dogmatical silence** vow of silence, lasting five years among the Pythagoreans 36 **obstreperous** noisy 39 **moyle** mule

Androgyno. Into a very strange beast, by some writers called an ass;
By others, a precise, pure, illuminate° brother,
Of those devour flesh, and sometimes one another,
And will drop you forth a libel, or a sanctified lie,
Betwixt every spoonful of a nativity pie.°
Nano. Now quit thee, for heaven, of that profane nation,
And gently report thy next transmigration.
Androgyno. To the same that I am.
Nano. A creature of delight,
And what is more than a fool, an hermaphrodite?
Now, 'pray thee, sweet soul, in all thy variation,
Which body wouldst thou choose to take up thy station?
Androgyno. Troth, this I am in, even here would I tarry.
Nano. 'Cause here the delight of each sex thou canst vary?
Androgyno. Alas, those pleasures be stale and forsaken;
No, 'tis your fool wherewith I am so taken,
The only one creature that I can call blessèd,
For all other forms I have proved most distressèd.
Nano. Spoke true, as thou wert in Pythagoras still.
This learned opinion we celebrate will,
Fellow eunuch,° as behooves us, with all our wit and art,
To dignify that° whereof ourselves are so great and special a part.
Volpone. Now, very, very pretty! Mosca, this
Was thy invention?
Mosca. If it please my patron,
Not else.
Volpone. It doth, good Mosca.
Mosca. Then it was, sir.

Song.°

Fools, they are the only nation
Worth men's envy or admiration;
Free from care or sorrow-taking,

43 **precise, pure, illuminate** puritanical, rigorous, visionary (ironic) 46 **nativity pie** Christmas pie (the Puritans avoided the Popish implications of "mas") 61 **fellow eunuch** i.e., Castrone 62 **that** i.e., folly 65 **Song** (singers not designated, probably they are the three grotesques, Nano, Androgyno, and Castrone)

Selves and others merry making,
All they speak or do is sterling.
Your fool, he is your great man's dearling,°
And your ladies' sport and pleasure;
Tongue and bable° are his treasure.
E'en his face begetteth laughter,
And he speaks truth free from slaughter.°
He's the grace of every feast,
And, sometimes, the chiefest guest:
Hath his trencher° and his stool,
When wit waits upon the fool.°
O, who would not be
Hee, hee, hee?

One knocks without.

Volpone. Who's that? Away!

[*Exeunt Nano, Castrone.*]

Look, Mosca.

Mosca. Fool, begone! [*Exit Androgyno.*]
'Tis Signior Voltore, the advocate;
I know him by his knock.

Volpone. Fetch me my gown,
My furs,° and night-caps; say my couch is changing,
And let him entertain himself awhile
Without i' th' gallery. [*Exit Mosca.*] Now, now, my clients
Begin their visitation! Vulture, kite,
Raven, and gorcrow,° all my birds of prey,
That think me turning carcass, now they come.
I am not for 'em° yet.

[*Enter Mosca.*]

How now? the news?

Mosca. A piece of plate, sir.

Volpone. Of what bigness?

Mosca. Huge,
Massy, and antique, with your name inscribed,
And arms engraven.

71 **dearling** darling 73 **bable** bauble, the fool's scepter (with phallic allusion) 75 **slaughter** retaliation (the professional fool was allowed free rein to speak) 78 **trencher** dish 79 **wit . . . fool** wise man serves the fool 85 **furs** (worn by sick to keep warm) 89 **gorcrow** carrion crow 91 **for 'em** i.e., he doesn't yet have the furs and nightcap he asked for

Volpone. Good! and not a fox
Stretched on the earth, with fine delusive sleights
Mocking a gaping crow? ha, Mosca!
Mosca. Sharp, sir.
Volpone. Give me my furs. Why dost thou laugh so, man?
Mosca. I cannot choose, sir, when I apprehend
What thoughts he has, without, now, as he walks:
That this might be the last gift he should give;
That this would fetch you; if you died today,
And gave him all, what he should be tomorrow;
What large return would come of all his ventures;°
How he should worshipped be, and reverenced;
Ride with his furs, and foot-cloths; waited on
By herds of fools and clients; have clear way
Made for his moyle, as lettered as himself;
Be called the great and learnèd advocate:
And then concludes, there's nought impossible.
Volpone. Yes, to be learnèd, Mosca.
Mosca. O, no; rich
Implies it. Hood an ass with reverend purple,°
So you can hide his two ambitious ears,
And he shall pass for a cathedral doctor.
Volpone. My caps, my caps, good Mosca. Fetch him in.
Mosca. Stay, sir; your ointment for your eyes.
Volpone. That's true;
Dispatch, dispatch. I long to have possession
Of my new present.
Mosca. That, and thousands more,
I hope to see you lord of.
Volpone. Thanks, kind Mosca.
Mosca. And that, when I am lost in blended dust,
And hundreds such as I am, in succession—
Volpone. Nay, that were too much, Mosca.
Mosca. You shall live
Still to delude these harpies.
Volpone. Loving Mosca!
'Tis well.° My pillow now, and let him enter.
[*Exit Mosca.*]

103 ventures speculations, i.e., the gifts to Volpone **111 reverend purple** crimson hood for Doctor of Divinity **123 'Tis well** (Volpone is now prepared and may now check his makeup in a mirror)

Now. my feigned cough, my phthisic,° and my gout,
My apoplexy, palsy, and catarrhs,
Help, with your forcèd functions, this my posture,°
Wherein, this three year, I have milked their hopes.
He comes, I hear him—uh, uh, uh, uh, O.

Act I, Scene iii

[*Enter*] *Mosca* [*with*] *Voltore. Volpone* [*in bed.*]

Mosca. You still are what you were, sir. Only you,
Of all the rest, are he commands his love,
And you do wisely to preserve it thus,
With early visitation, and kind notes
Of your good meaning° to him, which, I know,
Cannot but come most grateful. Patron, sir.
Here's Signior Voltore is come—
Volpone. What say you?
Mosca. Sir, Signior Voltore is come this morning
To visit you.
Volpone. I thank him.
Mosca. And hath brought
A piece of antique plate, bought of St. Mark,°
With which he here presents you.
Volpone. He is welcome.
Pray him to come more often.
Mosca. Yes.
Voltore. What says he?
Mosca. He thanks you and desires you see him often.
Volpone. Mosca.
Mosca. My patron?
Volpone. Bring him near, where is he?
I long to feel his hand.
Mosca. The plate is here, sir.
Voltore. How fare you, sir?
Volpone. I thank you, Signor Voltore.
Where is the plate? mine eyes are bad.

124 **phthisic** consumption, also asthma 126 **posture** imposture, role I.iii.4-5 **notes of your good meaning** marks of your good intentions 10 **of St. Mark** from the square of St. Mark (where goldsmith shops were located)

Voltore. [*gives it to Volpone.*] I'm sorry
To see you still thus weak.
Mosca. [*Aside.*] That he is not weaker.
Volpone. You are too munificent.
Voltore. No, sir; would to heaven
I could as well give health to you as that plate!
Volpone. You give, sir, what you can. I thank you. Your love
Hath taste in this,° and shall not be unanswered.
I pray you see me often.
Voltore. Yes, I shall, sir.
Volpone. Be not far from me.
Mosca. [*to Voltore.*] Do you observe that, sir?
Volpone. Hearken unto me still; it will concern you.
Mosca. You are a happy man, sir; know your good.
Volpone. I cannot now last long—
Mosca. You are his heir, sir.
Voltore. Am I?
Volpone. I feel me going, uh, uh, uh, uh.
I am sailing to my port, uh, uh, uh, uh?
And I am glad I am so near my haven.
Mosca. Alas, kind gentleman. Well, we must all go—
Voltore. But, Mosca—
Mosca. Age will conquer.
Voltore. Pray thee, hear me.
Am I inscribed his heir for certain?
Mosca. Are you?
I do beseech you, sir, you will vouchsafe
To write me i' your family.° All my hopes
Depend upon your worship. I am lost
Except the rising sun do shine on me.
Voltore. It shall both shine and warm thee, Mosca.
Mosca. Sir,
I am a man that have not done your love
All the worst offices. Here I wear your keys,
See all your coffers and your caskets locked,
Keep the poor inventory of your jewels,
Your plate, and monies; am your steward, sir,
Husband your goods here.

22 **Hath taste in this** is indicated by this, i.e., the plate 35 **write me i' your family** put my name in your household book, i.e., take me under your patronage

Voltore. But am I sole heir?
Mosca. Without a partner, sir, confirmed this morning;
The wax is warm yet, and the ink scarce dry
Upon the parchment.
Voltore. Happy, happy me!
By what good chance, sweet Mosca?
Mosca. Your desert, sir;
I know no second cause.
Voltore. Thy modesty
Is loth to know it;° well, we shall requite it.
Mosca. He ever liked your course,° sir; that first took him.°
I oft have heard him say how he admired
Men of your large° profession, that could speak
To every cause, and things mere contraries,°
Till they were hoarse again, yet all be law;
That, with most quick agility, could turn,
And re-turn; make knots, and undo them;
Give forkèd° counsel; take provoking gold
On either hand, and put it up.° These men,
He knew, would thrive with their humility.
And, for his part, he thought he should be bless'd
To have his heir of such a suffering spirit,
So wise, so grave, of so perplexed° a tongue,
And loud withal, that would not wag, nor scarce
Lie still, without a fee; when every word
Your worship but lets fall, is a chequin!°
Another knocks.
Who's that? One knocks. I would not have you seen, sir.
And yet—pretend you came and went in haste;
I'll fashion an excuse. And, gentle sir,
When you do come to swim in golden lard,
Up to the arms in honey, that your chin
Is borne up stiff with fatness of the flood,
Think on your vassal; but remember me:
I ha' not been your worst of clients.

50 know it admit it **51 course** way of acting, i.e., as a lawyer **51 took him** caught his attention **53 large** liberal and eloquent **53-4 speak . . . contraries** argue all sides and even matters that contradict each other **58 forkèd** fork-tongued, equivocal **58-9 take . . . put it up** take gold from both parties to initiate a legal action, and then pocket it **63 perplexed** confused by the intricacy of his argument **66 chequin** gold coin

Voltore. Mosca—
Mosca. When will you have your inventory brought, sir?
Or see a copy of the will? [*one knocks again.*] Anon.
I'll bring 'em to you, sir. Away, be gone,
Put business i' your face. [*Exit Voltore.*]
Volpone. Excellent, Mosca!
Come hither, let me kiss thee.
Mosca. Keep you still, sir.
Here is Corbaccio.
Volpone. Set the plate away.
The vulture's gone, and the old raven's come.

Act I, Scene iv

Mosca. Betake you, to your silence, and your sleep.
[*sets down the plate.*]
Stand there and multiply. Now shall we see
A wretch who is indeed more impotent
Than this° can feign to be, yet hopes to hop
Over his grave. [*Enter Corbaccio.*] Signior Corbaccio!
You're very welcome, sir.
Corbaccio. How does your patron?
Mosca. Troth, as he did, sir; no amends.
Corbaccio. What? mends he?
Mosca. No, sir. He is rather worse.
Corbaccio. That's well. Where is he?
Mosca. Upon his couch, sir, newly fall'n asleep.
Corbaccio. Does he sleep well?
Mosca. No wink, sir, all this night,
Nor yesterday, but slumbers.°
Corbaccio. Good! he should take
Some counsel of physicians. I have brought him
An opiate here, from mine own doctor—
Mosca. He will not hear of drugs.
Corbaccio. Why? I myself
Stood by while 't was made, saw all th' ingredients,
And know it cannot but most gently work.
My life for his, 'tis but to make him sleep.
Volpone. [*Aside.*] Ay, his last sleep, if he would take it.

I.iv.4 this i.e., Volpone **11 but slumbers** only dozes

Mosca. Sir,
He has no faith in physic.°
Corbaccio. Say you, say you?
Mosca. He has no faith in physic: he does think
Most of your doctors° are the greater danger,
And worst disease t' escape. I often have
Heard him protest that your physician
Should never be his heir.
Corbaccio. Not I his heir?
Mosca. Not your physician, sir.
Corbaccio. O, no, no, no,
I do not mean it.
Mosca. No, sir, nor their fees
He cannot brook; he says they flay a man
Before they kill him.
Corbaccio. Right, I do conceive° you.
Mosca. And then, they do it by experiment,
For which the law not only doth absolve 'em,
But gives them great reward; and he is loth
To hire his death so.
Corbaccio. It is true, they kill
With as much license as a judge.
Mosca. Nay, more;
For he but kills, sir, where the law condemns,
And these can kill him too.
Corbaccio. Ay, or me,
Or any man. How does his apoplex?
Is that strong on him still?
Mosca. Most violent.
His speech is broken, and his eyes are set,
His face drawn longer than 't was wont—
Corbaccio. How? how?
Stronger than he was wont?
Mosca. No, sir; his face
Drawn longer than 't was wont.
Corbaccio. O, good.
Mosca. His mouth
Is ever gaping, and his eyelids hang.
Corbaccio. Good.

19 **physic** medicine 21 **your doctors** i.e., doctors in general
28 **conceive** intend

Mosca. A freezing numbness stiffens all his joints,
And makes the color of his flesh like lead.
Corbaccio. 'Tis good.
Mosca. His pulse beats slow and dull.
Corbaccio. Good symptoms still.
Mosca. And from his brain—
Corbaccio. Ha? How? not from his brain?
Mosca. Yes, sir. and from his brain°—
Corbaccio. I conceive you; good.
Mosca. Flows a cold sweat, with a continual rheum,
Forth the resolvèd° corners of his eyes.
Corbaccio. Is't possible? Yet I am better, ha!
How does he with the swimming of his head?
Mosca. O, sir, 'tis past the scotomy;° he now
Hath lost his feeling, and hath left° to snort;
You hardly can perceive him that he breathes.
Corbaccio. Excellent, excellent; sure I shall outlast him!
This makes me young again, a score of years.
Mosca. I was a-coming for you, sir.
Corbaccio. Has he made his will?
What has he given me?
Mosca. No, sir.
Corbaccio. Nothing? ha?
Mosca. He has not made his will, sir.
Corbaccio. Oh, oh, oh.
What then did Voltore, the lawyer, here?
Mosca. He smelled a carcass, sir, when he but heard
My master was about his testament;
As I did urge him to it for your good—
Corbaccio. He came unto him, did he? I thought so.
Mosca. Yes, and presented him this piece of plate.
Corbaccio. To be his heir?
Mosca. I do not know, sir.
Corbaccio. True,
I know it too.
Mosca. By your own scale,° sir.
Corbaccio. Well,
I shall prevent° him yet. See, Mosca, look,

47 **from his brain** (in the last stage of apoplexy, fluid was thought to flow from the brain) 49 **resolvèd** slackened 52 **scotomy** dizziness accompanied by dimness of sight 53 **left** ceased 67 **By . . . scale** according to your own standards 68 **prevent** thwart by getting ahead

Here I have brought a bag of bright chequins,
Will quite weigh down° his plate.
Mosca. Yea, marry, sir.
This is true physic, this your sacred medicine;
No talk of opiates to this great elixir.°
Corbaccio. 'Tis aurum palpabile, if not potabile.°
Mosca. It shall be ministered to him, in his bowl?
Corbaccio. Ay, do, do, do.
Mosca. Most blessed cordial!°
This will recover him.
Corbaccio. Yes, do, do, do.
Mosca. I think it were not best, sir.
Corbaccio. What?
Mosca. To recover him.
Corbaccio. O, no, no, no; by no means.
Mosca. Why, sir, this
Will work some strange effect if he but feel it.
Corbaccio. 'Tis true, therefore forbear; I'll take my venture;°
Give me 't again.
Mosca. At no hand. Pardon me.
You shall not do yourself that wrong, sir. I
Will so advise you, you shall have it all.
Corbaccio. How?
Mosca. All, sir; 'tis your right, your own; no man
Can claim a part; 'tis yours without a rival,
Decreed by destiny.
Corbaccio. How, how, good Mosca?
Mosca. I'll tell you, sir. This fit he shall recover°—
Corbaccio. I do conceive you.
Mosca. And on first advantage
Of his gained sense,° will I re-importune him
Unto the making of his testament,
And show him this.°

70 **weigh down** outweigh, figuratively and literally 72 **to this great elixir** in comparison to this marvelous drug (fabled to make life eternal) 73 **aurum . . . potabile** gold capable of being touched, if not drunk (particles of gold in a volatile oil were actually used as medicine) 75 **cordial** medicine to invigorate the heart 80 **venture** i.e., the bag of gold 87 **recover** recover from 88-9 **on first . . . sense** at the first favorable moment after he has regained his senses 91 **this** i.e., the bag of chequins

Corbaccio. Good, good.
Mosca. 'Tis better yet,
If you will hear, sir.
Corbaccio. Yes, with all my heart.
Mosca. Now would I counsel you, make home with speed;
There, frame° a will whereto° you shall inscribe
My master your sole heir.
Corbaccio. And disinherit
My son?
Mosca. O, sir, the better; for that color°
Shall make it much more taking.°
Corbaccio. O, but color?
Mosca. This will, sir, you shall send it unto me.
Now, when I come to enforce,° as I will do,
Your cares, your watchings, and your many prayers,
Your more than many gifts, your this day's present,
And, last, produce your will; where, without thought
Or least regard unto your proper issue,°
A son so brave and highly meriting,
The stream of your diverted love hath thrown you
Upon my master, and made him your heir:
He cannot be so stupid, or stone dead,
But out of conscience and mere° gratitude—
Corbaccio. He must pronounce me his?
Mosca. 'Tis true.
Corbaccio. This plot
Did I think on before.
Mosca. I do believe it.
Corbaccio. Do you not believe it?
Mosca. Yes, sir.
Corbaccio. Mine own project.
Mosca. Which, when he hath done, sir—
Corbaccio. Published me his heir?
Mosca. And you so certain to survive him—
Corbaccio. Ay.
Mosca. Being so lusty a man—
Corbaccio. 'Tis true.
Mosca. Yes, sir—

94 **frame** compose 94 **whereto** wherein 96 **color** appearance, here a mock disinheritance 97 **taking** convincing 99 **enforce** urge 103 **proper issue** own child 108 **mere** simple

Corbaccio. I thought on that too. See, how he° should be
The very organ to express my thoughts!
Mosca. You have not only done yourself a good—
Corbaccio. But multiplied it on my son?
Mosca. 'Tis right, sir.
Corbaccio. Still my invention.°
Mosca. 'Las, sir, heaven knows
It hath been all my study, all my care.
(I e'en grow grey withtal) how to work things—
Corbaccio. I do conceive, sweet Mosca.
Mosca. You are he
For whom I labor here.
Corbaccio. Ay, do, do, do.
I'll straight about it.°
[*Mosca now speaks too softly for Corbaccio to hear.*]
Mosca. Rook go with you,° raven.
Corbaccio. I know thee honest.
Mosca. You do lie, sir.
Corbaccio. And—
Mosca. Your knowledge is no better than your ears,° sir.
Corbaccio. I do not doubt to be a father to thee.
Mosca. Nor I to gull° my brother° of his blessing.
Corbaccio. I may ha' my youth restored to me, why not?
Mosca. Your worship is a precious ass—
Corbaccio. What sayst thou?
Mosca. I do desire your worship to make haste, sir.
Corbaccio. 'Tis done, 'tis done, I go. [*Exit.*]
Volpone. O, I shall burst!
Let out my sides, let out my sides.
Mosca. Contain
Your flux° of laughter, sir. You know this hope°
Is such a bait it covers any hook.
Volpone. O, but thy working, and they placing it!

115 **See, how he** Look, isn't it wonderful how he, i.e., Mosca 119 **Still my invention** (Corbaccio repeatedly claims to have first thought of the idea of using the will as bait) 124 **I'll straight about it** I'll get right to it (making the new will) 124 **rook go with you** may you be rooked, i.e., fooled 126 **ears** hearing 128 **gull** cheat 128 **my brother** i.e., Corbaccio's son (ironic) 134 **flux** flow, here a flood or discharge 134 **this hope** i.e., Corbaccio's to become Volpone's heir

I cannot hold; good rascal, let me kiss thee.
I never knew thee in so rare a humor.
Mosca. Alas, sir, I but do as I am taught;
Follow your grave instruction; give 'em words;
Pour oil into their ears, and send them hence.
Volpone. 'Tis true, 'tis true. What a rare punishment
Is avarice to itself!
Mosca. Ay, with our help, sir.
Volpone. So many cares, so many maladies,
So many fears attending on old age.
Yea, death so often called on as no wish
Can be more frequent with 'em. Their limbs faint,
Their senses dull, their seeing, hearing, going,°
All dead before them;° yea, their very teeth,
Their instruments of eating, failing them.
Yet this is reckoned life! Nay, here was one,
Is now gone home, that wishes to live longer!
Feels not his gout, nor palsy; feigns himself
Younger by scores of years, flatters his age
With confident belying it; hopes he may
With charms, like Aeson° have his youth restored;
And with these thoughts so battens,° as if fate
Would be as easily cheated on as he,
Another knocks.
And all turns air! Who's that, there, now? a third?
Mosca. Close to your couch again; I hear his voice.
It is Corvino, our spruce merchant.
Volpone. [*Lies down.*] Dead.
Mosca. Another bout, sir, with your eyes.° Who's there?

Act I, Scene v

Mosca [*welcomes*] *Corvino. Volpone* [*in bed.*]

Mosca. Signior Corvino! come most wished for! O,
How happy were you, if you knew it, now!

148 **going** ability to walk 149 **before them** i.e., their functions are dead before they are 156 **Aeson** Jason's father (with magic charms Medea restored him to youth) 157 **battens** grows fat (figuratively) 162 **Another bout . . . eyes** (Mosca applies the ointment again)

Corvino. Why? what? wherein?
Mosca. The tardy hour is come, sir.
Corvino. He is not dead?
Mosca. Not dead, sir, but as good;
He knows no man.
Corvino. How shall I do then?
Mosca. Why, sir?
Corvino. I have brought him here a pearl.
Mosca Perhaps he has
So much remembrance left as to know you, sir.
He still calls on you, nothing but your name
Is in his mouth. Is your pearl orient,° sir?
Corvino. Venice was never owner of the like.
Volpone. Signior Corvino.
Mosca. Hark.
Volpone. Signior Corvino.
Mosca. He calls you; step and give it him. He is here, sir.
And he has brought you a rich pearl.
Corvino. How do you, sir?
Tell him it doubles the twelfth caract.°
Mosca. Sir,
He cannot understand, his hearing's gone,
And yet it comforts him to see you—
Corvino. Say
I have a diamond for him, too.
Mosca. Best show 't, sir,
Put it into his hand; 'tis only there
He apprehends, he has his feelings yet.
[*Volpone seizes the pearl.*]
See how he grasps it!
Corvino. 'Las, good gentleman!
How pitiful the sight is!
Mosca. Tut, forget, sir.
The weeping of an heir should still be laughter
Under a visor.°
Corvino. Why? am I his heir?
Mosca. Sir, I am sworn, I may not show the will
Till he be dead. But here has been Corbaccio,
Here has been Voltore, here were others too,
I cannot number 'em, they were so many;

I.v.9 orient from the far east, hence more precious **14 caract** carat **23 visor** mask

All gaping here for legacies; but I,
Taking the vantage of his naming you,
"Signior Corvino, Signior Corvino," took
Paper, and pen, and ink, and there I asked him
Whom he would have his heir? *"Corvino."* Who
Should be executor? *"Corvino."* And
To any question he was silent to,
I still interpreted the nods he made,
Through weakness, for consent; and sent home th' others,
Nothing bequeathed them but to cry and curse.
They embrace.

Corvino. O, my dear Mosca. Does he not perceive us?

Mosca. No more than a blind harper.° He knows no man,
No face of friend, nor name of any servant,
Who 't was that fed him last, or gave him drink;
Not those he hath begotten, or brought up,
Can he remember.

Corvino. Has he children?

Mosca. Bastards,
Some dozen, or more, that he begot on beggars,
Gypsies, and Jews, and black-moors when he was drunk.
Knew you not that, sir? 'Tis the common fable,
The dwarf, the fool, the eunuch are all his;°
He's the true father of his family,
In all save me, but he has given 'em nothing.

Corvino. That's well, that's well. Art sure he does not hear us?

Mosca. Sure, sir? why, look you, credit your own sense.
[*Shouts in Volpone's ear.*]
The pox° approach and add to your diseases,
If it would send you hence the sooner, sir,
For, your incontinence, it hath deserved it°
Throughly and throughly, and the plague to boot.
(You may come near, sir) Would you would once close
Those filthy eyes of yours that flow with slime
Like two frog-pits, and those same hanging cheeks,
Covered with hide instead of skin—Nay, help, sir—
That look like frozen dish-clouts° set on end.

39 blind harper a nameless figure in the crowd (proverbial) **47 all his** i.e., his offspring **52 pox** the great pox, i.e., syphilis **54 incontinence . . . it** lack of control has deserved the pox **60 dish-clouts** rags

Corvino. Or, like an old smoked wall, on which the rain
Ran down in streaks
Mosca. Excellent, sir, speak out.
You may be louder yet; a culverin°
Dischargèd in his ear would hardly bore it.
Corvino. His nose is like a common sewer, still running.
Mosca. 'Tis good! And what his mouth?
Corvino. A very draught.°
Mosca. O, stop it up—°
Corvino. By no means.
Mosca. Pray you, let me.
Faith I could stifle him rarely° with a pillow,
As well as any woman that should keep him.
Corvino. Do as you will, but I'll be gone.
Mosca. Be so.
It is your presence makes him last so long.
Corvino. I pray you, use no violence.
Mosca. No, sir? why?
Why should you be thus scrupulous, pray you, sir?
Corvino. Nay, at your discretion.
Mosca. Well, good sir, be gone.
Corvino. I will not trouble him now to take my pearl?
Mosca. Puh! nor your diamond. What a needless care
Is this afflicts you! Is not all here yours?
Am not I here, whom you have made? Your creature?
That owe my being to you?
Corvino. Grateful Mosca!
Thou art my friend, my fellow, my companion,
My partner, and shalt share in all my fortunes.
Mosca. Excepting one.
Corvino. What's that?
Mosca. Your gallant° wife, sir.
[*Exit Corvino.*]
Now is he gone; we had no other means
To shoot him hence° but this.
Volpone. My divine Mosca!
Thou hast today outgone thyself.
Another knocks.

63 **culverin** type of cannon 66 **draught** cesspool 67 **stop it up** (here Mosca may start to smother Volpone) 68 **rarely** finely, with finesse 82 **gallant** here, beautiful 84 **shoot him hence** get rid of him

Who's there?
I will be troubled with no more. Prepare
Me music, dances, banquets, all delights;
The Turk is not more sensual in his pleasures
Than will Volpone. [*Exit Mosca.*]
Let me see: a pearl?
A diamond? plate? chequins? good morning's purchase.°
Why, this is better than rob churches, yet,
Or fat, by eating once a month a man.°

[*Enter Mosca.*]

Who is 't?
Mosca. The beauteous Lady Wouldbe, sir,
Wife to the English knight, Sir Politic Wouldbe—
This is the style, sir, is directed me—°
Hath sent to know how you have slept tonight,
And if you would be visited?
Volpone. Not now.
Some three hours hence—
Mosca. I told the squire so much.
Volpone. When I am high with mirth and wine, then, then.
'Fore heaven, I wonder at the desperate valor
Of the bold English, that they dare let loose°
Their wives to all encounters!
Mosca. Sir, this knight
Had not his name for nothing; he is *politic,*
And knows, howe'er his wife affect strange airs,
She hath not yet the face to be dishonest.°
But had she Signior Corvino's wife's face—
Volpone. Has she so rare a face?
Mosca. O, sir, the wonder,
The blazing star of Italy! a wench
O' the first year! a beauty ripe as harvest!
Whose skin is whiter than a swan, all over!
Than silver, snow, or lilies! a soft lip,

90 **purchase** business, here slangy: haul 92 **eating . . . man** cheating one man a month of his estate 95 **style . . . me** the style in which the message was delivered to me 101 **dare let loose** (Italians were astonished at the freedom the English allowed their wives) 105 **the face to be dishonest** the looks to be unchaste

Would tempt you to eternity of kissing!
And flesh that melteth, in the touch, to blood!°
Bright as your gold! and lovely as your gold!
Volpone. Why had not I known this before?
Mosca. Alas, sir,
Myself but yesterday discovered it.
Volpone. How might I see her?
Mosca. O, not possible;
She's kept as warily as is your gold,
Never does come abroad,° never takes air
But at a window. All her looks are sweet
As the first grapes or cherries, and are watched
As near° as they are.
Volpone. I must see her—
Mosca. Sir,
There is a guard, of ten spies thick, upon her;
All his whole household; each of which is set
Upon° his fellow, and have all their charge,°
When he goes out, when he comes in, examined.
Volpone. I will go see her, though but at her window.
Mosca. In some disguise then.
Volpone. That is true. I must
Maintain mine own shape° still the same: we'll think.
[*Exeunt.*]

Act II, Scene i

Politic Wouldbe [*and*] *Peregrine* [*in a public square in front of Corvino's house.*]

Sir Politic. Sir, to a wise man, all the world's his soil.°
It is not Italy, nor France, nor Europe,
That must bound me, if my fates call me forth.
Yet, I protest, it is no salt° desire
Of seeing countries, shifting a religion,
Nor any disaffection to the state

113 to blood to blushes **119 abroad** out of the house **122 near** closely **124-5 set Upon** set to spy on **125 all their charge** everything they are responsible for **129 maintain . . . shape** i.e., the image of a dying man **II.i.1 soil** land **4 salt** wanton

Where I was bred, and unto which I owe
My dearest plots,° hath brought me out; much less
That idle, antique, stale, grey-headed project
Of knowing men's minds, and manners, with Ulysses;°
But a peculiar humor° of my wife's,
Laid for this height° of Venice, to observe,
To quote,° to learn the language, and so forth.
I hope you travel, sir, with license?°

Peregrine. Yes.

Sir Politic. I dare the safelier converse—How long, sir,
Since you left England?

Peregrine. Seven weeks.

Sir Politic. So lately!
You ha' not been with my lord ambassador?°

Peregrine. Not yet, sir.

Sir Politic. 'Pray you, what news, sir, vents our climate?°
I heard, last night, a most strange thing reported
By some of my lord's followers, and I long
To hear how 'twill be seconded.

Peregrine. What was't, sir?

Sir Politic. Marry, sir, of a raven, that should build
In° a ship royal of the King's.

Peregrine. [*Aside.*]—This fellow,
Does he gull° me, trow?° or is gulled?—Your name, sir?

Sir Politic. My name is Politic Wouldbe.

Peregrine. [*Aside.*]—O, that speaks him—°
A knight, sir?

Sir Politic. A poor knight, sir.

Peregrine. Your lady
Lies° here, in Venice, for intelligence

8 **plots** ideas of projects (throughout Sir Politic inflates his speech) 10 **with Ulysses** which was Ulysses's aim (as expressed at the opening of *Odyssey*) 11 **humor** inclination, possibly obsession (an instance of Sir Politic's inflated speech) 12 **Laid . . . height** directed towards this latitude 13 **quote** make note 14 **license** approval of Privy Council 17 **my lord ambassador** (from 1604 to 1612 the ambassador was Sir Henry Wotton, known as an intriguer; Sir Politic may be a caricature of him) 18 **vents our climate** issues forth from our land (strained usage) 22-3 **should build In** who, it is said, builds a nest in the shrouds of 24 **gull** make a fool of 24 **trow** do you think? 25 **that speaks him** that name describes him precisely 27 **lies** stays

Of tires,° and fashions, and behavior
Among the courtesans?° The fine Lady Wouldbe?
Sir Politic. Yes, sir, the spider and the bee° ofttimes
Suck from one flower.
Peregrine. Good Sir Politic!
I cry you mercy;° I have heard much of you.
'Tis true, sir, of your raven.
Sir Politic. On your knowledge?
Peregrine. Yes, and your lion's° whelping in the Tower.°
Sir Politic. Another whelp!
Peregrine. Another, sir,
Sir Politic. Now heaven!
What prodigies° be these? The fires at Berwick!°
And the new star!° These things concurring, strange!
And full of omen! Saw you those meteors?°
Peregrine. I did, sir.
Sir Politic. Fearful! Pray you, sir, confirm me,
Were there three porpoises seen above the bridge,°
As they give out?°
Peregrine. Six, and a sturgeon, sir.
Sir Politic. I am astonished!
Peregrine. Nay, sir, be not so;
I'll tell you a greater prodigy than these—
Sir Politic. What should these things portend?
Peregrine. The very day
(Let me be sure) that I put forth from London,
There was a whale° discovered in the river,
As high as Woolwich, that had waited there,

27-8 **for intelligence Of tires** to learn about clothes (attires) and headdresses 29 **courtesans** high-class prostitutes 30 **the spider and the bee** here, the spider = the courtesan, the bee = Lady Wouldbe 31 **I cry you mercy** I beg your pardon 34 **your lion's** i.e., the lion you know of 34 **the Tower** (James I kept lions in the Tower, where he set dogs against a lion) 36 **prodigies** unusual events (in 1604 and again in 1605 the lioness Elizabeth birthed cubs) 36 **fires at Berwick** ghostly armies in battle reportedly seen near Berwick in 1604 37 **new star** (in 1606 Kepler reported discovery of a nova (?), new star (?) in the constellation Serpentarius seen September 30, 1604) 38 **meteors** disturbances in the cosmos, hence ill omens 40 **above the bridge** upstream of London bridge 41 **give out** report 46 **whale** (early in 1606 a porpoise and later a whale came up river toward London)

Few know how many months, for the subversion
Of the Stode fleet.°
Sir Politic. Is't possible? Believe it,
'Twas either sent from Spain, or the Archdukes!°
Spinola's° whale, upon my life, my credit!
Will they not leave these projects? Worthy sir,
Some other news.
Peregrine. Faith, Stone° the fool is dead,
And they do lack a tavern fool extremely.
Sir Politic. Is Mas'° Stone dead?
Peregrine. He's dead, sir; why, I hope
You thought him not immortal? [*Aside.*]—O, this knight,
Were he well known, would be a precious thing
To fit our English stage. He that should write
But such a fellow, should be thought to feign
Extremely, if not maliciously.
Sir Politic. Stone dead!
Peregrine. Dead. Lord! how deeply, sir, you apprehend° it.
He was no kinsman to you?
Sir Politic. That I know of.°
Well, that same fellow was an unknown fool.°
Peregrine. And yet you know him, it seems?
Sir Politic. I did so. Sir,
I knew him one of the most dangerous heads°
Living within the state, and so I held° him.
Peregrine. Indeed, sir?
Sir Politic While he lived, in action.
He has received weekly intelligence,
Upon my knowledge, out of the Low Countries,
For all parts of the world, in cabbages;
And those dispensed, again, t' ambassadors,
In oranges, musk-melons, apricots,

49 **Stode fleet** the fleet that sailed between London and Stode or Stade (a city on the Elbe river where the English Merchant Adventurers were settled at this time) 50 **Archdukes** the rulers of the Spanish Netherlands 51 **Spinola** Spanish commander in the Netherlands, regarded by the gullible as capable of monstrous feats 53 **Stone** popular clown of the day, whipped for ridiculing the Lord Admiral in 1605 55 **Mas'** master 61 **apprehend** (1) feel, (2) understand 62 **That I know of** Not that I know of 63 **unknown fool** being a fool was a cover for his real person 65 **heads** plotters 66 **held** regarded

Lemons, pome-citrons,° and suchlike; sometimes
In Colchester oysters, and your Selsey cockles.°
Peregrine. You make me wonder.
Sir Politic Sir, upon my knowledge.
Nay, I have observed him at your public ordinary°
Take his advertisement° from a traveler,
A concealed statesman,° in a trencher° of meat;
And, instantly, before the meal was done,
Convey an answer in a toothpick.
Peregrine. Strange!
How could this be, sir?
Sir Politic. Why, the meat was cut
So like his charàcter, and so laid as he
Must easily read the cipher.°
Peregrine. I have heard
He could not read, sir.
Sir Politic. So 'twas given out,
In policy,° by those that did employ him;
But he could read, and had your languages,
And to 't, as sound a noddle°—
Peregrine. I have heard, sir,
That your baboons were spies, and that they were
A kind of subtle nation near to China.
Sir Politic. Ay, ay, your Mamuluchi.° Faith, they had
Their hand in a French plot, or two; but they
Were so extremely given to° women as
They made discovery° of all; yet I
Had my advices° here, on Wednesday last,
From one of their own coat,° they were returned,
Made their relations,° as the fashion is,
And now stand fair° for fresh employment.

73 **pome-citrons** citrons or limes 74 **cockles** type of mollusc 76 **ordinary** tavern providing food at fixed prices 77 **Take his advertisement** get his information 78 **concealed statesman** secret government agent 78 **trencher** wooden platter 81-3 **the meat . . . cipher** the meat was cut to match his handwriting, and so arranged that he might easily read the code 85 **In policy** for political purposes 87 **And . . . noddle** And in addition, as sharp a mind 90 **Mamuluchi** plural of Mameluke, first slaves, then rulers of Egypt 92 **given to** had a weakness for 93 **discovery** disclosure 94 **advices** dispatches 95 **coat** party 96 **relations** reports 97 **stand fair** are available

Peregrine. [*Aside.*]—'Heart!°
This Sir Pol will be ignorant of nothing—
It seems, sir, you know all.
Sir Politic. Not all, sir. But
I have some general notions; I do love
To note and to observe: though I live out,°
Free from the active torrent, yet I'd mark
The currents and the passages of things
For mine own private use; and know the ebbs
And flows of state.
Peregrine. Believe it, sir, I hold
Myself in no small tie° unto my fortunes
For casting me thus luckily upon you,
Whose knowledge, if your bounty equal it,°
May do me great assistance in instruction
For my behavior, and my bearing, which
Is yet so rude and raw.
Sir Politic. Why? came you forth
Empty of rules for travel?
Peregrine. Faith, I had
Some common ones, from out that vulgar grammar,°
Which he that cried° Italian to me, taught me.
Sir Politic. Why, this it is that spoils all our brave bloods,°
Trusting our hopeful gentry unto pedants,
Fellows of outside, and mere bark.° You seem
To be a gentleman, of ingenuous race°—
I not profess it,° but my fate hath been
To be where I have been consulted with
In this high kind,° touching° some great men's sons,
Persons of blood and honor—
Peregrine. Who be these, sir?

97 **'Heart** i.e., by God's heart 101 **live out** remain aloof, i.e., stay out of politics 106 **tie** debt 108 **if . . . it** if your generosity equals it, i.e., your knowledge 113 **vulgar grammar** grammar in vulgar tongue, i.e., not Latin 114 **cried** intoned in speaking, hence taught 115 **brave bloods** fine young gentlemen 117 **bark** (1) of tree, (2) of dog with echo of "cried Italian" 118 **ingenuous race** noble birth 118 **it** i.e., educating young men 121 **high kind** important matter 121 **touching** having to do with

Act II, Scene ii

[*Enter Mosca and Nano, disguised, with materials to erect a scaffold stage.*]

Mosca. Under that window, there 't must be. The same.
Sir Politic. Fellows to mount a bank!° Did your instructor
In the dear° tongues, never discourse to you
Of the Italian mountebanks?
Peregrine. Yes, sir.
Sir Politic. Why,
Here shall you see one.
Peregrine. They are quacksalvers,°
Fellows that live by venting° oils and drugs.
Sir Politic. Was that the character he gave you of them?
Peregrine. As I remember.
Sir Politic. Pity his ignorance.
They are the only knowing men of Europe!
Great general scholars, excellent physicians,
Most admired statesmen, professed favorites
And cabinet counselors° to the greatest princes!
The only languaged men of all the world!
Peregrine. And I have heard they are most lewd° impostors,
Made all of terms and shreds;° no less beliers
Of° great men's favors than their own vile medicines;
Which they will utter upon monstrous oaths,
Selling that drug for twopence, ere they part,
Which they have valued at twelve crowns before.
Sir Politic. Sir, calumnies are answered best with silence.
Yourself shall judge. Who is it mounts, my friends?
Mosca. Scoto of Mantua,° sir.
Sir Politic. Is't he? Nay, then

II.ii.2 **mount a bank** from Italian *monta in banco,* banco or bench here being a raised scaffold, probably boards placed on trestles 3 **dear** esteemed 5 **quacksalvers** quackers or sellers of salves (from the Dutch) 6 **venting** vending 12 **cabinet counselors** close advisers 14 **lewd** ignorant 15 **terms and shreds** jargon and catch phrases 15-16 **beliers Of** liars about 22 **Scoto of Mantua** (famous Italian performer known in England as a juggler from his visit of 1576)

I'll proudly promise, sir, you shall behold
Another man than has been phantasied° to you.
I wonder, yet, that he should mount his bank
Here, in this nook, that has been wont t' appear
In the face of° the Piazza! Here he comes.

[*Enter Volpone disguised as a Mountebank. A crowd follows.*]

Volpone. [*to Nano.*] Mount, zany.°
Grege.° Follow, follow, follow, follow, follow.
Sir Politic. See how the people follow him! He's a man
May write ten thousand crowns in bank here. [*Volpone mounts stage.*] Note,
Mark but his gesture. I do use to observe
The state he keeps in getting up!°
Peregrine. 'Tis worth it, sir.

Volpone. Most noble gentlemen, and my worthy patrons, it may seem strange that I, your Scoto Mantuano, who was ever wont to fix my bank in face of the public Piazza, near the shelter of the Portico to the Procuratia,° should now, after eight months' absence from this illustrious city of Venice, humbly retire myself into an obscure nook of the Piazza.

Sir Politic. Did not I now object the same?
Peregrine. Peace, sir.

Volpone. Let me tell you: I am not, as your Lombard proverb saith, cold on my feet,° or content to part with my commodities at a cheaper rate than I accustomed. Look not for it. Nor that the calumnious reports of that impudent detractor, and shame to our profession, Allessandro Buttone° I mean, who gave out, in public, I was condemned *a sforzato*° to the galleys, for poisoning

24 **phantasied** described in fancy 27 **in face of** at the front or face of 28 **zany** clown 28 **Grege** crowd 32 **The state . . . getting up** the ceremony he employs in mounting the bank 36 **Portico to the Procuratia** arched portico on the north side of the Piazza di San Marco, before the residence of the Procurators 42 **cold on my feet** Ital., *aver freddo a piedi* forced to sell cheap 46 **Buttone** rival mountebank (no person of this name is known historically) 47 **a sforzato** by force, i.e., as a slave

the Cardinal Bembo's—cook,° hath at all attached,° much less deiected me. No, no, worthy gentlemen; to tell you true, I cannot endure to see the rabble of these ground *ciarlitani*° that spread their cloaks on the pavement as if they meant to do feats of activity,° and then come in lamely with their moldy tales out of Boccaccio, like stale Tabarin, the fabulist:° some of them discoursing their travels, and of their tedious captivity in the Turk's galleys, when, indeed, were the truth known, they were the Christian's galleys, where very temperately they ate bread, and drunk water, as a wholesome penance enjoined them by their confessors, for base pilferies.

Sir Politic. Note but his bearing and contempt of these.

Volpone. These turdy-facy-nasty-paty-lousy-fartical rogues, with one poor groatsworth° of unprepared° antimony, finely wrapped up in several *scartoccios,*° are able, very well, to kill their twenty a week, and play; yet these meager, starved spirits, who have half stopped the organs of their minds with earthy oppilations,° want not their favorers among your shriveled salad-eating artisans,° who are overjoyed that they may have their half-pe'rth of physic;° though it purge 'em into another world, 't makes no matter.

Sir Politic. Excellent! ha' you heard better language, sir?

Volpone. Well, let 'em go. And, gentlemen, honorable gentlemen, know that for this time our bank, being thus removed from the clamors of the *canaglia,*° shall be the scene of pleasure and delight; for I have nothing to sell, little or nothing to sell.

46 **Bembo's—cook** (dash before cook indicates Volpone is about to refer to someone else, perhaps mistress; Pietro Bembo was famed as a humanist) 48 **attached** constrained 51 **ground ciarlitani** street charlatans (too poor to have a platform 52 **feats of activity** tumbling 54 **Tabarin, the fabulist** (Tabarin was a renowned zany, but here the reference seems to be to him as an outworn storyteller) 63 **groatsworth** (a groat was worn fourpence) 63 **unprepared** unfit 64 **several scartoccios** separate scraps of paper to hold spices 67 **oppilations** obstructions 68-9 **salad-eating artisans** raw-vegetable-eating workers (sarcastic) 70 **half-pe'rth of physic** half a penny's worth of medicine 75 **canaglia** canaille, rabble

Sir Politic. I told you, sir, his end.

Peregrine. You did so, sir.

Volpone. I protest, I and my six servants are not able to make of this precious liquor so fast as it is fetched away from my lodging by gentlemen of your city, strangers of the Terra Firma,° worshipful merchants, ay, and senators too, who, ever since my arrival, have detained me to their uses by their splendidous liberalities. And worthily. For what avails your rich man to have his magazines° stuft with *moscadelli,*° or of the purest grape, when his physicians prescribe him, on pain of death, to drink nothing but water cocted° with aniseeds? O health! health! the blessing of the rich! the riches of the poor! who can buy thee at too dear a rate, since there is no enjoying this world without thee? Be not then so sparing of your purses, honorable gentlemen, as to abridge the natural course of life—

Peregrine. You see his end?°

Sir Politic. Ay, is't not good?

Volpone. For, when a humid flux, or catarrh, by the mutability of air falls from your head into an arm or shoulder, or any other part, take you a ducat, or your chequin of gold, and apply to the place affected: see, what good effect it can work. No, no, 'tis this blessed *unguento,*° this rare extraction, that hath only power to disperse all malignant humors° that proceed either of hot, cold, moist, or windy causes—

Peregrine. I would he had put in dry too.

Sir Politic. 'Pray you, observe.

Volpone. To fortify the most indigest and crude° stomach, ay, were it of one that through extreme weakness vomited blood, applying only a warm napkin to the place, after the unction and fricace;° for the vertigine° in the head, putting but a drop into your nostrils, likewise behind the ears; a most sovereign and approved

83 **Terra Firma** that part of Venice on the mainland 87 **magazines** storehouses 87 **moscadelli** muscatel 89 **cocted** boiled 95 **end** aim 101 **unguento** ointment 102 **humors** (in medieval thought the four humors of the body: blood, phlegm, choler, bile cirresponded to the four elements of air, water, fire, and earth) 105 **crude** sour 108 **unction and fricace** lubrication and massage 108 **vertigine** dizziness

remedy: the *mal caduco,*° cramps, convulsions, paralyses, epilepsies, *tremor cordia,*° retired nerves,° ill vapours of the spleen, stoppings of the liver, the stone, the strangury,° *hernia ventosa,*° *iliaca passio;*° stops a *dysenteria* immediately; caseth the torsion of the small guts; and cures *melancholia hypocondriaca,*° being taken and applied according to my printed receipt.° (*Pointing to his bill*° *and his glass.*) For, this is the physician, this the medicine; this counsels, this cures, this gives the direction, this works the effect; and, in sum, both together° may be termed an abstract of the theoric and practic° in the Aesculapian art.° 'Twill cost you eight crowns. And, Zan Fritada,° pray thee sing a verse, extempore, in honor of it.

Sir Politic. How do you like him, sir?
Peregrine. Most strangely, I!
Sir Politic. Is not his language rare?
Peregrine. But° alchemy
I never heard the like, or Broughton's books.°

Song.

Had old Hippocrates, or Galen,°
That to their books put med'cines all in,
But known this secret, they had never,
Of which they will be guilty ever,
Been murderers of so much paper,
Or wasted many a hurtless° taper.

111 **mal caduco** falling sickness (epilepsy) 112 **tremor cordia** heart palpitations 112 **retired nerves** shrunken sinews 114 **strangury** painful urination 114 **hernia ventosa** hernia causing flatulence 114 **iliacra passio** pains in the small intestines 116 **melancholia hypocondriaca** melancholy arising from the hypochondria (seat of liver, gallbladder, and spleen) 117 **receipt** recipe 118 s.d. **bill** prescription with directions 120-1 **both together** directions and medicine 121-2 **abstract . . . practice** summation of the theory and practice 122 **Aesculapian art** medicine 123 **Zan Fritada** a famous comedian, here Nano 126 **But** except for 127 **Broughton's books** (books of the rabbinical scholar and Puritan minister, Hugh Broughton, d. 1612) 128 **Hippocrates, or Galen** Greek physicians, inventor and expounder respectively of the theory of humors 133 **hurtless** harmless

No Indian drug had e'er been famèd,
Tobacco, sassafras not namèd;
Ne° yet of guacum° one small stick, sir,
Nor Raymond Lully's° great elixir.
Ne had been known the Danish Gonswart,°
Or Paracelsus, with his long sword.°

Peregrine. All this, yet, will not do; eight crowns is high.

Volpone. No more. Gentlemen, if I had but time to discourse to you the miraculous effects of this my oil, surnamed *Oglio del Scoto,*° with the countless catalogue of those I have cured of th'aforesaid, and many more diseases; the patents and privileges of all the princes and commonwealths of Christendom; or but the depositions of those that appeared on my part, before the signiory of the *Sanita*° and most learned college of physicians; where I was authorized, upon notice taken of the admirable virtues of my medicaments, and mine own excellency in matter of rare and unknown secrets, not only to disperse them publicly in this famous city, but in all the territories that happily joy under the government of the most pious and magnificent states of Italy. But may some other gallant fellow say, "O, there be divers° that make profession to have as good and as experimented receipts as yours." Indeed, very many have assayed, like apes, in imitation of that, which is really and essentially in me, to make of this oil; bestowed great cost in furnaces, stills, alembics,° continual fires, and preparation of the ingredients (as indeed there goes to it six hundred several simples,° besides some quantity of human fat, for the conglutina-

136 **Ne** nor 136 **guacum** a drug extracted from resin of guaiacum tree 137 **Raymond Lully** medieval sage, falsely thought to be an alchemist 138 **Gonswart** unidentified 139 **Paracelsus . . . sword** (Paracelsus, philosopher and physician, supposedly kept drugs and secret substances in the hollow pommel of his sword) 143 **Oglio del Scoto** Scoto's oil 148 **signiory of the Sanita** committee that licensed physicians, drug-sellers, and mountebanks in Venice 156 **divers** many different people 160 **furnaces, stills, alembics** items of alchemical equipment 162 **several simples** separate herbal remedies

tion, which we buy of the anatomists), but, when these practitioners come to the last decoction,° blow, blow, puff, puff,° and all flies in fumo.° Ha, ha, ha! Poor wretches! I rather pity their folly and indiscretion than their loss of time and money; for those may be recovered by industry; but to be a fool born is a disease incurable. For myself, I always from° my youth have endeavoured to get the rarest secrets, and book° them, either in exchange° or for money; I spared nor cost nor labor where anything was worthy to be learned. And gentlemen, honorable gentlemen, I will undertake, by virtue of chemical° art, out of the honorable hat that covers your head to extract the four elements,° that is to say, the fire, air, water, and earth, and return you your felt without burn or stain. For, whilst others have been at the balloo,° I have been at my book, and am now past the craggy paths of study, and come to the flowery plains of honor and reputation.

Sir Politic. I do assure you, sir, that is his aim.

Volpone. But to our price—

Peregrine. And that withal, Sir Pol.

Volpone. You all know, honorable gentlemen, I never valued this *ampulla*, or vial, at less than eight crowns, but for this time I am content to be deprived of it for six; six crowns is the price, and less in courtesy I know you cannot offer me; take it or leave it, howsoever, both it and I am at your service. I ask you not as the value° of the thing, for then I should demand of you a thousand crowns; so the Cardinals Montalto, Farnese, the great Duke of Tuscany,° my gossip,° with divers other princes have given me; but I despise money. Only to show

165 **decoction** boiling down to extract essences 165-6 **blow . . . puff** (Volpone imitates the alchemist at his work) 166 **fumo** smoke 170 **from** since 171 **book** put them into writing 171-2 **in exchange** by trading one secret for another 175 **chemical** i.e., alchemical 176 **four elements** air, water, fire, and earth 179 **balloo** balloon, a Venetian game played by a group of men with an inflated ball 189 **as the value** according to the value 191-2 **Cardinals . . . Tuscany** Montalto, later Pope Sixtus V; Farnese, possibly Alessandro Farnese, later Pope Paul III; Duke of Tuscany, Cosimo de' Medici after 1569 192 **gossip** godfather

my affection to you, honorable gentlemen, and your illustrious state here, I have neglected the messages of these princes, mine own offices,° framed° my journey hither, only to present you with the fruits of my travels. [*To Nano and Mosca.*] Tune your voices once more to the touch of your instruments, and give the honorable assembly some delightful recreation.

Peregrine. What monstrous and most painful° circumstance
Is here, to get some three or four *gazets*!°
Some threepence i' th' whole,° for that 'twill come to.

Song.

You that would last long, list to my song,
Make no more coil,° but buy of this oil.
Would you be ever fair? and young?
Stout of teeth? and strong of tongue?
Tart° of palate? quick of ear?
Sharp of sight? of nostril clear?
Moist of hand? and light of foot?
Or I will come nearer to't,
Would you live free from all diseases?
Do the act your mistress pleases;
Yet fright all aches from your bones?
Here's a med'cine for the nones.°

Volpone. Well, I am in a humor, at this time, to make a present of the small quantity my coffer contains to the rich, in courtesy, and to the poor, for God's sake. Wherefore, now mark: I asked you six crowns, and six crowns at other times you have paid me; you shall not give me six crowns, nor five, nor four, nor three, nor two, nor one; nor half a ducat; no, nor a *moccenigo.*° Six-pence it will cost you, or six hundred pound—expect no lower price, for by the banner of my front,° I will

196 **offices** duties 196 **framed** arranged 201 **painful** painstaking 202 **gazets** Venetian pennies 203 **i' th' whole** total 205 **coil** fuss 208 **tart** keen 215 **nones** nonce, occasion 222 **moccenigo** coin worth about nine gazets 224 **banner of my front** banner hanging in front of the scaffold listing diseases and remedies

not bate a bagatine;° that I will have, only, a pledge of your loves, to carry something from amongst you to show I am not contemned by you. Therefore, now, toss your handkerchiefs,° cheerfully, cheerfully; and be advertised° that the first heroic spirit that deigns to grace me with a handkerchief, I will give it° a little remembrance of something beside, shall please it better than if I had presented it with a double pistolet.°

Peregrine. Will you be that heroic spark,° Sir Pol?

Celia at the window throws down her handkerchief

O see! the window has prevented you.

Volpone. Lady, I kiss your bounty, and for this timely grace you have done your poor Scoto of Mantua, I will return you, over and above my oil, a secret of that high and inestimable nature shall° make you forever enamored on that minute wherein your eye first descended on so mean, yet not altogether to be despised, an object. Here is a poulder° concealed in this paper of which, if I should speak to° the worth, nine thousand volumes were but as one page, that page as a line, that line as a word: so short is this pilgrimage of man, which some call life, to the expressing of it. Would I reflect on the price? Why, the whole world were but as an empire, that empire as a province, that province as a bank, that bank as a private purse to the purchase of it. I will, only, tell you: it is the poulder that made Venus a goddess (given her by Apollo), that kept her perpetually young, cleared her wrinkles, firmed her gums, filled her skin, colored her hair. From her derived to Helen,° and at the sack of Troy unfortunately lost; till now, in this our age, it was as happily recovered by a studious antiquary out of some ruins of Asia, who sent a moiety° of it to the court of France (but much sophisticated°),

225 **bate a bagatine** cut the price by a bagatine (a small coin worth less than a farthing) 228 **handkerchiefs** (normally the money was knitted in one corner of a handkerchief) 228 **be advertised** be it known 230 **it** i.e., the person of heroic spirit 232 **pistolet** Spanish coin of gold 233 **spark** gallant fellow 238 **shall** i.e., that shall 241 **poulder** powder 242 **to** of 252 **Helen** i.e., Helen of Troy 255 **moiety** part 256 **sophisticated** adulterated

wherewith the ladies there now color their hair. The rest, at this present, remains with me; extracted to a quintessence, so that wherever it but touches in youth it perpetually preserves, in age restores the complexion; seats your teeth, did they dance like virginal jacks,° firm as a wall; makes them white as ivory, that were black as—

Act II, Scene iii

[*Enter Corvino.*]

Corvino. Spite o' the devil,° and my shame!
Come down here;
Come down! No house but mine to make your scene?
He beats away the mountebank, &c.
Signior Flaminio,° will you down, sir? down?
What, is my wife your Franciscina,° sir?
No windows on the whole Piazza, here,
To make your properties,° but mine? but mine?
Heart! ere tomorrow, I shall be new christened,
And called the Pantolone di Besogniosi°
About the town. [*Exit.*]
Peregrine. What should this mean, Sir Pol?
Sir Politic. Some trick of state, believe it. I will home.
Peregrine. It may be some design on you.
Sir Politic. I know not.
I'll stand upon my guard.
Peregrine. It is your best, sir.
Sir Politic. This three weeks all my advices, all my letters,
They have been intercepted.
Peregrine. Indeed, sir?
Best have a care.

261 **virginal jacks** (the virginal was a keyboard instrument; the jacks were movable pieces of wood with quills which plucked the strings) II.iii.1 **Spite o' the devil** malicious mark of the devil (Corvino refers either to Celia or to the mountebank) 3 **Flaminio** Flaminio Scala, a leading actor in the improvisatory *commedia dell'arte* 4 **Franciscina** a servant maid (stock figure in the *commedia*) 6 **properties** i.e., stage furniture and set 8 **Pantalone di Besogniosi** old man in the *commedia* often cuckolded by a young wife

Sir Politic. Nay, so I will. [*Exit.*]
Peregrine. This knight,
I may not lose him for my mirth, till night. [*Exit.*]

Act II, Scene iv

[*Enter*] *Volpone, Mosca* [*as themselves.*]

Volpone. O, I am wounded!
Mosca. Where, sir.
Volpone. Not without;°
Those blows° were nothing, I could bear them ever.
But angry Cupid, bolting from her eyes,
Hath shot himself° into me like a flame;
Where, now, he flings about his burning heat,
As in a furnace an ambitious fire°
Whose vent° is stopped. The fight is all within me.
I cannot live except thou help me, Mosca;
My liver° melts, and I, without the hope
Of some soft air from her refreshing breath,
Am but a heap of cinders.
Mosca. 'Las, good sir!
Would you had never seen her!
Volpone. Nay, would thou
Hadst never told me of her.
Mosca. Sir, 'tis true;
I do confess I was unfortunate,
And you unhappy; but I'm bound in conscience,
No less than duty, to effect my best
To your release of torment, and I will, sir.
Volpone. Dear Mosca, shall I hope?
Mosca. Sir, more than dear,
I will not bid you to despair of aught
Within a human compass.
Volpone. O, there spoke
My better angel. Mosca, take my keys,

II.iv.8 **without** on my body 2 **Those blows** Corvino's blows 3-4 **Cupid . . . himself** ("Cupid's bolt" is Cupid's arrow, here Cupid himself becomes the arrow) 6 **ambitious fire** mounting flame 7 **vent** outlet 9 **liver** supposedly the seat of intense emotion such as love

Gold, plate, and jewels, all's at thy devotion;°
Employ them how thou wilt; nay, coin me° too,
So thou in this but crown° my longings—Mosca?

Mosca. Use but your patience.

Volpone. So I have.

Mosca. I doubt not
To bring success to your desires.

Volpone. Nay, then,
I not repent me of my late disguise.

Mosca. If you can horn him,° sir, you need not.

Volpone. True.
Besides, I never meant him for my heir.
Is not the color° o' my beard and eyebrows
To make me known?

Mosca. No jot.

Volpone. I did it well.

Mosca. So well, would I could follow you in mine,
With half the happiness;° and, yet, I would
Escape your epilogue.°

Volpone. But were they gulled
With a belief that I was Scoto?

Mosca. Sir,
Scoto himself could hardly have distinguished!
I have not time to flatter you now; we'll part,
And as I prosper, so applaud my art. [*Exeunt.*]

Act II, Scene v

[*Corvino's House.*
Enter] *Corvino, Celia.*

Corvino. Death of mine honor, with the city's fool?
A juggling, tooth-drawing,° prating mountebank?
And at a public window? where, whilst he,

22 **devotion** disposal 23 **coin me** make me into coin (money) 24 **crown** satisfy (with pun on coin) 28 **horn him** cuckold him 30 **color** i.e., red, the fox's color 32-3 **mine . . . happiness** i.e., my performance with half the success 34 **epilogue** i.e., the end of your play (Corvino's beating) II.v.2 **tooth-drawing** (one of the services of mountebanks)

With his strained action,° and his dole of faces,°
To his drug-lecture draws your itching ears,
A crew of old, unmarried, noted lechers
Stood leering up like satyrs:° and you smile
Most graciously, and fan your favors forth,
To give your hot spectators satisfaction!
What, was your mountebank their call?° their whistle?
Or were y' enamored on his copper rings?
His saffron jewel, with the toad stone° in 't?
Or his embroidered suit, with the cope-stitch,
Made of a hearse cloth?° or his old tilt-feather?
Or his starched beard! Well, you shall have him, yes.
He shall come home and minister unto you
The fricace for the mother.° Or, let me see,
I think you'd rather mount?° would you not mount?
Why, if you'll mount, you may; yes truly, you may,
And so you may be seen, down to th' foot.
Get you a cittern,° Lady Vanity,°
And be a dealer with the virtuous man;°
Make one.° I'll but protest° myself a cuckold,
And save your dowry.° I am a Dutchman,° I!
For if you thought me an Italian,
You would be damned ere you did this, you whore!
Thou'dst tremble to imagine that the murder
Of father, mother, brother, all thy race,
Should follow as the subject of my justice!

Celia. Good sir, have patience!

4 **strained action** exaggerated performance 4 **dole of faces** repertoire of facial expressions (mugging) 7 **satyrs** lascivious demigods 10 **their call** their (the lechers') bird call 12 **toad stone** (found in the head of a toad, it supposedly had magical properties) 13-14 **suit . . . cloth** a suit made of used coffin drapery, marked by a stitch for decorating a border 17 **fricace for the mother** massage for hysteria (with lewd innuendo intended) 18 **mount** i.e., the mountebank's stage; also in a sexual sense, the mountebank himself 21 **cittern** zither 21 **Lady Vanity** an abstract character in the English morality play 22 **dealer . . . man** i.e., join the act (prostitute yourself?) with that virtuous (here sarcastic) fellow 23 **make one** become one of them 23 **protest** declare 24 **save your dowry** keep your dowry (since you are unfaithful) 24 **Dutchman** i.e., phlegmatic, not easily angered

Corvino. What couldst thou propose
Less to thyself than in this heat of wrath,
And stung with my dishonor, I should strike
[*Brandishes sword.*]
This steel into thee, with as many stabs
As thou wert gazed upon with goatish eyes?
Celia. Alas, sir, be appeased! I could not think
My being at the window should more now
Move your impatience than at other times.
Corvino. No? not to seek and entertain a parley°
With a known knave? before a multitude?
You were an actor with your handkerchief!
Which he, most sweetly, kissed in the receipt.°
And might, no doubt, return it with a letter,
And point° the place where you might meet: your sister's,
Your mother's, or your aunt's might serve the turn.°
Celia. Why, dear sir, when do I make these excuses?
Or ever stir abroad but to the church?
And that so seldom—
Corvino. Well, it shall be less;
And thy restraint before was liberty
To° what I now decree, and therefore mark me.
First, I will have this bawdy light° dammed up;
And till't be done, some two, or three yards off
I'll chalk a line, o'er which if thou but chance
To set thy desp'rate foot, more hell, more horror,
More wild, remorseless rage shall seize on thee
Than on a conjurer that had heedless left
His circle's safety ere his devil was laid.°
Then, here's a lock° which I will hang upon thee,
And, now I think on 't, I will keep thee backwards;°
Thy lodging shall be backwards, they walks backwards,
Thy prospect°—all be backwards, and no pleasure,
That thou shalt know but backwards. Nay, since you force

38 **parley** conversation 41 **in the receipt** on receiving it 43 **point** appoint 44 **the turn** (1) the purpose, (2) as the place to do the trick 49 **To** compared to 50 **light** (1) window, (2) daylight 55-6 **conjurer . . . laid** (a magician who raised a devil was safe only in his circle until he sent the spirit back to hell) 57 **lock** chastity belt 58 **backwards** i.e., in the back of the house (this time with unconscious innuendo by Corvino) 60 **prospect** view, lit. looking forward

My honest nature, know it is your own
Being too open makes me use you thus.
Since you will not contain your subtle° nostrils
In a sweet room, but they must snuff the air
Of rank and sweaty passengers°— *Knock within.*
One knocks.
Away, and be not seen, pain of thy life;
Not look toward the window; if thou dost—
(Nay, stay, hear this) let me not prosper, whore,
But I will make thee an anatomy,°
Dissect thee mine own self, and read a lecture
Upon thee to the city, and in public.
Away! [*Exit Celia.*]
Who's there?
[*Enter Servant.*]

Servant. 'Tis Signior Mosca, sir.

Act II, Scene vi

Corvino. Let him come in, his master's dead. There's yet
Some good to help the bad.

Enter Mosca.

My Mosca, welcome,
I guess your news.
Mosca. I fear you cannot, sir.
Corvino. Is't not his death?
Mosca. Rather the contrary.
Corvino. Not his recovery?
Mosca. Yes, sir.
Corvino. I am cursed,
I am bewitched, my crosses° meet to vex me.
How? how? how? how?
Mosca. Why, sir, with Scoto's oil!
Corbaccio and Voltore brought of it,
Whilst I was busy in an inner room—

64 **subtle** cunning 65-6 **snuff . . . passengers** sniff out the odor of smelly and sweating (lusting) passersby 70 **anatomy** skeleton or mummy II.vi.6 **crosses** afflictions

Corvino. Death! that damned mountebank! but for the law,
Now, I could kill the rascal; 't cannot be
His oil should have that virtue. Ha' not I
Known him a common rogue, come fiddling in
To th' *osteria,*° with a tumbling° whore,
And, when he has done all his forced tricks, been glad
Of a poor spoonful of dead wine, with flies in 't?
It cannot be. All his ingredients
Are a sheep's gall, a roasted bitch's marrow,
Some few sod earwigs,° pounded caterpillars,
A little capon's grease, and fasting spittle;°
I know 'em to a dram.
Mosca. I know not, sir;
But some on 't,° there, they poured into his ears,
Some in his nostrils, and recovered him,
Applying but the fricace.
Corvino. Pox o' that fricace.
Mosca. And since, to seem the more officious°
And flatt'ring of his health, there they have had,
At extreme° fees, the college of physicians
Consulting on him how they might restore him;
Where one would have a cataplasm° of spices,
Another a flayed ape clapped to his breast,
A third would ha' it a dog, a fourth an oil
With wild cats' skins. At last, they all resolved
That to preserve him was no other means
But some young woman must be straight° sought out,
Lusty, and full of juice, to sleep by him;
And to this service, most unhappily
And most unwillingly, am I now employed,
Which here I thought to pre-acquaint you with,
For your advice, since it concerns you most,
Because I would not do that thing might cross
Your ends,° on whom I have my whole dependence, sir.
Yet, if I do it not they may delate°

14 **osteria** inn 14 **tumbling** somersaulting (again with double meaning) 19 **sod earwigs** boiled insects 20 **fasting spittle** starving man's saliva, possibly Scoto's 22 **on 't** of it 25 **officious** zealous 27 **extreme** the highest 29 **cataplasm** plaster 34 **straight** immediately 40-41 **cross Your ends** conflict with your aims 42 **delate** report

My slackness to my patron, work me out
Of his opinion;° and there all your hopes,
Ventures, or whatsoever, are all frustrate.
I do but tell you, sir. Besides, they are all
Now striving who shall first present him.° Therefore,
I could entreat you, briefly, conclude somewhat.°
Prevent 'em° if you can.

Corvino. Death to my hopes!
This is my villainous fortune! Best to hire
Some common courtesan?

Mosca. Ay, I thought on that, sir.
But they are all so subtle, full of art,
And age again doting and flexible,°
So as—I cannot tell—we may perchance
Light on a quean° may cheat us all.

Corvino. 'Tis true.

Mosca. No, no; it must be one that has no tricks, sir,
Some simple thing, a creature made unto it;°
Some wench you may command. Ha' you no kinswoman?
God's so°—Think, think, think, think, think, think, think, sir.
One o' the doctors offered there his daughter.

Corvino. How!

Mosca. Yes, Signior Lupo,° the physician.

Corvino. His daughter!

Mosca. And a virgin, sir. Why, alas,
He knows the state of's body, what it is;
That nought can warm his blood, sir, but a fever;
Nor any incantation raise his spirit;
A long forgetfulness hath seized that part.°
Besides, sir, who shall know it? Some one or two—

Corvino. I pray thee give me leave. [*To himself.*]
If any man

44 **his opinion** i.e., his good opinion of me 47 **present him** i.e., with a young woman 48 **briefly, conclude somewhat** quickly, decide something 49 **prevent 'em** (1) hinder them, (2) get ahead of them 53 **And age . . . flexible** And (moreover) old age on the other hand doting and easily manipulated 55 **quean** whore 57 **made unto it** suited for the task or coerced to do it 59 **God's so** God's soul (?), corruption of **cazzo** Italian for male organ (?) 61 **Signior Lupo** Mr. Wolf 65-6 **Nor . . . part** (Mosca assures Corvino that Volpone is impotent now)

But I had had this luck—The thing in 't self,
I know, is nothing—Wherefore should not I
As well command my blood° and my affections
As this dull doctor? In the point of honor
The cases are all one of wife and daughter.
Mosca. [*Aside.*] I hear him coming.°
Corvino. She shall do't. 'Tis done.
'Slight,° if this doctor, who is not engaged,°
Unless 't be for his counsel, which is nothing,
Offer his daughter, what should I that am
So deeply in? I will prevent him; Wretch!
Covetous wretch! Mosca, I have determined.
Mosca. How, sir?
Corvino. We'll make all sure. The party you wot of°
Shall be mine own wife, Mosca.
Mosca. Sir, the thing
But that I would not seem to counsel you,
I should have motioned° to you at the first.
And make your count,° you have cut all their throats.
Why, 'tis directly taking a possession!°
And in his next fit, we may let him go.
'Tis but to pull the pillow from his head,
And he is throttled; 't had been done before
But for your scrupulous doubts.
Corvino. Ay, a plague on 't,
My conscience fools my wit!° Well, I'll be brief,
And so be thou, lest they should be before° us.
Go home, prepare him, tell him with what zeal
And willingness I do it; swear it was
On the first hearing, as thou mayst do, truly,
Mine own free motion.°
Mosca. Sir, I warrant you,
I'll so possess him with it that the rest
Of his starved clients° shall be banished all;

71 **blood** kin 74 **coming** i.e., taking the bait 75 **'Slight** God's light 75 **engaged** concerned in this business 80 **you wot of** you know about, i.e., you are seeking 83 **motioned** suggested, pointed that solution out 84 **make your count** i.e., you can start counting Volpone's money 85 **taking a possession** taking title legally 90 **wit** good sense 91 **be before** get ahead of 95 **free motion** unforced proposal 97 **starved clients** hangers-on who have gained nothing

And only you received. But come not, sir,
Until I send, for I have something else
To ripen for your good, you must not know 't.
Corvino. But do not you forget to send now.
Mosca. Fear not.
[*Exit Mosca.*]

Act II, Scene vii

Corvino. Where are you, wife? My Celia? wife?

[*Enter Celia crying.*]

What, blubbering?
Come, dry those tears. I think thou thought'st me in earnest?
Ha? by this light I talked so but to try° thee.
Methinks the lightness of the occasion°
Should ha' confirmed° thee. Come, I am not jealous.
Celia. No?
Corvino. Faith° I am not, I, nor never was;
It is a poor unprofitable humor.
Do not I know if women have a will°
They'll do 'gainst all the watches o'° the world?
And that the fiercest spies are tamed with gold?
Tut, I am confident in thee, thou shalt see 't;
And see I'll give thee cause too, to believe it.
Come, kiss me. Go, and make thee ready straight
In all thy best attire, thy choicest jewels,
Put 'em all on, and, with 'em, thy best looks.
We are invited to a solemn° feast
At old Volpone's, where it shall appear
How far I am free from jealousy or fear. [*Exeunt.*]

II.vii.3 **try** test 4 **lightness of the occasion** triviality of the circumstance at the window 5 **confirmed** convinced 6 **Faith** in faith 8 **will** sexual desire 9 **watches o'** either watchmen of or watching in 16 **solemn** formal

Act III, Scene i

Mosca [*alone.*]

Mosca. I fear I shall begin to grow in love
With my dear self and my most prosp'rous parts,°
They do so spring and burgeon; I can feel
A whimsy° i' my blood. I know not how,
Success hath made me wanton. I could skip
Out of my skin, now, like a subtle° snake,
I am so limber. O! your parasite
Is a most precious thing, dropped from above,
Not bred 'mongst clods and clodpolls,° here on earth.
I muse the mystery° was not made a science,°
It is liberally professed!° Almost
All the wise world is little else in nature
But parasites or sub-parasites. And yet,
I mean not those that have your bare town-art,°
To know who's fit to feed 'em; have no house,
No family, no care, and therefore mold
Tales° for men's ears, to bait that sense; or get
Kitchen-invention,° and some stale receipts°
To please the belly, and the groin;° nor those,
With their court-dog-tricks, that can fawn and fleer,°
Make their revènue out of legs and faces,°
Echo my lord, and lick away a moth.°
But your fine, elegant rascal, that can rise
And stoop, almost together, like an arrow;
Shoot through the air as nimbly as a star;
Turn short as doth a swallow; and be here,
And there, and here, and yonder, all at once;

III.i.2 **parts** abilities 4 **whimsy** dizziness 6 **subtle** shrewd and sinuous 9 **clodpolls** thick-headed fools 10 **mystery** trade, profession 10 **a science** a branch of learning 11 **liberally professed** widely practiced 14 **bare town-art** meager ability to survive in the city 16-17 **mold Tales** devise stories, perhaps slanderous 18 **kitchen-invention** backstairs gossip 18 **stale receipts** old recipes 19 **groin** (the recipes may include love potions) 20 **fleer** smile obsequiously 21 **legs and faces** bows and smirks 22 **lick away a moth** groom the lord subserviently, even to cleaning vermin from him

Present to any humor, all occasion;°
And change a visor° swifter than a thought,
This is the creature had the art born with him;
Toils not to learn it, but doth practice it
Out of most excellent nature: and such sparks
Are the true parasites, others but their zanies.°

Act III, Scene ii

[Enter] Bonario.

Mosca. Who's this? Bonario? Old Corbaccio's son?
The person I was bound° to seek. Fair sir,
You are happ'ly met.
Bonario. That cannot be by thee.
Mosca. Why, sir?
Bonario. Nay, 'pray thee know thy way and leave me:
I would be loth to interchange discourse
With such a mate as thou art.
Mosca. Courteous sir,
Scorn not my poverty.
Bonario. Not I, by heaven;
But thou shalt give me leave to hate thy baseness.
Mosca. Baseness?
Bonario. Ay, answer me, is not thy sloth
Sufficient argument? thy flattery?
Thy means of feeding?
Mosca. Heaven be good to me!
These imputations are too common, sir,
And eas'ly stuck on virtue when she's poor.
You are unequal° to me, and howe'er
Your sentence may be righteous, yet you are not,
That ere you know me, thus proceed in censure.°
St. Mark bear witness 'gainst you, 'tis inhuman.
[He weeps.]

28 **present . . . occasion** ready for any mood, always alert to the situation 29 **visor** mask, here "appearance" 33 **zanies** supporting clowns III.ii.2 **bound** on my way 14 **unequal** (1) above me in rank, (2) unfair 15-16 **Your sentence . . . censure** Your judgment may be morally based, but you are not being just to condemn me before knowing me

Bonario. [*Aside.*] What? does he weep? the sign is soft, and good!
I do repent me, that I was so harsh.
Mosca. 'Tis true that swayed by strong necessity,
I am enforced to eat my carefull bread°
With too much obsequy; 'tis true, beside,
That I am fain° to spin mine own poor raiment
Out of my mere° observance,° being not born
To a free fortune; but that I have done
Base offices, in rending friends asunder,
Dividing families, betraying counsels,
Whispering false lies, or mining° men with praises,
Trained° their credulity with perjuries,
Corrupted chastity, or am in love
With mine own tender ease, but would not rather
Prove° the most rugged and laborious course,
That might redeem my present estimation,
Let me here perish, in all hope of goodness.
Bonario. [*Aside.*]—This cannot be a personated° passion!
I was to blame, so to mistake thy nature;
Pray thee forgive me and speak out thy business.
Mosca. Sir, it concerns you, and though I may seem
At first to make a main° offence in manners,
And in my gratitude unto my master,
Yet, for the pure love which I bear all right,
And hatred of the wrong, I must reveal it.
This very hour your father is in purpose
To disinherit you—
Bonario. How!
Mosca. And thrust you forth
As a mere stranger to his blood; 'tis true, sir.
The work no way engageth me, but as
I claim an interest in the general state
Of goodness and true virtue, which I hear
T' abound in you, and for which mere respect,
Without a second aim, sir, I have done it.

21 carefull bread food earned in pain **23 fain** obliged **24 mere** (here and later Jonson uses "mere" to signify a completed or singular condition) **24 observance** service **28 mining** undermining **29 Trained** misled **32 Prove** test **35 personated** impersonated, pretended **39 main** major

Bonario. This tale hath lost thee much of the late trust
Thou hadst with me; it is impossible.
I know not how to lend it any thought°
My father should be so unnatural.
Mosca. It is a confidence that well becomes
Your piety,° and formed, no doubt, it is
From your own simple innocence, which makes
Your wrong more monstrous and abhorred. But, sir,
I now will tell you more. This very minute
It is, or will be doing; and if you
Shall be but pleased to go with me, I'll bring you,
I dare not say where you shall see, but where
Your ear shall be a witness of the deed;
Hear yourself written bastard and professed°
The common issue of the earth.
Bonario. I'm mazed!°
Mosca. Sir, if I do it not, draw your just sword
And score your vengeance on my front° and face;
Mark me your villian. You have too much wrong,
And I do suffer for you, sir. My heart
Weeps blood in anguish—
Bonario. Lead. I follow thee.

[*Exeunt.*]

Act III, Scene iii

Volpone [*at home; enter*] *Nano, Androgyno, Castrone.*

Volpone. Mosca stays long, methinks. Bring forth your sports
And help to make the wretched time more sweet.
Nano. Dwarf, fool, and eunuch, well met here we be.
A question it were now, whether° of us three,

53 **lend . . . thought** give it any credence 56 **piety** filial love 64 **professed** proclaimed 65 **mazed** stunned 67 **front** forehead III.iii.4 **whether** which

Being, all, the known delicates° of a rich man,
In pleasing him, claim the precedency can?

Castrone. I claim for myself.

Androgyno. And so doth the fool.

Nano. 'Tis foolish indeed, let me set you both to school.
First for your dwarf, he's little and witty,
And everything, as it is little, is pretty;
Else, why do men say to a creature of my shape,
So soon as they see him, "It's a pretty little ape"?
And, why a pretty ape? but for pleasing imitation
Of greater men's action, in a ridiculous fashion.
Beside, this feat° body of mine doth not crave
Half the meat, drink, and cloth one of your bulks will have.
Admit your fool's face be the mother of laughter,
Yet, for his brain, it must always come after;°
And though that° do feed him, it's a pitiful case
His body is beholding to such a bad face.

One knocks.

Volpone. Who's there? My couch, away, look, Nano, see;
Give me my caps first—go, inquire.

[*Exit Nano; Castrone and Androgyno follow. Volpone takes to his bed.*]

Now Cupid
Send it be Mosca, and with fair return.° *Enter Nano.*

Nano. It is the beauteous madam—

Volpone. Wouldbe—is it?

Nano. The same.

Volpone. Now, torment on me; squire her in,
For she will enter, or dwell here forever.
Nay, quickly, that my fit were past. I fear

[*Exit Nano.*]

A second hell too: that my loathing this°
Will quite expel my appetite to the other.°
Would she were taking, now, her tedious leave.
Lord, how it threats me, what I am to suffer!

5 **known delicates** acknowledged pleasures 15 **feat** neat, trim 18 **come after** be second in importance 19 **that** i.e., the face 23 **fair return** good profit 28 **this** i.e., Lady Wouldbe 29 **other** i.e., Celia

Act III, Scene iv

[*Enter Nano and Lady Wouldbe followed by her two women.*]

Lady Wouldbe. [*To Nano.*] I thank you, good sir. Pray you signify
Unto your patron I am here—This band°
Shows not my neck enough.—I trouble you, sir;
Let me request you bid one of my women
[*Nano signals to 1st woman.*]
Come hither to me. In good faith, I am dressed
Most favourably° today! It is no matter;
'Tis well enough. Look, see these petulant things!°
How they have done this!

Volpone. [*Aside.*] —I do feel the fever
Ent'ring in at mine ears. O for a charm
To fight it hence—

Lady Wouldbe. Come nearer. Is this curl
In his right place? or this? Why is this higher
Than all the rest? You ha' not washed your eyes yet?
Or do they not stand even i' your head?
Where's your fellow? Call her.
[*1st woman signals to 2nd woman.*]

Nano. Now, St. Mark
Deliver us! Anon° she'll beat her women
Because her nose is red.

Lady Wouldbe. I pray you, view.
This tire,° forsooth; are all things apt, or no?

1st Woman. One hair a little, here, sticks out, forsooth.

Lady Wouldbe. Dost so, forsooth? And where was your dear sight
When it did so, forsooth? What now! Bird-eyed?°
And you too? Pray you both approach and mend it.
Now, by that light, I muse you're not ashamed!
I, that have preached these things, so oft, unto you,
Read you the principles, argued all the grounds,

III.iv.2 **band** ruff 5-6 **I . . . favourably** (caustically directed at her maids) 7 **petulant things** i.e., her maids 15 **anon** in a moment 17 **tire** hairdressing 20 **bird-eyed** pop-eyed

Disputed every fitness, every grace,
Called you to counsel of so frequent dressings°—
Nano. [*Aside.*] More carefully than of your fame° or honor.
Lady Wouldbe. Made you acquainted what an ample dowry
The knowledge of these things would be unto you,
Able, alone, to get you noble husbands
At your return;° and you, thus, to neglect it?
Besides, you seeing what a curious° nation
Th' Italians are, what will they say of me?
"The English lady cannot dress herself."
Here's a fine imputation to our country!
Well, go your ways, and stay i' the next room.
This fucus° was too coarse, too; it's no matter.
Good sir, you'll give 'em entertainment?°
[*Exit Nano with Women.*]
Volpone. The storm comes toward me.
Lady Wouldbe. How does my Volp?
Volpone. Troubled with noise, I cannot sleep; I dreamt
That a strange fury entered, now, my house,
And, with the dreadful tempest of her breath,
Did cleave my roof asunder.
Lady Wouldbe. Believe me, and I
Had the most *fearful* dream, could I remember 't—
Volpone. [*Aside.*] Out on my fate! I ha' giv'n her the occasion
How to torment me. She will tell me hers.
Lady Wouldbe. Methought the golden mediocrity,°
Polite, and delicate—
Volpone: Oh, if you do love me,
No more; I sweat, and suffer, at the mention
Of *any* dream; feel how I tremble yet.
[*Placing her hand on his heart.*]
Lady Wouldbe. Alas, good soul! the passion of the heart,°
Seed-pearl were good now, boiled with syrup of apples,
Tincture of gold, and coral, citron-pills,
Your elecampane root, myrobalanes—

23-6 I . . . dressing (Lady Wouldbe resorts to terms for a learned exposition **27 fame** reputation **31 return** i.e., to England from the Continent **32 curious** fastidious **37 fucus** makeup for beautifying the skin **38 entertainment** attention **47 golden mediocrity** (a mistake or a pretentious expression for the golden mean) **51 passion of the heart** heartburn

Volpone. [*Aside.*] Ay me, I have ta'en a grasshopper by the wing!
Lady Wouldbe. Burnt silk and amber. You have muscadel
Good in the house—
Volpone. You will not drink and part?
Lady Wouldbe. No, fear not that. I doubt° we shall not get
Some English saffron, half a dram would serve,
Your sixteen cloves, a little musk, dried mints,
Bugloss, and barley-meal°—
Volpone. [*Aside.*] She's in again.
Before I feigned diseases, now I have one.
Lady Wouldbe. And these applied with a right scarlet cloth.°
Volpone. [*Aside.*] Another flood of words! a very torrent!
Lady Wouldbe. Shall I, sir, make you a poultice?
Volpone. No, no, no.
I'm very well, you need prescribe no more.
Lady Wouldbe. I have, a little, studied physic;° but now
I'm all for music, save, i' the forenoons
An hour or two for painting. I would have
A lady, indeed, to have all letters and arts,
Be able to discourse, to write, to paint,
But principal, as Plato holds, your music,
And so does wise Pythagoras, I take it,
Is your true rapture, when there is concent°
In face, in voice, and clothes, and is, indeed,
Our sex's chiefest ornament.
Volpone. The poet°
As old in time as Plato, and as knowing,
Says that your highest female grace is silence.
Lady Wouldbe. Which o' your poets? Petrarch? or Tasso? or Dante?
Guarini? Ariosto? Aretine?
Cieco di Hadria?° I have read them all.
Volpone. [*Aside.*] Is everything a cause to my destruction?
Lady Wouldbe. I think I ha' two or three of 'em about me.

52-61 **Seed-pearl . . . barley-meal** (assorted remedies of the period) 58 **doubt** fear 63 **scarlet cloth** wrapping for a patient with smallpox 67 **physic** medicine 74 **concent** harmony 76 **The poet** i.e., Sophocles in *Ajax* 293 79-81 **Petrarch . . . Cieco di Hadria** (Lady Wouldbe confuses the first four major Italian poets with Pietro Aretino, noted for his obscene verses, and Cieco di Hadria or Luigi Grito, a minor writer)

Volpone. [*Aside.*] The sun, the sea, will sooner both stand still
Than her eternal tongue! Nothing can scape it.
Lady Wouldbe. Here's *Pastor Fido*°—
Volpone. [*Aside.*] Profess obstinate silence;
That's now my safest.
Lady Wouldbe. All our English writers,
I mean such as are happy° in th' Italian,
Will deign to steal out of this author, mainly;
Almost as much as from Montagniè.°
He has so modern and facile a vein,
Fitting the time, and catching the court-ear.°
Your Petrarch is more passionate, yet he,
In days of sonneting, trusted 'em° with much.
Dante is hard, and few can understand him.
But for a desperate° wit, there's Aretine!
Only, his pictures° are a little obscene—
You mark me not.
Volpone. Alas, my mind's perturbed.
Lady Wouldbe. Why, in such cases, we must cure ourselves,
Make use of our philosophy—
Volpone. O'y me!
Lady Wouldbe. And as we find our passions do rebel,
Encounter 'em with reason, or divert 'em
By giving scope unto some other humor
Of lesser danger: as, in politic bodies°
There's nothing more doth overwhelm the judgment,
And clouds the understanding, than too much
Settling and fixing, and, as 'twere, subsiding
Upon one object. For the incorporating

86 **Pastor Fido** i.e., Guarini's pastoral play (1590), known in English as *The Faithful Shepherd* 88 **happy** fluent 90 **Montagniè** i.e., Michel de Montaigne, the sixteenth-century French writer 92 **court-ear** ear of those at court 94 **'em** i.e., his imitators in the composition of sonnet sequences 96 **desperate** outrageous 97 **his pictures** (actually engravings from designs by Giulio Romano accompanying Aretino's poems) 104 **politic bodies** political states 105-12 **There's . . . knowledge** (Lady Wouldbe jumbles one of the most familiar of Renaissance commonplaces, that is, the similarity of the commonwealth to the human body by arguing that fixation on one thing leads to mental constipation)

Of these same outward things° into that part
Which we call mental, leaves some certain feces
That stop the organs, and, as Plato says,
Assassinates our knowledge.°
Volpone. [*Aside.*] Now, the spirit
Of patience help me!
Lady Wouldbe. Come, in faith, I must
Visit you more adays and make you well;
Laugh and be lusty.
Volpone. [*Aside.*] My good angel save me!
Lady Wouldbe. There was but one sole man in all the world
With whom I e'er could sympathize; and he
Would lie you° often, three, four hours together
To hear me speak, and be sometimes so rapt,
As he would answer me quite from the purpose,
Like you, and you are like him, just. I'll discourse,
An 't be but only, sir, to bring you asleep,
How we did spend our time and loves together,
For some six years.
Volpone. Oh, oh, oh, oh, oh, oh.
Lady Wouldbe. For we were *coaetanei,*° and brought up—
Volpone. Some power, some fate, some fortune rescue me!

Act III, Scene v

[*Enter Mosca.*]

Mosca. God save you, madam!
Lady Wouldbe. Good sir.
Volpone. Mosca? welcome,
Welcome to my redemption.
Mosca. Why, sir?
Volpone. Oh,
Rid me of this my torture quickly, there,
My madam with the everlasting voice;
The bells in time of pestilence° ne'er made
Like noise, or were in that perpetual motion;
The cock-pit° comes not near it. All my house,

109 outward things i.e., passions **118 lie you** lie **125 coaetanei** at the same age **III.v.5 bells . . . pestilence** (allusion to the death knells which were rung almost continuously during a plague) **7 cock-pit** arena for cockfights

But now, steamed like a bath with her thick breath.
A lawyer could not have been heard; nor scarce
Another woman, such a hail of words
She has let fall. For hell's sake, rid her hence.

Mosca. Has she presented?°

Volpone. Oh, I do not care;
I'll take her absence upon any price,
With any loss.

Mosca. Madam—

Lady Wouldbe. I ha' brought your patron
A toy, a cap here, of mine own work.

Mosca. 'Tis well.
I had forgot to tell you I saw your knight
Where you'd little think it.

Lady Wouldbe. Where?

Mosca. Marry,
Where yet, if you make haste, you may apprehend him,
Rowing upon the water in a gondole,
With the most cunning courtesan of Venice.

Lady Wouldbe. Is't true?

Mosca. Pursue 'em, and believe your eyes.
Leave me to make your gift. [*Exit Lady Wouldbe.*] I knew 'twould take.
For lightly,° they that use° themselves most license,
Are still° most jealous.

Volpone. Mosca, hearty thanks
For thy quick fiction and delivery of me.
Now to my hopes, what sayst thou?

[*Enter Lady Wouldbe.*]

Lady Wouldbe. But do you hear, sir?

Volpone. Again! I fear a paroxysm.

Lady Wouldbe Which way
Rowed they together?

Mosca. Toward the Rialto.

Lady Wouldbe. I pray you lend me your dwarf.

Mosca. I pray you, take him.

[*Exit Lady Wouldbe.*]

Your hopes, sir, are like happy blossoms: fair,
And promise timely fruit, if you will stay
But the maturing; keep you at your couch.

12 **presented** offered a gift 23 **lightly** usually 23 **use** allow
24 **still** always

Corbaccio will arrive straight with the will;
When he is gone, I'll tell you more. [*Exit Mosca.*]

Volpone. My blood,
My spirits are returned; I am alive;
And, like your wanton gamester at primero,
Whose thought had whispered to him, not go less,
Methinks I lie, and draw°—for an encounter.
[*He draws the curtains across his bed.*]

Act III, Scene vi

[*Mosca leads Bonario to a place of concealment.*]

Mosca. Sir, here concealed you may hear all. But pray you
[*One knocks.*]
Have patience, sir; the same's your father knocks.
I am compelled to leave you.

Bonario. Do so. Yet
Cannot my thought imagine this a truth.
[*Bonario stands aside.*]

Act III, Scene vii

[*Enter Corvino and Celia.*]

Mosca. Death on me! you are come too soon, what meant you?
Did not I say I would send?°

Corvino. Yes, but I feared
You might forget it, and then they° prevent us.

Mosca. Prevent? [*Aside.*]—Did e'er man haste so for his horns?°
A courtier would not ply it so° for a place.—

36-8 **primero . . . draw** (primero was a card game similar to poker; "go less," "lie," and "draw" seem to be playing or betting terms here applied to the game of winning Celia) III.vii.2 **send** i.e., for you 3 **they** i.e., his rivals for Volpone's fortune 4 **horns** the customary sign of a cuckold 5 **ply it so** press so hard, i.e., for a post at court

Well, now there's no helping it, stay here;
I'll presently return. *[He goes toward Bonario.]*
Corvino. Where are you, Celia?
You know not wherefore I have brought you hither?
Celia. Not well, except° you told me.
Corvino. Now I will:
Hark hither. *[He speaks apart to Celia.]*
Mosca. To Bonario. Sir, your father hath sent word,
It will be half an hour ere he come;
And therefore, if you please to walk the while
Into that gallery—at the upper end
There are some books to entertain the time.
And I'll take care no man shall come unto you, sir.
Bonario. Yes, I will stay there, I do doubt° this fellow.
[Exit.]
Mosca. There, he is far enough; he can hear nothing.
And for his father, I can keep him off.
[Goes to Volpone.]
Corvino. Nay, now there is no starting back, and therefore
Resolve upon it: I have so decreed.
It must be done. Nor would I move° 't afore,
Because I would avoid all shifts and tricks,
That might deny me.
Celia. Sir, let me beseech you,
Affect not° these strange trials; if you doubt
My chastity, why, lock me up forever;
Make me the heir of darkness. Let me live
Where I may please your fears, if not your trust.
Corvino. Believe it, I have no such humor, I.
All that I speak I mean; yet I am not mad;
Not horn-mad,° see you? Go to, show yourself
Obedient, and a wife.
Celia. O heaven!
Corvino. I say it,
Do so.
Celia. Was this the train?°
Corvino. I've told you reasons:
What the physicians have set down; how much

9 **except** unless 16 **doubt** suspect, fear 21 **move** propose 24 **Affect not** Do not adopt 30 **Not horn-mad** not mad enough to let myself be cuckolded 32 **train** trick

It may concern me; what my engagements are;
My means, and the necessity of those means
For my recovery;° wherefore, if you be
Loyal and mine, be won, respect my venture.°
Celia. Before your honor?
Corvino. Honor! tut, a breath.
There's no such thing in nature; a mere term
Invented to awe fools. What, is my gold
The worse for touching? Clothes for being looked on?
Why, this 's no more. An old, decrepit wretch,
That has no sense,° no sinew; takes his meat
With others' fingers; only knows to gape
When you do scald his gums; a voice, a shadow;
And what can this man hurt you?
Celia. Lord! what spirit
Is this hath entered him?°
Corvino. And for your fame,
That's such a jig; as if I would go tell it,
Cry it, on the Piazza! Who shall know it
But he that cannot speak it, and this fellow,°
Whose lips are i' my pocket, save yourself.
—If you'll proclaim 't, you may—I know no other
Should come to know it.
Celia. Are heaven and saints then nothing?
Will they be blind, or stupid?
Cervino. How?
Celia. Good sir,
Be jealous still, emulate them, and think
What hate they burn with toward every sin.
Corvino. I grant you. If I thought it were a sin
I would not urge you. Should I offer this
To some young Frenchman, or hot Tuscan blood
That had read Aretine, conned all his prints,°
Knew every quirk within lust's labyrinth,
And were professed critic° in lechery;
And I would° look upon him, and applaud him,

35-6 My means . . . recovery my potential resources, and the need for those resources in order to restore my finances **37 venture** business deal **43 sense** sensory feeling **47 him** i.e., her husband **50 this fellow** i.e., Mosca **60 prints** i.e., Aretino's obscene pictures **62 professed critic** self-proclaimed expert **63 And I would** if I were to

This were a sin; but here, 'tis contrary,
A pious work, mere charity, for physic
And honest policy to assure mine own.°
Celia. O heaven! canst thou suffer such a change?
Volpone. Thou art mine honor, Mosca, and my pride,
My joy, my tickling, my delight! Go, bring 'em.
Mosca. Please you draw near, sir.
Corvino. Come on, what—
[*She does not follow.*]
You will not be rebellious? By that light—
Mosca. [*To Volpone.*] Sir, Signior Corvino, here, is come to see you.
Volpone. Oh.
Mosca. And hearing of the consultation had,
So lately, for your health, is come to offer,
Or rather, sir, to prostitute—
Corvino. Thanks, sweet Mosca.
Mosca. Freely, unasked, or unentreated—
Corvino. Well.
Mosca. As the true, fervent instance of his love,
His own most fair and proper wife, the beauty
Only of price° in Venice—
Corvino. 'Tis well urged.
Mosca. To be your comfortress, and to preserve you.
Volpone. Alas, I'm past already! Pray you, thank him
For his good care and promptness; but for that,
'Tis a vain labor e'en to fight 'gainst heaven;
Applying fire to a stone: uh, uh, uh, uh.
Making a dead leaf grow again. I take
His wishes gently, though; and you may tell him
What I've done for him. Marry, my state is hopeless!
Will him to pray for me, and t' use his fortune
With reverence when he comes to't.
Mosca. Do you hear, sir?
Go to him with your wife.
Corvino. [*To Celia.*] Heart of my father!
Wilt thou persist thus? Come, I pray thee, come.
Thou seest 'tis nothing, Celia. By this hand
I shall grow violent. Come, do 't, I say.

66 mine own i.e., Volpone's wealth, which is as good as mine
79 Only of price one without price

Celia. Sir, kill me rather. I will take down poison,
Eat burning coals, do anything—
Corvino. Be damned!
Heart, I will drag thee hence home by the hair,
Cry thee a strumpet through the streets, rip up
Thy mouth unto thine ears, and slit thy nose,
Like a raw rotchet°—Do not tempt me, come.
Yield, I am loth—Death, I will buy some slave
Whom I will kill, and bind thee to him, alive;
And at my window hang you forth, devising
Some monstrous crime, which I, in capital letters,
Will eat into thy flesh with aquafortis,°
And burning cor'sives,° on this stubborn breast.
Now, by the blood thou hast incensed, I'll do 't.
Celia. Sir, what you please, you may; I am your martyr.
Corvino. Be not thus obstinate, I ha' not deserved it.
Think who it is entreats you. Pray thee, sweet;
Good faith, thou shalt have jewels, gowns, attires,
What thou wilt, think and ask. Do, but go kiss him.
Or touch him, but.° For my sake. At my suit.
This once. No? Not? I shall remember this.
Will you disgrace me thus? D' you thirst my undoing?
Mosca. Nay, gentle lady, be advised.
Corvino. No, no.
She has watched her time. God's precious,° this is scurvy,
'Tis very scurvy; and you are—
Mosca. Nay, good sir.
Corvino. An errant,° locust, by heaven, a locust! Whore,
Crocodile,° that hast thy tears prepared,
Expecting how thou'lt bid 'em flow.
Mosca. Nay, pray you, sir!
She will consider.
Celia. Would my life would serve
To satisfy.
Corvino. 'Sdeath! if she would but speak to him,
And save my reputation, 'twere somewhat;
But spitefully to affect my utter ruin!
Mosca. Ay, now you've put your fortune in her hands.

99 **rotchet** a red gurnard (fish) 104 **aquafortis** nitric acid used for etching 105 **cor'sives** corrosives 112 **but** only that 116 **God's precious** by God's precious blood 118 **errant** arrant (?) 119 **Crocodile** (said to attract victims by its weeping)

Why i' faith, it is her modesty, I must quit° her.
If you were absent, she would be more coming;
I know it, and dare undertake for her.
What woman can before her husband? Pray you,
Let us depart and leave her here.
Corvino. Sweet Celia.
Thou may'st redeem all yet; I'll say no more.
If not, esteem yourself as lost.
[*She begins to leave with him.*]
Nay, stay there.
[*Exit Mosca and Corvino.*]
Celia. O God, and his good angels! whither, whither,
Is shame fled human breasts? that with such ease
Men dare put off your honors, and their own?
Is that, which ever was a cause of life,
Now placed beneath the basest circumstance,
And modesty an exile made, for money?
Volpone. Ay, in Corvino, and such earth-fed minds,
He leaps off from the couch.
That never tasted the true heaven of love.
Assure thee, Celia, he that would sell thee,
Only for hope of gain, and that uncertain,
He would have sold his part of Paradise
For ready money, had he met a cope-man.°
Why art thou mazed to see me thus revived?
Rather applaud thy beauty's miracle;
'Tis thy great work, that hath, not now alone,
But sundry times raised me in several shapes,
And, but this morning, like a mountebank,
To see thee at thy window. Ay, before
I would have left my practice° for thy love,
In varying figures° I would have contended
With the blue Proteus,° or the hornèd flood.°
Now, art thou welcome.
Celia. Sir!
Volpone. Nay, fly me not.
Nor let thy false imagination

126 **quit** acquit, excuse 144 **cope-man** chapman or buyer 151 **practice** scheming 152 **figures** shapes 153 **Proteus** (the mythical old man of the sea who could alter his shape unceasingly) 153 **flood** (the river god Achelous, termed "hornèd" because he fought Hercules in the shape of a bull)

That I was bed-rid, make thee think I am so:
Thou shalt not find it. I am, now, as fresh,
As hot, as high, and in as jovial plight°
As when in that so celebrated scene
At recitation of our comedy,
For entertainment of the great Valois,°
I acted young Antinous,° and attracted
The eyes and ears of all the ladies present,
T' admire each graceful gesture, note, and footing.

Song.

Come, my Celia, let us prove
While we can, the sports of love;
Time will not be ours forever,
He, at length, our good will sever;
Spend not then his gifts in vain.
Suns that set may rise again;
But if once we lose this light,
'Tis with us perpetual night.
Why should we defer our joys?
Fame and rumor are but toys.°
Cannot we delude the eyes
Of a few poor household spies?
Or his easier ears beguile,
Thus removèd by our wile?
'Tis no sin love's fruits to steal,
But the sweet thefts to reveal:
To be taken, to be seen,
These have crimes accounted been.

Celia. Some serene° blast me, or dire lightning strike
This my offending face.
Volpone. Why droops my Celia?
Thou hast in place of a base husband found
A worthy lover; use thy fortune well,
With secrecy and pleasure. See, behold,
[*Points to his treasure.*]

158 **plight** condition 161 **Valois** i.e., Henry of Valois, later Henry III of France, entertained at Venice in 1574 162 **Antinous** Emperor Hadrian's favorite, renowned for his beauty 174 **toys** trifles 183 **serene** noxious dew

What thou art queen of; not in expectation,
As I feed others, but possessed and crowned.
See, here, a rope of pearl, and each more orient°
Than that the brave Egyptian queen caroused;°
Dissolve and drink 'em. See, a carbuncle
May put out both the eyes of our St. Mark;°
A diamond would have bought Lollia Paulina°
When she came in like star-light, hid with jewels
That were the spoils of provinces; take these,
And wear, and lose 'em; yet remains an earring
To purchase them again, and this whole state.
A gem but worth a private patrimony
Is nothing; we will eat such at a meal.
The heads of parrots, tongues of nightingales,
The brains of peacocks, and of estriches
Shall be our food, and, could we get the phoenix,°
Though nature lost her kind, she were our dish.

Celia. Good sir, these things might move a mind affected
With such delights; but I, whose innocence
Is all I can think wealthy, or worth th' enjoying,
And which, once lost, I have nought to lose beyond it,
Cannot be taken with these sensual baits.
If you have conscience—

Volpone. 'Tis the beggar's virtue;
If thou hast wisdom, hear me, Celia.
Thy baths shall be the juice of July-flowers,°
Spirit of roses, and of violets,
The milk of unicorns, and panthers' breath°
Gathered in bags and mixed with Cretan wines.
Our drink shall be preparèd gold and amber,
Which we will take until my roof whirl round
With the vertigo; and my dwarf shall dance,
My eunuch sing, my fool make up the antic.°
Whilst we, in changèd shapes, act Ovid's tales,°

190 **orient** precious 191 **Egyptian queen caroused** i.e., Cleopatra drank 192-3 **a carbuncle . . . St. Mark** (lost allusion to a rich gem) 194 **Lollia Paulina** (famous for the rich jewels in which she clothed herself) 203 **phoenix** mythical bird reborn from its own ashes 212 **July-flowers** gilly flowers 214 **panthers' breath** (supposed to be exceptionally sweet) 219 **antic** grotesque dance 220 **Ovid's tales** i.e., from *Metamorphoses*

Thou like Europa° now, and I like Jove,
Then I like Mars, and thou like Erycine;°
So of the rest, till we have quite run through,
And wearied all the fables of the gods.
Then will I have thee in more modern forms,
Attirèd like some sprightly dame of France,
Brave Tuscan lady, or proud Spanish beauty;
Sometimes unto the Persian Sophy's° wife,
Or the Grand Signior's° mistress; and, for change,
To one of our most artful courtesans,
Or some quick° Negro, or cold Russian;
And I will meet thee in as many shapes;
Where we may, so, transfuse our wand'ring souls
Out at our lips and score up sums of pleasures,
That the curious shall not know
How to tell° them as they flow;
And the envious, when they find
What their number is, be pined.°

Celia. If you have ears that will be pierced, or eyes
That can be opened, a heart may be touched,
Or any part that yet sounds man° about you;
If you have touch of holy saints, or heaven,
Do me the grace to let me 'scape. If not,
Be bountiful and kill me. You do know
I am a creature hither ill betrayed
By one whose shame I would forget it were.
If you deign me neither of these graces,
Yet feed your wrath, sir, rather than your lust,
It is a vice comes nearer manliness,
And punish that unhappy crime of nature,
Which you miscall my beauty: flay my face,
Or poison it with ointments for seducing
Your blood to this rebellion. Rub these hands
With what may cause an eating leprosy,
E'en to my bones and marrow; anything
That may disfavour° me, save in my honor,

221 **Europa** (Jupiter, in the shape of a bull, carried her off) 222 **Erycine** Venus 228 **Sophy's** Shah's 229 **Grand Signior** Sultan of Turkey 231 **quick** lively 236 **tell** count 238 **be pined** pine away with envy 241 **sounds man** proclaims you a man 256 **disfavour** disfigure

And I will kneel to you, pray for you, pay down
A thousand hourly vows, sir, for your health;
Report, and think you virtuous—

Volpone. Think me cold,
Frozen, and impotent, and so report me?
That I had Nestor's hernia° thou wouldst think.
I do degenerate and abuse my nation
To play with opportunity thus long;
I should have done the act, and then have parleyed.
Yield, or I'll force thee.

Celia. O! just God.

Volpone. In vain—

Bonario. Forbear, foul ravisher! libidinous swine!

He [Bonario] leaps out from where Mosca had placed him.

Free the forced lady, or thou diest, impostor.
But that I am loth to snatch thy punishment
Out of the hand of justice, thou shouldst yet
Be made the timely sacrifice of vengeance,
Before this altar, and this dross, thy idol.
Lady, let's quit the place, it is the den
Of villainy; fear nought, you have a guard;
And he° ere long shall meet his just reward.

[Exeunt Bonario & Celia.]

Volpone. Fall on me, roof, and bury me in ruin!
Become my grave, that wert my shelter! O!
I am unmasked, unspirited, undone,
Betrayed to beggary, to infamy—

Act III, Scene viii

[Enter Mosca, bleeding.]

Mosca. Where shall I run, most wretched shame of men,
To beat out my unlucky brains?

Volpone. Here, here.
What! dost thou bleed?

Mosca. O, that his well-driven sword
Had been so courteous to have cleft me down

261 **Nestor's hernia** the impotence of aged Nestor, one of the Greek leaders at Troy 274 **he** i.e., Volpone

Unto the navel, ere I lived to see
My life, my hopes, my spirits, my patron, all
Thus desperately engagèd° by my error.
Volpone. Woe on thy fortune.
Mosca. And my follies, sir.
Volpone. Th' hast made me miserable.
Mosca. And myself, sir.
Who would have thought he° would have hearkened so?
Volpone. What shall we do?
Mosca. I know not; if my heart
Could expiate the mischance, I'd pluck it out.
Will you be pleased to hang me, or cut my throat?
And I'll requite you, sir. Let's die like Romans,
Since we have lived like Grecians.°

They knock without.

Volpone. Hark, who's there?
I hear some footing;° officers, the *Saffi*,°
Come to apprehend us! I do feel the brand
Hissing already at my forehead; now,
Mine ears are boring.°
Mosca. To your couch, sir; you
Make that place good, however.° Guilty men
Suspect what they deserve still.

[*Mosca turns to face newcomer.*]

Signior Corbaccio!

Act III, Scene ix

Enter Corbaccio.

Corbaccio. Why, how now, Mosca?
Mosca. O, undone, amazed, sir.
Your son, I know not by what accident,
Acquainted with your purpose to my patron,
Touching your will, and making him your heir,
Entered our house with violence, his sword drawn,

III.viii.7 **engagèd** ensnarled 10 **he** i.e., Bonario 14-5 **Let's die . . . Grecians** Let's die stoically like Romans since we have lived dissolutely as Greeks 16 **footing** footsteps 16 **Saffi** bailiffs 17-9 **brand . . . boring** (common punishments for criminals) 20 **however** whatever happens

Sought for you, called you wretch, unnatural,
Vowed he would kill you.
Corbaccio. Me?
Mosca. Yes, and my patron.
Corbaccio. This act shall disinherit him indeed.°
Here is the will.
Mosca. 'Tis well, sir.
Corbaccio. Right and well.
Be you as careful now for me.
[*Enter Voltore unseen.*]
Mosca. My life, sir.
Is not more tendered;° I am only yours.
Corbaccio. How does he? Will he die shortly, think'st thou?
Mosca. I fear
He'll outlast May.
Corbaccio. Today?
Mosca. No, last out May, sir.
Corbaccio. Couldst thou not gi' him a dram?°
Mosca. O, by no means, sir.
Corbaccio. Nay, I'll not bid you.
Voltore. [*Aside.*] This is a knave, I see.
Mosca. [*Aside.*] How, Signior Voltore! Did he hear me?
Voltore. Parasite.
Mosca. Who's that? O, sir, most timely welcome.
Voltore. Scarce
To the discovery of your tricks, I fear.
You are his, only? And mine, also, are you not?
[*Corbaccio stands aside.*]
Mosca. Who? I, sir?
Voltore. You, sir. What device° is this
About a will?
Mosca. A plot for you, sir.
Voltore. Come,
Put not your foists° upon me; I shall scent 'em.
Mosca. Did you not hear it?
Voltore. Yes, I hear Corbaccio
Hath made your patron, there, his heir.

III.ix.8 **disinherit him indeed** in actuality, i.e., not merely as a ploy to get Volpone's estate 11 **more tendered** treated more tenderly 14 **dram** drop of poison 20 **device** scheme 22 **foists** deceptions (also a glance at "musty odors")

Mosca. 'Tis true,
By my device, drawn to it by my plot,
With hope—
Voltore. Your patron should reciprocate?
And you have promised?
Mosca. For your good I did, sir.
Nay, more, I told his son, brought, hid him here,
Where he might hear his father pass the deed;
Being persuaded to it by this thought, sir:
That the unnaturalness, first, of the act,
And then his father's oft disclaiming in him,°
Which I did mean t' help on, would sure enrage him
To do some violence upon his parent.
On which the law should take sufficient hold,
And you be stated° in a double hope.
Truth be my comfort, and my conscience,
My only aim was to dig you a fortune
Out of these two old, rotten sepulchres—
Voltore. I cry thee mercy, Mosca.
Mosca. Worth your patience,
And your great merit, sir. And see the change!
Voltore. Why, what success?
Mosca. Most hapless! you must help, sir.
Whilst we expected th' old raven, in comes
Corvino's wife, sent hither by her husband—
Voltore. What, with a present?
Mosca. No, sir, on visitation;
I'll tell you how anon—and staying long,
The youth he grows impatient, rushes forth,
Seizeth the lady, wounds me, makes her swear—
Or he would murder her, that was his vow—
T' affirm my patron to have done her rape,
Which how unlike it is, you see! and hence,
With that pretext he's gone t' accuse his father,
Defame my patron, defeat you—
Voltore. Where's her husband.
Let him be sent for straight.
Mosca. Sir, I'll go fetch him.
Voltore. Bring him to the *Scrutineo.*°
Mosca. Sir, I will.

32 **in him** i.e., kinship with him 36 **stated** instated 55 **Scrutineo** law court in Senate House

Voltore. This must be stopped.
Mosca. O, you do nobly, sir.
Alas, 'twas labored all, sir, for your good;
Nor was there want of counsel in the plot.
But Fortune can, at any time, o'erthrow
The projects of a hundred learned clerks,° sir.
Corbaccio. What's that?
Voltore. [*To Corbaccio.*] Will 't please you, sir, to go along?
[*Exeunt Corbaccio and Voltore.*]
Mosca. Patron, go in and pray for our success.
Volpone. Need makes devotion; heaven your labor bless.
[*Exeunt.*]

Act IV, Scene i

[*Enter*] *Sir Politic, Peregrine.*

Sir Politic. I told you, sir, it° was a plot; you see
What observation is! You mentioned° me
For some instructions: I will tell you sir,
Since we are met here in this height° of Venice,
Some few particulars I have set down
Only for this meridian, fit to be known
Of your crude traveler; and they are these.
I will not touch, sir, at your phrase,° or clothes,
For they are old.
Peregrine. Sir, I have better.
Sir Politic. Pardon,
I meant as they are themes.°
Peregrine. O, sir, proceed.
I'll slander you no more of wit, good sir.
Sir Politic. First, for your garb,° it must be grave and serious,
Very reserved and locked; not tell a secret
On any terms, not to your father; scarce
A fable but with caution; make sure choice

60 **clerks** scholars IV.i.1 **it** i.e., the mountebank scene 2 **mentioned** asked (?) 4 **height** latitude 8 **at your phrase** upon people's manner of speaking 10 **themes** topics for conversation 12 **garb** behavior

Both of your company and discourse; beware
You never speak a truth—
Peregrine. How!
Sir Politic. Not to strangers,
For those be they you must converse with most;
Others I would not know,° sir, but at distance,
So as I still might be a saver in 'em.°
You shall have tricks, else, passed upon you hourly.
And then, for your religion, profess none,
But wonder at the diversity of all;
And, for your part, protest were there no other
But simply the laws o' th' land, you could content you.°
Nick Machiavel and Monsieur Bodin° both
Were of this mind. Then must you learn the use
And handling of your silver fork° at meals,
The metal° of your glass (these are main matters
With your Italian), and to know the hour
When you must eat your melons and your figs.
Peregrine. Is that a point of state too?
Sir Politic Here it is.
For your Venetian, if he see a man
Preposterous° in the least, he has him straight;°
He has, he strips him. I'll acquaint you, sir.
I now have lived here 'tis some fourteen months;
Within the first week of my landing here,
All took me for a citizen of Venice,
I knew the forms so well—
Peregrine. [*Aside.*] And nothing else.
Sir Politic. I had read Contarini,° took me a house,
Dealt with my Jews to furnish it with movables°—
Well, if I could but find one man, one man
To mine own heart, whom I durst trust, I would—

19 **know** acknowledge 20 **be a saver in 'em** keep myself safe from them 24-5 **protest . . . you** affirm that if there were no other religion except the law of the land, you would be satisfied 26 **Machiavel . . . Bodin** (here Sir Politic oversimplifies the views of Niccolo Machiavelli and Jean Bodin) 28 **fork** (still new in England at this time) 29 **metal** material in its molten state 34 **preposterous** i.e., doing things in the wrong order 34 **he . . . straight** "he has his number" 40 **Contarini** Cardinal Gasparo Contarini (whose book on Venice was translated into English in 1599) 41 **movables** furniture

Peregrine. What, what, sir?
Sir Politic. Make him rich, make him a fortune:
He should not think again. I would command it.
Peregrine. As how?
Sir Politic. With certain projects that I have,
Which I may not discover.°
Peregrine. [*Aside.*] If I had
But one° to wager with, I would lay odds, now,
He tells me instantly.
Sir Politic. One is, and that
I care not greatly who knows, to serve the state
Of Venice with red herrings for three years,
And at a certain rate, from Rotterdam,
Where I have correspondence.° There's a letter
Sent me from one o' th' States,° and to° that purpose;
He cannot write his name, but that's his mark.
Peregrine. He is a chandler?°
Sir Politic. No, a cheesemonger.
There are some other too with whom I treat
About the same negotiation;
And I will undertake it: for 'tis thus
I'll do 't with ease, I've cast° it all. Your hoy°
Carries but three men in her, and a boy;
And she shall make me three returns a year.
So, if there come but one of three, I save;
If two, I can defalk.° But this is now
If my main project fail.
Peregrine. Then you have others?
Sir Politic. I should be loath to draw the subtle air
Of such a place without my thousand aims.
I'll not dissemble, sir; where'er I come
I love to be considerative,° and 'tis true
I have at my free hours thought upon
Some certain goods unto° the state of Venice,
Which I do call my cautions; and, sir, which

47 **discover** reveal 48 **But one** only one penny 53 **correspondence** contacts 54 **one o' th' States** a member of the States-General in the Netherlands 54 **and to** especially for 56 **chandler** seller of candles (a jab at the greasiness of Sir Politic's letter) 60 **cast** reckoned 60 **hoy** Dutch boat 64 **defalk** allow a deduction (in price?) 69 **to be considerative** think through carefully 71 **goods unto** i.e., good things for

I mean, in hope of pension, to propound
To the Great Council, then unto the Forty,
So to the Ten.° My means° are made already—
Peregrine. By whom?
Sir Politic. Sir, one that though his place be obscure,
Yet he can sway, and they will hear him. He's
A *commendatore.*
Peregrine. What, a common sergeant?
Sir Politic. Sir, such as they are, put it in their mouths
What they should say,° sometimes, as well as greater.
I think I have my notes to show you—
Peregrine. Good sir.
Sir Politic. But you shall swear unto me, on your gentry,
Not to anticipate—
Peregrine. I, sir?
Sir Politic. Nor reveal
A circumstance—My paper is not with me.
Peregrine. O, but you can remember, sir.
Sir Politic. My first is
Concerning tinderboxes. You must know
No family is here without its box.
Now, sir, it being so portable a thing,
Put case° that you or I were ill affected
Unto the state; sir, with it in our pockets
Might not I go into the *arsenale*?°
Or you? Come out again? And none the wiser?
Peregrine. Except yourself, sir.
Sir Politic. Go to, then. I therefore
Advertise to° the state how fit it were
That none but such as were known patriots,
Sound lovers of their country, should be suffered
T' enjoy them° in their houses; and even those
Sealed° at some office, and at such a bigness
As might not lurk in pockets.
Peregrine. Admirable!

74-5 Great Council . . . Ten the ruling hierarchy of Venice **75 means** contacts **79-80 put it . . . say** influence what rulers say **89 Put case** suppose **91 arsenale** the Venetian armory **94 Advertise to** advise **97 them** i.e., tinderboxes **98 Sealed** registered

Sir Politic. My next° is, how t' inquire, and be resolved
By present° demonstration, whether a ship
Newly arrivèd from Syria, or from
Any suspected part of all the Levant,
Be guilty of the plague. And where they use
To lie out forty, fifty days, sometimes,
About the *Lazaretto*° for their trial,
I'll save that charge and loss unto the merchant,
And in an hour clear the doubt.
Peregrine. Indeed, sir!
Sir Politic. Or——I will lose my labor.
Peregrine. My faith, that's much.
Sir Politic. Nay, sir, conceive me. 'Twill cost me, in onions,°
Some thirty livres°—
Peregrine. Which is one pound sterling.
Sir Politic. Beside my waterworks. For this I do, sir:
First, I bring in your ship 'twixt two brick walls—
But those the state shall venture.° On the one
I strain° me a fair tarpaulin, and in that
I stick my onions, cut in halves; the other
Is full of loopholes, out at which I thrust
The noses of my bellows; and those bellows
I keep, with waterworks, in personal motion,
Which is the easiest matter of a hundred.
Now, sir, your onion, which doth naturally
Attract th' infection, and your bellows blowing
The air upon him, will show instantly
By his° changed color if there be contagion,
Or else remain as fair as at the first.
Now 'tis known, 'tis nothing.
Peregrine. You are right, sir.
Sir Politic. I would I had my note.
Peregrine. Faith, so would I.
But you ha' done well for once, sir.
Sir politic. Were I false,°
Or would be made so, I could show you reasons

100 My next i.e., project **101 present** immediate **106 Lazaretto** quarantine hospital **110 onions** (considered the best protection against the plague) **111 livres** French coins **114 venture** contribute the money for **115 strain** stretch **124 his** i.e., the onion's **128 false** traitorous

How I could sell this state, now to the Turk—
Spite of their galleys, or their—
Peregrine. Pray you, Sir Pol.
Sir Politic. I have 'em not about me.
Peregrine. That I feared.
They're there, sir?
[*Points to book in Sir Pol's pocket.*]
Sir Politic. No, this is my diary,
Wherein I note my actions of the day.
Peregrine. Pray you let's see, sir. [*Opens diary.*] What is here?—"*Notandum,*
A rat had gnawn my spur leathers; notwithstanding,
I put on new and did go forth; but first
I threw three beans over the threshold. Item,
I went and bought two toothpicks, whereof one
I burst, immediately, in a discourse
With a Dutch merchant 'bout *ragion del stato*.°
From him I went and paid a *moccenigo*
For piecing my silk stockings; by the way
I cheapened° sprats, and at St. Mark's I urined."
Faith, these are politic notes!
Sir Politic. Sir, I do slip
No action of my life, thus but I quote it.°
Peregrine. Believe me it is wise!
Sir Politic. Nay, sir, read forth.

Act IV, Scene ii

[*Enter Lady Wouldbe, Nano, and two women.*]

Lady Wouldbe. Where should this loose knight be, trow? Sure, he's housed.°
Nano. Why, then he's fast.°
Lady Wouldbe. Ay, he plays both° with me.
I pray you stay. This heat will do more harm
To my complexion than his heart is worth.

141 **ragion del stato** reasons of state 144 **cheapened** bargained for 146 **quote it** make a note of it IV.ii.1 **housed** i.e., with the supposed courtesan 2 **fast** caught 2 **plays both** i.e., fast and loose

I do not care to hinder, but to take him.
How it° comes off!
1st Woman. My master's yonder.
Lady Wouldbe. Where?
2nd Woman. With a young gentleman.
Lady Wouldbe. That same's the party!
In man's apparel! Pray you, sir, jog° my knight.
I will be tender to his reputation,
However he demerit.°
Sir Politic. My lady!
Peregrine. Where?
Sir Politic. 'Tis she indeed; sir, you shall know her. She is,
Were she not mine, a lady of that merit
For fashion, and behavior, and for beauty
I durst compare—
Peregrine It seems you are not jealous,
That dare commend her.
Sir Politic. Nay, and for discourse—
Peregrine. Being your wife, she cannot miss° that.
Sir Politic. [*The parties join.*] Madam,
Here is a gentleman; pray you, use him fairly;
He seems a youth, but he is—
Lady Wouldbe. None?
Sir Politic. Yes, one
Has put his face as soon into the world—
Lady Wouldbe. You mean, as early? But today?
Sir Politic How's this?
Lady Wouldbe. Why, in this habit,° sir; you apprehend me!
Well, Master Wouldbe, this doth not become you.
I had thought the odor, sir, of your good name
Had been more precious to you; that you would not
Have done this dire massàcre on your honor,
One of your gravity, and rank besides!
But knights, I see, care little for the oath
They make to ladies, chiefly their own ladies.
Sir Politic. Now, by my spurs, the symbol of my knighthood—
Peregrine. [*Aside.*] Lord! how his brain is humbled for an oath.

6 it i.e., her makeup **8 jog** nudge **10 demerit** is unworthy of it **16 miss** lack **21 habit** clothing

Sir Politic. I reach° you not.
Lady Wouldbe. Right sir, your polity
May bear it through° thus. [*To Peregrine*.] Sir, a word with you,
I would be loath to contest publicly
With any gentlewoman, or to seem
Froward,° or violent, as *The Courtier*° says.
It comes too near rusticity in a lady.
Which I would shun by all means. And, however
I may deserve from Master Wouldbe, yet
T' have one fair gentlewoman, thus, be made
And one she knows not, ay, and to persèver,
Th' unkind instrument to wrong another,
In my poor judgment, is not warranted
From being a solecism° in our sex,
If not in manners.
Peregrine. How is this!
Sir Politic. Sweet madam,
Come nearer to your aim.
Lady Wouldbe. Marry, and will, sir.
Since you provoke me with your impudence
And laughter of your light° land-siren here,
Your Sporus,° your hermaphrodite—
Peregrine. What's here?
Poetic fury and historic storms!
Sir Politic. The gentleman, believe it, is of worth,
And of our nation.
Lady Wouldbe. Ay, your Whitefriars nation?°
Come, I blush for you, Master Wouldbe, ay;
And am ashamed you should ha' no more forehead
Than thus to be the patron, or St. George,
To a lewd harlot, a base fricatrice,°
A female devil in a male outside.
Sir Politic. [*To Peregrine*.] Nay,

31 reach understand **31-2 your polity . . . through** your craftiness holds to its course **35 froward** perverse **35 The Courtier** Castiglione's well-known book on courtly conduct **43 From being a solecism** because it is a breach of good conduct **47 light** immoral **48 Sporus** youth castrated and "wed" by Nero **51 Whitefriars nation** a "liberty" or district outside London city control infamous as a gathering place for the lawless **55 fricatrice** whore

And you° be such a one, I must bid adieu
To your delights. The case appears too liquid.°
[*Exit.*]

Lady Wouldbe. Ay, you may carry't clear, with your state-face!°
But for your carnival concupiscence,°
Who here is fled for liberty of conscience,
From furious persecution of the marshal,°
Her will I disc'ple.°

Peregrine. This is fine, i' faith!
And do you use this° often? Is this part
Of your wit's exercise, 'gainst you have occasion?
Madam—

Lady Wouldbe. Go to sir.

Peregrine. Do you hear me, lady?
Why, if your knight have set you to beg shirts,
Or to invite me home, you might have done it
A nearer° way by far.

Lady Wouldbe. This cannot work you
Out of my snare.

Peregrine. Why, am I in it, then?
Indeed, your husband told me you were fair,
And so you are; only your nose inclines—
That side that's next the sun—to the queen-apple.°

Lady Wouldbe. This cannot be endured by any patience.

Act IV, Scene iii

[*Enter Mosca.*]

Mosca. What's the matter, madam?

Lady Wouldbe. If the Senate
Right not my quest° in this, I will protest° 'em
To all the world no aristocracy.

57 you i.e., Peregrine (some editors argue that Sir Politic addresses Lady Wouldbe here) **58 liquid** clear, apparent **59 state-face** grave countenance **60 carnival concupiscence** carnal (?) loose woman **62 marshal** prison officer **63 disc'ple** discipline **64 use this** act like this **69 nearer** more direct **73 queen-apple** an early variety of apple, perhaps markedly red on one side **IV.iii.2 quest** petition **2 protest** proclaim

Mosca. What is the injury, lady?
Lady Wouldbe. Why, the callet°
You told me of, here I have ta'en disguised.
Mosca. Who? This! What means your ladyship? The creature
I mentioned to you is apprehended, now
Before the Senate. You shall see her—
Lady Wouldbe. Where?
Mosca. I'll bring you to her. This young gentleman,
I saw him land this morning at the port.
Lady Wouldbe. Is't possible? How has my judgment wandered!
Sir, I must, blushing, say to you, I have erred;
And plead your pardon.
Peregrine. What! more changes yet?
Lady Wouldbe. I hope y' ha' not the malice to remember
A gentlewoman's passion. If you stay
In Venice, here, please you to use me,° sir—
Mosca. Will you go, madam?
Lady Wouldbe. Pray you, sir, use me. In faith,
The more you see me, the more I shall conceive
You have forgot our quarrel.
[*Exeunt Lady Wouldbe, Mosca, Nano and Women.*]
Peregrine. This is rare!
Sir Politic Wouldbe? No, Sir Politic Bawd!
To bring me, thus, acquainted with his wife!
Well, wise Sir Pol, since you have practiced thus
Upon my freshmanship,° I'll try your salt-head,°
What proof it is against a counterplot. [*Exit.*]

4 callet prostitute **16 use me** make use of my acquaintance socially (with unintentional sexual meaning) **22-3 practiced . . . freshmanship** played a joke in this way on my inexperience **23 try your salt-head** test your seasoned wisdom (ironic)

Act IV, Scene iv

[*Enter*] *Voltore, Corbaccio, Corvino, Mosca* [*to the Scrutineo.*]

Voltore. Well, now you know the carriage° of the business,
Your constancy is all that is required,
Unto the safety of it.
Mosca. Is the lie
Safely conveyed amongst us? Is that sure?
Knows every man his burden?°
Corvino. Yes.
Mosca. Then shrink not.
Corvino. [*Aside to Mosca.*] But knows the advocate the truth?
Mosca. O sir,
By no means. I devised a formal° tale
That salved° your reputation. But be valiant, sir.
Corvino. I fear no one but him, that this his pleading
Should make him stand for a co-heir—
Mosca. Co-halter!
Hang him, we will but use his tongue, his noise,
As we do Croaker's° here. [*Points to Corbaccio.*]
Corvino. Ay, what shall he do?
Mosca. When we ha' done, you mean?
Corvino. Yes.
Mosca. Why, we'll think:
Sell him for mummia,° he's half dust already.
To Voltore. Do not you smile to see this buffalo,°
How he doth sport it with his head?—I should,°
If all were well and past. *To Corbaccio.* Sir, only you
Are he that shall enjoy the crop of all,
And these not know for whom they toil.
Corbaccio. Ay, peace.

IV.iv.1 **carriage** management 5 **burden** refrain in a song, hence "lines" 7 **formal** elaborately constructed 8 **salved** spread healing salve over 12 **Croaker's** i.e., Corbaccio's or the Raven's cawing 14 **mummia** a mummy's excrescence used as medicine 15 **buffalo** i.e., Corvino, the wouldbe cuckold 16 **I should** i.e., play upon Corvino's cuckoldry (perhaps indicating Mosca's designs on Celia)

Mosca. To Corvino. But you shall eat it.°—Much!—
then to Voltore again. Worshipful sir,
Mercury sit upon your thund'ring tongue,
Or the French Hercules,° and make your language
As conquering as his club, to beat along,
As with a tempest, flat, our adversaries;
But much more yours, sir.
Voltore. Here they come, ha' done.
Mosca. I have another witness if you need, sir,
I can produce.
Voltore. Who is it?
Mosca. Sir, I have her.°

Act IV, Scene v

[*Enter four Avocatori, Bonario, Celia, Notario, Commendatori, and Others.*]

1st Avocatore. The like of this the Sentate never heard of.
2nd Avocatore. 'Twill come most strange to them when we report it.
4th Avocatore. The gentlewoman has been ever held
Of unreprovèd name.
3rd Avocatore. So the young man.
4th Avocatore. The more unnatural part, that of his father.
2nd Avocatore. More of the husband.
1st Avocatore. I not know to give
His act a name, it is so monstrous!
4th Avocatore. But the impostor, he is a thing created
T' exceed example.°
1st Avocatore. And all after-times!
2nd Avocatore. I never heard a true voluptuary
Described but him.
3rd Avocatore. Appear yet those were cited?°
Notario. All but the old magnifico,° Volpone.
1st Avocatore. Why is not he here?

20 eat it i.e., digest the legacy **21-2 Mercury . . . Hercules** symbols of eloquence **27 her** i.e., Lady Wouldbe **IV.v.9 example . . . after-times** known cases and any in the future **11 cited** summoned **12 magnifico** nobleman

Mosca. Please your fatherhoods,°
Here is his advocate. Himself's so weak,
So feeble—
4th Avocatore. Where are you?
Bonario. His parasite,
His knave, his pander! I beseech the court
He may be forced to come, that your grave eyes
May bear strong witness of his strange impostures.
Voltore. Upon my faith and credit with your virtues,
He is not able to endure the air.
2nd Avocatore. Bring him, however.
3rd Avocatore. We will see him.
4th Avocatore. Fetch him.
Voltore. Your fatherhoods' fit pleasures be obeyed,
But sure the sight will rather move your pities
Than indignation. May it please the court,
In the meantime he may be heard in me!
I know this place most void of prejudice,
And therefore crave it, since we have no reason
To fear our truth should hurt our cause.
3rd Avocator. Speak free.
Voltore. Then know, most honored fathers, I must now
Discover to your strangely abusèd ears
The most prodigious and most frontless° piece
Of solid impudence, and treachery,
That ever vicious nature yet brought forth
To shame the state of Venice. This lewd woman,
[*Points to Celia.*]
That wants° no artificial° looks or tears
To help the visor° she has now put on,
Hath long been known a close° adulteress
To that lascivious youth, there [*Points to Bonario.*];
not suspected,
I say, but known, and taken, in the act,
With him; and by this man, the easy husband,
[*Points to Corvino.*]
Pardoned; whose timeless bounty makes him now
Stand here, the most unhappy, innocent person
That ever man's own goodness made accused.

14 **fatherhoods'** (proper form of address to judges) 31 **frontless** shameless 35 **wants** lacks 35 **artificial** artful 36 **visor** mask, here pretense 37 **close** secret

For these, not knowing how to owe° a gift
Of that dear grace but with their shame, being placed
So above all powers of their gratitude,
Began to hate the benefit,° and in place
Of thanks, devise t' extirp° the memory
Of such an act. Wherein, I pray your fatherhoods
To observe the malice, yea, the rage of creatures
Discovered in their evils; and what heart°
Such take, even from their crimes. But that anon
Will more appear. This gentleman, the father,
[*Points to Corbaccio.*]
Hearing of this foul fact, with many others,
Which daily struck at his too tender ears,
And grieved in nothing more than that he could not
Preserve himself a parent (his son's ills°
Growing to that strange flood) at last decreed
To disinherit him.

1st Avocatore. These be strange turns!°

2nd Avocatore. The young man's fame° was ever fair and honest.

Voltore. So much more full of danger is his vice,
That can beguile so under shade of virtue.
But as I said, my honored sires, his father
Having this settled purpose—by what means
To him° betrayed, we know not—and this day
Appointed for the deed, that parricide,
I cannot style him better, by confederacy°
Preparing this his paramour to be there,
Entered Volpone's house—who was the man,
Your fatherhoods must understand, designed
For the inheritance—there sought his father.
But with what purpose sought he him, my lords?
I tremble to pronounce it, that a son
Unto a father, and to such a father,
Should have so foul, felonious intent:
It was, to murder him! When, being prevented
By his more happy absence, what then did he?
Not check his wicked thoughts? No, now new deeds—

44 **owe** own or recognize 47 **benefit** i.e., Corvino's forgiveness 48 **extirp** eradicate 51 **heart** boldness 57 **ills** evils 59 **turns** i.e., of events 60 **fame** reputation 65 **him** i.e., Bonario 67 **confederacy** conspiracy

Mischief doth ever end where it begins—
An act of horror, fathers! He dragged forth
The agèd gentleman, that had there lain bed-rid
Three years, and more, out off his innocent couch,
Naked, upon the floor, there left him; wounded
His servant in the face; and, with this strumpet,
The stale° to his forged practice,° who was glad
To be so active—I shall here desire
Your fatherhoods to note but my collections°
As most remarkable—thought at once to stop
His father's ends,° discredit his free choice
In the old gentleman,° redeem themselves
By laying infamy upon this man,°
To whom, with blushing, they should owe their lives.

1st Avocatore. What proofs have you of this?

Bonario. Most honored fathers,
I humbly crave there be no credit given
To this man's mercenary tongue.

2nd Avocatore. Forbear.

Bonario. His soul moves in his fee.

3rd Avocatore. O, sir.

Bonario. This fellow,
For six sols° more would plead against his Maker.

1st Avocatore. You do forget yourself.

Voltore. Nay, nay, grave fathers,
Let him have scope. Can any man imagine
That he will spare's accuser, that would not
Have spared his parent?

1st Avocatore. Well, produce your proofs.

Celia. I would I could forget I were a creature.°

Voltore. Signor Corbaccio.

4th Avocatore. What is he?

Voltore. The father.

2nd Avocatore. Has he had an oath?

Notario. Yes.

Corbaccio. What must I do now?

85 **stale** lure or decoy 85 **forged practice** previously formulated scheme 87 **collections** conclusions 89 **ends** aims 90 **gentleman** i.e., Volpone 91 **this man** i.e., Corvino 97 **sols** French coins of little value 102 **creature** (sense uncertain: Celia either wishes she were dead or that she were not of the same species as her accusers)

Notario. Your testimony's craved.
Corbaccio. Speak to the knave?
I'll ha' my mouth first stopped with earth. My heart
Abhors his knowledge.° I disclaim in° him.
1st Avocatore. But for what cause?
Corbaccio. The mere portent° of nature.
He is an utter stranger to my loins.
Bonario. Have they made you to° this?
Corbaccio. I will not hear thee,
Monster of men, swine, goat, wolf, parricide!
Speak not, thou viper.
Bonario. Sir, I will sit down,
And rather wish my innocence should suffer,
Than I resist the authority of a father.
Voltore. Signor Corvino.
2nd Avocatore. This is strange!
1st Avocatore. Who's this?
Notario. The husband.
4th Avocatore. Is he sworn?
Notario. He is.
3rd Avocatore. Speak, then.
Corvino. This woman, please your fatherhoods, is a whore
Of most hot exercise, more than a partridge,°
Upon recòrd—
1st Avocatore. No more.
Corvino. Neighs like a jennet.
Notario. Preserve the honor of the court.
Corvino. I shall,
And modesty of your most reverend ears.
And, yet, I hope that I may say these eyes
Have seen her glued unto that piece of cedar,
That fine, well-timbered° gallant; and that here
The letters may be read, thorough the horn,°
That make the story perfect.
Mosca. Excellent, sir.
Corvino. There is no shame in this now, is there?

107 **his knowledge** any knowledge of him 107 **disclaim in** deny 108 **portent** sign of calamity 110 **made you to** turned you into 118 **patridge** thought to be lustful 124 **well-timbered** well-built 125 **The letters . . . horn** (here Corvino holds forked fingers to his head, thus making a sign of horns as well as a Vee, a letter one can read in a hornbook)

Mosca. None.
Corvino. Or if I said I hoped that she were onward°
To her damnation, if there be a hell
Greater than whore and woman; a good Catholic
May make the doubt.
3rd Avocatore. His grief hath made him frantic.
1st Avocatore. Remove him hence. *She* [*Celia*] *swoons.*
2nd Avocatore. Look to the woman.
Corvino. Rare!
Prettily feigned! Again!
4th Avocatore. Stand from about her.
1st Avocatore. Give her the air.
3rd Avocatore. [*To Mosca.*] What can you say?
Mosca. My wound,
May 't please your wisdoms, speaks for me, received
In aid of my good patron, when he° missed
His sought-for-father, when that well-taught dame
Had her cue given her to cry out a rape.
Bonario. O most laid° impudence! Fathers—
3rd Avocatore. Sir, be silent,
You had your hearing free, so must they theirs.
2nd Avocatore. I do begin to doubt th' imposture here.
4th Avocatore. This woman has too many moods.
Voltore. Grave fathers,
She is a creature of a most professed
And prostituted lewdness.
Corvino. Most impetuous,
Unsatisfied, grave fathers!
Voltore. May her feignings
Not take your wisdoms; but° this day she baited°
A stranger, a grave knight, with her loose eyes
And more lascivious kisses. This man saw 'em
Together on the water in a gondola.
Mosca. Here is the lady herself that saw 'em too,
Without;° who, then, had in the open streets
Pursued them, but for saving her knight's honor.
1st Avocatore. Produce that lady. [*Exit Mosca.*]
2nd Avocatore. Let her come.

128 **onward** well on the way 136 **he** i.e., Bonario 139 **laid** well laid, i.e., nicely plotted 146 **but** only 146 **baited** enticed 151 **Without** outside

4th Avocatore. These things.
They strike with wonder!
3rd Avocatore. I am turned a stone!

Act IV, Scene vi

[*Enter Mosca with Lady Wouldbe.*]

Mosca. Be resolute, madam.
Lady Wouldbe Ay, this same is she.
Out, thou chameleon harlot! Now thine eyes
Vie tears with the hyena.° Dar'st thou look
Upon my wrongèd face? I cry your pardons.
I fear I have forgettingly transgressed
Against the dignity of the court—
2nd Avocatore. No, madam.
Lady Wouldbe. And been exorbitant°—
4th Avocatore. You have not, lady.
These proofs are strong.
Lady Wouldbe. Surely, I had no purpose
To scandalize your honors, or my sex's.
3rd Avocatore. We do believe it.
Lady Wouldbe. Surely, you may believe it.
2nd Avocatore. Madam, we do.
Lady Wouldbe. Indeed, you may; my breeding
Is not so coarse—
4th Avocatore. We know it.
Lady Wouldbe. To offend
With pertinacy°—
3rd Avocatore. Lady—
Lady Wouldbe. Such a presence.
No, surely,
1st Avocatore. We well think it.
Lady Wouldbe. You may think it.
1st Avocatore. Let her o'ercome.° [*To Bonario.*] What witnesses have you
To make good your report?

IV.vi.2-3 **chameleon . . . hyena** figures of change and treachery 7 **exorbitant** outrageous 13 **pertinacy** error for impertinency (?) 15 **o'ercome** i.e., have the last word

Bonario. Our consciences.
Celia. And heaven, that never fails the innocent.
4th Avocatore. These are no testimonies.
Bonario. Not in your courts,
Where multitude° and clamor overcomes.
1st Avocatore. Nay, then you do wax insolent.

Volpone is brought in, as impotent.°

Voltore. Here, here,
The testimony comes that will convince,
And put to utter dumbness their bold tongues.
See here, grave fathers, here's the ravisher,
The rider on men's wives, the great impostor,
The grand voluptuary! Do you not think
These limbs should affect venery?° Or these eyes
Covet a concubine? Pray you, mark these hands.
Are they not fit to stroke a lady's breasts?
Perhaps he doth dissemble!
Bonario. So he does.
Voltore. Would you ha' him tortured?
Bonario. I would have him proved.°
Voltore. Best try him, then, with goads, or burning irons;
Put him to the strappado.° I have heard
The rack hath cured the gout. Faith, give it him
And help° him of a malady; be courteous.
I'll undertake, before these honored fathers,
He shall have yet as many left diseases
As she has known adulterers, or thou strumpets.
O my most equal hearers,° if these deeds,
Acts of this bold and most exorbitant strain,°
May pass with sufferance, what one citizen
But owes the forfeit of his life, yea, fame,
To him that dares traduce him?° which of you
Are safe, my honored fathers? I would ask,

19 **multitude** the number (of voices) 20 s.d. **as impotent** i.e., as an invalid 26 **affect venery** delight in sexual play 30 **proved** put to the test 32 **strappado** a form of torture 34 **help** rid 38 **equal hearers** fair judges 39 **exorbitant strain** outrageous nature 40-2 **what one . . . traduce him** will there be one citizen who will not owe his very life, yes, his reputation, to whoever dares to slander him?

With leave of your grave fatherhoods, if their plot
Have any face or color like to truth?
Or if, unto the dullest nostril here,
It smell not rank and most abhorrèd slander?
I crave your care of this good gentleman,
Whose life is much endangered by their fable;°
And as for them, I will conclude with this:
That vicious persons when they are hot and fleshed°
In impious acts, their constancy° abounds:
Damned deeds are done with greatest confidence.

1st Avocatore. Take 'em to custody, and sever them.

[*Celia and Bonario are taken out.*]

2nd Avocatore. 'Tis pity two such prodigies° should live.

1st Avocatore. Let the old gentleman be returned with care.
I'm sorry our credulity wronged him.

[*Officers bear Volpone off.*]

4th Avocatore. These are two creatures!

3rd Avocatore. I have an earthquake in me!

2nd Avocatore. Their shame, even in their cradles, fled their faces.

4th Avocatore. [*To Voltore.*] You've done a worthy service to the state, sir,
In their discovery.

1st Avocatore. You shall hear ere night
What punishment the court decrees upon 'em.

Voltore. We thank your fatherhoods.—

[*Exeunt Avocatori, Notario, Commendatori, and others.*]

How like you it?

Mosca. Rare.
I'd ha' your tongue, sir, tipped with gold for this;
I'd ha' you be the heir to the whole city;
The earth I'd have want men, ere you want living.°
They're bound to erect your statue in St. Mark's.
Signor Corvino, I would have you go
And show yourself, that you have conquered.

Corvino. Yes.

49 fable false tale 51 hot and fleshed impetuous and hardened 52 constancy determination 55 prodigies monsters 66 want living lack income

Mosca. It was much better that you should profess
Yourself a cuckold, thus, than that the other°
Should have been proved.
Corvino. Nay, I considered that.
Now, it is her fault.
Mosca. Then, it had been yours.
Corvino. True. I do doubt this advocate still.
Mosca. I' faith,
You need not; I dare ease you of that care.
Corvino. I trust thee, Mosca.
Mosca. As your own soul, sir.
[*Exit Corvino.*]
Corbaccio. Mosca!
Mosca. Now for your business, sir.
Corbaccio. How! Ha' you business?
Mosca. Yes, yours, sir.
Corbaccio. O, none else?
Mosca. None else, not I.
Corbaccio. Be careful then.
Mosca. Rest you with both your eyes,° sir.
Corbaccio. Dispatch it.
Mosca. Instantly.
Corbaccio. And look that all
Whatever be put in:° jewels, plate, moneys,
Household stuff, beddings, curtains.
Mosca. Curtain-rings, sir;
Only the advocate's fee must be deducted.
Corbaccio. I'll pay him now; you'll be too prodigal.
Mosca. Sir, I must tender° it.
Corbaccio. Two chequins is well?
Mosca. No, six, sir.
Corbaccio. 'Tis too much.
Mosca. He talked a great while,
You must consider that, sir.
Corbaccio. Well, there's three—
Mosca. I'll give it him.
Corbaccio. Do so, and there's for thee.
[*Exit Corbaccio.*]

71 other i.e., pander for Volpon **79 Rest . . . eyes** Close both eyes, i.e., you may sleep easy **80-1 And look . . . put in** And be sure that every item is listed **85 tender** give

Mosca. Bountiful bones!° What horrid, strange offense
Did he commit 'gainst nature in his youth,
Worthy this age?° [*To Voltore.*] You see, sir, how I work
Unto your ends; take you no notice.°
Voltore. No,
I'll leave you.
Mosca. All is yours, [*Exit Voltore.*]—the devil and all,
Good advocate— Madam, I'll bring you home.
Lady Wouldbe. No, I'll go see your patron.
Mosca. That you shall not.
I'll tell you why: my purpose is to urge
My patron to reform° his will, and for
The zeal you've shown today, whereas before
You were but third or fourth, you shall be now
Put in the first; which would appear as begged
If you were present. Therefore—
Lady Wouldbe. You shall sway° me.
[*Exeunt.*]

Act V, Scene i

Volpone [*alone.*]

Volpone. Well, I am here, and all this brunt° is past.
I ne'er was in dislike with my disguise
Till this fled° moment. Here, 'twas good, in private,
But in your public—*Cave,*° whilst I breathe.
'Fore God, my left leg 'gan to have the cramp,
And I apprehended, straight,° some power had struck me
With a dead palsy. Well, I must be merry
And shake it off. A many of these fears
Would put me into some villainous disease
Should they come thick upon me. I'll prevent 'em.

89 **Bountiful bones!** generous bag of bones (ironic) 91 **Worthy this age** deserving this sort of old age 92 **take you no notice** don't pay attention to me (a warning perhaps?) 97 **reform** redo 101 **sway** persuade V.i.1 **brunt** crisis 3 **fled** past 4 **Cavè** beware 6 **apprehended, straight** felt, suddenly

Give me a bowl of lusty wine to fright
This humor from my heart. Hum, hum, hum!
He drinks.
'Tis almost gone already; I shall conquer.
Any device, now, of rare, ingenious knavery
That would possess me with a violent laughter,
Would make me up° again. So, so, so, so.
Drinks again.
This heat is life; 'tis blood by this time!° Mosca!

Act V, Scene ii

[*Enter Mosca.*]

Mosca. How now, sir? Does the day look clear again?
Are we recovered? and wrought out of error
Into our way, to see our path before us?
Is our trade free once more?
Volpone. Exquisite Mosca!
Mosca. Was it not carried learnedly?
Volpone. And stoutly.
Good wits are greatest in extremities.°
Mosca. It were a folly beyond thought to trust
Any grand act unto a cowardly spirit.
You are not taken with it° enough, methinks?
Volpone. O, more than if I had enjoyed the wench.
The pleasure of all womankind's not like it.
Mosca. Why, now you speak, sir! We must here be fixed;
Here we must rest. This is our masterpiece;
We cannot think to go beyond this.
Volpone. True,
Th'ast played thy prize, my precious Mosca.
Mosca. Nay, sir,
To gull° the court—
Volpone. And quite divert the torrent
Upon the innocent.

16 up whole **17 This heat . . . time** (debased allusion to the Renaissance idea of how the body's vital heat is generated) **V.ii.6 extremities** emergencies **9 taken with it** pleased with our game **16 gull** trick

Mosca. Yes, and to make
So rare a music out of discords—
Volpone. Right.
That yet to me 's the strangest; how th'ast borne it!°
That these, being so divided 'mongst themselves,
Should not scent somewhat, or in me or thee,
Or doubt their own side.
Mosca. True, they will not see't.
Too much light blinds 'em, I think. Each of 'em
Is so possessed and stuffed with his own hopes
That anything unto the contrary,
Never so true, or never so apparent,
Never so palpable, they will resist it—
Volpone. Like a temptation of the devil.
Mosca. Right, sir.
Merchants may talk of trade, and your great signiors
Of land that yields well; but if Italy
Have any glebe° more fruitful than these fellows,
I am deceived. Did not your advocate rare?°
Volpone. O—"My most honored fathers, my grave fathers,
Under correction of your fatherhoods,
What face of truth is here? If these strange deeds
May pass, most honored fathers"—I had much ado
To forbear laughing.
Mosca. 'T seemed to me you sweat,° sir.
Volpone. In troth, I did a little.
Mosca. But confess, sir;
Were you not daunted?
Volpone. In good faith, I was
A little in a mist,° but not dejected;
Never but still myself.
Mosca. I think° it, sir.
Now, so truth help me, I must needs say this, sir,
And out of conscience for your advocate:
He's taken pains, in faith, sir, and deserved,
In my poor judgment, I speak it under favor,°
Not to contrary you, sir, very richly—
Well—to be cozened.°

19 **borne it** carried it off 31 **glebe** soil 32 **rare** i.e., behave rarely 37 **sweat** sweated 40 **in a mist** confused 41 **think** believe 45 **under favor** with permission 47 **cozened** cheated

Volpone. Troth, and I think so too,
By that I heard him in the latter end.
Mosca. O, but before, sir, had you heard him first
Draw it to certain heads,° then aggravate,°
Then use his vehement figures°—I looked still
When he would shift a shirt;° and doing this
Out of pure love, no hope of gain—
Volpone. 'Tis right.
I cannot answer° him, Mosca, as I would,
Not yet; but for thy sake, at thy entreaty,
I will begin e'en now to vex 'em all,
This very instant.
Mosca. Good, sir.
Volpone. Call the dwarf
And eunuch forth.
Mosca. Castrone, Nano.

[*Enter Castrone and Nano.*]

Nano. Here.
Volpone. Shall we have a jig° now?
Mosca. What you please, sir.
Volpone. Go,
Straight give out about the streets, you two,
That I am dead; do it with constancy,
Sadly,° do you hear? Impute it to the grief
Of this late slander. [*Exeunt Castrone and Nano.*]
Mosca. What do you mean, sir?
Volpone. O,
I shall have instantly my vulture, crow,
Raven, come flying hither on the news
To peck for carrion, my she-wolf and all,
Greedy and full of expectation—
Mosca. And then to have it ravished from their mouths?
Volpone. 'Tis true. I will ha' thee put on a gown,
And take upon thee as° thou wert mine heir;

50 **Draw it to certain heads** lead up to certain topics 50 **aggravate** emphasize the gravity (of the case) 51 **vehement figures** intensive figures of speech 52 **shift a shirt** change his shirt (damp from his exertion?) 54 **answer** repay 59 **jig** dance, trick 62 **Sadly** seriously 70 **take upon thee as** assume the manner as if

Show 'em a will. Open that chest and reach
Forth one of those that has the blanks. I'll straight
Put in thy name.
Mosca. It will be rare, sir.
Volpone. Ay,
When they e'en gape, and find themselves deluded—
Mosca. Yes.
Volpone. And thou use them scurvily! Dispatch,
Get on thy gown.
Mosca. But what, sir, if they ask
After the body?
Volpone. Say it was corrupted.
Mosca. I'll say it stunk, sir; and was fain° t' have it
Coffined up instantly and sent away.
Volpone. Anything, what thou wilt. Hold, here's my will.
Get thee a cap, a count-book,° pen and ink,
Papers afore thee; sit as thou wert taking
An inventory of parcels.° I'll get up
Behind the curtain, on a stool, and hearken;
Sometime peep over, see how they do look,
With what degrees their blood doth leave their faces.
O, 'twill afford me a rare meal of laughter!
Mosca. Your advocate will turn stark dull° upon it.
Volpone. It will take off his oratory's edge.
Mosca. But your *clarissimo*,° old round-back, he
Will crump you° like a hog-louse with the touch.
Volpone. And what Corvino?
Mosca. O sir, look for him
Tomorrow morning with a rope and dagger°
To visit all the streets; he must run mad.
My lady too, that came into the court
To bear false witness for your worship—
Volpone. Yes,
And kissed me 'fore the fathers, when my face
Flowed all with oils—
Mosca. And sweat, sir. Why, your gold
Is such another med'cine, it dries up

78 fain obliged **81 count-book** account book, ledger **83 parcels** items **88 turn stark dull** be struck dumb completely **90 clarissimo** high-ranking Venetian **91 crump you** crumple up **93 rope and dagger** (stage properties for characters driven mad by despair)

All those offensive savors! It transforms
The most deformèd, and restores 'em lovely
As 'twere the strange poetical girdle.° Jove
Could not invent t' himself a shroud more subtle
To pass Acrisius' guards.° It is the thing
Makes all the world her grace, her youth, her beauty.
Volpone. I think she loves me.
Mosca. Who? The lady, sir?
She's jealous of you.
Volpone Dost thou say so?
[*Knocking without.*]
Mosca. Hark,
There's some already.
Volpone. Look!
Mosca. It is the vulture;
He has the quickest scent.
Volpone. I'll to my place,
Thou to thy posture.°
Mosca. I am set.
Volpone. But Mosca,
Play the artificer° now, torture 'em rarely.

Act V, Scene iii

[*Enter Voltore.*]

Voltore. How now, my Mosca?
Mosca. [*Writing.*] Turkey carpets,° nine—
Voltore. Taking an inventory? That is well.
Mosca. Two suits of bedding, tissue°—
Voltore. Where's the will?
Let me read that the while.

[*Enter bearers carrying Corbaccio in a chair.*]

102 **girdle** (Cestus, the girdle of Venus, could beautify the ugly and arouse the aged) 102-4 **Jove . . . guards** (To reach Danaë Jove came to her in a shower of gold in order to penetrate her father Acrisius' brass tower) 110 **posture** pose 111 **artificer** schemer V.iii.1 **Turkey carpets** used for tables as well as walls 3 **tissue** cloth woven with gold or silver

Corbaccio. So, set me down,
And get you home. [*Exeunt bearers.*]
Voltore. Is he come now, to trouble us?
Mosca. Of cloth of gold, two more—
Corbaccio. Is it done, Mosca?
Mosca. Of several vellets,° eight—
Voltore. I like his care.
Corbaccio. Dost thou not hear?

[*Enter Corvino.*]

Corvino. Ha? Is the hour come, Mosca?
Volpone. [*Aside.*] Ay, now they muster.
[*Volpone*] *peeps from behind a traverse.*°
Corvino. What does the advocate here,
Or this Corbaccio?
Corbaccio. What do these here?

[*Enter Lady Wouldbe.*]

Lady Wouldbe. Mosca!
Is his thread° spun?
Mosca. Eight chests of linen—
Volpone. [*Aside.*] O,
My fine Dame Wouldbe, too!
Corvino. Mosca, the will,
That I may show it these and rid 'em hence.
Mosca. Six chests of diaper,° four of damask—There.
[*Gives them the will.*]
Corbaccio. Is that the will?
Mosca. Down-beds, and bolsters—
Volpone. [*Aside.*] Rare!
Be busy still. Now they begin to flutter;
They never think of me. Look, see, see, see!
How their swift eyes run over the long deed
Unto the name, and to the legacies,
What is bequeathed them there.

7 **several vellets** separate velvet hangings 9 **s.d. traverse** curtain or screen 11 **thread** i.e., of life, spun by the Fates 14 **diaper** patterned fabric

Mosca. Ten suits of hangings°—
Volpone. [*Aside.*] Ay, i' their garters,° Mosca. Now their hopes
Are at the gasp.°
Voltore. Mosca the heir!
Corbaccio. What's that?
Volpone. [*Aside.*] My advocate is dumb; look to my merchant.
He has heard of some strange storm, a ship is lost,
He faints; my lady will swoon. Old glazen-eyes°
He hath not reached his despair, yet.
Corbaccio. All these
Are out of hope; I'm sure the man.
Corvino. But, Mosca—
Mosca. Two cabinets—
Corvino. Is this in earnest?
Mosca. One
Of ebony—
Corvino. Or do you but delude me?
Mosca. The other, mother of pearl—I am very busy.
Good faith, it is a fortune thrown upon me—
Item, one salt° of agate—not my seeking.
Lady Wouldbe. Do you hear, sir?
Mosca. A perfumed box—Pray you forbear,
You see I'm troubled—made of an onyx—
Lady Wouldbe. How?
Mosca Tomorrow, or next day, I shall be at leisure
To talk with you all.
Corvino. Is this my large hope's issue?
Lady Wouldbe. Sir, I must have a fairer answer.
Mosca. Madam!
Marry, and shall: pray you, fairly quit my house.
Nay, raise no tempest with your looks; but hark you,
Remember what your ladyship offered me
To put you in an heir; go to, think on 't.
And what you said e'en your best madams did
For maintenance, and why not you? Enough.

20 suits of hangings sets of tapestries **21 i' their garters** (Volpone completes the proverbial phrase, "Hang oneself in one's own garters.") 22 **gasp** last gasp 25 **glazen-eyes** i.e., Corbaccio, who wears glasses 32 **salt** salt cellar

Go home and use the poor Sir Pol, your knight, well,
For fear I tell some riddles.° Go, be melancholic.
[*Exit Lady Wouldbe.*]

Volpone. [*Aside.*] O my fine devil!
Corvino. Mosca, pray you a word.
Mosca. Lord! Will not you take your dispatch hence yet?
Methinks of all you should have been th' example.°
Why should you stay here? With what thought? What promise?
Hear you: do not you know I know you an ass,
And that you would most fain have been a wittol°
If fortune would have let you? That you are
A declared cuckold, on good terms? This pearl,
You'll say, was yours? Right. This diamond?
I'll not deny't, but thank you. Much here else?
It may be so. Why, think that these good works
May help to hide your bad. I'll not betray you,
Although you be but extraordinary,
And have it only in title, it sufficeth.°
Go home, be melancholic too, or mad.
[*Exit Corvino.*]

Volpone. [*Aside.*] Rare, Mosca! How his villainy becomes him!
Voltore. Certain he doth delude all these for me.
Corbaccio. Mosca the heir?
Volpone. [*Aside.*] O, his four eyes have found it!
Corbaccio. I'm cozened, cheated, by a parasite slave!
Harlot,° th'ast gulled me.
Mosca. Yes, sir. Stop your mouth,
Or, I shall draw the only tooth is left.
Are not you he, that filthy, covetous wretch
With the three legs,° that here, in hope of prey,
Have, any time this three year, snuffed about
With your most grov'ling nose, and would have hired
Me to the pois'ning of my patron, sir?
Are not you he that have, today, in court,
Professéd the disinheriting of your son?

45 **riddles** secrets 48 **example** i.e., of leaving first 51 **wittol** willing cuckold 57-9 **I'll . . . sufficeth** I'll not reveal that you are an extraordinary cuckold, being one in name only, yet that's enough 65 **Harlot** originally a rogue 68 **three legs** i.e., two legs and a cane

Perjured yourself? Go home, and die, and stink.
If you but croak a syllable, all comes out.
Away, and call your porters! Go, go, stink.
[*Exit Corbaccio.*]

Volpone. [*Aside.*] Excellent varlet!
Voltore. Now, my faithful Mosca,
I find thy constancy.
Mosca. Sir?
Voltore. Sincere.
Mosca. A table.
Of porphyry—I mar'l° you'll be thus troublesome.
Voltore. Nay, leave off now, they are gone.
Mosca. Why, who are you?
What! Who did send for you? O, cry you mercy,
Reverend sir! Good faith, I am grieved for you,
That any chance° of mine should thus defeat
Your—I must needs say—most deserving travails.
But I protest, sir, it was cast upon me,
And I could, almost, wish to be without it,
But that the will o' th' dead must be observed.
Marry, my joy is that you need it not;
You have a gift, sir—thank your education—
Will never let you want while there are men
And malice to breed causes.° Would I had
But half the like, for all my fortune, sir.
If I have any suits—as I do hope,
Things being so easy and direct, I shall not—
I will make bold with your obstreperous aid;
Conceive me, for your fee,° sir. In meantime,
You that have so much law, I know ha' the conscience
Not to be covetous of what is mine.
Good sir, I thank you for my plate;° 'twill help
To set up a young man. Good faith, you look
As you were costive;° best go home and purge, sir.
[*Exit Voltore.*]

Volpone. Bid him eat lettuce° well! My witty mischief,
[*Coming from behind the traverse.*]

79 **mar'l** marvel 83 **chance** i.e., lucky chance 91 **causes** lawsuits 96 **Conceive . . . fee** Understand me, I expect to pay your usual fee 99 **plate** i.e., that Voltore previously gave to Volpone 101 **costive** constipated 102 **lettuce** a laxative

Let me embrace thee. O that I could now
Transform thee to a Venus—Mosca, go,
Straight take my habit of *clarissimo*,°
And walk the streets; be seen, torment 'em more.
We must pursue as well as plot. Who would
Have lost this feast?
Mosca. I doubt it will lose them.°
Volpone. O, my recovery shall recover all.
That I could now but think on some disguise
To meet 'em in, and ask 'em questions.
How I would vex 'em still at every turn!
Mosca. Sir, I can fit you.
Volpone. Canst thou?
Mosca. Yes, I know
One o' th' *commendatori*,° sir, so like you;
Him will I straight make drunk, and bring you his habit.
Volpone. A rare disguise, and answering° thy brain!
O, I will be a sharp disease unto 'em.
Mosca. Sir, you must look for cures—
Volpone. Till they burst;
The fox fares ever best when he is cursed.
[*Exeunt.*]

Act V, Scene iv

[*Sir Politic's house. Enter Peregrine disguised, and three Merchants.*]

Peregrine. Am I enough disguised?
1st Merchant. I warrant° you.
Peregrine. All my ambition is to fright him only.
2nd Merchant. If you could ship him away, 'twere excellent.
3rd Merchant. To Zant,° or to Aleppo?
Peregrine. Yes, and ha' his
Adventures put i' th' book of voyages,
And his gulled story registered for truth?

105 habit of Clarissimo distinctive robe of a nobleman **108 I . . . them** I have no doubt it will get rid of them **114 commendatori** minor law court officers **116 answering** resembling (the rareness of Mosca's brain) **V.iv.1 warrant** assure **4 Zant** an Ionian island

Well, gentlemen, when I am in a while,
And that you think us warm in our discourse,
Know your approaches.°
1st Merchant. Trust it to our care.
[*Exeunt Merchants.*]

[*Enter Woman.*]

Peregrine. Save you, fair lady. Is Sir Pol within?
Woman. I do not know, sir.
Peregrine. Pray you say unto him,
Here is a merchant, upon earnest business,
Desires to speak with him.
Woman. I will see, sir.
Peregrine. Pray you.
[*Exit Woman.*]
I see the family is all female here.

[*Enter Woman.*]

Woman. He says, sir, he has weighty affairs of state
That now require him whole;° some other time
You may possess him.
Peregrine. Pray you, say again,
If those require him whole, these will exact him,°
Whereof I bring him tidings. [*Exit Woman.*] What might be
His grave affair of state now? How to make
Bolognian sausages here in Venice, sparing°
One o' th' ingredients?

[*Enter Woman.*]

Woman. Sir, he says he knows
By your word "tidings"° that you are no statesman,
And therefore wills you stay.
Peregrine. Sweet, pray you return him:°

9 **Know your approaches** make your entrance 16 **require him whole** demand his full attention 18 **exact him** probably, extract something from him 21 **sparing** omitting 23 **tidings** rather than the code word "intelligences" 24 **return him** i.e., return this message to him

I have not read so many proclamations
And studied them for words, as he has done,
But—Here he deigns to come.

[*Enter Sir Politic.*]

Sir Politic. Sir, I must crave
Your courteous pardon. There hath chanced today
Unkind disaster 'twixt my lady and me,
And I was penning my apology
To give her satisfaction, as you came now.
Peregrine. Sir, I am grieved I bring you worse disaster:
The gentleman you met at th' port today,
That told you he was newly arrived—
Sir Politic. Ay, was
A fugitive punk?°
Peregrine. No, sir, a spy set on you,
And he has made relation to the Senate
That you professed to him to have a plot
To sell the state of Venice to the Turk.
Sir Politic. O me!
Peregrine. For which warrants are signed by this time
To apprehend you and to search your study
For papers—
Sir Politic. Alas, sir, I have none but notes
Drawn out of play-books—
Peregrine. All the better, sir.
Sir Politic. And some essays. What shall I do?
Peregrine. Sir, best
Convey yourself into a sugar-chest,
Or, if you could lie round,° a frail° were rare,
And I could send you aboard.
Sir Politic. Sir, I but talked so
For discourse' sake merely. *They knock without.*
Peregrine. Hark, they are there.
Sir Politic. I am a wretch, a wretch!
Peregrine. What will you do, sir?
Ha' you ne'er a currant-butt° to leap into?
They'll put you to the rack, you must be sudden.

35 punk prostitute **45 lie round** curl up **45 frail** rush basket for packing figs **49 currant-butt** cask for currants

Sir Politic. Sir, I have an engine°—
3rd Merchant. [*Off-stage.*] Sir Politic Wouldbe!
2nd Merchant. Where is he?
Sir Politic. That I have thought upon beforetime.
Peregrine. What is it?
Sir Politic. I shall ne'er endure the torture!
Marry, it is, sir, of a tortoise-shell,
Fitted for these extremities. Pray you, sir, help me.
Here I've a place, sir, to put back my legs;
Please you to lay it on, sir. With this cap
And my black gloves, I'll lie, sir, like a tortoise,
Till they are gone.
Peregrine. And call you this an engine?
Sir Politic. Mine own device—Good sir, bid my wife's women
To burn my papers.
They [*the three Merchants*] *rush in.*
1st Merchant. Where's he hid?
3rd Merchant. We must,
And will, sure, find him.
2nd Merchant. Which is his study?
1st Merchant. What
Are you, sir?
Peregrine. I'm a merchant that came here
To look upon this tortoise.
3rd Merchant. How!
1st Merchant. St. Mark!
What beast is this?
Peregrine. It is a fish.
2nd Merchant. Come out here!
Peregrine. Nay, you may strike him, sir, and tread upon him.
He'll bear a cart.
1st Merchant. What, to run over him?
Peregrine. Yes.
3rd Merchant. Let's jump upon him.
2nd Merchant. Can he not go?
Peregrine. He creeps, sir.
1st Merchant. Let's see him creep. [*Prods him.*]
Peregrine. No, good sir, you will hurt him.
2nd Merchant. Heart, I'll see him creep, or prick his guts.

51 **engine** device

3rd Merchant. Come out here!
Peregrine. [*To Sir Politic.*] Pray you, sir, creep a little.
1st Merchant. Forth.
2nd Merchant. Yet further.
Peregrine. [*To Sir Politic.*] Good sir, creep.
2nd Merchant. We'll see his legs.
They pull off the shell and discover him.
3rd Merchant. Godso, he has garters!
1st Merchant. Ay, and gloves!
2nd Merchant. Is this
Your fearful tortoise?
Peregrine. Now, Sir Pol, we are even;
[*Throwing off his disguise.*]
For your next project I shall be prepared.
I am sorry for the funeral° of your notes, sir.
1st Merchant. 'Twere a rare motion° to be seen in Fleet Street.
2nd Merchant. Ay, i' the term.°
1st Merchant. Or Smithfield, in the fair.°
3rd Merchant. Methinks 'tis but a melancholic sight.
Peregrine. Farewell, most politic tortoise.
[*Exeunt Peregrine and Merchants.*]
Sir Politic. Where's my lady?
Knows she of this?
Woman. I know not, sir.
Sir Politic. Inquire.
[*Exit Woman.*]
O, I shall be the fable of all feats,
The freight of the *gazetti,*° ship-boys' tale,
And, which is worst, even talk for ordinaries.°

[*Re-enter Woman.*]

Woman. My lady's come most melancholic home,
And says, sir, she will straight to sea, for physic.°
Sir Politic. And I, to shun this place and clime forever,

76 **funeral** i.e., the burning of his papers 77 **motion** puppet show 78 **i' the term** i.e., when courts are in session 78 **the fair** Bartholomew Fair at Smithfield 83 **freight of the gazetti** topic of the newspapers 84 **ordinaries** taverns 86 **physic** cure

Creeping with house on back, and think it well
To shrink my poor head in my politic shell.
[*Exeunt.*]

Act V, Scene v

[*Enter*] *Volpone, Mosca, the first in the habit of a Commendatore; the other, of a Clarissimo.*

Volpone. Am I then like him?°
Mosca. O sir, you are he;
No man can sever° you.
Volpone. Good.
Mosca. But what am I?
Volpone. 'Fore heav'n, a brave *clarissimo,* thou becom'st it!
Pity thou wert not born one.
Mosca. If I hold
My made one,° 'twill be well.
Volpone. I'll go and see
What news, first, at the court [*Exit.*]
Mosca. Do so. My fox
Is out on° his hole, and ere he shall re-enter,
I'll make him languish in his borrowed case,°
Except° he come to composition° with me.
Androgyno, Castrone, Nano.

[*Enter Androgyno, Castrone, and Nano.*]

All. Here.
Mosca. Go recreate° yourselves abroad, go sport.
[*Exeunt the three.*]
So, now I have the keys and am possessed.°
Since he will needs be dead afore his time,
I'll bury him, or gain by him. I'm his heir,
And so will keep me, till he share at least.
To cozen him of all were but a cheat

V.v.1 him i.e., the commendatore **2 sever** distinguish **4-5 hold My made one** (1) hold up my role, (2) hold on to my new status **7 on** of **8 case** disguise **9 Except** unless **9 composition** agreement **11 recreate** amuse **12 possessed** in possession

Well placed; no man would construe it a sin.
Let his sport pay for 't.° This is called the fox-trap.
[*Exit.*]

Act V, Scene vi

[*Enter Corbaccio and Corvino.*]

Corbaccio. They say the court is set.
Corvino. We must maintain
Our first tale good, for both our reputations.
Corbaccio. Why, mine's no tale! My son would, there, have killed me.
Corvino. That's true, I had forgot. Mine is, I am sure.
But for your will, sir.
Corbaccio. Ay, I'll come upon him°
For that hereafter, now his patron's dead.

[*Enter Volpone in disguise.*]

Volpone. Signor Corvino! And Corbaccio! Sir,
Much joy unto you.
Corvino. Of what?
Volpone. The sudden good
Dropped down upon you—
Corbaccio. Where?
Volpone. And none knows how,
From old Volpone, sir.
Corbaccio. Out, arrant knave!
Volpone. Let not your too much wealth, sir, make you furious.
Corbaccio. Away, thou varlet.
Volpone. Why, sir?
Corbaccio. Dost thou mock me?
Volpone. You mock the world, sir; did you not change° wills?
Corbaccio. Out, harlot!
Volpone. O! Belike you are the man,

18 **Let . . . for't** Let his fooling around pay for his pleasure
V.vi.5 **him** i.e., Mosca 13 **change** exchange

Signor Corvino? Faith, you carry it well;
You grow not mad withal. I love your spirit.
You are not over-leavened° with your fortune.
You should ha' some would swell now like a wine-fat°
With such an autumn°—Did he gi' you all, sir?

Corvino. Avoid,° you rascal.

Volpone. Troth, your wife has shown
Herself a very woman!° But you are well,
You need not care, you have a good estate
To bear it out, sir, better by this chance.
Except Corbaccio have a share?

Corbaccio. Hence, varlet.

Volpone. You will not be a'known,° sir? Why, 'tis wise.
Thus do all gamesters, at all games, dissemble.
No man will seem to win.

[*Exeunt Corvino and Corbaccio.*]

Here comes my vulture,
Heaving his beak up i' the air, and snuffing.

Act V, Scene vii

[*Enter*] *Voltore* [*to*] *Volpone.*

Voltore. Outstripped thus, by a parasite! A slave,
Would run on errands, and make legs for crumbs?
Well, what I'll do—

Volpone. The court stays for your worship.
I e'en rejoice, sir, at your worship's happiness,
And that it fell into so learned hands,
That understand the fingering—

Voltore. What do you mean?

Volpone. I mean to be a suitor to your worship
For the small tenement, out of reparations,°
That at the end of your long row of houses,
By the *Piscaria;*° it was, in Volpone's time,
Your predecessor, ere he grew diseased,

17 **over-leavened** puffed up 18 **wine-fat** wine-vat 19 **autumn** harvest 20 **Avoid** get away 21 **a very woman** a typical woman, i.e., loose 25 **a'known** publicly known as the heir 8 **reparations** repairs 10 **Piscaria** fish market

A handsome, pretty, customed° bawdy-house
As any was in Venice—none dispraised—
But fell with him. His body and that house
Decayed together.
Voltore. Come, sir, leave your prating.
Volpone. Why, if your worship give me but your hand,
That I may ha' the refusal,° I have done.
'Tis a mere toy to you, sir, candle-rents.°
As your learned worship knows—
Voltore. What do I know?
Volpone. Marry, no end of your wealth, sir, God decrease° it.
Voltore. Mistaking knave! What, mock'st thou my misfortune?
Volpone. His blessing on your heart, sir; would 'twere more! [*Exit Voltore.*]
Now, to my first again, at the next corner.

Act V, Scene viii

[*Enter*] *Corbaccio, Corvino,* (*Mosca passant*°). *Volpone* [*remains.*]

Corbaccio. See, in our habit! See the impudent varlet!
Corvino. That I could shoot mine eyes at him, like gunstones!°
Volpone. But is this true, sir, of the parasite?
Corbaccio. Again t' afflict us? Monster!
Volpone. In good faith, sir,
I'm heartily grieved a beard of your grave length°
Should be so over-reached. I never brooked
That parasite's hair; methought his nose should cozen.
There still° was somewhat in his look did promise
The bane° of a *clarissimo.*
Corbaccio. Knave.

12 **customed** well patronized 17 **refusal** i.e., first refusal or option 18 **candle-rents** slum rents 20 **decrease** (deliberate malaprop for "increase") V.viii. s.d. **passant** i.e., Mosca passes across the stage 2 **gunstones** stone cannonballs 5 **beard . . . length** a man of your age 8 **still** always 9 **bane** ruin

Volpone. Methinks
Yet you, that are so traded° i' the world,
A witty merchant, the fine bird Corvino,
That have such moral emblems° on your name,
Should not have sung your shame, and dropped your cheese,
To let the fox laugh at your emptiness.
Corvino. Sirrah, you think the privilege of the place,°
And your red, saucy cap, that seems to me
Nailed to your jolt-head with those two chequins,°
Can warrant your abuses. Come you hither:
You shall perceive, sir, I dare beat you. Approach.
Volpone. No haste, sir. I do know your valor well,
Since you durst publish what you are, sir.
Corvino. Tarry,
I'd speak with you.
Volpone. Sir, sir, another time—
Corvino. Nay, now.
Volpone. O God, sir! I were a wise man
Would stand the fury of a distracted cuckold.
Mosca walks by 'em.
Corbaccio. What, come again!
Volpone. Upon 'em, Mosca; save me.
Corbaccio. The air's infected where he breathes.
Corvino. Let's fly him.
[*Exeunt Corvino and Corbaccio.*]
Volpone. Excellent basilisk!° Turn upon the vulture.

Act V, Scene ix

[*Enter Voltore.*]

Voltore. Well, flesh-fly,° it is summer with you now;
Your winter will come on.
Mosca. Good advocate,
Pray thee not rail, nor threaten out of place thus;

10 **traded** experienced 12 **moral emblems** (alluding to the fable of the crow and the fox) 15 **the place** your position 17 **chequins** gold coins 27 **basilisk** fabled serpent whose glance was deadly V.ix.1. **flesh-fly** the meaning of "Mosca"

Thou'lt make a solecism, as Madam says.
Get you a biggen° more; your brain breaks loose.
[*Exit.*]

Voltore. Well, sir.
Volpone. Would you ha' me beat the insolent slave?
Throw dirt upon his first good clothes?
Voltore. This same
Is doubtless some familiar!°
Volpone. Sir, the court,
In troth, stays for you. I am mad;° a mule
That never read Justinian,° should get up
And ride an advocate! Had you no quirk°
To avoid gullage,° sir, by such a creature?
I hope you do but jest; he has not done 't;
This's but confederacy to blind the rest.
You are the heir?
Voltore. A strange, officious,
Troublesome knave! Thou dost torment me.
Volpone. —I know—
It cannot be, sir, that you should be cozened;
'Tis not within the wit of man to do it.
You are so wise, so prudent, and 'tis fit
That wealth and wisdom still should to together.

Act V, Scene x

[*Enter*] *four Avocatori, Notario, Commendatori, Bonario, Celia, Corbaccio, Corvino.*

1st Avocatore. Are all the parties here?
Notario. All but the advocate.
2nd Avocatore. And here he comes.

[*Enter Voltore, Volpone following him.*]

Avocatori. Then bring 'em° forth to sentence.
Voltore. O my most honored fathers, let your mercy

5 biggen lawyer's skull cap **8 familiar** dependent possessed of an evil spirit **9 mad** furious **10 Justinian** Roman code of law prepared at the order of Justinian I **11 quirk** trick or quibble **12 gullage** being made a fool of V.x.2 **'em** i.e., Celia and Bonario

Once win upon° your justice, to forgive—
I am distracted—
Volpone. [*Aside.*] What will he do now?
Voltore. O,
I know not which t' address myself to first,
Whether your fatherhoods, or these innocents—
Corvino. [*Aside.*] Will he betray himself?
Voltore. Whom equally
I have abused, out of most covetous ends—
Corvino. The man is mad!
Corbaccio. What's that?
Corvino. He is possessed.°
Voltore. For which, now struck in conscience, here I prostrate
Myself at your offended feet, for pardon.
[*He kneels.*]
1st, 2nd Avocatori. Arise.
Celia. O heav'n, how just thou art!
Volpone. [*Aside.*] I'm caught
I' mine own noose.
Corvino. [*Aside to Corbaccio.*] Be constant,° sir, nought now
Can help but impudence.
1st Advocatore. Speak forward.
Commendatore. [*To the Courtroom.*] Silence!
Voltore. It is not passion° in me, reverend fathers,
But only conscience, conscience, my good sires,
That makes me now tell the truth. That parasite,
That knave, hath been the instrument of all.
Avocatori. Where is that knave? Fetch him.
Volpone. I go.
[*Exit.*]
Corvino. Grave fathers,
This man's distracted, he confessed it now,
For, hoping to be old Volpone's heir,
Who now is dead—
3rd Avocatore. How!
2nd Avocatore. Is Volpone dead?
Corvino. Dead since, grave fathers—
Bonario. O sure vengeance!

4 **upon** over 10 **possessed** i.e., by the devil 14 **constant** steadfast 16 **passion** frenzy

1st Avocatore. Stay.
Then he was no deceiver.
Voltore. O, no, none;
The parasite, grave fathers.
Corvino. He does speak
Out of mere envy, 'cause the servant's made
The thing he gaped for. Please your fatherhoods,
This is the truth; though I'll not justify
The other, but he may be some-deal° faulty.
Voltore. Ay, to your hopes, as well as mine, Corvino.
But I'll use modesty.° Pleaseth your wisdoms
To view these certain notes, and but confer° them;
[*Gives them papers.*]
As I hope favor, they shall speak clear truth.
Corvino. The devil has entered him!
Bonario. Or bides in you.
4th Avocatore. We have done ill, by a public officer°
To send for him, if he be heir.
2nd Avocatore. For whom?
4th Avocatore. Him that they call the parasite.
3rd Avocatore. 'Tis true,
He is a man of great estate now left.
4th Avocatore. Go you, and learn his name, and say the court
Entreats his presence here, but to the clearing
Of some few doubts. [*Exit Notario.*]
2nd Avocatore. This same's a labyrinth!
1st Avocatore. Stand you unto your first report?
Corvino. My state,
My life, my fame—
Bonario. Where is't?
Corvino. Are at the stake.
1st Avocatore. Is yours so too?
Corbaccio. The advocate's a knave,
And has a forkèd tongue—
2nd Avocatore. Speak to the point.
Corbaccio. So is the parasite too.
1st Avocatore. This is confusion.

30 **some-deal** somewhat 32 **modesty** moderation 33 **confer** compare 36 **by a public officer** i.e., the commendatore (Mosca's new rank merits the Notario)

Voltore. I do beseech your fatherhoods, read but those.°
Corvino. And credit nothing the false spirit hath writ.
  It cannot be but he is possessed, grave fathers.

Act V, Scene xi

[*Enter*] *Volpone.*

Volpone. To make a snare for mine own neck! And run
  My head into it wilfully, with laughter!
  When I had newly 'scaped, was free and clear!
  Out of mere wantonness! O, the dull devil
  Was in this brain of mine when I devised it,
  And Mosca gave it second;° he must now
  Help to sear° up this vein, or we bleed dead.

[*Enter Nano, Androgyno, and Castrone.*]

  How now! Who let you loose? Whither go you now?
  What, to buy gingerbread, or to drown kitlings?°
Nano. Sir, Master Mosca called us out of doors,
  And bid us all go play, and took the keys.
Androgyno. Yes.
Volpone. Did Master Mosca take the keys? Why, so!
  I am farther in. These are my fine conceits!°
  I must be merry, with a mischief to me!
  What a vile wretch was I, that could not bear
  My fortune soberly; I must ha' my crotchets
  And my conundrums!° Well, go you and seek him.
  His meaning may be truer than my fear.
  Bid him, he straight come to me to the court;
  Thither will I, and if't be possible,
  Unscrew° my advocate, upon new hopes.
  When I provoked him, then I lost myself.

[*Exeunt.*]

48 **those** i.e., the notes V.xi.6 **gave it second** seconded it 7 **sear** cauterize or seal a cut with a hot iron 9 **kitlings** kittens 13 **conceits** notions 16-17 **crotchets . . . conundrums** whims and riddles 21 **Unscrew** reverse the course of

Act V, Scene xii

Avocatori, &c. [Notario, Commendatori, Bonario, Celia, Corbaccio, Corvino, Voltore.]

1st Avocatore. [Holding Voltore's notes.] These things can ne'er be reconciled. He here
Professeth that the gentleman was wronged,
And that the gentlewoman was brought thither,
Forced by her husband, and there left.
Voltore. Most true.
Celia. How ready° is heav'n to those that pray!
1st Avocator. But that
Volpone would have ravished her, he holds
Utterly false, knowing his impotence.
Corvino. Grave fathers, he is possessed; again, I say,
Possessed. Nay, if there be possession
And obsession, he has both.
3rd Avocatore. Here comes our officer.

[Enter Volpone, disguised.]

Volpone. The parasite will straight be here, grave fathers.
4th Avocatore. You might invent some other name, sir varlet.
3rd Avocatore. Did not the notary meet him?
Volpone. Not that I know.
4th Avocatore. His coming will clear all.
2nd Avocatore. Yet, it is misty.
Voltore. May't please your fatherhoods—
Volpone. Sir, the parasite
Volpone whispers [to] the Advocate.
Willed me to tell you that his master lives;
That you are still the man; your hopes the same;
And this was only a jest—
Voltore. How?
Volpone. Sir, to try
If you were firm, and how you stood affected.
Voltore. Art sure he lives?
Volpone. Do I live,° sir?

V.xii.5 **ready** responsive 21 **Do I live** (probably Volpone reveals himself to Voltore)

Voltore. O me!
I was too violent.
Volpone. Sir, you may redeem it:
They said you were possessed: fall down, and seem so.
I'll help to make it good. God bless the man!
Voltore falls.
[*Aside to Voltore.*]
—Stop your wind° hard, and swell—See, see, see, see!
He vomits crooked pins! His eyes are set
Like a dead hare's hung in a poulter's shop!°
His mouth's running away!° Do you see, signior?
Now, 'tis in his belly.
Corvino. Ay, the devil!
Volpone. Now, in his throat.
Corvino. Ay, I perceive it plain.
Volpone. 'Twill out, 'twill out! Stand clear. See where it flies!
In a shape of a blue toad, with a bat's wings!
Do you not see it, sir?
Corbaccio. What? I think I do.
Corvino. 'Tis too manifest.
Volpone. Look! He comes t' himself.
Voltore. Where am I?
Volpone. Take good heart, the worst is past, sir.
You are dispossessed.
1st Avocatore. What accident is this?
2nd Avocatore. Sudden, and full of wonder!
3rd Avocatore. If he were
Possessed, as it appears, all this is nothing.
[*Waving notes.*]
Corvino. He has been often subject to these fits.
1st Avocatore. Show him that writing.—Do you know it, sir?
Volpone. [*Aside.*] Deny it sir, forswear it, know it not.
Voltore. Yes, I do know it well, it is my hand;°
But all that it contains is false.
Bonario. O practice!°
2nd Avocatore. What maze is this!

24 Stop your wind hold your breath **26 poulter's shop** poultry shop **27 running away** moving violently **41 hand** handwriting **42 practice** intrigue

1st Avocatore. Is he not guilty then,
Whom you, there, name the parasite?
Voltore. Grave fathers,
No more than his good patron, old Volpone.
4th Avocatore. Why, he is dead.
Voltore. O, no, my honored fathers.
He lives—
1st Avocatore. How! Lives?
Voltore. Lives.
2nd Avocatore. This is subtler yet!°
3rd Avocatore. You said he was dead.
Voltore. Never.
3rd Avocatore. You said so!
Corvino. I heard so.
4th Avocatore. Here comes the gentleman, make him way.°

[*Enter Mosca.*]

3rd Avocatore. A stool!
4th Avocatore. A proper man and, were Volpone dead,
A fit match for my daughter.
3rd Avocatore. Give him way.
Volpone. [*Aside to Mosca.*] Mosca, I was almost lost; the advocate
Had betrayed all; but now it is recovered.
All's o' the hinge° again. Say I am living.
Mosca. What busy° knave is this? Most reverend fathers,
I sooner had attended your grave pleasures,
But that my order for the funeral
Of my dear patron did require me—
Volpone. [*Aside.*] Mosca!
Mosca. Whom I intend to bury like a gentleman.
Volpone. [*Aside.*] Ay, quick,° and cozen me of all.
2nd Avocator. Still stranger!
More intricate!
1st Avocatore. And come about° again!
4th Avocator. [*Aside.*] It is a match, my daughter is bestowed.
Mosca. [*Aside to Volpone.*] Will you gi' me half?

47 **subtler yet** more bewildering still 49 **make him way** make way for him 54 **o' the hinge** i.e., swinging smoothly 55 **busy** interfering 60 **quick** alive 61 **come about** reversed

Volpone. [*aloud.*] First I'll be hanged.
Mosca. [*Aside.*] I know
Your voice is good, cry not so loud.
1st Avocatore. Demand°
The advocate. Sir, did not you affirm
Volpone was alive?
Volpone. Yes, and he is;
This gent'man told me so. [*Aside to Mosca.*] Thou shalt have half.
Mosca. Whose drunkard is this same? Speak, some that know him.
I never saw his face. [*Aside to Volpone.*] I cannot now
Afford it you so cheap.
Volpone. [*Aside.*] No?
1st Avocatore. [*To Voltore.*] What say you?
Voltore. The officer told me.
Volpone. I did, grave fathers,
And will maintain he lives with mine own life,
And that this creature° told me. [*Aside.*] I was born
With all good stars my enemies!
Mosca. Most grave fathers,
If such an insolence as this must pass
Upon me, I am silent; 'twas not this
For which you sent, I hope.
2nd Avocatore. Take him away.
Volpone. [*Aside.*] Mosca!
3rd Avocatore. Let him be whipped.
Volpone. [*Aside.*] Wilt thou betray me?
Cozen me?
3rd Avocatore. And taught to bear himself
Toward a person of his rank.
4th Avocatore. [*The Officers seize Volpone.*] Away.
Mosca. I humbly thank your fatherhoods.
Volpone. [*Aside.*] Soft, soft. Whipped?
And lose all that I have? If I confess,
It cannot be much more.
4th Avocatore. [*To Mosca.*] Sir, are you married?
Volpone. [*Aside.*] They'll be allied° anon; I must be resolute:
The fox shall here uncase.°

64 **Demand** question 73 **this creature** i.e., Mosca 84 **allied** i.e., in marriage 85 **uncase** take off disguise

He puts off his disguise.

Mosca. Patron!

Volpone. Nay, now
My ruins shall not come alone; your match
I'll hinder sure. My substance shall not glue you,
Nor screw you, into a family.

Mosca. Why, patron!

Volpone. I am Volpone, and this is my knave;
This, his own knave; this, avarice's fool;
This, a chimera° of wittol, fool, and knave.°
And, reverend fathers, since we all can hope
Nought but a sentence, let's not now despair it.°
You hear me brief.

Corvino. May it please your fatherhoods—

Commendatore. Silence.

1st Avocatore. The knot is now undone by miracle!

2nd Avocatore. Nothing can be more clear.

3rd Avocatore. Or can more prove
These innocent.

1st Avocatore. Give 'em their liberty.

Bonario. Heaven could not long let such gross crimes be hid.

2nd Avocatore. If this be held the highway to get riches,
May I be poor!

3rd Avocatore. This's not the gain, but torment.

1st Avocatore. These possess wealth as sick men possess fevers,
Which trulier may be said to possess them.

2nd Avocatore. Disrobe that parasite.

Corvino, Mosca. Most honored fathers—

1st Avocatore. Can you plead aught to stay the course of justice?
If you can, speak.

Corvino, Voltore. We beg favor.

Celia. And mercy.

1st Avocatore. You hurt your innocence, suing for the guilty.
Stand forth; and first the parasite. You appear

89-91 **This . . . knave** (At each "this" Volpone indicates Mosca, Voltore, Corbaccio, and Corvino in order) 91 **chimera** mythical monster 93 **despair it** delay it (?)

T'have been the chiefest minister,° if not plotter,
In all these lewd impostures; and now, lastly,
Have with your impudence abused the court,
And habit of a gentleman of Venice,
Being a fellow of no birth or blood.
For which our sentence is, first thou be whipped;
Then live perpetual prisoner in our galleys.

Volpone. I thank you for him.

Mosca. Bane to° thy wolfish nature.

1st Avocatore. Deliver him to the *Saffi.*° [*Mosca is taken out.*] Thou Volpone,
By blood and rank a gentleman, canst not fall
Under like censure; but our judgment on thee
Is that thy substance all be straight confiscate
To the hospital of the *Incurabili.*°
And since the most was gotten by imposture,
By feigning lame, gout, palsy, and such diseases,
Thou art to lie in prison, cramped with irons,
Till thou be'st sick and lame indeed. Remove him.

Volpone. This is called mortifying° of a fox.

1st Avocatore. Thou, Voltore, to take away the scandal
Thou hast giv'n all worthy men of thy profession,
Art banished from their fellowship, and our state.
Corbaccio, bring him near! We here possess
Thy son of all thy state,° and confine thee
To the monastery of *San' Spirito*;°
Where, since thou knew'st not how to live well here,
Thou shalt be learned to die well.

Corbaccio. Ha! What said he?

Commendatore. You shall know anon, sir.

1st Avocatore. Thou, Corvino, shalt
Be straight embarked from thine own house, and rowed
Round about Venice, through the Grand Canal,
Wearing a cap with fair long ass's ears
Instead of horns; and so to mount, a paper
Pinned on thy breast, to the *Berlina*°—

108 **minister** agent 115 **Bane to** destruction on 116 **Saffi** bailiffs 120 **Incurabili** incurables 125 **mortifying** killing the flesh in both a physical and spiritual sense 130 **state** estate 131 **San' Spirito** i.e., of the Holy Spirit 139 **Berlina** the pillory

Corvino. Yes,
And have mine eyes beat out° with stinking fish,
Bruised fruit, and rotten eggs—'Tis well, I'm glad
I shall not see my shame yet.
1st Avocatore. And to expiate
Thy wrongs done to thy wife, thou art to send her
Home to her father, with her dowry trebled.
And these are all your judgments.
All. Honored fathers!
1st Avocatore. Which may not be revoked. Now you begin,
When crimes are done and past, and to be punished,
To think what your crimes are. Away with them!
Let all that see these vices thus rewarded,
Take heart, and love to study 'em. Mischiefs feed
Like beasts, till they be fat, and then they bleed.
[*Volpone comes forward.*]
Volpone. The seasoning of a play is the applause.
Now, though the fox be punished by the laws,
He yet doth hope there is no suff'ring due
For any fact° which he hath done 'gainst you.
If there be, censure him; here he doubtful stands.
If not, fare jovially, and clap your hands.

140 eyes beat out i.e., from objects thrown at those pilloried
155 fact crime

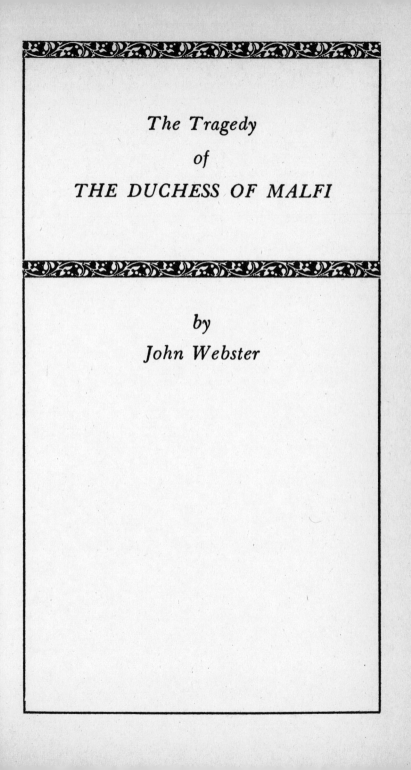

The Tragedy
of
THE DUCHESS OF MALFI

by

John Webster

JOHN WEBSTER

In the story of the English stage, John Webster is a shadowy figure. Yet seldom has so indistinct a person made so large an impression. His impact stems from two plays, *The White Devil* and *The Duchess of Malfi,* and even then, it is the second play that glorifies the first. These two plays, which are among the few that Webster wrote entirely by himself, stand out in contrast to a scattering of works on which he collaborated over many years.

Neither Webster's date of birth nor time of death is known precisely. He was born about 1580 and died, it is supposed, in the 1630s. As a playwright he was active through the first quarter of the seventeenth century. Considering the length of his writing career, it is surprising that he produced so little, particularly if he worked regularly as a professional dramatist. This has been doubted, and one supposition is that he wrote intermittently, mainly between the years 1602-1605, 1609-1614, and after 1624. If so, he may have had other resources for his sustenance.

Among the few things known about Webster, one is that his father was a member of the Merchant Taylors guild, and that he was therefore born "free" of it, that is, born into the guild with a hereditary right. As one of the principal guilds of London, the Merchant Taylors was prosperous, contributing its share of alderman and lord mayors to city life. A recent biographer also suggests that the John Webster who attended the Middle Temple was the dramatist. If so, then he read law there and could have participated in its literary life. The poet's frequent resort to legal terminology supports that contention. He seems to have ceased writing for a time before 1624, a gap attributed to his succession to the Merchant Taylors guild at the death of his father. But even these few details stretch our knowledge into the realm of conjecture, for beyond the probability of his middle-class birth, nothing is known with certainty.

About his work as a playwright, however, there is some hard evidence. He did most of his writing in collaboration with others. In 1602 his name appears five times in the payment records of the theater banker, Philip Henslowe, in connection with four different plays. In each note his name appears alongside others, most frequently that of Thomas Dekker. In 1604 he wrote an Induction to John Marston's play *The Malcontent,* and collaborated again with Dekker on a play entitled *Westward Ho!* He may have done the same with *Northward Ho!* a year later. During these early years as a playwright, he does not seem to have written a single work by himself alone. He shared the satiric bite of John Marston and George Chapman, and in Thomas Dekker he had one of the most popular and active dramatists as partner. But nothing in this early writing suggested the high-tempered fierceness of his two female tragedies.

The first of these, *The White Devil,* appeared in 1612. Produced by one of the three principal acting companies of London, the Queen's men, the play had an unfortunate debut. In his preface to the play, Webster attributes its failure to the fact that "it was acted, in so dull a time of winter . . . in so open and black a theatre." The play was printed the year it was performed, as though Webster hoped to recover through print what was lost on the stage.

Almost immediately after the appearance of his first tragedy, he began his second, a companion piece, yet more finished and better received. He completed *The Duchess of Malfi* and saw it performed successfully before the end of 1614. In this production Webster was fortunate. The acting itself was in the hands of the King's men, the foremost English troupe. The leading roles were played by well-seasoned players. Bosola fell to the lot of John Lowin, admired hitherto for his performance as Volpone and a successor to most of Shakespeare's major tragic roles. The original Hamlet, Richard Burbage, leading actor of the age, played Ferdinand. To a boy actor fell the role of Duchess, but in a company in which boy actors had played Cleopatra and Lady Macbeth.

Nor was the production doomed to a black and open playhouse. *The Duchess of Malfi* appeared in both theaters where the King's men customarily performed: the more intimate indoor house of Blackfriars and the far larger, outdoor playhouse of the Globe. The intimacy of the action and especially the reliance on lighting effects must mean, one editor argues, that the play was first given at Blackfriars. If that were so, then Webster could delight in conditions which helped assure a favorable reception. But it is mainly to the play itself that we must look for its acceptance. In accord with the usual history of a successful play of the time, *The Duchess of Malfi* was revived periodically, and continued to be played with acclaim until the end of the seventeenth century.

Concurrently with writing the tragedies, Webster produced an elegy entitled *A Monumental Column* (1613) on the death of Henry, Prince of Wales, and contributed to the collection of character sketches issued in Sir Thomas Overbury's name in 1615. Sometime in this period he also wrote at least one more play under his sole authorship. Dated between 1610 and 1619, *The Devil's Law Case* was different in tone from the two tragedies, on the one hand being a tragicomedy, on the other being didactic in manner. Otherwise, Webster returned to collaboration, never again endeavoring to scale the heights of tragedy.

The White Devil and *The Duchess of Malfi* are both Italian-type revenge plays. Both are based upon historical incidents. Yet neither is merely a play of revenge, nor is either truly a history. In each play the action revolves about an extraordinary woman. Vittoria Corrombona, the White Devil, is bold, defiant, dazzling, a victim of masculine intrigue, but also a match for that intrigue. Her fall is inevitable because the jealous powers of court life can allow no independence, even a criminal independence. The Duchess of Malfi—she has no other name—is impetuous, passionate, yet essentially passive, a person without any power but the capacity to endure the afflictions of the world about her, a world of male duplicity. Whatever authority is attached to her title, her actual authority is pitifully limited, and when she tries to exercise that little for her own satisfaction, she lights a fuse that blows her to destruction.

The events treated in *The Duchess of Malfi* occurred in sixteenth-century Italy. First told by Matteo Bandello, possibly the model for Delio, the story reached Webster by way of William Painter's *Palace of Pleasure*. Left widowed by the death of her first husband, the youthful Duchess of Malfi, a descendant of the house of Aragon, falls in love with Antonio Bologna. She engages him as her majordomo, marries him secretly, and bears him two children. At this point her brothers, the Cardinal of Aragon and the Duke, learn of her offspring. They send men to the Duchess' court to spy on her. By then she is pregnant with a third child. To thwart the snooping, Antonio and the Duchess decide to separate temporarily, he to go to Ancona.

Thereafter, fearful that the spies will soon learn of her pregnancy, she travels to the shrine of Our Lady of Loretto and from thence to join Antonio in Ancona. There she informs her servants of her secret marriage. They are dismayed by the news, and lest they be implicated in her disgrace, leave her, taking care, moreover, to send word to the Cardinal of his sister's confession. The Cardinal causes the couple to be driven from Ancona and subsequently from Siena. In flight toward Venice, they are overtaken by the Cardinal's men. Antonio and his eldest child escape to Milan. The Duchess and her two babies are imprisoned at Malfi, then murdered. Some years later a hired assassin, Daniel de Bozola, kills Antonio in Milan. Thus concludes Painter's tale with its ambiguous instruction. Although Painter repeatedly condemns Antonio for social climbing and the Duchess for lustful passions, his recital ultimately arouses sympathy for the unfortunate pair while it condemns the cruelty of the Aragonian brethren.

These pathetic incidents provided Webster with the raw material out of which he fashioned a seething tale of sadistic power and desperate passions. Webster's method, however, was not merely to convert his source into a play in a straightforward manner. Like his fellow playwrights, he was an assiduous collector of ideas and phrases. None of the writers of the time hesitated to borrow from one another and from dozens of other sources any characters, events, or images that might serve their turn. In this matter of borrowing, however, Webster's appetite was gargantuan. He culled expressions and moral sentences from a wide assortment of documents. These he grafted to his story so adroitly that the final result appears unified and spontaneous. Out of his many borrowings emerges a distinctive atmosphere that belongs entirely to Webster.

In Painter's story, the Cardinal is a remote figure, exerting his will over the Duchess, but only rarely coming to life in action. His brother has one passage of uncontrolled rage. But the predatory temper of these two proud men, one cool, the other hot at heart, is wholly Webster's work. He infuses them with a watchfulness over their sister and a steady pursuit of her destruction. Painter treats the story as a tragedy, but if it is a tragedy as he tells it, then it is a domestic one, its catastrophe brought about by the vulnerability and temerity of the lovers. Webster transforms this material into what appears on the surface to be a play of revenge, but which in its most inward nature is a dramatization of martyr-like endurance.

The revenge play has a curious and ironic history. *Hamlet* depicts the trials of a hero who is bound to revenge his father's murder. In *Hamlet*'s predecessor, *The Spanish Tragedy*, the revenge is for a murdered son. Although the rightness of revenge is suggested, the righteousness of the hero cannot be consequently assumed. In the twelve or fourten years between *Hamlet* and *The Duchess of Malfi*, a variety of revenge plays appeared. No longer, however, is the hero's case untainted. In *The Revenger's Tragedy* (1607), Vindice—that is, vindictiveness itself—is a hero with a justifiable cause but a frightening unjustifiable delight in avenging that cause. Between himself and the villain, moral difference disappears. By the time *The Duchess of Malfi* arrives, the avenger is no longer the hero but the fraternal villains. They repair their honor by destroying their sister. Since, as a woman and a prince, she is helpless before them, she can only absorb their blows, not avoid the pain. To be their instrument and yet their severest critic, Webster created the malcontent Bosola out of the Lombard ruffian of the same name. Bosola invests every nook and cranny of the play, bitter in his scorn of human vanity, contemptuous not only of his superiors but of himself for seeking their favor. He embodies the moral confusion that infects the world of the play, the only defense against which seems to be a personal code of conduct that Antonio and finally the Duchess practice.

As a revenge play, *The Duchess of Malfi* is simple. As a tragedy of love and of the integrity required to sustain love, it is far from simple. Both in reading and in performance, the play has an elusive, often dense texture. The events do not unfold at a steady pace, but appear to leap and lurch spasmodically from one occasion to the next. Details of narrative are ignored. Instead, scenes flash out with little preparation but with extraordinary vividness. Bosola suspects that the Duchess is pregnant and devises a plan to discover the truth while we have yet to learn that Antonio and she are "long since married." Not some cosmological force that connects the present to the past but chance and impulse seem to propel events.

The same disjointedness informs the language. Dramatic speech in the play swings wildly. The satiric prose of Bosola with its caustic tone and pungent imagery plays off the moral idealism of Antonio's verse. Yet Bosola and Antonio's expressions are equally rhetorical, and contrast sharply with the utter simplicity—and elegance—of the wooing scene (I. ii) and, above all, the Duchess' death scene (IV. ii). These moments distill what is most direct and open in human discourse. They approach the time in *Lear* when art and nature lose their identities in each other.

Yet despite the abruptness with which one scene succeeds another, the play has a tragic coherence. From the very beginning, the action unfolds in dreamlike motion. Although events commence at the court of Malfi, ceremonial life is minimal. People come and go like shadows on a screen. Gradually there emerges the felt, ominous fixation of the brothers upon their sister's behavior. Because their motives are hazy, never satisfactorily elucidated, their obsession with her honor becomes a fetid miasma. She does not so much struggle against it as project a counter-spirit, a spirit of loving, physical and ideal at the same time. It is that spirit which the events test and refine in the fires of revenge; it is that spirit which the Aragonian brethren seek to extinguish. And it is that spirit which so disturbs Bosola. Between the pride of the brothers and the humility of the sister wallows Bosola's mechanical villainy parading under the banner of satiric superiority. When he tests the Duchess to the uttermost and fails to shake her spirit—however grotesque the means he uses—he becomes haunted as much as Ferdinand is haunted by the dead duchess.

That the play goes on after her death—with Bosola turned revenger and the confused killings of good and bad alike—seems arbitrary at first, devoid as the ending is of the simple nobility of the Duchess' final moments. Rather, the finale is a baroque melange of plot, counterplot, and mistaken identity. None of the victims faces death so knowingly and forthrightly as did the Duchess. Antonio's accidental assault only leaves him time to reflect on the futility of life and commend himself to his friend Delio and to his son, who, he wishes, would "fly the courts of princes." Ironically, at the very end Delio leads Antonio's son before the survivors so that he may become a prince himself. Thus, it may seem that the mother's spirit is being renewed. Yet nothing in the final horrors can rival the radiance of the Duchess' integrity. Antonio and to a lesser extent Bosola have touches of it. Ferdinand and the Cardinal can do little but condemn themselves in spasms of contrition. It is Delio who speaks for the Duchess when he concludes the play with the couplet:

> Integrity of life is fame's best friend,
> Which nobly, beyond death, shall crown the end.
> (V. v. 120-21)

Webster's play was not printed until 1623, the same year in which Shakespeare's Folio was issued. The copy of the text reveals care, probably at the hands of the author. It displays both theatrical and literary concerns. On the verso of the title page, it supplies a double cast list for what is likely to have been the initial performance and then a later revival. This is the first such list to include both the names of the characters as well as the actors playing the roles.

At the same time the copy has literary features, specifically, the systematic designation of the acts and scenes and the use of block entries. Block entries occur at the head of each scene. They list the names of all characters to appear in the scene, whether from the beginning or by a later entrance. Actual entrances are not designated. Such block entries follow the traditional style of literary drama, and therefore dignify the publication of popular plays. In print, then, *The Duchess of Malfi* testifies to its twin nature, as a stage show and as a text. Encompassing both aspects in performance, however, proves to be an immense challenge. This play demands a small but extremely able group of actors who combine rare vocal skill with fine intensity of feeling in order to capture the dark and golden spirit of Webster's haunted people.

The Actors' Names

Bosola
Ferdinand [Duke of Calabria]
Cardinal [his brother]
Antonio [steward to the Duchess]
Delio [his friend]
Forobosco
[Count] Malateste
The Marquis of Pescara
Silvio [a lord]
Several mad men
[Castruchio, an old lord, husband of Julia]
[Roderigo]
[Grisolan]
The Duchess
The Cardinal's Mistress [Julia]
The Doctor
Cariola [the Duchess' woman]
Court Officers
Three young Children [of the Duchess and Antonio]
Two Pilgrims
[An Old Lady]
[Attendants, Ladies, Executioners]

To the Right Honourable George Harding, Baron Berkeley, of Berkeley Castle and Knight of the Order of the Bath to the illustrious Prince Charles.

My Noble Lord,

That I may present my excuse why, being a stranger to your Lordship, I offer this poem to your patronage, I plead this warrant; men, who never saw the sea, yet desire to behold that regiment of waters, choose some eminent river to guide them thither; and make that as it were, their conduct, or postilion. By the like ingenious means has your fame arrived at my knowledge, receiving it from some of worth, who both in contemplation, and practice, owe to your Honour their clearest service. I do not altogether look up at your title: The ancientest nobility, being but a relic of time past, and the truest honour indeed being for a man to confer honour on himself, which your learning strives to propagate, and shall make you arrive at the dignity of a great example. I am confident this work is not unworthy your Honour's perusal for by such poems as this, poets have kissed the hands of great princes, and drawn their gentle eyes to look down upon their sheets of paper, when the poets themselves were bound up in their winding sheets. The like courtesy from your Lordship, shall make you live in your grave, and laurel spring out of it, when the ignorant scorners of the Muses, that like worms in libraries, seem to live only to destroy learning shall wither, neglected and forgotten. This work and myself I humbly present to your approved censure.° It being the utmost of my wishes, to have your honourable self my weighty and perspicuous comment: which grace so done me, shall ever be acknowledged

By your Lordship's
in all duty and
observance,
John Webster.

27-8 **approved censure** proven judgment

In the just worth, of that well deserver,
MR. JOHN WEBSTER, and upon this
masterpiece of tragedy.

In this thou imitat'st one rich, and wise,
That sees his good deed done before he dies;
As he by works, thou by this work of fame,
Hast well provided for thy living name;
To trust to others' honorings, is worth's crime,
Thy monument is rais'd in thy life time;
And 'tis most just; for every worthy man
Is his own marble; and his merit can
Cut him to any figure, and express
More art, than Death's cathedral palaces,
Where royal ashes keep their court: thy note
Be ever plainness, 'tis the richest coat:
Thy epitaph only the title be,
Write, *Duchess*, that will fetch a tear for thee,
For who e'er saw this *Duchess* live, and die,
That could get off under a bleeding eye?

In Tragædiam.

Ut lux ex tenebris ictu percussa tonantis;
Illa, (ruina malis) claris sit vita poetis.°
Thomas Middletonus,
Poëta & Chron:
Londinensis.°

20-22 In . . . poetis "To Tragedy./As light out of darkness is struck by the thunderer's blow,/So may it bring ruin to evil, life to famous poets" **23-5 Thomas . . . Londinensis** (Thomas Middleton received an appointment as City Chronologer of London in 1620)

To his friend Mr. John Webster
Upon his Duchess
of Malfi.

I never saw thy Duchess, till the day,
That she was lively body'd° in thy play;
Howe'er she answer'd° her low-rated love,
Her brothers' anger did so fatal prove,
Yet my opinion is, she might speak more;
But never (in her life) so well before.
WIL: ROWLEY

To the reader of the author,
and his Duchess of Malfi

Crown him a poet, whom nor Rome, nor Greece,
Transcend in all theirs, for a masterpiece:
In which, whiles words and matter change, and men
Act one another; he, from whose clear pen
They all took life, to memory hath lent
A lasting fame, to raise his monument.
JOHN FORD

5 body'd embodied **6 answer'd** justified

THE DUCHESS OF MALFI

Act I, Scene i

[*Enter Antonio and Delio.*]

Delio. You are welcome to your country, dear Antonio,
You have been long in France, and you return
A very formal Frenchman, in your habit.°
How do you like the French court?
Antonio. I admire it;
In seeking to reduce both State and people
To a fix'd order, their judicious King
Begins at home. Quits° first his royal palace
Of flatt'ring sycophants, of dissolute,
And infamous persons, which° he sweetly terms
His Master's master-piece, the work of Heaven,
Consid'ring duly, that a Prince's court
Is like a common fountain, whence should flow
Pure silver-drops in general.° But if't chance
Some curs'd example poison't near the head,
Death and diseases through the whole land spread.
And what is't makes this blessed government,
But a most provident Council, who dare freely
Inform him, the corruption of the times?
Though some o'th' court hold it presumption
To instruct Princes what they ought to do,
It is a noble duty to inform them
What they ought to foresee. Here comes Bosola

[*Enter Bosola.*]

The only court-gall:° yet I observe his railing°
Is not for simple love of piety:
Indeed he rails at those things which he wants,
Would be as lecherous, covetous, or proud,
Bloody, or envious, as any man,
If he had means to be so. Here's the Cardinal.

3 **habit** dress 7 **Quits** rids 9 **which** i.e., which action (?) 13 **in general** universally 23 **court-gall** i.e., one who "galls" or abuses the court 23 **railing** reviling (of sin)

[*Enter Cardinal.*]

Bosola. I do haunt you still.

Cardinal. So.

Bosola. I have done you better service than to be slighted thus. Miserable age, where only the reward° of doing well, is the doing of it!

Cardinal. You enforce° your merit too much.

Bosola. I fell into the galleys in your service, where, for two years together, I wore two towels instead of a shirt, with a knot on the shoulder, after the fashion of a Roman mantle. Slighted thus? I will thrive some way: blackbirds fatten best in hard weather: why not I, in these dog days?°

Cardinal. Would you could become honest,—

Bosola. With all your divinity, do but direct me the way to it. I have known many travel far for it, and yet return as arrant° knaves, as they went forth; because they carried themselves always along with them. [*Exit Cardinal*] Are you gone? Some fellows, they say, are possessed with the devil, but this great fellow were able to possess the greatest devil, and make him worse.

Antonio. He hath denied thee some suit?

Bosola. He and his brother are like plum trees, that grow crooked over standing° pools, they are rich, and o'erladen with fruit, but none but crows, pies,° and caterpillars feed on them. Could I be one of their flatt'ring panders, I would hang on their ears like a horse-leech°, till I were full, and then drop off. I pray leave me. Who would rely upon these miserable dependences, in expectation to be advanc'd° tomorrow? What creature ever fed worse, than hoping Tantalus;° nor ever died any man more fearfully, than he that hop'd for a pardon? There are rewards for hawks, and dogs, when they have done us service; but for a soldier, that hazards his limbs in a

32 **only the reward** the only reward 34 **enforce** insist on 40 **dog days** i.e., the hottest days at the end of summer, also evil times 44 **arrant** notorious 51 **standing** stagnant 52 **pies** magpies 54 **horse-leech** i.e., blood-sucker 57 **advanc'd** raised in rank 58 **Tantalus** (punished in Hades with perpetual thirst)

battle, nothing but a kind of geometry is his last supportation.

Delio. Geometry?

Bosola. Ay, to hang in a fair pair of slings, take his latter swing in the world, upon an honourable pair of crutches, from hospital to hospital: fare ye well sir. And yet do not you scorn us, for places in the court are but like beds in the hospital, where this man's head lies at that man's foot, and so lower and lower. [*Exit Bosola.*]

Delio. I knew this fellow seven years in the galleys,
For a notorious murther, and 'twas thought
The Cardinal suborn'd it: he was releas'd
By the French general, Gaston de Foix
When he recover'd Naples.

Antonio. 'Tis great pity
He should be thus neglected, I have heard
He's very valiant. This foul melancholy
Will poison all his goodness, for, I'll tell you,
If too immoderate sleep be truly said
To be an inward rust unto the soul;
It then doth follow want of action
Breeds all black malcontents, and their close rearing,
Like moths in cloth, do hurt for want of wearing.

Scene ii°

[*Enter Castruchio, Silvio, Roderigo and Grisolan.*]

Delio. The presence° gins to fill. You promis'd me
To make me the partaker of the natures
Of some of your great courtiers.

Antonio. The Lord Cardinal's
And other strangers', that are now in court?
I shall. Here comes the great Calabrian Duke.

[*Enter Ferdinand.*]

Ferdinand. Who took the ring° oft'nest?

Silvio. Antonio Bologna, my lord.

Scene ii marked so in quartos although the action is continuous
1 presence audience chamber **6 took the ring** i.e., in jousting

Ferdinand. Our sister Duchess' great master of her household? Give him the jewel: when shall we leave this sportive action, and fall to action indeed?

Castruchio. Methinks, my lord, you should not desire to go to war, in person.

Ferdinand [*aside*]. Now, for some gravity: why, my lord?

Castruchio. It is fitting a soldier arise to be a prince, but not necessary a prince descend to be a captain!

Ferdinand. No?

Castruchio. No, my lord, he were far better do it by a deputy.

Ferdinand. Why should he not as well sleep, or eat, by a deputy? This might take idle, offensive, and base office from him, whereas the other deprives him of honour.

Castruchio. Believe my experience: that realm is never long in quiet, where the ruler is a soldier.

Ferdinand. Thou told'st me thy wife could not endure fighting.

Castruchio. True, my lord.

Ferdinand. And of a jest she broke,° of a captain she met full of wounds: I have forgot it.

Castruchio. She told him, my lord, he was a pitiful fellow, to lie, like the children of Ismael, all in tents.°

Ferdinand. Why, there's a wit were able to undo all the chirurgeons° o' the city, for although gallants should quarrel, and had drawn their weapons, and were ready to go to it; yet her persuasions would make them put up.°

Castruchio. That she would, my lord.
How do you like my Spanish jennet?°

Roderigo. He is all fire.

Ferdinand. I am of Pliny's opinion, I think he was begot by the wind; he runs as if he were ballasted with quicksilver.

Silvio. True, my lord, he reels° from the tilt often.

Roderigo and *Grisolan.* Ha, ha, ha!

Ferdinand. Why do you laugh? Methinks you that are courtiers should be my touchwood, take fire when I give

27 **jest she broke** joke she made 30 **tents** (1) common meaning, (2) dressings for wounds 32 **chirurgeons** surgeons 34 **put up** sheathe their weapons 37 **jennet** a small Spanish horse 42 **reels** staggers

fire; that is, laugh when I laugh, were the subject never so witty,—

Castruchio. True, my lord, I myself have heard a very good jest, and have scorn'd to seem to have so silly° a wit, as to understand it.

Ferdinand. But I can laugh at your fool, my lord.

Castruchio. He cannot speak, you know, but he makes faces; my lady cannot abide him.

Ferdinand. No?

Castruchio. Nor endure to be in merry company: for she says too much laughing, and too much company, fills her too full of the wrinkle.

Ferdinand. I would then have a mathematical instrument made for her face, that she might not laugh out of compass.° I shall shortly visit you at Milan, Lord Silvio.

Silvio. Your Grace shall arrive most welcome.

Ferdinand. You are a good horseman, Antonio; you have excellent riders in France, what do you think of good horsemanship?

Antonio. Nobly, my lord: as out of the Grecian horse° issued many famous princes: so out of brave horsemanship, arise the first sparks of growing resolution, that raise the mind to noble action.

Ferdinand. You have bespoke it worthily.

[*Enter Duchess, Cardinal, Cariola and Julia.*]

Silvio. Your brother, the Lord Cardinal, and sister Duchess.

Cardinal. Are the galleys come about?

Grisolan. They are, my lord.

Ferdinand. Here's the Lord Silvio, is come to take his leave.

Delio [*aside to Antonio*]. Now sir, your promise: what's that Cardinal? I mean his temper? They say he's a brave fellow, will play his five thousand crowns at tennis, dance, court ladies, and one that hath fought single combats.

Antonio. Some such flashes° superficially hang on him, for form:° but observe his inward character: he is a melancholy churchman. The spring° in his face is nothing but the engend'ring of toads: where he is jealous of any

49 **silly** simple 59-60 **out of compass** immoderately 65 **Grecian horse** i.e., the so-called Trojan horse 79 **flashes** ostentatious acts 80 **form** mere appearance 81 **spring** i.e., of water

man, he lays worse plots for them, than ever was impos'd on Hercules: for he strews in his way flatterers, panders, intelligencers,° atheists: and a thousand such political° monsters: he should have been Pope: but instead of coming to it by the primitive decency of the Church, he did bestow bribes, so largely, and so impudently, as if he would have carried it away without Heaven's knowledge. Some good he hath done.

Delio. You have given too much of him: what's his brother?

Antonio. The Duke there? a most perverse and turbulent nature;
What appears in him mirth, is merely outside,
If he laugh heartily, it is to laugh
All honesty out of fashion.

Delio Twins?

Antonio. In quality:
He speaks with others' tongues, and hears men's suits°
With others' ears: will seem to sleep o'th' bench
Only to entrap offenders in their answers;
Dooms men to death by information,
Rewards, by hearsay.

Delio. Then the law to him
Is like a foul black cobweb to a spider,
He makes it his dwelling, and a prison
To entangle those shall feed him.

Antonio. Most true:
He nev'r pays debts, unless they be shrewd turns,°
And those he will confess, that he doth owe.
Last: for his brother, there, the Cardinal,
They that do flatter him most, say oracles
Hang at his lips: and verily I believe them:
For the devil speaks in them.
But for their sister, the right noble Duchess,
You never fix'd your eye on three fair medals,
Cast in one figure,° of so different temper.°
For her discourse, it is so full of rapture,
You only will begin, then to be sorry
When she doth end her speech: and wish, in wonder,

85 **intelligencers** spies, informers 85 **political** scheming 96 **hears men's suits** i.e., as a judge 104 **shrewd turns** malicious deeds 112 **figure** shape 112 **temper** quality

She held it less vainglory to talk much
Than your penance, to hear her: whilst she speaks,
She throws upon a man so sweet a look,
That it were able to raise one to a galliard°
That lay in a dead palsy; and to dote
On that sweet countenance: but in that look
There speaketh so divine a continence,
As cuts off all lascivious, and vain hope.
Her days are practis'd in such noble virtue,
That, sure her nights, nay more, her very sleeps,
Are more in heaven, than other ladies' shrifts.°
Let all sweet ladies break their flatt'ring glasses,
And dress themselves in her.

Delio. Fie Antonio,
You play the wire-drawer° with her commendations.

Antonio. I'll case the picture up: only thus much:
All her particular worth grows to this sum:
She stains° the time past: lights the time to come.

Cariola. You must attend my lady, in the gallery,
Some half an hour hence.

Antonio. I shall.

[*Exeunt Antonio and Delio.*]

Ferdinand. Sister, I have a suit to you.

Duchess. To me, sir?

Ferdinand. A gentleman here: Daniel de Bosola:
One, that was in the galleys.

Duchess. Yes, I know him.

Ferdinand. A worthy fellow h'is: pray let me entreat for
The provisorship of your horse.

Duchess. Your knowledge of him
Commends him, and prefers° him.

Ferdinand. Call him hither.

[*Exit Attendant.*]

We are now upon parting. Good Lord Silvio
Do us commend to all our noble friends
At the leaguer.°

Silvio. Sir, I shall.

Duchess. You are for Milan?

119 **galliard** a lively dance 126 **shrifts** confessions 129 **wire-drawer** one who draws out and distorts the truth 132 **stains** puts in the shade, outshines 140 **prefers** promotes (to a position or office) 143 **leaguer** military camp

Silvio. I am.
Duchess. Bring the caroches:° we'll bring you down to the haven.
[*Exeunt Duchess, Cariola, Silvio, Castruchio, Roderigo, Grisolan and Julia.*]
Cardinal. Be sure you entertain that Bosola
For your intelligence:° I would not be seen in't.
And therefore many times I have slighted him,
When he did court our furtherance: as this morning.
Ferdinand. Antonio, the great master of her household
Had been far fitter.
Cardinal. You are deceiv'd in him,
His nature is too honest for such business.
He comes: I'll leave you.

[*Enter Bosola.*]

Bosola. I was lur'd to you.
[*Exit Cardinal.*]
Ferdinand. My brother here, the Cardinal, could never
Abide you.
Bosola. Never since he was in my debt.
Ferdinand. May be some oblique character in your face
Made him suspect you?
Bosola. Doth he study physiognomy?
There's no more credit to be given to th' face,
Than to a sick man's urine, which some call
The physician's whore, because she cozens° him.
He did suspect me wrongfully.
Ferdinand. For that
You must give great men leave to take their times:
Distrust doth cause us seldom be deceiv'd;
You see, the oft shaking of the cedar tree
Fastens it more at root.
Bosola. Yet take heed:
For to suspect a friend unworthily
Instructs him the next way to suspect you,
And prompts him to deceive you.
Ferdinand. There's gold.
Bosola. So:

145 caroches stately coaches 147 For your intelligence as your informer 160 cozens cheats

What follows? (Never rain'd such showers as these
Without thunderbolts i'th' tail of them;)
Whose throat must I cut?
Ferdinand. Your inclination to shed blood rides post°
Before my occasion to use you. I give you that°
To live i'th' court, here: and observe the Duchess,
To note all the particulars of her haviour:°
What suitors do solicit her for marriage
And whom she best affects:° she's a young widow,
I would not have her marry again.
Bosola. No, sir?
Ferdinand. Do not you ask the reason: but be satisfied,
I say I would not.
Bosola. It seems you would create me
One of your familiars.
Ferdinand. Familiar? what's that?
Bosola. Why, a very quaint invisible devil in flesh:
An intelligencer.
Ferdinand. Such a kind of thriving thing
I would wish thee: and ere long, thou mayst arrive
At a higher place by't.
Bosola. Take your devils
Which hell calls angels:° these curs'd gifts would make
You a corrupter, me an impudent traitor,
And should I take these they'll'd take me to hell.
Ferdinand. Sir, I'll take nothing from you that I have given.
There is a place that I procur'd for you
This morning, the provisorship o'th' horse,
Have you heard on't?
Bosola. No.
Ferdinand. 'Tis yours, is't not worth thanks?
Bosola. I would have you curse yourself now, that your bounty,
Which makes men truly noble, e'er should make
Me a villain: oh, that to avoid ingratitude
For the good deed you have done me, I must do
All the ill man can invent. Thus the devil

172 **post** too hastily 173 **that** (probably a purse of gold) 175 **haviour** behavior 177 **affects** likes, favors 186 **angels** gold coins

Candies all sins o'er: and what Heaven terms vild,
That names he complemental.°

Ferdinand. Be yourself:
Keep your old garb of melancholy: 'twill express
You envy those that stand above your reach,
Yet strive not to come near 'em. This will gain
Access to private lodgings, where yourself
May, like a politic dormouse,—

Bosola. As I have seen some,
Feed in a lord's dish, half asleep, not seeming
To listen to any talk: and yet these rogues
Have cut his throat in a dream: what's my place?
The provisorship o'th' horse? say then my corruption
Grew out of horse dung. I am your creature.

Ferdinand. Away!

Bosola. Let good men, for good deeds, covet good fame,
Since place and riches oft are bribes of shame;
Sometimes the devil doth preach. [*Exit Bosola.*]

[*Enter Cardinal, Duchess and Cariola.*]

Cardinal. We are to part from you: and your own discretion
Must now be your director.

Ferdinand. You are a widow:
You know already what man is: and therefore
Let not youth: high promotion, eloquence,—

Cardinal. No, nor any thing without the addition, Honour,
Sway your high blood.

Ferdinand. Marry? they are most luxurious,°
Will wed twice.

Cardinal. O fie!

Ferdinand. Their livers are more spotted
Than Laban's sheep.°

Duchess. Diamonds are of most value
They say, that have pass'd through most jewellers' hands.

Ferdinand. Whores, by that rule, are precious.

Duchess. Will you hear me?
I'll never marry—

199 **complemental** i.e., a polite accomplishment 219 **luxurious** lascivious 221 **Laban's sheep** (allusion to Jacob's breeding of spotted sheep, Genesis, xxx, 31-42)

Cardinal. So most widows say:
But commonly that motion° lasts no longer
Than the turning of an hourglass; the funeral sermon
And it, end both together.
Ferdinand. Now hear me:
You live in a rank° pasture here, i'th' court,
There is a kind of honey-dew that's deadly:
'Twill poison your fame; look to't; be not cunning:
For they whose faces do belie their hearts
Are witches, ere they arrive at twenty years,
Ay: and give the devil suck.
Duchess. This is terrible good counsel.
Ferdinand. Hypocrisy is woven of a fine small thread,
Subtler than Vulcan's engine:° yet, believe't,
Your darkest actions: nay, your privat'st thoughts,
Will come to light.
Cardinal. You may flatter yourself,
And take your own choice: privately be married
Under the eaves of night—
Ferdinand. Think't the best voyage
That e'er you made; like the irregular crab,
Which, though't goes backward, thinks that it goes right,
Because it goes its own way: but observe:
Such weddings may more properly be said
To be executed, than celebrated.°
Cardinal. The marriage night
Is the entrance into some prison.
Ferdinand. And those joys,
Those lustful pleasures, are like heavy sleeps
Which do forerun man's mischief.
Cardinal. Fare you well.
Wisdom begins at the end: remember it. [*Exit Cardinal.*]
Duchess. I think this speech between you both was studied,
It came so roundly off.
Ferdinand. You are my sister,
This was my father's poniard: do you see,
I'll'd be loath to see't look rusty, 'cause 'twas his.

225 **motion** proposal, inclination 228 **rank** overly ripe, licentious 235 **Vulcan's engine** the device through which Vulcan caught his wife, Venus, with Mars 244 **executed, than celebrated** legally carried out (with pun on "put to death") rather than performed joyfully

I would have you to give o'er these chargeable° revels;
A visor and a mask are whispering-rooms
That were nev'r built for goodness: fare ye well:
And women like that part, which, like the lamprey,
Hath nev'r a bone in't.

Duchess. Fie sir!

Ferdinand. Nay,
I mean the tongue: variety of courtship;
What cannot a neat° knave with a smooth tale
Make a woman believe? Farewell, lusty widow.
[*Exit Ferdinand.*]

Duchess. Shall this move me? If all my royal kindred
Lay in my way unto this marriage:
I'll'd make them my low foot-steps.° And even now,
Even in this hate, (as men in some great battles
By apprehending danger, have achiev'd
Almost impossible actions: I have heard soldiers say so,)
So I, through frights and threat'nings, will assay
This dangerous venture. Let old wives° report
I winked,° and chose a husband. Cariola,
To thy known secrecy I have given up
More than my life, my fame.

Cariola. Both shall be safe:
For I'll conceal this secret from the world
As warily as those that trade in poison,
Keep poison from their children.

Duchess. Thy protestation
Is ingenious and hearty: I believe it.
Is Antonio come?

Cariola. He attends you.

Duchess. Good dear soul,
Leave me: but place thyself behind the arras,°
Where thou mayst overhear us: wish me good speed
For I am going into a wilderness,
Where I shall find nor path, nor friendly clew
To be my guide. [*Cariola goes behind the arras.*]

[*Enter Antonio.*]

253 **chargeable** costly 259 **neat** fashionably dressed 263 **low foot-steps** altar steps 268 **old wives** (noted for telling tales) 269 **winked** shut eyes to (my brothers' warnings?) 277 **arras** tapestry, used as wall hanging or curtain

I sent for you. Sit down:
Take pen and ink, and write. Are you ready?
Antonio. Yes.
Duchess. What did I say?
Antonio. That I should write somewhat.
Duchess. Oh, I remember:
After these triumphs° and this large expense
It's fit, like thrifty husbands,° we inquire
What's laid up for tomorrow.
Antonio. So please your beauteous excellence.
Duchess. Beauteous?
Indeed I thank you: I look young for your sake.
You have tane my cares upon you.
Antonio. I'll fetch your Grace
The particulars of your revenue and expense.
Duchess. Oh, you are an upright treasurer: but you mistook,
For when I said I meant to make inquiry
What's laid up for tomorrow: I did mean
What's laid up yonder for me.
Antonio. Where?
Duchess. In heaven.
I am making my will, as 'tis fit princes should
In perfect memory, and I pray sir, tell me
Were not one better make it smiling, thus?
Than in deep groans, and terrible ghastly looks,
As if the gifts we parted with, procur'd
That violent distraction?
Antonio. Oh, much better.
Duchess. If I had a husband now, this care were quit:
But I intend to make you overseer;
What good deed shall we first remember? Say.
Antonio. Begin with that first good deed, begin i'th' world,
After man's creation, the sacrament of marriage.
I'd have you first provide for a good husband,
Give him all.
Duchess. All?
Antonio. Yes, your excellent self.
Duchess. In a winding sheet?°

285 **triumphs** festivities (such as jousts mentioned earlier) 286 **husbands** managers (of estates) 309 **In a winding sheet** in a burial shroud

Antonio. In a couple.°
Duchess. St. Winifred!° that were a strange will.
Antonio. 'Twere strange
If there were no will in you to marry again.
Duchess. What do you think of marriage?
Antonio. I take't, as those that deny purgatory,
It locally contains or heaven, or hell;
There's no third place in't.
Duchess. How do you affect° it?
Antonio. My banishment, feeding my melancholy,
Would often reason thus:—
Duchess. Pray let's hear it.
Antonio. Say a man never marry, nor have children,
What takes that from him? only the bare name
Of being a father, or the weak delight
To see the little wanton° ride a-cock-horse
Upon a painted stick, or hear him chatter
Like a taught starling.
Duchess. Fie, fie, what's all this?
One of your eyes is bloodshot, use my ring to't,
They say 'tis very sovereign:° 'twas my wedding ring.
And I did vow never to part with it,
But to my second husband.
Antonio. You have parted with it now.
Duchess. Yes, to help your eyesight.
Antonio. You have made me stark blind.
Duchess. How?
Antonio. There is a saucy and ambitious devil
Is dancing in this circle.
Duchess. Remove him.
Antonio. How?
Duchess. There needs small conjuration, when your finger
May do it: thus, is it fit?
[*She puts the ring on his finger; he kneels.*]
Antonio. What said you?
Duchess. Sir,
This goodly roof of yours, is too low built,
I cannot stand upright in't, nor discourse,

309 In a couple in wedlock **310 St. Winifred** (decapitated by a rejectd suitor, but latr restored to life) **315 affect** feel about **321 wanton** rascal **325 sovereign** effective as a cure

Without I raise it higher: raise yourself,
Or if you please, my hand to help you: so. [*Raises him.*]

Antonio. Ambition, Madam, is a great man's madness,
That is not kept in chains, and close-pent rooms,
But in fair lightsome lodgings, and is girt
With the wild noise of prattling visitants,
Which makes it lunatic, beyond all cure.
Conceive not, I am so stupid, but I aim°
Whereto your favours tend. But he's a fool
That, being a-cold, would thrust his hands i'th' fire
To warm them.

Duchess. So, now the ground's broke,
You may discover what a wealthy mine
I make you lord of.

Antonio. O my unworthiness!

Duchess. You were ill to sell yourself;
This dark'ning of your worth is not like that
Which tradesmen use i'th' city; their false lights°
Are to rid bad wares off: and I must tell you
If you will know where breathes a complete man,
(I speak it without flattery), turn your eyes,
And progress° through yourself.

Antonio. Were there nor heaven,
nor hell,
I should be honest: I have long serv'd virtue,
And nev'r tane wages of her.

Duchess. Now she pays it.
The misery of us, that are born great,
We are forc'd to woo, because none dare woo us:
And as a tyrant doubles with° his words,
And fearfully equivocates: so we
Are forc'd to express our violent passions
In riddles, and in dreams, and leave the path
Of simple virtue, which was never made
To seem the thing it is not. Go, go brag
You have left me heartless, mine is in your bosom,
I hope 'twill multiply love there. You do tremble:
Make not your heart so dead a piece of flesh
To fear, more than to love me. Sir, be confident,

343 **aim** guess, conjecture 351 **false lights** dark windows 355 **progress** make a progress, i.e., a regal visit 360 **doubles with** gives double meanings to

What is't distracts you? This is flesh, and blood,
sir,
'Tis not the figure cut in alabaster
Kneels at my husband's tomb. Awake, awake, man,
I do here put off all vain ceremony,
And only do appear to you, a young widow
That claims you for her husband, and like a widow,
I use but half a blush in't.

Antonio. Truth speak for me,
I will remain the constant sanctuary
Of your good name.

Duchess. I thank you, gentle love,
And 'cause you shall not come to me in debt,
Being now my steward, here upon your lips
I sign your *Quietus est.*° [*kisses him.*] This you should
have begg'd now:
I have seen children oft eat sweetmeats thus,
As fearful to devour them too soon.

Antonio. But for your brothers?

Duchess. Do not think of them:
All discord, without this circumference,°
Is only to be pitied, and not fear'd.
Yet, should they know it, time will easily
Scatter the tempest.

Antonio. These words should be mine,
And all the parts you have spoke, if some part of it
Would not have savour'd flattery.

Duchess. Kneel.

[*Enter Cariola from behind the arras.*]

Antonio. Ha?

Duchess. Be not amaz'd, this woman's of my counsel.
I have heard lawyers say, a contract in a chamber,
Per verba de presenti,° is absolute marriage.

381 **Quietus est** "he is quit," i.e., his account is settled (used in discharging business matters as well as in speaking of the dying) 385 **circumference** i.e., of their embrace 393 **Per verba de presenti** (a valid but not entirely approved form of marriage by which the partners contract themselves to each other with or without witnesses)

Bless, Heaven, this sacred Gordian, which let violence
Never untwine.°
Antonio. And may our sweet affections, like the spheres,°
Be still° in motion.
Duchess. Quick'ning,° and make
The like soft music.
Antonio. That we may imitate the loving palms,°
Best emblem of a peaceful marriage,
That nev'r bore fruit divided.
Duchess. What can the Church force° more?
Antonio. That Fortune may not know an accident
Either of joy or sorrow, to divide
Our fixed wishes.
Duchess. How can the Church build faster?
We now are man and wife, and 'tis the Church
That must but echo this. Maid, stand apart,
I now am blind.
Antonio. What's your conceit in this?
Duchess. I would have you lead your fortune by the hand,
Unto your marriage bed:
(You speak in me this, for we now are one)
We'll only lie, and talk together, and plot
T'appease my humorous° kindred; and if you please,
Like the old tale, in *Alexander and Lodowick*,°
Lay a naked sword between us, keep us chaste.
Oh, let me shroud° my blushes in your bosom,
Since 'tis the treasury of all my secrets.
Cariola. Whether the spirit of greatness, or of woman
Reign most in her, I know not, but it shows
A fearful madness: I owe her much of pity. *Exeunt.*

394-5 **sacred Gordian . . . untwine** (the knot that defied all efforts to untie it was finally cut by the youthful Alexander the Great) 396 **spheres** (the heavenly spheres revolved about the earth producing a celestial harmony) 397 **still** always 397 **quick'ning** coming to life 399 **palms** i.e., palm trees 402 **force** urge, require 413 **humorous** ill-humored, capricious 414 **Alexander and Lodowick** (a medieval tale of ideal friendship) 416 **shroud** veil

Act II, Scene i

[*Enter Bosola and Castruchio.*]

Bosola. You say you would fain be taken for an eminent courtier?

Castruchio. 'Tis the very main° of my ambition.

Bosola. Let me see, you have a reasonable good face for't already, and your nightcap° expresses your ears sufficient largely; I would have you learn to twirl the strings of your band° with a good grace; and in a set speech, at th' end of every sentence, to hum, three or four times, or blow your nose, till it smart again, to recover your memory. When you come to be a president° in criminal causes, if you smile upon a prisoner, hang him, but if you frown upon him, and threaten him, let him be sure to scape the gallows.

Castruchio. I would be a very merry president,—

Bosola. Do not sup a nights; 'twill beget you an admirable wit.

Castruchio. Rather it would make me have a good stomach to quarrel, for they say your roaring boys° eat meat seldom, and that makes them so valiant: but how shall I know whether the people take me for an eminent fellow?

Bosola. I will teach a trick to know it: give out you lie a-dying, and if you hear the common people curse you, be sure you are taken for one of the prime nightcaps.

[*Enter Old Lady.*]

You come from painting° now?

Old Lady. From what?

Bosola. Why, from your scurvy face physic:° To behold thee not painted inclines somewhat near a miracle. These in thy face here, were deep ruts and foul sloughs, the last progress. There was a lady in France, that having had the smallpox, flayed the skin off her face, to

II.i.3 **main** i.e., height 5 **nightcap** white coif worn by sergeants at law 6-7 **strings of your band** white tabs worn by sergeants 10 **president** presiding officer 18 **roaring** bullies 25 **painting** applying makeup 27 **physic** medicine

make it more level; and whereas before she look'd like a nutmeg grater, after she resembled an abortive hedge-hog.

Old Lady. Do you call this painting?

Bosola. No, no but you call it careening of an old morphew'd lady, to make her disembogue° again. There's roughcast phrase to your plastic.°

Old Lady. It seems you are well acquainted with my closet?°

Bosola. One would suspect it for a shop of witchcraft, to find in it the fat of serpents; spawn of snakes, Jews' spittle, and their young children's ordure, and all these for the face. I would sooner eat a dead pigeon, taken from the soles of the feet of one sick of the plague, than kiss one of you fasting. Here are two of you, whose sin of your youth is the very patrimony of the physician, makes him renew his footcloth with the spring,° and change his high-priz'd courtesan with the fall of the leaf: I do wonder you do not loathe yourselves. Observe my meditation now:

What thing is in this outward form of man
To be belov'd? We account it ominous,
If nature do produce a colt, or lamb,
A fawn, or goat, in any limb resembling
A man; and fly from't as a prodigy.
Man stands amaz'd to see his deformity,
In any other creature but himself.
But in our own flesh, though we bear diseases
Which have their true names only tane from beasts,
As the most ulcerous wolf, and swinish measles;°
Though we are eaten up of lice, and worms,
And though continually we bear about us
A rotten and dead body, we delight
To hide it in rich tissue: all our fear,
Nay, all our terror, is lest our physician

36-7 **careening . . . disembogue** scraping the paint off an old foul-skinned lady, to enable her to put to sea again, i.e., seek new adventures 38 **plastic** fine modeling 40 **closet** private chamber 46-8 **Here are . . . spring** any two of you painted ladies, whose diseases gotten in youthful sexual games are enough to provide an inheritance for a doctor, and so enable him to replace his horse's rich coverlet in the spring 61 **ulcerous wolf . . . measle** (names of diseases)

Should put us in the ground, to be made sweet,
Your wife's gone to Rome: you two couple, and get you
To the wells at Lucca,° to recover your aches.

[*Exeunt Castruchio and Old Lady.*]

I have other work on foot: I observe our Duchess
Is sick a-days, she pukes, her stomach seethes,
The fins° of her eyelids look most teeming° blue,
She wanes i'the' cheek, and waxes fat i'th' flank;
And, contrary to our Italian fashion,
Wears a loose-bodied gown: there's somewhat in't.
I have a trick, may chance discover it,
A pretty one; I have bought some apricocks,°
The first our spring yields.

[*Enter Antonio and Delio.*]

Delio. And so long since married?
You amaze me.
Antonio. Let me seal your lips for ever,
For did I think that anything but th' air
Could carry these words from you, I should wish
You had no breath at all. [*To Bosola.*] Now sir, on your contemplation?
You are studying to become a great wise fellow?

Bosola. Oh sir, the opinion of wisdom is a foul tetter,° that runs all over a man's body: if simplicity direct us to have no evil, it directs us to a happy being. For the subtlest folly proceeds from the subtlest wisdom. Let me be simply honest.

Antonio. I do understand your inside.
Bosola. Do you so?
Antonio. Because you would not seem to appear to th' world
Puff'd up with your preferment, you continue
This out of fashion melancholy; leave it, leave it.

Bosola. Give me leave to be honest in any phrase, in any compliment whatsoever: shall I confess myself to you? I look no higher than I can reach: they are the gods, that must ride on winged horses, a lawyer's mule of a slow pace will both suit my disposition and business. For,

69 **Lucca** famous as a health spa 72 **fins** edges 72 **teeming** pregnant 77 **apricocks** apricots 84 **tetter** skin sore such as eczema

mark me, when a man's mind rides faster than his horse can gallop they quickly both tire.

Antonio. You would look up to Heaven, but I think The devil, that rules i'th' air, stands in your light.

Bosola. Oh, sir, you are lord of the ascendant,° chief man with the Duchess: a duke was your cousin-german,° remov'd. Say you were lineally descended from King Pippin,° or he himself, what of this? Search the heads of the greatest rivers in the world, you shall find them but bubbles of water. Some would think the souls of princes were brought forth by some more weighty cause, than those of meaner persons; they are deceiv'd, there's the same hand to them: the like passions sway them; the same reason, that makes a vicar go to law for a tithe-pig,° and undo his neighbours, makes them spoil a whole province, and batter down goodly cities with the cannon.

[*Enter Duchess, Old Lady, Ladies.*]

Duchess. Your arm Antonio, do I not grow fat?
I am exceeding short-winded. Bosola,
I would have you, sir, provide for me a litter,
Such a one, as the Duchess of Florence rode in.

Bosola. The duchess us'd one, when she was great with child.

Duchess. I think she did. Come hither, mend my ruff,
Here; when?° thou art such a tedious lady; and
Thy breath smells of lemon pills;° would thou hadst done;
Shall I sound° under thy fingers? I am
So troubled with the mother.°

Bosola [*aside.*] I fear too much.

Duchess. I have heard you say that the French courtiers
Wear their hats on 'fore the king.

Antonio. I have seen it.

Duchess. In the presence?

103 **lord of the ascendant** in astrology, the dominant planet at a particular time 104 **cousin-german** first cousin 105-6 **King Pippin** Pepin, king of the Franks (d. 768) 112 **tithe-pig** pig due as tithe or tenth to the church 121 **when?** an exclamation of impatience 122 **pills** peels 123 **sound** swoon 124 **mother** form of hysteria

Antonio. Yes.
Duchess. Why should not we bring up that fashion?
'Tis ceremony more than duty, that consists
In the removing of a piece of felt:
Be you the example to the rest o'th' court,
Put on your hat first.
Antonio. You must pardon me:
I have seen, in colder countries than in France,
Nobles stand bare° to th' prince; and the distinction
Methought show'd reverently.
Bosola. I have a present for your Grace.
Duchess. For me sir?
Bosola. Apricocks, Madam.
Duchess. O sir, where are they?
I have heard of none to-year.°
Bosola [*aside*]. Good, her colour rises.
Duchess. Indeed I thank you: they are wondrous fair ones.
What an unskilful fellow is our gardener!
We shall have none this month.
Bosola. Will not your Grace pare them?
Duchess. No, they taste of musk, methinks; indeed they do.
Bosola. I know not: yet I wish your Grace had par'd 'em.
Duchess. Why?
Bosola. I forgot to tell you the knave gard'ner,
Only to raise his profit by them the sooner,
Did ripen them in horse-dung.
Duchess. Oh you jest.
[*to Antonio.*] You shall judge: pray taste one.
Antonio. Indeed Madam,
I do not love the fruit.
Duchess. Sir, you are loth
To rob us of our dainties: 'tis a delicate fruit,
They say they are restorative?
Bosola. 'Tis a pretty art,
This grafting.
Duchess. 'Tis so: a bett'ring of nature.
Bosola. To make a pippin grow upon a crab,°
A damson° on a black-thorn: [*aside.*] How greedily she eats them!

134 **bare** bare-headed 138 **to-year** this year 153 **a crab** crab-apple tree 154 **damson** small plum

A whirlwind strike off these bawd farthingales,°
For, but for that, and the loose-bodied gown,
I should have discover'd apparently°
The young springal° cutting a caper in her belly.

Duchess. I thank you, Bosola: they were right good ones,
If they do not make me sick.

Antonio. How now Madam?

Duchess. This green fruit: and my stomach are not friends.
How they swell me!

Bosola [*aside.*] Nay, you are too much swell'd already.

Duchess. Oh, I am in an extreme cold sweat.

Bosola. I am very sorry.

Duchess. Lights to my chamber! O, good Antonio,
I fear I am undone.

Exit Duchess.°

Delio. Lights there, lights!

Antonio. O my most trusty Delio, we are lost:
I fear she's fall'n in labour: and there's left
No time for her remove.°

Delio. Have you prepar'd
Those ladies to attend her? and procur'd
That politic safe conveyance for the midwife
Your duchess plotted?

Antonio. I have.

Delio. Make use then of this forc'd occasion:
Give out that Bosola hath poison'd her,
With these apricocks: that will give some colour
For her keeping close.

Antonio. Fie, fie, the physicians
Will then flock to her.

Delio. For that you may pretend
She'll use some prepar'd antidote of her own,
Lest the physicians should repoison her.

Antonio. I am lost in amazement: I know not what to think on't.

Ex[*eunt.*]

155 **farthingales** hooped petticoats 157 **apparently** clearly 158 **springal** stripling 165 s.d. **Exit Duchess** The Duchess' ladies follow her; so may Bosola 168 **remove** i.e., to a place where she can give birth secretly

Scene ii

[*Enter Bosola and Old Lady.*]

Bosola. So, so: there's no question but her tetchiness° and most vulturous eating of the apricocks, are apparent signs of breeding, now?

Old Lady. I am in haste, sir.

Bosola. There was a young waiting-woman, had a monstrous desire to see the glass-house°—

Old Lady. Nay, pray let me go:

Bosola. And it was only to know what strange instrument it was, should swell up a glass to the fashion of a woman's belly.

Old Lady. I will hear no more of the glass-house, you are still abusing women!

Bosola. Who, I? no, only, by the way now and then, mention your frailties. The orange tree bears ripe and green fruit and blossoms altogether. And some of you give entertainment for pure love: but more, for more precious reward. The lusty spring smells well: but drooping autumn tastes well. If we have the same golden showers, that rained in the time of Jupiter the Thunderer: you have the same Danaes° still, to hold up their laps to receive them: didst thou never study the mathematics?

Old Lady. What's that, sir?

Bosola. Why, to know the trick how to make a many lines meet in one centre. Go, go; give your foster-daughters good counsel: tell them, that the devil takes delight to hang at a woman's girdle, like a false rusty watch, that she cannot discern how the time passes.

[*Exit Old Lady; enter Antonio, Delio, Roderigo, Grisolan.*]

Antonio. Shut up the court gates.

Roderigo. Why sir? what's the danger?

Antonio. Shut up the posterns presently:° and call
All the officers o'th' court.

Grisolan. I shall instantly. [*Exit.*]

Antonio. Who keeps the key o'th' park-gate?

II.ii.1 tetchiness irritability 6 **glass-house** glass factory 19-20 **Jupiter . . . Danaes** (Jupiter appeared to Danae in a shower of gold) 29 **posterns presently** back and side gates at once

Roderigo. Forobosco.
Antonio. Let him bring't presently.

[*Enter Officers, Gentlemen of the Court.*]

1 Gentleman. Oh, gentlemen o'th' court, the foulest treason!
Bosola. [*aside.*] If that these apricocks should be poison'd, now;
Without my knowledge!
1 Gentleman. There was taken even now
A Switzer° in the Duchess' bedchamber.
2 Gentleman. A Switzer?
1 Gentleman. With a pistol in his great cod-piece.°
Bosola. Ha, ha, ha.
1 Gentleman. The cod-piece was the case for't.
2 Gentleman. There was a cunning traitor.
Who would have search'd his cod-piece?
1 Gentleman. True, if he had kept out of the ladies' chambers:
And all the moulds of his buttons were leaden bullets.
2 Gentleman. Oh wicked cannibal:° a fire-lock° in's cod-piece?
1 Gentleman. 'Twas a French plot upon my life.
2 Gentleman. To see what the devil can do.
Antonio. All the officers here?
Gentlemen. We are.
Antonio. Gentlemen,
We have lost much plate you know; and but this evening
Jewels, to the value of four thousand ducats
Are missing in the Duchess' cabinet.
Are the gates shut?
1 Gentleman. Yes.
Antonio. 'Tis the Duchess' pleasure
Each officer be lock'd into his chamber
Till the sun-rising; and to send the keys

36 **Switzer** Swiss mercenary soldier 37 **cod-piece** a flap, often ornamented, worn over the crotch by a man 42 **cannibal** blood-thirsty savage 42 **fire-lock** gun-lock for igniting gun powder

Of all their chests, and of their outward° doors
Into her bedchamber. She is very sick.

Roderigo. At her pleasure.

Antonio. She entreats you take't not ill. The innocent
Shall be the more approv'd° by it.

Bosola. Gentleman o'th' wood-yard,° where's your Switzer now?

1 Servant. By this hand 'twas credibly reported by one o'th' black-guard.°

[*Exeunt Bosola, Roderigo and Officers.*]

Delio. How fares it with the Duchess?

Antonio. She's expos'd
Unto the worst of torture, pain, and fear.

Delio. Speak to her all happy comfort.

Antonio. How I do play the fool with mine own danger!
You are this night, dear friend, to post to Rome,
My life lies in your service.

Delio. Do not doubt me.

Antonio. Oh, 'tis far from me: and yet fear presents me
Somewhat that looks like danger.

Delio. Believe it,
'Tis but the shadow of your fear, no more:
How superstitiously we mind our evils!
The throwing down salt, or crossing of a hare;
Bleeding at nose, the stumbling of a horse:
Or singing of a cricket, are of power
To daunt whole man in us. Sir, fare you well:
I wish you all the joys of a bless'd father;
And, for my faith, lay this unto your breast,
Old friends, like old swords, still are trusted best.

[*Exit Delio.*]

[*Enter Cariola.*]

Cariola. Sir, you are the happy father of a son,
Your wife commends him to you.

Antonio. Blessed comfort!
For heaven' sake tend her well: I'll presently
Go set a figure° for's nativity. *Exeunt.*

51 **outward** outer 55 **approv'd** commended 56 **wood-yard** yard for firewood (sarcastic) 58 **th' black-guard** the household drudges 79 **figure** horoscope

Scene iii

[*Enter Bosola with a dark lanthorn.*°]

Bosola. Sure I did hear a woman shriek: list, ha?
And the sound came, if I receiv'd it right,
From the Duchess' lodgings: there's some stratagem
In the confining all our courtiers
To their several wards.° I must have part of it,
My intelligence° will freeze else. List again,
It may be 'twas the melancholy bird,
Best friend of silence, and of solitariness,
The owl, that scream'd so: ha! Antonio?

[*Enter Antonio with a candle, his sword drawn.*]

Antonio. I heard some noise: who's there? What art thou?
Speak.
Bosola. Antonio! Put not your face nor body
To such a forc'd expression of fear,
I am Bosola; your friend.
Antonio. Bosola!
[*aside.*] This mole does undermine me—heard you not
A noise even now?
Bosola. From whence?
Antonio. From the Duchess' lodging.
Bosola. Not I: did you?
Antonio. I did: or else I dream'd.
Bosola. Let's walk towards it.
Antonio. No. It may be 'twas
But the rising of the wind.
Bosola. Very likely.
Methinks 'tis very cold, and yet you sweat.
You look wildly.
Antonio. I have been setting a figure
For the Duchess' jewels.
Bosola. Ah: and how falls your question?
Do you find it radical?°

II.iii. s.d. **a dark lanthorn** a lantern with means for concealing the light 5 **wards** apartments 6 **intelligence** surveillance 22 **radical** fit to be judged

Antonio. What's that to you?
'Tis rather to be question'd what design,
When all men were commanded to their lodgings,
Makes you a night-walker.
Bosola. In sooth I'll tell you:
Now all the court's asleep, I thought the devil
Had least to do here; I come to say my prayers,
And if it do offend you, I do so,
You are a fine courtier.
Antonio [*aside.*] This fellow will undo me.
You gave the Duchess apricocks to-day,
Pray heaven they were not poison'd!
Bosola. Poison'd! a Spanish fig°
For the imputation.
Antonio. Traitors are ever confident,
Till they are discover'd. There were jewels stol'n too,
In my conceit,° none are to be suspected
More than yourself.
Bosola. You are a false steward.
Antonio. Saucy slave! I'll pull thee up by the roots.
Bosola. May be the ruin will crush you to pieces.
Antonio. You are an impudent snake indeed, sir,
Are you scarce warm, and do you show your sting?
[*Bosola.*] . . .
Antonio. You libel well, sir.
Bosola. No sir, copy it out:
And I will set my hand to't.
Antonio. [*aside.*] My nose bleeds.
One that were superstitious, would count
This ominous: when it merely comes by chance.
Two letters, that are wrought° here for my name
Are drown'd in blood!
Mere accident: for you, sir, I'll take order:
I'th' morn you shall be safe: [*aside.*] 'tis that must colour
Her lying-in: sir, this door you pass not:
I do not hold it fit, that you come near

31 **a Spanish fig** (a term of contempt in which the speaker also makes an obscene gesture known as "giving the finger") 34 **conceit** opinion 44 **wrought** embroidered (in a handkerchief)

The Duchess' lodgings, till you have quit yourself;
[*aside.*] *The great are like the base; nay, they are the same,*
When they seek shameful ways to avoid shame. *Ex*[*it.*]

Bosola. Antonio here about did drop a paper,
Some of your help, false friend:° oh, here it is.
What's here? a child's nativity calculated?
[*reads:*].*The Duchess was deliver'd of a son, 'tween the hours twelve and one, in the night: Anno Dom: 1504. (that's this year)* decimo nono Decembris, *(that's this night) taken according to the Meridian of Malfi (that's our Duchess: happy discovery). The Lord of the first house, being combust° in the ascendant, signifies short life: and* Mars *being in a human sign, join'd to the tail of the Dragon, in the eight house, doth threaten a violent death;* Cætera non scrutantur.°
Why now 'tis most apparent. This precise° fellow
Is the Duchess' bawd: I have it to my wish.
This is a parcel of intelligency
Our courtiers were cas'd up for! It needs must follow,
That I must be committed, on pretence
Of poisoning her: which I'll endure, and laugh at.
If one could find the father now: but that
Time will discover. Old Castruchio
I'th' morning posts to Rome; by him I'll send
A letter, that shall make her brothers' galls
O'erflow their livers. This was a thrifty way.
Though lust do masque° in ne'er so strange disguise
She's oft found witty, but is never wise. [*Exit.*]

Scene iv

[*Enter Cardinal and Julia.*]

Cardinal. Sit: thou art my best of wishes; prithee tell me
What trick didst thou invent to come to Rome,
Without thy husband?

54 **false friend** i.e., the lanthorn 61 **combust** burnt up, i.e., approaching the sun and consequently ineffective 64 **Caetera non scrutantur** "the rest is not investigated" 65 **precise** over-scrupulous (scornful) 76 **masque** i.e., mask

Julia. Why, my Lord, I told him
I came to visit an old anchorite°
Here, for devotion.
Cardinal. Thou art a witty false one:
I mean to him.
Julia. You have prevailed with me
Beyond my strongest thoughts: I would not now
Find you inconstant.
Cardinal. Do not put thyself
To such a voluntary torture, which proceeds
Out of your own guilt.
Julia. How, my Lord?
Cardinal. You fear
My constancy, because you have approv'd
Those giddy and wild turnings in yourself.
Julia. Did you e'er find them?
Cardinal. Sooth, generally for women:
A man might strive to make glass malleable,
Ere he should make them fixed.
Julia. So, my Lord.
Cardinal. We had need go borrow that fantastic glass
Invented by Galileo the Florentine,
To view another spacious world i'th' moon,
And look to find a constant woman there.
Julia. This is very well, my Lord.
Cardinal. Why do you weep?
Are tears your justification? The selfsame tears
Will fall into your husband's bosom, lady,
With a loud protestation that you love him
Above the world. Come, I'll love you wisely,
That's jealously, since I am very certain
You cannot make me cuckold.
Julia. I'll go home
To my husband.
Cardinal. You may thank me, lady,
I have taken you off your melancholy perch,
Bore you upon my fist, and show'd you game,
And let you fly at it.° I pray thee kiss me.
When thou wast with thy husband, thou wast watch'd

II.iv.4 anchorite hermit **28-30 perch . . . fly at it** (terms from falconry)

Like a tame elephant: (still you are to thank me.)
Thou hadst only kisses from him, and high feeding,
But what delight was that? 'Twas just like one
That hath a little fing'ring on the lute,
Yet cannot tune it: (still you are to thank me.)
Julia. You told me of a piteous wound i'th' heart,
And a sick liver,° when you wooed me first,
And spake like one in physic.
Cardinal. Who's that?

[*Enter Servant.*]

Rest firm, for my affection to thee,
Lightning moves slow to't.°
Servant. Madam, a gentleman
That's come post from Malfi, desires to see you.
Cardinal. Let him enter, I'll withdraw. *Exit.*
Servant. He says
Your husband, old Castruchio, is come to Rome,
Most pitifully tir'd with riding post. [*Exit Servant.*]

[*Enter Delio.*]

Julia. Signior Delio! [*aside.*] 'tis one of my old suitors.
Delio. I was bold to come and see you.
Julia. Sir, you are welcome.
Delio. Do you lie here?
Julia. Sure, your own experience
Will satisfy you no; our Roman prelates
Do not keep lodging for ladies.
Delio. Very well.
I have brought you no commendations from your husband,
For I know none by him.
Julia. I hear he's come to Rome?
Delio. I never knew man and beast, of a horse and a knight,
So weary of each other; if he had had a good back,
He would have undertook to have borne his horse,
His breach° was so pitifully sore.

38 **liver** (thought to be the seat of amorous passion) 41 **to't** in comparison to it 56 **breach** here, battered seat

Julia. Your laughter
Is my pity.
Delio. Lady, I know not whether
You want money, but I have brought you some.
Julia. From my husband?
Delio. No, from mine own allowance.
Julia. I must hear the condition, ere I be bound to take it.
Delio. Look on't, 'tis gold, hath it not a fine colour?
Julia. I have a bird more beautiful.
Delio. Try the sound on't.
Julia. A lute-string far exceeds it;
It hath no smell, like cassia° or civet,°
Nor is it physical,° though some fond doctors
Persuade us, seethe't° in cullises.° I'll tell you,
This is a creature bred by—

[*Enter Servant.*]

Servant. Your husband's come,
Hath deliver'd a letter to the Duke of Calabria,
That, to my thinking, hath put him out of his wits.
[*Exit Servant.*]
Julia. Sir, you hear,
Pray let me know your business and your suit,
As briefly as can be.
Delio. With good speed. I would wish you,
At such time, as you are non-resident
With your husband, my mistress.
Julia. Sir, I'll go ask my husband if I shall,
And straight return your answer. *Exit.*
Delio. Very fine,
Is this her wit, or honesty° that speaks thus?
I heard one say the Duke was highly mov'd
With a letter sent from Malfi. I do fear
Antonio is betray'd: how fearfully
Shows his ambition now; unfortunate Fortune!
They pass through whirlpools, and deep woes do shun,
Who the event weigh, ere the action's done. *Exit.*

64 **cassia** a coarse kind of cinnamon, but here a plant of great fragrance 64 **civet** perfume 65 **physical** medicinal 66 **seethe't** i.e., the gold 66 **culisses** broths 77 **honesty** chastity

Scene v

[*Enter*] *Cardinal, and Ferdinand, with a letter.*

Ferdinand. I have this night digg'd up a mandrake.°
Cardinal. Say you?
Ferdinand. And I am grown mad with't.
Cardinal. What's the prodigy?
Ferdinand. Read there, a sister damn'd, she's loose, i'th' hilts:°
Grown a notorious strumpet.
Cardinal. Speak lower.
Ferdinand. Lower?
Rogues do not whisper't now, but seek to publish't,
As servants do the bounty of their lords,
Aloud; and with a covetous searching eye,
To mark who note them. Oh confusion seize her,
She hath had most cunning bawds to serve her turn,
And more secure conveyances for lust,
Than towns of garrison, for service.°
Cardinal. Is't possible?
Can this be certain?
Ferdinand. Rhubarb, oh for rhubarb
To purge this choler;° here's the cursed day°
To prompt my memory, and here't shall stick
Till of her bleeding heart I make a sponge
To wipe it out.
Cardinal. Why do you make yourself
So wild a tempest?
Ferdinand. Would I could be one,
That I might toss her palace 'bout her ears,
Root up her goodly forests, blast her meads,
And lay her general territory as waste,
As she hath done her honors.

II.v.1 mandrake a medicinal though poisonous plant whose root, when forked, had a human shape **3 loose i'th' hilts** unchaste **11 service** (1) military service (2) sexual opportunity **13 choler** fury (rhubarb was considered an antidote) **13 here's the cursed day** reference to horoscope sent by Bosola (?)

Cardinal. Shall our blood,
The royal blood of Aragon and Castile,
Be thus attainted?
Ferdinand. Apply desperate physic,
We must not now use balsamum,° but fire,
The smarting cupping-glass,° for that's the mean
To purge infected blood, such blood as hers.
There is a kind of pity in mine eye,
I'll give it to my handkercher; and now 'tis here,
I'll bequeath this to her bastard.
Cardinal. What to do?
Ferdinand. Why, to make soft lint for his mother's wounds,
When I have hewed her to pieces.
Cardinal. Curs'd creature!
Unequal° nature, to place women's hearts
So far upon the left side.°
Ferdinand. Foolish men,
That e'er will trust their honour in a bark,
Made of so slight, weak bulrush, as is woman,
Apt every minute to sink it!
Cardinal. Thus ignorance, when it hath purchas'd° honour,
It cannot wield it.
Ferdinand. Methinks I see her laughing,
Excellent hyena! Talk to me somewhat, quickly,
Or my imagination will carry me
To see her in the shameful act of sin.
Cardinal. With whom?
Ferdinand. Happily,° with some strong thigh'd bargeman;
Or one o'th' wood-yard, that can quoit the sledge°
Or toss the bar, or else some lovely squire
That carries coals up to her privy° lodgings.
Cardinal. You fly beyond your reason.
Ferdinand. Go to, mistress!
'Tis not your whore's milk, that shall quench my wild-fire
But your whore's blood.

24 **balsamum** balm (an ointment) 25 **cupping-glass** i.e., for drawing blood surgically 32 **unequal** unjust (?), disorderly (?) 33 **left side** i.e., the wrong or deceitful side 37 **purchas'd** obtained 43 **Happily** haply 44 **quoit the sledge** throw the sledge-hammer 46 **privy** private

Cardinal. How idly shows this rage! which carries you,
As men convey'd by witches, through the air
On violent whirlwinds: this intemperate noise
Fitly resembles deaf men's shrill discourse,
Who talk aloud, thinking all other men
To have their imperfection.

Ferdinand. Have not you
My palsy?

Cardinal. Yes, I can be angry
Without this rupture; there is not in nature
A thing, that makes man so deform'd, so beastly
As doth intemperate anger; chide yourself:
You have divers men, who never yet express'd
Their strong desire of rest but by unrest,
By vexing of themselves. Come, put yourself
In tune.

Ferdinand. So, I will only study to seem
The thing I am not. I could kill her now,
In you, or in myself, for I do think
It is some sin in us, Heaven doth revenge
By her.

Cardinal. Are you stark mad?

Ferdinand. I would have their bodies
Burnt in a coal-pit, with the ventage stopp'd,
That their curs'd smoke might not ascend to Heaven:
Or dip the sheets they lie in, in pitch or sulphur,
Wrap them in't, and then light them like a match:
Or else to boil their bastard to a cullis,°
And give't his lecherous father, to renew
The sin of his back.

Cardinal. I'll leave you.

Ferdinand. Nay, I have done;
I am confident, had I been damn'd in hell,
And should have heard of this, it would have put me
Into a cold sweat. In, in, I'll go sleep:
Till I know who leaps my sister, I'll not stir:
That known, I'll find scorpions to string my whips,
And fix her in a general° eclipse. *Exeunt.*

72 cullis broth 80 general total

Act III, Scene i

[*Enter Antonio and Delio.*]

Antonio. Our noble friend, my most beloved Delio,
Oh, you have been a stranger long at court,
Came you along with the Lord Ferdinand?
Delio. I did, sir, and how fares your noble Duchess?
Antonio. Right fortunately well. She's an excellent
Feeder of pedigrees: since you last saw her,
She hath had two children more, a son and daughter.
Delio. Methinks 'twas yesterday. Let me but wink,
And not behold your face, which to mine eye
Is somewhat leaner, verily I should dream
It were within this half hour.
Antonio. You have not been in law, friend Delio,
Nor in prison, nor a suitor at the court,
Nor begg'd the reversion of some great man's place,
Nor troubled with an old wife, which doth make
Your time so insensibly hasten.
Delio. Pray sir tell me,
Hath not this news arriv'd yet to the ear
Of the Lord Cardinal?
Antonio. I fear it hath;
The Lord Ferdinand, that's newly come to court,
Doth bear himself right dangerously.
Delio. Pray why?
Antonio. He is so quiet, that he seems to sleep
The tempest out, as dormice do in winter;
Those houses, that are haunted, are most still,
Till the devil be up.
Delio. What say the common people?
Antonio. The common rabble do directly say
She is a strumpet.
Delio. And your graver heads,
Which would be politic, what censure° they?
Antonio. They do observe I grow to infinite purchase°
The left-hand° way, and all suppose the Duchess
Would amend it, if she could. For, say they,

III.i.27 **censure** judge 28 **purchase** acquisition, hence wealth 29 **left-hand** sinister

Great princes, though they grudge their officers
Should have such large and unconfined means
To get wealth under them, will not complain
Lest thereby they should make them odious
Unto the people: for other obligation
Of love, or marriage, between her and me,
They never dream of.

[*Enter Ferdinand, Duchess and Bosola.*]

Delio. The Lord Ferdinand
Is going to bed.
Ferdinand. I'll instantly to bed,
For I am weary: I am to bespeak
A husband for you.
Duchess. For me, sir! pray who is't?
Ferdinand. The great Count Malateste.
Duchess. Fie upon him,
A count? He's a mere stick of sugar-candy,
You may look quite thorough him: when I choose
A husband, I will marry for your honour.
Ferdinand. You shall do well in't. How is't, worthy
Antonio?
Duchess. But, sir, I am to have private conference with you,
About a scandalous report is spread
Touching mine honour.
Ferdinand. Let me be ever deaf to't:
One of Pasquil's° paper bullets, court calumny,
A pestilent air, which princes' palaces
Are seldom purg'd of. Yet, say that it were true,
I pour it in your bosom,° my fix'd love
Would strongly excuse, extenuate, nay deny
Faults were they apparent in you. Go, be safe
In your own innocency.
Duchess. Oh bless'd comfort,
This deadly air is purg'd.

Exeunt [*Duchess, Antonio, Delio.*]

Ferdinand. Her guilt treads on
Hot burning cultures.° Now Bosola,
How thrives our intelligence?

49 **Pasquil's paper bullets** pasquinades or satirical verses 52 **pour . . . bosom** confide in you 57 **cultures** coulters, i.e., blades of a ploughshare (some editors place Bosola's entrance at this point)

Bosola. Sir, uncertainly:
'Tis rumour'd she hath had three bastards, but
By whom, we may go read i'th' stars.
Ferdinand. Why some
Hold opinion, all things are written there.
Bosola. Yes, if we could find spectacles to read them;
I do suspect, there hath been some sorcery
Us'd on the Duchess.
Ferdinand. Sorcery, to what purpose?
Bosola. To make her dote on some desertless fellow,
She shames to acknowledge.
Ferdinand. Can your faith give way
To think there's power in potions, or in charms,
To make us love, whether we will or no?
Bosola. Most certainly.
Ferdinand. Away, these are mere gulleries,° horrid things
Invented by some cheating mountebanks
To abuse us. Do you think that herbs, or charms
Can force the will? Some trials have been made
In the foolish practice; but the ingredients
Were lenative° poisons, such as are of force
To make the patient mad; and straight the witch
Swears, by equivocation, they are in love.
The witchcraft lies in her rank blood: this night
I will force confession from her. You told me
You had got, within these two days, a false key
Into her bed-chamber.
Bosola. I have.
Ferdinand. As I would wish.
Bosola. What do you intend to do?
Ferdinand. Can you guess?
Bosola. No.
Ferdinand. Do not ask then.
He that can compass me, and know my drifts,
May say he hath put a girdle 'bout the world,
And sounded all her quick-sands.
Bosola. I do not
Think so.
Ferdinand. What do you think then, pray?
Bosola. That you

70 **gulleries** impostures 75 **lenative** sweet or apparently soothing

Are your own chronicle too much: and grossly
Flatter yourself.
Ferdinand. Give me thy hand; I thank thee.
I never gave pension but to flatterers,
Till I entertained thee: farewell,
That friend a great man's ruin strongly checks,
Who rails into his belief° all his defects. *Exeunt.*

Scene ii

[*Enter Duchess, Antonio and Cariola.*]

Duchess. Bring me the casket hither, and the glass;
You get no lodging here to-night, my lord.
Antonio. Indeed, I must persuade one.
Duchess. Very good:
I hope in time 'twill grow into a custom,
That noblemen shall come with cap and knee,°
To purchase a night's lodging of their wives.
Antonio. I must lie here.
Duchess. Must? you are a lord of mis-rule.°
Antonio. Indeed, my rule is only in the night.
Duchess. To what use will you put me?
Antonio. We'll sleep together.
Duchess. Alas, what pleasure can two lovers find in sleep?
Cariola. My lord, I lie with her often: and I know
She'll much disquiet you.
Antonio. See, you are complain'd of.
Cariola. For she's the sprawling'st bedfellow.
Antonio. I shall like her the better for that.
Cariola. Sir, shall I ask you a question?
Antonio. I pray thee Cariola.
Cariola. Wherefore still, when you lie with my lady
Do you rise so early?
Antonio. Labouring men,
Count the clock oft'nest Cariola,
Are glad when their task's ended.

93 **rails into his belief** nags him into recognizing III.ii.5 **with cap and knee** with cap in hand and bended knee, humbly 7 **lord of mis-rule** (1) person elevated to reign over courtly revels, (2) lord ruling over a miss or mistress

Duchess. I'll stop your mouth [*kisses him.*]
Antonio. Nay, that's but one, Venus had two soft doves
To draw her chariot: I must have another [*kisses her*].
When wilt thou marry, Cariola?
Cariola. Never, my lord.
Antonio. O fie upon this single life: forgo it.
We read how Daphne, for her peevish flight
Became a fruitless bay-tree; Sirinx turn'd
To the pale empty reed; Anaxarete
Was frozen into marble:° whereas those
Which married, or prov'd kind unto their friends
Were, by a gracious influence, transhap'd
Into the olive, pomegranate, mulberry:
Became flowers, precious stones, or eminent stars.
Cariola. This is vain poetry; but I pray you tell me,
If there were propos'd me wisdom, riches, and beauty,
In three several young men, which should I choose?
Antonio. 'Tis a hard question. This was Paris' case
And he was blind in't, and there was great cause:
For how was't possible he could judge right,
Having three amorous goddesses in view,
And they stark naked? 'Twas a motion°
Were able to benight the apprehension
Of the severest counsellor of Europe.
Now I look on both your faces, so well form'd
It puts me in mind of a question, I would ask.
Cariola. What is't?
Antonio. I do wonder why hard favour'd ladies
For the most part, keep worse-favour'd waiting-women,
To attend them, and cannot endure fair ones.
Duchess. Oh, that's soon answer'd.
Did you ever in your life know an ill painter
Desire to have his dwelling next door to the shop
Of an excellent picture-maker? 'Twould disgrace
His face-making, and undo him. I prithee
When we were so merry? My hair tangles.
Antonio [*aside to Cariola.*] Pray thee, Cariola, let's steal forth the room,

25-8 **Daphne . . . marble** (for fleeing Apollo, Daphne was changed into a bay-tree, for refusing Pan Sirinx was turned into a reed, and for her hardness toward Iphis Anaxarete was made a stone) 40 **motion** proposal, spectacle

And let her talk to herself: I have divers times
Serv'd her the like, when she hath chaf'd extremely.
I love to see her angry: softly Cariola.

Exeunt [*Antonio and Cariola.*]

Duchess. Doth not the colour of my hair 'gin to change?
When I wax grey, I shall have all the court
Powder their hair with arras,° to be like me:
You have cause to love me, I ent'red you into my heart,
Before you would vouchsafe to call for the keys.

[*Enter Ferdinand, unseen.*]

We shall one day have my brothers take you napping.
Methinks his presence, being now in court,
Should make you keep your own bed: but you'll say
Love mix'd with fear is sweetest. I'll assure you
You shall get no more children till my brothers
Consent to be your gossips.° Have you lost your tongue?

She sees Ferdinand holding a poniard.

'Tis welcome:°
For know, whether I am doom'd to live, or die,
I can do both like a prince.

Ferdinand gives her a poniard.

Ferdinand. Die then, quickly.
Virtue, where art thou hid? What hideous thing
Is it, that doth eclipse thee?
Duchess. Pray sir hear me—
Ferdinand. Or is it true, thou art but a bare name,
And no essential thing?
Duchess. Sir—
Ferdinand. Do not speak.
Duchess. No sir:
I will plant my soul in mine ears, to hear you.
Ferdinand. Oh most imperfect light of human reason,
That mak'st us so unhappy, to foresee
What we can least prevent. Pursue thy wishes:
And glory in them: there's in shame no comfort,
But to be past all bounds and sense of shame.

60 **arras** here, orris, a root whose white powder was used to whiten and perfume hair 68 **your gossips** godfathers to your children 69 **'Tis welcome** i.e., the poniard or dagger that Ferdinand holds

Duchess. I pray sir, hear me: I am married—
Ferdinand. So.
Duchess. Happily,° not to your liking: but for that
Alas: your shears do come untimely now
To clip the bird's wings, that's already flown.
Will you see my husband?
Ferdinand. Yes, if I could change
Eyes with a basilisk.
Duchess. Sure, you came hither
By his confederacy.
Ferdinand. The howling of a wolf
Is music to thee, screech-owl; prithee peace.
Whate'er thou art, that hast enjoy'd my sister,
(For I am sure thou hear'st me), for thine own sake
Let me not know thee. I came hither prepar'd
To work thy discovery: yet am now persuaded
It would beget such violent effects
As would damn us both. I would not for ten millions
I had beheld thee; therefore use all means
I never may have knowledge of thy name;
Enjoy thy lust still, and a wretched life,
On that condition. And for thee, vild woman,
If thou do wish thy lecher may grow old
In thy embracements, I would have thee build
Such a room for him, as our anchorites
To holier use inhabit. Let not the sun
Shine on him, till he's dead. Let dogs and monkeys
Only converse with him, and such dumb things
To whom nature denies use to sound his name.
Do not keep a paraquito,° lest she learn it;
If thou do love him, cut out thine own tongue
Lest it bewray him.
Duchess. Why might not I marry?
I have not gone about, in this, to create
Any new world, or custom.
Ferdinand. Thou art undone:
And thou hast tane that massy sheet of lead
That hid thy husband's bones, and folded it
About my heart.
Duchess. Mine bleeds for't.

84 happily haply, perhaps 108 paraquito parakeet

Ferdinand. Thine? thy heart?
What should I name't, unless a hollow bullet°
Fill'd with unquenchable wild-fire?°
Duchess. You are in this
Too strict: and were you not my princely brother
I would say too wilful. My reputation
Is safe.
Ferdinand. Dost thou know what reputation is?
I'll tell thee, to small purpose, since th'instruction
Comes now too late:
Upon a time Reputation, Love and Death
Would travel o'er the world: and it was concluded
That they should part, and take three several ways.
Death told them, they should find him in great battles:
Or cities plagu'd with plagues. Love gives them counsel
To inquire for him 'mongst unambitious shepherds,
Where dowries were not talk'd of: and sometimes
'Mongst quiet kindred, that had nothing left
By their dead parents. 'Stay', quoth Reputation,
'Do not forsake me: for it is my nature
If once I part from any man I meet
I am never found again.' And so, for you:
You have shook hands with Reputation,
And made him invisible. So fare you well.
I will never see you more.
Duchess. Why should only I,
Of all the other princes of the world
Be cas'd up, like a holy relic? I have youth,
And a little beauty.
Ferdinand. So you have some virgins,
That are witches. I will never see thee more. *Exit.*

Enter [Cariola and] Antonio with a pistol.

Duchess. You saw this apparition?
Antonio. Yes: we are
Betray'd; how came he hither? I should turn
This, to thee, for that. [*points the pistol at Cariola.*]
Cariola. Pray sir do: and when

116 hollow bullet cannon ball 117 wild-fire virtually unextinguishable materials used in warfare

That you have cleft my heart, you shall read there,
Mine innocence.
Duchess. That gallery gave him entrance.
Antonio. I would this terrible thing would come again,
That, standing on my guard, I might relate
My warrantable love. Ha! what means this?
Duchess. He left this with me. *she shows the poniard.*
Antonio. And it seems, did wish
You would use it on yourself?
Duchess. His action seem'd
To intend so much.
Antonio. This hath a handle to't,
As well as a point: turn it towards him, and
So fasten the keen edge in his rank gall. [*knocking*]
How now? Who knocks? More earthquakes?
Duchess. I stand
As if a mine, beneath my feet, were ready
To be blown up.
Cariola. 'Tis Bosola.
Duchess. Away!
Oh misery, methinks unjust actions
Should wear these masks and curtains; and not we.
You must instantly part hence: I have fashion'd it
already. *Ex*[*it*] *Ant*[*onio.*]

[*Enter Bosola.*]

Bosola. The Duke your brother is tane up in a whirlwind;
Hath took horse, and's rid post to Rome.
Duchess. So late?
Bosola. He told me, as he mounted into th' saddle,
You were undone.
Duchess. Indeed, I am very near it.
Bosola. What's the matter?
Duchess. Antonio, the master of our household
Hath dealt so falsely with me, in's° accounts:
My brother stood engag'd with me for money
Tane up of certain Neapolitan Jews,
And Antonio lets the bonds be forfeit.
Bosola. Strange: [*aside.*] This is cunning.

167 in's in his

Duchess. And hereupon
My brother's bills at Naples are protested
Against. Call up our officers.
Bosola. I shall. *Exit.*

[*Enter Antonio.*]

Duchess. The place that you must fly to, is Ancona,
Hire a house there. I'll send after you
My treasure, and my jewels: our weak safety
Runs upon enginous° wheels: short syllables
Must stand for periods. I must now accuse you
Of such a feigned crime, as Tasso calls
Magnanima mensogna: a noble lie,
'Cause it must shield our honours: hark, they are coming.

[*Enter Bosola and Officers.*]

Antonio. Will your Grace hear me?
Duchess. I have got well by you: you have yielded me
A million of loss; I am like to inherit
The people's curses for your stewardship.
You had the trick, in audit time to be sick,
Till I had sign'd your *Quietus*; and that cur'd you
Without help of a doctor. Gentlemen,
I would have this man be an example to you all:
So shall you hold my favour. I pray let him;°
For h'as° done that, alas! you would not think of,
And, because I intend to be rid of him,
I mean not to publish. Use your fortune elsewhere.
Antonio. I am strongly arm'd to brook my overthrow,
As commonly men bear with a hard year:
I will not blame the cause on't; but do think
The necessity of my malevolent star
Procures this, not her humour. O the inconstant
And rotten ground of service, you may see;
'Tis ev'n like him that, in a winter night,
Takes a long slumber, o'er a dying fire
As loth to part from't: yet parts thence as cold,
As when he first sat down.

177 **enginous** crafty 190 **let him** let him go 191 **h'as** he has

Duchess. We do confiscate,
Towards the satisfying of your accounts,
All that you have.
Antonio. I am all yours; and 'tis very fit
All mine should be so.
Duchess. So, sir; you have your pass.
Antonio. You may see, gentlemen, what 'tis to serve
A prince with body and soul. *Exit.*

Bosola. Here's an example for extortion; what moisture is drawn out of the sea, when foul weather comes, pours down, and runs into the sea again.

Duchess. I would know what are your opinions
Of this Antonio.

2 *Officer.* He could not abide to see a pig's head gaping, I thought your Grace would find him a Jew:

3 *Officer.* I would you had been his officer, for your own sake.

4 *Officer.* You would have had more money.

1 *Officer.* He stopp'd his ears with black wool:° and to those came to him for money said he was thick of hearing.°

2 *Officer.* Some said he was an hermaphrodite, for he could not abide a woman.

4 *Officer.* How scurvy proud he would look, when the treasury was full. Well, let him go.

1 *Officer.* Yes, and the chippings° of the butt'ry fly after him, to scour his gold chain.°

Duchess. Leave us. [*Exeunt Officers.*] What do you think of these?

Bosola. That these are rogues, that in's° prosperity,
But to have waited on his fortune, could have wish'd
His dirty stirrup riveted through their noses:
And follow'd after's mule, like a bear in a ring.
Would have prostituted their daughters to his lust;
Made their first born intelligencers; thought none happy
But such as were born under his bless'd planet;
And wore his livery: and do these lice drop off now?
Well, never look to have the like again;

219 **black wool** a cure for ear-ache 220 **thick of hearing** i.e., hard of hearing 226 **chippings** paring of a crust of bread 227 **gold chain** the steward's badge of office 230 **in's** in his, i.e., Antonio's

He hath left a sort of flatt'ring rogues behind him,
Their doom must follow. Princes pay flatterers,
In their own money. Flatterers dissemble their vices,
And they dissemble their lies, that's justice.
Alas, poor gentleman,—
Duchess. Poor! he hath amply fill'd his coffers.
Bosola. Sure he was too honest. Pluto° the god of riches,
When he's sent, by Jupiter, to any man
He goes limping, to signify that wealth
That comes on God's name, comes slowly; but when he's sent
On the devil's errand, he rides post, and comes in by scuttles.°
Let me show you what a most unvalu'd° jewel
You have, in a wanton humour, thrown away.
To bless the man shall find him. He was an excellent
Courtier, and most faithful; a soldier, that thought it
As beastly to know his own value too little,
As devilish to acknowledge it too much;
Both his virtue and form deserv'd a far better fortune:
His discourse rather delighted to judge itself, than show itself.
His breast was fill'd with all perfection,
And yet it seem'd a private whisp'ring room:
It made so little noise of't.
Duchess. But he was basely descended.
Bosola. Will you make yourself a mercenary herald,°
Rather to examine men's pedigrees, than virtues?
You shall want° him:
For know an honest statesman to a prince,
Is like a cedar, planted by a spring,
The spring bathes the tree's root, the grateful tree
Rewards it with his shadow: you have not done so;
I would sooner swim to the Bermoothas° on
Two politicians' rotten bladders, tied
Together with an intelligencer's heart string
Than depend on so changeable a prince's favour.
Fare thee well, Antonio, since the malice of the world

245 **Pluto** actually Plutus; Pluto was the god of the underworld 249 **by scuttles** scuttling (?) 250 **unvalu'd** (1) invaluable, (2) unappreciated 261 **mercenary herald** herald who sells coats of arms 263 **want** lack, miss 268 **Bermoothas** Bermudas

Would needs down with thee, it cannot be said yet
That any ill happened unto thee,
Considering thy fall was accomplished with virtue.
Duchess. Oh, you render me excellent music.
Bosola. Say you?
Duchess. This good one that you speak of, is my husband.
Bosola. Do I not dream? Can this ambitious age
Have so much goodness in't, as to prefer
A man merely for worth: without these shadows
Of wealth, and painted honours? possible?
Duchess. I have had three children by him.
Bosola. Fortunate lady,
For you have made your private nuptial bed
The humble and fair seminary° of peace.
No question but many an unbenefic'd° scholar
Shall pray for you, for this deed, and rejoice
That some preferment in the world can yet
Arise from merit. The virgns of your land,
That have no dowries, shall hope your example
Will raise them to rich husbands. Should you want
Soldiers, 'twould make the very Turks and Moors
Turn Christians, and serve you for this act.
Last, the neglected poets of your time,
In honour of this trophy of a man,
Rais'd by that curious engine, your white hand,
Shall thank you in your grave for't; and make that
More reverend than all the cabinets
Of living princes. For Antonio,
His fame shall likewise flow from many a pen,
When heralds shall want coats,° to sell to men.
Duchess. As I taste comfort, in this friendly speech,
So would I find concealment—
Bosola. Oh the secret of my prince,
Which I will wear on th'inside of my heart.
Duchess. You shall take charge of all my coin, and jewels,
And follow him, for he retires himself
To Ancona.
Bosola. So.
Duchess. Whither, within few days,
I mean to follow thee.

284 **seminary** seed bed, nursery 285 **unbenefic'd** without a benefice i.e., a church endowment 300 **coats** i.e., of arms

Bosola. Let me think:
I would wish your Grace to feign a pilgrimage
To Our Lady of Loretto, scarce seven leagues
From fair Ancona, so may you depart
Your country with more honour, and your flight
Will seem a princely progress, retaining
Your usual train about you.
Duchess. Sir, your direction
Shall lead me, by the hand.
Cariola. In my opinion,
She were better progress to the baths at Lucca,
Or go visit the Spa
In Germany:° for, if you will believe me,
I do not like this jesting with religion,
This feigned pilgrimage.
Duchess. Thou art a superstitious fool:
Prepare us instantly for our departure.
Past sorrows, let us moderately lament them,
For those to come, seek wisely to prevent them.
Exit [*Duchess with Cariola.*]
Bosola. A politician° is the devil's quilted anvil,
He fashions all sins on him, and the blows
Are never heard; he may work in a lady's chamber,
As here for proof. What rests, but I reveal
All to my lord? Oh, this base quality
Of intelligencer! Why, every quality i'th' world
Prefers but gain, or commendation:
Now for this act. I am certain to be rais'd,
And men that paint weeds to the life are prais'd. *Exit.*

Scene iii

[*Enter*] *Cardinal, Ferdinand, Malateste, Pescara, Silvio, Delio.*

Cardinal. Must we turn soldier then?
Malateste. The Emperor,°
Hearing your worth that way, ere you attain'd
This reverend garment, joins you in commission

317 **Germany** (actually Spa was in Belgium) 323 **politician** intriguer III.iii.1 **The Emperor** Charles V

With the right fortunate soldier, the Marquis of Pescara
And the famous Lannoy.°
Cardinal. He that had the honour
Of taking the French king prisoner?
Malateste. The same.
Here's a plot° drawn for a new fortification
At Naples.
Ferdinand. This great Count Malateste, I perceive
Hath got employment.
Delio. No employment, my lord;
A marginal note in the muster book, that he is
A voluntary lord.
Ferdinand. He's no soldier?
Delio. He has worn gunpowder, in's hollow tooth,
For the tooth-ache.
Silvio. He comes to the leaguer° with a full intent
To eat fresh beef, and garlic; means to stay
Till the scent be gone, and straight return to court.
Delio. He hath read all the late service,°
As the City chronicle relates it,
And keeps two painters going, only to express
Battles in model.
Silvio. Then he'll fight by the book.
Delio. By the almanac, I think,
To choose good days, and shun the critical.
That's his mistress' scarf.
Silvio. Yes, he protests
He would do much for that taffeta,—
Delio. I think he would run away from a battle
To save it from taking° prisoner.
Silvio. He is horribly afraid
Gunpowder will spoil the perfume on't,—
Delio. I saw a Dutchman break his pate once
For calling him pot-gun;° he made his head
Have a bore in't, like a musket.
Silvio. I would he had made a touch-hole to't.

5 **Lannoy** Charles de Lannoy, Viceroy of Naples 7 **plot** plan 14 **leaguer** military camp 17 **read . . . service** read all about the recent military action 26 **taking** being taken 29 **pot-gun** pop-gun

He is indeed a guarded sumpter-cloth°
Only for the remove of the court.

[*Enter Bosola.*]

Pescara. Bosola arriv'd? What should be the business?
Some falling out amongst the cardinals.
These factions amongst great men, they are like
Foxes, when their heads are divided:
They carry fire in their tails, and all the country
About them goes to wrack for't.

Silvio. What's that Bosola?

Delio. I knew him in Padua, a fantastical scholar, like such who study to know how many knots was in Hercules' club; of what colour Achilles' beard was, or whether Hector were not troubled with the toothache. He hath studied himself half blear-ey'd, to know the true symmetry of Caesar's nose by a shoeing-horn: and this he did to gain the name of a speculative man.

Pescara. Mark Prince Ferdinand,
A very salamander lives in's eye,
To mock the eager violence of fire.

Silvio. That cardinal hath made more bad faces with his oppression than ever Michael Angelo made good ones: he lifts up's nose, like a foul porpoise before a storm,—

Pescara. The Lord Ferdinand laughs.

Delio. Like a deadly cannon, that lightens ere it smokes.

Pescara. These are your true pangs of death,
The pangs of life, that struggle with great statesmen,—

Delio. In such a deformed silence, witches whisper their charms.

Cardinal. Doth she make religion her riding hood
To keep her from the sun and tempest?

Ferdinand. That:
That damns her. Methinks her fault and beauty
Blended together, show like leprosy,
The whiter, the fouler. I make it a question
Whether her beggarly brats were ever christ'ned.

Cardinal. I will instantly solicit the state° of Ancona
To have them banish'd.

32 guarded sumpter-cloth ornamentally lined saddle cloth **65 state** nobles, rulers

Ferdinand. You are for Loretto?
I shall not be at your ceremony; fare you well:
Write to the Duke of Malfi, my young nephew
She had by her first husband, and acquaint him
With's mother's honesty.
Bosola. I will.
Ferdinand. Antonio!
A slave, that only smell'd of ink and counters,°
And nev'r in's life look'd like a gentleman,
But in the audit time: go, go presently,
Draw me out an hundred and fifty of our horse,
And meet me at the fort-bridge. *Exeunt.*

Scene iv

[*Enter*] *Two Pilgrims to the Shrine of Our Lady of Loretto.*

1 Pilgrim. I have not seen a goodlier shrine than this,
Yet I have visited many.
2 Pilgrim. The Cardinal of Aragon
Is this day to resign his cardinal's hat;
His sister duchess likewise is arriv'd
To pay her vow of pilgrimage. I expect
A noble ceremony.
1 Pilgrim. No question.—They come.

Here the ceremony of the Cardinal's instalment in the habit of a soldier: perform'd in delivering up his cross, hat, robes, and ring at the shrine; and investing him with sword, helmet, shield, and spurs. Then Antonio, the Duchess and their children, having presented themselves at the shrine, are (by a form of banishment in dumb-show expressed towards them by the Cardinal, and the State of Ancona) banished. During all which ceremony this ditty is sung to very solemn music, by divers churchmen; and then *Exeunt.*

Arms and honours deck thy story,
To thy fame's eternal glory,

71 **counters** tokens used in making calculations

Adverse fortune ever fly thee,
No disastrous fate come nigh thee.
The Author disclaims this Ditty to be his.

I alone will sing thy praises,
Whom to honour virtue raises;
And thy study that divine is,
Bent to martial discipline is:
Lay aside all those robes lie by thee,
Crown thy arts with arms: they'll beautify thee.

O worthy of worthiest name, adorn'd
in this manner,
Lead bravely thy forces on, under war's
warlike banner:
O mayst thou prove fortunate in all
martial courses,
Guide thou still by skill, in arts and forces:
Victory attend thee nigh, whilst fame sings
loud thy powers,
Triumphant conquest crown thy head, and
blessings pour down showers.

1 Pilgrim. Here's a strange turn of state: who would have thought
So great a lady would have match'd herself
Unto so mean a person? Yet the Cardinal
Bears himself much too cruel.

2 Pilgrim. They are banish'd.

1 Pilgrim. But I would ask what power hath this state
Of Ancona, to determine of° a free prince?

2 Pilgrim. They are a free state° sir, and her brother show'd
How that the Pope, forehearing of her looseness,
Hath seiz'd into th' protection of the Church
The dukedom which she held as dowager.

1 Pilgrim. But by what justice?

2 Pilgrim. Sure I think by none,
Only her brother's instigation.

1 Pilgrim. What was it, with such violence he took
Off from her finger?

III.iv.28 determine of make a decision about 29 free state i.e., a republic

2 Pilgrim. 'Twas her wedding-ring,
Which he vow'd shortly he would sacrifice
To his revenge.
1 Pilgrim. Alas Antonio!
If that a man be thrust into a well,
No matter who sets hand to't, his own weight
Will bring him sooner to th' bottom. Come, let's hence.
Fortune makes this conclusion general,
All things do help th'unhappy man to fall. [*Exeunt.*]

Scene v

[*Enter*] *Antonio, Duchess, Children, Cariola, Servants.*

Duchess. Banish'd Ancona?
Antonio. Yes, you see what power
Lightens in great men's breath.
Duchess. Is all our train
Shrunk to this poor remainder?
Antonio. These poor men,
Which have got little in your service, vow
To take your fortune. But your wiser buntings°
Now they are fledg'd are gone.
Duchess. They have done wisely;
This puts me in mind of death: physicians thus,
With their hands full of money, use to give o'er
Their patients.
Antonio. Right° the fashion of the world:
From decay'd fortunes every flatterer shrinks,
Men cease to build where the foundation sinks.
Duchess. I had a very strange dream tonight.
Antonio. What was't?
Duchess. Methought I wore my coronet of state,
And on a sudden all the diamonds
Were chang'd to pearls.
Antonio. My interpretation
Is, you'll weep shortly; for to me, the pearls
Do signify your tears.
Duchess. The birds, that live i'th' field

III.v.5 buntings small birds **9 Right** just

On the wild benefit of nature, live
Happier than we; for they may choose their mates,
And carol their sweet pleasures to the spring.

Enter Bosola with a letter.

Bosola. You are happily o'ertane.
Duchess. From my brother?
Bosola. Yes, from the Lord Ferdinand; your brother,
All love, and safety—
Duchess. Thou dost blanch mischief;°
Wouldst make it white. See, see; like to calm weather
At sea before a tempest, false hearts speak fair
To those they intend most mischief. [*She reads.*] *A Letter:*
Send Antonio to me; I want his head in a business.
(A politic equivocation°)
He doth not want your counsel, but your head;
That is, he cannot sleep till you be dead.
And here's another pitfall, that's strew'd o'er
With roses: mark it, 'tis a cunning one:
I stand engaged for your husband for several debts at Naples: let not that trouble him, I had rather have his heart than his money.
And I believe so too.
Bosola. What do you believe?
Duchess. That he so much distrusts my husband's love,
He will by no means believe his heart is with him
Until he see it. The devil is not cunning enough
To circumvent us in riddles.
Bosola. Will you reject that noble and free league
Of amity and love which I present you?
Duchess. Their league is like that of some politic kings
Only to make themselves of strength and power
To be our after-ruin: tell them so.
Bosola. And what from you?
Antonio. Thus tell them: I will not come.
Bosola. And what of this?
Antonio. My brothers° have dispers'd
Bloodhounds abroad; which till I hear are muzzl'd

23 **blanch mischief** whitewash (black) mischief 28 **politic equivocation** crafty double meaning 47 **brothers** i.e., brothers-in-law

No truce, though hatch'd with ne'er such politic skill
Is safe, that hangs upon our enemies' will.
I'll not come at them.

Bosola. This proclaims your breeding.
Every small thing draws a base mind to fear;
As the adamant° draws iron: fare you well sir,
You shall shortly hear from's. *Exit.*

Duchess. I suspect some ambush:
Therefore by all my love; I do conjure you
To take your eldest son, and fly towards Milan;
Let us not venture all this poor remainder
In one unlucky bottom.°

Antonio. You counsel safely.
Best of my life, farewell. Since we must part
Heaven hath a hand in't: but no otherwise
Than as some curious artist takes in sunder
A clock, or watch, when it is out of frame
To bring't in better order.

Duchess. I know not which is best,
To see you dead, or part with you. Farewell boy,
Thou art happy, that thou hast not understanding
To know thy misery. For all our wit
And reading brings us to a truer sense
Of sorrow. In the eternal Church, sir,
I do hope we shall not part thus.

Antonio. O be of comfort,
Make patience a noble fortitude:
And think not how unkindly° we are us'd.
Man, like to cassia, is prov'd best being bruis'd.

Duchess. Must I like to a slave-born Russian,
Account it praise to suffer tyranny?
And yet, O Heaven, thy heavy hand is in't.
I have seen my little boy oft scourge his top,
And compar'd myself to't: nought made me e'er go right,
But Heaven's scourge-stick.°

Antonio. Do not weep:
Heaven fashion'd us of nothing; and we strive
To bring ourselves to nothing. Farewell Cariola,
And thy sweet armful. [*To the Duchess.*] If I do never see thee more,

53 adamant loadstone **58 bottom** hold of a ship **71 unkindly** unnaturally **78 scourge-stick** whip used for child's top

Be a good mother to your little ones,
And save them from the tiger: fare you well.

Duchess: Let me look upon you once more: for that speech
Came from a dying father: your kiss is colder
Than I have seen an holy anchorite
Give to a dead man's skull.

Antonio. My heart is turn'd to a heavy lump of lead,
With which I sound° my danger: fare you well.

Exit [*with elder Son.*]

Duchess. My laurel° is all withered.

Cariola. Look, Madam, what a troop of armed men
Make toward us.

Enter Bosola with a guard [*with vizards°*].

Duchess. O, they are very welcome:
When Fortune's wheel is over-charg'd with princes,
The weight makes it move swift. I would have my ruin
Be sudden. I am your adventure,° am I not?

Bosola. You are: you must see your husband no more,—

Duchess. What devil art thou, that counterfeits Heaven's thunder?

Bosola. Is that terrible? I would have you tell me whether
Is that note worse that frights the silly birds
Out of the corn; or that which doth allure them
To the nets? You have heark'ned to the last too much.

Duchess. O misery! like to a rusty o'ercharg'd cannon,
Shall I never fly in pieces? Come: to what prison?

Bosola. To none.

Duchess. Whither then?

Bosola. To your palace.

Duchess. I have heard that Charon's boat serves to convey
All o'er the dismal lake, but brings none back again.

Bosola. Your brothers mean you safety and pity.

Duchess. Pity!
With such a pity men preserve alive
Pheasants and quails, when they are not fat enough
To be eaten.

89 **sound** measure the depth of 90 **laurel** (a sign of victory)
92 **s.d. vizards** masks 95 **adventure** quest

Bosola. These are your children?
Duchess. Yes.
Bosola. Can they prattle?
Duchess. No:
But I intend, since they were born accurs'd;
Curses shall be their first language.
Bosola. Fie, Madam!
Forget this base, low fellow.
Duchess. Were I a man,
I'll'd beat that counterfeit face° into thy other—
Bosola. One of no birth.
Duchess. Say that he was born mean,
Man is most happy, when's own actions
Be arguments and examples of his virtue.
Bosola. A barren, beggarly virtue.
Duchess. I prithee, who is greatest, can you tell?
Sad tales befit my woe: I'll tell you one.
A Salmon, as she swam unto the sea,
Met with a Dog-fish; who encounters her
With this rough language: 'Why art thou so bold
To mix thyself with our high state of floods
Being no eminent courtier, but one
That for the calmest and fresh time o'th' year
Dost live in shallow rivers, rank'st thyself
With silly Smelts and Shrimps? And darest thou
Pass by our Dog-ship without reverence?'
'O', quoth the Salmon, 'sister, be at peace:
Thank Jupiter, we both have pass'd the Net,
Our value never can be truly known,
Till in the Fisher's basket we be shown;
I'th' Market then my price may be the higher,
Even when I am nearest to the Cook, and fire.
So, to great men, the moral may be stretched.
Men oft are valued high, when th'are most wretch'd.
But come: whither you please. I am arm'd 'gainst misery:
Bent to all sways of the oppressor's will.
There's no deep valley, but near some great hill.
Ex[*eunt.*]

117 counterfeit face i.e., the vizard

Act IV, Scene i

[*Enter Ferdinand and Bosola.*]

Ferdinand. How doth our sister Duchess bear herself
In her imprisonment?
Bosola. Nobly: I'll describe her:
She's sad, as one long us'd to't: and she seems
Rather to welcome the end of misery
Than shun it: a behaviour so noble,
As gives a majesty to adversity:
You may discern the shape of loveliness
More perfect in her tears, than in her smiles;
She will muse four hours together: and her silence,
Methinks, expresseth more than if she spake.
Ferdinand. Her melancholy seems to be fortifi'd
With a strange disdain.
Bosola. 'Tis so: and this restraint
(Like English mastiffs, that grow fierce with tying)
Makes her too passionately apprehend
Those pleasures she's kept from.
Ferdinand. Curse upon her!
I will no longer study in the book
Of another's heart: inform her what I told you. *Exit.*

[*Enter Duchess and Servants.*]

Bosola. All comfort to your Grace;—
Duchess. I will have none.
'Pray-thee, why dost thou wrap thy poison'd pills
In gold and sugar?
Bosola. Your elder brother the Lord Ferdinand
Is come to visit you: and sends you word
'Cause once he rashly made a solemn vow
Never to see you more; he comes i'th' night;
And prays you, gently, neither torch nor taper
Shine in your chamber: he will kiss your hand;
And reconcile himself: but, for his vow,
He dares not see you.
Duchess. At his pleasure.
Take hence the lights: he's come.
[*Exeunt Servants with lights.*]

[*Enter Ferdinand.*]

Ferdinand. Where are you?
Duchess. Here sir.
Ferdinand. This darkness suits you well.
Duchess. I would ask your pardon.
Ferdinand. You have it;
For I account it the honorabl'st revenge
Where I may kill, to pardon: where are your cubs?
Duchess Whom?
Ferdinand. Call them your children;
For though our national law distinguish bastards
From true legitimate issue, compassionate nature
Makes them all equal.
Duchess. Do you visit me for this?
You violate a sacrament° o'th' Church
Shall make you howl in hell for't.
Ferdinand. It had been well,
Could you have liv'd thus always: for indeed
You were too much i'th' light.° But no more;
I come to seal my peace with you: here's a hand,
gives her a dead man's hand.
To which you have vow'd much love: the ring upon't
You gave.
Duchess. I affectionately kiss it.
Ferdinand. Pray do: and bury the print of it in your heart.
I will leave this ring with you, for a love-token:
And the hand, as sure as the ring: and do not doubt
But you shall have the heart too. When you need a friend
Send it to him that ow'd° it: you shall see
Whether he can aid you.
Duchess. You are very cold.
I fear you are not well after your travel:
Ha! Lights: O horrible!
Ha! Lights: [*Enter Servants with lights.*] O horrible!
Ferdinand. Let her have lights enough. *Exit.*
Duchess. What witchcraft doth he practise, that he hath left

IV.i.39 sacrament of marriage (?), of penance (?) 42 i'th' light in the public gaze 50 ow'd owned

A dead man's hand here?—

Here is discover'd,° behind a traverse, the artificial figures of Antonio and his children; appearing as if they were dead.

Bosola. Look you: here's the piece from which 'twas tane;
He doth present you this sad spectacle,
That now you know directly they are dead,
Hereafter you may, wisely, cease to grieve
For that which cannot be recovered.
Duchess. There is not between heaven and earth one wish
I stay for after this: it wastes me more,
Than were't my picture, fashion'd out of wax,
Stuck with a magical needle, and then buried
In some foul dunghill: and yond's an excellent property
For a tyrant, which I would account mercy,—
Bosola. What's that?
Duchess. If they would bind me to that lifeless trunk,
And let me freeze to death.
Bosola. Come, you must live.
Duchess. That's the greatest torture souls feel in hell,
In hell: that they must live, and cannot die.
Portia,° I'll new kindle thy coals again,
And revive the rare and almost dead example
Of a loving wife.
Bosola. O fie! despair? remember
You are a Christian.
Duchess. The Church enjoins fasting:
I'll starve myself to death.
Bosola. Leave this vain sorrow;
Things being at the worst, begin to mend:
The bee when he hath shot his sting into your hand
May then play with your eyelid.
Duchess. Good comfortable fellow
Persuade a wretch that's broke upon the wheel°
To have all his bones new set: entreat him live,
To be executed again. Who must dispatch me?
I account this world a tedious theatre,
For I do play a part in't 'gainst my will.

55 s.d. **discover'd** i.e., revealed by drawing of a curtain or traverse 72 **Portia** wife of Brutus; on learning of her husband's death, she kept hot coals in her mouth and so choked to death 80 **the wheel** an instrument of torture

Bosola. Come, be of comfort, I will save your life.
Duchess. Indeed I have not leisure to tend so small a
business.
Bosola. Now, by my life, I pity you.
Duchess. Thou are a fool then,
To waste thy pity on a thing so wretch'd
As cannot pity itself. I am full of daggers.
Puff! let me blow these vipers from me.
[*To one of the Servants.*]
What are you?
Servant. One that wishes you long life.
Duchess. I would thou wert hang'd for the horrible curse
Thou hast given me: I shall shortly grow one
Of the miracles of pity. I'll go pray. No,
I'll go curse.
Bosola. Oh fie!
Duchess. I could curse the stars.
Bosola. Oh fearful!
Duchess. And those three smiling seasons of the year
Into a Russian winter: nay the world
To its first chaos.
Bosola. Look you, the stars shine still.
Duchess. Oh, but you must
Remember, my curse hath a great way to go:
Plagues, that make lanes through largest families,
Consume them.
Bosola. Fie lady!
Duchess. Let them like tyrants
Never be rememb'red, but for the ill they have done:
Let all the zealous prayers of mortified
Churchmen forget them,—
Bosola. O uncharitable!
Duchess. Let Heaven, a little while, cease crowning martyrs
To punish them.
Go, howl them this: and say I long to bleed.
It is some mercy when men kill with speed. *Exit.*

[*Enter Ferdinand.*]

Ferdinand. Excellent; as I would wish: she's plagu'd in art.
These presentations are but fram'd in wax
By the curious master in that quality,

Vincentio Lauriola,° and she takes them
For true substantial bodies.
Bosola. Why do you do this?
Ferdinand. To bring her to despair.
Bosola. 'Faith,° end here;
And go no farther in your cruelty,
Send her a penitential garment,° to put on
Next to her delicate skin, and furnish her
With beads and prayerbooks.
Ferdinand. Damn her! that body of hers,
While that my blood ran pure in't, was more worth
Than that which thou wouldst comfort, call'd a soul.
I will send her masques° of common courtesans,
Have her meat serv'd up by bawds and ruffians,
And, 'cause she'll needs be mad, I am resolv'd
To remove forth° the common hospital
All the mad folk, and place them near her lodging:
There let them practise together, sing, and dance,
And act their gambols to the full o'th' moon:
If she can sleep the better for it, let her.
Your work is almost ended.
Bosola. Must I see her again?
Ferdinand. Yes.
Bosola. Never.
Ferdinand. You must.
Bosola. Never in mine own shape;
That's forfeited by my intelligence,
And this last cruel lie: when you send me next,
The business shall be comfort.
Ferdinand. Very likely:
Thy pity is nothing of kin to thee. Antonio
Lurks about Milan; thou shalt shortly thither,
To feed a fire as great as my revenge,
Which nev'r will slack, till it have spent his fuel;
Intemperate agues make physicians cruel. *Exeunt.*

113 Vincentio Lauriola unknown or fictional person **115 'Faith** in faith **117 penitential garment** of an adultress (?) **122 masques** courtly entertainments, mainly of dancing **125 forth** from

Scene ii

[*Enter Duchess and Cariola.*]

Duchess. What hideous noise was that?
Cariola. 'Tis the wild consort°
Of madmen, lady, which your tyrant brother
Hath plac'd about your lodging. This tyranny,
I think, was never practis'd till this hour.
Duchess. Indeed I thank him: nothing but noise, and folly
Can keep me in my right wits, whereas reason
And silence make me stark mad. Sit down,
Discourse to me some dismal tragedy.
Cariola. O 'twill increase your melancholy.
Duchess. Thou art deceiv'd;
To hear of greater grief would lessen mine.
This is a prison?
Cariola. Yes, but you shall live
To shake this durance° off.
Duchesss. Thou art a fool:
The robin red-breast and the nightingale
Never live long in cages.
Cariola. Pray dry your eyes.
What think you of Madam?
Duchess. Of nothing:
When I muse thus, I sleep.
Cariola. Like a madman, with your eyes open?
Duchess. Dost thou think we shall know one another
In th'other world?
Cariola. Yes, out of question.
Duchess. O that it were possible we might
But hold some two days' conference with the dead,
From them I should learn somewhat, I am sure
I never shall know here. I'll tell thee a miracle,
I am not mad yet, to my cause of sorrow.
Th'heaven o'er my head seems made of molten brass,
The earth of flaming sulphur, yet I am not mad.
I am acquainted with sad misery,
As the tann'd galley-slave is with his oar.

IV.ii.1 **consort** group, usually of musicians 12 **durance** confinement

Necessity makes me suffer constantly.
And custom makes it easy. Who do I look like now?
Cariola. Like to your picture in the gallery,
A deal of life in show, but none in practice:°
Or rather like some reverend monument
Whose ruins are even pitied.
Duchess. Very proper:
And Fortune seems only to have her eyesight,
To behold my tragedy.
How now! what noise is that?

[*Enter Servant.*]

Servant. I am come to tell you,
Your brother hath intended you some sport.
A great physician when the Pope was sick
Of a deep melancholy, presented him
With several sorts of madmen, which wild object,
Being full of change and sport, forc'd him to laugh,
And so th'imposthume° broke: the selfsame cure
The Duke intends on you.
Duchess. Let them come in.
Servant. There's a mad lawyer, and a secular priest,°
A doctor that hath forfeited his wits
By jealousy; an astrologian,
That in his works said such a day o'th' month
Should be the day of doom; and, failing of't,
Ran mad; an English tailor, craz'd i'th' brain
With the study of new fashion; a gentleman usher°
Quite beside himself with care to keep in mind
The number of his lady's salutations,
Or 'How do you?' she employ'd him in each morning:
A farmer too, an excellent knave in grain,°
Mad, 'cause he was hind'red transportation;°
And let one broker,° that's mad, loose to these,
You'ld think the devil were among them.

33 A deal . . . practice very lifelike in appearance, but not at all in action **44 imposthume** abscess **46 secular priest** one ministering in the world, not secluded in a monastery **52 gentleman usher** a gentleman acting as usher to a superior **56 knave in grain** an ingrained knave **57 transportation** export **58 broker** pawnbroker

Duchess. Sit Cariola: let them loose when you please, For I am chain'd to endure all your tyranny.

[*Enter Madmen.*]

Here, by a madman, this song is sung to a dismal kind of music.

O let us howl, some heavy note,
some deadly-dogged howl,
Sounding, as from the threat'ning throat,
of beasts, and fatal fowl.
As ravens, screech-owls, bulls, and bears,
We'll bill,° and bawl our parts,
Till yerksome° noise, have cloy'd your ears,
and corrosiv'd° your hearts.
At last when as our quire wants° breath,
our bodies being blest,
We'll sing like swans, to welcome death,
and die in love and rest.

Mad Astrologer. Doomsday not come yet? I'll draw it nearer by a perspective,° or make a glass, that shall set all the world on fire upon an instant. I cannot sleep, my pillow is stufft with a litter of porcupines.

Mad Lawyer. Hell is a mere glass-house,° where the devils are continually blowing up women's souls on hollow irons, and the fire never goes out.

Mad Priest. I will lie with every woman in my parish the tenth night: I will tithe them over like haycocks.

Mad Doctor. Shall my pothecary outgo me, because I am a cuckold? I have found out his roguery: he makes allum of his wife's urine, and sells it to Puritans, that have sore throats with over-straining.

Mad Astrologer. I have skill in heraldry.

Mad Lawyer. Hast?

Mad Astrologer. You do give for your crest a woodcock's head, with the brains pick'd out on't. You are a very ancient gentleman.

67 **bill** bellow 68 **yerksome** irksome 69 **corrosiv'd** corroded 70 **quire wants** choir lacks 75 **perspective** telescope 78 **glass-house** glass factory

Mad Priest. Greek is turn'd Turk; we are only to be sav'd by the Helvetian translation.°

Mad Astrologer [*to Lawyer.*]. Come on sir, I will lay° the law to you.

Mad Lawyer. Oh, rather lay a corrosive, the law will eat to the bone.

Mad Priest. He that drinks but to satisfy nature is damn'd.

Mad Doctor. If I had my glass here, I would show a sight should make all the women here call me mad doctor.

Mad Astrologer [*pointing to Priest.*]. What's he, a rope-maker?°

Mad Lawyer. No, no, no, a snuffling knave, that while he shows the tombs, will have his hand in a wench's placket.°

Mad Priest. Woe to the caroche that brought home my wife from the masque, at three o'clock in the morning; it had a large feather bed in it.

Mad Doctor. I have pared the devil's nails forty times, roasted them in raven's eggs, and cur'd agues with them.

Mad Priest. Get me three hundred milch bats, to make possets° to procure sleep.

Mad Doctor. All the college may throw their caps at° me, I have made a soap-boiler costive:° it was my master-piece:—

Here the dance consisting of 8 madmen, with music answerable thereunto, after which Bosola, like an old man, enters.

Duchess. Is he mad too?

Servant. Pray question him; I'll leave you.

[*Exeunt Servant and Madmen.*]

Bosola. I am come to make thy tomb.

Duchess. Ha! my tomb?
Thou speak'st as if I lay upon my death-bed,
Gasping for breath: dost thou perceive me sick?

92-3 **Greek . . . translation** (the mad priest, representing a Puritan parson, charges that the recent translations of the Greek New Testament [e.g., the King James version, 1611] have "turned Turk," i.e., faithless, and that the only salvation is in the Calvinist Genevan Bible of 1560) 94 **lay** expound 101-2 **ropemaker** i.e., one who makes the hangman's tool 105 **placket** slit in skirt 112 **possets** beverage of hot milk laced with wine and spices 114 **throw their caps at** emulate 114 **soap-boiler costive** soap-maker constipated

Bosola. Yes, and the more dangerously, since thy sickness is insensible.°

Duchess. Thou art not mad, sure; dost know me?

Bosola. Yes.

Duchess. Who am I?

Bosola. Thou art a box of worm seed, at best, but a salvatory of green mummy:° what's this flesh? a little cruded milk, fantastical puff-paste:° our bodies are weaker than those paper prisons boys use to keep flies in: more contemptible; since ours is to preserve earth-worms: didst thou ever see a lark in a cage? such is the soul in the body: this world is like her little turf of grass, and the heaven o'er our heads, like her looking-glass, only gives us a miserable knowledge of the small compass of our prison.

Duchess. Am not I thy Duchess?

Bosola. Thou art some great woman, sure; for riot begins to sit on thy forehead (clad in grey hairs) twenty years sooner than on a merry milkmaid's. Thou sleep'st worse, than if a mouse should be forc'd to take up her lodging in a cat's ear: a little infant, that breeds its teeth, should it lie with thee, would cry out, as if thou wert the more unquiet bedfellow.

Duchess. I am Duchess of Malfi still.

Bosola. That makes thy sleeps so broken:
Glories, like glow-worms, afar off shine bright,
But look'd to near, have neither heat nor light.

Duchess. Thou art very plain.

Bosola. My trade is to flatter the dead, not the living;
I am a tomb-maker.

Duchess. And thou com'st to make my tomb?

Bosola. Yes.

Duchess. Let me be a little merry;
Of what stuff wilt thou make it?

Bosola. Nay, resolve me first, of what fashion?

Duchess. Why, do we grow fantastical in our death-bed?
Do we affect fashion in the grave?

Bosola. Most ambitiously. Princes' images on their tombs
Do not lie as they were wont, seeming to pray

121 **insensible** unfelt 126 **salvatory of green mummy** box of unripe mummia (a medicine prepared from mummies) 127 **puff-paste** a light pastry

Up to Heaven: but with their hands under their cheeks,
As if they died of the tooth-ache; they are not carved
With their eyes fix'd upon the stars; but as
Their minds were wholly bent upon the world,
The self-same way they seem to turn their faces.
Duchess. Let me know fully therefore the effect
Of this thy dismal preparation,
This talk, fit for a charnel.
Bosola. Now I shall;

[*Enter Executioners with*] *a coffin, cords, and a bell.*

Here is a present from your princely brothers,
And may it arrive welcome, for it brings
Last benefit, last sorrow.
Duchess. Let me see it.
I have so much obedience, in my blood,
I wish it in their veins, to do them good.
Bosola. This is your last presence chamber.
Cariola. O my sweet lady!
Duchess. Peace; it affrights not me.
Bosola. I am the common bellman,
That usually is sent to condemn'd persons,
The night before they suffer.
Duchess. Even now thou said'st
Thou wast a tomb-maker?
Bosola. 'Twas to bring you
By degrees to mortification. Listen: [*rings the bell.*]
Hark, now every thing is still,
The screech-owl and the whistler° shrill
Call upon our Dame, aloud,
And bid her quickly don her shroud.
Much you had of land and rent,°
Your length in clay's now competent.°
A long war disturb'd your mind,
Here your perfect peace is sign'd.
Of what is't fools make such vain keeping?
Sin their conception, their birth, weeping:
Their life, a general mist of error,
Their death, a hideous storm of terror.

180 **whistler** one of several birds of ill omen, having a piercing cry 183 **rent** revenue 184 **competent** sufficient

Strew your hair with powders sweet:
Don clean linen, bath your feet,
And, the foul fiend more to check,
A crucifix let bless your neck.
'Tis now full tide 'tween night and day,
End your groan, and come away.

Cariola. Hence villains, tyrants, murderers. Alas!
What will you do with my lady? Call for help.
Duchess. To whom, to our next neighbors? They are madfolks.
Bosola. Remove that noise. [*Attendants seize Cariola.*]
Duchess. Farewell Cariola,
In my last will I have not much to give;
A many hungry guests have fed upon me,
Thine will be a poor reversion.°
Cariola. I will die with her.
Duchess. I pray thee look thou giv'st my little boy
Some syrup for his cold, and let the girl
Say her prayers, ere she sleep.
[*Attendants take Cariola out.*]
Now what you please,
What death?
Bosola. Strangling: here are your executioners.
Duchess. I forgive them:
The apoplexy, catarrh,° or cough o'th' lungs
Would do as much as they do.
Bosola. Doth not death fright you?
Duchess. Who would be afraid on't?
Knowing to meet such excellent company
In th'other world.
Bosola. Yet, methinks,
The manner of your death should much afflict you,
This cord should terrify you?
Duchess. Not a whit:
What would it pleasure me, to have my throat cut
With diamonds? or to be smothered
With cassia? or to be shot to death, with pearls?
I know death hath ten thousand several doors
For men to take their *Exits*: and 'tis found

203 **reversion** succession 209 **catarrh** cerebral hemorrhage

They go on such strange geometrical hinges,
You may open them both ways: any way, for Heaven sake,
So I were out of your whispering. Tell my brothers
That I perceive death, now I am well awake,
Best gift is, they can give, or I can take.
I would fain put off my last woman's fault,
I'll'd not be tedious to you.
Executioners. We are ready.
Duchess. Dispose my breath how please you, but my body
Bestow upon my women, will you?
Executioners. Yes.
Duchess. Pull, and pull strongly, for your able strength
Must pull down heaven upon me:
Yet stay, heaven gates are not so highly arch'd
As princes' palaces: they that enter there
Must go upon their knees. [*kneels.*] Come violent death,
Serve for mandragora to make me sleep;
Go tell my brothers, when I am laid out,
They then may feel in quiet. *They strangle her.*
Bosola. Where's the waiting woman?
Fetch her. [*Exeunt several Executioners.*]
Some other strangle the children.
[*Exit Executioner; the others bring in Cariola.*]
Look you, there sleeps your mistress.
Cariola. O you are damn'd
Perpetually for this. My turn is next,
Is't not so ordered?
Bosola. Yes, and I am glad
You are so well prepar'd for't.
Cariola. You are deceiv'd sir,
I am not prepar'd for't. I will not die,
I will first come to my answer;° and know
How I have offended.
Bosola. Come, dispatch her.
You kept her counsel, now you shall keep ours.
Cariola. I will not die, I must not, I am contracted
To a young gentleman.
Executioner [*showing the noose.*]. Here's your wedding-ring.

244 **come to my answer** make a legal defense

Cariola. Let me but speak with the Duke. I'll discover
Treason to his person.
Bosola. Delays: throttle her.
Executioner. She bites: and scratches.
Cariola. If you kill me now
I am damn'd. I have not been at confession
This two years.
Bosola. When!
Cariola. I am quick with child.
Bosola. Why then,
Your credit's sav'd: [*They strangle her.*]
bear her into th' next room.
Let this° lie still.
[*Exeunt Executioners with Cariola's body.*]

[*Enter Ferdinand.*]

Ferdinand. Is she dead?
Bosola. She is what
You'd have her. But here begin your pity,
Shows° the children strangled.
Alas, how have these offended?
Ferdinand. The death
Of young wolves is never to be pitied.
Bosola. Fix your eye here.
Ferdinand. Constantly.
Bosola. Do you not weep?
Other sins only speak; murther shrieks out:
The element of water moistens the earth,
But blood flies upwards, and bedews the heavens.
Ferdinand. Cover her face. Mine eyes dazzle: she di'd young.
Bosola. I think not so: her infelicity
Seem'd to have years too many.
Ferdinand. She and I were twins:
And should I die this instant, I had liv'd
Her time to a minute.
Bosola. It seems she was born first:
You have bloodily approv'd° the ancient truth,

252 **this** i.e., the Duchess' body 255 s.d. **Shows** (probably Bosola draws a curtain to reveal the children's bodies) 268 **approv'd** proved

That kindred commonly do worse agree
Than remote strangers.
Ferdinand. Let me see her face again;
Why didst not thou pity her? What an excellent
Honest man might'st thou have been
If thou hadst borne her to some sanctuary!
Or, bold in a good cause, oppos'd thyself
With thy advanced sword above thy head,
Between her innocence and my revenge!
I bad thee, when I was distracted of my wits,
Go kill my dearest friend, and thou hast done't.
For let me but examine well the cause;
What was the meanness of her match to me?
Only I must confess, I had a hope,
Had she continu'd widow; to have gain'd
An infinite mass of treasure by her death:
And that was the main cause; her marriage,
That drew a stream of gall quite through my heart;
For thee, (as we observe in tragedies
That a good actor many times is curs'd
For playing a villain's part) I hate thee for't:
And, for my sake, say thou hast done much ill, well.
Bosola. Let me quicken your memory: for I perceive
You are falling into ingratitude. I challenge
The reward due to my service.
Ferdinand. I'll tell thee,
What I'll give thee—
Bosola. Do.
Ferdinand. I'll give thee a pardon
For this murther.
Bosola. Ha?
Ferdinand. Yes: and 'tis
The largest bounty I can study to do thee.
By what authority didst thou execute
This bloody sentence?
Bosola. By yours.
Ferdinand. Mine? Was I her judge?
Did any ceremonial form of law
Doom her to not-being? did a complete jury
Deliver her conviction up i'th' court?
Where shalt thou find this judgment register'd
Unless in hell? See: like a bloody fool
Th'hast forfeited thy life, and thou shalt die for't.

Bosola. The office of justice is perverted quite
When one thief hangs another: who shall dare
To reveal this?
Ferdinand. Oh, I'll tell thee:
The wolf shall find her grave, and scrape it up;
Not to devour the corpse, but to discover
The horrid murther.
Bosola. You; not I shall quake for't.
Ferdinand. Leave me.
Bosola. I will first receive my pension.
Ferdinand. You are a villain.
Bosola. When your ingratitude
Is judge, I am so—
Ferdinand. O horror!
That not the fear of him which binds the devils
Can prescribe man obedience.
Never look upon me more.
Bosola. Why fare thee well:
Your brother and yourself are worthy men;
You have a pair of hearts are hollow graves,
Rotten, and rotting others: and your vengeance,
Like two chain'd bullets,° still goes arm in arm;
You may be brothers: for treason, like the plague,
Doth take much in a blood.° I stand like one
That long hath tane a sweet and golden dream.
I am angry with myself, now that I wake.
Ferdinand. Get thee into some unknown part o'th' world
That I may never see thee.
Bosola. Let me know
Wherefore I should be thus neglected? Sir,
I served your tyranny: and rather strove
To satisfy yourself, than all the world;
And though I loath'd the evil, yet I lov'd
You that did counsel it: and rather sought
To appear a true servant than an honest man.
Ferdinand. I'll go hunt the badger by owl-light:
'Tis a deed of darkness. *Exit.*
Bosola. He's much distracted. Off my painted honour!°

319 **chain'd bullets** cannon balls chained together 321 **take much in a blood** runs in families 334 **painted honour** false honor (in the Duchess' household) or false appearance (of honoring Ferdinand)

While with vain hopes our faculties we tire,
We seem to sweat in ice and freeze in fire;
What would I do, were this to do again?
I would not change my peace of conscience
For all the wealth of Europe. She stirs; here's life.
Return, fair soul, from darkness, and lead mine
Out of this sensible° hell. She's warm, she breathes:
Upon thy pale lips I will melt my heart
To store them with fresh colour. Who's there?
Some cordial drink! Alas! I dare not call:
So pity would destroy pity: her eye opes,
And heaven in it seems to ope, that late was shut,
To take me up to mercy.

Duchess. Antonio!

Bosola. Yes, Madam, he is living,
The dead bodies you saw were but feign'd statues;
He's reconcil'd to your brothers: the Pope hath wrought
The atonement.°

Duchess. Mercy. *she dies.*

Bosola. Oh, she's gone again: there the cords of life broke.
Oh sacred innocence, that sweetly sleeps
On turtles'° feathers: whilst a guilty conscience
Is a black register, wherein is writ
All our good deeds and bad; a perspective°
That shows us hell; that we cannot be suffer'd
To do good when we have a mind to it!
This is manly sorrow:
These tears, I am very certain, never grew
In my mother's milk. My estate is sunk
Below the degree of fear: where were
These penitent fountains while she was living?
Oh, they were frozen up: here is a sight
As direful to my soul as is the sword
Unto a wretch hath slain his father. Come,
I'll bear thee hence,
And execute thy last will; that's deliver
Thy body to the reverend dispose
Of some good women: that the cruel tyrant
Shall not deny me. Then I'll post to Milan,

341 **sensible** palpable 351 **atonement** reconciliation 354 **turtles'** turtledoves, 356 **perspective** i.e., magnifying glass

Where somewhat I will speedily enact
Worth my dejection. *Exit [with body of the Duchess.]*

Act V, Scene i

[Enter Antonio and Delio.]

Antonio. What think you of my hope of reconcilement
To the Aragonian brethren?
Delio. I misdoubt it
For though they have sent their letters of safe conduct
For your repair° to Milan, they appear
But nets to entrap you. The Marquis of Pescara,
Under whom you hold certain land in cheat,°
Much 'gainst his noble nature, hath been mov'd
To seize those lands, and some of his dependants
Are at this instant making it their suit
To be invested in your revenues.
I cannot think they mean well to your life,
That do deprive you of your means of life,
Your living.
Antonio. You are still an heretic.
To any safety I can shape myself.
Delio. Here comes the Marquis. I will make myself
Petitioner for some part of your land,
To know whither it is flying.
Antonio. I pray do.

[Enter Pescara.]

Delio. Sir, I have a suit to you.
Pescara. To me?
Delio. An easy one:
There is the citadel of St. Bennet,°
With some demenses,° of late in the possession
Of Antonio Bologna; please you bestow them on me?

V.i.4 **repair** stay 6 **in cheat** i.e., subject to "escheat" (chance); land so held reverted to the lord of the fee in the event the landholder died without heirs or committed a crime 19 **St. Bennet** St. Benedict 20 **demenses** properly demesnes, land occupied by its owner

Pescara. You are my friend. But this is such a suit
Nor fit for me to give, nor you to take.
Delio. No sir?
Pescara. I will give you ample reason for't
Soon, in private. Here's the Cardinal's mistress.

[*Enter Julia.*]

Julia. My lord, I am grown your poor petitioner,
And should be an ill beggar, had I not
A great man's letter here, the Cardinal's
To court you in my favour. [*She gives him letter.*]
Pescara. He entreats for you
The citadel of Saint Bennet, that belong'd
To the banish'd Bologna.
Julia. Yes.
Pescara. I could not have thought of a friend I could
Rather pleasure with it: 'tis yours.
Julia. Sir, I thank you:
And he shall know how doubly I am engag'd
Both in your gift, and speediness of giving,
Which makes your grant the greater. *Exit.*
Antonio [*aside.*]. How they fortify
Themselves with my ruin!
Delio. Sir, I am
Little bound to you.
Pescara. Why?
Delio. Because you deni'd this suit to me, and gave't
To such a creature.
Pescara. Do you know what it was?
It was Antonio's land: not forfeited
By course of law; but ravish'd from his throat
By the Cardinal's entreaty: it were not fit
I should bestow so main a piece of wrong
Upon my friend: 'tis a gratification
Only due to a strumpet; for it is injustice.
Shall I sprinkle the pure blood of innocents
To make those followers I call my friends
Look ruddier upon me? I am glad
This land, tane from the owner by such wrong.
Returns again unto so foul an use,
As salary for his lust. Learn, good Delio,

To ask noble things of me, and you shall find
I'll be a noble giver.
Delio. You instruct me well.
Antonio [*aside.*]. Why, here's a man, now, would fright impudence
From sauciest beggars.
Pescare. Prince Ferdinand's come to Milan
Sick, as thy give out, of an apoplexy:
But some say 'tis a frenzy; I am going
To visit him. *Exit.*
Antonio. 'Tis a noble old fellow:
Delio. What course do you mean to take, Antonio?
Antonio. This night I mean to venture all my fortune,
Which is no more than a poor ling'ring life,
To the Cardinal's worst of malice. I have got
Private access to his chamber: and intend
To visit him, about the mid of night,
As once his brother did our noble Duchess.
It may be that the sudden apprehension
Of danger (for I'll go in mine own shape)
When he shall see it fraught with love and duty,
May draw the poison out of him, and work
A friendly reconcilement: if it fail,
Yet it shall rid me of this infamous calling,
For better fall once, than be ever falling.
Delio. I'll second you in all danger: and, howe'er,
My life keeps rank with yours.
Antonio. You are still my lov'd and best friend. *Exeunt.*

Scene ii

[*Enter Pescara and Doctor.*]

Pescara. Now doctor, may I visit your patient?
Doctor. If't please your lordship: but he's instantly
To take the air here in the gallery,
By my direction.
Pescara. Pray thee, what's his disease?
Doctor. A very pestilent disease, my lord,
They call lycanthropia.°

V.ii.6 **lycanthropia** (the Doctor describes a disease which, despite fables about it, was a genuine mania)

Pescara. What's that?
I need a dictionary to't.
Doctor. I'll tell you:
In those that are possess'd with't there o'erflows
Such melancholy humour, they imagine
Themselves to be transformed into wolves.
Steal forth to churchyards in the dead of night,
And dig dead bodies up: as two nights since
One met the Duke, 'bout midnight in a lane
Behind St. Mark's church, with the leg of a man
Upon his shoulder; and he howl'd fearfully:
Said he was a wolf: only the difference
Was, a wolf's skin was hairy on the outside,
His on the inside: bad them take their swords,
Rip up his flesh, and try: straight I was sent for,
And having minister'd to him, found his Grace
Very well recovered.
Pescara. I am glad on't.
Doctor. Yet not without some fear
Of a relapse: if he grow to his fit again
I'll go a nearer° way to work with him
Than ever Paracelsus° dream'd of. If
They'll give me leave, I'll buffet his madness out of him.
Stand aside: he comes.

[*Enter Ferdinand, Cardinal, Malateste with Bosola following.*]

Ferdinand. Leave me.
Malateste. Why doth your lordship love this solitariness?
Ferdinand. Eagles commonly fly alone. They are crows, daws, and starlings that flock together. Look, what's that follows me?
Malateste. Nothing, my lord.
Ferdinand. Yes.
Malateste. 'Tis your shadow.
Ferdinand. Stay it; let it not haunt me.
Malateste. Impossible, if you move, and the sun shine.
Ferdinand. I will throttle it.
[*Throws himself upon his shadow.*]

24 **nearer** more direct 25 **Paracelsus** notable early-sixteenth-century physician-magician

Malateste. Oh, my lord: you are angry with nothing.

Ferdinand. You are a fool. How is't possible I should catch my shadow unless I fall upon't? When I go to hell, I mean to carry a bribe: for look you, good gifts evermore make way for the worst persons.

Pescara. Rise, good my lord.

Ferdinand. I am studying the art of patience.

Pescara. 'Tis a noble virtue;—

Ferdinand. To drive six snails before me, from this town to Moscow; neither use goad nor whip to them, but let them take their own time: (the patient'st man i'th' world match me for an experiment) and I'll crawl after like a sheep-biter.°

Cardinal. Force him up. [*They raise Ferdinand.*]

Ferdinand. Use me well, you were best.
What I have done, I have done: I'll confess nothing.

Doctor. Now let me come to him. Are you mad, my lord?
Are you out of your princely wits?

Ferdinand. What's he?

Pescara. Your doctor.

Ferdinand. Let me have his beard saw'd off, and his eye-brows
Fil'd more civil.°

Doctor. I must do mad tricks with him,
For that's the only way on't. I have brought
Your Grace a salamander's skin, to keep you
From sun-burning.

Ferdinand. I have cruel sore eyes.

Doctor. The white of a cockatrice's° egg is present° remedy.

Ferdinand. Let it be a new-laid one, you were best.
Hide me from him. Physicians are like kings,
They brook no contradiction.

Doctor. Now he begins
To fear me; now let me alone with him.

Cardinal. How now, put off your gown?

Doctor. Let me have some forty urinals filled with rose-water: he and I'll go pelt one another with them; now he begins to fear me. Can you fetch a frisk,° sir?

51 **sheep-biter** dog that harries sheep, hence a sneaking thief 58 **civil** decent, polite 62 **cockatrice's** cockatrice = basilisk, a fabled serpent whose glance was deadly 62 **present** immediate 70 **fetch a frisk** cut a caper

Let him go, let him go upon my peril. I find by his eye, he stands in awe of me: I'll make him as tame as a dormouse.

Ferdinand. Can you fetch your frisks, sir! I will stamp him into a cullis;° flay off his skin, to cover one of the anatomies,° this rogue hath set i'th' cold yonder, in Barber-Chirurgeons' Hall.° [*beats Doctor.*] Hence, hence! you are all of you like beasts for sacrifice, there's nothing left of you, but tongue and belly, flattery and lechery. [*Exit.*]

Pescara. Doctor, he did not fear you throughly.

Doctor. True, I was somewhat too forward.

Bosola [*aside.*]. Mercy upon me, what a fatal judgment
Hath fall'n upon this Ferdinand!

Pescara. Knows your Grace
What accident hath brought unto the Prince
This strange distraction?

Cardinal [*aside.*]. I must feign somewhat. Thus they say it grew:
You have heard it rumour'd for these many years,
None of our family dies, but there is seen
The shape of an old woman, which is given
By tradition, to us, to have been murther'd
By her nephews, for her riches. Such a figure
One night, as the Prince sat up late at's book,
Appear'd to him; when crying out for help,
The gentlemen of's chamber found his Grace
All on a cold sweat, alter'd much in face
And language. Since which apparition
He hath grown worse and worse, and I much fear
He cannot live.

Bosola. Sir, I would speak with you.

Pescara. We'll leave your Grace,
Wishing to the sick Prince, our noble lord,
All health of mind and body.

Cardinal. You are most welcome.
[*Exeunt Pescara, Malateste and Doctor.*]
[*aside.*] Are you come? So: this fellow must not know
By any means I had intelligence

75 **cullis** broth 76 **anatomies** skeletons used in medical studies
76-7 **Barber-Chirurgeons' Hall** the meeting place for barbers and surgeons, men of the same profession at that time

In our Duchess' death. For, though I counsell'd it,
The full of all the engagement° seem'd to grow
From Ferdinand. Now sir, how fares our sister?
I do not think but sorrow makes her look
Like to an oft-dy'd garment. She shall now
Taste comfort from me: why do you look so wildly?
Oh, the fortune of your master here, the Prince
Dejects you, but be you of happy comfort:
If you'll do one thing for me I'll entreat,
Though he had a cold tombstone o'er his bones,
I'll'd make you what you would be.

Bosola. Any thing;
Give it me in a breath, and let me fly to't:
They that think long, small expedition win,
For musing much o'th' end, cannot begin.

[*Enter Julia.*]

Julia. Sir, will you come in to supper?

Cardinal. I am busy, leave me.

Julia [*aside.*]. What an excellent shape hath that fellow!
Exit.

Cardinal. 'Tis thus: Antonio lurks here in Milan;
Inquire him out, and kill him: while he lives
Our sister cannot marry, and I have thought
Of an excellent match for her: do this, and style me
Thy advancement.°

Bosola. But by what means shall I find him out?

Cardinal. There is a gentleman, call'd Delio
Here in the camp, that hath been long approv'd
His loyal friend. Set eye upon that fellow,
Follow him to mass; may be Antonio,
Although he do account religion
But a school-name, for fashion of the world,
May accompany him: or else go inquire out
Delio's confessor, and see if you can bribe
Him to reveal it: there are a thousand ways
A man might find to trace him: as, to know

106 The full . . . engagement the full responsibility for engaging Bosola as a spy **124 style me . . . advancement** name how I shall reward you

What fellows haunt the Jews for taking up
Great sums of money, for sure he's in want;
Or else go to th' picture-makers, and learn
Who brought her picture lately: some of these
Happily may take—

Bosola. Well, I'll not freeze i'th' business,
I would see that wretched thing, Antonio,
Above all sights i'th' world.

Cardinal. Do, and be happy. *Exit.*

Bosola. This fellow doth breed basalisks in's eyes,
He's nothing else but murder: yet he seems
Not to have notice of the Duchess' death.
'Tis his cunning: I must follow his example;
There cannot be a surer way to trace,
Than that of an old fox.

[*Enter Julia with a pistol.*]

Julia. So, sir, you are well met.

Bosola. How now?

Julia. Nay, the doors are fast enough.
Now sir, I will make you confess your treachery.

Bosola. Treachery?

Julia. Yes, confess to me
Which of my women 'twas you hir'd, to put
Love-powder into my drink?

Bosola. Love-powder?

Julia. Yes, when I was at Malfi;
Why should I fall in love with such a face else?
I have already suffer'd for thee so much pain,
The only remedy to do me good
Is to kill my longing.

Bosola. Sure, your pistol holds
Nothing but perfumes or kissing-comfits:° excellent lady,
You have a pretty way on't to discover
Your longing. Come, come, I'll disarm you
And arm you thus: [*embraces her.*] yet this is wondrous strange.

Julia. Compare thy form and my eyes together,
You'll find my love no such great miracle.
Now you'll say

159 kissing-comfits breath sweeteners

I am a wanton. This nice modesty in ladies
Is but a troublesome familiar°
That haunts them.
Bosola. Know you me, I am a blunt soldier.
Julia. The better:
Sure, there wants fire where there are no lively sparks
Of roughness.
Bosola. And I want compliment.°
Julia. Why, ignorance
In courtship cannot make you do amiss,
If you have a heart to do well.
Bosola. You are very fair.
Julia. Nay, if you lay beauty to my charge,
I must plead unguilty.
Bosola. Your bright eyes
Carry a quiver of darts in them, sharper
Than sunbeams.
Julia. You will mar me with commendation,
Put yourself to the charge of courting me,
Whereas now I woo you.
Bosola [*aside*.].I have it, I will work upon this creature—
Let us grow most amorously familiar.
If the great Cardinal now should see me thus,
Would he not count me a villain?
Julia. No, he might count me a wanton,
Not lay a scruple° of offence on you:
For if I see, and steal a diamond,
The fault is not i'th' stone, but in me the thief
That purloins it. I am sudden with you;
We that are great women of pleasure, use to cut off
These uncertain wishes and unquiet longings,
And in an instant join the sweet delight
And the pretty excuse together: had you been i'th' street,
Under my chamber window, even there
I should have courted you.
Bosola. Oh, you are an excellent lady.
Julia. Bid me do somewhat for you presently
To express I love you.
Bosola. I will, and if you love me,
Fail not to effect it.

167 **familiar** devilish spirit 171 **want compliment** lack refined manners 185 **scruple** minutest bit

The Cardinal is grown wondrous melancholy,
Demand the cause, let him not put you off
With feign'd excuse; discover the main ground on't.
Julia. Why would you know this?
Bosola. I have depended on him,
And I hear that he is fall'n in some disgrace
With the Emperor: if he be, like the mice
That forsake falling houses, I would shift
To other dependence.
Julia. You shall not need follow the wars:
I'll be your maintenance.
Bosola. And I your loyal servant;
But I cannot leave my calling.
Julia. Not leave an
Ungrateful general for the love of a sweet lady?
You are like some, cannot sleep in feather-beds,
But must have blocks for their pillows.
Bosola. Will you do this?
Julia. Cunningly.
Bosola. Tomorrow I'll expect th'intelligence.
Julia. Tomorrow? get you into my cabinet,
You shall have it with you: do not delay me,
No more than I do you. I am like one
That is condemn'd: I have my pardon promis'd,
But I would see it seal'd. Go, get you in,
You shall see me wind my tongue about his heart
Like a skein of silk. [*Bosola withdraws.*]

[*Enter Cardinal followed by Servants.*]

Cardinal. Where are you?
Servants. Here.
Cardinal. Let none upon your lives
Have conference with the Prince Ferdinand,
Unless I know it. [*Exeunt Servants.*] In this distraction
He may reveal the murther.
Yond's my ling'ring consumption:
I am weary of her; and by any means
Would be quit of—
Julia. How now, my Lord?
What ails you?
Cardinal. Nothing.
Julia. Oh, you are much alter'd:

Come, I must be your secretary,° and remove
This lead from off your bosom; what's the matter?
Cardinal. I may not tell you.
Julia. Are you so far in love with sorrow,
You cannot part with part of it? or think you
I cannot love your Grace when you are sad,
As well as merry? or do you suspect
I, that have been a secret to your heart
These many winters, cannot be the same
Unto your tongue?
Cardinal. Satisfy thy longing.
The only way to make thee keep my counsel
Is not to tell thee.
Julia. Tell your echo this,
Or flatterers, that, like echoes, still report
What they hear, though most imperfect, and not me:
For, if that you be true unto yourself,
I'll know.
Cardinal. Will you rack me?
Julia. No, judgment shall
Draw it from you. It is an equal fault,
To tell one's secrets unto all, or none.
Cardinal. The first argues folly.
Julia. But the last tyranny.
Cardinal. Very well; why, imagine I have committed
Some secret deed which I desire the world
May never hear of!
Julia. Therefore may not I know it?
You have conceal'd for me as great a sin
As adultery. Sir, never was occasion
For perfect trial of my constancy
Till now. Sir, I beseech you.
Cardinal. You'll repent it.
Julia. Never.
Cardinal. It hurries thee to ruin: I'll not tell thee.
Be well advis'd, and think what danger 'tis
To receive a prince's secrets: they that do,
Had need have their breasts hoop'd with adamant
To contain them. I pray thee yet be satisfi'd,
Examine thine own frailty; 'tis more easy

229 secretary confidant

To tie knots, than unloose them: 'tis a secret
That, like a ling'ring poison, may chance lie
Spread in thy veins, and kill thee seven year hence.
Julia. Now you dally with me.
Cardinal. No more; thou shalt know it:
By my appointment the great Duchess of Malfi
And two of her young children, four nights since
Were strangled.
Julia. Oh Heaven! Sir, what have you done?
Cardinal. How now? how settles this?° Think you your bosom
Will be a grave dark and obscure enough
For such a secret?
Julia. You have undone yourself, sir.
Cardinal. Why?
Julia. It lies not in me to conceal it.
Cardinal. No?
Come, I will swear you to't upon this book.
Julia. Most religiously.
Cardinal. Kiss it. [*She kisses the book.*°]
Now you shall never utter it; thy curiosity
Hath undone thee; thou'rt poison'd with that book.
Because I knew thou couldst not keep my counsel,
I have bound thee to't by death.

[*Enter Bosola.*]

Bosola. For pity-sake, hold.
Cardinal. Ha, Bosola!
Julia. I forgive you
This equal piece of justice you have done:
For I betray'd your counsel to that fellow;
He overheard it; that was the cause I said
It lay not in me to conceal it.
Bosola. Oh foolish woman,
Couldst not thou have poison'd him?
Julia. 'Tis weakness,
Too much to think what should have been done. I go,
I know not whither. [*Dies.*]
Cardinal. Wherefore com'st thou hither?

267 **how settles this?** how does this sink in? 272 s.d. **book** (probably a Bible)

Bosola. That I might find a great man, like yourself,
Not out of his wits, as the Lord Ferdinand,
To remember my service.
Cardinal. I'll have thee hew'd in pieces.
Bosola. Make not yourself such a promise of that life
Which is not yours to dispose of.
Cardinal. Who plac'd thee here?
Bosola. Her lust, as she intended.
Cardinal. Very well;
Now you know me for your fellow murderer.
Bosola. And wherefore should you lay fair marble colours
Upon your rotten purposes° to me?
Unless you imitate some that do plot great treasons,
And when they have done, go hide themselves i'th' graves
Of those were actors in't.
Cardinal. No more: there is a fortune attends thee.
Bosola. Shall I go sue to Fortune any longer?
'Tis the fool's pilgrimage.
Cardinal. I have honours in store for thee.
Bosola. There are a many ways that conduct to seeming
Honour, and some of them very dirty ones.
Cardinal. Throw to the devil
Thy melancholy; the fire burns well,
What need we keep a stirring of't, and make
A greater smother? Thou wilt kill Antonio?
Bosola. Yes.
Cardinal. Take up that body.
Bosola. I think I shall
Shortly grow the common bier for churchyards!
Cardinal. I will allow thee some dozen of attendants,
To aid thee in the murther.
Bosola. Oh, by no means: physicians that apply horse-leeches to any rank swelling, use to cut off their tails, that the blood may run through them the faster. Let me have no train, when I go to shed blood, lest it make me have a greater, when I ride to the gallows.
Cardinal. Come to me after midnight, to help to remove that body

292-3 lay fair marble . . . purposes (alludes to the painting of wood to imitate marble; here the wood, i.e., purposes, is rotten)

To her own lodging. I'll give out she di'd o'th' plague;
'Twill breed the less inquiry after her death.
Bosola. Where's Castruchio her husband?
Cardinal. He's rode to Naples to take possession
Of Antonio's citadel.
Bosola. Believe me, you have done a very happy turn.
Cardinal. Fail not to come. There is the master-key
Of our lodgings: and by that you may conceive
What trust I plant in you. ***Exit.***
Bosola. You shall find me ready.
Oh poor Antonio, though nothing be so needful
To thy estate, as pity, yet I find
Nothing so dangerous. I must look to my footing;
In such slipper ice-pavements men had need
To be frost-nail'd well: they may break their necks else.
The precedent's here afore me: how this man°
Bears up in blood! seems fearless! Why, 'tis well:
Security° some men call the suburbs of hell,
Only a dead wall between. Well, good Antonio,
I'll seek thee out; and all my care shall be
To put thee into safety from the reach
Of these most cruel biters, that have got
Some of thy blood already. It may be,
I'll join with thee in a most just revenge.
The weakest arm is strong enough, that strikes
With the sword of justice. Still methinks the Duchess
Haunts me: there, there: t'is nothing but my
melancholy.
O penitence, let me truly taste thy cup,
That throws men down, only to raise them up. ***Exit.***

Scene iii

[*Enter*] *Antonio and Delio;* [*there is an*] *Echo from the Duchess' grave.*

Delio. Yond's the Cardinal's window. This fortification
Grew from the ruins of an ancient abbey:
And to yond side o'th' river lies a wall,

330 this man i.e., the Cardinal 332 Security overconfidence in one's safety

Piece of a cloister, which in my opinion
Gives the best echo that you ever heard;
So hollow, and so dismal, and withal
So plain in the distinction of our words,
That many have suppos'd it is a spirit
That answers.

Antonio. I do love these ancient ruins:
We never tread upon them, but we set
Our foot upon some reverend history,
And, questionless,° here in this open court,
Which now lies naked to the injuries
Of stormy weather, some men lie interr'd
Lov'd the church so well, and gave so largely to't,
They thought it should have canopi'd their bones
Till doomsday. But all things have their end:
Churches and cities, which have diseases like to men,
Must have like death that we have.

Echo. *Like death that we have.*

Delio. Now the echo hath caught you.

Antonio. It groan'd, methought, and gave
A very deadly accent!

Echo. *Deadly accent.*

Delio. I told you 'twas a pretty one. You may make it
A huntsman, or a falconer, a musician
Or a thing of sorrow.

Echo. *A thing of sorrow.*

Antonio. Ay sure: that suits it best.

Echo. *That suits it best.*

Antonio. 'Tis very like my wife's voice.

Echo. *Ay, wife's voice.*

Delio. Come: let's walk farther from't:
I would not have you go to th' Cardinal's tonight:
Do not.

Echo. Do not.

Delio. Wisdom doth not more moderate wasting sorrow
Than time: take time for't: be mindful of thy safety.

Echo. Be mindful of thy safety.

Antonio. Necessity compels me:
Make scrutiny throughout the passages
Of your own life you'll find it impossible
To fly your fate.

V.iii.12 questionless doubtless

Echo. *O fly your fate.*
Delio. Hark: the dead stones seem to have pity on you
And give you good counsel.
Antonio. Echo, I will not talk with thee;
For thou art a dead thing.
Echo. *Thou art a dead thing.*
Antonio. My Duchess is asleep now,
And her little ones, I hope sweetly: oh Heaven
Shall I never see her more?
Echo. *Never see her more.*
Antonio. I mark'd not one repetition of the Echo
But that: and on the sudden, a clear light
Presented me a face folded in sorrow.
Delio. Your fancy; merely.
Antonio. Come: I'll be out of this ague;
For to live thus, is not indeed to live:
It is a mockery, and abuse of life.
I will not henceforth save myself by halves;
Lose all, or nothing.
Delio. Your own virtue save you.
I'll fetch your eldest son; and second you:
It may be that the sight of his own blood
Spread in so sweet a figure, may beget
The more compassion.
Antonio. However, fare you well.
Though in our miseries Fortune hath a part
Yet, in our noble sufferings, she hath none:
Contempt of pain, that we may call our own. *Exe[unt.]*

Scene iv

[*Enter*] *Cardinal, Pescara, Malateste, Roderigo, Grisolan.*

Cardinal. You shall not watch tonight by the sick Prince;
His Grace is very well recover'd.
Malateste. Good my lord, suffer us.
Cardinal. Oh, by no means:
The noise and change of object in his eye
Doth more distract him. I pray, all to bed,
And though you hear him in his violent fit,
Do not rise, I entreat you.

Pescara. So sir, we shall not—
Cardinal. Nay, I must have you promise
Upon your honours, for I was enjoin'd to't
By himself; and he seem'd to urge it sensibly.
Pescara. Let our honours bind this trifle.
Cardinal. Nor any of your followers.
Pescara. Neither.
Cardinal. It may be to make trial of your promise
When he's asleep, myself will rise, and feign
Some of his mad tricks, and cry out for help,
And feign myself in danger.
Malateste. If your throat were cutting,
I'll'd not come at you, now I have protested against it.
Cardinal. Why, I thank you. [*Withdraws.*]
Grisolan. 'Twas a foul storm tonight.
Roderigo. The Lord Ferdinand's chamber shook like an osier.°
Malateste. 'Twas nothing but pure kindness in the devil,
To rock his own child.
Exeunt [*Roderigo, Malateste, Pescara, Grisolan.*]
Cardinal. The reason why I would not suffer these
About my brother, is because at midnight
I may with better privacy convey
Julia's body to her own lodging. O, my conscience!
I would pray now: but the devil takes away my heart
For having any confidence in prayer.
About this hour I appointed Bosola
To fetch the body: when he hath serv'd my turn,
He dies. *Exit.*

[*Enter Bosola.*]

Bosola. Ha! 'twas the Cardinal's voice. I heard him name
Bosola, and my death: listen, I hear one's footing.

[*Enter Ferdinand.*]

Ferdinand. Strangling is a very quiet death.
Bosola. Nay then I see, I must stand upon my guard.
Ferdinand. What say' to that? Whisper, softly: do you agree to't?

V.iv.19 **osier** species of willow tree

So it must be done i'th' dark: the Cardinal
Would not for a thousand pounds the doctor should see it. *Exit.*

Bosola. My death is plotted; here's the consequence of murther.
We value not desert, nor Christian breath,
When we know black deeds must be cur'd with death.
[*Withdraws.*]

[*Enter Antonio and a Servant.*]

Servant. Here stay sir, and be confident, I pray:
I'll fetch you a dark lanthorn. *Exit.*

Antonio. Could I take him
At his prayers, there were hope of pardon.

Bosola. Fall right my sword: [*strikes Antonio.*]
I'll not give thee so much leisure as to pray.

Antonio. Oh, I am gone. Thou hast ended a long suit,
In a minute.

Bosola. What art thou?

Antonio. A most wretched thing
That only have thy benefit in death,
To appear myself.°

[*Enter Servant with a dark lanthorn.*]

Servant. Where are you sir?

Antonio. Very near my home. Bosola?

Servant. Oh misfortune!

Bosola [*to Servant.*]. Smother thy pity, thou art dead else. Antonio!
The man I would have sav'd 'bove mine own life!
We are merely the stars' tennis-balls, struck and banded°
Which way please them: oh good Antonio,
I'll whisper one thing in thy dying ear,
Shall make thy heart break quickly. Thy fair Duchess
And two sweet children—

Antonio. Their very names
Kindle a little life in me.

Bosola. Are murder'd!

49 appear myself appear like myself **53 banded** bandied

Antonio. Some men have wish's to die
At the hearing of sad tidings: I am glad
That I shall do't in sadness:° I would not now
Wish my wounds balm'd, nor heal'd: for I have no use
To put my life to. In all our quest of greatness,
Like wanton boys, whose pastime is their care,
We follow after bubbles, blown in th'air.
Pleasure of life, what is't? only the good hours
Of an ague: merely a preparative to rest,
To endure vexation. I do not ask
The process of my death: only commend me
To Delio.
Bosola. Break, heart!
Antonio. And let my son fly the courts of princes. [*Dies.*]
Bosola. Thou seem'st to have lov'd Antonio?
Servant. I brought him hither,
To have reconcil'd him to the Cardinal.
Bosola. I do not ask thee that.
Take him up, if thou tender° thine own life,
And bear him where the Lady Julia
Was wont to lodge. Oh, my fate moves swift.
I have this Cardinal in the forge already,
Now I'll bring him to th' hammer. (O direful misprision°)
I will not imitate things glorious,
No more than base: I'll be mine own example.
On, on: and look thou represent, for silence,
The thing thou bear'st.° *Exeunt.*

Scene v

[*Enter*] *Cardinal with a book.*

Cardinal. I am puzzl'd in a question about hell:
He says, in hell there's one material fire,
And yet it shall not burn all men alike.
Lay him by. How tedious is a guilty conscience!
When I look into the fishponds, in my garden,

61 **sadness** earnest 75 **tender** care for 79 **misprision** mistake, misperception 82 **On, on . . . bear'st** (spoken to the servant carrying Antonio's body)

Methinks I see a thing arm'd with a rake
That seems to strike at me. Now? Art thou come?

[*Enter Bosola and Servant with Antonio's body.*]

Thou look'st ghastly:
There sits in thy face some great determination,
Mix'd with some fear.
Bosola. Thus it lightens° into action:
I am come to kill thee.
Cardinal. Ha? Help! our guard!
Bosola. Thou art deceiv'd:
They are out of thy howling.
Cardinal. Hold: and I will faithfully divide
Revenues with thee.
Bosola. Thy prayers and proffers
Are both unseasonable.
Cardinal. Raise the watch:
We are betray'd!
Bosola. I have confin'd your flight:
I'll suffer° your retreat to Julia's chamber,
But no further.
Cardinal. Help: we are betray'd!

[*Enter Pescara, Malateste, Roderigo and Grisolan, above.*]

Malateste. Listen.
Cardinal. My dukedom for rescue!
Roderigo. Fie upon his counterfeiting.
Malateste. Why, 'tis not the Cardinal.
Roderigo. Yes, yes, 'tis he:
But I'll see him hang'd, ere I'll go down to him.
Cardinal. Here's a plot upon me; I am assaulted. I am lost,
Unless some rescue!
Grisolan. He doth this pretty well:
But it will not serve to laugh me out of mine honour.
Cardinal. The sword's at my throat!
Roderigo. You would not bawl so loud then.
Malateste. Come, come: let's go to bed: he told us thus much aforehand.

V.vi.10 **lightens** flashes 18 **suffer** allow

Pescara. He wish'd you should not come at him: but believ't,
The accent of the voice sounds not in jest.
I'll go down to him, howsoever, and with engines
Force ope the doors. [*Exit.*]
Roderigo. Let's follow him aloof,
And note how the Cardinal will laugh at him.
[*Exeunt above.*]
Bosola. There's for you first:
'Cause you shall not unbarricade the door
To let in rescue. *He kills the Servant.*
Cardinal. What cause hast thou to pursue my life?
Bosola. Look there.
Cardinal. Antonio!
Bosola. Slain by my hand unwittingly.
Pray, and be sudden: when thou kill'd'st thy sister,
Thou took'st from Justice her most equal balance,
And left her naught but her sword.
Cardinal. O mercy!
Bosola. Now it seems thy greatness was only outward:
For thou fall'st faster of thyself than calamity
Can drive thee. I'll not waste longer time. There.
[*Stabs the Cardinal.*]
Cardinal. Thou hast hurt me.
Bosola. Again. [*Stabs him again.*]
Cardinal. Shall I die like a leveret°
Without any resistance? Help, help, help!
I am slain.

[*Enter Ferdinand.*]

Th'alarum? give me a fresh horse.
Rally the vaunt-guard;° or the day is lost.
Yield, yield! I give you the honour of arms,
Shake my sword over you, will you yield?
Cardinal. Help me, I am your brother.
Ferdinand. The devil?
My brother fight upon the adverse party?
He wounds the Cardinal and, in the scuffle, gives Bosola his death wound.
There flies your ransome.

44 **leveret** young hare 47 **vaunt-guard** vanguard

Cardinal. Oh Justice:
I suffer now for what hath former been
Sorrow is held the eldest child of sin.

Ferdinand. Now you're brave fellows, Caesar's fortune was harder than Pompey's: Caesar died in the arms of prosperity, Pompey at the feet of disgrace: you both died in the field, the pain's nothing. Pain many times is taken away with the apprehension of greater, as the toothache with the sight of a barber that comes to pull it out: there's philosophy for you.

Bosola. Now my revenge is perfect: sink, thou main cause
Of my undoing: the last part of my life
Hath done me best service. *He kills Ferdinand.*

Ferdinand. Give me some wet hay, I am broken winded.
I do account this world but a dog-kennel:
I will vault credit, and affect high pleasures
Beyond death.

Bosola. He seems to come to himself,
Now he's so near the bottom.

Ferdinand. My sister, oh! my sister, there's the cause on't.
Whether we fall by ambition, blood, or lust,
Like diamonds we are cut with our own dust. [*Dies.*]

Cardinal. Thou hast thy payment too.

Bosola. Yes, I hold my weary soul in my teeth;
'Tis ready to part from me. I do glory
That thou, which stood'st like a huge pyramid
Begun upon a large and ample base,
Shalt end in a little point, a kind of nothing.

[*Enter Pescara, Malateste, Roderigo and Grisolan.*]

Pescara. How now, my lord?

Malateste. O sad disaster!

Roderigo. How comes this?

Bosola. Revenge, for the Duchess of Malfi, murdered
By th' Aragonian brethren; for Antonio,
Slain by this hand; for lustful Julia,
Poison'd by this man; and lastly, for myself,
That was an actor in the main of all,
Much 'gainst mine own good nature, yet i'th' end
Neglected.

Pescara. How now, my lord?

Cardinal. Look to my brother:
He gave us these large wounds, as we were struggling
Here i'th'rushes. And now, I pray, let me
Be laid by, and never thought of. [*Dies.*]
Pescara. How fatally, it seems, he did withstand
His own rescue!
Malateste. Thou wretched thing of blood,
How came Antonio by his death?
Bosola. In a mist: I know not how;
Such a mistake as I have often seen
In a play. Oh, I am gone:
We are only like dead walls, or vaulted graves
That, ruin'd, yields no echo. Fare you well;
It may be pain: but no harm to me to die
In so good a quarrel. Oh this gloomy world,
In what a shadow, or deep pit of darkness
Doth, womanish, and fearful, mankind live?
Let worthy minds ne'er stagger in distrust
To suffer death or shame for what is just:
Mine is another voyage. [*Dies.*]
Pescara. The noble Delio, as I came to th'palace,
Told me of Antonio's being here, and show'd me
A pretty gentleman his son and heir.

[*Enter Delio with Antonio's son.*]

Malateste. O sir, you come too late.
Delio. I heard so, and
Was arm'd for't ere I came. Let us make noble use
Of this great ruin; and join all our force
To establish this young hopeful gentleman
In's mother's right. These wretched eminent things
Leave no more fame behind 'em, than should one
Fall in a frost, and leave his print in snow,
As soon as the sun shines, it ever melts
Both form and matter. I have ever thought
Nature doth nothing so great for great men,
As when she's pleas'd to make them lords of truth:
Integrity of life is fame's best friend,
Which nobly, beyond death, shall crown the end.
Exeunt.

FINIS.

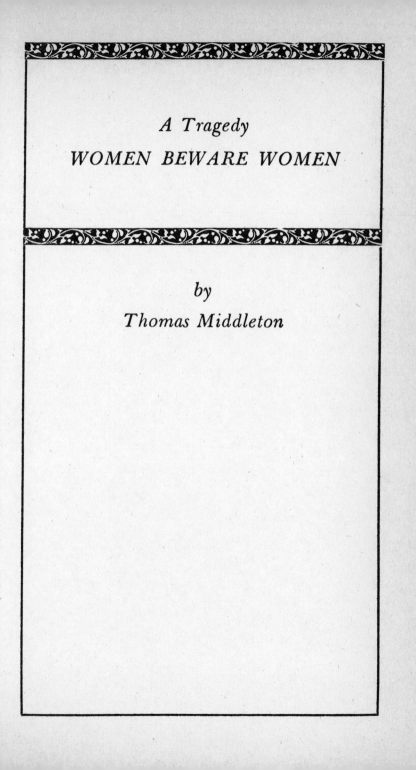

A Tragedy
WOMEN BEWARE WOMEN

by

Thomas Middleton

THOMAS MIDDLETON

In the competitive and lively world of the London theater, Thomas Middleton was one of those active, free-lance writers upon whom actors depended for their material. He was productive for nearly a quarter of a century, beginning in 1602. Unlike John Webster, who seems to have written intermittently, Middleton worked constantly, supplying scripts to a wide variety of companies and changing his style to fit the times. He wrote at least thirty plays, alone and in collaboration, as well as twenty or more civic entertainments and masques. His stature as a writer, however, was modest. In his lifetime he received little commendation, and insofar as we know, he had no exalted opinion of himself in the manner of Ben Jonson or Webster. It was not until Charles Lamb and the romantic poets expressed their admiration for him that Middleton's reputation began to mount.

As with almost every playwright of the time, nothing in Thomas Middleton's family background tied him to players or playhouses. He was born in April 1580 to a prosperous middle-class couple, William and Ann Middleton. His father was a bricklayer, though that name has an inappropriate connotation; probably he was what we would now call a builder or contractor. These prosperous circumstances were shattered by his father's death and his mother's remarriage when Thomas was about five years of age. During his adolescence his mother and stepfather, and later a brother-in-law, were in bitter and recurrent dispute over domestic arrangements and the control of William Middleton's will. How deeply involved Thomas was in these arguments and the lawsuits they generated is not readily apparent. Nevertheless, he managed to secure sufficient albeit exceedingly slender means to attend Oxford University, and indeed mortgaged his modest inheritance to his brother-in-law in order to get the funds for his stay at the university.

His life at Oxford is mirrored in one of his early pamphlets, *Father Hubbard's Tale*. In it he describes an impoverished young scholar pursuing his studies avidly, only to yield to "the lickerish study of poetry, that sweet honey-poison." Shortly before his twenty-first birthday in 1601, a witness of one of the recurrent family lawsuits reports that Thomas was in London "accompanying the players." If so, it is unlikely that he graduated from the university. Instead, he seems to have begun some sort of association with one or another acting troupe. But whether he himself acted (of which there is no later sign) or handled offstage duties (which may have included writing), we cannot tell. Within a year after that, he is collaborating with Dekker and Webster, turning out a new play, and writing additions to Robert Greene's *Friar Bacon and Friar Bungay* for a performance at court.

Rapidly, he became a working professional and maintained a steady output. Married in April 1601 to Mary Marbeck, and a father in 1603 or 1604, Middleton spent the next ten or twelve years writing for both children and adult companies. Some of his most noted work in this period was done in collaboration with Thomas Dekker. Their share in *The Honest Whore* (1604) and *The Roaring Girl* (1604-10) is, however, in dispute. Middleton certainly contributed to the first part of *The Honest Whore* and probably had a hand in *The Roaring Girl,* although in the composition of both plays he was undoubtedly the junior partner. Concurrently, Middleton wrote three or four comedies for the Children of Paul's and others. Contemporary in setting and gently satiric in tone, these plays treat the business world of sharpers and potential marks. Along with George Chapman and Jonson, Middleton is one of the leading writers in this novel genre, commonly known as city comedy. In 1613 he produced what is regarded as his best work of this type, *A Chaste Maid in Cheapside.*

Although Middleton continued to collaborate on comedies throughout his career, after 1613 he became regularly engaged in writing and supervising entertainments and masques for the Lord Mayor's pageant and other London civic occasions. He had full responsibility for conceiving the entertainment, hiring workers, and overseeing the preparation of displays, costumes, music, and whatever else was needed. This regular employment eventually led to his appointment as City Chronologer in 1620, an appointment that required continuing attention to the civic entertainments as well as recording the important historical events of the year. He retained this post until his death in 1627 despite charges against him in 1626 that he had failed to carry out his duties properly.

His engagement in city pageants did not lessen his involvement in theatrical writing. The writing changed, however. Alone and with others, he began to concentrate on tragedies and tragicomedies. By the second decade of the seventeenth century the children's companies were things of the past, and Middleton then did his work for the Lady Elizabeth's men, the Queen's men, and the King's men. Early in the 1620s he collaborated with William Rowley on *The Changeling,* long regarded as a major tragedy and possibly his best. We can say *his* best despite the collaboration, since Rowley is thought to have written the comic subplot and Middleton the tragic main plot.

In 1624 Middleton wrote a play that become a *cause célèbre.* The play, *A Game of Chess,* was a thinly veiled attack on the proposed Spanish alliance and particularly on the former Spanish ambassador, Gondomar. Within the frame of a chess game Middleton tells of the moves of the English (the White House) against the Spanish or Black House. The opening of the play at the Globe immediately became the talk of London. Thousands flocked to see it, and its popularity made it the ancestor of long-run hits. In an unprecedented move, the King's men played the controversial piece for nine consecutive performances before the protests of the Spanish ambassador pressured the Privy Council to close down the playhouse. Considering the uproar, the actors escaped lightly. How severely Middleton suffered for his presumption is not clear. He avoided immediate punishment, but may have endured a lasting prohibition, since *A Game of Chess* is his last play.

Where *Women Beware Women* fits into this chronology is by no means certain. The play was not published until 1657. Neither document nor allusion records its first appearance in the theater. Therefore, dating must depend on internal evidence. On the basis of its tragic yet bitter tone, its affinity to *The Changeling,* and its simpler yet deft use of chess as a satiric analogy, most scholars put its composition between *The Changeling* in 1622 and *A Game of Chess* in 1624. It shares *The Changeling*'s portrayal of sexual indulgence in exotic circumstances, though it lacks the bold, straightforward depiction of corruption, embodied so ruthlessly in DeFlores, the villain of *The Changeling. Women Beware Women,* on the other hand, reveals a more intricate, perverted disturbance of morality, one that increasingly fascinates readers, leading them to see in *Women Beware Women* Middleton's greatest tragedy.

Women Beware Women is in the line of Italianate intrigue plots with features of the revenge play. By using these popular elements, Middleton tells a sophisticated story of the corruption of women, partly by men but mainly through the complicity of other women. Unfolding in mid-sixteenth-century Italy, the tragedy treats the real-life affair between the beauteous and notorious Bianca Capello and Francesco I di Medici, the Grand Duke of Florence. Bianca, a Venetian noblewoman, had run off with a bank clerk, Pietro Buonaventuri. In Florence, where they settled, she met the Duke, apparently conspired in her husband's murder, married the Duke, and died with him, possibly of poison. Her bitter enemy, the Duke's brother, Cardinal Ferdinando, may have played a part in her death.

With these events as the source of his main plot, Middleton drew upon *The True History of the Tragicke Lives of Hipolito and Isabella Neapolitans* for his subplot. Middleton must have seen the story in manuscript, since it was not published in English until 1628, the year after his death. Skillfully, he tied the subplot to the main plot through a character of his own invention, Livia. In Livia he created one of his most brilliant characterizations, a woman of wit, amoral, passionate, inventive, and vindictive. She is aptly named after the shrewd, ruthless, and handsome wife of the Emperor Augustus. By acting as the corrupter of Bianca and the deceiver of Isabella, Livia precipitates the tragedy that engulfs them all.

In source and genre, *Women Beware Women* is not atypical. What makes this play different from others in its class is Middleton's reshaping of the traditional elements to produce novel effects. This play, like the two tragedies of Webster, sets events at one of the near-legendary Italian ducal courts that so fascinated the English. But while *The White Devil* and *The Duchess of Malfi* are centered at their respective courts, *Women Beware Women* follows a slightly tangential course. Its first scenes open in the humble quarters of an impecunious merchant's clerk, Leantio. It next moves to the grander residence of a noble lady, Livia. By the end of the play, the masque unfolds in the Grand Duke's palace. Thus, as the locale ascends in grandeur, the action proceeds to greater and greater debasement. This kind of purposeful use of space is uncommon in Renaissance drama, a tribute to Middleton's inventive genius and perhaps a result of his experience as a producer of civic pageants.

Middleton also modifies his received materials in another way. Admittedly, he depicts a clutch of burghers and nobles, all of whom are corrupted and debased in the course of the play. But their corruption is not mere sensual indulgence. An atmosphere of lust hangs over the events, and yet the impulses that propel the characters are genuine. Leantio loves Bianca possessively, and yields to Livia's importunities only when Bianca is completely lost to him. The Duke is truly devoted to Bianca, Hippolito to Isabella, even Livia to Leantio. They are not merely giving way to sexual pleasure, but rather idealize their lovers. Their passion is thus deeply rooted, not inevitably perverted at the source. What is perverted is their moral sense. They do not hesitate to transgress social norms and moral standards to satisfy their passions. Leantio steals Bianca from her family, the Duke steals her from Leantio. In their eyes, love justifies their acts. Hippolito violates kinship taboos to gratify his love for Isabella. Livia ignores family honor to court Leantio. Although this last act does not seem heinous in our eyes, it is of the same nature as Hippolito's feeding on his own blood. As for Bianca and Isabella, who are the objects of violent passion, their initial instinct is for moral restraint. When, however, the Duke forces Bianca's affection and Livia dupes Isabella to commit incest, all stops are out. No longer do they exercise any control over their desires and feelings. All things are possible: scorn, shamelessness, hypocrisy, and finally murder. The tragedy comes to lie in the awful discrepancy between the untainted devotion people start with and the lengths to which their sexual appetite, however genuine it may be, will take them. That is why the portrayal of the Ward is not irrelevant, as some critics claim. He is incapable of such earnest yet terrible passion, and that capacity makes him a fool.

The full impact of Middleton's tragic vision, furthermore, is embedded in the presentational style of the play. One of its distinctive features is the alternation of engagement and detachment that the characters undergo. This oscillation is evident from the beginning. When the Mother greets Leantio with a heartfelt "Welcome" and "Welcome again," Leantio responds, not by answering her directly, face-to-face, but as though observing her from afar: " 'Las, poor affectionate soul, how her joys speak to me" (I. i. 8). That detachment appears again and again. Even as mother and son speak, they regard the silent Bianca, commenting on her as she stands to one side. When at last the Mother addresses Bianca, Leantio comments on his mother's manner of speech. These sequences of private thought and face-to-face exchanges become far more complicated as the play proceeds, reaching in Livia's wooing of Leantio a sharp division between Leantio absorbed in the turmoil of an interior monologue and Livia fruitlessly attempting to catch his attention (III. ii. 243-70).

In the present text the unquestionably detached speeches usually are marked as asides. But the reader should be alert to the many instances where the degree of detachment between one character and another is open to interpretation. Depending on how an actor delivers a speech, he can relate to a fellow actor or indicate self-absorption. At times *Women Beware Women* seems to be a forerunner of Eugene O'Neill's *Strange Interlude* where the characters alternate between speaking to others and speaking their thoughts.

The detachment in *Women Beware Women* serves to isolate the individuals, to make them observers as well as actors, and in that way witnesses of their own disasters. That lends a special irony to the masque, for in that horror-filled performance, each of the leading figures plays a part and yet watches to see the effect of that part. Isabella watches for the death of Livia, Livia and Guardiano for the death of Hippolito, Bianca for the death of the Cardinal. Those who do not know about the plots, namely, the Duke and Isabella's father, are entirely confused. This game of watching—crystallized in the chess match in which the Mother and Bianca are pawns—collapses in utter ruin.

Yet despite the ruin of all, a memory of love survives. Despite her hatred of the Cardinal, Bianca can still cry out before she dies,

> Yet this my gladness is, that I remove [die],
> Tasting the same death [as the Duke] in a cup of love.
> (V. ii. 218-19)

As Bianca's last words suggest, the tragic victim of *Women Beware Women* is love itself.

Of all the plays in this collection, *Women Beware Women* was the last to receive wide acclaim. While the romantics elevated Middleton's reputation in general, this play lagged in critical repute and especially in theatrical recognition. The tide is turning. In the last generation the play appears with increasing frequency on the stage, and with its familiarity, its latent power emerges. While it was not printed until 1657, at least a generation after it was written, and it was not presented again until the twentieth century, it speaks so directly to the present day that it is assured a sympathetic response.

TO THE READER

When these° amongst others of Mr. Thomas Middleton's excellent poems came to my hands, I was not a little confident but that his name would prove as great an inducement for thee to read, as me to print them, since those issues of his brain that have already seen the sun have by their worth gained themselves a free entertainment amongst all that are ingenious; and I am most certain that these will no way lessen his reputation, nor hinder his admission to any noble and recreative spirits. All that I require at thy hands, is to continue the author in his deserved esteem, and to accept of my endeavours which have ever been to please thee.

Farewell

Upon the Tragedy of My Familiar Acquaintance Tho. Middleton

Women beware Women: 'tis a true text
Never to be forgot. Drabs of state vexed
Have plots, poisons, mischiefs that seldom miss
To murther virtue with a venom kiss—
Witness this worthy tragedy, expressed
By him that well deserved amongst the best
Of poets in his time. He knew the rage,
Madness of women crossed; and for the stage
Fitted their humours, hell-bred malice, strife
Acted in state, presented to the life.
I that have seen't can say, having just cause,
Never came tragedy off with more applause.

Nath. Richards°

2 **these** (*Women Beware Women* and *More Dissemblers Besides Women* were published in the same volume in 1657) 26 **Richards** Nathaniel Richards, who wrote *The Tragedy of Messallina* (1635).

[Cast of Characters]

Duke of Florence
Lord Cardinal, brother to the Duke
Two Cardinals more
A Lord
Fabritio, father to Isabella
Hippolito, brother to Fabritio
Guardiano, uncle to the foolish Ward
The Ward, a rich young heir
Leantio, a factor,° husband to Bianca
Sordido, the Ward's man
Livia, sister to Fabritio
Isabella, niece to Livia
Bianca, Leantio's wife
The Widow, his [Leantio's] mother
States° of Florence, Citizens, a 'Prentice, Boys, Messenger, Servants
[Two Ladies, other Lords, Pages, Guard]

The Scene

Florence

9 **factor** a merchant's agent 15 **States** nobility

WOMEN BEWARE WOMEN

[Act I, Scene i]

Enter Leantio with Bianca, and Mother.

Mother. Thy sight was never yet more precious to me;
Welcome with all the affection of a mother,
That comfort can express° from natural love.
Since thy birth-joy—a mother's chiefest gladness
After sh'as undergone her curse of sorrows—
Thou wast not more dear to me than this hour
Presents thee to my heart. Welcome again.
Leantio. [*Aside.*] 'Las, poor affectionate soul, how her joys speak to me!
I have observed it often, and I know it is
The fortune commonly of knavish children
To have the loving'st mothers.
Mother. What's this gentlewoman?
Leantio. Oh you have named the most unvalued'st° purchase,°
That youth of man had ever knowledge of.
As often as I look upon that treasure,
And know it to be mine—there lies the blessing—
It joys me that I ever was ordained
To have a being, and to live 'mongst men;
Which is a fearful living, and a poor one,
Let a man truly think on't,
To have the toil and griefs of fourscore years
Put up in a white sheet, tied with two knots.°
Methinks it should strike earthquakes in adulterers,
When ev'n the very sheets they commit sin in,
May prove, for aught they know, all their last garments.
Oh what a mark were there for women then!
But beauty able to content a conqueror,°

3 **express** distill 12 **unvalued'st** invaluable 12 **purchase** acquisition, theft (?) 21 **two knots** a shroud fastened with a knot at head and feet 26 **conqueror** (allusion to Alexander the Great, who, it was reported, wept because earth afforded no new worlds to conquer)

Whom earth could scarce content, keeps me in compass;°
I find no wish in me bent sinfully
To this man's sister, or to that man's wife:
In love's name let 'em keep their honesties,
And cleave to their own husbands, 'tis their duties.
Now when I go to church, I can pray handsomely;
Nor come like gallants only to see faces,
As if lust went to market still on Sundays.
I must confess I am guilty of one sin, mother,
More than I brought into the world with me;
But that I glory in: 'tis theft, but noble
As ever greatness yet shot up withal.

Mother. How's that?

Leantio. Never to be repented, mother,
Though sin be death! I had died, if I had not sinned,
And here's my masterpiece. Do you now behold her!
Look on her well, she's mine. Look on her better.
Now say, if't be not the best piece of theft
That ever was committed. And I have my pardon for't:
'Tis sealed from Heaven by marriage.

Mother. Married to her!

Leantio. You must keep council mother, I am undone else;
If it be known, I have lost her. Do but think now
What that loss is—life's but a trifle to't.
From Venice her consent and I have brought her,
From parents great in wealth, more now in rage;
But let storms spend their furies. Now we have got
A shelter o'er our quiet innocent loves,
We are contented. Little money sh'as brought me:
View but her face, you may see all her dowry,
Save that which lies locked up in hidden virtues,
Like jewels kept in cabinets.

Mother. Y'are to blame,
If your obedience will give way to a check,
To wrong such a perfection.

Leantio. How?

Mother. Such a creature,
To draw her from her fortune, which no doubt,
At the full time, might have proved rich and noble:
You know not what you have done. My life can give you
But little helps, and my death lesser hopes;

27 **in compass** within limits

And hitherto your own means has but made shift
To keep you single, and that hardly too.
What ableness have you to do her right, then,
In maintenance fitting her birth and virtues,
Which ev'ry woman of necessity looks for,
And most to go above it, not confined
By their conditions, virtues, bloods, or births,
But flowing to affections, wills and humours?

Leantio. Speak low sweet mother; you are able to spoil as many
As come within the hearing; if it be not
Your fortune to mar all, I have much marvel.
I pray do not you teach her to rebel,
When she's in a good way to obedience;
To rise with other women in commotion
Against their husbands, for six gowns a year,
And so maintain their cause, when they're once up,
In all things else that require cost enough.
They are all of 'em a kind of spirits, soon raised,°
But not so soon laid, mother. As for example,
A woman's belly is got up in a trice:
A simple charge° ere it be laid down again:
So ever in all their quarrels, and their courses.°
And I'm a proud man, I hear nothing of 'em;
They're very still, I thank my happiness,
And sound asleep; pray let not your tongue wake 'em.
If you can but rest quiet, she's contented
With all conditions that my fortunes bring her to:
To keep close as a wife that loves her husband;
To go after the rate of my ability,
Not the licentious swinge° of her own will,
Like some of her old schoolfellows. She intends
To take out other works in a new sampler,°
And frame the fashion of an honest love,
Which knows no wants but, mocking poverty,
Brings forth more children, to make rich men wonder
At divine Providence, that feeds mouths of infants,
And sends them° none to feed, but stuffs their rooms

80 **raised** i.e., conjured up, as ghostly spirits 83 **A simple charge** a nice expense (ironic) 84 **courses** actions 92 **swinge** sway 94 **To take . . . sampler** to copy other art work in a new embroidered sampler 99 **them** i.e., the rich men

With fruitful bags, their beds with barren wombs.
Good mother, make not you things worse than they are
Out of your too much openness—pray take heed on't—
Nor imitate the envy of old people,
That strive to mar good sport, because they are perfect.°
I would have you more pitiful to youth,
Especially to your own flesh and blood.
I'll prove an excellent husband—here's my hand—
Lay in provision, follow my business roundly,
And make you a grandmother in forty weeks!
Go, pray salute° her, bid her welcome cheerfully.

Mother. Gentlewoman, thus much is a debt of courtesy
Which fashionable strangers pay each other
At a kind of meeting; [*kisses Bianca.*] then there's more than one,
Due to the knowledge I have of your nearness;
[*kisses her again.*]
I am bold to come again, and now salute you
By th'name of daughter, which may challenge more
Than ordinary respect. [*kisses her a third time.*]

Leantio. [*Aside.*] Why, this is well now,
And I think few mothers of threescore will mend it.

Mother. What I can bid you welcome to, is mean;
But make it all your own: we are full of wants,
And cannot welcome worth.

Leantio. Now this is scurvy,
And spoke as if a woman lacked her teeth.°
These old folks talk of nothing but defects,
Because they grow so full of 'em themselves.

Bianca. Kind mother, there is nothing can be wanting
To her that does enjoy all her desires.
Heaven send a quiet peace with this man's love,
And I am as rich, as virtue can be poor,
Which were enough, after the rate° of mind,
To erect temples for content placed here.
I have forsook friends, fortunes, and my country;
And hourly I rejoice in't. Here's my friends,
And few is the good number. Thy successes,
Howe'er they look, I will still name my fortunes;

104 perfect contented **110 salute her** kiss her **121-2 scurvy . . . teeth** (one of the consequences of scurvy is loss of teeth) **129 after the rate** according to the measure or quality

Hopeful or spiteful, they shall all be welcome:
Who invites many guests, has of all sorts
As he that traffics much, drinks of all fortunes:
Yet they must all be welcome, and used well.
I'll call this place the place of my birth now,
And rightly too, for here my love was born,
And that's the birthday of a woman's joys.
You have not bid me welcome since I came.
Leantio. That I did, questionless.
Bianca. No, sure, how was't?
I have quite forgot it.
Leantio. Thus. [*kisses her.*]
Bianca. Oh sir, 'tis true,
Now I remember well: I have done thee wrong,
Pray take't again, sir. [*kisses him.*]
Leantio. How many of these wrongs
Could I put up in an hour? and turn up the glass°
For twice as many more.
Mother. Will't please you to walk in, daughter?
Bianca. Thanks, sweet mother;
The voice of her that bare me is not more pleasing.
Exeunt [*Mother and Bianca.*]
Leantio. Though my own care and my rich master's trust
Lay their commands both on my factorship,°
This day and night I'll know no other business
But her and her dear welcome. 'Tis a bitterness
To think upon tomorrow, that I must leave her
Still to the sweet hopes of the week's end.
That pleasure should be so restrained and curbed
After the course of a rich workmaster,
That never pays till Saturday night!
Marry, it comes together in a round sum then,
And does more good; you'll say. Oh fair-eyed Florence!
Didst thou but know what a most matchless jewel
Thou now art mistress of, a pride would take thee
Able to shoot destruction through the bloods
Of all thy youthful sons! But 'tis great policy
To keep choice treasures in obscurest places:

147 turn up the glass reverse the hour-glass **152 factorship** position as a merchant's employee

Should we show thieves our wealth, 'twould make 'em bolder.
Temptation is a devil will not stick
To fasten upon a saint: take heed of that.
The jewel is cased up from all men's eyes:
Who could imagine now a gem were kept
Of that great value, under this plain roof?
But how in times of absence, what assurance
Of this restraint then? yes, yes—there's one with her:
Old mothers know the world; and such as these,
When sons lock chests, are good to look to keys.

Exit.

[Act I, Scene ii]

Enter Guardiano, Fabritio, and Livia [*with Servant.*]

Guardiano. What, has your daughter seen him yet? know you that?
Fabritio. No matter—she shall love him.
Guardiano. Nay, let's have fair play;
He has been now my ward some fifteen year,
And 'tis my purpose, as time calls upon me,
By custom seconded, and such moral virtues,
To tender him a wife; now, sir, this wife
I'ld fain elect out of a daughter of yours.
You see my meaning's fair. If now this daughter,
So tendered—let me come to your own phrase, sir—
Should offer to refuse him, I were hanselled.°
[*Aside.*] Thus am I fain to calculate all my words
For the meridian° of a foolish old man,
To take his understanding! What do you answer, sir?
Fabritio. I say still, she shall love him.
Guardiano. Yet again?
And shall she have no reason for this love?

I.ii.10 hanselled (a hansel is a gift, normally proffered to launch the new year or a fresh enterprise. Here Fabritio's daughter is the "hansel" which is offered ["tendered"]) **12 meridian** peak of capacity

Fabritio. Why, do you think that women love with reason?
Guardiano. I perceive fools are not at all hours foolish,
No more than wisemen wise.
Fabritio. I had a wife;
She ran mad for me; she had no reason for't
For aught I could perceive. What think you,
Lady sister?
Guardiano. [*Aside.*] 'Twas a fit match that,
Being both out of their wits! A loving wife, 'seemed,
She strove to come as near you as she could.
Fabritio. And if her daughter prove not mad for love too,
She takes not after her; nor after me,
If she prefer reason before my pleasure.
[*To Livia.*] You're an experienced widow, lady sister;
I pray let your opinion come amongst us.
Livia. I must offend you then, if truth will do't,
And take my niece's part, and call't injustice
To force her love to one she never saw.
Maids should both see and like; all little enough:
If they love truly after that, 'tis well.
Counting the time, she takes one man till death,
That's a hard task, I tell you; but one may
Enquire at three years' end amongst young wives,
And mark how the game goes.
Fabritio. Why, is not man
Tied to the same observance, lady sister,
And in one woman?
Livia. 'Tis enough for him;
Besides, he tastes of many sundry dishes
That we poor wretches never lay our lips to—
As obedience, forsooth, subjection, duty, and such kickshaws,°
All of our making, but served in to them;
And if we lick a finger then, sometimes,
We are not to blame; your best cooks use it.°
Fabritio. Th'art a sweet lady, sister, and a witty.
Livia. A witty! Oh, the bud of commendation,
Fit for a girl of sixteen. I am blown,° man.
I should be wise by this time; and, for instance,

42 **kickshaws** fancy dishes 45 **use it** make a habit of it, i.e., licking their fingers 48 **blown** fully in bloom

I have buried my two husbands in good fashion,
And never mean more to marry.
Guardiano. No, why so, lady?
Livia. Because the third shall never bury me:
I think I am more than witty. How think you, sir?
Fabritio. I have paid often fees to a counsellor
Has had a weaker brain.
Livia. Then I must tell you,
Your money was soon parted.
Guardiano. Light her now, brother.°
Livia. Where is my niece? let her be sent for straight.
[*Exit Servant.*]
If you have any hope 'twill prove a wedding,
'Tis fit i'faith she should have one sight of him,
And stop upon't, and not be joined in haste,
As if they went to stock a new found land.°
Fabritio. Look out her uncle, and y'are sure of her,
Those two are nev'r asunder; they've been heard
In argument at midnight, moonshine nights
Are noondays with them; they walk out their sleeps,
Or rather at those hours appear like those
That walk in 'em, for so they did to me.
Look you, I told you truth: they're like a chain,
Draw but one link, all follows.

Enter Hippolito and Isabella the niece.

Guardiano. Oh affinity,
What piece of excellent workmanship art thou?
'Tis work clean wrought, for there's no lust, but love in't,
And that abundantly—when in stranger things,
There is no love at all, but what lust brings.
Fabritio. On with your mask, for 'tis your part to see now,
And not be seen. Go to, make use of your time;
See what you mean to like—nay, and I charge you,
Like what you see. Do you hear me? there's no dallying.

56 **Light her now, brother** (no one has either explained this line satisfactorily or offered an emendation that is generally accepted) 61 **stock a new found land** (allusion to colonization of the new lands in America, possibly of Newfoundland between 1610 and 1618)

The gentleman's almost twenty, and 'tis time
He were getting lawful heirs, and you a-breeding on 'em.
Isabella. Good father!
Fabritio. Tell not me of tongues and rumours!
You'll say the gentleman is somewhat simple—
The better for a husband, were you wise:
For those that marry fools, live ladies' lives.
On with the mask, I'll hear no more; he's rich:
The fool's hid under bushels.
Livia. Not so hid neither,
But here's a foul great piece of him, methinks:
What will he be, when he comes altogether?

Enter the Ward with a trapstick,° and Sordido his man.

Ward. Beat him? I beat him out o'th'field with his own cat-stick,
Yet gave him the first hand.°
Sordido. Oh strange!
Ward. I did it,
Then he set jacks° on me.
Sordido. Nay, that's no wonder,
He's used to beating.°
Ward. Nay, I tickled him
When I came once to my tippings.°
Sordido. Now you talk on 'em,
there was a poulterer's wife made a great complaint of you last night to your guardianer, that you struck a bump in her child's head, as big as an egg.

Ward. An egg may prove a chicken, then in time the poulterer's wife will get by't. When I am in game, I am furious; came my mother's eyes in my way, I would not lose a fair end. No, were she alive, but with one tooth in her head, I should venture the striking out of that. I think of nobody, when I am in play, I am so earnest.

87 s.d. **trapstick** the stick used in the game of tip-cat to strike the wooden "cat" or piece of wood tapered at both ends; the player tries to strike the "cat" again while it is in the air 90 **first hand** first strike 91 **jacks** fellows 93 **He's used to beating** (he, the tailor, is acquainted with "beaten" or embroidered cloth) 94 **tippings** (a term in the game of tip-cat)

Coads me, my guardiner! Prithee lay up my cat and cat-stick safe.

Sordido. Where sir, i'th'chimney-corner?

Ward. Chimney-corner!

Sordido. Yes, sir, your cats° are always safe i'th'chimney-corner, unless they burn their coats.

Ward. Marry, that I am afraid on.

Sordido. Why then, I will bestow your cat i'th'gutter, and there she's safe, I am sure.

Ward. If I but live to keep a house, I'll make thee a great man—if meat and drink can do't. I can stoop gallantly, and pitch out° when I list; I'm dog at° a hole. I mar'l° my guardiner does not seek a wife for me; I protest, I'll have a bout with the maids else, or contract myself at midnight to the larder-woman in presence of a fool° or a sack-posset.°

Guardiano. Ward!

Ward. I feel myself after any exercise horribly prone:° let me but ride, I'm lusty—a cockhorse° straight, i'faith.

Guardiano. Why, ward I say.

Ward. I'll forswear eating eggs in moon-shine nights;° there's nev'r a one I eat, but turns into a cock in four-and-twenty hours; if my hot blood be not took down in time, sure 'twill crow shortly.

Guardiano. Do you hear, sir? follow me; I must new school you.

Ward. School me? I scorn that now; I am past schooling. I am not so base to learn to write and read; I was born to better fortunes in my cradle.

Exit [Ward, Sordido, and Guardiano.]

108 **cats** (a double pun, on a feline as well as a woman; Sordido may be playing on the Ward's simplicity by seeming to suggest the animal while he also makes obscene jokes about diseased ["burned"] and clean ["safe"] whores) 114-5 **stoop gallantly and pitch out** (possibly terms in tip-cat; "stoop gallant" may refer to venereal disease) 115 **dog at** adept at 115 **mar'l** marvel 118 **fool** a delicacy of cream and fruit 119 **sack-posset** beverage made with sack (wine), eggs, and sugar 121 **prone** i.e., to lechery 122 **cockhorse** hobby horse, here a slang term for whore 124 **eggs in moonshine-nights** (eggs were considered to be aphrodisiac; "moonshine-nights" may refer to a type of poached egg; throughout his speech the Ward boasts of his sexual prowess

Fabritio. How do you like him, girl? this is your husband.
Like him or like him not, wench, you shall have him,
And you shall love him.
Livia. Oh, soft there, brother! Though you be a justice,
Your warrant cannot be served out of your liberty.°
You may compel, out of the power of father,
Things merely harsh to a maid's flesh and blood;
But when you come to love, there the soil alters;
Y'are in another country, where your laws
Are no more set by,° than the cacklings of geese
In Rome's great Capitol.°
Fabritio. Marry him she shall then;
Let her agree upon love afterwards. [*Exit.*]
Livia. You speak now, brother, like an honest mortal
That walks upon th'earth with a staff;
You were up i'th'clouds before; you'ld command love—
And so do most old folks that go without it.
[*To Hippolito.*] My best and dearest brother, I could dwell here;°
There is not such another seat on earth
Where all good parts better express themselves.
Hippolito. You'll make me blush anon.
Livia. 'Tis but like saying grace before a feast, then,
And that's most comely; thou art all a feast,
And she that has thee, a most happy guest.
Prithee cheer up thy niece with special counsel.
[*Exit.*]
Hippolito. [*Aside.*] I would 'twere fit to speak to her what I would, but
'Twas not a thing ordained; Heaven has forbid it,
And 'tis most meet that I should rather perish
Than the decree divine receive least blemish.
Feed inward, you my sorrows, make no noise;
Consume me silent, let me be stark dead
Ere the world know I'm sick. You° see my honesty;
If you befriend me, so.

137 **liberty** district within which a justice of the peace is entitled to preside 142 **set by** valued 142-3 **crackling . . . Capitol** (sacred geese on Capitoline Hill once warned the Romans of invading Gauls (the analogy is obscure) 149 **here** (either refers to Hippolito or some part of him) 163 **You** i.e., his sorrows

Isabella. [*Aside.*] Marry a fool!
Can there be greater misery to a woman
That means to keep her days true to her husband,
And know no other man, so virtue wills it!
Why, how can I obey and honour him,
But I must needs commit idolatry?°
A fool is but the image of a man,
And that but ill made neither. Oh the heartbreakings
Of miserable maids, where love's enforced!
The best condition is but bad enough:
When women have their choices, commonly
They do but buy their thraldoms, and bring great portions°
To men to keep 'em in subjection:
As if a fearful prisoner should bribe
The keeper to be good to him, yet lies in° still.
And glad of a good usage, a good look sometimes.
By'r Lady, no misery surmounts a woman's.
Men buy their slaves, but women buy their masters.
Yet honesty and love makes all this happy
And, next to angels', the most blest estate.
That Providence, that has made ev'ry poison
Good for some use, and sets four warring elements°
At peace in man, can make a harmony
In things that are most strange to human reason.
Oh, but this marriage! [*To Hippolito.*] What, are you sad too, uncle?
'Faith, then there's a whole household down together:
Where shall I go to seek my comfort now
When my best friend's distressed? What is't afflicts you, sir?

Hippolito. 'Faith, nothing but one grief that will not leave me,
And now 'tis welcome; ev'ry man has something
To bring him to his end, and this will serve,
Joined with your father's cruelty to you—
That helps it forward.

169 **idolatry** here, the worship of a senseless object 175 **portions** doweries 178 **lies in** remains in prison 185 **four warring elements** (the four conflicting elements in man correspond to those in nature: fire, air, earth, and water according to the Ptolemaic system)

Isabella. Oh be cheered, sweet uncle!
How long has't been upon you? I nev'r spied it;
What a dull sight have I! how long, I pray sir?
Hippolito. Since I first saw you, niece, and left Bologna.
Isabella. And could you deal so unkindly with my heart,
To keep it up so long hid from my pity?
Alas, how shall I trust your love hereafter.
Have we passed through so many arguments,°
And missed of that still, the most needful one?
Walked out whole nights together in discourses,
And the main point forgot? We are to blame both;
This is an obstinate wilful forgetfulness,
And faulty on both parts. Let's lose no time now.
Begin, good uncle, you that feel't; what is it?
Hippolito. You of all creatures, niece, must never hear on't;
'Tis not a thing ordained for you to know.
Isabella. Not I, sir! all my joys that word cuts off;
You made profession once you loved me best—
'Twas but profession!
Hippolito. Yes, I do't too truly,
And fear I shall be chid for't. Know the worst then:
I love thee dearlier than an uncle can.
Isabella. Why, so you ever said, and I believed it.
Hippolito. So simple is the goodness of her thoughts
They understand not yet th'unhallowed language
Of a near sinner.° I must yet be forced
(Though blushes be my venture)° to come nearer.
As a man loves his wife, so love I thee.
Isabella. What's that?
Methought I heard ill news come toward me,
Which commonly we understand too soon,
Than over-quick at hearing. I'll prevent it,
Though my joys fare the harder; welcome it—
It shall nev'r come so near mine ear again.°
Farewell all friendly solaces and discourses;
I'll learn to live without ye, for your dangers

203 **arguments** subjects 220 **near sinner** (1) person verging on sin, (2) a sinner who is closely related 221 **blushes . . . venture** blushes are the reward of my enterprise 223-27 **Methought . . . again** (although the passage is elusive, in it Isabella has the sensation that bad news, which one normally grasps immediately, is approaching gradually)

Are greater than your comforts. What's become
Of truth in love, if such we cannot trust—
When blood that should be love is mixed with lust!
Exit.

Hippolito. The worst can be but death, and let it come;
He that lives joyless, every day's his doom. *Exit.*

[Act I, Scene iii]

Enter Leantio alone.

Leantio. Methinks I'm ev'n as dull now at departure
As men observe great gallants the next day
After a revels; you shall see 'em look
Much of my fashion, if you mark 'em well.
'Tis ev'n a second hell to part from pleasure
When man has got a smack° on't. As many holidays
Coming together makes your poor heads idle
A great while after, and are said to stick
Fast in their fingers' ends; ev'n so does game
In a new-married couple for the time;
It spoils all thrift, and indeed lies a-bed

[*Enter*] *Bianca and Mother above.*

To invest all the new ways for great expenses.
See, and she be not got on purpose now
Into the window to look after me!
I have no power to go now and° I should be hanged.
Farewell all business! I desire no more
Than I see yonder. Let the goods at quay
Look to themselves; why should I toil my youth out?
It is but begging two or three year sooner,
And stay with her continually: is't a match?
Oh fie, what a religion have I leaped into!
Get out again, for shame! The man loves best
When his care's most—that shows his zeal to love.
Fondness is but the idiot to affection,°

I.iii.6 **smack** taste 15 **and** if 24 **Fondness . . . affection** doting plays the fool to true love

That plays at hot-cockles° with rich merchants' wives;
Good to make sport withal when the chest's full,
And the long warehouse cracks.° 'Tis time of day
For us to be more wise; 'tis early with us,
And if they° lose the morning of their affairs
They commonly lose the best part of the day.
Those that are wealthy and have got enough,
'Tis after sunset with 'em; they may rest,
Grow fat with ease, banquet, and toy and play,
When such as I enter the heat o'th'day;
And I'll do't cheerfully.

Bianca. I perceive, sir,
Y'are not gone yet; I have good hope you'll stay now.

Leantio. Farewell, I must not.

Bianca. Come, come; pray return.
Tomorrow, adding but a little care more,
Will dispatch all as well—believe me, 'twill sir.

Leantio. I could well wish myself where you would have me;
But love that's wanton must be ruled awhile
By that that's careful, or all goes to ruin.
As fitting is a government° in love
As in a kingdom; where 'tis all mere lust
'Tis like an insurrection in the people
That, raised in self-will, wars against all reason:
But love that is respective° of increase
Is like a good king, that keeps all in peace.
Once more, farewell.

Bianca. But this one night, I prithee.

Leantio. Alas, I'm in for twenty, if I stay.
And then for forty more, I have such luck to flesh:
I never bought a horse, but he bore double.°
If I stay any longer, I shall turn
An everlasting spendthrift; as you love
To be maintained well, do not call me again,
For then I shall not care which end goes forward.
Again, farewell to thee. *Exit.*

25 **hot-cockles** a game similar to blindman's buff, here a reference to sexual play 27 **warehouse cracks** i.e., from all the goods stored in them 29 **they** i.e., people 43 **a government** self-discipline 47 **is respective of** has respect for 52 **bore double** carried two riders (?), able to carry the weight of two (?)

Bianca. Since it must, farewell too.
Mother. 'Faith daughter, y'are to blame; you take the course
To make him an ill husband, troth you do,
And that disease is catching, I can tell you—
Ay, and soon taken by a young man's blood,
And that with little urging. Nay, fie, see now,
What cause have you to weep? would I had no more,
That have lived threescore years; there were a cause
And 'twere well thought on. Trust me, y'are to blame;
His absence cannot last five days at utmost.
Why should those tears be fetched forth? cannot love
Be ev'n as well expressed in a good look,
But it must see her face still in a fountain?
It shows like a country maid dressing her head
By a dish of water. Come, 'tis an old custom
To weep for love.

Enter two or three Boys, and a Citizen or two, with an Apprentice.

Boys. Now they come, now they come.
2 Boy. The duke!
3 Boy. The state!°
Citizen. How near, boy?
1 Boy. I'th'next street sir, hard at hand.
Citizen. You sirra, get a standing° for your mistress,
The best in all the city.
Apprentice. I have't for her, sir.
'Twas a thing I provided for her over-night,
'Tis ready at her pleasure.
Citizen. Fetch her to't then; away sir!
Bianca. What's the meaning of this hurry,
Can you tell, mother?
Mother. What a memory
Have I! I see by that years come upon me.
Why, 'tis a yearly custom and solemnity,°
Religiously observed by th'duke and state,
To St. Mark's temple, the fifteenth of April.°

73 state the nobles **75 standing** a place to stand **83 solemnity** festival **85 the fifteenth of April** (the Feast of St. Mark actually occurred on the 25th of April)

See if my dull brains had not quite forgot it!
'Twas happily questioned of thee; I had gone down else,
Sat like a drone below,° and never thought on't.
I would not to be ten years younger again
That you had lost the sight; now you shall see
Our duke, a goodly gentleman of his years.

Bianca. Is he old then?

Mother. About some fifty-five.

Bianca. That's no great age in man; he's then at best
For wisdom and for judgement.

Mother. The lord cardinal,
His noble brother—there's a comely gentleman,
And greater in devotion than in blood.°

Bianca. He's worthy to be marked.

Mother. You shall behold
All our chief states of Florence; you came fortunately
Against this solemn day.

Bianca. I hope so always.

Music.

Mother. I hear 'em near us now; do you stand easily?

Bianca. Exceeding well, good mother.

Mother. Take this stool.

Bianca. I need it not, I thank you.

Mother. Use your will, then.

Enter in great solemnity six Knights bare-headed, then two Cardinals, and then the Lord Cardinal, then the Duke; after him the States of Florence by two and two, with variety of music and song.

Exit.

Mother. How like you, daughter?

Bianca. 'Tis a noble state.
Methinks my soul could dwell upon the reverence
Of such a solemn and most worthy custom.
Did not the duke look up? me-thought he saw us.

Mother. That's everyone's conceit that sees a duke:
If he look steadfastly, he looks straight at them;
When he perhaps, good careful° gentleman,

88 **below** in the kitchen probably 96 **blood** noble birth 109 **careful** full of cares

Never minds any, but the look he casts
Is at his own intentions, and his object
Only the public good.
Bianca. Most likely so.
Mother. Come, come, we'll end this argument° below.
Exeunt.

[Act II, Scene i]

Enter Hippolito and Lady Livia the widow.

Livia. A strange affection, brother, when I think on't!
I wonder how thou cam'st by't.
Hippolito. Ev'n as easily
As man comes by destruction, which oft-times
He wears in his own bosom.
Livia. Is the world
So populous in women, and creation
So prodigal in beauty and so various,
Yet does love turn thy point to thine own blood?
'Tis somewhat too unkindly.° Must thy eye
Dwell evilly on the fairness of thy kindred,
And seek not where it should? It is confined
Now in a narrower prison than was made for't:
It is allowed a stranger; and where bounty
Is made the great man's honour, 'tis ill husbandry
To spare, and servants shall have small thanks for't.
So he Heaven's bounty seems to scorn and mock,
That spares free means,° and spends of his own stock.
Hippolito. Never was man's misery so soon sewed up,
Counting how truly.
Livia. Nay, I love you so,
That I shall venture much to keep a change from you
So fearful as this grief will bring upon you.
'Faith, it even kills me, when I see you faint
Under a reprehension;° and I'll leave it,
Though I know nothing can be better for you.

113 **argument** subject of discussion II.i.8 **unkindly** with pun on kind = family 16 **spares free means** refrains from using freely available resources, here women in general 22 **reprehension** reprimand

Prithee, sweet brother, let not passion waste
The goodness of thy time, and of thy fortune;
Thou keep'st the treasure of that life I love
As dearly as mine own; and if you think
My former words too bitter, which were ministered
By truth and zeal. 'Tis but a hazarding°
Of grace and virtue, and I can bring forth
As pleasant fruits as sensuality wishes
In all her teeming longings. This I can do.

Hippolito. Oh nothing that can make my wishes perfect!

Livia. I would that love of yours were pawned to't, brother,
And as soon lost that way as I could win.°
Sir, I could give as shrewd a lift to° chastity
As any she that wears a tongue in Florence:
Sh'ad need be a good horsewoman and sit fast
Whom my strong argument could not fling at last.
Prithee take courage, man; though I should counsel
Another to despair, yet I am pitiful
To thy afflictions, and will venture hard—
I will not name for what, 'tis not handsome;
Find you the proof, and praise me.

Hippolito. Then I fear me,
I shall not praise you in haste.

Livia. This is the comfort,
You are not the first, brother, has attempted
Things more forbidden than this seems to be.
I'll minister all cordials° now to you,
Because I'll cheer you up, sir.

Hippolito. I am past hope.

Livia. Love, thou shalt see me do a strange cure then,
As e'er was wrought on a disease so mortal
And near akin to shame. When shall you see her?

Hippolito. Never in comfort more.

Livia. Y'are so impatient too.

29 **but a hazarding** only a matter of risking 34-5 **I would . . . win** "I wish I could make you forget your love for Isabella as easily as I could, if I wished, cause her to return it" (Mulryne) 36 **give . . . a lift to** offer a helping hand (ironic), attack (?) 48 **cordials** medicinal stimulants for the heart

Hippolito. Will you believe—'death,° sh'as forsworn my company,
And sealed it with a blush.
Livia. So, I perceive
All lies upon my hands, then; well, the more glory
When the work's finished.

Enter Servant.

How now, sir, the news?
Servant. Madam, your niece, the virtuous Isabella,
Is 'lighted° now to see you.
Livia. That's great fortune.
Sir, your stars bless you simply. Lead her in.
Exit Servant.
Hippolito. What's this to me?
Livia. Your absence, gentle brother;
I must bestir my wits for you.
Hippolito. Ay, to great purpose.
Exit Hippolito.
Livia. Beshrew you, would I loved you not so well!
I'll go to bed, and leave this deed undone;
I am the fondest° where I once affect,
The carefull'st of their healths, and of their ease, forsooth,
That I look still but slenderly to mine own.
I take a course to pity him so much now,
That I have none left for modesty and myself.
This 'tis to grow so liberal—y'have few sisters
That love their brother's ease 'bove their own honesties:
But if you question my affections,
That will be found my fault.

Enter Isabella the niece.

Niece, your love's welcome.
Alas, what draws that paleness to thy cheeks?
This enforced marriage towards?°

54 **'death** by God's death 59 **Is 'lighted** has arrived 65 **fondest** most foolish 75 **towards** approaching 81 **entailed** by inheritance

Isabella. It helps, good aunt,
Amongst some other griefs—but those I'll keep
Locked up in modest silence; for they're sorrows
Would shame the tongue more than they grieve the thought.
Livia. Indeed, the ward is simple.
Isabella. Simple! that were well:
Why, one might make good shift with such a husband.
But he's a fool entailed,° he halts downright in't.°
Livia. And knowing this, I hope 'tis at your choice
To take or refuse, niece.
Isabella. You see it is not.
I loathe him more than beauty can hate death,
Or age, her spiteful neighbour.
Livia. Let 't appear, then.
Isabella. How can I, being born with that obedience
That must submit unto a father's will?
If he command, I must of force° consent.
Livia. Alas, poor soul! Be not offended, prithee,
If I set by the name of niece awhile,
And bring in pity in a stranger fashion.
It lies here in this breast, would cross this match.
Isabella. How, cross it, aunt?
Livia. Ay, and give thee more liberty
Than thou hast reason yet to apprehend.°
Isabella. Sweet aunt, in goodness keep not hid from me
What may befriend my life.
Livia. Yes, yes, I must,
When I return to reputation,
And think upon the solemn vow I made
To your dead mother, my most loving sister°—
As long as I have her memory 'twixt mine eyelids,
Look for no pity, now.
Isabella. Kind, sweet, dear aunt—
Livia. No, 'twas a secret I have took special care of,
Delivered by your mother on her deathbed—
That's nine years now—and I'll not part from 't yet,
Though nev'r was fitter time nor greater cause for 't.

81 **halts . . . in't** falls right into it (foolishness) 88 **of force** by necessity 94 **apprehend** understand 99 **sister** sister-in-law, in actuality

Isabella. As you desire the praises of a virgin—
Livia. Good sorrow!° I would do thee any kindness,
Not wronging secrecy or reputation.
Isabella. Neither of which, as I have hope of fruitfulness,
Shall receive wrong from me.
Livia. Nay, 'twould be your own wrong
As much as any's, should it come to that once.
Isabella. I need no better means to work persuasion then.
Livia. Let it suffice, you may refuse this fool,
Or you may take him, as you see occasion
For your advantage: the best wits will do't.
Y'have liberty enough in your own will;
You cannot be enforced: there grows the flower,
If you could pick it out, makes whole life sweet to you.
That which you call your father's command's nothing:
Then your obedience must needs be as little.
If you can make shift here to taste your happiness,
Or pick out aught that likes you, much good do you.
You see your cheer,° I'll make you no set dinner.
Isabella. And trust me, I may starve for all the good
I can find yet in this! Sweet aunt, deal plainlier.
Livia. Say I should trust you now upon an oath,
And give you in a secret that would start you;°
How am I sure of you, in faith and silence?
Isabella. Equal assurance may I find in mercy,
As you for that in me.
Livia. It shall suffice.
Then know, however custom has made good,
For reputation's sake, the names of niece
And aunt 'twixt you and I, w'are nothing less.
Isabella. How's that!
Livia. I told you I should start your blood.
You are no more allied to any of us,
Save what courtesy of opinion casts
Upon your mother's memory and your name,
Than the mer'st stranger is, or one begot
At Naples when the husband lies at Rome;
There's so much odds betwixt us.° Since your knowledge

107 **sorrow** i.e., Isabella 123 **cheer** here, food 127 **that . . . you** something that would startle you 140 **so much . . . us** that degree of separation, i.e, in blood, between us

Wished more instruction, and I have your oath
In pledge for silence, it makes me talk the freelier.
Did never the report of that famed Spaniard,
Marquess of Coria, since your time was ripe
For understanding, fill your ear with wonder?

Isabella. Yes, what of him? I have heard his deeds of honour
Often related when we lived in Naples.

Livia. You heard the praises of your father then.

Isabella. My father!

Livia. That was he; but all the business
So carefully and so discreetly carried
That fame received no spot by't, not a blemish.
Your mother was so wary to her end;
None knew it but her conscience, and her friend,
Till penitent confession made it mine,
And now my pity, yours: it had been long else,
And I hope care and love alike in you,
Made good by oath, will see it take no wrong now.
How weak his commands now, whom you call father?
How vain all his enforcements, your obedience?
And what a largeness in your will and liberty
To take or to reject, or to do both?
For fools will serve to father wise men's children—
All this y'have time to think on. Oh my wench,
Nothing o'erthrows our sex but indiscretion!
We might do well else of a brittle people°
As any under the great canopy.°
I pray forget not but to call me aunt still—
Take heed of that, it may be marked in time else.
But keep your thoughts to yourself, from all the world,
Kindred or dearest friend—nay, I entreat you,
From him that all this while you have called uncle;
And though you love him dearly, as I know
His deserts claim as much ev'n from a stranger,
Yet let not him know this, I prithee do not;
As ever thou hast hope of second pity
If thou shouldst stand in need on't, do not do't.

165 of a brittle people "for a frail, mortal race" (Mulryne) **166 the great canopy** the sky or heavens

Isabella. Believe my oath, I will not.
Livia. Why, well said.
[*Aside.*] Who shows more craft t'undo a maidenhead,
I'll resign my part to her.

Enter Hippolito.

She's thin own, go. *Exit.*
Hippolito. [*Aside.*] Alas, fair flattery cannot cure my sorrows!
Isabella. [*Aside.*] Have I passed so much time in ignorance,
And never had the means to know myself
Till this blest hour! Thanks to her virtuous pity
That brought it now to light—would I had known it
But one day sooner! he had then received
In favours what, poor gentleman, he took
In bitter words—a slight and harsh reward
For one of his deserts.
Hippolito. [*Aside.*] There seems to me now
More anger and distraction in her looks.
I'm gone, I'll not endure a second storm;
The memory of the first is not past yet.
Isabella. [*Aside.*] Are you returned, you comforts of my life,
In this man's presence? I will keep you fast now,
And sooner part eternally from the world
Than my good joys in you. [*To Hippolito.*] Prithee, forgive me.
I did but chide in jest; the best loves use it
Sometimes; it sets an edge upon affection.°
When we invite our best friends to a feast
'Tis not all sweetmeats that we set before them,
There's somewhat sharp and salt, both to whet appetite,
And make 'em taste their wine well: so, methinks,
After a friendly, sharp, and savoury chiding,
A kiss tastes wondrous well and full o'th'grape—
[*kisses him.*]
—How think'st thou, does't not?

196-7 the best loves . . . affection those who love best do it, i.e., scold in jest, because it stimulates the appetite of feeling

Hippolito. 'Tis so excellent,
I know not how to praise it, what to say to't.
Isabella. This marriage shall go forward.
Hippolito. With the ward?
Are you in earnest?
Isabella. 'Twould be ill for us else.
Hippolito. For us! how means she that?
Isabella. Troth, I begin
To be so well, methinks, within this hour—
For all this match able to kill one's heart—
Nothing can pull me down now; should my father
Provide a worse fool yet (which I should think
Were a hard thing to compass) I'ld have him either:
The worse the better; none can come amiss now
If he want° wit enough. So discretion love me,
Desert and judgement, I have content sufficient.
She that comes once to be a housekeeper
Must not look every day to fare well, sir,
Like a young waiting gentlewoman in service;
For she feels commonly as her lady does,
No good bit passes her but she gets a taste on't;
But when she comes to keep house for herself,
She's glad of some choice cates° then once a week,
Or twice at most, and glad if she can get 'em:
So must affection learn to fare with thankfulness.
Pray make your love no stranger, sir, that's all.
Though you be one yourself, and know not on't,
And I have sworn you must not. *Exit.*
Hippolito. This is beyond me!
Never came joys so unexpectedly
To meet desires in man. How came she thus?
What has she done to her, can any tell?
'Tis beyond sorcery, this, drugs or love-powders;
Some art that has no name, sure; strange to me
Of all the wonders I ere met withal
Throughout my ten years' travels. But I'm thankful for't.
This marriage now must of necessity forward:
It is the only veil wit can devise
To keep our acts hid from sin-piercing eyes.
Exit.

215 want lack 223 cates delicacies

[Act II, Scene ii]

Enter Guardiano and Livia.

Livia. How, sir, a gentlewoman so young, so fair,
As you set forth, spied from the widow's window?
Guardiano. She!
Livia. Our Sunday-dinner woman?
Guardiano. And Thursday-supper woman,° the same still.
I know not how she came by her, but I'll swear
She's the prime gallant for a face in Florence,
And no doubt other parts follow their leader.°
The duke himself first spied her at the window,
Then in a rapture, as if admiration
Were poor when it were single, beckoned me,
And pointed to the wonder warily,
As one that feared she would draw in her splendour
Too soon, if too much gazed at. I nev'r knew him
So infinitely taken with a woman;
Nor can I blame his appetite, or tax
His raptures of slight folly; she's a creature
Able to draw a state from serious business,
And make it their best piece to do her service.
What course shall we devise? h'as spoke twice now.
Livia. Twice.
Guariano. 'Tis beyond your apprehension
How strangely that one look has catched his heart!
'Twould prove but too much worth in wealth and favour
To those should work his peace.°
Livia. And if I do't not,
Or at least come as near it (if your art
Will take a little pains and second me)
As any wench in Florence of my standing,
I'll quite give o'er, and shut up shop in cunning.
Guardiano. 'Tis for the duke; and if I fail your purpose,
All means to come, by riches or advancement,
Miss me and skip me over!

II.ii.4-5 **Our . . . Thursday-supper woman** (although the exact meaning is unclear, the lines suggest that the widow is a dependent of Livia in some way) 8 **leader** i.e., her face 24 **work his peace** bring him peace of mind, i.e., by satisfying his desires

Livia. Let the old woman then
Be sent for with all speed; then I'll begin.
Guardiano. A good conclusion follow, and a sweet one,
After this stale beginning with old ware.
Within there!

Enter Servant.

Servant. Sir, do you call?
Guardiano. Come near, list hither.
Livia. [*Aside.*] I long myself to see this absolute° creature
That wins the heart of love and praise so much.
Guardiano. Go sir, make haste.
Livia. Say I entreat her company;
Do you hear, sir?
Servant. Yes, madam. *Exit.*
Livia. That brings her quickly.
Guardiano. I would 'twere done; the duke waits the good hour,
And I wait the good fortune that may spring from't:
I have had a lucky hand these fifteen year
At such court-passage° with three dice in a dish.

Enter Fabritio.

Signor Fabritio!
Fabritio. Oh sir, I bring an alteration in my mouth now.
Guardiano. An alteration! [*Aside.*] no wise speech, I hope;
He means not to talk wisely does he, trow?
[*To him.*] Good! what's the change, I pray sir?
Fabritio. A new change.
Guardiano. [*Aside.*] Another yet! 'faith, there's enough already.
Fabritio. My daughter loves him now.
Guardiano. What, does she, sir?
Fabritio. Affects him beyond thought—who but the ward, forsooth!

36 absolute perfect **43 such court-passage** (passage is a game played with three dice; "such court-passage" suggests that Guardiano has often managed affairs for the Duke so as to secure an attractive woman and deceive an elderly chaperon)

No talk but of the ward; she would have him
To choose 'bove all the men she ever saw.
My will goes not so fast as her consent now;
Her duty gets before my command still.°

Guardiano. Why then sir, if you'll have me speak my thoughts, I smell 'twill be a match.

Fabritio. Ay, and a sweet young couple
If I have any judgement.

Guardiano. [*Aside.*] 'Faith, that's little.
[*To Fabritio.*] Let her be sent tomorrow before noon,
And handsomely tricked up,° for 'bout that time
I mean to bring her in and tender her to him.

Fabritio. I warrant you for handsome; I will see
Her things laid ready, every one in order,
And have some part of her tricked up tonight.

Guardiano. Why, well said.

Fabritio. 'Twas a use her mother had
When she was invited to an early wedding;
She'ld dress her head o'ernight, sponge up herself,
And give her neck three lathers.

Guardiano. [*Aside.*] Ne'er a halter?°

Fabritio. On with her chain of pearl, her ruby bracelets,
Lay ready all her tricks and jiggambobs.°

Guardiano. So must your daughter.

Fabritio. I'll about it straight, sir.

Exit Fabritio.

Livia. How he sweats in the foolish zeal of fatherhood
After six ounces° an hour, and seems
To toil as much as if his cares were wise ones!

Guardiano. Y'have let his folly blood in the right vein, lady.

Livia. And here comes his sweet son-in-law that shall be.
They're both allied in wit before the marriage;
What will they be hereafter, when they are nearer?
Yet they can go further than the fool:
There's the world's end in both of 'em.

55 **gets . . . still** is always anticipating my command to her 60 **tricked up** dressed, decked out 68 **halter** (Guardiano puns on "lather" = leather out of which a halter is made) 70 **tricks and jiggambobs** trinkets and doodads 73 **After six ounces** at the rate of six ounces, i.e., of perspiration

Enter Ward and Sordido, one with a shuttlecock, the other a battledore.°

Guardiano. Now, young heir!

Ward. What's the next business after shuttlecock, now?

Guardiano. Tomorrow you shall see the gentlewoman must be your wife.

Ward. There's ev'n another thing° too must be kept up with a pair of battledores. My wife! what can she do?

Guardiano. Nay, that's a question you should ask yourself, ward, when y'are alone together.

Ward. That's as I list. A wife's to be asked anywhere, I hope; I'll ask her in a congregation,° if I have a mind to't, and so save a license.—My guardiner has no more wit than an herb-woman, that sells away all her sweet herbs and nosegays, and keeps a stinking breath for her own pottage.

Sordido. Let me be at the choosing of your beloved, if you desire a woman of good parts.

Ward. Thou shalt, sweet Sordido.

Sordido. I have a plaguey guess; let me alone to see what she is. If I but look upon her—'way,° I know all the faults to a hair that you may refuse her for.

Ward. Dost thou? I prithee let me hear 'em Sordido.

Sordido. Well, mark 'em then; I have 'em all in rhyme.

The wife your guardiner ought to tender,
Should be pretty, straight and slender;
Her hair not short, her foot not long,
Her hand not huge, nor too too loud her tongue;
No pearl in eye° nor ruby° in her nose,
No burn or cut but what the catalogue shows.
She must have teeth, and that no black ones,
And kiss most sweet when she does smack once:
Her skin must be both white and plumpt,
Her body straight, not hopper-rumped,°

80 s.d. **battledore** a small racket used to strike the shuttlecock 84 **another thing** i.e., a wife, here equated with "shuttlecock," a term sometimes used for "harlot" 89 **ask her in a congregation** i.e., ask the banns in church (without which, a special license to wed was required) 98 **'way** away, leave it to me 106 **pearl in eye** cataract in eye 106 **ruby** pimple 111 **hopper-rumped** having wide buttocks like the hopper of a mill

Or wriggle sideways like a crab.
She must be neither slut nor drab,
Nor go too splay-foot with her shoes
To make her smock lick up the dews.
And two things more which I forgot to tell ye:
She neither must have bump in back nor belly.
These are the faults that will not make her pass.

Ward. And if I spy not these I am a rank ass.

Sordido. Nay, more; by right, sir, you should see her naked,°
For that's the ancient order.

Ward. See her naked?
That were good sport, i'faith. I'll have the books turned over,
And if I find her naked on record
She shall not have a rag on. But stay, stay,
How if she should desire to see me so too?
I were in a sweet case then; such a foul skin.

Sordido. But y'have a clean shirt, and that makes amends, sir.

Ward. I will not see her naked for that trick, though.
Exit.

Sordido. Then take her with all faults with her clothes on,
And they may hide a number with a bum-roll.°
'Faith, choosing of a wench in a huge farthingale
Is like the buying of ware under a great penthouse:°
What with the deceit of one,
And the false° light of th'other, mark my speeches,
He may have a diseased wench in's bed
And rotten stuff in's breeches. *Exit.*

Guardiano. It may take° handsomely.

Livia. I see small hindrance.

Enter [Servant followed by] Mother.

How now, so soon returned?

Guardiano. She's come.

Livia. That's well.

120 see her naked (a custom proposed by Thomas More in *Utopia*) **131 bum-roll** roll of padding to hold out a skirt **133 penthouse** sloping roof attached to the wall of a building **135 false** meager **138 take** succeed

[*Exit Servant.*]

Widow, come, come; I have a great quarrel to you,
'Faith, I must chide you, that you must be sent for!
You make yourself so strange, never come at us,
And yet so near a neighbour, and so unkind,
Troth, y'are too blame; you cannot be more welcome
To any house in Florence, that I'll tell you.

Mother. My thanks must needs acknowledge so much, madam.

Livia. How can you be so strange then? I sit here
Sometime whole days together without company
When business draws this gentleman from home,
And should be happy in society
Which I so well affect as that of yours.
I know y'are alone too; why should not we,
Like two kind neighbours, then, supply the wants
Of one another, having tongue-discourse,°
Experience in the world, and such kind helps
To laugh down time, and meet age merrily?

Mother. Age, madam! you speak mirth; 'tis at my door,
But a long journey from your ladyship yet.

Livia. My faith, I'm nine-and-thirty, ev'ry stroke, wench;
And 'tis a general observation
'Mongst knights' wives or widows, we account
Ourselves then old, when young men's eyes leave looking at's:
'Tis a true rule amongst us, and ne'er failed yet
In any but in one that I remember;
Indeed, she had a friend° at nine-and-forty!
Marry, she paid well for him; and in th'end
He kept a quean° or two with her own money,
That robbed her of her plate and cut her throat.

Mother. She had her punishment in this world, madam;
And a fair warning to all other women
That they live chaste at fifty.

Livia. Ay, or never, wench.
Come, now I have thy company I'll not part with't
Till after supper.

Mother. Yes, I must crave pardon, madam.

154 tongue-discourse the facility to converse pleasantly **165 friend** lover **167 quean** whore

Livia. I swear you shall stay supper; we have no strangers, woman,
None but my sojourners° and I, this gentleman
And the young heir, his ward. You know our company.
Mother. Some other time I will make bold with you, madam.
Guardiano. Nay, pray stay widow.
Livia. 'Faith, she shall not go.
Do you think I'll be forsworn?
Table and chess [*set out.*]
Mother. 'Tis a great while
Till supper-time; I'll take my leave, then, now madam,
And come again i'th'evening, since your ladyship
Will have it so.
Livia. I'th'evening! By my troth, wench,
I'll keep you while I have you; you have great business, sure,
To sit alone at home. I wonder strangely
What pleasure you take in't! were't to me now,°
I should be ever at one neighbour's house
Or other all day long, having no charge,
Or none to chide you if you go or stay.
Who may live merrier, ay, or more at heart's ease?
Come, we'll to chess or draughts; there are an hundred tricks
To drive out time till supper, never fear't, wench.
Mother. I'll but make one step home and return straight, madam.
Livia. Come, I'll not trust you; you use more excuses
To your kind friends than ever I knew any.
What business can you have, if you be sure
Y'have locked the doors? and that being all you have,
I know y'are careful on't. One afternoon
So much to spend here! say I should entreat you now
To lie a night or two, or a week, with me,
Or leave your own house for a month together—
It were a kindness that long neighbourhood°
And friendship might well hope to prevail in.

175 **sojourners** lodgers or guests 185 **were't to me now** were this my situation 201 **neighbourhood** being neighbors

Would you deny such a request? i'faith,
Speak truth, and freely.
Mother. I were then uncivil, madam.
Livia. [*pointing to chess set.*]
Go to then, set your men;° we'll have whole nights
Of mirth together ere we be much older, wench.
Mother. [*Aside.*] As good now tell her, then, for she will know't;
I have always found her a most friendly lady.
Livia. Why widow, where's your mind?
Mother. Troth, ev'n at home, madam.
To tell you truth, I left a gentlewoman
Ev'n sitting all alone, which is uncomfortable,
Especially to young bloods.
Livia. Another excuse!
Mother. No, as I hope for health madam, that's a truth.
Please you to send and see.
Livia. What gentlewoman? Pish!
Mother. Wife to my son, indeed, but not known, madam,
To any but yourself.
Livia. Now I beshrew you,
Could you be so unkind to her and me,
To come and not bring her? 'Faith, 'tis not friendly!
Mother. I feared to be too bold.
Livia. Too bold? Oh what's become
Of the true hearty love was wont to be
'Mongst neighbours in old time!
Mother. And she's a stranger, madam.
Livia. The more should be her welcome. When is courtesy
In better practice, than when 'tis employed
In entertaining strangers? I could chide, i'faith.
Leave her behind, poor gentlewoman, alone too!
Make some amends, and send for her betimes; go.
Mother. Please you command one of your servants, madam.
Livia. Within there!

Enter Servant.

Servant. Madam?
Livia. Attend the gentlewoman.
Mother. It must be carried wondrous privately

205 men chessmen

From my son's knowledge; he'll break out in storms else.
Hark you sir.
[*She speaks apart to Servant.*]
Livia. Now comes in the heat of your part.
Guardiano. True, I know it, lady; and if I be out,°
May the duke banish me from all employments,
Wanton or serious. [*Exit Servant.*]
Livia. So, have you sent, widow?
Mother. Yes madam, he's almost at home by this.
Livia. And 'faith, let me entreat you, that henceforward
All such unkind faults may be swept from friendship,
Which does but dim the lustre. And think thus much:
It is wrong to me, that have ability
To bid friends welcome, when you keep 'em from me;
You cannot set greater dishonour near me,
For bounty is the credit and the glory
Of those that have enough. I see y'are sorry,
And the good 'mends° is made by't.
Mother. Here she' [i]s, madam.

Enter Bianca, and Servant.

Bianca. I wonder how she comes to send for me now?
[*Exit Servant.*]
Livia. Gentlewoman, y'are most welcome, trust me y'are,
As courtesy can make one, or respect
Due to the presence of you.
Bianca. I give you thanks, lady.
Livia. I heard you were alone, and 't had appeared
An ill condition in me, though I knew you not,
Nor ever saw you (yet humanity
Thinks ev'ry case her own) to have kept your company
Here from you and left you all solitary.
I rather ventured upon boldness then
As the least fault, and wished your presence here—
A thing most happily motioned of° that gentleman,
Whom I request you, for his care and pity,
To honour and reward with your acquaintance;

232 **be out** forget lines, as in a play 244 **'mends** amends 256 **motioned of** suggested by

A gentleman that ladies' rights stands for:
That's his profession.°
Bianca. 'Tis a noble one,
And honours my acquaintance.
Guardiano. All my intentions
Are servants to such mistresses.
Bianca. 'Tis your modesty,
It seems, that makes your deserts speak so low, sir.
Livia. Come widow. [*They play at chess.*] Look you, lady, here's our business;
Are we not well employed, think you? an old quarrel
Between us, that will never be at an end.
Bianca. No?
And methinks there's men° enough to part you, lady.
Livia. Ho—but they set us on, let us come off
As well as we can, poor souls; men care no farther.
I pray sit down, forsooth, if you have the patience
To look upon two weak and tedious gamesters.
Guardiano. 'Faith madam, set these by till evening;
You'll have enough on't then. The gentlewoman,
Being a stranger, would take more delight
To see your rooms and pictures.
Livia. Marry, good sir,
And well remembered! I beseech you show 'em her,
That will beguile time well; pray heartily, do sir,
I'll do as much for you; here, take these keys,
Show her the monument° too—and that's a thing
Everyone sees not; you can witness that, widow.
Mother. And that's worth sight indeed, madam.
Bianca. Kind lady.
I fear I came to be a trouble to you.
Livia. Oh, nothing less, forsooth.
Bianca. And to this courteous gentleman,
That wears a kindness in his breast so noble
And bounteous to the welcome of a stranger.
Guardiano. If you but give acceptance to my service,
You do the greatest grace and honour to me
That courtesy can merit.
Bianca. I were to blame else,
And out of fashion much; I pray you lead, sir.

260 **profession** claim, possibly also adopted role 267 **men** i.e., the chessmen 279 **monument** here, a statue (see l. 313)

Livia. After a game or two we'are for you, gentlefolks.
Guardiano. We wish no better seconds in society
Than your discourses, madam, and your partner's there.
Mother. I thank your praise. I listened to you, sir,
Though when you spoke there came a paltry rook°
Full in my way, and chokes up all my game.
Exit Guardiano and Bianca.
Livia. Alas, poor widow, I shall be too hard for thee.
Mother. Y'are cunning at the game, I'll be sworn, madam.
Livia. It will be found so, ere I give you over.°
She that can place her man well—
Mother. As you do, madam—
Livia. As I shall wench—can never lose her game.
Nay, nay, the black king's mine.
Mother. Cry you mercy, madam.
Livia. And this my queen.
Mother. I see't now.
Livia. Here's a duke
Will strike a sure stroke for the game anon;
Your pawn° cannot come back to relieve itself.
Mother. I know that, madam.
Livia. You play well the whilst;
How she belies her skill! I hold° two ducats
I give you check and mate to your white king,
Simplicity itself, your saintish king there.
Mother. Well, ere now, lady,
I have seen the fall of subtlety. Jest on.
Livia. Ay, but simplicity receives two for one.°
Mother. What remedy but patience!

Enter above Guardiano and Bianca.

Bianca. Trust me, sir,
Mine eye nev'r met with fairer ornaments.
Guardiano. Nay, livelier,° I'm persuaded, neither Florence
Nor Venice can produce.

295 rook (now the castle, this place was also known as the duke at one time) **299 give you over** am through with you **305 pawn** (the pawn, here an allusion to Bianca, can only move forward) **307 hold** bet you **312 two for one** two blows or checks for one **315 livelier** more lifelike

Bianca. Sir, my opinion
Takes your part highly.
Guardiano. There's a better piece
Yet than all these. *Duke above.*°
Bianca. Not possible, sir.
Guardiano. Believe it;
You'll say so when you see't. Turn but your eye now,
Y'are upon it presently. *Exit.*
Bianca. Oh sir!
Duke. He's gone, beauty!
Pish, look not after him, he's but a vapour
That when the sun° appears is seen no more.
Bianca. Oh treachery to honour!
Duke. Prithee tremble not.
I feel thy breast shake like a turtle° panting
Under a loving hand that makes much on't.
Why art so fearful? as I'm friend to brightness,
There's nothing but respect and honour near thee.
You know me, you have seen me; here's a heart
Can witness I have seen thee.
Bianca. The more's my danger.
Duke. The more's thy happiness. Pish, strive not, sweet!
This strength were excellent employed in love, now,
But here 'tis spent amiss. Strive not to seek
Thy liberty and keep me still in prison.
I'faith, you shall not out till I'm released now,
We'll both be freed together, or stay still by't;
So is captivity pleasant.
Bianca. Oh my lord.
Duke. I am not here in vain: have but the leisure
To think on that, and thou'lt be soon resolved.
The lifting of thy voice is but like one
That does exalt his enemy, who, proving high,
Lays all the plots to confound him that raised him.
Take warning, I beseech thee; thou seem'st to me
A creature so composed of gentleness
And delicate meekness, such as bless the faces
Of figures that are drawn for goddesses
And make art proud to look upon her work.

318 s.d. **above** i.e., at the same level as Bianca and Guardiano
322 **the sun** i.e., the prince 324 **turtle** turtledove

I should be sorry the least force should lay
An unkind touch upon thee.
Bianca. Oh my extremity!
My lord, what seek you?
Duke. Love.
Bianca. 'Tis gone already;
I have a husband.
Duke. That's a single comfort;
Take a friend to him.°
Bianca. That's a double mischief,
Or else there's no religion.
Duke Do not tremble
At fears of thine own making.
Bianca. Nor, great lord,
Make me not bold with death and deeds of ruin
Because they fear not you; me they must fright,
Then am I best in health. Should thunder speak
And none regard it, it had lost the name,
And were as good be still. I'm not like those
That take their soundest sleeps in greatest tempests;
Then wake I most, the weather fearfullest,
And call for strength to virtue.
Duke. Sure I think
Thou know'st the way to please me. I affect
A passionate pleading 'bove an easy yielding;
But never pitied any—they deserve none
That will not pity me. I can command:
Think upon that. Yet if thou truly knewest
The infinite pleasure my affection takes
In gentle, fair entreatings, when love's businesses
Are carried courteously 'twixt heart and heart,
You'ld make more haste to please me.
Bianca. Why should you seek, sir,
To take away that you can never give?
Duke. But I give better in exchange: wealth, honour.
She that is fortunate in a duke's favour
Lights on a tree that bears all women's wishes:
If your own mother saw you pluck fruit° there,
She would commend your wit, and praise the time

351 **Take a friend to him** take a lover in addition to him 375 **pluck fruit** (an allusion to the Fall of Man caused by Eve plucking the apple of knowledge)

Of your nativity. Take hold of glory.
Do not I know y'have cast away your life
Upon necessities, means merely doubtful
To keep you in indifferent health and fashion
(A thing I heard too lately and soon pitied).
And can you be so much your beauty's enemy
To kiss away a month or two in wedlock,
And weep whole years in wants for ever after?
Come, play the wise wench, and provide for ever:
Let storms come when they list, they find thee sheltered;
Should any doubt arise, let nothing trouble thee.
Put trust in our love for the managing
Of all to thy heart's peace. We'll walk together,
And show a thankful joy for both our fortunes.

Exit [both] above.

Livia. Did not I say my duke would fetch you over, widow?
Mother. I think you spoke in earnest when you said it, madam.
Livia. And my black king makes all the haste he can, too.
Mother. Well, madam, we may meet with him in time yet.
Livia. I have given thee blind mate° twice.
Mother. You may see, madam,
My eyes begin to fail.
Livia. I'll swear they do, wench.

Enter Guardiano.

Guardiano. [*Aside.*] I can but smile as often as I think on't!
How prettily the poor fool was beguiled,
How unexpectedly! It's a witty age;
Never were finer snares for women's honesties
Than are devised in these days; no spider's web
Made of a daintier thread, than are now practised
To catch love's flesh-fly by the silver wing.
Yet to prepare her stomach° by degrees
To Cupid's feast, because I saw 'twas queasy,
I showed her naked pictures by the way:
A bit to stay the appetite. Well, advancement,
I venture hard to find thee; if thou com'st

395 **blind mate** a checkmate in which a player calls check without realizing that he has actually mated his opponent 404 **stomach** appetite

With a greater title° set upon thy crest,
I'll take that first cross patiently, and wait
Until some other comes greater than that.
I'll endure all.

Livia. The game's ev'n at the best now; you may see, widow,
How all things draw to an end.

Mother. Ev'n so do I, madam.

Livia. I pray take some of your neighbours along with you.°

Mother. They must be those are almost twice your years, then,
If they be chose fit matches for my time, madam.

Livia. Has not my duke bestirred himself?

Mother. Yes, 'faith madam,
H'as done me all the mischief in this game.

Livia. H'as showed himself in's kind.

Mother. In's kind, call you it?
I may swear that.

Livia. Yes 'faith, and keep your oath.

Guardiano. Hark, list! there's somebody coming down; 'tis she.

Enter Bianca.

Bianca. [*Aside.*] Now bless me from a blasting! I saw that now
Fearful for any woman's eye to look on.
Infectious mists and mildews hang at's eyes,
The weather of a doomsday dwells upon him.
Yet since mine honour's leprous, why should I
Preserve that fair that caused the leprosy?
Come, poison all at once! Thou in whose business
The bane of virtue broods, I'm bound in soul
Eternally to curse thy smooth-browed treachery
That wore the fair veil of a friendly welcome,
And I a stranger; think upon't, 'tis worth it.
Murders piled up upon a guilty spirit
At his last breath will not lie heavier

409 **a greater title** pander (Gill) 415 **I pray . . . you** meaning: If you are so near to your end (death) as you say, so are some of your neighbors, as, for instance, myself

Than this betraying act upon thy conscience.
Beware of off'ring the first-fruits to sin:
His weight is deadly who commits° with strumpets
After they have been abased and made for use;
If they offend to th'death, as wise men know,
How much more they, then, that first make 'em so?
I give thee that to feed on. I'm made bold now,
I thank thy treachery; sin and I'm acquainted,
No couple greater; and I'm like that great one°
Who, making politic use of a base villain,
'He likes the treason well, but hates the traitor';
So I hate thee, slave.

Guardiano. [*Aside.*] Well, so the duke love me
I fare not much amiss then; two great feasts
Do seldom come together in one day,
We must not look for 'em.

Bianca. What, at it still, mother?

Mother. You see we sit by't; are you so soon returned?

Livia. So lively and so cheerful! a good sign, that.

Mother. You have not seen all since, sure?

Bianca. That have I, mother,
The monument and all: I'm so beholding
To this kind, honest, courteous gentleman.
You'ld little think it, mother—showed me all,
Had me from place to place so fashionably;
The kindness of some people, how't exceeds!
'Faith, I have seen that I little thought to see
I'th'morning when I rose.

Mother. Nay, so I told you
Before you saw't, it would prove worth your sight.
I give you great thanks for my daughter, sir,
And all your kindness towards her.

Guardiano. Oh good widow!
Much good may't do her [*aside.*] forty weeks hence, i'faith.

Enter Servant.

438 **commits** fornicates 444 **that great one** e.g., such as a king

Livia. Now sir?
Servant. May't please you, madam, to walk in;
Supper's upon the table.
Livia. Yes, we come.
Will't please you, gentlewoman?
Bianca. Thanks, virtuous lady
Y'are a damned bawd—I'll follow you, forsooth;
Pray take my mother in—an old ass go with you—
This gentleman and I vow not to part.
Livia. Then get you both before.
Bianca. —There lies his art.
Exeunt [Bianca and Guardiano.]
Livia. Widow, I'll follow you. *[Exit Mother.]*
Is't so, 'damned bawd'!
Are you so bitter? 'Tis but want of use;
Her tender modesty is sea-sick a little,
Being not accustomed to the breaking billow
Of woman's wavering faith, blown with temptations.
'Tis but a qualm of honour, 'twill away;
A little bitter for the time, but lasts not.
Sin tastes at the first draught like wormwood water,°
But drunk again, 'tis nectar ever after. *Exit.*

[Act III, Scene i]

Enter Mother.

Mother. I would my son either keep at home
Or I were in my grave.
She was but one day abroad, but ever since
She's grown so cutted,° there's no speaking to her.
Whether the sight of great cheer at my lady's,
And such mean fare at home, work discontent in her,
I know not; but I'm sure she's strangely altered.
I'll ne'er keep daughter-in-law i'th'house with me
Again, if I had an hundred. When read I of any
That agreed long together, but she and her mother
Fell out in the first quarter—nay, sometime

479 **Wormwood water** a drink made from wormwood, hence bitter III.i.4 **cutted** querulous

A grudging° of a scolding the first week, by'r Lady.
So takes the new disease,° methinks, in my house.
I'm weary of my part, there's nothing likes her;
I know not how to please her here o' late.
And here she comes.

Enter Bianca.

Bianca. This is the strangest house
For all defects, as ever gentlewoman
Made shift withal, to pass away her love in.
Why is there not a cushion-cloth of drawn work,°
Or some fair cut-work° pinned up in my bed-chamber,
A silver-and-gilt casting-bottle° hung by't?
Nay, since I am content to be so kind to you,
To spare you for a silver basin and ewer,
Which one of my fashion looks for of duty
She's never offered under, where she sleeps.

Mother She talks of things here my whole state's° not worth.

Bianca. Never a green silk quilt is there i'th'house, mother,
To cast upon my bed?

Mother. No by troth is there,
Nor orange-tawny neither.

Bianca. Here's a house
For a young gentlewoman to be got with child in!

Mother. Yes, simple though you make it, there has been three
Got in a year in't—since you move me to't—
And all as sweet-faced children and as lovely
As you'll be mother of: I will not spare you.
What, cannot children be begot, think you,
Without gilt casting-bottles? Yes, and as sweet ones:
The miller's daughter brings forth as white boys°
As she that bathes herself with milk and bean-flour.
'Tis an old saying 'one may keep good cheer

12 **grudging** bit 13 **the new disease** "an uncertainly diagnosed fever that made its appearance in England in the latter half of the sixteenth century" (Mulryne) 19 **drawn work** patterns of threads pulled out from a woven cloth 20 **cut-work** lace 21 **casting-bottle** bottle for sprinkling scent 26 **state's** estate's 37 **white boys** darlings

In a mean house': so may true love affect
After the rate of princes,° in a cottage.

Bianca. Troth, you speak wondrous well for your old house here;
'Twill shortly fall down at your feet to thank you,
Or stoop when you go to bed, like a good child,
To ask you blessing. Must I live in want,
Because my fortune matched me with your son?
Wives do not give away themselves to husbands
To the end to be quite cast away; they look
To be the better used and tendered rather,
Highlier respected, and maintained the richer;
They're well rewarded else for the free gift
Of their whole life to a husband. I ask less now
Than what I had at home when I was a maid
And at my father's house; kept short of that
Which a wife knows she must have—nay, and will,
Will, mother, if she be not a fool born;
And report went of me that I could wrangle
For what I wanted when I was two hours old;
And by that copy,° this land still I hold.
You hear me, mother. *Exit.*

Mother. Ay, too plain, methinks;
And were I somewhat deafer when you spake
'Twere nev'r a whit the worse for my quietness.
'Tis the most sudden'st, strangest alteration,
And the most subtlest that ev'r wit at threescore
Was puzzled to find out. I know no cause for't; but
She's no more like the gentlewoman at first
Than I am like her that nev'r lay with man yet,
And she's a very young thing where'er she be.
When she first lighted here, I told her then
How mean she should find all things; she was pleased, forsooth,
None better: I laid open all defects to her;
She was contented still. But the devil's in her,
Nothing contents her now. Tonight my son
Promised to be at home; would he were come once,°
For I'm weary of my charge, and life too.
She'ld be served all in silver, by her good will,

40-41 affect . . . princes feel as deeply as princes do **59 copy** copyhold **74 once** at once

By night and day; she hates the name of pewter
More than sick men the noise,° or diseased bones
That quake at fall o'th'hammer, seeming to have
A fellow-feeling with't at every blow.
What course shall I think on? she frets me so.
[*Mother stands aside.*]

Enter Leantio.

Leantio. How near am I now to a happiness
That earth exceeds not—not another like it!
The treasures of the deep are not so precious
As are the concealed comforts of a man,
Locked up in woman's love. I scent the air
Of blessings when I come but near the house.
What a delicious breath marriage sends forth;
The violet-bed's not sweeter. Honest wedlock
Is like a banqueting-house built in a garden,°
On which the spring's chaste flowers take delight
To cast their modest odours when base lust,
With all her powders, paintings and best pride,
Is but a fair house built by a ditch side.
When I behold a glorious dangerous strumpet,
Sparkling in beauty and destruction too,
Both at a twinkling, I do liken straight°
Her beautified body to a goodly temple
That's built on vaults where carcasses lie rotting:
And so by little and little I shrink back again,
And quench desire with a cool meditation;
And I'm as well, methinks. Now for a welcome
Able to draw men's envies upon man:
A kiss now that will hang upon my lip
As sweet as morning dew upon a rose,
And full as long. After a five days' fast
She'll be so greedy now, and cling about me,
I take care° how I be rid of her;
And here't begins.

78 **the noise** sounds preceding death 90 **banqueting-house . . . garden** (semipermanent, much admired feature of Jacobean gardens) 97 **liken straight** compare immediately 108 **I take care** I'll have a deal of trouble (ironic)

[*Enter Bianca.*]

Bianca. Oh sir, y'are welcome home.
Mother. [*noticing Leantio.*] Oh is he come? I am glad on't.
Leantio. Is that all?
Why this? as dreadful now as sudden death
To some rich man that flatters all his sins
With promise of repentance when he's old,
And dies in the midway before he comes to't.
Sure y'are not well Bianca! How dost, prithee?
Bianca. I have been better than I am at this time.
Leantio. Alas, I thought so.
Bianca. Nay, I have been worse too
Than now you see me sir.
Leantio. I'm glad thou mend'st yet;
I feel my heart mend too. How came it to thee?
Has anything disliked thee in my absence?
Bianca. No, certain; I have had the best content
That Florence can afford.
Leantio. Thou makest the best on't;
Speak mother, what's the cause? you must needs know.
Mother. Troth, I know none, son; let her speak herself.
[*Aside.*] Unless it be the same gave Lucifer
A tumbling-cast,° that's pride.
Bianca. Methinks this house stands nothing to my mind,
I'ld have some pleasant lodgings i'th'high street, sir;
Or if 'twere near the court, sir, that were much better:
'Tis a sweet recreation for a gentlewoman
To stand in a bay-window and see gallants.
Leantio. Now I have another temper,° a mere stranger
To that of yours, it seems; I should delight
To see none but yourself.
Bianca. I praise not that:
Too fond is as unseemly as too churlish.
I would not have a husband of that proneness
To kiss me before company, for a world.
Beside, 'tis tedious to see one thing still, sir,
Be it the best that ever heart affected—
Nay, were't yourself, whose love had power, you know,
To bring me from my friends, I would not stand thus
And gaze upon you always; troth, I could not, sir.

126 **tumbling-cast** wrestling throw 132 **temper** temperament

As good be blind and have no use of sight
As look on one thing still: what's the eye's treasure
But change of objects? You are learned, sir,
And know I speak not ill. 'Tis full as virtuous
For woman's eye to look on several men,
As for her heart, sir, to be fixed on one.

Leantio. Now thou com'st home to me; a kiss for that word.

Bianca. No matter for a kiss, sir; let it pass;
'Tis but a toy, we'll not so much as mind it.
Let's talk of other business and forget it.
What news now of the pirates; any stirring?
Prithee discourse a little.

Mother. I am glad he's here yet
To see her tricks himself; I had lied monstrously
If I had told 'em first.

Leantio. Speak, what's the humour, sweet,
You make your lip so strange?° this was not wont.

Bianca. Is there no kindness betwixt man and wife
Unless they make a pigeon-house of friendship
And be still billing? 'tis the idlest fondness
That ever was invented, and 'tis pity
It's grown a fashion for poor gentlewomen;
There's many a disease kissed in a year by't,
And a French curtsy° made to't. Alas, sir,
Think of the world, how we shall live, grow serious;
We have been married a whole fortnight now.

Leantio. How? a whole fortnight! why, is that so long?

Bianca. 'Tis time to leave off dalliance; 'tis a doctrine
Of your own teaching, if you be remembered,
And I was bound to obey it.

Mother. Here's one fits him;
This was well catched, i'faith son, like a fellow
That rids another country of a plague
And brings it home with him to his own house.
Who knocks? *Knock within.*

Leantio. Who's there now? Withdraw you, Bianca;
Thou art a gem no stranger's eye must see,
Howe'er thou please now to look dull on me.
Exit [Bianca.]

157 strange unfriendly 164 French curtsy (1) elegant manners of the French, (2) the pox or syphilis, the "French disease"

Enter Messenger.

Y'are welcome sir; to whom your business pray?
Messenger. To one I see not here now.
Leantio. Who should that be, sir?
Messenger. A young gentlewoman I was sent to.
Leantio. A young gentlewoman?
Messenger. Ay sir, about sixteen.
Why look you wildly sir?
Leantio. At your strange error;
Y'have mistook the house, sir, there's none such here,
I assure you.
Messenger. I assure you too:
The man that sent me cannot be mistook.
Leantio. Why, who is't sent you, sir?
Messenger. The duke.
Leantio. The duke!
Messenger. Yes, he entreats her company at a banquet
At Lady Livia's house.
Leantio. Troth, shall I tell you, sir,
It is the most erroneous business
That ere your honest pains was abused with.
I pray forgive me if I smile a little—
I cannot choose, i'faith sir, at an error
So comical as this (I mean no harm, though).
His grace has been most wondrous ill informed;
Pray so return it, sir. What should her name be?
Messenger. That I shall tell you straight too: Bianca Capella.
Leantio. How sir, Bianca? what do you call th'other?
Messenger. Capella. Sir, it seems you know no such, then?
Leantio. Who should this be? I never heard o'th'name.
Messenger. Then 'tis a sure mistake.
Leantio. What if you enquired
In the next street, sir? I saw gallants there
In the new houses that are built of late.
Ten to one, there you find her.
Messenger. Nay, no matter,
I will return° the mistake and seek no further.
Leantio. Use your own will and pleasure sir; y'are welcome.
Exit Messenger.
What shall I think of first? Come forth Bianca.

203 return report

[*Enter Bianca.*]

Thou art betrayed, I fear me.
Bianca. Betrayed—how sir?
Leantio. The duke knows° thee.
Bianca. Knows me! how know you that, sir?
Leantio. Has got thy name.
Bianca. Ay, and my good name too,
That's worse o'th'twain.
Leantio. How comes this work about?
Bianca. How should the duke know me? can you guess, mother?
Mother. Not I with all my wits; sure, we kept house close.
Leantio. Kept close! not all the locks in Italy
Can keep you women so. You have been gadding,
And ventured out at twilight to th'court-green° yonder,
And met with the gallant bowlers coming home—
Without your masks° too, both of you; I'll be hanged else!
Thou hast been seen, Bianca, by some stranger;
Never excuse it.
Bianca. I'll not seek the way, sir.
Do you think y'have married me to mew me up
Not to be seen; what would you make of me?
Leantio. A good wife, nothing else.
Bianca. Why, so are some
That are seen ev'ry day, else the devil take 'em.
Leantio. No more then: I believe all virtuous in thee
Without an argument. 'Twas but thy hard chance
To be seen somewhere; there lies all the mischief,
But I have devised a riddance.
Mother. Now I can tell you, son,
The time and place.
Leantio. When? where?
Mother. What wits have I!
When you last took your leave, if you remember,
You left us both at window.
Leantio. Right, I know that.

207 **knows** (1) knows about, (2) has sexual knowledge of 214 **court-green** bowling green 216 **Without your masks** (the opposite of what was proper for young Italian wives to do)

Mother. And not the third part of an hour after
The duke passed by in a great solemnity
To St Mark's temple; and to my apprehension
He looked up twice to th'window.
Leantio. Oh, there quickened°
The mischief of this hour.
Bianca. [*Aside.*] If you call't mischief,
It is a thing I fear I am conceived with.
Leantio. Looked he up twice, and could you take no warning!
Mother. Why, once may do as much harm, son, as a thousand:
Do not you know one spark has fired an house
As well as a whole furnace?
Leantio. My heart flames for't.
Yet let's be wise and keep all smothered closely;
I have bethought a means. Is the door fast?
Mother. I locked it myself after him.
Leantio. You know, mother,
At the end of the dark parlour there's a place
So artificially° contrived for a conveyance°
No search could ever find it—when my father
Kept in for manslaughter, it was his sanctuary:
There will I lock my life's best treasure up.
Bianca?
Bianca. Would you keep me closer yet?
Have you the conscience? Y'are best ev'n choke me up, sir!
You make me fearful of your health and wits,
You cleave to such wild courses. What's the matter?
Leantio. Why, are you so insensible of your danger
To ask that now? The duke himself has sent for you
To Lady Livia's, to a banquet forsooth.
Bianca. Now I beshrew you heartily, has he so!
And you the man would never yet vouchsafe
To tell me on't till now. You show your loyalty
And honesty at once; and so farewell, sir.
Leantio. Bianca, whither now?

233 **quickened** came to life (with a double meaning) 244 **artificially** artfully 244 **conveyance** secret passage

Bianca. Why, to the duke, sir.
You say he sent for me.
Leantio. But thou dost not mean
To go, I hope.
Bianca. No? I shall prove unmannerly,
Rude and uncivil, mad, and imitate you?
Come, mother, come; follow his humour no longer.
We shall be all executed for treason shortly.
Mother. Not I, i'faith; I'll first obey the duke,
And taste of a good banquet; I'm of thy mind.
I'll step but up and fetch two handkerchiefs
To pocket up some sweetmeats, and o'ertake thee.
[*Exit.*]
Bianca. [*Aside.*] Why, here's an old wench would trot into° a bawd now
For some dry sucket° or a colt in marchpane.°
[*Exit.*]
Leantio. Oh thou the ripe time of man's misery, wedlock,
When all his thoughts, like over-laden trees,
Crack with the fruits they bear, in cares, in jealousies.
Oh that's a fruit that ripens hastily
After 'tis knit to marriage: it begins
As soon as the sun shines upon the bride
A little to show colour. Blessed powers!
Whence comes this alteration? the distractions,
The fears and doubts it brings are numberless;
And yet the cause I know not. What a peace
Has he that never marries! if he knew
The benefit he enjoyed, or had the fortune
To come and speak with me, he should know then
The infinite wealth he had, and discern rightly
The greatness of his treasure by my loss.
Nay, what a quietness has he 'bove mine,
That wears his youth out in a strumpet's arms,
And never spends more care upon a woman
Than at the time of lust; but walks away,
And if he finds her dead at his return,
His pity is soon done: he breaks a sigh
In many parts, and gives her but a piece on't.

269 **trot into** rush into becoming 270 **dry sucket** a kind of glazed food, usually fruit 270 **marchpane** marzipan, here in the shape of a colt

But all the fears, shames, jealousies, costs and troubles,
And still renewed cares of a marriage bed
Live in the issue when the wife is dead.

Enter Messenger.

Messenger. A good perfection° to your thoughts.
Leantio. The news, sir?
Messenger. Though you were pleased of late to pin an error on me,
You must not shift another in your stead too:
The duke has sent me for you.
Leantio. How, for me, sir?
[*Aside.*] I see then 'tis my theft; w're both betrayed.
Well, I'm not the first has stol'n away a maid:
My countrymen have used it. [*To Messenger.*]
I'll along with you, sir. *Exeunt.*

[Act III, Scene ii]

A banquet prepared:

Enter Guardiano and Ward.

Guardiano. Take you especial note of such a gentlewoman,
She's here on purpose; I have invited her,
Her father and her uncle, to this banquet.
Mark her behaviour well, it does concern you;
And what her good parts are, as far as time
And place can modestly require a knowledge of,
Shall be laid open to your understanding.
You know I'm both your guardian and your uncle:
My care of you is double, ward and nephew,
And I'll express it here.
Ward. 'Faith, I should know her
Now, by her mark,° among a thousand women:
A little, pretty, deft and tidy thing, you say?
Guardiano. Right.

296 **perfection** finishing off (the Messenger may overhear Leantio's last words) III.ii.11 **mark** distinguishing appearance

Ward. With a lusty sprouting sprig in her hair?
Guardiano. Thou goest the right way still; take one mark more:
Thou shalt nev'r find her hand out of her uncle's,
Or else his out of hers, if she be near him:
The love of kindred never yet stuck closer
Than their's to one another; he that weds her
Marries her uncle's heart too. *Cornets.*
Ward. Say you so, sir;
Then I'll be asked i'th'church to both of 'em.
Guardiano. Fall back, here comes the duke.
Ward. He brings a gentlewoman,
I should fall forward° rather.

Enter Duke, Bianca, Fabritio, Hippolito, Livia, Mother, Isabella, and Attendants.

Duke. Come Bianca,
Of purpose sent into the world to show
Perfection once in woman; I'll believe
Henceforward they have ev'ry one a soul° too,
'Gainst all the uncourteous opinions
That man's uncivil rudeness ever held of 'em.
Glory of Florence, light° into mine arms!

Enter Leantio.

Bianca. Yon comes a grudging man will chide you, sir.
The storm is now in's heart, and would get nearer
And fall here° if it durst; it pours down yonder.
Duke. If that be he, the weather shall soon clear;
List and I'll tell thee how. [*Whispers to Bianca.*]
Leantio. [*Aside.*] A kissing too?
I see 'tis plain lust now, adultery boldened.
What will it prove anon, when 'tis stuffed full
Of wine and sweetmeats, being so impudent fasting?
Duke. [*To Leantio.*] We have heard of your good parts, sir, which we honour

24 fall forward i.e., upon her **28 ev'ry one a soul** (whether or not women had souls was a matter of dispute going back to medieval times) **31 light** leap **34 here** (Bianca indicates either herself or the Duke)

With our embrace and love. [*To Gentleman.*] Is not the captainship
Of Rouans'° citadel, since the late deceased,
Supplied by any yet?
Gentleman. By none, my lord.
Duke. Take it, the place is yours then [*Leantio kneels.*] and as faithfulness
And desert grows, our favour shall grow with't:
Rise now the captain of our fort at Rouans.
Leantio. The service of whole life give your grace thanks.
Duke. Come, sit Bianca.
Leantio. [*Aside.*] This is some good yet,
And more than ev'r I looked for; a fine bit
To stay a cuckold's stomach.° All preferment
That springs from sin and lust, it shows up quickly,
As gardeners' crops do in the rotten'st grounds:
So is all means raised from base prostitution
Ev'n like a sallet° growing upon a dunghill.
I'm like a thing that never was yet heard of,
Half merry and half mad—much like a fellow
That eats his meat with a good appetite,
And wears a plague-sore that would fright a country;
Or rather like the barren° hardened ass,
That feeds on thistles till he bleeds again°—
And such is the condition of my misery.
Livia. Is that your son, widow?
Mother. Yes, did your ladyship
Never know that till now?
Livia. No, trust me, did I.
[*Aside.*] Nor ever truly felt the power of love
And pity to a man, till now I knew him.
I have enough to buy me my desires,
And yet to spare, that's one good comfort. [*To Leantio.*] Hark you?
Pray let me speak with you, sir, before you go.
Leantio. With me, lady? you shall; I am at your service.
[*Aside.*] What will she say now, trow? more goodness yet?
Ward. I see her now, I'm sure; the ape's so little, I shall scarce feel her! I have seen almost as tall as she sold in

42 **Rouans'** (the existence of such a citadel is uncertain) 50 **To stay . . . stomach** To appease a cuckold's hunger (for revenge) 54 **sallet** salad 59 **barren** stupid 60 **again** as a result

the fair for tenpence. See how she simpers it—as if marmalade would not melt in her mouth! She might have kindness, i'faith, to send me a gilded bull from her own trencher, a ram, a goat,° or somewhat to be nibbling; these women, when they come to sweet things once, they forget all their friends, they grow so greedy—nay, oftentimes their husbands.

Duke. Here's a health now, gallants,
To the best beauty at this day in Florence.
Bianca. Whoe'er she be, she shall not go unpledged, sir.
Duke. Nay, you're excused for this.
Bianca. Who, I my lord?
Duke. Yes, by the law of Bacchus; plead your benefit:°
You are not bound to pledge your own health, lady.
Bianca. That's a good way, my lord, to keep me dry.
Duke. Nay then, I will not offend Venus so much;
Let Bacchus seek his 'mends in another court.
Here's to thyself, Bianca.
Bianca. Nothing comes
More welcome to that name than your grace.
Leantio. [*Aside*.] So, so!
Here stands the poor thief now that stole the treasure,
And he's not thought on. Ours° is near kin now
To a twin misery born into the world:
First the hard-conscienced wordling, he hoards wealth up;
Then comes the next, and he feasts all upon't—
One's damned for getting, th'other for spending on't.
Oh equal justice thou hast met my sin
With a full weight; I'm rightly now oppressed:
All her friends'° heavy hearts lie in my breast.
Duke. Methinks there is no spirit amongst us, gallants,
But what divinely sparkles from the eyes
Of bright Bianca; we sat all in darkness
But for that splendour. Who was't told us lately
Of a match-making rite, a marriage-tender?
Guardiano. 'Twas I, my lord.

75-6 **gilded bull . . . goat** figures carved in marchpane or marzipan, having lecherous connotations 84 **plead your benefit** claim exemption from obligation or punishment because of class status 92 **Ours** i.e., thieves such as himself 99 **friends** i.e., those left behind in Venice

Duke. 'Twas you indeed. Where is she?
Guardiano. This is the gentlewoman.
Fabritio. My lord, my daughter.
Duke. Why, here's some stirring yet.
Fabritio. She's a dear child to me.
Duke. That must needs be, you say she is your daughter.
Fabritio. Nay my good lord, dear to my purse, I mean,
Beside my person; I nev'r reckoned that.°
She has the full qualities of a gentlewoman;
I have brought her up to music, dancing, what not,
That may commend her sex and stir her husband.
Duke. And which is he now?
Guardiano. This young heir, my lord.
Duke. What is he brought up to?
Hippolito. [*Aside.*] To cat and trap.
Guardiano. My lord, he's a great ward, wealthy but simple;
His parts° consist in acres.
Duke. Oh, wise-acres!
Guardiano. Y'have spoke him in a word, sir.
Bianca. 'Las, poor gentlewoman,
She's ill bestead, unless sh'as dealt the wiselier
And laid in more provision for her youth:
Fools° will not keep in summer.
Leantio. No, nor such wives
From whores in winter.
Duke. Yea, the voice too, sir?
Fabritio. Ay, and a sweet breast° too, my lord, I hope,
Or I have cast away my money wisely;
She took her pricksong° earlier, my lord,
Than any of her kindred ever did.
A rare child, though I say't—but I'ld not have
The baggage hear so much; 'twould make her swell straight,
And maids of all things must not be puffed up.
Duke. Let's turn us to a better banquet, then;
For music bids the soul of man to a feast,
And that's indeed a noble entertainment

110 **reckoned that** included that in the reckoning 117 **parts** accomplishments 121 **Fools** desserts made of cream 123 **breast** singing voice 125 **pricksong** vocal music that is written out ("pricked down") on paper

Worthy Bianca's self. You shall perceive, beauty,
Our Florentine damsels are not brought up idlely.
Bianca. They're wiser of themselves, it seems, my lord,
And can take gifts, when goodness offers 'em.

Music.

Leantio. [*Aside*.] True; and damnation has taught you that wisdom,
You can take gifts too. Oh that music mocks me!
Livia. [*Aside*.] I am as dumb to any language now
But love's, as one that never learned to speak!
I am not yet so old, but he may think of me.
My own fault—I have been idle a long time;
But I'll begin the week and paint° tomorrow,
So follow my true labour day by day:
I never thrived so well as when I used it.
Isabella.

Song°

What harder chance can fall to woman,
Who was born to cleave to some man,
Than to bestow her time, youth, beauty,
Life's observance,° honour, duty,
On a thing for no use good,
But to make physic work, or blood
Force fresh in an old lady's cheek?°
She that would be
Mother of fools, let her compound with me.

Ward. Here's a tune indeed! Pish! I had rather hear one ballad sung i'th'nose now, of the lamentable drowning of fat sheep and oxen, than all these simpering tunes played upon cat-guts and sung by little kitlings.
Fabritio. How like you her breast now, my lord?
Bianca. [*Aside*.] Her breast?
He talks as if his daughter had given suck

143 paint apply cosmetics **146-58 Song** (originally the song was printed on the left of the page and the Ward's speech on the right, indicating simultaneous performance) 149 **observance** dutiful service 151-2 **But . . . cheek** Exciting enough only to make a laxative work or an old lady blush 158 **kitlings** kittens

Before she were married, as her betters have;
The next he praises sure will be her nipples.
Duke. [*Aside*.] Methinks now, such a voice to such a husband
Is like a jewel of unvalued worth
Hung at a fool's ear.
Fabritio. May it please your grace
To give her leave to show another quality?
Duke. Marry, as many good ones as you will, sir,
The more the better welcome.
Leantio. [*Aside*.] But the less
The better practised. That soul's black indeed
That cannot commend virtue. But who keeps it?
The extortioner will say to a sick beggar
'Heaven comfort thee', though he give none himself.
This good is common.
Fabritio. Will it please you now, sir,
To entreat your ward to take her by the hand
And lead her in a dance before the duke?
Guardiano. That will I, sir; 'tis needful.° Hark you, nephew.
Fabritio. Nay you shall see, young heir, what y'have for your money,
Without fraud or imposture.
Ward. Dance with her!
Not I, sweet guardiner, do not urge my heart to't,
'Tis clean against my blood;° dance with a stranger!
Let whos' will do't, I'll not begin first with her.
Hippolito. [*Aside*.] No, fear't not, fool; sh'as took a better order.
Guardiano. Why, who shall take her, then?
Ward. Some other gentleman—
Look, there's her uncle, a fine-timbered° reveller;
Perhaps he knows the manner of her dancing too;
I'll have him do't before me. I have sworn, guardiner;
Then may I learn the better.
Guardiano. Thou'lt be an ass still.
Ward. Ay, all that 'uncle' shall not fool me out:
Pish, I stick closer° to myself than so.

176 **needful** (apparently it was a custom for the bridal couple to dance together as a sign of concord) 180 **blood** natural bent 184 **fine-timbered** well-built 189 **stick closer** remain truer

Guardiano. I must entreat you, sir, to take your niece
And dance with her; my ward's a little wilful,
He would have you show him the way.
Hippolito. Me sir?
He shall command it at all hours; pray tell him so.
Guardiano. I thank you for him; he has not wit himself, sir.
Hippolito. Come, my life's peace, I have a strange office on't here.
'Tis some man's luck to keep the joys he likes
Concealed for his own bosom; but my fortune
To set 'em out now for another's liking:
Like the mad misery of necessitous man,
That parts from his good horse with many praises,
And goes on foot himself. Need must be obeyed
In ev'ry action, it mars man and maid.

Music. A dance, [with Hippolito and Isabella] making honours to the Duke and curtsy to themselves, both before and after.

Duke. Signor Fabritio, y'are a happy father;
Your cares and pains are fortunate; you see
Your cost bears noble fruits. Hippolito, thanks.
Fabritio. Here's some amends for all my charges yet;
She wins both prick and praise° where'er she comes.
Duke. How lik'st, Bianca?
Bianca. All things well, my lord,
But this poor gentlewoman's fortune, that's the worst.
Duke. There is no doubt, Bianca, she'll find leisure
To make that good enough; he's rich and simple.
Bianca. She has the better hope o'th'upper hand, indeed,
Which women strive for most.
Guardiano. Do't when I bid you
Ward. I'll venture but a hornpipe° with her, guardiner,
Or some such married man's dance.
Guardiano. Well, venture something, sir.
Ward. I have rhyme for what I do.
Guardiano. But little reason, I think.

207 prick and praise praise for hitting the bull's eye (in archery the prick is the point at the center of the target) **214 hornpipe** a simple vigorous dance

Ward. Plain men dance the measures,° the cinquepace° the gay!
Cuckolds dance the hornpipe, and farmers dance the hay;°
Your soldiers dance the round,° and maidens that grow big
Your drunkards, the canaries;° your whore and bawd, the jig.°
Here's your eight kind of dancers—he that finds the ninth,
Let him pay the minstrels.
Duke. Oh, here he appears once in his own person;
I thought he would have married her by attorney,°
And lain with her so too.
Bianca. Nay, my kind lord,
There's very seldom any found so foolish
To give away his part there.
Leantio. [*Aside*.] Bitter scoff!
Yet I must do't. With what a cruel pride
The glory° of her sin strikes by° my afflictions!

Music. Ward and Isabella dance; he ridiculously imitates Hippolito.

Duke. This thing will make shift, sirs, to make a husband,
For aught I see in him; how think'st, Bianca?
Bianca. 'Faith, an ill-favoured shift, my lord. Methinks
If he would take some voyage when he's married,
Dangerous or long enough, and scarce be seen
Once in nine year together, a wife then
Might make indifferent shift to be content with him.
Duke. A kiss! that wit deserves to be made much on.
Come, our caroche!°
Guardiano. Stands ready for your grace.
Duke. My thanks to all your loves. Come, fair Bianca;
We have took special care of you, and provided
Your lodging near us now.

217 **measures** a stately dance 217 **cinquepace** a lively French dance, early form of the galliard 218 **hay** a country dance 219 **round** a circling dance, appropriate for soldiers who make rounds 220 **canaries** a sprightly dance, said to originate in the Canary Islands 220 **jig** a raucous, somewhat lewd dance 224 **attorney** proxy 228 **glory** glorification 228 **strikes by** obliterates 238 **caroche** a rich coach

Bianca. Your love is great, my lord.
Duke. Once more, our thanks to all.
Omnes. All blest honours guard you.
Cornets flourish.
Exeunt all but Leantio and Livia.
Leantio. [*Aside.*] Oh, hast thou left me then, Bianca, utterly!
Bianca! now I miss thee—Oh return,
And save the faith of woman. I nev'r felt
The loss of thee till now; 'tis an affliction
Of greater weight than youth was made to bear—
As if a punishment of after-life
Were fallen upon man here, so new it is
To flesh and blood; so strange, so insupportable
A torment—ev'n mistook, as a body
Whose death were drowning, must needs therefore suffer it
In scalding oil.
Livia. Sweet sir!
Leantio. [*Aside.*] As long as mine eye saw thee,
I half enjoyed thee.
Livia. Sir?
Leantio. [*Aside.*] Canst thou forget
The dear pains my love took, how it has watched°
Whole nights together in all weathers for thee,
Yet stood in heart more merry than the tempests
That sung about mine ears, like dangerous flatterers
That can set all their mischiefs to sweet tunes;
And then received thee from thy father's window
Into these arms at midnight, when we embraced
As if we had been statues only made for't,
To show art's life, so silent were our comforts;
And kissed as if our lips had grown together.
Livia. [*Aside.*] This makes me madder to enjoy him now.
Leantio. [*Aside.*] Canst thou forget all this? and better joys
That we met after this, which then new kisses
Took pride to praise?
Livia. [*Aside.*] I shall grow madder yet. [*To Leantio.*] Sir!
Leantio. [*Aside.*] This cannot be but of some close° bawd's working.

255 watched kept watch **269 close** secretive

[*To Livia.*] Cry mercy, lady! what would you say to me?
My sorrow makes me so unmannerly,
So comfort bless me, I had quite forgot you.
Livia. Nothing, but ev'n in pity to that passion,
Would give your grief good counsel.
Leantio. Marry, and welcome, lady;
It never could come better.
Livia. Then first, sir,
To make away all your good thoughts at once of her,
Know most assuredly she is a strumpet.
Leantio. Ha! most assuredly! Speak not a thing
So vilde° so certainly; leave it more doubtful.
Livia. Then I must leave all truth, and spare my knowledge
A sin which I too lately found and wept for.
Leantio. Found you it?
Livia. Ay, with wet eyes.
Leantio. Oh perjurious friendship!
Livia. You missed your fortunes when you met with her, sir.
Young gentlemen that only love for beauty,
They love not wisely; such a marriage rather
Proves the destruction of affection:
It brings on want, and want's the key of whoredom.
I think y'had small means with her?
Leantio. Oh, not any, lady.
Livia. Alas, poor gentleman! What mean'st thou, sir,
Quite to undo thyself with thine own kind heart?
Thou art too good and pitiful to woman.
Marry sir, thank thy stars for this blest fortune
That rids the summer of thy youth so well
From many beggars, that had lain a-sunning
In thy beams only else, till thou hadst wasted
The whole days of thy life in heat and labour.
What would you say now to a creature found
As pitiful to you, and as it were
Ev'n sent on purpose from the whole sex general°
To requite all that kindness you have shown to't?
Leantio. What's that, madam?
Livia. Nay, a gentlewoman,
And one able to reward good things; ay,

279 vilde vile 299 the whole sex general womankind

And bears a conscience to't. Couldst thou love such a one
That, blow all fortunes,° would never see thee want?
Nay more, maintain thee to thine enemy's envy;
And shalt not spend a care for't, stir a thought,
Nor break a sleep—unless love's music waked thee,
No storm of fortune should. Look upon me,
And know that woman.

Leantio. Oh my life's wealth, Bianca!

Livia. [*Aside.*] Still with her name? will nothing wear it out?
[*To Leantio.*] That deep sigh went but for a strumpet, sir.

Leantio. It can go for no other that loves me.

Livia. [*Aside.*] He's vexed in mind. I came too soon to him;
Where's my discretion now, my skill, my judgement?
I'm cunning in all arts but my own love.
'Tis as unseasonable to tempt him now,
So soon, as a widow to be courted
Following her husband's corse, or to make bargain
By their grave-side, and take a young man there:
Her strange departure stands like a hearse° yet
Before her eyes, which time will take down shortly.

Exit.

Leantio. Is she my wife till death, yet no more mine?
That's a hard measure. Then what's marriage good for?
Methinks by right I should not now be living,
And then 'twere all well. What a happiness
Had I been made of, had I never seen her!
For nothing makes man's loss grievous to him
But knowledge of the worth of what he loses:
For what he never had, he never misses.
She's gone for ever—utterly; there is
As much redemption of a soul from hell
As a fair woman's body from his palace.
Why should my love last longer than her truth?
What is there good in women to be loved
When only that which makes her so has left her?
I cannot love her now, but I must like
Her sin and my own shame too, and be guilty

304 blow all fortunes despite whatever fortune may blow, as in a storm **320 hearse** here a wooden structure temporarily raised about a coffin

Of law's breach with her, and mine own abusing;
All which were monstrous. Then my safest course,
For health of mind and body, is to turn
My heart and hate her, most extremely hate her;
I have no other way. Those virtuous powers
Which were chaste witnesses of both our troths
Can witness she breaks first—and I'm rewarded
With captainship o'th'fort! a place of credit,
I must confess, but poor; my factorship
Shall not exchange means with't; he that died last in't,
He was no drunkard, yet he died a beggar
For all his thrift. Besides, the place not fits me:
It suits my resolution, not my breeding.

Enter Livia.

Livia. [*Aside.*] I have tried all ways I can, and have not power
To keep from sight of him. [*To Leantio.*] How are you now, sir?

Leantio. I feel a better ease, madam.

Livia. Thanks to blessedness.
You will do well, I warrant you, fear it not, sir.
Join but your own good will to't; he's not wise
That loves his pain or sickness, or grows fond
Of a disease whose property is to vex him
And spitefully drink his blood up. Out upon't, sir,
Youth knows no greater loss. I pray let's walk, sir.
You never saw the beauty of my house yet,
Nor how abundantly fortune has blessed me
In worldly treasure; trust me, I have enough, sir,
To make my friend a rich man in my life,
A great man at my death—yourself will say so.
If you want anything and spare to speak,
Troth, I'll condemn you for a wilful man, sir.

Leantio. Why sure, this can be but the flattery of some dream.

Livia. Now by this kiss, my love, my soul and riches.
'Tis all true substance. [*kisses him.*]
Come, you shall see my wealth, take what you list;
The gallanter you go, the more you please me.
I will allow you, too, your page and footman,
Your racehorses, or any various pleasure

Exercised youth delights in: but to me
Only, sir, wear your heart of constant stuff.
Do but you love enough, I'll give enough.

Leantio. Troth then, I'll love enough and take enough.

Livia. Then we are both pleased enough.

Exeunt.

[Act III, Scene iii]

Enter Guardiano and Isabella at one door, and the Ward and Sordido at another.

Guardiano. Now nephew, here's the gentlewoman again.

Ward. Mass, here she's come again; mark her now, Sordido.

Guardiano. This is the maid my love and care has chose
Out for your wife, and so I tender her to you.
Yourself has been eye witness of some qualities
That speak a courtly breeding and are costly.
I bring you both to talk together now,
'Tis time you grew familiar in your tongues:
Tomorrow you join hands, and one ring ties you,
And one bed holds you; if you like the choice.
Her father and her friends are i'th'next room
And stay to see the contract ere they part;
Therefore dispatch, good ward, be sweet and short.
Like her or like her not, there's but two ways:
And one your body, th'other your purse pays.°

Ward. I warrant you guardiner, I'll not stand all day thrumming,°
But quickly shoot my bolt° at your next coming.

Guardiano. Well said! Good fortune to your birding then.

[*Exit.*]

Ward. I never missed mark yet.

Sordido. Troth I think, master, if the truth were known, you never shot at any but the kitchen-wench, and that was a she-woodcock, a mere innocent, that was oft lost and cried at eight-and-twenty.°

III.iii.15 **purse pays** i.e., by loss of her dowery 16 **thrumming** trifling 17 **shoot my bolt** make my decision ("bolt" = arrow) 22-3 **cried at eight-and-twenty** (small children were "cried" out for if they strayed; this wench is still "cried" at twenty-eight years of age)

Ward. No more of that meat, Sordido, here's eggs o'th'spit° now; we must turn gingerly. Draw out the catalogue of all the faults of women.

Sordido. How, all the faults! have you so little reason to think so much paper will lie in my breeches? Why, ten carts will not carry it, if you set down but the bawds. All the faults! pray let's be content with a few of 'em; and if they were less, you would find 'em enough, I warrant you. Look you, sir.

Isabella. [*Aside.*] But that I have the advantage of the fool
As much as woman's heart can wish and joy at,
What an infernal torment 'twere to be
Thus bought and sold and turned and pried into; when alas
The worst bit is too good for him! And the comfort is,
H'as but a cater's° place on't, and provides
All for another's table—yet how curious
The ass is, like some nice professor° on't,
That buys up all the daintiest food i'th'markets
And seldom licks his lips after a taste on't.

Sordido. Now to her, now y'have scanned all her parts over.

Ward. But at what end shall I begin now, Sordido?

Sordido. Oh, ever at a woman's lip, while you live, sir; do you ask that question?

Ward. Methinks, Sordido, sh'as but a crabbed face to begin with.

Sordido. A crabbed face? that will save money.

Ward. How, save money, Sordido?

Sordido. Ay sir; for having a crabbed face of her own, she'll eat the less verjuice° with her mutton—'twill save verjuice at year's end, sir.

Ward. Nay, and your jests begin to be saucy once, I'll make you eat your meat without mustard.

Sordido. And that in some kind is a punishment.

Ward. Gentlewoman, they say 'tis your pleasure to be my wife; and you shall know shortly whether it be mine or no to be your husband. And thereupon thus I first enter upon you. [*Kisses her.*] Oh most delicious scent! methinks it tasted as if a man had stepped into a

24-5 **ggs o'th'spit** careful business to attend to 39 **cater's** buyer of cates (delicacies) 41 **nice professor** precise specialist 52 **verjuice** crab-apple sauce

comfit-maker's shop° to let a cart go by, all the while I kissed her. It is reported, gentlewoman, you'll run mad for me, if you have me not.

Isabella. I should be in great danger of my wits, sir,
For being so forward—should this ass kick backward
now.

Ward. Alas, poor soul. And is that hair your own?

Isabella. Mine own? yes sure, sir; I owe nothing for't.

Ward. 'Tis a good hearing; I shall have the less to pay when I have married you. Look, does her eyes stand well?

Sordido. They cannot stand better than in her head, I think; where would you have them? and for her nose, 'tis of a very good last.°

Ward. I have known as good as that has not lasted a year, though.

Sordido. That's in the using of a thing; will not any strong bridge fall down in time, if we do nothing but beat at the bottom? A nose of buff would not last always, sir, especially if it came into th' camp once.°

Ward. But Sordido, how shall we do to make her laugh, that I may see what teeth she has—for I'll not bate her a tooth, nor take a black one into th'bargain.

Sordido. Why, do but you fall in talk with her; you cannot choose but one time or other make her laugh, sir.

Ward. It shall go hard, but I will. Pray what qualities have you beside singing and dancing? can you play at shuttlecock, forsooth?

Isabella. Ay, and at stool-ball° too, sir; I have great luck at it.

Ward. Why, can you catch a ball well?

Isabella. I have catched two in my lap at one game.

Ward. What, have you, woman? I must have you learn to play at trap too, then y'are full and whole.

62 **comfit-maker's shop** (comfit is a sweetmeat, usually of fruit, preserved with sugar) 73 **last** form, derived from cobbler's last 76-9 **any strong bridge . . . camp once** any bridge of the nose will collapse (due to syphilis) if we do nothing but attack the lower part (of a woman); even a nose of strong leather would not last forever, especially if it was that of a camp follower (whore) 89 **stool ball** a game played mainly by women, where one player defends a stool against a ball thrown by an opponent

Isabella. Anything that you please to bring me up to I shall take pains to practise.

Ward. 'Twill not do, Sordido; we shall never get her mouth opened wide enough.

Sordido. No sir? that's strange; then here's a trick for your learning.

He yawns [Isabella yawns too, but covers her mouth with a handkerchief.]

Look now, look now! quick, quick there.

Ward. Pox of that scurvy mannerly trick with handkerchief; it hindered me a little, but I am satisfied. When a fair woman gapes and stops her mouth so, it shows like a cloth stopple° in a cream-pot. I have fair hope of her teeth now, Sordido.

Sordido. Why, then y'have all well, sir, for aught I see. She's right and straight enough now, as she stands—they'll commonly lie crooked, that's no matter; wise gamesters never find fault with that, let 'em lie still so.

Ward. I'ld fain mark how she goes, and then I have all—for of all creatures I cannot abide a splay-footed woman:° she's an unlucky thing to meet in a morning; her heels keep together so, as if she were beginning an Irish dance still, and the wriggling of her bum° playing the tune to't. But I have bethought a cleanly shift to find it: dab° down as you see me, and peep of one side when her back's toward you; I'll show you the way.

Sordido. And you shall find me apt enough to peeping.
I have been one of them has seen mad sights
Under your scaffolds.°

Ward. Will it please you walk, forsooth,
A turn or two by yourself? you are so pleasing to me,
I take delight to view you on both sides.

Isabella. I shall be glad to fetch a walk to your love, sir;
'Twill get affection a good stomach, sir
[*Aside.*] Which I had need have, to fall to such coarse victuals. [*She walks about.*]

Ward. Now go thy ways for a clean-treading wench,
As ever man in modesty peeped under.

Sordido. I see the sweetest sight to please my master:

104 stopple stopper made of cloth **111-12 splay-footed woman** a witch known by the splay foot **114 bum** buttocks **116 dab** bend **120 scaffolds** platforms for spectators or performers

Never went Frenchman righter upon ropes°
Than she on Florentine rushes.°

Ward. 'Tis enough, forsooth.

Isabella. And how do you like me now, sir?

Ward. 'Faith, so well
I never mean to part with thee, sweetheart,
Under some sixteen children, and all boys.

Isabella. You'll be at simple pains, if you prove kind,
And breed 'em all in your teeth.°

Ward. Nay, by my faith,
What serves your belly for? 'twould make my cheeks
Look like blown bagpipes.

Enter Guardiano.

Guardiano. How now, ward and nephew,
Gentlewoman and niece! speak, is it so or not?

Ward. 'Tis so; we are both agreed, sir.

Guardiano. In to your kindred, then;
There's friends, and wine and music, waits to welcome you.

Ward. Then I'll be drunk for joy.

Sordido. And I for company;
I cannot break my nose in a better action.

Exeunt.

[Act IV, Scene i]

Enter Bianca attended by two Ladies.

Bianca. How goes your watches, ladies; what's o'clock now?

1 Lady. By mine, full nine.

2 Lady. By mine, a quarter past.

1 Lady. I set mine by St. Mark's.

2 Lady. St. Antony's,
They say, goes truer.

128 **ropes** tightropes 129 **rushes** used on the floor as covering 134-5 **pains . . . teeth** "In allusion to a superstitious idea, that an affectionate husband had the toothache while his wife was breeding" (Dilke)

1 Lady. That's but your opinion, madam,
Because you love a gentleman o'th'name.
2 Lady. He's a true gentleman, then.
1 Lady. So may he be
That comes to me tonight, for aught you know.
Bianca. I'll end this strife straight. I set mine by the sun;
I love to set by th' best, one shall not then
Be troubled to set often.°
2 Lady. You do wisely in't.
Bianca. If I should set my watch as some girls do
By ev'ry clock i'th'town, 'twould nev'r go true;
And too much turning of the dial's point,
Or tamp'ring with the spring, might in small time
Spoil the whole work too.° Here it wants of nine now.
1 Lady. It does indeed, forsooth; mine's nearest truth yet.
2 Lady. Yet I have found her lying with an advocate, which showed
Like two false clocks together in one parish.
Bianca. So now I thank you ladies. I desire
Awhile to be alone.
1 Lady. And I am nobody,
Methinks, unless I have one or other with me;
'Faith, my desire and hers will nev'r be sisters.
Exeunt Ladies.
Bianca. How strangely woman's fortune comes about!
This was the farthest way to come to me,
All would have judged, that knew me born in Venice
And there with many jealous eyes brought up,
That never thought they had me sure enough
But when they were upon me; yet my hap
To meet it here, so far off from my birthplace,
My friends or kindred. 'Tis not good, in sadness,°
To keep a maid so strict in her young days.
Restraint breeds wand'ring thoughts, as many fasting days
A great desire to see flesh stirring again.

IV.i.1-10 **How . . . often** (employing the oft-used comparison of clock and woman or clock and love, this passage reveals Bianca's sense of superiority since she sets her clock by the sun, i.e., heaven's dial, the Duke) 11-15 **If I . . . work too** (the sexual innuendo is obvious) 30 **in sadness** seriously

I'll nev'r use any girl of mine so strictly;
Howev'r they're kept, their fortunes find 'em out;
I see't in me. If they be got in court
I'll never forbid 'em the country; nor the court,
Though they be born i'th'country. They will come to't,
And fetch their falls° a thousand mile about,
Where one would little think on't.

Enter Leantio.

Leantio. I long to see how my despiser looks
Now she's come here to court; these are her lodgings;
She's simply° now advanced! I took her out
Of no such window, I remember, first;
That was a great deal lower, and less carved.

Bianca. How now? what silkworm's this, i'th'name of pride;
What, is it he?

Leantio. A bow i'th'ham to your greatness;
You must have now three legs,° I take it, must you not?

Bianca. Then I must take another, I shall want° else
The service° I should have; you have but two there.

Leantio. Y'are richly placed.

Bianca. Methinks y'are wondrous brave,° sir.

Leantio. A sumptuous lodging!

Bianca. Y'have an excellent suit there.

Leantio. A chair of velvet!

Bianca. Is your cloak lined through, sir?

Leantio. Y'are very stately here.

Bianca. 'Faith, something proud, sir.

Leantio. Stay, stay; let's see your cloth-of-silver slippers.

Bianca. Who's your shoemaker? h'as made you a neat boot.

Leantio. Will you have a pair? the duke will lend you spurs.

Bianca. Yes, when I ride.

Leantio. 'Tis a brave life you lead.

Bianca. I could nev'r see you in such good clothes
In my time.

Leantio. In your time?

Bianca. Sure I think, sir,

39 **falls** i.e., into sin 43 **simply** absolutely 48 **legs** bows 49 **want** lack 50 **service** (1) courtesy, (2) lovemaking 51 **brave** well-dressed

We both thrive best asunder.
Leantio. Y'are a whore.
Bianca. Fear nothing, sir.
Leantio. An impudent, spiteful strumpet.
Bianca. Oh sir, you give me thanks for your captainship;
I thought you had forgot all your good manners.
Leantio. And to spite thee as much, look there, there read!
Vex, gnaw! thou shalt find there I am not love-starved.
The world was never yet so cold or pitiless
But there was ever still more charity found out
Than at one proud fool's door; and 'twere hard, 'faith,
If I could not pass that. Read to thy shame, there—
A cheerful and a beauteous benefactor too,
As ev'r erected the good works of love.
Bianca. [*Aside.*] Lady Livia!
Is't possible? Her worship was my pandress.
She dote and send and give, and all to him;
Why, here's a bawd plagued home. [*To Leantio.*] Y'are simply happy, sir,
Yet I'll not envy you.
Leantio. No, court-saint, not thou!
You keep some friend of a new fashion.
There's no harm in your devil, he's a suckling;
But he will breed teeth° shortly, will he not?
Bianca. Take heed you play not then too long with him.
Leantio. Yes, and the great one too. I shall find time
To play a hot religious bout with some of you,
And perhaps drive you and your course° of sins
To their eternal kennels. I speak softly now,
'Tis manners in a noblewoman's lodgings.
And I well know all my degrees of duty.
But come I to your everlasting parting once,
Thunder shall seem soft music to that tempest.
Bianca. 'Twas said last week there would be change of weather
When the moon hung so; and belike you heard it.
Leantio. Why, here's sin made, and nev'r a conscience put to't,°
A monster with all forehead and no eyes!°

79 **breed teeth** cut his teeth, i.e., be able to bite 83 **course** pack, as of dogs 91 **put to't** troubled 92 **with all forehead . . . eyes** with no shame and blind, i.e., to virtue

Why do I talk to thee of sense or virtue,
That art as dark as death? and as much madness
To set light before thee, as to lead blind folks
To see the monuments which they may smell as soon
As they behold—marry, oft-times their heads,
For want of light, may feel the hardness of 'em:
So shall thy blind pride my revenge and anger,
That canst not see it now; and it may fall
At such an hour when thou least see'st of all.
So to an ignorance darker than thy womb
I leave thy perjured soul. A plague will come.
Exit.

Bianca. Get you gone first, and then I fear no greater—
Nor thee will I fear long! I'll have this sauciness
Soon banished from these lodgings, and the rooms
Perfumed well after the corrupt air it leaves.
His breath has made me almost sick, in troth.
A poor base start-up!° 'Life—because h'as got
Fair clothes by foul means, comes to rail and show 'em.

Enter the Duke.

Duke. Who's that?
Bianca. Cry you mercy, sir.
Duke. Prithee, who's that?
Bianca. The former thing, my lord, to whom you gave
The captainship; he eats his meat with grudging still.
Duke. Still!
Bianca. He comes vaunting here of his new love
And the new clothes she gave him. Lady Livia—
Who but she now his mistress!
Duke. Lady Livia?
Be sure of what you say.
Bianca. He showed me her name, sir,
In perfumed paper—her vows, her letter—
With an intent to spite me: so his heart said,
And his threats made it good; they were as spiteful
As ever malice uttered; and as dangerous,
Should his hand follow the copy.°
Duke. But that must not.

109 **start-up** upstart, social climber 122 **copy** example in a copy-book, here the idea in his mind

Do not you vex your mind; prithee to bed, go.
All shall be well and quiet.
Bianca. I love peace, sir.
Duke. And so do all that love; take you no care for't,
It shall be still provided to your hand.
Exit [Bianca.]
Who's near us there?

Enter Messenger.

Messenger. My lord?
Duke. Seek out Hippolito,
Brother to Lady Livia, with all speed.
Messenger. He was the last man I saw, my lord.
Duke. Make haste.
Exit.
He is a blood° soon stirred; and as he's quick
To apprehend a wrong, he's bold and sudden
In bringing forth a ruin. I know likewise
The reputation of his sister's honour's
As dear to him as life-blood to his heart;
Beside, I'll flatter him with a goodness to her
Which I now thought on—but nev'r meant to practise
Because I know her base; and that wind° drives him.
The ulcerous reputation feels the poise°
Of lightest wrongs, as sores are vexed with flies.
He comes. *Enter Hippolito.* Hippolito, welcome.
Hippolito. My loved lord.
Duke. How does that lusty widow, thy kind sister?
Is she not sped yet of° a second husband?
A bed-fellow she has, I ask not that;
I know she's sped of him.
Hippolito. Of him, my lord?
Duke. Yes, of a bed-fellow. Is the news so strange to you?
Hippolito. I hope 'tis so to all.
Duke. I wish it were, sir,
But 'tis confessed° too fast. Her ignorant pleasures,
Only by lust instructed, have received
Into their services an impudent boaster,

130 **blood** fiery young man 137 **wind** motive 138 **poise** weight 142 **sped yet of** successfully furnished with 147 **confessed** revealed

One that does raise his glory from her shame,
And tells the midday sun what's done in darkness.
Yet blinded with her appetite, wastes her wealth;
Buys her disgraces at a dearer rate
Than bounteous housekeepers purchase their honour.
Nothing sads me so much, as that in love
To thee and to thy blood, and I had picked out
A worthy match for her, the great Vincentio,
High in our favour and in all men's thoughts.

Hippolito. Oh thou destruction of all happy fortunes,
Unsated blood! Know you the name, my lord,
Of her abuser?

Duke. One Leantio.

Hippolito. He's a factor.

Duke. He nev'r made so brave a voyage
By his own talk.

Hippolito. The poor old widow's son;
I humbly take my leave.

Duke. [*Aside*.] I see 'tis done.
[*To Hippolito*.] Give her good counsel, make her see her error;
I know she'll harken to you.

Hippolito. Yes, my lord,
I make no doubt—as I shall take the course
Which she shall never know till it be acted;
And when she wakes to honour, then she'll thank me for't.
I'll imitate the pities of old surgeons°
To this lost limb, who ere they show their art
Cast one asleep, then cut the diseased part:
So out of love to her I pity most,
She shall not feel him going till he's lost;
Then she'll commend the cure. *Exit*.

Duke. The great cure's past.
I count this done already; his wrath's sure,
And speaks an injury deep. Farewell, Leantio;
This place will never hear thee murmur more.

Enter Lord Cardinal, attended.

Our noble brother, welcome!

170 the pities of old surgeons (Mulryne notes that as early as the thirteenth century Theodoric of Lucca, a Dominican friar, recommended the use of narcotics before surgery)

Cardinal. Set those lights down.
Depart till you be called. [*Exit Attendants.*]
Duke. [*Aside.*] There's serious business
Fixed in his look; nay, it inclines a little
To the dark colour of a discontentment.
—Brother, what is't commands your eye so powerfully?
Speak, you seem lost.°
Cardinal. The thing I look on seems so,
To my eyes lost for ever.
Duke. You look on me.
Cardinal. What a grief 'tis to a religious feeling
To think a man should have a friend so goodly,
So wise, so noble—nay, a duke, a brother;
And all this certainly damned!
Duke. How!
Cardinal. 'Tis no wonder,
If your great sin can do't. Dare you look up,
For thinking of a vengeance? dare you sleep,
For fear of never waking but to death?
And dedicate unto a strumpet's love
The strength of your affections, zeal and health?
Here you stand now: can you assure your pleasures
You shall once more enjoy her—but once more?
Alas, you cannot! What a misery 'tis, then,
To be more certain of eternal death
Than of a next embrace. Nay, shall I show you
How more unfortunate you stand in sin,
Than the low private man: all his offences,
Like enclosed grounds, keep but about himself
And seldom stretch beyond his own soul's bounds;
And when a man grows miserable, 'tis some comfort
When he's no further charged than with himself:
'Tis a sweet ease to wretchedness. But, great man,
Ev'ry sin thou commit'st shows like a flame
Upon a mountain; 'tis seen far about,
And with a big wind made of popular breath°
The sparkles fly through cities; here one takes,
Another catches there, and in short time
Waste all to cinders: but remember still,
What burnt the valleys, first came from the hill.

184 **lost** i.e., in thought 209 **popular breath** opinion of the common people

Ev'ry offence draws his particular pain;
But 'tis example proves the great man's bane.
The sins of mean men lie like scattered parcels°
Of an unperfect bill;° but when such° fall,
Then comes example, and that sums up all.
And this your reason grants: if men of good lives,
Who by their virtuous actions stir up others
To noble and religious imitation,
Receive the greater glory after death—
As sin must needs confess—what may they feel
In height of torments and in weight of vengeance;
Not only they themselves not doing well,
But sets a light up to show men to hell?

Duke. If you have done, I have. No more, sweet brother.

Cardinal. I know time spent in goodness is too tedious;
This had not been a moment's space in lust, now.
How dare you venture on eternal pain,
That cannot bear a minute's reprehension?
Methinks you should endure to hear that talked of
Which you so strive to suffer. Oh my brother!
What were you, if you were taken now?
My heart weeps blood to think on't; 'tis a work
Of infinite mercy you can never merit,
That yet you are not death struck—no, not yet—
I dare not stay you long, for fear you should not
Have time enough allowed you to repent in.
There's but this wall° betwixt you and destruction
When y'are at strongest; and but poor thin clay.
Think upon't, brother! Can you come so near it
For a fair strumpet's love, and fall into
A torment that knows neither end nor bottom
For beauty but the deepness of a skin,
And that not of their own neither? Is she a thing
Whom sickness dare not visit, or age look on,
Or death resist? does the worm shun her grave?
If not (as your soul knows it) why should lust
Bring man to lasting pain, for rotten dust?

Duke. Brother of spotless honour, let me weep

216 **parcels** parts, items 217 **unperfect bill** incomplete bill of particulars 217 **such** great men, as opposed to the "mean men" 240 **wall** i.e., the body

The first of my repentance in thy bosom,
And show the blest fruits of a thankful spirit;
And if I ere keep woman more unlawfully,
May I want penitence at my greatest need:
And wise men know there is no barren place
Threatens more famine, than a dearth in grace.

Cardinal. Why, here's a conversion is at this time, brother,
Sung for a hymn in Heaven; and at this instant,
The powers of darkness groan, makes all hell sorry.
First, I praise Heaven; then in my work I glory.
Who's there attends without?

Enter Servants.

Servant. My lord?

Cardinal. Take up those lights; there was a thicker darkness
When they came first. The peace of a fair soul
Keep with my noble brother. *Exit Cardinal, etc.*

Duke. Joys be with you, sir.
She lies alone tonight for't; and must still,
Though it be hard to conquer. But I have vowed
Never to know her as a strumpet more,
And I must save° my oath. If fury fail not,
Her husband dies tonight, or at the most
Lives not to see the morning spent tomorrow;
Then will I make her lawfully mine own,
Without this sin and horror. Now I'm chidden
For what I shall enjoy then unforbidden,
And I'll not freeze in stoves; 'tis but a while
Live like a hopeful bridegroom, chaste from flesh,
And pleasure then will seem new, fair and fresh. *Exit.*

[Act IV, Scene ii]

Enter Hippolito.

Hippolito. The morning so far wasted, yet his baseness
So impudent? See if the very sun do not blush at him!
Dare he do thus much, and know me alive!

269 save keep

Put case° one must be vicious, as I know myself
Monstrously guilty, there's a blind time made for't;
He might use only that, 'twere conscionable—
Art, silence, closeness, subtlety and darkness
Are fit for such a business: but there's no pity
To be bestowed on an apparent sinner,°
An impudent daylight lecher! The great zeal
I bear to her advancement in this match
With Lord Vincentio, as the duke has wrought it,
To the perpetual honour of our house,
Puts fire into my blood, to purge the air
Of this corruption, fear it spread too far
And poison the whole hopes of this fair fortune.
I love her good so dearly, that no brother
Shall venture farther for a sister's glory
Than I for her preferment.

Enter Leantio and a Page.

Leantio. I'll see that glist'ring whore shines like a serpent,
Now the court sun's upon her. Page!
Page. Anon sir!
Leantio. I'll go in state too. See the coach be ready.
[*Exit Page.*]
I'll hurry away presently.
Hippolito. Yes, you shall hurry,
And the devil after you; take that at setting forth!
[*Strikes him.*]
Now, and° you'll draw, we are upon equal terms, sir.
Thou took'st advantage of my name in honour
Upon my sister; I nev'r saw the stroke
Come, till I found my reputation bleeding;
And therefore count it I no sin to valour
To serve thy lust so. Now we are of even hand,
Take your best course against me. You must die.
Leanito. How close sticks envy to man's happiness!
When I was poor, and little cared for life,
I had no such means offered me to die,
No man's wrath minded me. [*draws sword.*] Slave, I turn
this to thee,

IV.ii.4 **Put case** assuming 9 **apparent sinner** one who flaunts his sinfulness openly 25 **and** if

To call thee to account for a wound lately
Of a base stamp upon me.

Hippolito. 'Twas most fit
For a base mettle.° Come and fetch one now,
More noble, then; for I will use thee fairer
Than thou hast done thine own soul or our honour.
[*They fight.*]
And there I think 'tis for thee.

Voices. [*Within.*] Help, help! oh part 'em.

Leantio. False wife, I feel now th'hast paid heartily for me.
Rise, strumpet, by my fall! Thy lust may reign now;
My heart-string and the marriage-knot that tied thee
Breaks both together.

Hippolito. There I heard the sound on't,
And never liked string better.

Enter Guardino, Livia, Isabella, Ward, and Sordido.

Livia. 'Tis my brother!
Are you hurt, sir?

Hippolito. Not anything.

Livia. Blessed fortune!
Shift for thyself; what is he thou hast killed?

Hippolito. Our honour's enemy.

Guardiano. Know you this man, lady?

Livia. Leantio! My love's joy! [*To Hippolito.*] Wounds
stick upon thee
As deadly as thy sins! art thou not hurt?
The devil take that fortune. And he dead!
Drop plagues into thy bowels without voice,°
Secret and fearful. [*To others.*] Run for officers,
Let him be apprehended with all speed,
For fear he 'scape away; lay hands on him,
We cannot be too sure. 'Tis wilful murder!
You do Heaven's vengeance and the law just service;
You know him not as I do—he's a villain,
As monstrous as a prodigy, and as dreadful.

Hippolito. Will you but entertain a noble patience
Till you but hear the reason, worthy sister!

Livia. The reason! that's a jest hell falls a-laughing at!
Is there a reason found for the destruction

38 **mettle** with a pun on "metal" 53 **voice** noise, i.e., warning

Of our more lawful loves? and was there none
To kill the black lust 'twixt thy niece and thee
That has kept close° so long?

Guardiano. How's that, good madam?

Livia. Too true sir! There she stands, let her deny't;
The deed cries shortly in the midwife's arms,
Unless the parents' sins strike it still-born;
And if you be not deaf and ignorant,
You'll hear strange notes ere long. Look upon me, wench!
'Twas I betrayed thy honour subtilly to him
Under a false tale; it lights upon me now!
His arm has paid me home upon thy breast,
My sweet, beloved Leantio!

Guardiano. [*Aside.*] Was my judgement
And care in choice so dev'lishly abused,
So beyond-shamefully—all the world will grin at me.

Ward. Oh Sordido, Sordido, I'm damned, I'm damned!

Sordido. Damned! why, sir?

Ward. One of the wicked; dost not see't?
A cuckold, a plain reprobate cuckold!

Sordido. Nay, and you be damned for that, be of good cheer, sir—y'have gallant company for all professions; I'll have a wife next Sunday° too, because I'll along with you myself.

Ward. That will be some comfort yet.

Livia. [*To Guardiano.*] You, sir, that bear your load of injuries
As I of sorrows, lend me your grieved strength
To this sad burthen who, in life, wore actions
Flames were not nimbler. We will talk of things
May have the luck to break our hearts together.

Guardiano. I'll list to nothing but revenge and anger,
Whose counsels I will follow.

Exeunt Livia and Guardiano [*with Leantio's body.*]

Sordido. A wife, quoth'a! Here's a sweet plum-tree of your guardiner's grafting!

Ward. Nay, there's a worse name belongs to this fruit yet,

66 **close** secret 83-4 **wife next Sunday** "When she would be wearing her best clothes and looking deceptively virtuous" (Gill)

and you could hit on't; a more open one! For he that marries a whore looks like a fellow bound all his lifetime to a medlar-tree;° and that's good stuff—'tis no sooner ripe but it looks rotten;° and so do some queans at nineteen. A pox on't, I thought there was some knavery abroach, for something stirred in her belly the first night I lay with her.

Sordido. What, what sir!

Ward. This is she brought up so courtly! can sing and dance—and tumble too, methinks. I'll never marry wife again that has so many qualities.

Sordido. Indeed, they are seldom good, master. For likely when they are taught so many, they will have one trick more of their own finding out. Well, give me a wench but with one good quality, to lie with none but her husband, and that's bringing-up enough for any woman breathing.

Ward. This was the fault when she was tendered to me; you never looked to this.

Sordido. Alas, how would you have me see through a great farthingale, sir! I cannot peep through a millstone, or in the going, to see what's done i'th' bottom.°

Ward. Her father praised her breast! sh'ad the voice, forsooth! I marvell'd she sung so small, indeed, being no maid; now I perceive there's a young chorister in her belly—this breeds a singing in my head,° I'm sure.

Sordido. 'Tis but the tune of your wives' cinquepace danced in a featherbed. 'Faith, go lie down, master, but take heed your horns do not make holes in the pillowberes°—I would not batter brows with him for a hogshead of angels;° he would prick my skull as full of holes as a scrivener's sandbox.° *Exeunt Ward and Sordido.*

Isabella. [*Aside.*] Was ever maid so cruelly beguiled
To the confusion of life, soul and honour,
All of one woman's murd'ring! I'ld fain bring

99 **medlar-tree** a medlar is a type of pear, often a cant term for whore 100 **looks rotten** the ripened state of the medlar; also rotten—infected with venereal disease 117-8 **in the going . . . bottom** as its turning, see what is happening beneath the millstone 122 **singing in my head** i.e., from the cuckold's horns 125-6 **pillow beres** pillowcases 127 **angels** gold coins 128 **sand-box** (scriveners used fine sand for blotting ink)

Her name no nearer to my blood than woman,
And 'tis too much of that. Oh shame and horror!
In that small distance from yon man to me
Lies sin enough to make a whole world perish.
[*To Hippolito.*] 'Tis time we parted, sir, and left the sight
Of one another; nothing can be worse
To hurt repentance—for our very eyes
Are far more poisonous to religion
Than basilisks° to them. If any goodness
Rest in you, hope of comforts, fear of judgements,
My request is, I nev'r may see you more;
And so I turn me from you everlastingly,
So is my hope to miss you. [*Aside.*] But for her,
That durst so dally with a sin so dangerous,
And lay a snare so spitefully for my youth,
If the least means but favour my revenge,
That I may practise the like cruel cunning
Upon her life, as she has on mine honour,
I'll act it without pity.

Hippolito. Here's a care
Of reputation and a sister's fortune
Sweetly rewarded by her! Would a silence,
As great as that which keeps among the graves,
Had everlastingly chained up her tongue.
My love to her has made mine miserable.

Enter Guardiano and Livia.

Guardiano. If you can but dissemble your heart's griefs now,
Be but a woman so far.

Livia. Peace! I'll strive, sir.

Guardiano. As I can wear my injuries in a smile.
Here's an occasion offered, that gives anger
Both liberty and safety to perform
Things worth the fire it holds, without the fear
Of danger or of law; for mischiefs acted
Under the privilege° of a marriage-triumph°

140 basilisks a basilisk was a fabled serpent whose glance was deadly **163 privilege** immunity, here protection **163 marriage-triumph** spectacle to celebrate a wedding

At the duke's hasty nuptials, will be thought
Things merely accidental, all's° by chance,
Not got of their own natures.

Livia. I conceive you, sir,
Even to a longing for performance on't;
And here behold some fruits.
[*Kneels before Hippolito and Isabella.*]
Forgive me both.
What I am now, returned to sense and judgement,
Is not the same rage and distraction
Presented lately to you; that rude form
Is gone for ever. I am now myself,
That speaks all peace and friendship; and these tears
Are the true springs of hearty, penitent sorrow
For those foul wrongs which my forgetful fury
Slandered your virtues with. This gentleman
Is well resolved now.

Guardiano. I was never otherways.
I knew, alas, 'twas but your anger spake it,
And I nev'r thought on't more.

Hippolito. Pray rise, good sister.

Isabella. [*Aside.*] Here's ev'n as sweet amends made up for a wrong now
As one that gives a wound, and pays the surgeon;
All the smart's nothing, the great loss of blood,
Or time of hindrance!° Well, I had a mother,
I can dissemble too. [*To Livia.*] What wrongs have slipped
Through anger's ignorance, aunt, my heart forgives.

Guardiano. Why, this is tuneful now.

Hippolito. And what I did, sister,
Was all for honour's cause, which time to come
Will approve to you.

Livia. Being awaked to goodness,
I understand so much, sir, and praise now
The fortune of your arm and of your safety;
For by his death y'have rid me of a sin
As costly as ev'r woman doted on.
'T has pleased the duke so well too that, behold sir,

165 all's all as if **183 time of hindrance** i.e., time when laid up sick

H'as sent you here your pardon, which I kissed
With most affectionate comfort; when 'twas brought,
Then was my fit just past—it came so well, methought,
To glad my heart.
Hippolito. I see his grace thinks on me.
Livia. There's no talk now but of the preparation
For the great marriage.
Hippolito. Does he marry her, then?
Livia. With all speed, suddenly, as fast as cost
Can be laid on with many thousand hands.
This gentleman and I had once a purpose
To have honoured the first marriage of the duke
With an invention° of his own; 'twas ready,
The pains well past, most of the charge bestowed on't,°
Then came the death of your good mother, niece,
And turned the glory of it all to black.
'Tis a device would fit these times so well, too,
Art's treasury not better. If you'll join,
It shall be done the cost shall all be mine.
Hippolito. Y'have my voice° first; 'twill well approve my thankfulness
For the duke's love and favour.
Livia. What say you, niece?
Isabella. I am content to make one.°
Guardiano. The plot's full,° then;
Your pages, madam, will make shift for cupids.
Livia. That will they, sir.
Guardiano. You'll play your old part still?
Livia. What is't? good troth, I have ev'n forgot it.
Guardiano. Why, Juno Pronuba,° the marriage goddess.
Livia. 'Tis right, indeed.
Guardiano. And you shall play the nymph
That offers sacrifice to appease her wrath.
Isabella. Sacrifice, good sir?
Livia. Must I be appeased, then?
Guardiano. That's as you list yourself, as you see cause.
Livia. Methinks 'twould show the more state in her deity
To be incensed.

204 **invention** a show newly conceived 205 **charge bestowed on't** cost already paid for it 211 **voice** vote 213 **make one** play a part 213 **plot's full** all is set for the play 217 **Juno Pronuba** (one of the offices of Juno, wife of Jupiter)

Isabella. 'Twould—but my sacrifice
Shall take a course to appease you, or I'll fail in't,
And teach a sinful bawd to play a goddess.
Guardiano. [*To Hippolito.*] For our parts we'll not be ambitious, sir;
Please you walk in and see the project° drawn,
Then take your choice.
Hippolito. I weigh° not, so I have one.
Exeunt [*all except Livia.*]
Livia. How much ado have I to restrain fury
From breaking into curses! Oh how painful 'tis
To keep great sorrow smothered! sure I think
'Tis harder to dissemble grief than love.
Leantio, here the weight of thy loss lies,
Which nothing but destruction can suffice. *Exit.*

[Act IV, Scene iii]

Hoboys.°

Enter in great state the Duke and Bianca, richly attired, with Lords, Cardinals, Ladies, and other Attendants. They pass solemnly over. Enter Lord Cardinal in a rage, seeming to break off the ceremony.

Cardinal. Cease, cease! Religious honours done to sin
Disparage virtue's reverence, and will pull
Heaven's thunder upon Florence; holy ceremonies
Were made for sacred uses, not for sinful.
Are these the fruits of your repentance, brother?
Better it had been you had never sorrowed
Than to abuse the benefit, and return
To worse than where sin left you.
Vowed you then never to keep strumpet more,
And are you now so swift in your desires
To knit your honours and your life fast to her?
Is not sin sure enough to wretched man
But he must bind himself in chains to't? Worse!

227 project plan **228 weigh** care **IV.iii. s.d. Hoboys** oboes

Must marriage, that immaculate robe of honour
That renders virtue glorious, fair and fruitful
To her great Master,° be now made the garment
Of leprosy and foulness? is this penitence,
To sanctify hot lust? What is it otherways
Than worship done to devils? Is this the best
Amends that sin can make after her riots:
As if a drunkard, to appease Heaven's wrath,
Should offer up his surfeit for a sacrifice:
If that be comely, then lust's offerings are,
On wedlock's sacred altar.
Duke. Here y'are bitter
Without cause, brother: what I vowed, I keep
As safe as you your conscience; and this needs not.°
I taste more wrath in't than I do religion,
And envy more than goodness. The path now
I tread, is honest, leads to lawful love
Which virtue in her strictness would not check.
I vowed no more to keep a sensual woman:
'Tis done; I mean to make a lawful wife of her.
Cardinal. He° that taught you that craft,
Call him not master long, he will undo you.
Grow not too cunning for your soul, good brother.
Is it enough to use adulterous thefts,
And then take sanctuary in marriage?
I grant, so long as an offender keeps
Close in a privileged temple, his life's safe;
But if he ever venture to come out,
And so be taken, then he surely dies for't:
So now y'are safe; but when you leave this body,
Man's only privileged temple upon earth
In which the guilty soul takes sanctuary,
Then you'll perceive what wrongs chaste vows endure
When lust usurps the bed that should be pure.
Bianca. Sir, I have read you over all this while
In silence, and I find great knowledge in you,
And severe learning; yet 'mongst all your virtues
I see not charity written, which some call
The first-born of religion; and I wonder
I cannot see't in yours. Believe it, sir,

16 her great Master God **26 this needs not** this reproach is unjustified **33 He** the devil

There is no virtue can be sooner missed
Or later welcomed; it begins the rest,
And sets 'em all in order. Heaven and angels
Take great delight in a converted sinner:
Why should you, then, a servant and professor,
Differ so much from them? If ev'ry woman
That commits evil should be therefore kept
Back in desires of goodness, how should virtue
Be known and honoured? From a man that's blind
To take a burning taper, 'tis no wrong,
He never misses it; but to take light
From one that sees, that's injury and spite.
Pray, whether is religion better served:
When lives that are licentious are made honest,
Than° when they still run through a sinful blood?
'Tis nothing virtue's temple to deface:
But build the ruins, there's a work of grace.

Duke. I kiss thee for that spirit; thou hast praised thy wit
A modest way. On, on there! *Hoboys.*

Cardinal. Lust is bold,
And will have vengeance speak, ere't be controlled.
Exeunt.

[Act V, Scene i]

Enter Guardiano and Ward.

Guardiano. Speak, hast thou any sense of thy abuse? dost thou know what wrong's done thee?

Ward. I were an ass else; I cannot wash my face but I am feeling on't.°

Guardiano. Here, take this caltrop,° then; convey it secretly into the place I showed you. Look you, sir, this is the trap-door to't.

Ward. I know't of old, uncle, since the last triumph;° here rose up a devil with one eye, I remember, with a company of fireworks at's tail.

Guardiano. Prithee leave squibbing° now; mark me and

67 Than or V.i.3 **feeling on't** i.e., the cuckold's horns 5 **caltrop** spiked ball, used for defense against cavalry 7 **triumph** pageant 11 **squibbing** talking foolishly

fail not: But when thou hear'st me give a stamp, down with't; the villain's caught then.

Ward. If I miss you, hang me; I love to catch a villain, and your stamp shall go current, I warrant you. But how shall I rise up and let him down too, all at one hole? That will be a horrible puzzle. You know I have a part in't, I play Slander.

Guardiano. True, but never make you ready for't.

Ward. No?—but my clothes are bought and all, and a foul fiend's head with a long contumelious tongue i'th'chaps on't, a very fit shape for Slander i'th'out-parishes.°

Guardiano. It shall not come so far; thou understand'st it not.

Ward. Oh, oh?

Guardiano. He shall lie deep enough ere that time, and stick first upon those.°

Ward. Now I conceive you, guardiner.

Guardiano. Away; list to the privy stamp, that's all thy part.

Ward. Stamp my horns in a mortar if I miss you, and give the powder in white wine to sick cuckolds—a very present remedy for the headache. *Exit Ward.*

Guardiano. If this should any way miscarry now—
As, if the fool be nimble enough, 'tis certain—
The pages that present° the swift-winged cupids
Are taught to hit him with their shafts of love,
Fitting his part, which I have cunningly poisoned.
He cannot 'scape my fury; and those ills
Will be laid all on fortune, not our wills;
That's all the sport on't, for who will imagine
That at the celebration of this night
Any mischance that haps can flow from spite? *Exit.*

[Act V, Scene ii]

Flourish. Enter above Duke, Bianca, Lord Cardinal, Fabritio, and other Cardinals, Lords and Ladies in state.

22 **out-parishes** i.e., outside the city proper 27 **those** the spikes of the caltrop 36 **present** i.e., perform

Duke. Now our fair duchess, your delight shall witness
How y'are beloved and honoured: all the glories
Bestowed upon the gladness of this night
Are done for your bright sake.
Bianca. I am the more
In debt, my lord, to loves and courtesies,
That offer up themselves so bounteously
To do me honoured grace, without my merit.
Duke. A goodness set in greatness! how it sparkles
Afar off, like pure diamonds set in gold.
How perfect my desires were, might I witness
But a fair noble peace 'twixt your two spirits!°
The reconcilement would be more sweet to me
Than longer life to him that fears to die.
Good sir!
Cardinal. I profess peace, and am content.
Duke. I'll see the seal upon't, and then 'tis firm.
Cardinal. You shall have all you wish. [*Kisses Bianca.*]
Duke. I have all indeed now.
Bianca. [*Aside.*] But I have made surer work; this shall not blind me.
He that begins so early to reprove,
Quickly rid him, or look for little love:
Beware a brother's envy—he's next heir too.
Cardinal, you die this night; the plot's laid surely:
In time of sports death may steal in securely.
Then 'tis least thought on:
For he that's most religious, holy friend,
Does not at all hours think upon his end;
He has his times of frailty, and his thoughts
Their transportations too, through flesh and blood,
For all his zeal, his learning, and his light,
As well as we poor souls that sin by night.
Duke. [*Fabritio offers Duke a paper.*] What's this, Fabritio?
Fabritio. Marry, my lord, the model
Of what's presented.
Duke. Oh, we thank their loves.
Sweet Duchess, take your seat; list to the argument.°

V.ii.11 **your two spirits** i.e., the high-strung tempers of Bianca and the Lord Cardinal 32 **argument** here, the summary of the plot prefixed to a play

Reads:

There is a nymph that haunts the woods and springs
In love with two at once, and they with her;
Equal it runs; but to decide these things,
The cause to mighty Juno they refer,
She being the marriage-goddess. The two lovers,
They offer sighs; the nymph, a sacrifice;
All to please Juno, who by signs discovers
How the event shall be. So that strife dies.
Then springs a second; for the man refused
Grows discontent, and out of love abused
He raises Slander up, like a black friend,
To disgrace th'other, which pays him i'th'end.

Bianca. In troth, my lord, a pretty, pleasing argument,
And fits th'occasion well: envy and slander
Are things soon raised against two faithful lovers;
But comfort is, they are no long unrewarded. *Music.*
Duke. This music shows they're upon entrance now.
Bianca. Then enter all my wishes!

Enter Hymen in yellow,° Ganymede° in a blue robe powdered with stars, and Hebe in a white robe with golden stars, with covered cups in their hands. They dance a short dance, then bowing to the Duke etc., Hymen speaks:

Hymen. [*To Bianca.*] To thee, fair bride, Hymen offers up
Of nuptial joys this the celestial cup;
Taste it, and thou shalt ever find
Love in thy bed, peace in thy mind.
Bianca. We'll taste you, sure; 'twere pity to disgrace
So pretty a beginning.
Duke. 'Twas spoke nobly.
Ganymede. Two cups of nectar have we begged from Jove:
Hebe, give that to Innocence; I this to Love.

50 s.d. **Hymen in yellow** (Hymen, the god of marriage, traditionally wears yellow) 50 **Ganymede** cup-bearer to Jupiter

Take heed of stumbling more, look to your way;
Remember still the Via Lactea.°

Hebe. Well Ganymede, you have more faults, though not so known;
I spilled one cup, but you have filched many a one.

Hymen. No more, forbear for Hymen's sake;
In love we met, and so let's parting take. *Exeunt.*

Duke. But soft! here's no such persons in the argument
As these three, Hymen, Hebe, Ganymede;
The actors that this model here discovers
Are only four—Juno, a nymph, two lovers.

Bianca. This is some antemasque° belike, my lord,
To entertain time;—now my peace is perfect.
Let sports come on apace; now is their time, my lord, *Music.*
Hark you, you hear from 'em.

Duke. The nymph indeed.

Enter two dressed like nymphs, bearing two tapers lighted; then Isabella dressed with flowers and garlands, bearing a censer with fire in it. They set the censer and tapers on Juno's altar with much reverence, this ditty being sung in parts°

Ditty.

Juno, nuptial goddess, thou that rul'st o'er coupled bodies,
Tiest man to woman, never to forsake her; thou only powerful marriage-maker;
Pity this amazed° affection:
I love both and both love me;

59-60 **Take . . . Lactea** (according to a little-known myth, Hebe, while carrying a cup for Jupiter, stumbled over a star spilling the wine or milk in the heavens where now is the Milky Way. In the action Hebe gives a cup to the Cardinal and Ganymede one to the Duke. By line 70 the Duke and Cardinal drink, for then Bianca says, "Now my peace is perfect")
69 **antemasque** an introductory scene, comic or grotesque, before the masque 72 s.d. **in parts** i.e., in which each singer sings a different melodic line 75 **amazed** astonished, bewildered

Nor know I where to give rejection,
My heart likes so equally,
Till thou set'st right my peace of life,
And with thy power conclude this strife.

Isabella. Now with my thanks depart, you to the springs,
I to these wells of love. [*Exeunt Nymphs.*]
Thou sacred goddess,
And queen of nuptials, daughter to great Saturn,
Sister and wife to Jove, imperial Juno,
Pity this passionate conflict in my breast,
This tedious war 'twixt two affections;
Crown one with victory, and my heart's at peace.

Enter Hippolito and Guardiano like shepherds.

Hippolito. Make me that happy man, thou mighty goddess.
Guardiano. But I live most in hope, if truest love
Merit the greatest comfort.
Isabella. I love both
With such an even and fair affection,
I know not which to speak for, which to wish for,
Till thou, great arbitress 'twixt lovers' hearts,
By thy auspicious grace, design° the man:
Which pity I implore.
Hippolito and Guardiano. We all implore it.
Isabella. And after sighs, contrition's truest odours,
Livia descends like Juno.
I offer to thy powerful deity
This precious incense: may it ascend peacefully.
[*Aside.*] And if it keep true touch, my good aunt Juno,
'Twill try your immortality ere't be long;
I fear you'll never get so nigh Heaven again,
When you're once down.
Livia. Though you and your affections
Seem all as dark to our illustrious brightness
As night's inheritance, hell, we pity you,
And your requests are granted. You ask signs:
They shall be given you; we'll be gracious to you.
He of those twain which we determine for you,
Love's arrows shall wound twice; the later wound
Betokens love in age: for so are all

94 **design** designate

Whose love continues firmly all their lifetime
Twice wounded at their marriage, else affection
Dies when youth ends.—This savor° overcomes me!
—Now for a sign of wealth and golden days,
Bright-eyed prosperity which all couples love,
Ay, and makes love, take that—
[*Throws flaming gold upon Isabella who falls dead.*]
Our brother Jove
Never denies us of his burning treasure
T'express bounty.

Duke. She falls down upon't;
What's the conceit of that?

Fabritio. As over-joyed, belike:
Too much prosperity overjoys us all,
And she has her lapful, it seems, my lord.

Duke. This swerves a little from the argument, though:
Look you, my lords.

Guardiano. [*Aside.*] All's fast; now comes my part to toll° him hither;
Then, with a stamp given, he's dispatched as cunningly.
[*The trap-door opens; Guardiano falls through the trap.*]

Hippolito. [*of Isabella.*] Stark dead! Oh treachery, cruelly made away! how's that?

Fabritio. Look, there's one of the lovers dropped away too.

Duke. Why sure, this plot's drawn false; here's no such thing.

Livia. Oh, I am sick to th'death! let me down quickly.
This fume is deadly. Oh, 't has poisoned me!
My subtilty is sped; her art has quitted me.
My own ambition pulls me down to ruin. [*dies.*]

Hippolito. Nay, then I kiss thy cold lips, and applaud
This thy revenge in death.
Cupids shoot [*at Hippolito.*]

Fabritio. Look, Juno's down too.
What makes she there? her pride should keep aloft.
She was wont to scorn the earth in other shows.
Methinks her peacocks' feathers° are much pulled.

Hippolito. Oh, death runs through my blood in a wild flame too!

112 **savor** odor 123 **toll** entice 136 **peacock's feathers** (peacocks were sacred to Juno)

Plague of those cupids! some lay hold on 'em.
Let 'em not 'scape, they have spoiled me; the shaft's
deadly.

Duke. I have lost myself in this quite.

Hippolito. My great lords, we are all confounded.

Duke. How?

Hippolito. Dead; and I worse.

Fabritio. Dead? my girl dead? I hope
My sister Juno has not served me so.

Hippolito. Lust and forgetfulness has been amongst us,
And we are brought to nothing. Some blest charity
Lend me the speeding pity of his sword
To quench this fire in blood! Leantio's death
Has brought all this upon us—now I taste it—
And made us lay plots to confound each other:
The event so proves it; and man's understanding
Is riper at his fall than all his lifetime.
She,° in a madness for her lover's death,
Revealed a fearful lust in our near bloods,
For which I am punished dreadfully and unlooked for;
Proved her own ruin too: vengeance met vengeance
Like a set match: as if the plagues of sin
Had been agreed to meet here altogether.
But how her fawning partner fell, I reach° not,
Unless caught by some springe° of his own setting—
For on my pain, he never dreamed of dying;
The plot was all his own, and he had cunning
Enough to save himself: but 'tis the property
Of guilty deeds to draw your wise men downward.
Therefore the wonder ceases.—Oh this torment!

Duke. Our guard below there!

Enter a Lord with a Guard.

Lord. My lord?

Hippolito. Run and meet death
then,
And cut off time and pain. [*Runs on Guard's weapon.*]°

Lord. Behold, my lord,
H'as run his breast upon a weapon's point.

152 **She** i.e., Livia 158 **reach** understand 159 **springe** snare
166 s.d. **weapon** sword (?), halbert (?)

Duke. Upon the first night of our nuptial honours
Destruction plays her triumph, and great mischiefs
Mask in expected pleasures; 'tis prodigious!
They're things most fearfully ominous: I like 'em not.
Remove these ruined bodies from our eyes.
[*Guards bear away bodies.*]

Bianca. [*Aside.*] Not yet? no change? when falls he° to the earth?

Lord. Please but your excellence to peruse that paper,
Which is a brief confession from the heart
Of him that fell first, ere his soul departed;
And there the darkness of these deeds speaks plainly:
'Tis the full scope, the manner and intent.
His ward, that ignorantly let him° down,
Fear put to present flight at the voice of him.

Bianca. [*Aside.*] Nor yet?

Duke. Read, read; for I am lost in sight and strength.

Cardinal. My noble brother!

Bianca. Oh the curse of wretchedness!
My deadly hand is fal'n upon my lord.
Destruction take me to thee, give me way;
The pains and plagues of a lost soul upon him
That hinders me a moment!

Duke. My heart swells bigger yet; help here, break't ope,
My breast flies open next. [*dies.*]

Bianca. Oh, with the poison
That was prepared for thee, thee, Cardinal!
'Twas meant for thee!

Cardinal. Poor prince!

Bianca. Accursed error!

Bianca. Give me thy last breath, thou infected bosom,
And wrap two spirits in one poisoned vapour.
Thus, thus, reward thy murderer, and turn death
Into a parting kiss! My soul stands ready at my lips,
Ev'n vexed to stay one minute after thee.

Cardinal. The greatest sorrow and astonishment
That ever struck the general peace of Florence
Dwells in this hour.

Bianca. So my desires are satisfied,
I feel death's power within me!

173 **he** i.e., the Cardinal 179 **him** i.e., Guardiani

Thou hast prevailed in something, cursed poison,
Though thy chief force was spent in my lord's bosom.
But my deformity in spirit's more foul:
A blemished face best fits a leprous soul.
What make I here? these are all strangers to me,
Not known but by their malice, now th'art gone,
Nor do I seek their pities.

Cardinal. Oh restrain
Her ignorant, wilful hand.

[*Bianca seizes the poisoned cup and drinks from it.*]

Bianca. Now do; 'tis done.
Leantio, now I feel the breach of marriage
At my heart-breaking! Oh the deadly snares
That women set for women—without pity
Either to soul or honour! Learn by me
To know your foes. In this belief I die:
Like our own sex, we have no enemy, no enemy.

Lord. See, my lord,
What shift sh'as made to be her own destruction.

Bianca. Pride, greatness, honours, beauty, youth, ambition,
You must all down together; there's no help for't.
Yet this my gladness is, that I remove,
Tasting the same death in a cup of love. [*dies.*]

Cardinal. Sin, what thou art, these ruins show too
piteously!
Two kings on one throne cannot sit together
But one must needs down, for his title's wrong:
So where lust reigns, that prince cannot reign long.

Exeunt.

FINIS

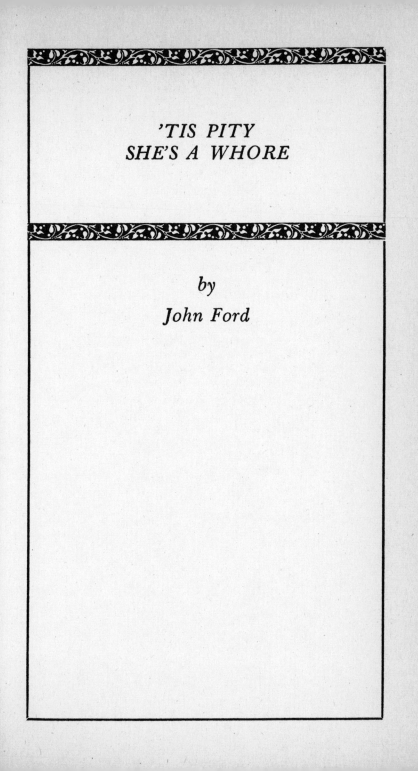

'TIS PITY SHE'S A WHORE

by

John Ford

JOHN FORD

We come to the reading of *'Tis Pity She's a Whore* with little of the explanatory context that surrounds other plays. There are neither biographical nor theatrical nor historical references to throw perspective on how John Ford wrote or what he sought to achieve. Instead the reader confronts this strange and disturbing tragedy uncertain whether it is one of the last Jacobean-Caroline grotesques or one of the first modern psychological dramas.

Although Ford was born while the Elizabethan age was in its prime, as a playwright he is wholly a figure of late Jacobean and Caroline time. The son of a prosperous Devonshire gentleman, he was baptized on April 17, 1586. As a younger son, he did not benefit greatly from his father's wealth, however great or small that was. He did, on the other hand, enter the Middle Temple in 1602, a lad of sixteen, and remain there, except for a period of expulsion, until 1617. His long residence at the Middle Temple indicates that he performed some kind of legal work during these years, though he fell short of being a full-fledged barrister.

So far as our meager information suggests, Ford had no connection with the theater during his years at Middle Temple. He did start writing in 1606, but confined himself to prose and verse. By 1620 he completed three pamphlets, two long poems, and several shorter poems. None of these have much distinction, and until 1620 there is nothing to hint at his future qualities as a dramatist.

As with so many playwrights of the time, he began his career in the theater by collaborating with an experienced writer. Once again, Thomas Dekker played midwife. Between 1620 and 1625 Ford collaborated with Dekker alone on the composition of three plays, and with Dekker and others on two plays. Two of these joint efforts are extant: *The Witch of Edmonton* (with Dekker and William Rowley) and *The Sun's Darling* (with Dekker alone). What exactly were Ford's contributions to these plays can not be determined now. But it appears that once he had gone through his belated apprenticeship, he did not write with partners again. After 1625, all of his plays are individual compositions.

John Ford's distinctive work thus coincides with the fateful reign of Charles I. Following the death of James I in 1625, life at court became more rarefied, politics more claustrophobic, and entertainments more idolatrous. Theatrically, the period is considered a ripening to decay of characteristics generated in earlier years. Comedy becomes more flippant, less moral. Tragedy becomes less horrifying, more languid and lush, continuing to mine the traditions of revenge, Italian luxuriousness, and intrigue. To a large extent the theatrical tone of these Caroline years is set by the work of Ford and James Shirley.

'Tis Pity She's a Whore is one of three tragedies that Ford composed between 1625 and 1639, the year after which we hear no more of him. The other two tragedies are *Love's Sacrifice* and *The Broken Heart.* In addition, he wrote the last history play of the pre-Restoration era, *Perkin Warbeck,* and three tragicomedies: *The Lover's Melancholy, The Lady's Trial,* and *The Fancies Chaste and Noble.* All of these are extant. Titles of two or three other plays, now lost, are also known. As is so often the case with Renaissance plays, dating these works is hazardous. The most broadly accepted chronology of the three tragedies puts *The Broken Heart* first with *Love's Sacrifice* and *'Tis Pity* somewhat later, all three appearing by 1633.

Coming late to stage writing, Ford does not seem to have had close connections with the players. After 1625 he wrote first for Shakespeare's old company, the King's men, and then for Christopher Beeston's companies at the Phoenix. The title page of *'Tis Pity* advertises that it was "acted by the Queen's Majesty's Servants, at the Phoenix in Drury Lane." Otherwise, nothing in Ford's dedicatory epistles or in allusions to him mention the stage. As in so much else about Ford and his writing, the play stands alone, isolated.

This impression of isolation is reinforced by the absence of any know source for *'This Pity She's a Whore.* Although the play follows the received pattern of Italian intrigue tragedy, it lacks the historical or documentary detailing that gives plays like *The Duchess of Malfi* and *Women Beware Women* their particularity. Rather, *'Tis Pity* conveys a quality of distillation, of familiar content abstracted and placed at the service of its starting subject.

No play of the period, or indeed of a later age, treats incest so directly and baldly. Ever since it was written, critics have found the encounter with the material unnerving. Ignoring

Ford's claim in his epistle to the Earl of Peterborough that "the Gravity of the Subject may easily excuse the lightness of the Title," they have charged the author with sensationalism, and from that objection attacked him as decadent. In his work they see exemplified the widespread deterioration of tragic sensibility, reflected not only in the extremity of the subject but in the reworking of outworn theatrical conventions.

But while it is true that Ford uses situations and devices from the great English Renaissance storehouse, he does so with sophistication. *'Tis Pity* deliberately echoes several late-sixteenth-century plays, notably *Romeo and Juliet, Tamburlaine,* and *Doctor Faustus.* The last, in particular, keynotes Ford's play. At the very beginning of *'Tis Pity,* the Friar alludes to Faustus' fall. In his first lines he admonishes Giovanni:

> wits that presumed
> On wit too much, by striving how to prove
> There was no God, with foolish grounds of art,
> Discovered first the nearest way to hell,
> And filled the world with devilish atheism.
> (I. i. 4-8)

This throwback to a sophisticated morality play, together with Ford's revival of the history play in *Perkin Warbeck,* suggests a knowing and purposeful use of the past for new ends. By utilizing the vocabulary of the older tragedy he sought to create a fresh image.

The initial insistence on a moral universe by the Friar only highlights the absence of moral perspective throughout *'Tis Pity*. By abstracting the action, Ford gives it an exemplary rather than a realistic quality. It emerges as a kind of theatrical postulate: let us take the most forbidden realm of love and explore how it thrives, in itself and in relation to the world. The coolness of the proposition is evident in the fact that the horror of incest appalls the audience far more than it ever does the characters. Even when Soranzo discovers the truth about Annabella and Giovanni, he is furious because he was made a scapegoat rather than shocked by the unnatural love affair.

In presenting the sibling lovers, Ford introduces none of the disgust that first assails Isabella in *Women Beware Women.*

In that play the disgust arises from an uncle's affection for a niece. But in *'Tis Pity* where sister responds to brother, Annabella's reception of Giovanni's avowal is subdued and free of horror. When Giovanni first declares his love, Annabella expresses slight dismay. Yet her words have as much to do with his plea that she stab him for presuming to love her as they do with her feelings about his confession.

> Forbid it, my just fears.
> If this be true, 'twere fitter I were dead.
> (I. ii. 215-16)

After he goes on to describe his torment at loving and not expressing his love, she asks, "Comes this in sadness [that is, seriously] from you?" (226) and advises him, "You are my brother Giovanni" (228). But he continues to urge his love, concluding with the question to her, "Must I now live, or die?" She replies:

> Live. Thou hast won
> The field, and never fought; what thou hast
> urged
> My captive heart had long ago resolved.
> (I. ii. 240-42)

Throughout the first half of the play, Ford paints Giovanni and Annabella's love in the most attractive colors. While sensual, it is also deeply spiritual, obsessive yet somehow idealized. In the entire play, it stands forth as the most worthy of the passions that possess the characters. Grimaldi's desire for Annabella is envious and criminal, Soranzo's abandonment of Hippolita curdles his interest in Annabella, Bergetto's simpleminded devotion to Philotis generates acceptance but not affection from Philotis. None of these desires has the heartfelt devotion of the forbidden passion.

What then is the source of tragedy in the play? Does it proceed from the disapproval of society? Does it come from the failure of the lovers? Is it a consequence of the moral lapse into incest? None and all of these causes contribute to the ultimate catastrophe. Florio's pressures on Annabella to marry do not have as strong a thirst for social climbing as we find in Fabritio's demands on Isabella (*Women Beware Women*). Rather, a natural inevitability is at work. In the ordinary passage of time, Annabella must marry. Once she discovers that she is pregnant, a new urgency, one that cannot be ignored, arises, and to meet this the Friar conspires in deceiving Soranzo, thus undermining his own moral position.

Finally, the lovers must choose between life and death. To defend herself, Annabella turns coarse. Her defiance of Soranzo vulgarizes her. She doubts the emotional purity of her passion. The incestuous love itself—which was consummated so radiantly—turns violent, and finally outrageously grotesque.

How are we to take that awesome-laughable Grand Guignol of Giovanni entering the banquet with Annabella's "heart upon his dagger"? The answer may be signaled in an earlier scene. To revenge herself on Soranzo, Hippolita presents a masque to him and his new bride, Annabella, at their wedding. Under the mask of reconciliation, she tries to poison her former lover. But Soranzo's servant, Vasques, has misled her, and it is she who is destroyed. Such a scene, with revenger acting under cover of a masque, is one of the staples of Jacobean tragedy: *The Revenger's Tragedy* has the double action of revengers triumphant and then unmasked; *Women Beware Women* has the reverberating mutuality of revenger slaying revenger. But these murderous masques occur in the final scene. By transferring this kind of concluding action to the middle of the play and furthermore by having the revenger defeated, Ford is commenting on the futility of conventional devices. He seems to be saying that extraordinary passions deserve extraordinary ends, that only the most horrid of acts can quench the thirst for love.

It is difficult for us to read or see this final scene without shrinking in disgust or guffawing in nervousness. Yet there is something appropriately ludicrous in the image of the heart on a dagger, and given the earlier masque, something ironic in its signification. Is Ford challenging us with a deeply black comedy, as though to ask, "If conventional bloodletting does not satisfy you, what do you think of horror piled on horror?" Giovanni's final bitterness stems not from social circumstance nor psychopathic obsession but from the searing irony of love too intimate, too precious, too all-consuming to survive the daily round of eixstence. By assaulting us with love turned in on itself, Ford casts doubt on the capacity of acceptable love to be as true as incest—challenges, in short, so-called normality.

TO MY FRIEND THE AUTHOR

With admiration I beheld this Whore
Adorned with beauty such as might restore
(If ever being as thy muse hath famed)
Her Giovanni, in his love unblamed:
The ready Graces lent their willing aid,
Pallas° herself now played the chambermaid,
And helped to put her dressings on. Secure
Rest thou that thy name herein shall endure
To th' end of age; and Annabella be
Gloriously fair, even in her infamy.

THOMAS ELLICE°

7 Pallas Pallas Athena, goddess of war and wisdom **12 Thomas Ellice** (Thomas Ellice is unknown, though Ford dedicated *The Lover's Melancholy* to Robert Ellice of Gray's Inn)

TO THE TRULY NOBLE JOHN, EARL OF PETERBOROUGH, LORD MORDAUNT, BARON OF TURVEY°

MY LORD,

Where a truth of merit hath a general warrant, there love is but a debt, acknowledgment a justice. Greatness cannot often claim virtue by inheritance; yet in this, yours appears most eminent, for that you are not more rightly heir to your fortunes than glory shall be to your memory. Sweetness of disposition ennobles a freedom of birth; in both, your lawful interest adds honour to your own name and mercy to my presumption. Your noble allowance° of these first fruits of my leisure° in the action° emboldens my confidence of your as noble construction in this presentment;° especially since my service must ever owe particular duty to your favours by a particular engagement. The gravity of the subject may easily excuse the lightness of the title: otherwise I had been a severe judge against mine own guilt. Princes have vouchsafed grace to trifles offered from a purity of devotion; your lordship may likewise please to admit into your good opinion, with these weak endeavours, the constancy of affection from the sincere lover of your deserts in honour.

JOHN FORD

2-3 John . . . Turvey John Mordaunt (1599-1642), favored by James I, created Earl of Peterborough by Charles I, fought on the side of Parliament in the civil war 10 **allowance** approbation 11 **fruits . . . leisure** (this phrase has not been satisfactorily explained) 11 **in the action** in performance 13 **presentment** form of presentation, i.e., print

The Actors' Names

Bonaventura, a friar.
A Cardinal, nuncio to the Pope.
Soranzo, a nobleman.
Florio, a citizen of Parma.
Donaldo, another citizen.
Grimaldi, a Roman gentleman.
Giovanni, son to Florio.
Bergetto, nephew to Donado.
Richardetto, a supposed physician.
Vasques, servant to Soranzo.
Poggio, servant to Bergetto.
Banditti, [Officers, Servants, etc.].

Women

Annabella, daughter to Florio.
Hippolita, wife to Richardetto.
Philotis, his niece.
Putana, tut'ress to Annabella.

The Scene

PARMA

'TIS PITY SHE'S A WHORE

[Act I, Scene i]

Enter Friar and Giovanni.

Friar. Dispute no more in this, for know, young man,
These are no school-points;° nice° philosophy
May tolerate unlikely arguments,
But Heaven admits no jest; wits that presumed
On wit too much, by striving how to prove
There was no God, with foolish grounds of art,°
Discovered first the nearest way to hell,
And filled the world with devilish atheism.
Such questions, youth, are fond.° For better 'tis,
To bless the sun than reason why it shines;
Yet He thou talk'st of is above the sun.
No more; I may not hear it.
Giovanni. Gentle father,
To you I have unclasped my burdened soul,
Emptied the storehouse of my thoughts and heart,
Made myself poor of secrets; have not left
Another word untold, which hath not spoke
All what I ever durst, or think, or know;
And yet is here the comfort I shall have,
Must I not do, what all men else may, love?
Friar. Yes, you may love, fair son.
Giovanni. Must I not praise
That beauty which, if framed anew, the gods
Would make a god of, if they had it there,
And kneel to it, as I do kneel to them?
Friar. Why, foolish madman!
Giovanni. Shall a peevish° sound,
A customary form, from man to man,
Of brother and of sister, be a bar
'Twixt my perpetual happiness and me?
Say that we had one father, say one womb

2 school-points academic points of argument **2 nice** full of narrow and trivial distinctions **6 art** knowledge **9 fond** foolish **24 peevish** trifling

(Curse to my joys) gave both us life, and birth;
Are we not therefore each to other bound
So much the more by nature? by the links
Of blood, of reason? nay, if you will have't,
Even of religion, to be ever one,
One soul, one flesh, one love, one heart, one all?

Friar. Have done, unhappy youth, for thou art lost.

Giovanni. Shall then, for that I am her brother born,
My joys be ever banished from her bed?
No, father; in your eyes I see the change
Of pity and compassion; from your age,
As from a sacred oracle, distils
The life of counsel: tell me, holy man,
What cure shall give me ease in these extremes.

Friar. Repentance, son, and sorrow for this sin:
For thou hast moved a Majesty above
With thy unranged° (almost) blasphemy.

Giovanni. O do not speak of that, dear confessor.

Friar. Art thou, my son, that miracle of wit
Who once, within these three months, wert esteemed
A wonder of thine age, throughout Bononia?°
How did the University applaud
Thy government,° behaviour, learning, speech,
Sweetness, and all that could make up a man!
I was proud of my tutelage, and chose
Rather to leave my books, than part with thee.
I did so: but the fruits of all my hopes
Are lost in thee, as thou art in thyself.
O Giovanni, hast thou left the schools
Of knowledge, to converse with lust and death?
For death waits on thy lust. Look through the world,
And thou shalt see a thousand faces shine
More glorious, than this idol ador'st:
Leave her, and take thy choice, 'tis much less sin,
Though in such games as those, they lose that win.°

Giovanni. It were more ease to stop the ocean
From floats° and ebbs, than to dissuade my vows.

Friar. Then I have done, and in thy wilful flames

45 **unranged** deranged 49 **Bononia** Bologna, famous for its university 51 **government** good conduct 62-63 **'tis much . . . that win** fornication is less sinful than incest though still damnable 65 **floats** flows (of the tide)

Already see thy ruin; Heaven is just,
Yet hear my counsel.

Giovanni. As a voice of life.

Friar. Hie to thy father's house, there lock thee fast
Alone within thy chamber, then fall down
On both thy knees, and grovel on the ground:
Cry to thy heart, wash every word thou utter'st
In tears (and if't be possible) of blood:
Beg Heaven to cleanse the leprosy of lust
That rots thy soul, acknowledge what thou art,
A wretch, a worm, a nothing: weep, sigh, pray
Three times a day, and three times every night.
For seven days' space do this, then if thou find'st
No change in thy desires, return to me:
I'll think on remedy. Pray for thyself
At home, whilst I pray for thee here.—Away,
My blessing with thee, we have need to pray.

Giovanni. All this I'll do, to free me from the rod
Of vengeance; else I'll swear, my fate's my god.

Exeunt.

[Act I, Scene ii]

Enter Grimaldi and Vasques ready to fight.

Vasques. Come sir, stand to your tackling;° if you prove craven, I'll make you run quickly.

Grimaldi. Thou art no equal match for me.

Vasques. Indeed I never went to the wars to bring home news, nor cannot play the mountebank for a meal's meat, and swear I got my wounds in the field. See you these grey hairs? They'll not flinch for a bloody nose. Wilt thou to this gear?°

Grimaldi. Why, slave, think'st thou I'll balance my reputation with a cast-suit?° Call thy master, he shall know that I dare—

Vasques. Scold like a cot-quean,° that's your profession, thou poor shadow of a soldier; I will make thee know

I.ii.1 **tackling** weapons 7 **gear** businss (i.e., fighting) 10 **cast-suit** one who wears cast-off clothing 12 **cot-quean** shrew my master keeps servants thy betters in quality and performance. Com'st thou to fight or prate?

Grimaldi. Neither with thee. I am a Roman, and a gentleman, one that have got mine honour with expense of blood.

Vasques. You are a lying coward and a fool. Fight, or by these hilts I'll kill thee—brave my lord!—you'll fight?

Grimaldi. Provoke me not, for if thou dost—

Vasques. Have at you!

They fight; Grimaldi hath the worst.

Enter Florio, Donado, Soranzo.

Florio. What mean these sudden broils so near my doors?
Have you not other places but my house
To vent the spleen of your disordered bloods?
Must I be haunted still with such unrest,
As not to eat or sleep in peace at home?
Is this your love, Grimaldi? Fie, 'tis naught.

Donado. And Vasques, I may tell thee 'tis not well
To broach these quarrels; you are ever forward
In seconding contentions.

Enter above° Annabella and Putana.

Florio. What's the ground?

Soranzo. That, with your patience, signors, I'll resolve:
This gentleman,° whom fame reports a soldier,
(For else I know not) rivals me in love
To Signor Florio's daughter; to whose ears
He still prefers his suit to my disgrace,
Thinking the way to recommend himself,
Is to disparage me in his report.
But know, Grimaldi, though, may be, thou art
My equal in thy blood, yet this bewrays°
A lowness in thy mind which, wert thou noble,
Thou wouldst as much disdain, as I do thee

31 s.d. **above** balcony overlooking the stage platform proper 34 **gentleman** (Soranzo indicates Grimaldi) 41 **bewrays** betrays, reveals

For this unworthiness; and on this ground
I willed my servant to correct his tongue,
Holding a man, so base, no match for me.

Vasques. And had not your sudden coming prevented us, I had let my gentleman blood under the gills; I should have wormed you sir, for running mad.°

Grimaldi. I'll be revenged, Soranzo.

Vasques. On a dish of warm broth to stay your stomach—do, honest innocence, do; spoon-meat is a wholesomer diet than a Spanish blade.

Grimaldi. Remember this.

Soranzo. I fear thee not, Grimaldi. *Exit Grimaldi.*

Florio. My Lord Soranzo, this is strange to me,
Why you should storm, having my word engaged:
Owing° her heart, what need you doubt her ear?
Losers may talk by law of any game.

Vasques. Yet the villainy of words, Signor Florio, may be such as would make any unspleened dove° choleric. Blame not my lord in this.

Florio. Be you more silent.
I would not for my wealth my daughter's love
Should cause the spilling of one drop of blood.
Vasques, put up,° let's end this fray in wine.
Exeunt [Florio, Donado, Soranzo and Vasques.]

Putana. How like you this, child? Here's threatening, challenging, quarreling, and fighting, on every side, and all is for your sake; you had need look to yourself, charge, you'll be stolen away sleeping else shortly.

Annabella. But, tut'ress, such a life gives no content
To me, my thoughts are fixed on other ends;
Would you would leave me.

Putana. Leave you? No marvel else. Leave me no leaving, charge; this is love outright. Indeed I blame you not, you have choice fit for the best lady in Italy.

Annabella. Pray do not talk so much.

Putana. Take the worst with the best, there's Grimaldi the soldier, a very well-timbered fellow. They say he is a

49 **wormed you . . . mad** wormed you (i.e., as though you were a dog) to prevent you from running mad 58 **Owing** owning 61 **unspleened dove** (popular but mistaken notion that this gentle bird has no gall) 66 **put up** put away your sword

Roman, nephew to the Duke Montferrato, they say he did good service in the wars against the Milanese, but 'faith, charge, I do not like him, an't be for nothing but for being a soldier; not one amongst twenty of your skirmishing captains but have some privy maim or other that mars their standing upright.° I like him the worse, he crinkles so much in the hams; though he might serve if there were no more men, yet he's not the man I would choose.

Annabella. Fie, how thou prat'st.

Putana. As I am a very woman, I like Signor Soranzo well; he is wise, and what is more, rich; and what is more than that, kind, and what is more than all this, a nobleman; such a one, were I the fair Annabella myself, I would wish and pray for. Then he is bountiful; besides, he is handsome, and by my troth, I think wholesome° (and that's news in a gallant of three and twenty); liberal, that I know; loving, that you know; and a man sure, else he could never ha' purchased such a good name with Hippolita, the lusty widow, in her husband's lifetime: and 'twere but for that report, sweetheart, would 'a° were thine. Commend a man for his qualities, but take a husband as he is a plain-sufficient, naked man: such a one is for your bed, and such a one is Signor Soranzo, my life for't.

Annabella. Sure the woman took her morning's draught too soon.

Enter Bergetto and Poggio.

Putana. But look, sweetheart, look what thing comes now: here's another of your ciphers to fill up the number. O brave old ape in a silken coat. Observe.

Bergetto. Didst thou think, Poggio, that I would spoil my new clothes, and leave my dinner to fight?

Poggio. No, sir, I did not take you for so arrant a baby.

Bergetto. I am wiser than so: for I hope, Poggio, thou

84-5 **have some privy maim . . . upright** have some hurt in a private place that mars their virility 95 **wholesome** free of venereal disease 101 **'a** he (this form appears frequently in the play scripts of the time) never heardst of an elder brother that was a coxcomb.° Didst, Poggio?

Poggio. Never indeed, sir, as long as they had either land or money left them to inherit.

Bergetto. Is it possible, Poggio? O monstrous! Why, I'll undertake with a handful of silver to buy a headful of wit at any time; but sirrah, I have another purchase in hand, I shall have the wench, mine uncle says. I will but wash my face, and shift socks, and then have at her i'faith.—Mark my pace, Poggio.

Poggio. Sir—[*Aside.*] I have seen an ass and a mule trot the Spanish pavin° with a better grace, I know not how often.

Exeunt [Bergetto and Poggio.]

Annabella. This idiot haunts me too.

Putana. Ay, ay, he needs no description; the rich magnifico that is below with your father, charge, Signor Donado his uncle, for that he means to make this his cousin° a golden calf, thinks that you will be a right Israelite° and fall down to him presently: but I hope I have tutored you better. They say a fool's bauble° is a lady's playfellow, yet you having wealth enough, you need not cast upon the dearth of flesh at any rate: hang him, innocent.°

Enter Giovanni.

Annabella. But see, Putana, see: what blessed shape
Of some celestial creature now appears?
What man is he, that with such sad aspect
Walks careless of himself?
Putana. Where?
Annabella. Look below.

114 elder . . . coxcomb (because the elder brother inherited the entire estate) 125 **pavin** pavane, a stately dance 130 **cousin** (a general term for any kinsman or kinswoman, here a nephew) **130-31 a golden calf . . . Israelite** (alludes to the incident in Exodus, xxxii, when the Jews in the desert made and worshiped a golden calf while Moses was receiving the tablet of the Ten Commandments on Mount Sinai) 133 **bauble** stick, here a phallic pun 136 **innocent** natural fool

Putana. O, 'tis your brother, sweet—
Annabella. Ha!
Putana. 'Tis your brother.
Annabella. Sure 'tis not he; this is some woeful thing
Wrapped up in grief, some shadow of a man.
Alas, he beats his breast, and wipes his eyes
Drowned all in tears: methinks I hear him sigh.
Let's down, Putana, and partake the cause;
I know my brother in the love he bears me,
Will not deny me partage° in his sadness.
My soul is full of heaviness and fear.
Exit [with Putana.]
Giovanni. Lost, I am lost. My fates have doomed my death.
The more I strive, I love; the more I love,
The less I hope: I see my ruin, certain.
What judgment or endeavours could apply
To my incurable and restless wounds
I throughly° have examined, but in vain.
O that it were not in religion sin
To make our love a god, and worship it.
I have even wearied Heaven with prayers, dried up
The spring of my continual tears, even starved
My veins with daily fasts: what wit or art
Could counsel, I have practised; but alas,
I find all these but dreams and old men's tales
To fright unsteady youth; I'm still the same.
Or I must speak, or burst. 'Tis not, I know,
My lust, but 'tis my fate that leads me on.
Keep fear° and low faint-hearted shame with slaves;
I'll tell her that I love her, though my heart
Were rated° at the price of that attempt.
O me! She comes.

Enter Annabella and Putana.

Annabella. Brother.
Giovanni. [*Aside.*] If such a thing
As courage dwell in men, ye heavenly powers,
Now double all that virtue in my tongue.
Annabella. Why, brother, will you not speak to me?

148 partage share **155 throughly** i.e., thoroughly **166 Keep fear** let fear keep or remain **168 rated** measured

Giovanni. Yes; how d'ee, sister?
Annabella. Howsoever I am, methinks you are not well.
Putana. Bless us, why are you so sad, sir?
Giovanni. Let me entreat you leave us a while, Putana.
Sister, I would be private with you.
Annabella. Withdraw, Putana.
Putana. I will [*Aside.*] If this were any other company for her, I should think my absence an office of some credit;° but I will leave them together. *Exit Putana.*
Giovanni. Come, sister, lend your hand, let's walk together.
I hope you need not blush to walk with me;
Here's none but you and I.
Annabella. How's this?
Giovanni. Faith, I mean no harm.
Annabella. Harm?
Giovanni. No, good faith; how is't with 'ee?
Annabella. [*Aside.*] I trust he be not frantic—I am very well, brother.
Giovanni. Trust me, but I am sick, I fear so sick,
'Twill cost my life.
Annabella. Mercy forbid it. 'Tis not so, I hope.
Giovanni. I think you love me, sister.
Annabella. Yes, you know I do.
Giovanni. I know't indeed—Y'are very fair.
Annabella. Nay then, I see you have a merry sickness.
Giovanni. That's as it proves. The poets feign, I read,
That Juno° for her forehead did exceed
All other goddesses: but I durst swear
Your forehead exceeds hers, as hers did theirs.
Annabella. Troth, this is pretty.
Giovanni. Such a pair of stars
As are thine eyes would, like Promethean fire,
If gently glanced, give life to senseless stones.
Annabella. Fie upon 'ee.
Giovanni. The lily and the rose, most sweetly strange,
Upon your dimpled cheeks do strive for change.
Such lips would tempt a saint; such hands as those
Would make an anchorite° lascivious.
Annabella. D'ee mock me, or flatter me?

181 **my absence . . . credit** my departure would be worth a bribe 200 **Juno** Juno, the wife of Jupiter, was also his sister 210 **anchorite** hermit

Giovanni. If you would see a beauty more exact°
Than art can counterfeit, or nature frame,
Look in your glass, and there behold your own.
Annabella. O you are a trim youth.
Giovanni. Here. *Offers his dagger to her.*
Annabella. What to do?
Giovanni. And here's my breast, strike home.
Rip up my bosom, there thou shalt behold
A heart in which is writ the truth I speak.
Why stand 'ee?
Annabella. Are you earnest?
Giovanni. Yes, most earnest.
You cannot love?
Annabella. Whom?
Giovanni. Me. My tortured soul
Hath felt affliction in the heat of death.
O Annabella, I am quite undone.
The love of thee, my sister, and the view
Of thy immortal beauty hath untuned
All harmony both of my rest and life.
Why d'ee not strike?
Annabella. Forbid it, my just fears.
If this be true, 'twere fitter I were dead.
Giovanni. True, Annabella; 'tis no time to jest.
I have too long suppressed the hidden flames
That almost have consumed me; I' have spent
Many a silent night in sighs and groans,
Ran over all my thoughts, despised my fate,
Reasoned against the reasons of my love,
Done all that smoothed-cheek virtue could advise,
But found all bootless;° 'tis my destiny
That you must either love, or I must die.
Annabella. Comes this in sadness° from you?
Giovanni. Let some mischief
Befall me soon, if I dissemble aught.
Annabella. You are my brother Giovanni.
Giovanni. You
My sister Annabella; I know this:
And could afford you instance why to love
So much the more for this; to which intent

212 exact perfect 239 bootless useless 241 in sadness seriously

Wise nature first in your creation meant
To make you mine; else't had been sin and foul
To share one beauty to a double soul.
Nearness in birth or blood doth he persuade
A nearer nearness in affection.
I have asked counsel of the holy church,
Who tells me I may love you, and 'tis just
That since I may, I should; and will, yes, will.
Must I now live, or die?

Annabella. Live. Thou hast won
The field, and never fought; what thou hast urged
My captive heart had long ago resolved.
I blush to tell thee—but I'll tell thee now—
For every sigh that thou hast spent for me
I have sighed ten; for every tear shed twenty:
And not so much for that° I loved, as that
I durst not say I loved, nor scarcely think it.

Giovanni. Let not this music be a dream, ye gods,
For pity's sake, I beg 'ee.

Annabella. On my knees, *She kneels.*
Brother, even by our mother's dust, I charge you,
Do not betray me to your mirth or hate,
Love me, or kill me, brother.

Giovanni. On my knees, *He kneels.*
Sister, even by my mother's dust, I charge you,
Do not betray me to your mirth or hate,
Love me, or kill me, sister.

Annabella. You mean good sooth° then?

Giovanni. In good troth I do,
And so do you, I hope: say, I'm in earnest.

Annabella. I'll swear't, I.

Giovanni. And I, and by this kiss, *Kisses her.*
(Once more, yet once more; now let's rise by this)
[*They rise.*]
I would not change this minute for Elysium.
What must we now do?

Annabella. What you will.

Giovanni. Come then,
After so many tears as we have wept,
Let's learn to court in smiles, to kiss, and sleep.
Exeunt.

261 for that because **271 sooth** truth

[Act I, Scene iii]

Enter Florio and Donado.

Florio. Signor Donado, you have said enough,
I understand you; but would have you know
I will not force my daughter 'gainst her will.
You see I have but two, a son and her;
And he is so devoted to his book,
As I must tell you true, I doubt° his health:
Should he miscarry, all my hopes rely
Upon my girl; as for worldly fortune,
I am, I thank my stars, blest with enough.
My care is how to match her to her liking:
I would not have her marry wealth, but love,
And if she like your nephew, let him have her.
Here's all that I can say.
Donado. Sir, you say well,
Like a true father, and for my part, I
If the young folks can like ('twixt you and me),
Will promise to assure my nephew presently
Three thousand florins yearly during life,
And after I am dead, my whole estate.
Florio. 'Tis a fair proffer, sir; meantime your nephew
Shall have free passage to commence his suit.
If he can thrive, he shall have my consent.
So for this time I'll leave you, signor. *Exit.*
Donado. Well,
Here's hope yet, if my nephew would have wit;
But he is such another dunce, I fear
He'll never win the wench. When I was young
I could have done't, i'faith, and so shall he
If he will learn of me; and in good time
He comes himself.

Enter Bergetto and Poggio.

How now, Bergetto, whither away so fast?
Bergetto. O uncle, I have heard the strangest
ever came out of the mint,° have I not, Poggio

I.iii.6 **doubt** fear for 31 **out of the mint** freshly made

Poggio. Yes indeed, sir.

Donado. What news, Bergetto?

Bergetto. Why, look ye, uncle, my barber told me just now that there is a fellow come to town who undertakes to make a mill go without the mortal help of any water or wind, only with sand-bags: and this fellow hath a strange horse, a most excellent beast, I'll assure you, uncle (my barber says), whose head, to the wonder of all Christian people, stands just behind where his tail is. Is't not true, Poggio?

Poggio. So the barber swore, forsooth.

Donado. And you are running thither?

Bergetto. Ay forsooth, uncle.

Donado. Wilt thou be a fool still? Come sir, you shall not go: you have more mind of a puppet-play than on the business I told ye; why, thou great baby, wilt never have wit, wilt make thyself a may-game° to all the world?

Poggio. Answer for yourself, master.

Bergetto. Why, uncle, should I sit at home still, and not go abroad to see fashions like other gallants?

Donado. To see hobby-horses! What wise talk, I pray, had you with Annabella, when you were at Signor Florio's house?

Bergetto. O, the wench! Uds sa' me,° uncle, I tickled her with a rare speech, that I made her almost burst her belly with laughing.

Donado. Nay, I think so; and what speech was't?

Bergetto. What did I say, Poggio?

Poggio. Forsooth, my master said that he loved her almost as well as he loved parmasent,° and swore (I'll be sworn for him) that she wanted but such a nose as his was to be as pretty a young woman as any was in Parma.

Donado. O gross.

Bergetto. Nay, uncle, then she asked me whether my father had any more children than myself: and I said 'No, 'twere better he should have had his brains knocked out first.'

Donado. This is intolerable.

Bergetto. Then said she 'Will Signor Donado your uncle leave you all his wealth?'

48 **may-game** laughingstock 55 **Uds sa' me** God save me 61 **parmasent** Parmesan, cheese of Parma

Donado. Ha! that was good; did she harp upon that string?

Bergetto. Did she harp upon that string? Ay, that she did. I answered 'Leave me all his wealth? Why, woman, he hath no other wit; if he had, he should hear on't to his everlasting glory and confusion: I know,' quoth I, 'I am his white boy,° and will not be gulled';° and with that she fell into a great smile, and went away. Nay, I did fit her.°

Donado. Ah, sirrah, then I see there is no changing of nature. Well, Bergetto, I fear thou wilt be a very ass still.

Bergetto. I should be sorry for that, uncle.

Donado. Come, come you home with me. Since you are no better a speaker, I'll have you write to her after some courtly manner, and enclose some rich jewel in the letter.

Bergetto. Ay marry, that will be excellent.

Donado. Peace, innocent.
Once in my time I'll set my wits to school,
If all fail, 'tis but the fortune of a fool.

Bergetto. Poggio, 'twill do, Poggio. *Exeunt.*

[Act II, Scene i]

Enter Giovanni and Annabella, as from their chamber.

Giovanni. Come Annabella, no more sister now,
But love, a name more gracious; do not blush,
Beauty's sweet wonder, but be proud to know
That yielding thou hast conquered, and inflamed
A heart whose tribute is thy brother's life.

Annabella. And mine is his. O, how these stol'n contents°
Would print a modest crimson on my cheeks,
Had any but my heart's delight prevailed.

Giovanni. I marvel why the chaster of your sex
Should think this pretty toy called maidenhead
So strange a loss, when, being lost, 'tis nothing,
And you are still the same.

77 **white boy** favorite 77 **gulled** made a fool of 78-9 **fit her** answer her aptly II.i.6 **contents** satisfactions, delights

Annabella. 'Tis well for you;
Now you can talk.
Giovanni. Music as well consists
In th' ear as in the playing.
Annabella. O, y'are wanton.
Tell on't, y'are best: do.
Giovanni. Thou wilt chide me then.
Kiss me —so. Thus hung Jove on Leda's neck,°
And sucked divine ambrosia from her lips.
I envy not the mightiest man alive,
But hold myself in being king of thee,
More great, than were I king of all the world.
But I shall lose you, sweetheart.
Annabella. But you shall not.
Giovanni. You must be married, mistress.
Annabella. Yes, to whom?
Giovanni. Someone must have you.
Annabella. You must.
Giovanni. Nay, some other.
Annabella. Now prithee do not speak so; without jesting,
You'll make me weep in earnest.
Giovanni. What, you will not?
But tell me, sweet, canst thou be dared to swear
That thou wilt live to me,° and to no other?
Annabella. By both our loves I dare, for didst thou know,
My Giovanni, how all suitors seem
To my eyes hateful, thou wouldst trust me then.
Giovanni. Enough, I take thy word. Sweet, we must part.
Remember what thou vowst; keep well my heart.
Annabella. Will you be gone?
Giovanni. I must.
Annabella. When to return?
Giovanni. Soon.
Annabella. Look you do.
Giovanni. Farewell. *Exit.*
Annabella. Go where thou wilt, in mind I'll keep thee here,
And where thou art, I know I shall be there.
Guardian!

16 **Jove on Leda's neck** (Jupiter in the form of a swan seduced Leda) 27 **live to me** live only for me

Enter Putana.

Putana. Child, how is't, child? Well, thank Heaven, ha!
Annabella. O guardian, what a paradise of joy
Have I passed over!

Putana. Nay, what a paradise of joy have you passed under. Why, now I commend thee, charge; fear nothing, sweetheart; what though he be your brother? Your brother's a man, I hope, and I say still, if a young wench feel the fit upon her, let her take anybody, father or brother, all is one.

Annabella. I would not have it known for all the world.

Putana. Nor I, indeed, for the speech of the people;° else 'twere nothing.

Florio within. Daughter Annabella.
Annabella. O me! my father,—Here sir,—Reach my work.
Florio within. What are you doing?
Annabella. So: let him come now.

Enter Florio, Richardetto like a doctor of physic, and Philotis with a lute in her hand.

Florio. So hard at work? That's well; you lose no time.
Look, I have brought you company; here's one,
A learned doctor, lately come from Padua,
Much skilled in physic, and for that I see
You have of late been sickly, I entreated
This reverend man to visit you some time.
Annabella. Y'are very welcome, sir.
Richardetto. I thank you, mistress.
Loud fame in large report hath spoke your praise
As well for virtue as perfection:
For which I have been bold to bring with me
A kinswoman of mine, a maid, for song
And music, one perhaps will give content;
Please you to know her.
Annabella. They are parts° I love,
And she for them most welcome.
Philotis. Thank you, lady.

48 **for the speech of the people** because of popular gossip 65 **parts** discrete abilities of a person

Florio. Sir, now you know my house, pray make not
strange,°
And if you find my daughter need your art,
I'll be your paymaster.
Richardetto. Sir, what I am
She shall command.
Florio. You shall bind me to you.
Daughter, I must have conference with you
About some matters that concerns us both.
Good master doctor, please you but walk in,
We'll crave a little of your cousin's cunning.°
I think my girl hath not quite forgot
To touch an instrument, she could have done't.
We'll hear them both.
Richardetto. I'll wait upon you, sir. *Exeunt.*

[Act II, Scene ii]

Enter Soranzo in his study reading a book.

Soranzo. 'Love's measure is extreme, the comfort, pain,
The life unrest, and the reward disdain.'
What's here? Look't o'er again: 'tis so, so writes
This smooth licentious poet in his rhymes.
But Sannazar,° thou liest, for had thy bosom
Felt such oppression as is laid on mine,
Thou wouldst have kissed the rod that made thee smart.
To work then, happy muse, and contradict
What Sannazar hath in his envy writ.
'Love's measure is the mean, sweet his annoys,
His pleasure's life, and his reward all joys.'
Had Annabella lived when Sannazar
Did in his brief encomium° celebrate
Venice, that queen of cities, he had left°
That verse which gained him such a sum of gold,
And for one only look from Annabel
Had writ of her and her diviner cheeks.
O how my thoughts are—

67 **make not strange** do not be a stranger 74 **cunning** skill II.ii.5 **Sannazar** Jacopo Sannazaro (c. 1456-1530), Neapolitan poet 13 **brief encomium** short Latin poem 14 **he had left** he would have abandoned

Vasques within. Pray forbear; in rules of civility, let me give notice on't: I shall be taxed of° my neglect of duty and service.

Soranzo. What rude intrusion interrupts my peace?
Can I be nowhere private?

Vasques within. Troth you wrong your modesty.

Soranzo. What's the matter, Vasques? Who is't?

Enter Hippolita and Vasques.

Hippolita. 'Tis I:
Do you know me now? Look, perjured man, on her
Whom thou and thy distracted lust have wronged.
Thy sensual rage of blood hath made my youth
A scorn to men and angels, and shall I
Be now a foil to thy unsated change?°
Thou knowst, false wanton, when my modest fame°
Stood free from stain or scandal, all the charms
Of hell or sorcery could not prevail
Against the honour of my chaster bosom.
Thine eyes did plead in tears, thy tongue in oaths
Such and so many, that a heart of steel
Would have been wrought to pity, as was mine:
And shall the conquest of my lawful bed,
My husband's death urged on by his disgrace,
My loss of womanhood, be ill rewarded
With hatred and contempt? No; know, Soranzo,
I have a spirit doth as much distaste
The slavery of fearing thee,° as thou
Dost loathe the memory of what hath passed.

Soranzo. Nay, dear Hippolita.

Hippolita. Call me not dear,
Nor think with supple words to smooth the grossness
Of my abuses; 'tis not your new mistress,
Your goodly Madam Merchant, shall triumph
On my dejection: tell her thus from me,
My birth was nobler, and by much more free.

Soranzo. You are too violent.

20 taxed of blamed for **31 foil . . . change** background for your insatiable fickleness **32 modest fame** well-known modesty **43-4 distaste . . . fearing thee** dislike being a slave to my fear for your love

Hippolita. You are too double
In your dissimulation. Seest thou this,
This habit,° these black mourning weeds of care?
'Tis thou art cause of this, and hast divorced
My husband from his life and me from him,
And made me widow in my widowhood.

Soranzo. Will you yet hear?

Hippolita. More of thy perjuries?
Thy soul is drowned too deeply in those sins,
Thou need'st not add to th' number.

Soranzo. Then I'll leave you;
You are past all rules of sense.

Hippolita. And thou of grace.

Vasques. Fie, mistress, you are not near° the limits of reason: if my lord had a resolution as noble as virtue itself, you take the course to unedge° it all. Sir, I beseech you, do not perplex her; griefs, alas, will have a vent. I dare undertake Madam Hippolita will now freely hear you.

Soranzo. Talk to a woman frantic! Are these the fruits of your love?

Hippolita. They are the fruits of thy untruth, false man.
Didst thou not swear, whilst yet my husband lived,
That thou wouldst wish no happiness on earth
More than to call me wife? Didst thou not vow,
When he should die, to marry me? For which,
The devil in my blood, and thy protests,
Caused me to counsel him to undertake
A voyage to Ligorn,° for that we heard
His brother there was dead, and left a daughter
Young and unfriended, who, with much ado,
I wished him to bring hither: he did so,
And went; and as thou know'st died on the way.
Unhappy man, to buy his death so dear
With my advice. Yet thou for whom I did it
Forget'st thy vows, and leav'st me to my shame.

Soranzo. Who could help this?

Hippolita. Who? Perjured man, thou couldst,
If thou hadst faith or love.

54 **habit** dress, attire 62 **not near** beyond 64 **unedge** blunt
77 **Ligorn** Leghorn (Italian *Livorno*

Soranzo. You are deceived.
The vows I made, if you remember well,
Were wicked and unlawful: 'twere more sin
To keep them than to break them. As for me,
I cannot mask my penitence. Think thou
How much thou hast digressed from honest shame
In bringing of a gentleman to death
Who was thy husband; such a one as he,
So noble in his quality, condition,
Learning, behaviour, entertainment, love,
As Parma could not show a braver man.

Vasques. You do not well; this was not your promise.

Soranzo. I care not; let her know her monstrous life.
Ere I'll be servile to so black a sin,
I'll be accursed. Woman, come here no more.
Learn to repent and die, for by my honour
I hate thee and thy lust: you have been too foul. [*Exit.*]

Vasques. This part has been scurvily played.°

Hippolita. How foolishly this beast contemns his fate,°
And shuns the use of that which I more scorn
Than I once loved, his love. But let him go;
My vengeance shall give comfort to this woe.
She offers to go away.

Vasques. Mistress, mistress Madam Hippolita, pray, a word or two.

Hippolita. With me, sir?

Vasques. With you, if you please.

Hippolita. What is't?

Vasques. I know you are infinitely moved° now, and you think you have cause; some I confess you have, but sure not so much as you imagine.

Hippolita. Indeed.

Vasques. O, you were miserably bitter, which you followed even to the last syllable. Faith, you were somewhat too shrewd;° by my life you could not have took my lord in a worse time, since I first knew him: tomorrow you shall find him a new man.

Hippolita. Well, I shall wait his leisure.

103 scurvily played performed wrongly **104 contemns his fate** scorns his fate (i.e., his tie to Hippolita) **112 infinitely moved** highly impassioned **118 shrewd** shrewish

Vasques. Fie, this is not a hearty patience, it comes sourly from you; troth, let me persuade you for once.

Hippolita. [*Aside.*] I have it, and it shall be so; thanks, opportunity!—Persuade me to what?

Vasques. Visit him in some milder temper. O if you could but master a little your female spleen, how might you win him.

Hippolita. He will never love me. Vasques, thou hast been a too trusty servant to such a master, and I believe thy reward in the end will fall out like mine.

Vasques. So perhaps too.

Hippolita. Resolve° thyself it will. Had I one so true, so truly honest, so secret to my counsels, as thou hast been to him and his, I should think it a slight acquittance,° not only to make him master of all I have, but even of myself.

Vasques. O you are a noble gentlewoman.

Hippolita. Wilt thou feed always upon hopes? Well, I know thou art wise, and seest the reward of an old servant daily, what it is.

Vasques. Beggary and neglect.

Hippolita. True, but Vasques, wert thou mine, and wouldst be private to me and my designs, I here protest myself and all what I can else call mine should be at thy dispose.

Vasques. [*Aside.*] Work you that way, old mole? Then I have the wind of you.°—I were not worthy of it by any desert that could lie within my compass; if I could—

Hippolita. What then?

Vasques. I should then hope to live in these my old years with rest and security.

Hippolita. Give me thy hand: now promise but thy silence,
And help to bring to pass a plot I have,
And here in sight of Heaven, that being done,
I make thee lord of me and mine estate.

Vasques. Come, you are merry; this is such a happiness that I can neither think or believe.

Hippolita. Promise thy secrecy, and 'tis confirmed.

Vasques. Then here I call our good genii for witnesses, whatsoever your designs are, or against whomsoever, I

133 Resolve assure **135 acquittance** payment of debt **148 have the wind of you** smell you out

will not only be a special actor therein, but never disclose it till it be effected.

Hippolita. I take thy word, and with that, thee for mine:
Come then, let's more confer of this anon.
On this delicious bane° my thoughts shall banquet,
Revenge shall sweeten what my griefs have tasted.

Exeunt.

[Act II, Scene iii]

Enter Richardetto and Philotis.

Richardetto. Thou seest, my lovely niece, these strange mishaps,
How all my fortunes turn to my disgrace,
Wherein I am but as a looker-on,
Whiles others act my shame, and I am silent.
Philotis. But uncle, wherein can this borrowed shape°
Give you content?
Richardetto. I'll tell thee, gentle niece:
Thy wanton aunt in her lascivious riots
Lives now secure, thinks I am surely dead
In my late journey to Ligorn for you
(As I have caused it to be rumoured out).
Now would I see with what an impudence
She gives scope to her loose adultery,
And how the common voice allows hereof:°
Thus far I have prevailed.
Philotis. Alas, I fear
You mean some strange revenge.
Richardetto. O, be not troubled;
Your ignorance shall plead for you° in all.
But to our business: what, you learned for certain
How Signor Florio means to give his daughter
In marriage to Soranzo?
Philotis. Yes, for certain.
Richardetto. But how find you young Annabella's love
Inclined to him?

166 **bane** poison II.iii.5 **borrowed shape** disguise 13 **voice allows hereof** opinion thinks of it 16 **ignorance shall plead for you** lack of knowledge shall excuse you

Philotis. For aught I could perceive,
She neither fancies him or any else.
Richardetto. There's mystery in that which time must show.
She used you kindly?
Philotis. Yes.
Richardetto. And craved your company?
Philotis. Often.
Richardetto. 'Tis well; it goes as I could wish.
I am the doctor now, and as for you,
None knows you; if all fail not, we shall thrive.
But who comes here?

Enter Grimaldi.

I know him: 'tis Grimaldi,
A Roman and a soldier, near allied
Unto the duke of Montferrato, one
Attending on the nuncio of the Pope
That now resides in Parma, by which means
He hopes to get the love of Annabella.
Grimaldi. Save you, sir.
Richardetto. And you, sir.
Grimaldi. I have heard
Of your approved° skill, which through the city
Is freely talked of, and would crave your aid.
Richardetto. For what, sir?
Grimaldi. Marry, sir, for this—
But I would speak in private.
Richardetto. Leave us, cousin.
Exit Philotis.
Grimaldi. I love fair Annabella, and would know
Whether in art there may not be receipts°
To move affection.
Richardetto. Sir, perhaps there may,
But these will nothing profit you.
Grimaldi. Not me?
Richardetto. Unless I be mistook, you are a man
Greatly in favour with the cardinal.
Grimaldi. What of that?
Richardetto. In duty to his grace,

35 **approved** proven 40 **receipts** recipes

I will be bold to tell you, if you seek
To marry Florio's daughter, you must first
Remove a bar 'twixt you and her.
Grimaldi. Who's that?
Richardetto. Soranzo is the man that hath her heart;
And while he lives, be sure you cannot speed.°
Grimaldi. Soranzo! What, mine enemy? Is't he?
Richardetto. Is he your enemy?
Grimaldi. The man I hate
Worse than confusion;
I'll kill him straight.
Richardetto. Nay then, take mine advice
(Even for his grace's sake, the cardinal):
I'll find a time when he and she do meet,
Of which I'll give you notice, and to be sure
He shall not 'scape you, I'll provide a poison
To dip your rapier's point in; if he had
As many heads as Hydra had, he dies.
Grimaldi. But shall I trust thee, doctor?
Richardetto. As yourself;
Doubt not in aught.—Thus shall the fates decree,
By me Soranzo falls, that ruined me. *Exeunt.*

[Act II, Scene iv]

Enter Donado, Bergetto and Poggio.

Donado. Well, sir, I must be content to be both your secretary and your messenger myself. I cannot tell what this letter may work, but as sure as I am alive, if thou come once to talk with her, I fear thou wilt mar whatsoever I make.

Bergetto. You make, uncle? Why, am not I big enough to carry mine own letter, I pray?

Donado. Ay, ay, carry a fool's head o' thy own. Why, thou dunce, wouldst thou write a letter and carry it thyself?

Bergetto. Yes, that I would, and read it to her with my own mouth; for you must think, if she will not believe

50 speed succeed

me myself when she hears me speak, she will not believe another's handwriting. O, you think I am a blockhead, uncle. No, sir, Poggio knows I have indited a letter myself, so I have.

Poggio. Yes truly, sir; I have it in my pocket.

Donado. A sweet one, no doubt; pray let's see't.

Bergetto. I cannot read my own hand very well, Poggio; read it, Poggio.

Donado. Begin.

Poggio reads. 'Most dainty and honey-sweet mistress, I could call you fair, and lie as fast as any that loves you, but my uncle being the elder man, I leave it to him, as more fit for his age, and the colour of his beard, I am wise enough to tell you I can bourd° where I see occasion, or if you like my uncle's wit better than mine, you shall marry me; if you like mine better than his, I will marry you in spite of your teeth; so commending my best parts to you, I rest. Yours upwards and downwards, or you may choose, Bergetto.'

Bergetto. Aha, here's stuff, uncle.

Donado. Here's stuff indeed to shame us all. Pray whose advice did you take in this learned letter?

Poggio. None, upon my word, but mine own.

Bergetto. And mine, uncle, believe it, nobody's else; 'twas mine own brain, I thank a good wit for't.

Donado. Get you home, sir, and look you keep within doors till I return.

Bergetto. How? that were a jest indeed; I scorn it i'faith.

Donado. What! You do not?

Bergetto. Judge me, but I do now.

Poggio. Indeed, sir, 'tis very unhealthy.

Donado. Well, sir, if I hear any of your apish running to motions° and fopperies, till I come back, you were as good no; look to't. *Exit Donado.*

Bergetto. Poggio, shall's steal to see this horse with the head in's tail?

Poggio. Ay, but you must take heed of whipping.

Bergetto. Dost take me for a child, Poggio? Come, honest Poggio. *Exeunt.*

II.iv.25 bourd jest **44 motions** puppet shows

[Act II, Scene v]

Enter Friar and Giovanni.

Friar. Peace. Thou hast told a tale, whose every word
Threatens eternal slaughter to the soul.
I'm sorry I have heard it; would mine ears
Had been one minute deaf, before the hour
That thou cam'st to me. O young man castaway,
By the religious number of mine order,
I day and night have waked my aged eyes,
Above my strength, to weep on thy behalf:°
But Heaven is angry, and be thou resolved,°
Thou art a man remarked° to taste a mischief.
Look for't; though it come late, it will come sure.
Giovanni. Father, in this you are uncharitable;
What I have done I'll prove both fit and good.
It is a principle (which you have taught
When I was yet your scholar), that the frame
And composition of the mind doth follow
The frame and composition of the body:
So where the body's furniture is beauty,
The mind's must needs be virtue; which allowed,°
Virtue itself is Reason but refined,°
And Love the quintessence of that. This proves
My sister's beauty being rarely fair
Is rarely virtuous; chiefly in her love,
And chiefly in that love, her love to me.
If hers to me, then so is mine to her;
Since in like causes are effects alike.
Friar. O ignorance in knowledge. Long ago,
How often have I warned thee this before?
Indeed, if we were sure there were no deity,
Nor Heaven nor hell, then to be led alone
By nature's light (as were philosophers
Of elder times°), might instance some defence.

II.v.5-8 **O young man . . . behalf** (the text is troublesome here and has occasioned various explanations. The sense is clear, however, although the oath by which the Friar swears is odd) 9 **resolved** assured, certain 10 **remarked** marked out 19 **allowed** conceded 20 **but refined** only made more fine 31-2 **philosophers Of elder times** pagan philosophers

But 'tis not so; then, madman, thou wilt find
That nature is in Heaven's positions° blind.
Giovanni. Your age o'errules you; had you youth like mine,
You'd make her love your Heaven, and her divine.
Friar. Nay then, I see th'art too far sold to hell,
It lies not in the compass of my prayers
To call thee back; yet let me counsel thee:
Persuade thy sister to some marriage.
Giovanni. Marriage? Why, that's to damn her. That's to prove
Her greedy of variety of lust.
Friar. O fearful! If thou wilt not, give me leave
To shrive° her, lest she should die unabsolved.
Giovanni. At your best leisure, father; then she'll tell you
How dearly she doth prize my matchless love.
Then you will know what pity 'twere we two
Should have been sundered from each other's arms.
View well her face, and in that little round
You may observe a world of variety:
For colour, lips; for sweet perfumes, her breath;
For jewels, eyes; for threads of purest gold,
Hair; for delicious choice of flowers, cheeks;
Wonder in every portion of that throne.
Hear her but speak, and you will swear the spheres
Make music to the citizens in Heaven.
But, father, what is else for pleasure framed,
Lest I offend your ears, shall go unnamed.
Friar. The more I hear, I pity thee the more,
That one so excellent should give those parts
All to a second death;° what I can do
Is but to pray: and yet I could advise thee,
Wouldst thou be ruled.
Giovanni. In what?
Friar. Why, leave her yet;
The throne of mercy is above your trespass;
Yet time is left you both—
Giovanni. To embrace each other,
Else let all time be struck quite out of number.
She is like me, and I like her, resolved.

34 positions doctrines **44 shrive** confess **61 second death** damnation

Friar. No more! I'll visit her. This grieves me most,
Things being thus, a pair of souls are lost. *Exeunt.*

[Act II, Scene vi]

Enter Florio, Donado, Annabella, Putana.

Florio. Where's Giovanni?
Annabella. Newly walked abroad,
And, as I heard him say, gone to the friar,
His reverend tutor.
Florio. That's a blessed man,
A man made up of holiness; I hope
He'll teach him how to gain another world.
Donado. Fair gentlewoman, here's a letter sent
To you from my young cousin; I dare swear
He loves you in his soul: would you could hear
Sometimes what I see daily, sighs and tears,
As if his breast were prison to his heart.
Florio. Receive it, Annabella.
Annabella. Alas, good man.
Donado. What's that she said?
Putana. An't please you, sir, she said, 'Alas, good man.' Truly I do commend him to her every night before her first sleep, because I would have her dream of him, and she hearkens to that most religiously.
Donado. Say'st so? God-a-mercy, Putana, there's something for thee, and prithee do what thou canst on his behalf; sha' not be lost labour, take my word for't.
Putana. Thank you most heartily, sir; now I have a feeling of your mind, let me alone to work.
Annabella. Guardian!
Putana. Did you call?
Annabella. Keep this letter.
Donado. Signor Florio, in any case bid her read it instantly.
Florio. Keep it for what? Pray read it me hereright.°
Annabella. I shall, sir. *She reads.*
Donado. How d'ee find her inclined, signor?
Florio. Troth, sir, I know not how; not all so well
As I could wish.

II.vi.27 **hereright** right away

Annabella. Sir, I am bound to rest your cousin's debtor.
The jewel I'll return; for if he love,
I'll count that love a jewel.
Donado. Mark you that?
Nay, keep them both, sweet maid.
Annabella. You must excuse me,
Indeed I will not keep it.
Florio. Where's the ring,
That which your mother in her will bequeathed,
And charged you on her blessing not to give't
To any but your husband? Send back that.
Annabella. I have it not.
Florio. Ha, have it not! Where is't?
Annabella. My brother in the morning took it from me,
Said he would wear't today.
Florio. Well, what do you say
To young Bergetto's love? Are you content
To match with him? Speak.
Donado. There's the point indeed.
Annabella. [*Aside.*] What shall I do? I must say something now.
Florio. What say? Why d'ee not speak?
Annabella. Sir, with your leave,
Please you to give me freedom?
Florio. Yes, you have it.
Annabella. Signor Donado, if your nephew mean
To raise his better fortunes in his match,
The hope of me will hinder such a hope;
Sir, if you love him, as I know you do,
Find one more worthy of his choice than me.
In short, I'm sure I sha' not be his wife.
Donado. Why, here's plain dealing; I commend thee for't,
And all the worst I wish thee is, Heaven bless thee!
Your father yet and I will still be friends,
Shall we not, Signor Florio?
Florio. Yes, why not?
Look, here your cousin comes.

Enter Bergetto and Poggio.

Donado. [*Aside.*] O coxcomb, what doth he make here?
Bergetto. Where's my uncle, sirs?
Donado. What's the news now?

Bergetto. Save you, uncle, save you. You must not think I come for nothing, masters; and how, and how is't? What, you have read my letter? Ah, there I—tickled you i'faith.

Poggio. But 'twere better you had tickled her in another place.

Bergetto. Sirrah sweetheart, I'll tell thee a good jest; and riddle what 'tis.

Annabella. You say you'd tell me.

Bergetto. As I was walking just now in the street, I met a swaggering fellow would needs take the wall of me,° and because he did thrust me, I very valiantly called him rogue. He hereupon bade me draw; I told him I had more wit than so, but when he saw that I would not, he did so maul me with the hilts of his rapier that my head sung whilst my feet capered in the kennel.°

Donado. [*Aside.*] Was ever the like ass seen?

Annabella. And what did you all this while?

Bergetto. Laugh at him for a gull,° till I see the blood run about mine ears, and then I could not choose but find in my heart to cry; till a fellow with a broad beard (they say he is a new-come doctor) called me into his house, and gave me a plaster—look you, here 'tis—and, sir, there was a young wench washed my face and hands most excellently, i'faith, I shall love her as long as I live for't, did she not, Poggio?

Poggio. Yes, and kissed him too.

Bergetto. Why, la now, you think I tell a lie, uncle, I warrant.

Donado. Would he that beat thy blood out of thy head had beaten some wit into it; for I fear thou never wilt have any.

Bergetto. O, uncle, but there was a wench would have done a man's heart good to have looked on her—by this light she had a face methinks worth twenty of you, Mistress Annabella.

Donado. Was ever such a fool born?

Annabella. I am glad she liked° you, sir.

Bergetto. Are you so? By my troth I thank you, forsooth.

70 **take the wall of me** walk nearest the wall, i.e., the cleanest part of a street 75 **kennel** gutter 78 **gull** dupe 97 **liked** pleased

Florio. Sure 'twas the doctor's niece, that was last day° with us here.

Bergetto. 'Twas she, 'twas she.

Donado. How do you know that, simplicity?

Bergetto. Why, does not he say so? If I should have said no, I should have given him the lie, uncle, and so have deserved a dry° beating again; I'll none of that.

Florio. A very modest well-behaved young maid
As I have seen.

Donado. Is she indeed?

Florio. Indeed
She is, if I have any judgment.

Donado. Well, sir, now you are free, you need not care for sending letters: now you are dismissed, your mistress here will none of you.

Bergetto. No. Why, what care I for that? I can have wenches enough in Parma for half-a-crown apiece, cannot I, Poggio?

Poggio. I'll warrant you, sir.

Donado. Signor Florio,
I thank you for your free recourse you gave
For my admittance; and to you, fair maid,
That jewel I will give you 'gainst° your marriage.
Come, will you go, sir?

Bergetto. Ay, marry will I. Mistress, farewell, mistress. I'll come again tomorrow. Farewell, mistress.

Exit Donado, Bergetto, and Poggio.

Enter Giovanni.

Florio. Son, where have you been? What, alone, alone still?
I would not have it so, you must forsake
This over-bookish humour. Well, your sister
Hath shook the fool off.

Giovanni. 'Twas no match for her.

Florio. 'Twas not indeed, I mean it nothing less;
Soranzo is the man I only like;
Look on him, Annabella. Come, 'tis supper-time,
And it grows late. *Exit Florio.*

Giovanni. Whose jewel's that?

99 **last day** yesterday 105 **dry** i.e., one that not bleed 119 **'gainst** looking toward

Annabella. Some sweetheart's.
Giovanni. So I think.
Annabella. A lusty youth,
Signor Donado, gave it me to wear
Against my marriage.
Giovanni. But you shall not wear it.
Send it him back again.
Annabella. What, you are jealous?
Giovanni. That you shall know anon, at better leisure.
Welcome, sweet night, the evening crowns the day.
Exeunt.

[Act III, Scene i]

Enter Bergetto and Poggio.

Bergetto. Does my uncle think to make me a baby still? No, Poggio, he shall know I have a sconce° now.

Poggio. Ay, let him not bob° you off like an ape with an apple.

Bergetto. 'Sfoot, I will have the wench if he were ten uncles, in spite of his nose, Poggio.

Poggio. Hold him to the grindstone and give not a jot of ground.
She hath in a manner promised you already.

Bergetto. True, Poggio, and her uncle the doctor swore I should marry her.

Poggio. He swore, I remember.

Bergetto. And I will have her, that's more; didst see the codpiece-point° she gave me and the box of marmalade?

Poggio. Very well; and kissed you, that my chops° watered at the sight on't. There's no way but to clap up a marriage in hugger-mugger.°

Bergetto. I will do't; for I tell thee, Poggio, I begin to grow valiant methinks, and my courage begins to rise.

Poggio. Should you be afraid of your uncle?

Bergetto. Hang him, old doting rascal. No, I say I will have her.

III.i.2 **sconce** brain 3 **bob** fob 14 **codpiece-point** lace for tying the codpiece, a flap, often ornamented, worn over the crotch by a man 15 **chops** mouth 16-17 **clap up . . . hugger-mugger** hastily arrange a marriage secretly

Poggio. Lose no time then.

Bergetto. I will beget a race of wise men and constables, that shall cart whores at their own charges,° and break the duke's peace ere I have done myself.—Come away.

Exeunt.

[Act III, Scene ii]

Enter Florio, Giovanni, Soranzo, Annabella, Putana and Vasques.

Florio. My lord Soranzo, though I must confess
The proffers that are made me have been great
In marriage of my daughter, yet the hope
Of your still rising honours have prevailed
Above all other jointures. Here she is;
She knows my mind, speak for yourself to her,
And hear you, daughter, see you use him nobly;
For any private speech I'll give you time.
Come, son, and you the rest, let them alone:
Agree they as they may.

Soranzo. I thank you, sir.

Giovanni. [*Aside.*] Sister, be not all woman, think on me.

Soranzo. Vasques.

Vasques. My lord?

Soranzo. Attend me without—

Exeunt omnes, manet Soranzo and Annabella.

Annabella. Sir, what's your will with me?

Soranzo. Do you not know
What I should tell you?

Annabella. Yes, you'll say you love me.

Soranzo. And I'll swear it too; will you believe it?

Annabella. 'Tis no point of faith.°

Enter Giovanni above.°

25 **cart whores . . . charges** parade whores in carts through the streets (a common punishment) for which the whores themselves will have to pay III.ii.18 s.d. **above** (as Giovanni watches Annabella and Soranzo from above, he makes comments that they cannot hear) 18 **point of faith** dogma necessary to salvation

Soranzo. Have you not will to love?
Annabella. Not you.
Soranzo. Whom then?
Annabella. That's as the fates infer.
Giovanni. Of those I'm regent now.
Soranzo. What mean you, sweet?
Annabella. To live and die a maid.
Soranzo. O, that's unfit.
Giovanni. Here's one can say that's but a woman's note.
Soranzo. Did you but see my heart, then would you swear—
Annabella. That you were dead.
Giovanni. That's true, or somewhat near it.
Soranzo. See you these true love's tears?
Annabella. No.
Giovanni. Now she winks.
Soranzo. They plead to you for grace.
Annabella. Yet nothing speak.
Soranzo. O grant my suit.
Annabella. What is't?
Soranzo. To let me live—
Annabella. Take it.—
Soranzo. Still yours—
Annabella. That is not mine to give.
Giovanni. One such another world would kill his hopes.
Soranzo. Mistress, to leave those fruitless strifes of wit,
Know I have loved you long and loved you truly;
Not hope of what you have, but what you are,
Have drawn me on; then let me not in vain
Still feel the rigour of your chaste disdain.
I'm sick, and sick to th' heart.
Annabella. Help, aqua-vitae.°
Soranzo. What mean you?
Annabella. Why, I thought you had been sick.
Soranzo. Do you mock my love?
Giovanni. There, sir, she was too nimble.
Soranzo. [*Aside.*] 'Tis plain, she laughs at me.—These scornful taunts
Neither become your modesty or years.

35 aqua-vitae liquor, here to be used as a restorative

Annabella. You are no looking glass; or if you were,
I'd dress my language by you.
Giovanni. I'm confirmed—
Annabella. To put you out of doubt, my lord, methinks
Your common sense should make you understand
That if I loved you, or desired your love,
Some way I should have given you better taste:
But since you are a nobleman, and one
I would not wish should spend his youth in hopes,
Let me advise you here to forbear your suit,
And think I wish you well, I tell you this.
Soranzo. Is't you speak this?
Annabella. Yes, I myself; yet know—
Thus far I give you comfort—if mine eyes
Could have picked out a man (amongst all those
That sued to me) to make a husband of,
You should have been that man. Let this suffice;
Be noble in your secrecy and wise.
Giovanni. Why, now I see she loves me.
Annabella. One word more:
As ever virtue lived within your mind,
As ever noble courses were your guide,
As ever you would have me know you loved me,
Let not my father know hereof by you;
If I hereafter find that I must marry,
It shall be you or none.
Soranzo. I take that promise.
Annabella. O, O, my head.
Soranzo. What's the matter? Not well?
Annabella. O, I begin to sicken.
Giovanni. Heaven forbid. *Exit from above.*
Soranzo. Help, help within there, ho!

Enter Florio, Giovanni, Putana.

Look to your daughter, Signor Florio.
Florio. Hold her up, she swoons.
Giovanni. Sister, how d'ee?
Annabella. Sick—brother, are you there?
Florio. Convey her to her bed instantly, whilst I send for a physician; quickly, I say.
Putana. Alas, poor child! *Exeunt, manet Soranzo.*

Enter Vasques.

Vasques. My lord.

Soranzo. O Vasques, now I doubly am undone
Both in my present and my future hopes.
She plainly told me that she could not love,
And thereupon soon sickened, and I fear
Her life's in danger.

Vasque. [*Aside.*] By'r lady, sir, and so is yours, if you knew all.—'Las sir, I am sorry for that; may be 'tis but the maid's-sickness,° an over-flux° of youth, and then, sir, there is no such present remedy as present marriage. But hath she given you an absolute denial?

Soranzo. She hath and she hath not; I'm full of grief,
But what she said I'll tell thee as we go. *Exeunt.*

[Act III, Scene iii]

Enter Giovanni and Putana.

Putana. O sir, we are all undone, quite undone, utterly undone, and shamed forever; your sister, O your sister.

Giovanni. What of her? For Heaven's sake, speak; how does she?

Putana. O that ever I was born to see this day.

Giovanni. She is not dead, ha? Is she?

Putana. Dead? No, she is quick;° 'tis worse, she is with child. You know what you have done; Heaven forgive 'ee. 'Tis too late to repent now, Heaven help us.

Giovanni. With child? How dost thou know't?

Putana. How do I know't? Am I at these years ignorant what the meanings of qualms and water-pangs be? Of changing of colours, queasiness of stomachs, pukings, and another thing that I could name? Do not, for her and your credit's sake, spend the time in asking how, and which way, 'tis so; she is quick, upon my word: if you let a physician see her water, y'are undone.

Giovanni. But in what case° is she?

83 maid's-sickness green-sickness, a form of anemia **83 over-flux** overflow **III.iii.7 quick** alive, here also pregnant **18 case** condition

Putana. Prettily amended; 'twas but a fit which I soon espied, and she must look for often henceforward.

Giovanni. Commend me to her, bid her take no care;°
Let not the doctor visit her, I charge you,
Make some excuse, till I return.—O me,
I have a world of business in my head.—
Do not discomfort her.—
How does this news perplex me!—If my father
Come to her, tell him she's recovered well,
Say 'twas but some ill diet; d'ee hear, woman?
Look you to't.

Putana. I will, sir. *Exeunt.*

[Act III, Scene iv]

Enter Florio and Richardetto.

Florio. And how d'ee find her, sir?

Richardetto. Indifferent° well;
I see no danger, scarce perceive she's sick,
But that she told me she had lately eaten
Melons, and, as she thought, those disagreed
With her young stomach.

Florio. Did you give her aught?

Richardetto. An easy surfeit-water,° nothing else.
You need not doubt her health; I rather think
Her sickness is a fulness of her blood—
You understand me?

Florio. I do; you counsel well,
And once, within these few days, will so order't
She shall be married ere she know the time.

Richardetto. Yet let not haste, sir, make unworthy choice;
That were dishonour.

Florio. Master Doctor, no;
I will not do so neither; in plain words,
My lord Soranzo is the man I mean.

Richardetto. A noble and a virtuous gentleman.

Florio. As any is in Parma. Not far hence
Dwells Father Bonaventure, a grave friar,

21 **take no care** not to worry III.iv.1 **Indifferent** moderately
6 **surfeit-water** cure for indigestion

Once tutor to my son; now at his cell
I'll have 'em married.
Richardetto. You have plotted wisely.
Florio. I'll send one straight to speak with him tonight.
Richardetto. Soranzo's wise, he will delay no time.
Florio. It shall be so.

Enter Friar and Giovanni.

Friar. Good peace be here and love.
Florio. Welcome, religious friar; you are one
That still° bring blessing to the place you come to.
Giovanni. Sir, with what speed I could, I did my best
To draw this holy man from forth his cell
To visit my sick sister, that with words
Of ghostly° comfort, in this time of need,
He might absolve her, whether she live or die.
Florio. 'Twas well done, Giovanni; thou herein
Hast showed a Christian' care, a brother's love.
Come, father, I'll conduct you to her chamber,
And one thing would entreat you.
Friar. Say on, sir.
Florio. I have a father's dear impression,°
And wish, before I fall into my grave,
That I might see her married, as 'tis fit;
A word from you, grave man, will win her more
Than all our best persuasions.
Friar. Gentle sir,
All this I'll say, that Heaven may prosper her.
Exeunt.

[Act III, Scene v]

Enter Grimaldi.

Grimaldi. Now if the doctor keep his word, Soranzo,
Twenty to one you miss your bride; I know
'Tis an unnoble act, and not becomes
A soldier's valour, but in terms of love,

25 still always **29 ghostly** spiritual **35 dear impression** an idea or belief impressed on the mind, dear to fathers

Where merit cannot sway, policy° must.
I am resolved; if this physician
Play not on both hands,° then Soranzo falls.

Enter Richardetto.

Richardetto. You are come as I could wish; this very night
Soranzo, 'tis ordained, must be affied°
To Annabella, and, for aught I know,
Married.
Grimaldi. How!
Richardetto. Yet your patience;
The place, 'tis Friar Bonaventure's cell.
Now I would wish you to bestow this night
In watching thereabouts; 'tis but a night:
If you miss now, tomorrow I'll know all.
Grimaldi. Have you the poison?
Richardetto. Here 'tis in this box.
Doubt nothing, this will do't; in any case,
As you respect your life, be quick and sure.
Grimaldi. I'll speed him.°
Richardetto. Do. Away; for 'tis not safe
You should be seen much here.—Ever my love!
Grimaldi. And mine to you. *Exit Grimaldi.*
Richardetto. So. If this hit,° I'll laugh and hug revenge;
And they that now dream of a wedding-feast
May chance to mourn the lusty bridegroom's ruin.
But to my other business: Niece Philotis!

Enter Philotis.

Philotis. Uncle?
Richardetto. My lovely niece.
You have bethought 'ee?
Philotis. Yes, and, as you counselled,
Fashioned my heart to love him; but he swears
He will tonight be married, for he fears

III.v.5 policy politic cunning 7 Play not on both hands doesn't work for both sides (an expression descriptive of the Vice or devil) 9 affied affianced, engaged 19 speed him hurry him on to his death 22 hit succeed

His uncle else, if he should know the drift,
Will hinder all, and call his coz to shrift.

Richardetto. Tonight? Why, best of all; but let me see,
I—ha—yes—so it shall be; in disguise
We'll early to the friar's, I have thought on't.

Enter Bergetto and Poggio.

Philotis. Uncle, he comes.

Richardetto. Welcome, my worthy coz.

Bergetto. Lass, pretty lass, come buss,° lass! [*Kisses her.*] Aha, Poggio!

Poggio.° There's hope of this yet.

Richardetto. [*to Bergetto.*] You shall have time enough; withdraw a little,
We must confer at large.°

Bergetto. [*to Philotis.*] Have you not sweetmeats or dainty devices for me?

Philotis. You shall have enough, sweetheart.

Bergetto. Sweetheart! Mark that, Poggio.—[*to Philotis.*] By my troth, I cannot choose but kiss thee once more for that word 'sweetheart.'—Poggio, I have a monstrous swelling about my stomach, whatsoever the matter be.

Poggio. You shall have physic for't, sir.

Richardetto. Time runs apace.

Bergetto. Time's a blockhead.

Richardetto. Be ruled; when we have done what's fit to do,
Then you may kiss your fill, and bed her too.

Exeunt.

[Act III, Scene vi]

Enter the Friar in his study sitting in a chair, Annabella kneeling and whispering to him; a table before them and wax-lights; she weeps and wrings her hands.

Friar. I am glad to see this penance; for, believe me,
You have unripped° a soul so foul and guilty

37 buss kiss 38 (line assigned to Philotis is Q. Early editors give it to Richardetto, recent editors to Poggio) 40 at large at length III.vi.2 unripped torn open

As I must tell you true, I marvel how
The earth hath borne you up; but weep, weep on,
These tears may do you good; weep faster yet,
Whiles I do read a lecture.°

Annabella. Wretched creature!

Friar. Ay, you are wretched, miserably wretched,
Almost condemned alive. There is a place—
List, daughter—in a black and hollow vault,
Where day is never seen; there shines no sun,
But flaming horror of consuming fires,
A lightless sulphur, choked with smoky fogs
Of an infected darkness; in this place
Dwell many thousand thousand sundry sorts
Of never-dying deaths; there damned souls
Roar without pity; there are gluttons fed
With toads and adders; there is burning oil
Poured down the drunkard's throat; the usurer
Is forced to sup whole draughts of molten gold;
There is the murderer forever stabbed,
Yet can he never die; there lies the wanton
On racks of burning steel, whiles in his soul
He feels the torment of his raging lust.

Annabella. Mercy, O mercy!

Friar. There stands these wretched things
Who have dreamed out whole years in lawless sheets
And secret incests, cursing one another.°
Then you will wish each kiss your brother gave
Had been a dagger's point; then you shall hear
How he will cry, 'O would my wicked sister
Had first been damned, when she did yield to lust!'—
But soft, methinks I see repentance work
New motions in your heart; say, how is't with you?

Annabella. Is there no way left to redeem my miseries?

Friar. There is, despair not; Heaven is merciful,
And offers grace even now. 'Tis thus agreed,
First, for your honour's safety, that you marry
The Lord Soranzo; next, to save your soul,
Leave off this life, and henceforth live to him.

Annabella. Ay me!

6 read a lecture deliver a reprimand **26 cursing one another** i.e., the punishment of incestuous sinners is to turn against their lover-kindred

Friar. Sigh not; I know the baits of sin
Are hard to leave. O, 'tis a death to do't.
Remember what must come. Are you content?
Annabella. I am.
Friar. I like it well; we'll take the time.°
Who's near us there?

Enter Florio [and] Giovanni.

Florio. Did you call, father?
Friar. Is Lord Soranzo come?
Florio. He stays below.
Friar. Have you acquainted him at full?
Florio. I have,
And he is overjoyed.
Friar. And so are we.
Bid him come near.
Giovanni. [*Aside.*] My sister weeping, ha?
I fear this friar's falsehood.—I will call him.
Exit.
Florio. Daughter, are you resolved?
Annabella. Father, I am.

Enter Giovanni, Soranzo, and Vasques.

Florio. My Lord Soranzo, here
Give me your hand; for that I give you this.°
Soranzo. Lady, say you so too?
Annabella. I do, and vow
To live with you and yours.
Friar. Timely resolved:
My blessing rest on both; more to be done,
You may perform it on the morning sun. *Exeunt.*

42 take the time seize the opportunity 52 this i.e., Annabella's hand

[Act III, Scene vii]

Enter Grimaldi with his rapier drawn and a dark lantern.°

Grimaldi. 'Tis early night° as yet, and yet too soon
To finish such a work; here I will lie
To listen who comes next. [*He lies down.*]

Enter Bergetto and Philotis disguised, and after Richardetto and Poggio.

Bergetto. We are almost at the place, I hope, sweetheart.

Grimaldi. [*Aside.*] I hear them near, and heard one say 'sweetheart'.
'Tis he; now guide my hand, some angry justice,
Home to his bosom.—Now have at you, sir!

Strikes Bergetto and exit.

Bergetto. O help, help, here's a stitch fallen in my guts. O for a flesh-tailor° quickly,—Poggio!

Philotis. What ails my love?

Bergetto. I am sure I cannot piss forward and backward, and yet I am wet before and behind.—Lights, lights! ho, lights!

Philotis. Alas some villain here has slain my love.

Richardetto. O Heaven forbid it. Raise up the next neighbours
Instantly, Poggio, and bring lights. *Exit Poggio.*
How is't, Bergetto? Slain? It cannot be;
Are you sure y'are hurt?

Bergetto. O my belly seethes like a porridge-pot; some cold water, I shall boil over else; my whole body is in a sweat, that you may wring my shirt; feel here—Why, Poggio!

Enter Poggio with Officers and lights and halberts.

Poggio. Here. Alas, how do you?

Richardetto. Give me a light. What's here? All blood! O sirs,
Signor Donado's nephew now is slain.

III.vii.1 s.d. **dark lantern** lantern with means for concealing the light 1 **early night** evening 9 **flesh-tailor** surgeon

Follow the murderer with all the haste
Up to the city, he cannot be far hence;
Follow, I beseech you.
Officers. Follow, follow, follow. *Exeunt Officers.*
Richardetto. Tear off thy linen, coz, to stop his wounds.—
Be of good comfort, man.
Bergetto. Is all this mine own blood? Nay then, good night with me. Poggio, commend me to my uncle, dost hear? Bid him for my sake make much of this wench. O!—I am going the wrong way sure, my belly aches so.—O farewell, Poggio —O —O — *Dies.*
Philotis. O, he is dead.
Poggio. How! Dead!
Richardetto. He's dead indeed.
'Tis now too late to weep; let's have him home,
And with what speed we may, find out the murderer.
Poggio. O my master, my master, my master.
Exeunt.

[Act III, Scene viii]

Enter Vasques and Hippolita.

Hippolita. Betrothed?
Vasques. I saw it.
Hippolita. And when's the marriage-day?
Vasques. Some two days hence.
Hippolita. Two days? Why, man, I would but wish two hours
To send him to his last, and lasting sleep.
And, Vasques, thou shalt see I'll do it bravely.
Vasques. I do not doubt your wisdom, nor, I trust, you my secrecy;
I am infinitely yours.
Hippolita. I will be thine in spite of my disgrace.
So soon? O, wicked man, I durst be sworn,
He'd laugh to see me weep.
Vasques. And that's a villainous fault in him.
Hippolita. No, let him laugh, I'm armed in my resolves;
Be thou still true.
Vasques. I should get little by treachery against so hopeful a preferment as I am like to climb to.

Hippolita. Even to my bosom, Vasques. Let my youth°
Revel in these new pleasures; if we thrive,
He now hath but a pair of days to live. *Exeunt.*

[Act III, Scene ix]

Enter Florio, Donado, Richardetto, Poggio and Officers.

Florio. 'Tis bootless° now to show yourself a child,
Signor Donado; what is done, is done.
Spend not the time in tears, but seek for justice.
Richardetto. I must confess, somewhat I was in fault
That had not first acquainted you what love
Passed 'twixt him and my niece; but, as I live,
His fortune grieves me as it were mine own.
Donado. Alas, poor creature, he meant no man harm,
That I am sure of.
Florio. I believe that too.
But stay, my masters, are you sure you saw
The murderer pass here?
Officer. And it please you, sir, we are sure we saw a ruffian, with a naked weapon in his hand all bloody, get into my lord cardinal's grace's gate, that we are sure of; but for fear of his grace (bless us) we durst go no further.
Donado. Know you what manner of man he was?
Officer. Yes, sure, I know the man; they say 'a is a soldier; he that loved your daughter, sir, an't please ye; 'twas he for certain.
Florio. Grimaldi, on my life.
Officer. Ay, ay, the same.
Richardetto. The cardinal is noble; he no doubt
Will give true justice.
Donado. Knock someone at the gate.
Poggio. I'll knock, sir. *Poggio knocks.*
Servant within. What would 'ee?
Florio. We require speech with the lord cardinal
About some present° business; pray inform
His grace that we are here.

III.viii.18 **my youth** i.e., Soranzo III.ix1 **bootless** pointless 27 **present** urgent

Enter Cardinal and Grimaldi.

Cardinal. Why, how now, friends! What saucy mates are you
That know nor duty nor civility?
Are we a person fit to be your host,
Or is our house become your common inn,
To beat our doors at pleasure? What such haste
Is yours as that it cannot wait fit times?
Are you the masters of this commonwealth,
And know no more discretion? O, your news
Is here before you; you have lost a nephew,
Donado, last night by Grimaldi slain:
Is that your business? Well, sir, we have knowledge on't.
Let that suffice.

Grimaldi. In presence of your grace,
In thought I never meant Bergetto harm.
But Florio, you can tell, with how much scorn
Soranzo, backed with his confederates,
Hath often wronged me; I, to be revenged,
(For that I could not win him else to fight)
Had thought by way of ambush to have killed him,
But was unluckily therein mistook;
Else he had felt what late Bergetto did:
And though my fault to him were merely chance,
Yet humbly I submit me to your grace,
To do with me as you please.

Cardinal. Rise up, Grimaldi.
You citizens of Parma, if you seek
For justice, know, as nuncio from the Pope,
For this offence I here receive Grimaldi
Into his holiness' protection.
He is no common man, but nobly born;
Of princes' blood, though you, Sir Florio,
Thought him too mean a husband for your daughter.
If more you seek for, you must go to Rome,
For he shall thither; learn more wit, for shame.
Bury your dead.—Away, Grimaldi—leave 'em.

Exeunt Cardinal and Grimaldi.

Donado. Is this a churchman's voice? Dwells justice here?

Florio. Justice is fled to Heaven and comes no nearer.
Soranzo. Was't for him? O impudence.

Had he the face to speak it, and not blush?
Come, come, Donado, there's no help in this,
When cardinals think murder's not amiss.
Great men may do their wills, we must obey;
But Heaven will judge them for't another day.

Exeunt.

[Act IV, Scene i]

A Banquet. Hautboys.° Enter the Friar, Giovanni, Annabella, Philotis, Soranzo, Donado, Florio, Richardetto, Putana, and Vasques.

Friar. These holy rites performed, now take your times
To spend the remnant of the day in feast;
Such fit repasts are pleasing to the saints,
Who are your guests, though not with mortal eyes
To be beheld. Long prosper in this day,
You happy couple, to each other's joy.

Soranzo. Father, your prayer is heard; the hand of goodness
Hath been a shield for me against my death;
And, more to bless me, hath enriched my life
With this most precious jewel; such a prize
As earth hath not another like to this.
Cheer up, my love, and gentlemen, my friends,
Rejoice with me in mirth; this day we'll crown
With lusty cups to Annabella's health.

Giovanni. [*Aside.*]. O torture. Were the marriage yet undone,
Ere I'd endure this sight, to see my love
Clipped° by another, I would dare confusion,
And stand the horror of ten thousand deaths.

Vasques. Are you not well, sir?

Giovanni. Prithee, fellow, wait;°
I need not thy officious diligence.

Florio. Signor Donado, come, you must forget
Your late mishaps, and drown your cares in wine.

Soranzo. Vasques.

Vasques. My lord?

IV.i.1 s.d. **Hautboys** oboes 17 **Clipped** embraced 19 **wait** wait on the guests

Soranzo. Reach me that weighty bowl.
Here, brother Giovanni, here's to you;
Your turn comes next, though now a bachelor.
Here's to your sister's happiness and mine.
Giovanni. I cannot drink.
Soranzo. What?
Giovanni. 'Twill indeed offend me.
Annabella. Pray do not urge him, if he be not willing.
[*Hautboys.*]
Florio. How now, what noise° is this?
Vasques. O, sir, I had forgot to tell you; certain young maidens of Parma, in honour to Madam Annabella's marriage, have sent their loves to her in a masque, for which they humbly crave your patience and silence.
Soranzo. We are much bound° to them, so much the more
As it comes unexpected; guide them in.

Hautboys. Enter Hippolita and Ladies in [*masks and*] *white robes, with garlands of willows. Music and a dance.*

Thanks, lovely virgins; now might we but know
To whom we have been beholding for this love,
We shall acknowledge it.
Hippolita. Yes you shall know;
[*Unmasks.*]
What think you now?
Omnes. Hippolita!
Hippolita. 'Tis she,
Be not amazed; nor blush, young lovely bride,
I come not to defraud you of your man.
'Tis now no time to reckon up the talk
What Parma long hath rumoured of us both:
Let rash report run on; the breath that vents it
Will, like a bubble, break itself at last.
But now to you, sweet creature: lend's your hand;
Perhaps it hath been said that I would claim
Some interest in Soranzo, now your lord.
What I have right to do, his soul knows best;
But in my duty to your noble worth,
Sweet Annabella, and my care of you,
Here take, Soranzo, take this hand from me:

29 noise here, music 34 bound obliged

I'll once more join what by the holy church
Is finished and allowed. Have I done well?

Soranzo. You have too much engaged us.°

Hippolita. One thing more.
That you may know my single charity,°
Freely I here remit all interest
I e'er could claim, and give you back your vows;
And to confirm't—reach me a cup of wine—
My Lord Soranzo, in this draught I drink
Long rest t'ee.—Look to it, Vasques.

Vasques. Fear nothing.

He gives her a poisoned cup: she drinks.

Soranzo. Hippolita, I thank you, and will pledge
This happy union as another life;
Wine, there.

Vasques. You shall have none, neither shall you pledge her.

Hippolita. How!

Vasques. Know now, Mistress She-Devil, your own mischievous treachery hath killed you; I must not marry you.

Hippolita. Villain.

Omnes. What's the matter?

Vasques. Foolish woman, thou art now like a firebrand that hath kindled others and burnt thyself; *troppo sperar, inganna,*° thy vain hope hath deceived thee, thou art but dead; if thou hast any grace, pray.

Hippolita. Monster.

Vasques. Die in charity, for shame.—This thing of malice, this woman, had privately corrupted me with promise of marriage, under this politic° reconciliation, to poison my lord, whiles she might laugh at his confusion on his marriage day. I promised her fair, but I knew what my reward should have been; and would willingly have spared her life, but that I was acquainted with the danger of her disposition, and now have fitted her a just payment in her own coin. There she is, she hath yet—and° end thy days in peace, vile woman; as for

55 **engaged us** placed us under obligation 56 **single charity** unique generosity 74-5 **troppo sperar inganna** "too much hope deceives" 80 **under this politic** under cover of this cunning 87 **yet—and** (there appears to be an omission in the text at this point)

life there's no hope, think not on't.
Omnes. Wonderful justice!
Richardetto. Heaven, thou art righteous.
Hippolita. O, 'tis true;
I feel my minute coming. Had that slave
Kept promise (O, my torment) thou this hour
Hadst died, Soranzo—heat above hell fire—
Yet ere I pass away—cruel, cruel flames—
Take here my curse amongst you: may thy bed
Of marriage be a rack unto thy heart,
Burn blood and boil in vengeance—O my heart,
My flame's intolerable—Mayst thou live
To father bastards, may her womb bring forth
Monsters, and die together in your sins,
Hated, scorned, and unpitied— O —O — *Dies.*
Florio. Was e'er so vile a creature?
Richardetto. Here's the end
Of lust and pride.
Annabella. It is a fearful sight.
Soranzo. Vasques, I know thee now a trusty servant,
And never will forget thee.—Come, my love,
We'll home, and thank the Heavens for this escape.
Father and friends, we must break up this mirth;
It is too sad a feast.
Donado. Bear hence the body.
Friar. Here's an ominous change;
Mark this, my Giovanni, and take heed.
I fear the event;° that marriage seldom's good,
Where the bride-banquet so begins in blood.
Exeunt.

[Act IV, Scene ii]

Enter Richardetto and Philotis.

Richardetto. My wretched wife, more wretched in her shame
Than in her wrongs to me, hath paid too soon
The forfeit of her modesty and life;
And I am sure, my niece, though vengeance hover,

111 event outcome, result

Keeping aloof yet from Soranzo's fall,
Yet he will fall, and sink with his own weight.
I need not now—my heart persuades me so—
To further his confusion; there is One
Above begins to work, for, as I hear,
Debates° already 'twixt his wife and him
Thicken and run to head;° she, as 'tis said,
Slightens° his love, and he abandons hers.
Much talk I hear. Since things go thus, my niece,
In tender love and pity of your youth,
My counsel is, that you should free your years
From hazard of these woes by flying hence
To fair Cremona, there to vow your soul
In holiness a holy votaress:
Leave me to see the end of these extremes.
All human worldly courses are uneven;
No life is blessed but the way to Heaven.

Philotis. Uncle, shall I resolve to be a nun?

Richardetto. Ay, gentle niece, and in your hourly prayers
Remember me, your poor unhappy uncle.
Hie to Cremona now, as fortune leads,
Your home and your cloister, your best friends your beads.
Your chaste and single life shall crown your birth;
Who dies a virgin lives a saint on earth.

Philotis. Then farewell, world, and worldly thoughts, adieu.
Welcome, chaste vows; myself I yield to you.

Exeunt.

[Act IV, Scene iii]

Enter Soranzo unbraced,° and Annabella dragged in.

Soranzo. Come, strumpet, famous whore! Were every drop
Of blood that runs in thy adulterous veins

IV.ii.10 **Debates** arguments 11 **Thicken and run to head** intensify and come to a point, like a ripe boil ready to burst 12 **slightens** slights, makes little of IV.iii.1 s.d. **unbraced** with opened doublet (an image of disorder; see Ophelia's description of Hamlet, II. i. 75)

A life, this sword (dost see't?) should in one blow
Confound them all. Harlot, rare, notable harlot,
That with thy brazen face maintainst thy sin,
Was there no man in Parma to be bawd
To your loose cunning whoredom else but I?
Must your hot itch and pleurisy° of lust,
The heyday of your luxury,° be fed
Up to a surfeit, and could none but I
Be picked out to be cloak to your close° tricks,
Your belly-sports? Now I must be the dad
To all that gallimaufry° that's stuffed
In thy corrupted bastard-bearing womb,
Say, must I?

Annabella. Beastly man, why, 'tis thy fate.
I sued not to thee; for, but that I thought
Your over-loving lordship would have run
Mad on denial, had ye lent me time,
I would have told 'ee in what case I was.
But you would needs be doing.

Soranzo. Whore of whores!
Dar'st thou tell me this?

Annabella. O yes, why not?
You were deceived in me; 'twas not for love
I chose you, but for honour; yet know this,
Would you be patient yet, and hide your shame,
I'd see whether I could love you.

Soranzo. Excellent quean!°
Why, art thou not with child?

Annabella. What needs all this
When 'tis superfluous? I confess I am.

Soranzo. Tell me by whom.

Annabella. Soft, sir, 'twas not in my bargain.
Yet somewhat, sir, to stay your longing stomach,
I am content t'acquaint you with; the man,
The more than man, that got this sprightly boy—
For 'tis a boy, and therefore glory, sir,
Your heir shall be a son—

Soranzo. Damnable monster!

Annabella. Nay, and you will not hear, I'll speak no more.

8 **pleurisy** excess 9 **luxury** lechery 11 **close** secret 13 **gallimaufry** hodgepodge, here unpleasant 25 **quean** whore

Soranzo. Yes, speak, and speak thy last.
Annabella. A match, a match!
This noble creature was in every part
So angel-like, so glorious, that a woman
Who had not been but human, as was I,
Would have kneeled to him, and have begged for love.
You! Why, you are not worthy once to name
His name without true worship, or, indeed,
Unless you kneeled, to hear another name him.
Soranzo. What was he called?
Annabella. We are not come to that.
Let it suffice that you shall have the glory
To father what so brave a father got.
In brief, had not this chance fallen out as't doth,
I never had been troubled with a thought
That you had been a creature; but for marriage,
I scarce dream yet of that.
Soranzo. Tell me his name.
Annabella. Alas, alas, there's all.
Will you believe?
Soranzo. What?
Annabella. You shall never know.
Soranzo. How!
Annabella. Never; if you do, let me be cursed.
Soranzo. Not know it, strumpet? I'll rip up thy heart,
And find it there.
Annabella. Do, do.
Soranzo. And with my teeth
Tear the prodigious lecher joint by joint.
Annabella. Ha, ha, ha, the man's merry!
Soranzo. Dost thou laugh?
Come, whore, tell me your lover, or, by truth,
I'll hew thy flesh to shreds; who is't?
Annabella sings. Che mortè piu dolce che morire per amore?°
Soranzo. Thus will I pull thy hair, and thus I'll drag
Thy lust-be-lepered body through the dust.
Yet tell his name.

59 Che morte . . . amore? "What death is sweeter than to die for love?"

Annabella sings. Morendo in gratia Dei, morirei senza dolore.°

Soranzo. Dost thou triumph? The treasure of the earth
Shall not redeem thee; were there kneeling kings
Did beg thy life, or angels did come down
To plead in tears, yet should not all prevail
Against my rage. Dost thou not tremble yet?

Annabella. At what? To die? No, be a gallant hangman.°
I dare thee to the worst: strike, and strike home;
I leave revenge behind, and thou shalt feel't.

Soranzo. Yet tell me ere thou diest, and tell me truly,
Knows thy old father this?

Annabella. No, by my life.

Soranzo. Wilt thou confess, and I will spare thy life?

Annabella. My life? I will not buy my life so dear.

Soranzo. I will not slack° my vengeance.

Enter Vasques.

Vasques. What d'ee mean, sir?

Soranzo. Forbear, Vasques; such a damned whore
Deserves no pity.

Vasques. Now the gods forfend!° And would you be her executioner, and kill her in your rage too? O, 'twere most unmanlike. She is your wife: what faults hath been done by her before she married you, were not against you; alas, poor lady, what hath she committed which any lady in Italy in the like case would not? Sir, you must be ruled by your reason and not by your fury; that were unhuman and beastly.

Soranzo. She shall not live.

Vasques. Come, she must. You would have her confess the author of her present misfortunes, I warrant 'ee; 'tis an unconscionable demand, and she should lose the estimation that I, for my part, hold of her worth, if she had done it. Why, sir, you ought not of all men living to know it. Good sir, be reconciled; alas, good gentlewoman.

63 Morendo . . . dolore "Dying in the grace of God, I should die without sorrow" (sources of these songs remain unknown) **69 hangman** executioner **76 slack** lessen **80 forfend** forbid

Annabella. Pish, do not beg for me; I prize my life
As nothing; if the man will needs be mad,
Why, let him take it.

Soranzo. Vasques, hear'st thou this?

Vasques. Yes, and commend her for it; in this she shows the nobleness of a gallant spirit, and beshrew my heart, but it becomes her rarely. [*Aside.*] Sir, in any case° smother your revenge; leave the scenting-out your wrongs to me; be ruled, as you respect your honour, or you mar all.—Sir, if ever my service were of any credit with you, be not so violent in your distractions. You are married now; what a triumph might the report of this give to other neglected suitors. 'Tis as manlike to bear extremities as godlike to forgive.

Soranzo. O Vasques, Vasques, in this piece of flesh,
This faithless face of hers, had I laid up
The treasure of my heart.—Hadst thou been virtuous,
Fair, wicked woman, not the matchless joys
Of life itself had made me wish to live
With any saint but thee; deceitful creature,
How hast thou mocked my hopes, and in the shame
Of thy lewd womb even buried me alive.
I did too dearly love thee.

Vasques. This is well; [*Aside.*] Follow this temper° with some passion. Be brief and moving;° 'tis for the purpose.

Soranzo. Be witness to my words thy soul° and thoughts,
And tell me, didst not think that in my heart
I did too superstitiously adore thee?

Annabella. I must confess I know you loved me well.

Soranzo. And wouldst thou use me thus? O, Annabella,
Be thou assured, whatsoe'er the villain was
That thus hath tempted thee to this disgrace,
Well he might lust, but never loved like me.
He doted on the picture that hung out
Upon thy cheeks, to please his humorous eye;°
Not on the part I loved, which was thy heart,
And, as I thought, thy virtues.

101 **in any case** by all means 118 **follow this temper** carry on in this manner 119 **moving** affecting 120 **thy soul** upon thy soul (?) 129 **humorous** casually idle, i.e., not deeply committed

Annabella O my lord!
These words wound deeper than your sword could do.

Vasques. Let me not ever take comfort, but I begin to weep myself, so much I pity him; why, madam, I knew when his rage was over-past, what it would come to.

Soranzo. Forgive me, Annabella. Though thy youth
Hath tempered thee above thy strength to folly,
Yet will not I forget what I should be,
And what I am, a husband; in that name
Is hid divinity; if I do find
That thou wilt yet be true, here I remit
All former faults, and take thee to my bosom.

Vasques. By my troth, and that's a point of noble charity.

Annabella. Sir, on my knees—

Soranzo. Rise up, you shall not kneel.
Get you to your chamber, see you make no show
Of alteration; I'll be with you straight.
My reason tells me now that 'tis as common
To err in frailty as to be a woman.
Go to your chamber. *Exit Annabella.*

Vasques. So, this was somewhat to the matter; what do you think of your heaven of happiness now, sir?

Soranzo. I carry hell about me; all my blood
Is fired in swift revenge.

Vasques. That may be, but know you how, or on whom? Alas, to marry a great woman, being made great in the stock to your hand,° is a usual sport in these days; but to know what ferret it was that haunted your cony-berry,° there's the cunning.

Soranzo. I'll make her tell herself, or—

Vasques. Or what? You must not do so. Let me yet persuade your sufferance a little while; go to her, use her mildly, win her if it be possible to a voluntary,° to a weeping tune; for the rest, if all hit, I will not miss my mark. Pray, sir, go in; the next news I tell you shall be wonders.

Soranzo. Delay in vengeance gives a heavier blow.
Exit.

155-6 **great woman . . . your hand** highborn woman, already made large in the body for you in advance 157-8 **cony-berry** rabbit warren 162 **voluntary** improvised music, here a pun for a willing confession

Vasques. Ah, sirrah, here's work for the nonce. I had a suspicion of a bad matter in my head a pretty whiles ago; but after my madam's scurvy looks here at home, her waspish perverseness and loud fault-finding, then I remembered the proverb, that where hens crow and cocks hold their peace there are sorry houses. 'Sfoot, if the lower parts of a she-tailor's cunning° can cover such a swelling in the stomach, I'll never blame a false stitch in a shoe whiles I live again. Up and up so quick? And so quickly too? 'Twere a fine policy to learn by whom; this must be known; and I have thought on't—

Enter Putana.

Here's the way, or none—What, crying, old mistress! Alas, alas, I cannot blame 'ee, we have a lord, Heaven help us, is so mad as the devil himself, the more shame for him.

Putana. Vasques, that ever I was born to see this day. Doth he use thee so too, sometimes, Vasques?

Vasques. Me? Why, he makes a dog of me. But if some were of my mind, I know what we would do; as sure as I am an honest man, he will go near to kill my lady with unkindness. Say she be with child, is that such a matter for a young woman of her years to be blamed for?

Putana. Alas, good heart, it is against her will full sore.

Vasques. I durst be sworn, all his madness is for that she will not confess whose 'tis, which he will know, and when he doth know it, I am so well acquainted with his humour, that he will forget all straight. Well, I could wish she would in plain terms tell all, for that's the way indeed.

Putana. Do you think so?

Vasques. Foh, I know't; provided that he did not win her to't by force. He was once in a mind that you could tell, and meant to have wrung it out of you, but I somewhat pacified him for that; yet sure you know a great deal.

Putana. Heaven forgive us all, I know a little, Vasques.

Vasques. Why should you not? Who else should? Upon my

173 she-tailor's cunning skill of a woman's tailor (to hide a pregnancy)

conscience, she loves you dearly, and you would not betray her to any affliction for the world.

Putana. Not for all the world, by my faith and troth, Vasques.

Vasques. 'Twere pity of your life if you should; but in this you should both relieve her present discomforts, pacify my lord. and gain yourself everlasting love and preferment.

Putana. Dost think so, Vasques?

Vasques. Nay, I know't; sure 'twas some near and entire friend.

Putana. 'Twas a dear friend indeed; but—

Vasques. But what? Fear not to name him; my life between you and danger. Faith, I think 'twas no base fellow.

Putana. Thou wilt stand between me and harm?

Vasques. 'Ud's° pity, what else? You shall be rewarded too, trust me.

Putana. 'Twas even no worse than her own brother.

Vasques. Her brother Giovanni, I warrant 'ee.

Putana. Even he, Vasques; as brave a gentleman as ever kissed fair lady. O, they love most perpetually.

Vasques. A brave gentleman indeed; why, therein I commend her choice.—Better and better.—You are sure 'twas he?

Putana. Sure and you shall see he will not be long from her too.

Vasques. He were to blame if he would: but may I believe thee?

Putana. Believe me! Why, dost think I am a Turk or a Jew? No, Vasques, I have known their dealings too long to belie them now.

Vasques. Where are you? There within, sirs.

Enter Banditti.

Putana. How now, what are these?

Vasques. You shall know presently.° Come, sirs, take me this old damnable hag, gag her instantly, and put out her eyes. Quickly, quickly!

Putana. Vasques, Vasques!

218 'Uds God's 236 presently at once

Vasques. Gag her, I say. 'Sfoot, d'ee suffer her to prate? What d'ee fumble about? Let me come to her; I'll help your old gums, you toad-bellied bitch. Sirs, carry her closely into the coalhouse, and put out her eyes instantly; if she roars, slit her nose: d'ee hear, be speedy and sure. Why, this is excellent and above expectation.

Exeunt [Banditti] with Putana.

Her own brother? O horrible! To what a height of liberty° in damnation hath the devil trained° our age. Her brother, well; there's yet but a beginning: I must to my lord, and tutor him better in his points of vengeance; now I see how a smooth tale goes beyond a smooth tail. But soft—What thing comes next?

Enter Giovanni.

Giovanni! As I would wish; my belief is strengthened, 'tis as firm as winter and summer.

Giovanni. Where's my sister?

Vasques. Troubled with a new sickness, my lord; she's somewhat ill.

Giovanni. Took too much of the flesh,° I believe.

Vasques. Troth, sir, and you, I think, have e'en hit it. But my virtuous lady—

Giovanni. Where's she?

Vasques. In her chamber; please you visit her; she is alone. [*Giovanni gives him money.*] Your liberality° hath doubly made me your servant, and ever shall, ever—

Exit Giovanni.

Enter Soranzo.

Sir, I am made a man, I have plied my cue with cunning and success; I beseech you let's be private.

Soranzo. My lady's brother's come; now he'll know all.

Vasques. Let him know't; I have made some of them fast enough. How have you dealt with my lady?

Soranzo. Gently, as thou hast counselled. O, my soul

247 **liberty** license, lack of restraint 247 **trained** lured 257 **Took . . . flesh** ate too much meat (with sexual allusion) 262 **liberality** generosity, also sexual license

Runs circular in sorrow for revenge.
But, Vasques, thou shalt know—

Vasques. Nay, I will know no more, for now comes your turn to know; I would not talk so openly with you. Let my young master take time enough, and go at pleasure; he is sold to death, and the devil shall not ransom him. Sir, I beseech you, your privacy.

Soranzo. No conquest can gain glory of my fear. *Exeunt.*

[Act V, Scene i]

Enter Annabella above.

Annabella. Pleasures, farewell, and all ye thriftless minutes
Wherein false joys have spun a weary life.
To these my fortunes now I take my leave.
Thou, precious Time, that swiftly rid'st in post°
Over the world, to finish up the race
Of my last fate, here stay thy restless course,
And bear to ages that are yet unborn
A wretched, woeful woman's tragedy.
My conscience now stands up° against my lust
With depositions charactered° in guilt,

Enter Friar [*below*].

And tells me I am lost: now I confess
Beauty that clothes the outside of the face
Is cursed if it be not clothed with grace.
Here like a turtle° (mewed up° in a cage)
Unmated, I converse with air and walls,
And descant on my vile unhappiness.
O Giovanni, that hast had the spoil
Of thine own virtues and my modest fame,
Would thou hadst been less subject to those stars
That luckless reigned at my nativity:
O would the scourge due to my black offence

V.i.4 **rid'st in post** rides posthorses, hastily 9 **stands up** bears witness 10 **charactered** inscribed 14 **turtle** turtledove 14 **mewed up** imprisoned

Might pass from thee, that I alone might feel
The torment of an uncontrolled flame.
Friar. [*Aside.*] What's this I hear?
Annabella. That man, that blessed friar,
Who joined in ceremonial knot my hand
To him whose wife I now am, told me oft
I trod the path to death, and showed me how.
But they who sleep in lethargies of lust
Hug their confusion, making Heaven unjust,
And so did I.
Friar. [*Aside.*] Here's music to the soul.
Annabella. Forgive me, my good genius, and this once
Be helpful to my ends. Let some good man
Pass this way, to whose trust I may commit
This paper double-lined with tears and blood:
Which being granted, here I sadly° vow
Repentance, and a leaving of that life
I long have died in.
Friar. Lady, Heaven hath heard you,
And hath by providence ordained that I
Should be his minister for your behoof.°
Annabella. Ha, what are you?
Friar. Your brother's friend, the friar;
Glad in my soul that I have lived to hear
This free confession 'twixt your peace and you.
What would you, or to whom? Fear not to speak.
Annabella. Is Heaven so bountiful? Then I have found
More favour than I hoped. Here, holy man—
Throws a letter.
Commend me to my brother; give him that,
That letter; bid him read it and repent.
Tell him that I (imprisoned in my chamber,
Barred of all company, even of my guardian,
Who gives me cause of much suspect)° have time
To blush at what hath passed; bid him be wise,
And not believe the friendship of my lord.
I fear much more than I can speak: good father,
The place is dangerous, and spies are busy;
I must break off—you'll do't?

35 sadly solemnly 39 for your behoof in your behalf 50 suspect suspicion

Friar. Be sure I will;
And fly with speed—my blessing ever rest
With thee, my daughter; live, to die more blessed.
Exit Friar.

Annabella. Thanks to the Heavens, who have prolonged my breath
To this good use: now I can welcome death. *Exit.*

[Act V, Scene ii]

Enter Soranzo and Vasques.

Vasques. Am I to be believed now? First marry a strumpet that cast herself away upon you but to laugh at your horns,° to feast on your disgrace, riot in your vexations, cuckold you in your bride-bed, waste your estate upon panders and bawds!

Soranzo. No more, I say, no more.

Vasques. A cuckold is a goodly tame beast, my lord.

Soranzo. I am resolved; urge not another word.
My thoughts are great, and all as resolute
As thunder; in mean time I'll cause our lady
To deck herself in all her bridal robes,
Kiss her, and fold her gently in my arms.
Begone—yet hear you, are the banditti ready
To wait in ambush?

Vasques. Good sir, trouble not yourself about other business than your own resolution; remember that time lost cannot be recalled.

Soranzo. With all the cunning words thou canst, invite
The states° of Parma to my birthday's feast;
Haste to my brother-rival and his father,
Entreat them gently, bid them not to fail.
Be speedy, and return.

Vasques. Let not your pity betray you till my coming back; think upon incest and cuckoldry.

Soranzo. Revenge is all the ambition I aspire:
To that I'll climb or fall; my blood's on fire. *Exeunt.*

V.ii.3 horns (conventional sign of the cuckold) 19 states nobles

[Act V, Scene iii]

Enter Giovanni.

Giovanni. Busy opinion is an idle fool,
That, as a school-rod keeps a child in awe,
Frights the unexperienced temper of the mind:
So did it me; who, ere my precious sister
Was married, thought all taste of love would die
In such a contract; but I find no change
Of pleasure in this formal law of sports.
She is still one to me, and every kiss
As sweet and as delicious as the first
I reaped, when yet the privilege of youth
Entitled her a virgin. O the glory
Of two united hearts like hers and mine!
Let poring book-men° dream of other worlds,
My world, and all of happiness, is here,
And I'd not change it for the best to come:
A life of pleasure is Elysium.

Enter Friar.

Father, you enter on the jubilee
Of my retired delights; now I can tell you,
The hell you oft have prompted° is nought else
But slavish and fond° superstitious fear;
And I could prove it too—
Friar. Thy blindness slays thee.
Look there, 'tis writ to thee. *Gives the letter.*
Giovanni. From whom?
Friar. Unrip the seals and see;
The blood's yet seething hot, that will anon
Be frozen harder than congealed coral.
Why d'ee change colour, son?
Giovanni. 'Fore Heaven, you make
Some petty devil factor° 'twixt my love
And your religion-masked sorceries.
Where had you this?

V.iii.13 **poring book-men** bookish scholars 19 **prompted** put forward (in your arguments) 20 **fond** foolish 28 **factor** go-between, as in trade

Friar. Thy conscience, youth, is seared,°
Else thou wouldst stoop to warning.
Giovanni. 'Tis her hand,
I know't; and 'tis all written in her blood.
She writes I know not what. Death? I'll not fear
An armèd thunderbolt aimed at my heart.
She writes, we are discovered—pox on dreams
Of low faint-hearted cowardice. Discovered?
The devil we are; which way is't possible?
Are we grown traitors to our own delights?
Confusion take such dotage, 'tis but forged;
This is your peevish chattering, weak old man.

Enter Vasques.

Now, sir, what news bring you?

Vasques. My lord, according to his yearly custom keeping this day a feast in honour of his birthday, by me invites you thither. Your worthy father, with the Pope's reverend nuncio, and other magnificoes of Parma, have promised their presence; will't please you to be of the number?

Giovanni. Yes, tell him I dare come.
Vasques. 'Dare come'?
Giovanni. So I said; and tell him more, I will come.
Vasques. These words are strange to me.
Giovanni. Say I will come.
Vasques. You will not miss?
Giovanni. Yet more? I'll come! Sir, are you answered?
Vasques. So I'll say.—My service to you. *Exit Vasques.*
Friar. You will not go, I trust.
Giovanni. Not go? For what?
Friar. O, do not go. This feast, I'll gage° my life,
Is but a plot to train° you to your ruin.
Be ruled, you sha' not go.
Giovanni. Not go? Stood Death
Threatening his armies of confounding plagues,
With hosts of dangers hot as blazing stars,
I would be there. Not go? Yes, and resolve
To strike as deep in slaughter as they all.
For I will go.

30 seared dried up, burnt out **57 gage** wager **58 train** lure

Friar. Go where thou wilt; I see
The wildness of thy fate draws to an end,
To a bad fearful end. I must not stay
To know thy fall; back to Bononia I
With speed will haste, and shun this coming blow.
Parma, farewell; would I had never known thee,
Or aught of thine. Well, young man, since no prayer
Can make thee safe, I leave thee to despair. *Exit Friar.*

Giovanni. Despair, or tortures of a thousand hells,
All's one to me; I have set up my rest.°
Now, now, work serious thoughts on baneful° plots,
Be all a man, my soul; let not the curse
Of old prescription rend from me the gall
Of courage,° which enrols a glorious death.
If I must totter like a well-grown oak,
Some under-shrubs shall in my weighty fall
Be crushed to splits:° with me they all shall perish.
Exit.

[Act V, Scene iv]

Enter Soranzo, Vasques, and Banditti.

Soranzo. You will not fail, or shrink in the attempt?

Vasques. I will undertake for their parts. Be sure, my masters, to be bloody enough, and as unmerciful as if you were preying upon a rich booty on the very mountains of Liguria; for your pardons, trust to my lord, but for reward you shall trust none but your own pockets.

Banditti Omnes. We'll make a murder.

Soranzo. Here's gold, here's more; want nothing; what you do
Is noble, and an act of brave revenge,
I'll make ye rich banditti, and all free.

Omnes. Liberty, liberty.

Vasques. Hold, take every man a vizard; when ye are withdrawn, keep as much silence as you can possibly.

73 **set up my rest** made up my mind 74 **baneful** poisonous 75-7 **let not . . . courage** let not the Old Testament curse against incest tear out of me my embittered courage 80 **splits** splinters

You know the watchword; till which be spoken, move not, but when you hear that, rush in like a stormy flood; I need not instruct ye in your own profession.

Omnes. No, no, no.

Vasques. In, then; your ends are profit and preferment.—away. *Exeunt Banditti.*

Soranzo. The guests will all come, Vasques?

Vasques. Yes, sir. And now let me a little edge your resolution. You see nothing is unready to this great work, but a great mind in you. Call to your remembrance your disgraces, your loss of honour, Hippolita's blood; and arm your courage in your own wrongs; so shall you best right those wrongs in vengeance, which you may truly call 'your own'.

Soranzo. 'Tis well; the less I speak, the more I burn,
And blood shall quench that flame.

Vasques. Now you begin to turn Italian. This beside; when my young incest-monger comes, he will be sharp set on° his old bit: give him time enough, let him have your chamber and bed at liberty; let my hot hare have law° ere he be hunted to his death, that if it be possible, he may post° to hell in the very act of his damnation.

Enter Giovanni.

Soranzo. It shall be so; and see, as we would wish,
He comes himself first. Welcome, my much-loved
brother,
Now I perceive you honour me; y'are welcome.
But where's my father?

Giovanni. With the other states,
Attending on the nuncio of the Pope,
To wait upon him hither. How's my sister?

Soranzo. Like a good housewife, scarcely ready yet;
Y'are best walk to her chamber.

Giovanni. If you will.

Soranzo. I must expect° my honourable friends;
Good brother, get her forth.

Giovanni. You are busy, sir.

Exit Giovanni.

V.iv.31 sharp set on have a fierce hunger for **33 law** (the start given a hare) **35 post** ride **44 expect** attend

Vasques. Even as the great devil himself would have it; let him go and glut himself in his own destruction.

Flourish.

Hark, the nuncio is at hand; good sir, be ready to receive him.

Enter Cardinal, Florio, Donado, Richardetto, and Attendants.

Soranzo. Most reverend lord, this grace hath made me proud,
That you vouchsafe° my house; I ever rest
Your humble servant for this noble favour.

Cardinal. You are our friend, my lord; his holiness
Shall understand how zealously you honour
Saint Peter's vicar in his substitute:
Our special love to you.

Soranzo. Signors, to you
My welcome, and my ever best of thanks
For this so memorable courtesy.
Pleaseth your grace to walk near?

Cardinal. My lord, we come
To celebrate your feast with civil mirth,
As ancient custom teacheth: we will go.

Soranzo. Attend his grace there; Signors, keep your way.

Exeunt.

[Act V, Scene v]

Enter Giovanni and Annabella lying on a bed.°

Giovanni. What, changed so soon? Hath your new sprightly lord
Found out a trick in night-games more than we
Could know in our simplicity? Ha! Is't so?
Or does the fit come on you, to prove treacherous
To your past vows and oaths?

51 **vouchsafe** deign to visit V.v.1 s.d. **lying on a bed** (to introduce a bed into a scene, the actors would either draw curtains to reveal it or more frequently, would thrust a bed out upon the platform)

Annabella. Why should you jest
At my calamity, without all sense
Of the approaching dangers you are in?
Giovanni. What danger's half so great as thy revolt?
Thou art a faithless sister, else thou know'st
Malice, or any treachery beside,
Would stoop to my bent brows; why, I hold fate
Clasped in my fist, and could command the course
Of time's eternal motion, hadst thou been
One thought more steady than an ebbing sea.
And what? You'll now be honest, that's resolved?
Annabella. Brother, dear brother, know what I have been,
And know that now there's but a dining-time
'Twixt us and our confusion: let's not waste
These precious hours in vain and useless speech.
Alas, these gay attires were not put on
But to some end; this sudden solemn feast
Was not ordained to riot in expense;
I, that have now been chambered here alone,
Barred of my guardian, or of any else,
Am not for nothing at an instant freed
To fresh access. Be not deceived, my brother,
This banquet is an harbinger of death
To you and me; resolve yourself it is,
And be prepared to welcome it.
Giovanni. Well, then;
The schoolmen° teach that all this globe of earth
Shall be consumed to ashes in a minute.
Annabella. So I have read too.
Giovanni. But 'twere somewhat strange
To see the waters burn; could I believe
This might be true, I could believe as well
There might be hell or Heaven.
Annabella. That's most certain.
Giovanni. A dream, a dream, else in this other world
We should know one another.
Annabella. So we shall.
Giovanni. Have you heard so?
Annabella. For certain.
Giovanni. But d'ee think
That I shall see you there, you look on me?

30 schoolmen scholastics, medieval theologians

May we kiss one another, prate or laugh,
Or do as we do here?
Annabella. I know not that.
But good,° for the present, what d'ee mean
To free yourself from danger? Some way think
How to escape; I'm sure the guests are come.
Giovanni. Look up, look here; what see you in my face?
Annabella. Distraction and a troubled countenance.
Giovanni. Death, and a swift repining wrath—yet look,
What see you in mine eyes?
Annabella. Methinks you weep.
Giovanni. I do indeed; these are the funeral tears
Shed on your grave; these furrowed up my cheeks
When first I loved and knew not how to woo.
Fair Annabella, should I here repeat
The story of my life, we might lose time.
Be record° all the spirits of the air,
And all things else that are, that day and night,
Early and late, the tribute which my heart
Hath paid to Annabella's sacred love
Hath been these tears, which are her mourners now.
Never till now did Nature do her best
To show a matchless beauty to the world,
Which in an instant, ere it scarce was seen,
The jealous Destinies required again.
Pray, Annabella, pray; since we must part,
Go thou, white in thy soul, to fill a throne
Of innocence and sanctity in Heaven.
Pray, pray, my sister.
Annabella. Then I see your drift—
Ye blessed angels, guard me.
Giovanni. So say I.
Kiss me. If ever after-times should hear
Of our fast-knit affections, though perhaps
The laws of conscience and of civil use
May justly blame us, yet when they but know
Our loves, that love will wipe away that rigour
Which would in other incests be abhorred.
Give me your hand; how sweetly life doth run
In these well-coloured veins. How constantly
These palms do promise health. But I could chide

42 **good** i.e., good brother 54 **Be record** be witness

With Nature for this cunning flattery.
Kiss me again—forgive me.
Annabella. With my heart.
Giovanni. Farewell.
Annabella. Will you be gone?
Giovanni. Be dark, bright sun,
And make this midday night, that thy gilt rays
May not behold a deed will turn their splendour
More sooty than the poets feign their Styx.°
One other kiss, my sister.
Annabella. What means this?
Giovanni. To save thy fame, and kill thee in a kiss.
Stabs her.
Thus die, and die by me, and by my hand.
Revenge is mine; honour doth love command.
Annabella. O brother, by your hand?
Giovanni. When thou art dead
I'll give my reasons for't; for to dispute
With thy (even in thy death) most lovely beauty,
Would make me stagger to perform this act,
Which I most glory in.
Annabella. Forgive him, Heaven—and me my sins; farewell.
Brother unkind, unkind.—Mercy, great Heaven—
O —O — *Dies.*
Giovanni. She's dead, alas, good soul. The hapless° fruit
That in her womb received its life from me
Hath had from me a cradle and a grave.
I must not dally. This sad marriage-bed,
In all her best, bore her alive and dead.
Soranzo, thou hast missed thy aim in this;
I have prevented now thy reaching° plots,
And killed a love, for whose each drop of blood
I would have pawned my heart. Fair Annabella,
How over-glorious art thou in thy wounds,
Triumphing over infamy and hate!
Shrink not, courageous hand, stand up, my heart,
And boldly act my last and greater part.
Exit with the body.

82 feign their Styx depict the river Styx artistically **94 hapless** luckless **100 reaching** far-reaching, cunning

[Act V, Scene vi]

A Banquet. Enter Cardinal, Florio, Donado, Soranzo, Richardetto, Vasques, and Attendants; they take their places.

Vasques. Remember, sir, what you have to do; be wise and resolute.

Soranzo. Enough—my heart is fixed.—Pleaseth your grace
To taste these coarse confections; though the use
Of such set entertainments more consists
In custom than in cause, yet, reverend sir,
I am still made your servant by your presence.

Cardinal. And we your friend.

Soranzo. But where's my brother Giovanni?

Enter Giovanni with a heart upon his dagger.

Giovanni. Here, here, Soranzo; trimmed in reeking blood,
That triumphs over death; proud in the spoil
Of love and vengeance! Fate or all the powers
That guide the motions of immortal souls
Could not prevent me.

Cardinal. What means this?

Florio. Son Giovanni!

Soranzo. Shall I be forestalled?

Giovanni. Be not amazed; if your misgiving hearts
Shrink at an idle sight, what bloodless fear
Of coward passion would have seized your senses,
Had you beheld the rape of life and beauty
Which I have acted? My sister, O my sister.

Florio. Ha! What of her?

Giovanni. The glory of my deed
Darkened the midday sun, made noon as night.
You came to feast, my lords, with dainty fare;
I came to feast too, but I digged for food
In a much richer mine than gold or stone
Of any value balanced; t'is a heart,
A heart, my lords, in which is mine entombed:
Look well upon't; d'ee know't?

Vasques. What strange riddle's this?

Giovanni. 'Tis Annabella's heart, 'tis; why d'ee startle?
I vow 'tis hers: this dagger's point ploughed up

Her fruitful womb, and left to me the fame
Of a most glorious executioner.

Florio. Why, madman, art thyself?

Giovanni. Yes, father; and that times to come may know
How as my fate I honoured my revenge,
List, father, to your ears I will yield up
How much I have deserved to be your son.

Florio. What is't thou say'st?

Giovanni. Nine moons have had their changes
Since I first throughly viewed and truly loved
Your daughter and my sister.

Florio. How!—Alas,
My lords, he's a frantic madman!

Giovanni. Father, no.
For nine months' space in secret I enjoyed
Sweet Annabella's sheets; nine months I lived
A happy monarch of her heart and her.
Soranzo, thou know'st this; thy paler cheek
Bears the confounding print of thy disgrace,
For her too fruitful womb too soon bewrayed
The happy passage of our stol'n delights,
And made her mother to a child unborn.

Cardinal. Incestuous villain?

Florio. O, his rage belies him.

Giovanni. It does not, 'tis the oracle of truth;
I vow it so.

Soranzo. I shall burst with fury.
Bring the strumpet forth.

Vasques. I shall, sir. *Exit Vasques.*

Giovanni. Do, sir.—Have you all no faith
To credit yet my triumphs? Here I swear
By all that you call sacred, by the love
I bore my Annabella whilst she lived,
These hands have from her bosom ripped this heart.

Enter Vasques.

Is't true or no, sir?

Vasques. 'Tis most strangely true.

Florio. Cursed man.—Have I lived to— *Dies.*

Cardinal. Hold up, Florio.—
Monster of children, see what thou hast done,

Broke thy old father's heart. Is none of you
Dares venture on him?
Giovanni. Let 'em.—O, my father,
How well his death becomes him in his griefs!
Why, this was done with courage; now survives
None of our house but I, gilt in the blood
Of a fair sister and a hapless father.
Soranzo. Inhuman scorn of men, hast thou a thought
T'outlive thy murders?
Giovanni. Yes, I tell thee, yes;
For in my fists I bear the twists of life.°
Soranzo, see this heart, which was thy wife's;
Thus I exchange it royally for thine, [*Stabs him.*]
And thus and thus. Now brave revenge is mine.

Vasques. I cannot hold any longer.—You, sir, are you grown insolent in your butcheries? Have at you.

[*They*] *fight.*

Giovanni. Come, I am unarmed to meet thee.

Vasques. No, will it not be yet? If this will not, another shall. Not yet? I shall fit you anon.—'Vengeance.'

Enter Banditti.

Giovanni. Welcome, come more of you whate'er you be,
I dare your worst—
O, I can stand no longer. Feeble arms,
Have you so soon lost strength?

Vasques. Now you are welcome, sir,—Away, my masters, all is done, shift for yourselves. Your reward is your own; shift for yourselves.

Banditti. Away, away. *Exeunt Banditti.*

Vasques. How d'ee, my lord; see you this? How is't?

Soranzo. Dead; but in death well pleased that I have lived
To see my wrongs revenged on that black devil.
O Vasques, to thy bosom let me give
My last of breath; let not that lecher live—O — [*Dies.*]

Vasques. The reward of peace and rest be with him, my ever dearest lord and master.

Giovanni. Whose hand gave me this wound?

Vasques. Mine, sir, I was your first man; have you enough?

Giovanni. I thank thee; thou hast done for me but what

V.vi.73 I bear . . . life I hold the threads of life (like the Fates or Parcae in Greek mythology)

I would have else done on myself. Art sure
Thy lord is dead?

Vasques. O impudent slave; as sure as I am sure to see thee die.

Cardinal. Think on thy life and end, and call for mercy.

Giovanni. Mercy? Why, I have found it in this justice.

Cardinal. Strive yet to cry to Heaven.

Giovanni. O, I bleed fast.
Death, thou art a guest long looked for; I embrace
Thee and thy wounds; O, my last minute comes.
Where'er I go, let me enjoy this grace,
Freely to view my Annabella's face. *Dies.*

Donado. Strange miracle of justice!

Cardinal. Raise up the city; we shall be murdered all.

Vasques. You need not fear, you shall not; this strange task being ended, I have paid the duty to the son which I have vowed to the father.

Cardinal. Speak, wretched villain, what incarnate fiend
Hath led thee on to this?

Vasques. Honesty, and pity of my master's wrongs; for know, my lord, I am by birth a Spaniard, brought forth my country in my youth by Lord Soranzo's father, whom whilst he lived I served faithfully; since whose death I have been to this man as I was to him. What I have done was duty, and I repent nothing but that the loss of my life had not ransomed his.

Cardinal. Say, fellow, know'st thou any yet unnamed
Of counsel in this incest?

Vasques. Yes, an old woman, sometimes° guardian to this murdered lady.

Cardinal. And what's become of her?

Vasques. Within this room° she is; whose eyes, after her confession, I caused to be put out, but kept alive, to confirm what from Giovanni's own mouth you have heard. Now, my lord, what I have done you may judge of, and let your own wisdom be a judge in your own reason.

Cardinal. Peace!—First this woman, chief in these effects,°

127 sometimes at one time **130 room** building (?) **136 this woman . . . effects** (although "this woman" is usually taken to refer to Putana, the apposition "chief in these effects" suggests that the Cardinal may be thinking of Annabella)

My sentence is, that forthwith she be ta'en
Out of the city, for example's sake,
There to be burnt to ashes.
Donado. 'Tis most just.
Cardinal. Be it your charge, Donado, see it done.
Donado. I shall.
Vasques. What for me? If death, 'tis welcome; I have been honest to the son as I was to the father.
Cardinal. Fellow, for thee, since what thou didst was done
Not for thyself, being no Italian,
We banish thee forever, to depart
Within three days; in this we do dispense
With grounds of reason, not of thine offence.
Vasques. 'Tis well; this conquest is mine, and I rejoice that a Spaniard outwent an Italian in revenge.
Exit Vasques.
Cardinal. Take up these slaughtered bodies, see them buried;
And all the gold and jewels, or whatsoever,
Confiscate by the canons of the church,
We seize upon to the Pope's proper use.
Richardetto. [*discovers himself.*] Your grace's pardon: thus long I lived disguised
To see the effect of pride and lust at once
Brought both to shameful ends.
Cardinal. What, Richardetto whom we thought for dead?
Donado. Sir, was it you—
Richardetto. Your friend.
Cardinal. We shall have time
To talk at large of all; but never yet
Incest and murder have so strangely met.
Of one so young, so rich in nature's store,
Who could not say, 'tis pity she's a whore? *Exeunt.*

SUGGESTED REFERENCES

Bibliography: *Tudor and Stuart Drama,* compiled by Irving Ribner (Golden Tree Bibliographies, 1966).

General Studies of Elizabethan Drama and Theater.

Beckerman, Bernard. *Shakespeare at the Globe* (1962).

Bentley, Gerald E. *The Profession of the Dramatist in Shakespeare's Time* (1971).

Bradbrook, M. C. *Themes and Conventions of Elizabethan Tragedy* (1935).

Cook, Ann J. *The Privileged Playgoers of Shakespeare's London, 1576-1642* (1981).

Doran, Madeleine. *Endeavors of Art: A Study of Form in Elizabethan Drama* (1954).

Ellis-Fermor, Una. *The Jacobean Drama* (rev. ed. 1958).

Gurr, Andrew. *The Shakespearean Stage, 1574-1642* (1970).

Harbage, Alfred. *Shakespeare's Audience* (1941).

Leech, Clifford, and T. W. Craik, gen. eds. *The Revels History of Drama in English,* Volume III, 1576-1613 (1975).

Ornstein, Robert. *The Moral Vision of Jacobean Tragedy* (1960).

Christopher Marlowe

Standard edition: *The Works and Life of Christopher Marlowe,* gen. ed. R. H. Case, 6 vols. (1930-33).

Modern editions of *Doctor Faustus:* Sylvan Barnet, ed. (1969); John D. Jump, ed. (1962); Fredson Bowers, ed. (1973).

Gregg, W. W., ed. *Marlowe's Doctor Faustus 1604-1616: Parallel Texts* (1950).

Hotson, Leslie. *The Death of Christopher Marlowe* (1925).

Kocher, Paul H. *Christopher Marlow: A Study of His Thought, Learning and Character* (1946).

Steane, J. B. *Marlowe: A Critical Study* (1964).

Ben Jonson

Standard edition: *Ben Jonson,* eds. C. H. Herford and Percy and Evelyn Simpson, 11 vols. (1925-52).

Modern editions of *Volpone:* Philip Brockbank, ed. (1968); David Cook, ed. (1962); Alvin B. Kernan, ed: (1962).

Barish, Jonas, ed. *Ben Jonson: A Collection of Critical Essays,* Twentieth Century Views (1963).

Barish, Jonas. *Ben Jonson and the Language of Prose Comedy* (1960).

Enck, J. J. *Jonson and the Comic Truth* (1957).

Knights, L. C. "Ben Jonson, Dramatist," *The Age of* Shakespeare, Vol. II, *A Guide to English Literature,* ed. Boris Ford (1955).

Knights, L. C. *Drama and Society in the Age of Jonson* (1937).

Parker, R. B. "*Volpone* in Performance: 1921-1972," *Renaissance Drama,* n.s. IX (1978), 147-73.

Partridge, Edward B. *The Broken Compass: A Study of the Major Comedies of Ben Jonson* (1958).

John Webster

Standard edition: *The Works of John Webster,* ed. F. L. Lucas, 4 vols. (1927).

Modern editions of *The Duchess of Malfi:* John Russell Brown, ed. (1964); F. L. Lucas, ed. (1959); George Rylands and Charles Williams, eds. (1945).

Bogard, Travis. *The Tragic Satire of John Webster* (1955).

Boklund, Gunnar. *The Duchess of Malfi: Sources, Themes, Characters* (1962).

Bradbrook, M. C. *John Webster: Citizen and Dramatist* (1980).

Dent, R. W. *John Webster's Borrowing* (1960).

Leech, Clifford. *John Webster: A Critical Study* (1951).

Rabkin, Norman, ed. *Twentieth Century Interpretations of The Duchess of Malfi* (1968).

Thomas Middleton

Standard edition: *The Works of Thomas Middleton,* ed. A. H. Bullen, 8 vols. (1885-86).

Modern editions of *Women Beware Women:* Roma Gill, ed. (1968); J. R. Mulryne, ed. (1975).

Barker, R. H. *Thomas Middleton* (1958).

Farr, Dorothy M. *Thomas Middleton and the Drama of Realism* (1973).

Schoenbaum, Samuel. *Middleton's Tragedies* (1955).

John Ford

Standard edition: *The Works of John Ford,* eds. William Gifford and Alexander Dyce, 3 vols. (1869).

Modern editions of *'Tis Pity She's a Whore:* N. W. Bawcutt, ed. (1966); Brian Morris, ed. (1968).

Leech, Clifford. *John Ford and the Drama of His Time* (1957).

Sargeaunt, M. J. *John Ford* (1935).

Sensabaugh, G. F. *The Tragic Muse of John Ford* (1944).

Stavig, Mark. *John Ford and the Traditional Moral Order* (1968).